The

Brides *of the*

OLD WEST

Five Romantic Adventures from the American Frontier

The *Brides* *of the* OLD WEST

Peggy Darty, Darlene Franklin,
Sally Laity, Nancy Lavo,
Kathleen Paul

BARBOUR BOOKS
An Imprint of Barbour Publishing, Inc.

Print ISBN 978-1-63058-886-1

eBook Editions:
Adobe Digital Edition (.epub) 978-1-63409-335-4
Kindle and MobiPocket Edition (.prc) 978-1-63409-336-1

Published by Barbour Books, an imprint of Barbour Publishing, Inc., P.O. Box 719, Uhrichsville, Ohio 44683, www.barbourbooks.com

Our mission is to publish and distribute inspirational products offering exceptional value and biblical encouragement to the masses.

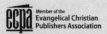
Member of the
Evangelical Christian
Publishers Association

Printed in the United States of America.

CONTENTS

Morning Mountain

by Peggy Darty

CHAPTER 1

S uzanne Waters withdrew her leather glove and swiped her bleeding thumb across her jeans. She hated barbed wire, even if Pa and other Colorado ranchers declared it to be the greatest invention of the 1870s. She sighed, checking her handiwork. Through dogged persistence, she had managed to twist a sagging strand of wire back in place, and now Pa would never know how close they had come to losing their horses.

Ever since her father's accident, she had been riding over the range, checking to be sure there were no breaks in the fence or other calamities to add to their list of disasters. With their only ranch hand gone and Pa laid up with cracked ribs and a sprained ankle, she was praying long and hard.

A strand of blond hair had escaped her felt hat, tickling her sunburned forehead as it dangled over worried gray eyes. If not for a promise to her mother to "remain ladylike," when Abigail Waters lay dying the past winter, she would grab the scissors and whack the long strands into a more practical style. A boys' cut, perhaps. After all, she was quickly falling into the role of the son her father wanted but never had.

Behind her, Nellie, her horse, nickered softly.

"We'll go soon," she promised, glancing over her shoulder to the beloved mare that had become her best friend in their new home. She had carried on some very serious conversations with patient Nellie, but Nellie, for once, was ignoring her.

"What's wrong?" Suzanne asked, noticing the way Nellie's ears were perked as the animal stared out across the valley.

Suzanne looked around, inspecting the landscape. At the base of Morning Mountain, the terrain spread into a valley, enclosed by walls of pine, cottonwood, and aspens. Beyond the woods lay the road to Wiley's Trading Post two miles down the road. Suzanne frowned. She could see a horse moving through the trees, toward the end of the woods. Soon the horse would reach the clearing and she'd be able to see the rider.

"Just someone headed to the post, Nellie." Suzanne stroked the mare's neck then turned her attention back to her sore thumb.

The bleeding had stopped and she pulled on her glove. As she wiggled her fingers into the warm leather, she glanced again toward the woods.

First the head, then the body of a black horse emerged. Suzanne frowned. There was something odd about the rider. She squinted, trying to determine what it was. Something about the rider bothered her. What? The rider sat on the horse, leaning forward like one afraid of falling—a rare sight in ranching country.

She pulled her hat brim lower on her forehead, shutting out the sun's rays for a better look.

The horse was in plain view now, and she realized the rider had slumped forward. Something was wrong with that rider.

Suzanne bit her lip, torn between Pa's warning to stay away from strangers and her own basic desire to help wherever she was needed. Glancing at the saddle scabbard that held her rifle, she felt safe enough to investigate. Gathering Nellie's reins, she swung astride and kneed her mare.

Nellie, sensitive to her rider, stretched her legs until the two were a gray streak across the upper end of the valley. Suzanne was an excellent rider, spending hours on Nellie's back. Horse and rider knew each other well, and now Nellie sensed a crisis.

"Whoa," Suzanne called as they drew near the black stallion.

By now, the man was barely hanging on. Even from a distance, she could see a trail of blood along the front of his shirt.

"What's happened?" she called, drawing rein. She jumped down and approached him cautiously.

The man was tall and well-built, dressed in a blue cotton shirt, dark pants, and leather boots. He wore a wide-brimmed, black hat, shading the face that slumped onto his chest.

She took a step closer. Dark hair tumbled over his forehead. His eyes were closed. Beneath a mustache, his mouth was partially open, as if asleep. But this man wasn't just asleep. He had lapsed into unconsciousness, unable to respond to her. She could see the mass of blood, clotting his shirt to his chest.

His horse stopped walking and turned wary eyes to Suzanne. She approached the horse, stroking the dark gray patch on his forehead. Then she looked up at the man. He was bleeding on the left side; his right hand had gone slack on the reins. Another minute and he'd be on the ground.

"Hold on," she called, reaching up to steady him. "Can you hear me?"

She stared bewildered at the dark hair and neatly trimmed mustache. He was a handsome man, probably in his middle to upper twenties, with high cheekbones, straight nose, and full lips beneath the mustache.

"Mister, I'm taking you to the ranch," she said, wondering if he would be alive by the time she got him there.

———◈———

Hank Waters thrust his handmade crutch solidly onto the board floor and hobbled from the living room back to the bedroom. He paused in the doorway, studying the stranger who now occupied his bed. His daughter stood at the bedside, adjusting the bandages she and Hank had just wrapped around the man's left side.

"Suzanne, your ma couldn't have stood by and watched me dig that bullet out of him like you did." Hank's voice was gruff, as usual, but Suzanne heard the unmistakable note of pride.

"Guess I'm more like you than Mom," she answered distractedly, her attention focused on her patient.

The man had turned his head on the pillow, as though aware of their words. Suzanne watched him closely. His dark lashes parted slowly, and the bluest eyes she'd ever seen stared into her face. Everything about this man had been a surprise. He had the broadest shoulders she'd ever touched, for starters, and beneath the firm skin, his muscles ware taut. She wondered what he did for a living; she wondered, even more, what had gotten him shot.

His dark brows drew together in confusion as he looked from Suzanne to her father, who was limping to the bed.

"Just lie still," she said, smiling at him. "Can you sip some water?"

A muffled sound drifted over his cracked lips, which she interpreted as yes. She reached for the tin cup of water on the bedside table.

"Here, I'll hold his head," Hank offered, cradling the man's head in his brawny hands. Hank was tall and wiry, muscular and strong for a man of sixty years.

Suzanne pressed the brim of the cup to the stranger's lips.

"Sip it slowly," she warned, gently tilting the cup.

She watched with concern as the water trickled over his tongue, and he began to gulp.

"No!" She withdrew the cup. "You'll be sick if you drink too quickly."

Hank's sharp eyes, the same steel gray as his hair and beard, swept to his daughter. "You oughta go back up to Denver and work in a hospital."

"Then who'd take care of you?" she shot back.

"I don't need—"

The stranger began to cough, interrupting their arguments. Their bantering was comfortable and frequent, as native to the cabin as the smell of beeswax, and coffee brewing on the stove.

"What's your name, mister?" Hank barked as the man's head sank into the pillow, and his eyes closed.

Suzanne put a hand on her father's arm and shook her head. "Let him sleep," she whispered.

"He's weak," Hank lowered his voice, "lost a lot of blood."

While Suzanne had restrained her father from asking questions, she found herself every bit as curious as Hank, perhaps even more. She checked the bandages—clean white strips of cloth improvised from an old sheet. The bleeding had stopped, thank God. She sighed with relief, pulling the quilt over his chest and motioning her father out of the room.

"Reckon I'll move my stuff out to the living room," Hank grumbled, hobbling to the pine wardrobe.

"Pa, I'll do that," Suzanne quickly offered. "You go lie down. At the moment, one patient is enough."

For once, Hank's stubborn streak refused to assert itself, allowing his daughter to take over. She stared after his thin frame, noticing how his shoulder blades jutted against his shirt. If not for a wide tight belt, his pants would never stay on. She wondered, worriedly, just how much weight he had lost since he'd begun working his daylight-to-dark regime, the labor backbreaking with no help.

God is our refuge and strength. The verse came to her mind; it was on the list she had made from her mother's Bible. Those verses had been all that had sustained her after her mother's death, and she found herself quoting them on a daily basis.

She followed her father out of the room, closing the door softly behind her. Hank had settled onto the front porch step and sat staring out at the valley, puffing on his pipe.

CHAPTER 2

Luke Thomason tried to wedge his mind from the nightmare that had gripped him for...he had no idea how long. There had been a woman—or had she been an angel? A woman with beautiful blond hair and a kind smile. Had she given him something to drink?

His mind tumbled backward and again he was trapped in that nightmare, unable to escape.

A kerosene lamp hung over the poker table, casting a yellow glow on the cards in Luke's hand. He couldn't believe his luck. He had another winning hand. With a pair of jacks and two eights and another card coming, he could end up with a full house; or if not, he still had two pairs. He glanced at the card lying facedown on the table. That card would tell the tale. Smoothly, he reached down, lifted it, and tucked the card among the others. *A jack!*

His mouth was dry, his palms were moist. He dared not move for fear of betraying his excitement. What was he doing here playing poker for high stakes when his experience had been limited to the bunkhouse at Godfrey's ranch?

Slowly, he lifted his eyes, studying the faces of the men at the table, trying to read their eyes. They had acquired the poker faces he'd heard about, but then he'd been told he had one, too. With him, the inscrutable expression had been stamped on years before, by a determination to hide the ache from a heart that had been ripped in two.

The two men, directly to his left and right, wore range clothes. He sensed their lives were similar to his—dirt-poor ranch hands dreaming of wealth at the tables. The man opposite him was from Denver and a thoroughly unlikable sort.

Dressed in a black frock coat and white linen shirt, he was a small man, barely over five feet tall, with a superior attitude and an insulting manner. A nervous twitch pulled at the man's thin face, and put constant movement into the close-set black eyes. Those eyes jumped from player to player, back to his cards, then to the chips on the table. The eyes shot to his dwindling stack of chips then sank again to the cards in his hand.

The city slicker with the money was losing badly. And Luke, drawing from instincts and a sharp mind, was winning it.

The two men beside him were down to a handful of chips. Luke studied the twin stacks of chips piled high before him.

He counted out an impressive stack and placed them in the center of the table. Their faces didn't betray them, but he could feel the disappointment settling over the other players. He had just upped the price of poker, forcing a show of hands.

"I'm out," the man next to him said, coming to his feet. "I'm not losing the rest of my money."

The other ranch hand stood slowly, grabbing his one remaining chip and pocketing it quickly.

"Me, too."

The city slicker stayed in the game, adding a stack of chips to the pile in the center.

Smoothly, Luke laid out his full house, and the little man's eyes bulged. He began to cough, looking and sounding as though someone were choking him to death. His wrist went limp, dropping the cards onto the table. Luke was looking at two pairs. He had won again.

Luke was not a gambler by nature, and while the game was a challenge, he knew the danger as well. He was a poor, hardworking cowhand who had hit a streak of luck. But he knew when to quit.

He stood, gathering up his winnings. "Think I'll cash in," he said, glancing at the red-faced man across the table.

The little man leaped to his feet, sputtering with rage. "You can't quit now!"

Luke towered over him, his blue eyes narrowed. "Beg your pardon," he drawled, "but I can quit anytime I want to. . ."

A soft touch moved across his forehead, and the vague aroma of wildflowers filled his nostrils. Was he lying in a meadow? If so, who was touching him? That touch had soothed him, calmed him, freed him at last from the nightmare. He sank deeper into the pillow and found the peaceful sleep he craved.

CHAPTER 3

Suzanne left the room again, closing the door softly behind her. Worriedly, she plodded out to the porch, where her father sat on the slab-log step, smoking his pipe.

"Pa, you've had experience with cowboys who took a bullet or got a bad injury riding bronc," Suzanne said, dropping down beside him. "Do you think an infection will set up in that man's shoulder?"

Hank squinted at her over a wisp of smoke. "Hard to tell. With all the alcohol we used, I'm guessing we've killed the germs."

"I rubbed down his horse then put him in the back corral so he and Rocky wouldn't tangle over the mares."

"Did you find a wallet on him or some identification?"

Suzanne shook her head. "Nope. There was a Colt revolver tucked in his bedroll and some personal items in his saddlebags, but nothing to tell us who he is."

"Wonder what happened?" Hank said, tapping the ashes from his pipe.

"I'm sure he'll tell us when he's able."

Hank frowned. "You say he had no money on him?"

Suzanne shook her head.

"He was robbed, then. Figured that when I saw he'd been shot in the back."

Suzanne lifted her eyes north to the sprawling mountain range of Pikes Peak. It was a wild and beautiful country, with its towering, snowcapped peaks and lush valleys of aspen and cottonwood. The problem was, everyone wanted to settle in Colorado, and men were killing each other over homestead claims and water rights.

"Suzanne," Hank said, drawing out her name the way he often did before making a point, "I'm saddling Rocky in the morning and getting back to work."

"Pa, you've got to give those cracked ribs time to heal. And your ankle is still too swollen for a day's punishment in the stirrups. I just hope you didn't do any damage to yourself when you helped me drag that man into the bedroom."

Hank turned and frowned at her. "Daughter, I'm getting tired of being bossed."

Suzanne jumped up from the step and began to pace the board porch. "Pa, I don't mean to be bossy, but you just won't take care of yourself. You should have known better than to try to break that mustang."

"Girl, I've broken more mustangs than you've counted years," he snapped. His gray eyes, faded by sun and wind, blazed with defiance. "When a musing lopes into my valley, with us desperate for horses...I ain't letting him get away if I can stop him."

But you couldn't stop him, Suzanne thought, biting her lip. *Not anymore, Pa.*

While she had wisely refrained from speaking the words, Hank Waters, nevertheless, seemed to read her mind. He heaved a sigh and dropped his head to stare at his bandaged ankle.

"Well, Wilbur's got to live with his conscience and that can't be easy," he said at last. "But sometimes it's hard work keeping the anger out of my soul."

Suzanne reached over and placed a gentle kiss on her father's bearded cheek. "Uncle Wilbur will pay for what he did, Pa. Anger would just harm us, not him."

Hank's thin face softened with tenderness as he slowly

turned to face his daughter. "You're so much like your ma. Just don't ever be as gullible."

Suzanne drew a deep breath. "Ma's love for her only brother blinded her to his faults."

Hank snorted. "And, like a fool, I took his word, sight unseen, that he had enough horses here to start a breeding ranch; and as for this cabin. . ." His voice trailed as he sank into silence.

"We'll make it work, Pa," Suzanne spoke with conviction, drawing upon her optimistic nature. They *would* make it work, somehow. "We've survived the winter and Ma. . ." She swallowed hard and plunged on, "The worst is over."

Hank shook his head, but he looked unconvinced.

"Come on, Pa, cheer up. I'm making dumplings tonight. Life can't be all bad."

For the first time in days, a tiny smile touched Hank Waters's thin lips. "Dumplings? You trying to impress that young buck in there?"

The defiance on Hank's face minutes before was now mirrored in the expression of his only child. Hank saw it and smiled to himself, secretly pleased by his daughter's spirit.

"I don't try to impress any man," she stated, before turning on her heel and hurrying inside the cabin.

She headed across the L-shaped room that served as living room and kitchen and fought the frustration she felt. In truth, her father had struck a nerve. How she'd like to impress this handsome stranger, but it would be a waste of time to let her mind wander in such a direction. Her eyes drifted toward the closed door of the bedroom as she recalled the items in his saddlebags: a compass, a few toiletries, and a gold wedding band.

Upon seeing the ring, a keen disappointment had filled her. While it was ridiculous to have any romantic notions about a stranger—one who had been shot—she had been unable to stop herself from speculating. And then she'd found the ring. Oh well, a woman somewhere would thank them for saving his life. *Some lucky woman!*

CHAPTER 4

Suzanne rolled over on the cot in her small bedroom and squinted at the daylight sifting through the muslin curtains above her bed. She reached up to part a curtain, curious about the weather. Gray clouds settled over Morning Mountain. She rubbed her eyes and tried to clear her mind, still fogged by sleep. Slowly, yesterday's strange events settled into her brain, and she bolted upright in bed, staring at the closed door of her bedroom. *The stranger!*

She swung her legs around and fumbled for her house shoes. The smell of coffee filled the cabin, a reminder of Hank's habit of rising early to drink a cup and watch the sunrise.

Suzanne reached into the wardrobe and removed a pair of clean pants and a cotton shirt. Her mother would roll over in her grave if she could see her dressed in the boys' clothes Suzanne had bought at the trading post. Still, there was no way she was going to muck out the stalls and ride over the range in a dress and petticoats. She shook her long blond hair back from her face, working the thickness into one fat braid at the nape. Her gray eyes ran over the clutter on her nightstand, wondering where the last grosgrain ribbon had landed. Abandoning the search, she grabbed a strip of leather and wound it around her braid.

She didn't care about clothes or being a lady right now; she had her father to think about. It was all she could do to keep him at home until he healed.

A muffled cough interrupted her thoughts. *The stranger!* The front door closed, and she could hear Pa's crutch stamping over the board floors to the bedroom.

Suzanne crossed the living room and stood looking through the open door of the bedroom. Hank was seated in a chair by the bed, talking to the stranger who was propped up on the pillow, sipping coffee. His dark hair was swept back from his face, and his blue eyes looked alert, rested.

"You were lucky the bullet passed through your shoulder without striking a bone," Hank was saying.

As Suzanne paused in the door, the stranger's eyes lifted to her and he nodded politely.

"Mr. Thomason. . ." Hank began.

"Just Luke. . ."

"This is my daughter, Suzanne."

Suzanne smiled. "Hello."

He nodded. "Hello. Your father was telling me how you saved my life. I'm grateful."

"He's from Kansas," Hank said, twisting in his chair to survey his daughter. "On his way to Colorado Springs. Any lowdown critter who'd shoot a man in the back. . ." Hank muttered, shaking his head.

Suzanne's eyes darted to the stranger, seeking his reaction. He had closed his eyes momentarily, as though trying to shut out some horrible memory. Then slowly he spoke.

"I should never have stopped in Bordertown."

"Bordertown?" Hank rasped. "No, son, you shouldn't have. That's an outlaws' hangout. You figure someone trailed you from there?"

Luke Thomason shook his head slowly as he stared across the room, obviously thinking back to two nights before. "The truth is, I got in a poker game. And I won. I rode out of town late at night. The guy I cleaned out must have followed me and waited till I made camp. I'd been in the saddle for two days; once

I crawled in the bedroll, a herd of cattle could have stampeded behind me, and I wouldn't have heard."

"He shot you in your bedroll? But how did you. . .?" Suzanne couldn't imagine someone would do such a thing. Maybe he didn't need to be talking about this. It had to have been a horrible experience.

"I hurt my back rodeoing this spring and—"

"Rodeoing?" Hank echoed, his gray eyes lighting up.

Suzanne studied her father's face, knowing he could barely contain his excitement. At last, he had someone under his roof who could talk rodeoing with him. These two could have a good time.

"Sleeping on the ground aggravated my back," the stranger continued, "so I put a pillow in my bedroll to support my shoulder."

"So the scoundrel sneaked up to shoot you in the back, not knowing about the pillow, and it slowed up the bullet," Hank finished, plowing a work-roughened hand through his gray hair.

"You think the man who shot you was the man from the poker table?" Suzanne asked.

Her mother would have said a lady did not pry, but she couldn't help it. After all, she'd invested quite a bit of time and effort in saving this man's life. She was curious to know just how he'd gotten himself into such a fix.

"I can't be sure," he answered. "I got shot, then I heard branches breaking and a horse taking off in the night. The man who lost his money to me looked like the kind who'd sneak up and shoot somebody in the back. And my wallet was the only thing missing." His eyes blazed with anger for a moment, then slowly the anger seemed to fade, replaced by an expression of. . .what? Suzanne wondered. Indifference? Yes, he looked indifferent to the conversation. It made her wonder how a person could slip from one emotion to another so quickly. Maybe he was the kind of man who tried to keep his thoughts private.

"He got your money?" Hank guessed.

"All of it." He stared into space for a moment then looked at

Hank. "Exactly where am I?" he asked.

"Geographically speaking, you're at the foot of Morning Mountain," Hank said, absently rubbing his healing ribs. "We're about half a day from Bordertown. Another day to Colorado Springs, but there's a trading post down the road that serves as stage stop, café, and general store. We can get a deputy out here. You'll be wanting to get a search on for the man who—"

"He's long gone by now," Luke sighed, staring into space.

Suzanne cleared her throat, trying to tactfully broach the subject. "Is there someone we should notify?"

He hesitated for a moment, studying his coffee cup. "No," he finally replied.

Suzanne was thinking of the gold wedding band. He had obviously decided not to alarm his wife now. "Then I'll get some breakfast," she said, heading for the door.

"Not for me," he called to her. "I'll be leaving as soon as—"

"Best not be thinking of getting on a horse just yet," Hank admonished. "You wouldn't make it far."

"Doc Browning stops by the post once a week, in case anyone in the area needs him," Suzanne said. "I'll leave word for him to come over."

"That won't be necessary," Luke replied. "You and your father have done a good job of patching me up. I'll be all right."

Suzanne studied his pale face and doubted he felt as healthy as he tried to appear. Her eyes moved to her father, who had fallen silent. Hank sat with his lips pursed, his eyes narrowed, looking at Luke Thomason.

"Pa, I'll get your breakfast," she said, turning from the room and walking back to the kitchen. Maybe the stranger wasn't hungry, but Hank would be wanting his biscuits and gravy, a ritual begun years ago by her mother and one he insisted on keeping.

CHAPTER 5

Luke stared at the closed door, hating the abruptness in his voice, but he didn't know how to behave around these people. Nobody had ever done anything for him without expecting something in return. That's why he had told them, straight out, about the poker game and then getting shot and having his wallet stolen. He didn't like other people knowing his business, but he liked even less people expecting something from him when he couldn't oblige.

He sank deeper into the pillow, staring at the ceiling. They were decent people, or at least they seemed to be. Once they knew he couldn't repay them, maybe they'd quit being so nice. It was making him nervous.

He closed his eyes, remembering how soft her fingers had felt on his skin, remembering the smell of the sachet she wore. She smelled as sweet as honeysuckle, and he knew he'd better get out of here fast. He was still running from the Godfrey woman; he wasn't about to let someone else get ideas in their head about settling him down.

Of course this woman was different. . . .

He twisted nervously, and the pain in his left shoulder ripped through him. He sank his teeth into his lower lip, cursing his luck. He'd lost all his money, plus the winnings from the poker game, and now he'd gotten shot and was trapped in this bed for another day or two.

He opened his eyes and looked around the room. Something on the dresser caught his eyes. He scowled, growing angrier.

———❖———

Balancing the tray of food, Suzanne paused before the bedroom door as she lifted her hand and knocked lightly.

"Come in."

She entered, looking shyly at Luke Thomason. He was propped up on the pillow, staring at the dresser.

"Do you believe that verse?" he asked in a low, toneless voice.

Suzanne saw that he was looking at the Bible verse her mother had done in calligraphy and framed.

"All things work together for good for those who love the Lord," she repeated, placing the tray on the nightstand. "I admit I've had occasions to wonder, but then I always come back to trusting God. It's all I can do."

"It's a noble thought," he drawled. There was no mistaking the sarcasm that dripped from his words.

Suzanne glanced covertly at his handsome face, and noticed that the muscles in his jaw were clenched as he avoided her face. This time he was staring at the ceiling.

"You don't agree?" she asked gently.

"I won't say that I disagree." He closed his eyes. "My mother was religious."

"Yes, mine was as well. She died this winter."

"I'm sorry to hear that," he said quietly, still staring at the ceiling.

"Thank you." She opened her mouth to ask about his mother, then pressed her lips together. He obviously didn't want to talk to her, so there was no point in trying to be friendly.

"Call me when you're finished," she said.

He ignored the food as he continued to stare at the ceiling. She turned to go.

"Thank you," he said quietly as she reached the door.

She glanced back over her shoulder. He had turned his head on the pillow, and was trying to force a smile as he looked at her. But all that followed was a mere twitch of his lips. Suzanne let a slow, wide smile spread over her lips. *There, let him see how it's done,* she thought.

"You're welcome," she said brightly.

He merely stared at her, saying nothing more. She walked out of the room, leaving him to ponder whatever had him so deep in thought.

———※———

"Everything all right?" Hank called from the porch as Suzanne hurried up the path from the stable the next afternoon.

"Everything's fine," she said, forcing a smile. In truth, the horses were almost out of feed, and their money was nearly gone.

Luke Thomason sat with her father on the porch. Luke looked rested and fresh in a change of clothes. She had left his belongings on the chair beside his bed, giving little thought to how he would manage to dress himself with only one hand. Apparently, he had accomplished the task with no problem. The bandage on his left side made a bulk through his blue denim shirt, but leaving the buttons undone allowed space. All in all, however, he looked just fine. Even his hair, she noted, was damp from grooming; his face was clean, his eyes blue—deep blue. She didn't really care for mustaches, but on him it looked okay.

She looked away, yanking her torn gloves from her fingers, hoping her father wouldn't notice their ragged condition. Her boots moved faster up the path, as she eagerly sought the shade and comfort of the cabin.

While this was her first spring in southern Colorado, she hadn't imagined it would be this warm. Summer was early, she decided, rolling up her shirtsleeves. A leisurely bath at the creek, that's what she needed. Or at least a quick swim.

"Mr. Waters, I've had some experience with horses," Luke was saying. "Maybe I could help out before I leave."

Hank snorted. "'Pears to me you're in worse shape than I am."

"There's nothing wrong with my hands. I can—"

"We're fine," Suzanne spoke up, shoving her gloves in her back pocket. "We don't need any help."

"How'd the back forty look?" Hank asked quickly.

Suzanne glanced at her father and saw the look of warning on his face. While Hank himself could be abrupt, he didn't like that trait in his daughter.

Sorry, she said with her eyes. Her optimism had been drained beneath a blazing sun while her mind had toiled over what tomorrow would bring.

"Looked fine," she repeated the words she had spoken earlier. Pa had to be constantly reassured that the horses, the fences, even the prairie dogs could survive without his close supervision.

She pushed the trailing strands of hair back from her face, trying to ignore Luke Thomason, who had taken an interest in her, now that she looked like a field hand. Who could figure men? Her brief experience with Walter Haddock in Denver had thoroughly bored her. Nevertheless, when she spotted one that interested her, he was either a renegade or...married, she thought, remembering the wedding band in the stranger's saddlebag.

"On Monday, I'm riding over to the trading post to replenish some supplies," she said to Hank.

"I'm coming with you," he said, pressing a hand to his rib cage as he moved to stand up.

"Pa, I don't need you to come with me!"

Suzanne regretted the impatience in her tone, but she was getting sick and tired of trying to avoid arguments with Hank.

"I'm not questioning whether you need me or not. I'm questioning my sanity if I don't get on Rocky and ride. This is the last day I'm gonna hole up here in this cabin like a prisoner!" Hank called after her as she hurried inside.

Suzanne knew he was venting his frustration, and she took no offense.

The cool dimness of the cabin was a welcome change as she crossed the board floors to the kitchen. After oversleeping, she had bolted out to do chores, leaving the breakfast dishes unwashed. She stopped, staring now at those dishes, washed and draining on the rack. It was not Hank's habit to wash dishes. On the rare occasions that he did, he simply piled everything haphazardly to drain. These dishes were neatly stacked. Was it possible Luke Thomason had cleaned up the kitchen?

She removed her wide-brimmed hat, and stared at the frayed ends of the leather sweatband. The poor old hat, left by someone on a nail in the barn, had been a blessing to her fair skin, and she was glad someone had abandoned it. As her eyes drifted over the battered hat, she couldn't help wondering what Luke Thomason thought of it.

Recalling his nice black hat with the smooth leather sweatband, she merely shook her head in frustration and hooked the hat on its peg on the wall.

She headed for the water bucket, wondering why she had been so defensive, moments before. Well, she knew the answer to that. All morning, as she had ridden over the pasture, she'd kept seeing those volatile blue eyes, angry, sad, worried, indifferent. She had kept wondering about him—what kind of life he had come from in Kansas, what he was going to in Colorado Springs.

She dipped a gourd into the bucket of water, gulping greedily to drown the dust in her throat. Well, if the man was ready to leave, let him go. They didn't need one more mouth to feed when they were facing starvation themselves.

She found her eyes wandering to the small looking glass on the wall, and tilted her head for a better view of herself. An oval face held delicate features and a small mouth. The sunburn on her fair skin had finally deepened to a healthy glow, leaving only a peeling nose as a reminder. Golden ringlets of hair had turned white around her forehead, having escaped her hat and bleached out beneath the sun.

She took a step closer, inspecting her image curiously. Her brows arched outward on the end, as though she were about to voice the questions always bubbling up in her inquisitive mind. Altogether it was a pleasant face, if not beautiful. Her chin was too long, her cheeks too hollow. Or so it seemed to her.

The door banged behind her and she turned to see Luke,

heading in her direction. He was looking at her with a serious expression on his face. She wondered what was on his mind.

"Your father has convinced me I need to stay on another day. I was wondering if you'd mind if I helped out at the stable. There's nothing I like better than working with animals. How many do you have?"

"We're down to four horses. We have one stud, Rocky, and three mares. One is about to foal. Incidentally, I put your stallion in a corral to himself. He and Rocky didn't seem to like the looks of one another."

"Your pa told me you took care of him. I appreciate that."

She nodded. "Thanks for your offer to help, but we can manage."

"I know you can," he snapped.

She stared at him, shocked by his rude tone. She was ready to give him a piece of her mind, when he lifted his right hand and raked through his thick dark hair, slowly shaking his head.

"Look," he said more civilly, "I've worked hard all my life. I can't lounge around on the porch, doing nothing, while you work like a man..."

His remark had stung. "Well, I don't know about the ladies where you come from, but out here, a woman has to work in order to survive."

He crammed his hands in his pants pockets and began to pace the kitchen floor. She realized then how tall he was, over six feet, yet he was lean and muscular. Yes, he did know something about work, she decided, so let him get on with his work, and leave them in peace. She had enough problems without dealing with another man. And why did men always want to argue?

What kind of woman did he leave behind? she wondered suddenly. *One who argued back, or sat with her hands folded demurely in her lap, while he sulked or argued?* Automatically, her eyes dropped to his broad hands, and she had a fleeting vision of the wedding ring around his right finger. *Why isn't there a thin white line there, showing where the ring had been?*

"Please, let me help," he said, leveling those blue eyes down into her upturned face. "Otherwise, I'll be leaving."

"You shouldn't ride until that wound heals," she protested.

Blue eyes bored into gray ones. From the front porch, Hank began to cough. At the sound of her father's repeated coughing, Suzanne looked toward the window, the tension of the moment broken.

She took a drink of water, trying to calm her scattered thoughts. Why was she being so defensive? What was wrong with her? If he wanted to help, why couldn't she accept his help and be grateful for it?

"All right, you can help," she said on a sigh. "I'm sure Pa would be relieved."

Luke turned and glanced toward the porch.

"He told me he loves this ranch and begrudges every minute he's not on the back of a horse," he said more civilly.

"Yes, he does," Suzanne responded.

A tightness clamped her throat as she fought against the sudden unexpected threat of tears. How could her father cope with losing this place, and their four pitiful horses? They didn't have much, but Hank had pinned his hopes on making a go of it.

Nervous and anxious, she leaned against the cabinet needing to talk. She looked at this stranger, who probably didn't care one way or another, and decided to be honest with him. She was getting tired of wailing her problems at Nellie's docile face.

"He was a cowhand when he met my mother in Denver," she said. "Ma's family owned a mercantile business, and he was persuaded to hang up his spurs and become a merchant. He was never happy. Ma used to say"—she smiled, remembering—"that Pa loved horses more than he loved her. It wasn't true, of course."

Luke was staring down at her, listening thoughtfully. "But he stayed in the mercantile business?" he asked.

"Yes. He did."

"Then you should be thankful for that," he said flatly. Bitterness edged his tone, an indifferent mask slipping over his face again.

She sauntered to the stove and shook the battered coffeepot to see if there was anything left. A slosh answered her question.

"We were thankful," she said, heating the coffee. "But Ma

wanted him to be happy. That's why she let her brother take advantage of them."

"What do you mean? Or maybe I shouldn't ask."

She shrugged. "My uncle was a dreamer, always chasing after get-rich-quick schemes. He never helped out in the family business. Finally Ma and Pa bought out his share after her parents died. Then, when he'd squandered everything, he came back to Denver with a real deal for them! He'd trade his horse ranch here for their share of the mercantile business. Pa jumped at the chance to have a small ranch, to go back to horses." She sighed. "It was a sorry bargain, but we've made the best of it."

"Made the best of it?" he echoed. "Why didn't your pa go back and thrash the daylights out of him?"

Suzanne laughed. "I guess Pa felt like doing that, but. . ." Her eyes swept over the living room, seeing in her mind's eye their nice living room in Denver: a room filled with Victorian furnishings, oil paintings, and Brussels carpets. That vision faded and she was looking at a horsehair couch, a straight-backed wooden chair, and a few plain end tables. A black iron stove and open shelves completed the kitchen. Only a few dishes and cooking utensils along with sparse cooking staples were visible on the shelves. Her gray eyes returned to the stranger in her kitchen. "My parents lived by Christian principles. They tried to believe that God had a reason for bringing them here."

"And what reason," he asked coldly, "did God have for letting your mother die?"

The harshness of his tone stunned her as much as the cruel question he had asked. She stared for a moment, shocked to the core. Before she could summon a reply, however, he had turned and stridden out of the room, back to the porch. Her eyes followed him through the door, as he bounded down the steps, his right hand extended over his wounded shoulder, as if he thought to protect it. But there seemed no way to protect, or to heal, the terrible wound he carried in his heart. And she began to suspect that wound had nothing to do with a bullet.

Chapter 6

Luke had gone for a walk, ending up down behind the house near a stream. He propped his shoulder against a cottonwood trunk and allowed the spring breeze to soothe his frustration.

He had no right to speak to her that way, he knew it. But he was getting sick of hearing them pour out all their goodness and mercy. They were living in another world, not the real one.

Maybe they were just being nice to him, hoping he would stay on and work for them for free. Their price for saving his life. He lifted a broad hand and plowed through his thick hair. If only he had some money to give them, but he had nothing.

He recalled how he had been suckered in at the Godfrey ranch. William Godfrey had been a decent man, generous with his ranch hands, and kind to Luke. Then Amanda Godfrey, the old maid daughter, had set her eyes and her hopes on him, and all the trouble had started. She had been determined to have him, and she really thought it would be easy to hook him. She'd even told him so.

He sighed and began to walk toward the corral where he spotted Smoky, prowling restlessly. He hadn't figured Mr. Godfrey would go back on his word, but then blood was thicker than water, as Ma used to say.

He looked back at the Waters' cabin and wondered if they were setting that kind of trap for him. They seemed like kind, decent folks, but so had the Godfreys.

No, he couldn't take any chances. He'd help them out for a day or two, he owed them that. Then he'd find a job along the route to Colorado Springs. He could get a job; he'd been working since he was twelve years old.

"Hey, boy," he called to his horse.

The big horse trotted to the fence, thrusting his head forward to nuzzle Luke.

"Glad to see me, aren't you?"

He stroked the horse's gleaming coat, looking him over. "Looks like someone's taking care of you all right. We'll be leaving soon. We don't stay cramped up long, do we?"

He drew a deep breath of fresh air into his lungs, enjoying the smell of evergreen that mingled on the breeze. He wouldn't lose his temper again; he wouldn't insult her. He had no right. But she got to him as no other woman had. He couldn't stop looking at her, and now she was popping up in his thoughts when he should be thinking of more important things. Like remembering the reason he was headed to Colorado Springs.

Sundays had always been special days for Suzanne and her parents. In Denver most of their Sundays had been the same: church services followed by large Sunday dinners where family and friends gathered to enjoy food and fellowship. While their surroundings had changed drastically when they had taken up ranch life, one thing had not changed. Sundays were days of worship.

In the beginning, Suzanne's mother had simply brought out the family Bible and read scripture. Sometimes they sang a hymn, other times they prayed quietly. Then, Iva Parkinson had come calling, inviting them to Trails End on Sunday for a service held on the front porch of their ranch home. Soon that had become the tradition for the community.

At first it had been difficult for Hank and Suzanne to go to Trails End Ranch without Abigail. But after that first dreadful Sunday, when they'd spent the day mourning Abigail, Hank had informed Suzanne that her mother would expect them to go to worship. Missing Abigail more than ever the next Sunday, they had dressed and gone to Trails End to join in community worship and had not missed a Sunday since.

"Will you be going over to the Parkinson's ranch today?" Hank asked as Suzanne stood at the stove, stirring the breakfast gravy.

She yawned. "Yes, but I think you could be excused."

"I think so, too," he quickly agreed.

Suzanne smiled. If she had suggested that he go, he would have joined her, but she thought it was best for him to stay home. "I'll tell them you'll be back next week," she said.

He glanced toward the closed door of the bedroom. "Luke is sleeping late."

Luke! Suzanne's fingers stiffened as she popped open a biscuit and spread gravy over it. She had not told her father the vicious words the man had spoken yesterday. He had avoided her ever since, and she was glad for that. She knew how to apply alcohol and cotton and bandage to an outer wound. But this man had something festering in his soul. It would take a mightier power than she to heal that kind of wound, but Luke Thomason didn't want to read their verses or hear anything about the love of God.

She sat down at the table, nibbling on a small biscuit. She had left a larger one on the stove, in case their grumpy guest decided he was hungry. She glanced across the table at Pa. *He is strangely quiet this morning, suspiciously quiet,* she thought.

"What time is it?" she asked.

He withdrew the gold watch Ma had given him and studied the numerals on its face.

"Eight o' clock."

"I'd better get dressed."

Later, as she hurried through the living room, grabbing up her Bible, she met Luke's stare from the bedroom door.

"Good morning," he said, his tone cool, reserved.

His hair was neatly combed and his face bore evidence of a recent shave. The mustache was gone. She liked his face even better without the mustache.

"Good morning," she said.

He was looking her up and down, his eyes lingering on the front of her dress. Was something wrong, she wondered, glancing down to see if she had popped a button. No. The dress looked pretty enough, all cleaned and pressed. She loved the color—blue like a spring sky—and it complimented her gold hair and gray eyes.

Her eyes returned to him, and now he was staring at her hair. Suzanne lifted a hand, absently smoothing the hair net covering the chignon she wore today. Why was he looking at her that way? Then it came to her: this was the first time he had seen her in a dress, rather than pants and a shirt. *Doing a man's work! Hadn't that been his expression?*

She felt her cheeks burn as he continued to stare at her, and a wave of indignation swept her. He had a wife somewhere; he had no right looking at her like that, making her feel self-conscious. It was time to put the man in his place.

"Mr. Thomason, could I ask you something?"

"What is it?"

"Are you married?"

His dark brows arched at her bold question. No doubt, he was wondering what had prompted her question. She held herself erect, her eyes never wavering from his face.

"No."

A simple word that told her nothing.

She opened her mouth to ask about the wedding band, then just as quickly she pressed her lips together. She couldn't bring herself to mention the ring; perhaps it was pride. She didn't want him to think she had been pilfering through his things. Actually, she had been looking for some identification, but there was no point in explaining that now.

"I left breakfast on the stove," she said, hurrying through the front door.

~~❦~~

The spring morning was warm, but not uncomfortable, as Suzanne cantered Nellie toward Trails End Ranch, as puzzled as ever about Luke Thomason. Then suddenly she solved the mystery of Luke and the wedding band. His wife had died! Of course. That was why he was so mad at the world, so angry and bitter. Her heart began to soften, and by the time she joined the small group assembled on the wide porch of the rambling ranch house and joined in singing "Rock of Ages," she had forgotten her troubles.

Arthur Parkinson Jr. a tall young man of twenty who still had not grown into his hands and feet, slipped into the chair beside Suzanne. He turned to grin at her, and she smiled politely, never missing a word of the hymn.

Why couldn't she feel something more than friendship for Art? she wondered as his pale blue eyes kept sneaking in her direction. He was nice, polite, well mannered. Single. And rich, Pa had reminded her. As the only son of the largest landowner in the area, Art had something to offer.

She sidled a glance at him. He sang in a clear tenor, but she didn't like the way his Adam's apple always bobbed against his collar. In fact, it was the largest Adam's apple she'd ever seen.

She turned her attention to Arthur Parkinson Sr., a tall, distinguished-looking man in his fifties. He stood with his Bible, ready to read scripture. She could see a vague resemblance between father and son; unfortunately, Art looked more like his mother. Suzanne scolded herself for the thought. Mrs. Parkinson was very nice—and she couldn't help it if her eyes bulged just a bit.

~~❦~~

Suzanne had settled Nellie in the corral, rewarding her with a handful of oats from the dwindling supply, and headed to the house. She had spotted Pa and Luke on the porch as she turned up the path. From the way Pa's mouth was moving, she figured he had filled Luke Thomason's head this morning.

Once she reached the house, she saw it was Luke who was

doing the talking. Hank, for once, was doing the listening.

"My grandfather bought land and cattle from the Mexicans in southeast Texas," Luke was saying. "He was an immigrant who came west with only a few dollars in his pockets."

"So did he get rich?" Hank inquired.

Again that pause that Suzanne had come to expect from Luke when questioned about a personal matter.

"No, he went broke. And he drifted north to Kansas."

"What happened there?" Hank asked, conversationally.

"He died a pauper."

An awkward silence followed. Then Hank turned to his daughter. "Did you pray for us, daughter?"

"Of course," she replied, allowing her smile to extend from her father to Luke for a brief moment. "Mrs. Parkinson was in true form this morning, missing all the high notes to 'Rock of Ages'."

Hank laughed heartily, appreciating her humor, but Luke's mouth merely twitched.

"And did Art sneak a seat beside you?" Hank demanded good-naturedly, winking at Luke. "Parkinson's son has a crush on Suzanne."

"Pa!" she reprimanded sharply, lifting her skirt to plant a kid leather slipper on the slab log step.

Slowly, her eyes slid to Luke as she reminded herself that she had asked God to forgive her for being so judgmental of the man. She was going to be more patient with him.

As Suzanne continued to the porch, Luke came to his feet. She might object to his grumpiness at times, but he had offered to help around the house. She supposed that he did have nice manners. She appreciated that. Her mother has always told her to seek a man with manners.

"Are you men hungry?" she asked.

"I could eat," Hank answered.

"No, I'm not hungry at all," Luke replied, turning his blue eyes toward the distant mountain range.

Good, Suzanne thought, *I won't have to add more gravy to the last of the venison roast.* She entered the house, humming "Rock of Ages," determined to hold on to her good mood for the rest of the day.

———※———

Luke Thomason proved to be more hungry than he'd thought, for after Hank nagged him into submission, he had joined them at the table. At first, he seemed to feel awkward and out of place—particularly when Suzanne said graces—but he began to relax as Hank broached the subject of rodeos.

"Yes, sir. I made most of my money rodeoing on weekends."

"Ever get hurt?" Hank asked.

"Just once. Nothing serious." He had glanced at Suzanne, who immediately pretended an interest in filling the water glasses. She had a feeling if he had broken both legs he'd never admit it. He was determined to appear as healthy as his horse.

"I've been meaning to ask," she whirled, water pitcher in hand. "What's your horse's name? I hate not being able to call him by his name when I talk to him. . ."

She had just given herself away. Her delight in petting the stallion, and imagining the life he and his master lived, had been her own secret until now. Now they knew she was in the habit of talking to animals!

"His name is Smoky. When people look at him, they wonder where I got the name."

"He has a smoky-looking patch on his forehead," Suzanne guessed. "I think it's a very good name."

Luke half-smiled. "You're right about the patch. That's where he got his name."

"And my bay is named after these wonderful mountains."

"Rocky." Luke nodded. "That, too, is a good name."

"But not as good as Nellie," Suzanne countered, enjoying the conversation now. She filled each glass, set the pitcher down, and took her seat again.

"And since we're comparing names," Luke said, "how did you settle on Nellie?"

Suzanne hesitated, glancing at her father. His gray eyes were amused as he looked across the table at her, obviously curious to see how she would answer.

"Because it suits her," she said with a smile. "And because that was her name when we bought her, sick, half-starved, and half-price, from a desperate rancher's wife."

It had turned into a pleasant meal. Luke had offered to help with the dishes but she had refused. Pa had gone to the sofa; Luke had wandered off somewhere, and Suzanne had dragged to her bed as soon as the kitchen was clean. Sunday had always been a day of rest for them, and today she was looking very forward to a long nap.

She was almost asleep when her father's voice echoed through the house.

"Suzanne!"

She heard the urgency in his tone and jumped out of bed, pulling an everyday dress on over her petticoats and chemise.

"Suzanne!" His voice came from the porch. "Hurry."

She bolted from her room, reaching the front door just in time to see Hank fall in the yard. He landed facedown on the ground, yelping in disgust as he tried to lift his ankle.

"What are you doing?" she cried.

"What does it look like I'm doing?" he snapped. "I was trying to get to the stable. . ."

"Pa, you know you can't go down there. The path is filled with gopher holes and you could turn your ankle again. But you just did! What am I going to do with you?" she cried in frustration,

"Will you quit babbling and listen to me?" Hank snapped, glaring at her. "Something's wrong with one of the horses. Hurry!" He bit the words out through clenched teeth as one hand shot to his rib cage. She wondered if he'd cracked another rib.

Suzanne leaped to her feet and saw Luke bounding out the door of the house. His eyes shot from Suzanne to Hank sprawled on the ground.

"Help him!" she cried as she tore out to the stable.

She could hear the cries of an animal in pain, and her heart jumped to her throat. She tried not to think about what she would find. From the animal's shrill cry she envisioned a grizzly in the barn, tearing into the mare's flesh...

She burst through the door of the stable, blinking against the dimness, giving no thought to what she would have done if, in fact, a grizzly *had* been loose in the barn. Instead, she came up short, her nose tingling from the tartness of straw and manure...and the mare in labor!

Blaze was down in the clean straw that Suzanne had lovingly provided the day before, her bulging abdomen heaving with the struggle of giving birth.

"Oh Blaze," Suzanne cried, rushing to the narrow stall.

She dropped down beside the brown mare and ran her palm up and down the white star on the mare's forehead. Like her father, Suzanne kept a special place in her heart for the horses. What if there was a complication, what if....The horror of losing Blaze was more than Suzanne could bear.

The mare rolled her head, peering up at Suzanne with wild, pain-filled eyes. She seemed to be begging for help, and feeling more helpless than ever, Suzanne sank her teeth in her lower lip. Of all times for her father to be laid up! He would know exactly what to do here, while Suzanne's knowledge was limited to comforting words. Why hadn't they discussed this? she wondered, as her frustration turned to panic.

The stable door creaked and she whirled to see Luke hurrying back to the stall. A wave of relief swept over her, even though she knew his assistance was limited to one good arm. He said nothing as he looked grimly at the mare. She needed desperately to hear something encouraging, but she doubted she would hear anything very encouraging from this man, who seemed to see only the dark side.

He knelt down beside the mare, using his right hand to gently prod her side. Then he moved to the mare's bottom to appraise the situation.

"The colt is coming," he announced matter-of-factly, "Do you have any instruments for..."

"Pa has a black bag up at the house."

"Please get it," he said, as he stretched out his right hand to gently stroke the mare's heaving side. "And tell him we can manage."

Could they? she wondered during her flight from the stable to the house. Hank, huddled on the porch step, was firing questions as fast as he could speak.

"Blaze is in labor," she said, rushing past him.

From inside she grabbed the black bag and a towel from the cupboard, then ran breathlessly for the stable.

Suzanne thrust the bag and towel toward Luke, then crumpled down, gasping for breath. She saw that Luke had managed to get both shirtsleeves rolled up, preparing for his role as veterinarian. Her eyes fell to his broad hand, his smooth long fingers, and her confidence was strengthened. Nevertheless, she felt compelled to ask the question that had popped into her mind during her frantic run.

"Have you ever done this?"

"Of course," he answered tersely.

Well, how did she know? She had a right to ask, didn't she? He shot a brief glance in her direction. "The mare does most of the work anyway," he added.

"Oh." She took a deep breath, trying to calm her nerves. She had no choice but to trust him; on the other hand, he could be a godsend.

"Try to keep her still," Luke instructed.

Suzanne placed her hand on the mare's neck and began to murmur words of comfort.

"It's okay," she spoke softly. "We're going to help you get the little one here."

The mare whinnied and made an effort to get up. Suzanne clung to her and began to chatter, saying whatever came to mind.

"We're halfway there," Luke called to her.

His voice floated over Blaze's suffering body, and she thought the man sounded calm, in control. Suddenly she was very glad to have him here with her, doing the work, helping Blaze. Maybe she could put up with his grumpiness a little while longer.

The mare tossed her head back and bared her teeth in a moan of anguish. "Hang on, sweetie," she said, wrapping her arms around the mare's neck, "it's almost over."

"It *is* over," Luke spoke confidently.

Suzanne looked across at him. A gleam of perspiration filled his handsome face, but the blue eyes glowed with pride. For the first time, a broad smile softened that serious mouth. "We have a hearty little male."

"*We do?*" Suzanne squealed, alarming the mare with her outburst. "I'm sorry, Blaze. I didn't mean to startle you, but you have a healthy baby."

The mare heaved one long quivering sigh and sank into the straw, as though she understood what Suzanne had said.

Suzanne unwound her arms from the mare and crawled around to Luke. He was wrapping a towel around the colt and Suzanne stared, feeling a wave of tenderness sweep over her.

"Could I hold him?"

"Careful," Luke instructed, placing the warm, wiggling bundle in her arms.

Suzanne touched the miniature blaze on his forehead. "He's just like his mother. Luke, he's the most beautiful creature I've ever seen," she said.

Luke grinned. "Yeah, he is."

She turned to Luke, smiling warmly. "I don't know how to thank you."

"Seeing the healthy colt is thanks enough," he said, trailing a finger down the colt's forehead. "I've always felt that animals are much kinder than people. I like helping them."

Suzanne opened her mouth to ask just why he felt that way, but something restrained her. He was such a private person, revealing so little about himself.

"I guess we should give him to his mother now," Luke said, "if you can bear to part with him."

Reluctantly, she handed over the colt, and Luke placed him next to Blaze. Suzanne watched, admiring how adeptly Luke managed with only his right hand. She wondered how soon he would be leaving. He had just proven he could fare for himself. He had also proven how desperate they were for help here.

A heaviness tugged at her heart as she stood, brushing the

straw from her dress. "I'll go deliver the news to Pa. He's probably crawling down the path to the stable."

She was surprised to hear Luke chuckle. So he was capable of laughter, after all.

"Then let me go meet him." Luke smiled as he trotted out the door.

Suzanne's heart was full of joy as she looked back at the new colt. She laughed as he searched eagerly for his first meal.

"Suzanne?" Luke called as she reached the door of the barn.

She turned, startled to hear her name on his lips. She hadn't been sure he even remembered it. She looked up as he came running down the path.

"Your pa has turned his ankle again, and he may have injured his ribs as well."

"Oh no! I don't know what I'm going to do with him!"

"Can't you find another ranch hand? You've got to have some help here." Again that irritable tone had crept back to his voice.

"Good help is hard to come by," she said, quoting Hank. Pride kept her from admitting the truth: there was no money for extra help. The only way they could survive was to do the work themselves. And even so, she was beginning to wonder how much longer they could hold on.

She looked at Luke and decided to be forthright. "Maybe we could work something out with you."

He shook his head, looking away. "I have to be on my way soon."

"Oh well." She turned her eyes toward the door, trying to conceal her disappointment. "It was just a thought. Anyway, maybe the colt is a good sign," she called over her shoulder then hurried out.

As she rushed up the path to check on Pa and tell him the good news, she thought again of the sturdy little colt. Sharing something so special had made her realize how lonely she was. She longed to share the joys and tears of life with someone besides her father.

She thought about Luke Thomason, wondering if there was some way they could persuade him to stay on. Even with a bandaged arm, he was far better help than any of the other drifters who hung around the post. He seemed so eager to leave, but maybe, just maybe, he would change his mind.

❈

Luke stared after Suzanne, turning the words she had spoken over and over in his mind. Maybe he had been wrong about her and her pa trying to sucker him into staying. If they were laying a trap for him, she wouldn't have been so nice about it when he'd said he was leaving. Would she?

He turned back to the little colt, smiling as he reached forward to gently touch him. The last hour had brought a warm and tender feeling to his heart. He was relieved to know he could still have such a feeling.

He sighed, leaning back against the straw, thinking about Suzanne again. With straw in her hair and perspiration on her upper lip, she was as appealing as ever. Her eyes had radiated such tenderness and love for the colt. He closed his eyes, wondering how he would feel if she had looked at him that way.

His eyes snapped open. Well, she wouldn't. As for trying to snag him for a husband, the rich rancher—Parkinson, was it?—was the one she was after. Why else would someone go all the way to another ranch for a worship service? It surprised him even more that Mr. Waters was accustomed to going with her.

He snorted. Parkinson didn't have a chance against both of them!

Chapter 7

Suzanne had sneaked quietly into the kitchen and removed the tin can from the top shelf of the cupboard. She didn't want Hank asking any questions. It occurred to her that she was having to sneak around her father a lot lately, but her intentions were good, and for the time being, he needed to be protected.

The tin can served as a bank for their cash. Each time she pulled the can down, it felt lighter and lighter. Today, it practically toppled from her hands. She closed her eyes for a moment, praying she had miscounted yesterday. Surely a couple of bills had been stuck together.

Please, God, she silently prayed as she sucked in her breath and gently eased the lid up. Her hopes sank. Only a few bills nestled in the bottom of the can. She had to think of something! She was no horse trader, but even if she were, Hank had put his foot down. He would hire on as a ranch hand over at Bar X, or mop floors at the trading post before another horse left their pasture.

What alternatives were left? She had never relished the idea of raising pigs or chickens, but she supposed she could learn. And that vegetable garden would have to be a reality now. She could learn anything she put her mind to; besides, what could be so hard about planting seeds in the ground, then watering and weeding?

That simple question prompted a glance out the kitchen window, and she knew there was nothing simple about a vegetable garden.

After much deliberation, she took half the money. She had no choice. The flour and sugar bins were empty, and Pa couldn't survive without his coffee. She'd grown adept at reusing coffee grounds, but there was no point in trying to serve thin brown water.

She sighed. Somehow, a way would be provided. She heard Luke's voice from the front porch and prayed he would change his mind about leaving. He was big and strong, obviously a hard worker, and he seemed to know a lot about horses. Two days had passed since they had worked side by side, delivering the colt. He hadn't mentioned leaving, and she had tiptoed around the subject. Since she had given him the job of feeding the animals, he seemed to take particular delight in his trips down to the stable, checking on Blaze and her colt. He was even offering to ride over the range on his black stallion, but Hank had balked at that.

"Back in my years, I tore open a wound bouncing around in the saddle. You gotta give yourself a couple more days," he had admonished Luke.

She turned back to the bills crumpled in her palm, and thrust them into her drawstring purse, along with the list she had spent hours devising. Only the bare essentials, and those trimmed even further.

Looping her purse strings over her arm, she headed for the front door. She was grateful that at last Pa had someone with whom to discuss land and horses—his favorite subjects. At least, this had kept him on the porch and off the back of Rocky. The rangy bay prowled his pen restlessly, as eager as his master to be streaking across the back forty. Maybe she'd ask Luke to exercise him tomorrow, if he felt up to it. Her eyes darted from Luke to her father as she stepped onto the porch.

"I'm riding over to the trading post for some supplies," she announced. "Also, I'm leaving word for Doc Browning to stop by when he makes the route." She looked at Luke. "It would be a good idea for him to see you too."

"I'm doing fine. Anyway, I'll be leaving soon," he added, looking away.

Those words were like a pinprick in her lungs, deflating all the air. She hadn't realized how much she had hoped, even depended, on him staying on until Pa was better.

Suzanne glanced at her father, thinking how little he knew about the tin can and its dwindling contents. Still, she was pleased to note that he looked cheerful this morning. His gray hair was neatly combed, his beard trimmed, and those gray eyes, faded by the sun and wind, looked rested.

"Luke tells me the colt's doing fine," Hank said.

Suzanne smiled. "Yes, he is."

She started down the steps and saw, to her amazement, that Nellie was already saddled and waiting. She whirled on Hank, ready to fuss at him.

"Hope you don't mind," Luke spoke up. "When your father mentioned you were going into town, I took the liberty of saddling your mare."

"But your shoulder. . . ?"

"I'm okay," he said, frowning at her. He seemed to take offense whenever she questioned his health, so she made up her mind never to mention it again.

"Well, you ain't up to riding all the way to Colorado Springs," Hank said gruffly.

Suzanne glanced sharply at her father. He liked having Luke around; that was obvious.

"Pa, we don't want to detain him when he's ready to leave."

Hank withdrew his pipe from his pocket, saying nothing more.

It was nice to have Nellie all saddled up and ready to go. She was glad Luke had saved her the time and effort. But they could get along without him, she reminded herself stoutly.

"Well, I'll be back in a couple of hours."

"You take care, missy," Hank called after her.

"I can do that better than you," she yelled back.

She mounted sidesaddle, waved to the men, and trotted Nellie down the road to Wiley's Post. Miles of level land stretched around her, bordered by the far-flung fences of Bar X, the biggest ranch in the area. Three smaller ranches made up the remaining territory before the terrain climbed to the Pikes Peak foothills.

It was a big robust land, and she could see why Hank had been so eager to settle here. Yet, this life was hard, requiring so much from them. It wouldn't be a bad life, if only their circumstances were different.

God is our refuge and strength, she told herself. She followed that one up with, *All things work together for good. . .*

Suzanne recalled Luke's suggestion of a ranch hand. Their one experience with hired help had been a disaster. Wally had been a drinker who was undependable and lazy, finally deserting them during a January blizzard. Quickly, she turned her eyes toward a cottonwood thicket, attempting to thwart the memory of the three of them—Pa, Ma, and herself—out, trying to get the horses rounded up. That night Ma had started running a fever and died before Doc Browning could get through the deep snow to see her.

Suzanne prodded her mind back to the present as she cantered Nellie up to the log-post rail. She always enjoyed chatting with Mattie, who managed to make everyone who came around feel better. She slipped down from Nellie and looped the reins around the log hitching rail. She hurried across the plank porch and pressed down the latch of the wide door.

Inside, half a dozen elk and moose racks overhung a blackened stone fireplace in a huge room. The front of the store was devoted to shelves and counters crammed with an assortment of general merchandise. At the rear, a long table, with two adjoining benches, served as dining table for the meals Mattie served to hungry customers. Two cowboys hunched over their coffee cups. Their felt hats sat low on their foreheads, and their range clothes were dusty and wrinkled.

Mary, Suzanne's best friend from Denver, had written letters inquiring if she had found herself a handsome cowboy. "You haven't seen *these* cowboys," Suzanne had written back.

"Well, look who's here," Mattie's strong voice rose above the clatter of dishes.

Suzanne hurried back to the kitchen, a small room filled to bursting, containing an iron cookstove, narrow shelves and counters, and dry goods stacked halfway up the wall.

"Hi, Mattie!" Suzanne called to the woman who was elbow-deep in a dishpan overflowing with soapsuds. The sight of Mattie made Suzanne feel better.

"I've been wondering when you'd come over for a visit," Mattie said, grabbing a cup towel to dry her hands.

Standing five feet ten inches tall, Mattie was the epitome of the sturdy pioneer woman. She joked that she wouldn't serve folks food she hadn't first tasted, and folks laughed with her and thought nothing of her extra pounds. Her fifty-odd years were written boldly in her round face, yet her brown eyes still held a youthful sparkle. The flavor of cinnamon drifted from her muslin apron and calico dress, and Suzanne found that comforting. Her thick brown hair, sprinkled with gray, was drawn into a bun.

"How's your pa?" she asked.

"As cranky as ever. I need the doc to come by and check on him. He had a bad fall this week."

Mattie looked concerned. "Doc Browning will be at Trails End tomorrow morning. They're having a meeting of cattlemen about a drive to Pueblo. He'll check in after the meeting, and I'll send him over. Anything else I can do?"

"No, Luke's keeping him company."

"Luke?" Mattie arched a brow.

It occurred to Suzanne that nobody knew about their strange guest.

"Yes, there's a man—"

"Stage is here," one of the cowboys yelled.

The arrival of the stage twice a week was a major event at the post, prompting Mattie into a frenzy. Mattie brushed past Suzanne with a force that nearly toppled her, had she not grabbed a chair for support, and then she hurried after Mattie.

Like everyone else, Suzanne was curious about the stage

and its passengers. Mattie jerked the door open, admitting the sound of thudding hoofbeats and jingling harness. Driver and team were engaged in a battle of strength, and Suzanne began to wonder who would win. When finally the horses had been wrestled to a halt, and the violently rocking stage had settled, the driver leaned back in the seat, planted a dusty boot on the brake, and tipped his frayed hat at Mattie.

"You're losing ground, Willie!" Mattie laughed.

"I was just teasing Robert," he said, baring tobacco-stained teeth in a wide grin as he turned to his companion, a young cowboy who served as shotgun messenger.

The younger man, not amused, dropped down and hobbled to the stage door, yanking it open. Dust cascaded like a waterfall before he unfolded the iron steps.

Two men, hats askew, tugged irritably at their rumpled clothing as they stumbled down the steps and stared bleary-eyed at the log trading post.

"Got any coffee?" Willie yelled.

"Always got coffee." Mattie motioned them inside. "Tom, put that bottle away," she admonished one of the cowboys at the table. "You know my rules. No drinking."

She turned back to the strangers, entering the post. "You men come inside: I've got beef stew and coffee."

Suzanne trailed after Mattie. "Can I help?"

Mattie, in full stride to the kitchen, merely smiled at Suzanne's offer. "No thanks, honey. I have everything under control, believe it or not."

"I believe it," Suzanne replied, watching in amazement as Mattie poured coffee, dipped stew, and dispensed utensils all at once. And she did it with grace. "I'll just gather up the supplies I need," Suzanne said feebly, aware that nobody was paying her any attention.

She took her time, sauntering around the store, pricing every item.

"Can you find what you need?" Mattie asked, joining her after the men were served.

"Oh sure. Mattie, don't you need some help here? You seem

awfully busy," Suzanne tried to keep her tone casual. She didn't want Mattie to know how desperate they were.

"My sister Lilly is coming soon."

"Is that right?" Suzanne smiled. "Well, I know you'll be glad to have her with you."

Mattie's husband had died the previous year, and Suzanne often wondered how Mattie could possibly do all the work. Yet she did, while maintaining a thriving business and keeping errant cowboys under control.

"Well, you got everything?" Mattie came around behind the board counter and looked at Suzanne.

"I think so. Mattie, I'd like to have a vegetable garden this year. When you have time, could you give me some pointers? You raise lots of vegetables, don't you?"

"I try, but the soil is not as good here as it was back in Dallas." She heaved a sigh. "It's hard work." She paused, as her brown eyes swept Suzanne. "I might just ride over to your place once Lilly comes to relieve me; I could take a look at the soil, tell you what might grow best. And maybe I'll argue a bit with your old man."

Something in the way Mattie spoke those words rang a bell in the back of Suzanne's mind. She recalled seeing Mattie and her pain a spirited political debate around the potbellied stove one winter day. Both had defended their opinions with fiendish delight. Pa had thoroughly enjoyed it.

"Where'd the stranger come from who's staying at your place?" Mattie asked.

"Kansas. He's on his way to Colorado Springs." She frowned. "He made the mistake of stopping in Bordertown and getting in a poker game. A poor loser followed him up the trail, shot, and robbed him. He managed to make it to our valley. I spotted him just before he fell off his horse."

Mattie's mouth fell open. "You don't say? What about the culprit who shot him?"

"He got away."

"A poker game," Mattie said, shaking her head. "There's usually a gun battle afterward. Too bad."

"But Luke isn't really a gambler."

Suzanne recognized the defensive tone in her voice as soon as she had spoken the words. And so had Mattie, whose brown eyes swung to Suzanne with a look of suspicion.

"Young lady, do we need to have a talk?"

Suzanne waved the suggestion aside. "No, he's leaving in a day or so. He's in a big hurry to get to Colorado Springs," Suzanne said, hoping to avoid a lecture from Mattie.

"What does this fellow look like?" she asked.

"Tall, with black hair and blue eyes." Mattie planted her elbows firmly on the counter and leaned forward. "Tall, dark, and handsome," Mattie said, eyeing Suzanne.

"Don't get any ideas," Suzanne scolded. Mattie laughed. "Why not? I'm an old romantic, you know. I don't have a husband anymore, so I just have to enjoy listening to someone else talk about a handsome man. . ."

"I didn't say handsome; you did!"

"But I believe you think so." Mattie grinned.

Suzanne opened her purse. "How much do I owe you?"

Mattie turned and began to tally the items Suzanne had lined up on the counter.

Suzanne waited, growing more nervous with each figure Mattie added to her tablet. Mattie would let her charge, but still. . . .

When Mattie gave her the sum, Suzanne stared at the figures. *That wasn't so bad, after all.*

Suzanne cleared her throat. "Did you add everything? I thought I would owe more."

Mattie grinned. "The good Lord looks out for us."

Suzanne nodded, counting out her money. She still had some change to spare. "Yes, He does. That's one thing I know for sure."

Mattie packaged the supplies while Suzanne said her good-byes and started for the door. The young stagehand rushed up. "Ma'am, let me help you with those packages."

"Why, thank you," she said, smiling at him.

He was polite and sort of handsome, she thought. Maybe it was time she started looking for a husband to help her and Pa run the ranch.

As she tied her bundle onto the saddle horn and waved to the young man, she decided he looked too young to be considered husband material. She sighed, digging her heels into Nellie's side. Maybe she was one of those women who were meant to remain single, although she had always longed for children and a husband who would look at her the way Pa had looked at Ma.

She sighed again, staring across the wide valley to the blazing sunset unfolding on the horizon. To her consternation, she found herself thinking of Luke Thomason again.

She arrived back at the ranch just as the evening shadows had begun to stretch over the valley. Luke stood at the stable door, watching her ride up.

"Make the trip okay?" he asked almost pleasantly.

"Just fine."

He stepped forward and extended his hand as she placed her heel in the stirrup and swung down. His strong grip on her elbow was reassuring, and she smiled her appreciation as he assisted with her packages.

"Your father's feeling a little tired. I insisted on sleeping on the couch tonight so he could go back to his bed. Maybe he'll rest better."

Suzanne nodded, listening as he spoke, and thinking he was being a chatterbox compared to the reserve he normally displayed in her presence.

"I'm going to fetch Doc Browning tomorrow to have a look at Pa. He'll be at the cattlemen's meeting at Trails End in the morning."

"Trails End?"

"The Parkinson ranch that adjoins ours. The ranchers are organizing a cattle drive to Pueblo, and Doc's a cattleman." It was several seconds before Suzanne realized they were staring at each other. "Well," she said, looking away, "I'll go on to the house. Thanks for your help."

"You're welcome," he said, leading her mare into the stable.

Despite her weariness, Suzanne's spirits lifted as she

sauntered up the path to the house. She paused along the way, glancing up at the pale stars already poking their heads through the blue curtain of sky. She took a deep breath of the fresh spring air, inhaling the flavor of the wildflowers blooming down behind the house.

She glanced back at the stable, hearing the sound of a bucket clanging as Luke tended to his chores. Encouraged by Luke's attitude, she decided things weren't really so bad after all. The colt *had* been a good sign.

Her soaring spirits crashed, however, when she walked through the front door and met Hank's angry face. He was seated at the kitchen table, staring down into the cookie tin.

"Why in the world did you spend so much money today?" he growled, eyeing her meager packages. "And what did you buy? Don't look like much."

Suzanne drew a deep breath, wishing she could have better prepared herself for this confrontation.

"I bought flour, sugar, and coffee. A few spices. That's all."

"Horse feed? No horse feed?" he asked in disbelief.

"We have enough for another week—"

"Suzanne, I demand to know when you've spent all this money."

Suzanne set the packages on the table and faced him squarely. "Pa, the money has been dwindling all winter. Ma stretched every dollar, and I've done the same. You shouldn't have bought that last mare. . ."

As the words tumbled out, she realized she had wanted to speak those words for weeks. Pa, as usual, had gotten carried away when it came to horses. His face flushed darkly as he came to his feet, flinched, then slumped back into the chair.

"How am I supposed to run a horse ranch without horses?" he demanded. "You and your ma want to spend all the money on—"

"On what?" Suzanne lashed out, furious now that he had not appreciated their frugality. "Food? Your coffee?"

He looked away, stung by her words. She knew she was inflicting more guilt, but he needed to understand her side of the matter. She should have discussed the situation with him sooner, rather than trying to protect him as Ma had.

"I can do without my coffee. And if our money's gone, I can do without food as well. I'm sending you back to Denver, where you can have a decent life!"

"And that'll solve everything, won't it?" she cried. "Just how do you propose to send me back to Denver when we don't have enough money left to buy oats for the horses?"

As their argument raged, their voices growing louder, they failed to notice Luke Thomason standing in the front door. The board had creaked beneath his boot as he came to an abrupt halt. Suzanne whirled, her cheeks flaming.

Anger was replaced by humiliation when she realized the man had heard everything.

Seeing his error, he turned and headed back to the porch, leaving them to their battle.

Tears filled Suzanne's eyes as she turned and fled to her room. Why did she and her pa always get into a shouting match? Why couldn't life take a turn for the better? Every time she thought it had, something cropped up again, making the situation worse than before.

Tears poured down her cheeks as she bit her trembling lip and decided maybe the argument was a good thing. The truth was out in the open now. Let Pa decide what to do!

A soft knock sounded on the door.

"What is it?" she said, trying to steady her voice.

"Daughter, I'm sorry," Hank said through the closed door. "I know you've done the best you could."

Suzanne grabbed an old bandanna from her dresser and dabbed at her eyes. She couldn't stay mad upon hearing the humility in her father's voice. One thing about Pa, he was never too proud to apologize, and she loved him for that.

She sniffled and cracked open the door.

Hank's cheeks were damp, too, and he seemed to have aged a few more years in the last ten minutes.

"I'm sorry, too," she said, opening the door wider as his thin arms encircled her shoulders, drawing her to him.

"We'll make it," he said, hugging her hard.

Suzanne nodded. "I know." She hugged him back, trying to sound confident. Beneath her fingers, her father's jutting shoulder blades reminded her he had lost more weight. His voice, always so strong, now sounded faint. She bit her lip, no longer confident about anything.

CHAPTER 8

Suzanne rolled over in her bed, squinting up at the shaft of sunlight. What time was it? Had she overslept? She lay there for a moment, trying to analyze why this particular morning seemed different from all the others. She sat up on her elbow, listening. The air felt cold, stale, and the smell of fresh coffee was missing.

She tossed the covers back and grabbed her robe while shoving her feet into her worn house slippers. Remembering Luke Thomason was a guest here, she paused at the door, buttoning her robe all the way to her chin. Then she smoothed her hair back, cracked the door, and peered into the living room.

Luke was nowhere in sight. The blanket was folded neatly at the end of the sofa. Her eyes flew to the closed door of her father's bedroom. Had Pa refused to make coffee because they had argued over the money spent for it? No, he didn't hold grudges or stay mad. She tiptoed across the living room to her father's bedroom and gently turned the knob.

He was still in bed, lying on his side, facing the wall. It wasn't like him to stay in bed so late. Was something wrong? A sudden panic overtook her. The pain of losing her mother was still fresh in her heart. She couldn't begin to comprehend what losing

Hank would mean. Her heart lunged to her throat and for a moment, she was paralyzed by fear. Her lips parted, but she couldn't force herself to call his name. What would she do if he didn't respond? Her eyes clung to his back as her breath froze.

His shoulders rose and fell, ever so slightly. He was breathing evenly; he was all right. She heaved a sigh, weak with relief. She remembered their argument, the worry over money. He'd probably not slept well.

She closed the door gently, not wanting to disturb him.

"Thank You, God," she said aloud, padding back across the living room. As long as Hank was alive, nothing seemed quite so bad. Passing the coffee table, she caught a flash of gold in the sunlight. She stopped, staring for several seconds before she realized what she was seeing. Slowly, she walked to the table and stared down at the wedding band, placed on a sheet of paper.

She sank onto the couch, not touching the ring or the paper, and sat there for a while. Then, drawing a deep breath, she reached forward, gently placing the wedding band on the table, and lifting the letter to read the masculine scrawl.

> I can't thank you enough for saving my life and sharing your home and food with me. I'm leaving the only thing of value that I own. Maybe you can sell it and get some money to tide you over. Thanks for your help.
> Luke Thomason

Suzanne lifted the gold wedding band and studied it thoughtfully. It was not shiny and new, but softly burnished and worn—lovingly worn, no doubt. She turned the ring over, inspecting the inner side as a miniature design caught her eye. Two dainty hearts were joined together, with each heart holding a tiny initial. *G* in one heart, *L* in the other.

Luke.

She stared into space, feeling numbness give way to disappointment. She glanced at the closed door of the bedroom, wondering how Hank would take the news that Luke had deserted them, just when they needed him most. As for the ring, where did he expect her to hock a wedding band?

She leaped from the sofa, pacing the floor. The man would rather part with this ring, a loving link to his wife, than put in a few days' work here, where he could see he was desperately needed!

Coward! She paced a wider circle, her steps moving quickly over the boards. She bit her lip, frustrated to tears, and another emotion battled her senses, frustrating her even more. She had been attracted to this man, and now she hated herself for it.

From the moment she'd found him, injured and bleeding to death, she had been struck by the fact that he was the most handsome man she'd ever seen. And later, as she had cleaned the wound, bound his shoulder, and prepared and served him food, she had felt drawn to him, despite his reserve, which often bordered on rudeness.

Then she had decided he was a widower coming to Colorado Springs to forget the sorrow of losing his wife. She had wanted him to stay here with them, to bring the smile back to Hank's face, to help her through this difficult time.

Her pacing ended at the table as she stared dumbly at the ring, then the letter. She leaned down, folded the letter over the wedding band, and wandered into her bedroom to place both in a drawer.

No way would she sell a wedding band with two hearts joined together just to buy a sack of oats for the horses! The man knew very little about Wiley's Trading Post. Mattie needed cash, not a wedding band; Mattie already had one of those, and she would starve to death before she'd part with it. She couldn't barter a wedding band for a ranch hand, which was what they needed most.

She yanked down her work clothes from a shelf, unable to stem the frustration boiling through her. Of course she could sell gold in Colorado Springs, but she didn't have the money to get there!

"Suzanne..."

"Coming," she called at the sound of her father's voice. She tugged on her clothes and hurried barefoot across the living room floor, poking her head into the bedroom.

"My chest is giving me some trouble this morning," Hank said, pushing himself up on the pillow. "Since you've got Luke to help you, maybe I'll just stay in bed awhile longer."

"Good idea, Pa."

Never could she recall her pa staying in bed. The old fear rose in her anew as she walked to his bed and looked down into his face. She didn't like the bluish tint to his skin. She pressed her palm against his forehead. No fever. She breathed a sigh of relief.

"My ribs are not as sore," he said, attempting a grin. "That's a blessing."

"A big one." She smiled, patting his shoulder. "You lie still while I go whip up the biscuits."

He shook his head. "Don't have any appetite this morning. But I need my coffee."

"You'll have it in a jiffy."

She hurried back to the kitchen, more grateful than ever that she'd bought coffee. There was no point in telling him that Luke had hightailed it. For now, she'd let him think Luke was checking out the back forty.

She grabbed the battered tin pot and reached for the water bucket. She was angrier than ever at Luke—they had saved his life, and yet he had deserted them just when he was needed most.

CHAPTER 9

It was early morning and Luke sat up with his back propped against an aspen tree. He closed his eyes, trying to tell himself he'd done the only thing he could do.

Just before daybreak, he had crept through the darkness to the stable, his bedroll and saddlebags clutched under his right arm. A pale gray light had begun to form on the horizon, and his steps had quickened. Hank would be getting up soon, making coffee. Luke would miss their conversations on the front porch.

He came upon Smoky in the small corral, and his spirits lifted. The big stallion was his best friend; they'd been through hell and high water together. He still counted it a blessing that the no-good thief and back shooter hadn't stolen Smoky. *A blessing*—he was beginning to sound like Suzanne.

He stepped inside the shed to retrieve Smoky's saddle and bridle. The big horse threw his head up and nickered. When Luke lifted the saddle onto Smoky's back, its weight brought a slight twinge of pain to Luke's sore shoulder. The Waterses had done a first-class job of patching him up; the wound was quickly healing.

He started to cinch up the girths, and almost before he

realized it, he was thinking of Suzanne again. She was good with horses; she sat one like she'd been born there.

What would she think when she awoke and found him gone? Would she care? He tried to tell himself that she and her pa would be disappointed that they'd lost a free hand, but those thoughts brought him shame now. His conscience jabbed at him, and the God he had run from had laid a message on his soul: the Waters were true Christians, setting an example of the way people should live. If all people had treated him as they had, he wouldn't have forsaken his faith. Maybe he hadn't forsaken it, after all.

He left the gate open as he entered the corral. Smoky was already pawing the ground. Luke planted a boot in the stirrup and pulled himself into the saddle, surprised not to feel more pain.

He kept a tight rein, walking the stallion slowly out of the corral. Once they reached the back meadow, he gave the big horse his head, and they tore across the valley toward the lowest knoll on Morning Mountain. Once there, he drew rein and shifted in the saddle. Far behind him, he could see the weathered little cabin outlined in gray light, nestled peacefully in the valley. There had been a few times, at that cabin, when he had experienced the kind of peace and contentment he had been seeking for a very long time.

He had known that kind of life once, but it seemed so long ago and far away that he scarcely remembered how he'd felt. He *did* recognize a longing for that kind of life; perhaps it was the reason he felt so restless and unhappy now. Perhaps it was what drove him, harder and harder, to find something worthwhile again.

Last night, hearing the words Suzanne had spoken in the kitchen, knowing for the first time how destitute they were, he couldn't take another bite of food from their table. It would be like taking food out of their mouths!

Lowering his hat over his forehead and shifting his weight in the saddle, he turned his eyes toward the road ahead. A soft ache settled around his heart, but he'd get over it. . .

Morning Mountain

The sound of a prairie dog scampering around the next tree awoke him. He stretched, being careful with his left shoulder, and came slowly to his feet.

He squinted at the road leading to the next ranch. Time to go; time to get on with his life.

CHAPTER 10

"I'm feeling better," Hank called from the kitchen table.

Suzanne was in her bedroom, putting on her riding boots.

"I know." She had been relieved to see that the bluish tint had faded from his skin, but he still looked pale. "I'm just going to make a quick trip over to Trails End to see if Doc Browning has some medicine he wants to send."

Hank was opening his mouth to protest as she hurried off, but she threw up her hand. "Don't waste your breath arguing about it. I'm going," she said and was off.

"Don't have any breath to waste," Hank muttered as the front door closed.

❧

The Little River Cattlemen's Association had been meeting at Trails End once a month to discuss cattle prices and markets. The purpose of today's meeting was to cover last-minute details of the cattle drive south to Pueblo.

Arthur Parkinson stood on his porch, looking from Arthur Junior, lounged against a post, to the ranchers gathered. There was Ben Graves, Harry Stockard, John Grayson, and now a tall, dark-haired stranger who had just ridden up, seeking work.

"What did you say your name was?" he asked.

"Luke Thomason." He looked Parkinson straight in the eye and spoke calmly. "I've been on cattle drives in Kansas. I know what has to be done."

Parkinson turned and looked at the other men, who nodded their approval.

"All right," he said, "you're hired. We'll be leaving tomorrow. In the meantime, you can put your gear in the bunkhouse and head to the cattle pens to help the hands."

"Thank you, sir." At that, Luke turned and left.

Arthur stared after him momentarily, noting the way he held his left arm close to his side. Still, he looked strong enough. He'd probably do as well as the others, maybe better.

"Here comes Doc Browning," one of the ranchers spoke up. "He's the last one to vote on the price we're accepting for the cattle. Now maybe we can finally get this thing settled and be on our way."

A white horse cantered up the driveway, and the men began to wave.

Nathaniel Browning was a native of St. Louis, attending medical school there, yet choosing the wide open spaces of Colorado to practice medicine. He was a short, rotund man with a giant heart and a penchant for raising cattle.

He had just arrived at the gathering and greeted the other ranchers when once again attention was diverted to another rider loping up the drive.

"It's Miss Waters," Art said, coming to life for the first time all day.

He bounded down the steps and waited at the hitching rail as Suzanne reined Nellie in. She accepted Art's hand as she tumbled from the horse, smiled briefly at him, then made a dash for the front porch.

"Miss Waters, what brings you over?" Art called to her.

"My father." She headed straight for Doc Browning. "Please, come over and take a look at him."

Doc Browning patted her shoulder. "Relax, young lady. Mattie told me about his fall, but he's too stubborn not to mend."

He turned to the other men. "Have you men got all the details in order?"

"Just need your vote on the price."

"You have it." he waved a hand dismissively. "Anything else?"

"We're short a cook. Ned's come down sick. Of course Rosa is still going," Arthur stated with a frown.

One of the ranchers groaned. "Without Ned there to keep the chili peppers out of everything, we'll be holding our stomachs."

"Why doesn't someone persuade Mattie to go along?" Doc suggested. "Mattie's a fine cook."

"Who'd keep the post open?" Parkinson frowned.

Suzanne had only half-listened to the conversation until now, but suddenly her attention was riveted to the subject at hand.

"I can cook," she offered, looking from one man to the other. "How much are you paying?" She knew she could work out the details if she could have an opportunity to earn some money for the ranch.

Art was at her side instantly. "Oh no, Miss Waters, you wouldn't want to consider anything like that."

The men turned startled faces to the pert young woman dressed like a cowhand, but looking quite feminine with flowing blond hair and fair skin.

"It'd be too hard on you, Suzanne," the older Parkinson cut the idea short. "We'll find someone. Doc, Mrs. Parkinson is overseeing a big lunch. Why don't you check on Hank and then come back and eat fried chicken?"

"Good idea," he nodded, rubbing his paunch. The subject of food was always of interest to him. "Let's go, young lady."

Doc Browning took his time placing his stethoscope back in his black bag, zipping the bag, then turning to Hank, lounged on the couch. Suzanne hurried in from the kitchen, bearing a tray. Doc rubbed his stomach, remembering he'd missed breakfast. He reached for the mug of coffee and began to munch the fluffy hot biscuit.

"Young lady, this may be the best biscuit I ever put in my mouth," he said, around a generous bite. "But don't tell Mrs. Browning." He winked.

Hank looked disinterestedly at the biscuits, then fixed a keen eye on the doctor. "Did I crack another rib?"

Hank was dressed in fresh clothes with his gray hair whisked back from his face, his beard neat. Suzanne had been relieved not to have to tangle with him about his appearance; in fact, he had been quietly cooperative when she'd informed him the doctor was coming. And this, too, worried Suzanne, knowing it was highly out of character for Hank. She wondered if he was depressed over Luke leaving. He'd had very little to say since she had broken that news.

"Your ribs will heal," Doc answered, "and your ankle's doing okay. That's not what has me worried."

Fear clutched Suzanne's heart. "What's wrong with him?"

Doc finished the biscuit and reached for his coffee. He seemed to be stalling for time as he gathered his thoughts. "I'd like Hank to see a doctor in Colorado Springs," he finally replied. "I'm afraid there might be a problem with his heart."

"His heart?" Suzanne repeated, dropping into the nearest chair.

"Aw, Doc, there's nothing wrong with my heart. My chest is just sore from the fall I took."

The doctor appraised him gravely. "Hank, your heart's beating too fast."

"It's 'cause I got all worked up yesterday," Hank said in a rush, glancing at Suzanne.

"Too fast?" Suzanne echoed. She had resorted to repeating everything the doctor said, but she couldn't seem to form her own words around the fear that was growing in her heart.

"Maybe it'll correct itself in a day or two," the doctor offered hopefully. "Maybe not." He sipped his coffee, staring at the floor for a few seconds. "I read in my medical journal about a new medicine that slows the heartbeat. And I know a special doctor in Colorado Springs who treats patients with heart conditions."

Suzanne took a deep breath, trying to rally her voice since

Hank had suddenly gone speechless.

"Well, of course we'll go to Colorado Springs," she said, hardly hearing her words above the fierce pounding of her heart. "We can—"

"I'm not going anywhere!" Hank protested. "If the old ticker's going out, there's nothing they can do. I lost a friend in Denver that way. It'd just be a waste of time and money..." His voice trailed, as he avoided Suzanne's face.

She stared at her father. Money, that was what was keeping him from seeing a doctor. Her father was a reasonable man, despite his gruffness. When Doc Browning thought his condition was serious enough to go to Colorado Springs, her father would be willing. It was that nearly empty cookie tin that brought this protest.

"Hank, your heartbeat is strong," Doc continued smoothly, "and you're in pretty good physical condition, considering how rough you treat yourself. That medicine may be all you need to get straightened out."

"What medicine?" Suzanne asked, seizing the hope Doc offered.

"The name wouldn't mean anything to you, but I hear it helps folks. Tell you what," he said, coming to his feet. "I have a colleague who'll be coming in from St. Louis in a day or two. I'll bring him out for a look at Hank. If he agrees with me, I'm going to insist you two go to Colorado Springs."

Silence settled over the room, broken only by the creak of a floorboard as Doc headed for the door.

"We'll think about this," Suzanne said, reaching for the bundle of biscuits and placing them in Doc's hands. He looked from the muslin-wrapped gift back to Suzanne and smiled, understanding this was his payment for seeing Hank.

"You take care," he called to Hank, as Suzanne walked him out the door. She followed him to the hitching rail, where his white horse pawed restlessly.

"Doc, I need your help," she blurted. Her outburst startled him. He was about to place a boot in the stirrup, but now he hesitated, looking at the young woman whose gray eyes were fixed worriedly on his face. "What can I do?" Doc asked earnestly.

"There's no money left for this medicine or a trip to Colorado Springs. If I can persuade Pa to go over and stay in one of Mattie's cabins, I want to go on that cattle drive and help Rosa cook."

He began to shake his head. "It would be too rough—"

"Doc," she cried, "who do you think runs this ranch now? And nothing could be rougher on me than watching Pa lie in there sick and helpless, knowing we can't afford the medicine he needs."

Doc lifted a hand to stroke his chin. "It's a good idea about him staying at Mattie's place. If he got worse, she could get word to me a lot quicker than if you two were over here by yourselves."

Suzanne nodded, already making plans. "I can pay Mattie back for her trouble."

"Mattie's got a heart of gold," Doc said, turning his eyes from Suzanne back to the cabin. Maybe it wasn't such a bad idea. Still, there had to be an easier way. "Young lady, don't you two have family up in Denver? Surely, there's somebody to help you."

She shook her head sadly. "No, there's no one. Ma's parents died years ago, and Pa was an orphan. There's only an uncle, and he's the one who cheated us." She bit her lip, fighting tears. "I have to do something, Doc. I'm the only one who can. Please put in a word for me with the ranchers. I can cook for them, you know I can."

He sighed. "Well, if the rest of your cooking matches these biscuits, those men'll be glad to have you along. And Rosa would be there. . ." He mulled the words over, obviously contemplating the prospect of Suzanne on a cattle drive.

"Doc, will you talk the ranchers into letting me come along? Please!"

She hated begging, but she would swallow her pride and do anything to help her father. He was all she had.

"Who'll take care of your horses?"

"Did I hear you say it was only a two-day trip?"

He nodded, stroking his chin. "Pedro owes me a favor. He's a bit slow but honest and dependable. He's been laid up at my place. Maybe I'll send him over here to see to things while you and Hank are away. We're talking four days at the most."

Suzanne grabbed his sleeve. "Doc, if you'll help me with this, I'll never forget it. God bless you!" She leaned up to plant a kiss on his cheek.

Doc Browning grinned down at the pretty young woman, who was about as desperate for help as anyone he'd encountered. How could he refuse? "All right, missy. But you don't know what you're letting yourself in for." He smiled tenderly. "Guess it wouldn't matter. You're about as stubborn as Hank!"

CHAPTER 11

It had taken both Mattie and Suzanne pleading, arguing, then resorting to threats, before Hank finally realized he was out-numbered and overpowered and gave in. Suzanne suspected it was Mattie's promise of lively conversation with cowboys and stage hands that had finally won him over.

Now, as she stood in the kitchen at Trails End, helping Rosa box up supplies, she felt a sense of relief. . .and adventure. She'd been stuck at the ranch for so long, she'd forgotten how excited she could get over a trip, even though this one was a bit different.

She grabbed a box and headed out the back door to the chuck wagon, humming softly. Just as she rounded a corner of the house, she almost collided with a tall cowboy with blazing blue eyes. She gasped, losing hold of the box. She would have spilled everything there in the dust, if he hadn't reached out to recover the tilting box.

"What are you doing here?" Luke stormed at her.

All the frustration that had been gathering since his departure erupted from her lips. "That's none of your business. Anyone who would run out in the middle of the night, without so much as a good-bye—" She broke off, realizing that she was betraying her emotions. She took a firm grip on the box and sidestepped him.

"Wait a minute." He caught up, grabbing her arm. "I didn't run out. I left a note. Besides, I told you I would be leaving."

"Miss Waters!" Art Parkinson's voice echoed from the opposite side of the yard. He was waving frantically.

She acknowledged him with a nod, smiling blankly.

Luke took a step closer, lowering his voice. "I couldn't take advantage of your hospitality any longer. I needed money. When you mentioned cowhands were being hired for this drive—"

"You're going, too?" she gasped, then tried to steady her voice. "Well, what you do is your business. You can pick up your wedding ring when we return." Her eyes sliced over his face. "I've never needed money badly enough to sell someone's wedding ring. But then," she added bitingly, "perhaps I have more respect for wedding vows than you do."

His dark brows shot up; then his blue eyes clamped into a scowl. She sensed she had gone too far, and now that she had vented her temper, her nerve was deserting her.

"If you'll step aside," she spoke calmly, "I have to get this to the wagon."

A bewildered look settled over Luke's features. "Did you take a job here?" he asked, falling in step beside her.

"I'm going on the cattle drive. I'll be helping Rosa cook."

His mouth fell open. "You can't be serious."

Again, Suzanne was struggling to keep her temper in tow. "Of course I'm serious! And from now on, I'd appreciate it if you'd do your job and let me do mine." She slid the box into the wagon while he stared at her. "Excuse me," she said, sidestepping him as she turned back up the path to the kitchen.

She was practically running by the time she reached the kitchen door. *Luke Thomason! Of all times and places!*

It occurred to her that she had never been so rude to anyone in her life, but she couldn't worry about that now, and she couldn't think about him. She had a job to do.

Rosa stood at the kitchen sink, scrubbing an iron kettle. She was a large Latin woman with warm brown eyes, an abundance of black hair, and a friendly, toothless smile.

Suzanne took a deep breath and smiled at Rosa. "Rosa, what's to go in the wagon next?" she asked, staring at the kettle while seeing Luke's blazing blue eyes.

⚬

Arthur Parkinson stood at the wagon, staring up at Rosa and Suzanne. Rosa gripped the reins with confidence, her ample body planted firmly on the wooden seat, one booted foot resting on the brake. Beneath her wide hat, Rosa smiled at Mr. Parkinson, assuring him they were ready.

So why does he look so worried? Suzanne pondered as he lingered, glancing once more at Suzanne. She felt a stab of guilt, knowing Mr. Parkinson didn't want her along. It had been the badgering of Doc, and probably Art Jr., that had forced him to give in.

He drew a breath and began to explain the hazards of their trip: dust, the threat of bad weather, even the possibility of rustlers along the way. He reminded the ladies they were solely in charge of the food wagon, preparing the meals and cleaning up afterward. With over a thousand head of cattle, the men had all they could do to keep the temperamental cattle watered, grazed, and moving in the right direction. They couldn't be worrying about the womenfolk.

Suzanne listened politely, watching the lines deepen in Mr. Parkinson's face as he detailed the problems. When finally he wound down, Suzanne gave him a reassuring smile.

"We'll do our part," she promised, remembering the generous salary they had agreed upon. It would be enough to get her and Hank to Colorado Springs for a doctor and medicine. "And don't concern yourself with me. I'll be just fine," she added.

Mr. Parkinson stared at her for a moment, looking unconvinced. Then he turned his attention to the wagon, checking over the supplies. Suzanne shifted on the seat and peered back into the wagon bed, literally a kitchen on wheels; tools, ropes, and a water barrel were attached to the outside. She couldn't imagine one more item being crammed aboard.

"See you up the trail," he concluded, climbing on his big horse, wheeling around, and cantering back to his men.

As Rosa clucked to the team, Suzanne clutched the edge of the seat and the wagon rocked from side to side, moving them out ahead of the herd. They were supposed to get a head start to ensure arrival at the campsite in time to set up for the meal.

As the wagon swung past the cowboys lined up at the corral waiting to herd the cattle, Suzanne spotted Luke in the rear. He was wearing leather chaps, spurs, and range clothes. His blue eyes watched from the narrow space between the low brim of his hat and the bandanna he was pulling over the lower half of his face.

She glanced at the other cowboys. They, too, had covered their faces to ward off the dust they would be eating along the trail.

"Be careful, Miss Waters," Art called to her. He had just arrived, tugging on a hat that looked too wide for his head.

"I will," she called, turning her attention to the road.

Everyone had a bandanna, she noticed, even Rosa. She took a deep breath, wondering why she hadn't thought of it. Well, she would manage, she vowed, watching the brown dust swirl up around the wagon wheels.

They stopped just past noon for a quick lunch while the cattle grazed and drank from a stream. She passed out the egg sandwiches that she and Rosa had packed, along with apples and tea cakes.

The cowboys had seemed self-conscious around her at first, but now they were eyeing her more boldly when Mr. Parkinson's back was turned. Art was clearly irritated by their impudence, and he glared at one, then the other, as he strode through the group to catch up with Suzanne.

"Miss Waters!"

Suzanne turned.

Art's long, gangly legs ate up the distance between them. "I thought you might need this." He proudly extended a clean bandanna.

"Why, Art, how thoughtful of you."

"I was afraid you wouldn't think of that," he said with a laugh, setting his Adam's apple in motion.

"Thank you. . ." Her voice trailed as Luke stood before her, his hand outstretched for his lunch.

His blue eyes held a look of irritation, as if he was angry with her again. But then she saw that his eyes were sliding toward Art, who was jauntily walking back to his horse.

She dropped the wrapped sandwich into his broad palm, her hand accidentally brushing his. She felt a nervous jolt. Averting her eyes, she moved on, distributing the remaining lunches.

She scarcely had time to gulp down her own sandwich before Rosa motioned for her to help repack the wagon. Suzanne quickly complied, and soon they were back on the trail again.

Far in the distance behind them came the herd, spreading across the plains like a giant brown wave, kicking up clods of dust that seemed to float forward, reaching Rosa and Suzanne. She glanced down at her clothes and saw that they were now rumpled and layered with dust.

Suzanne glanced again at the enormous herd that bawled and bellowed and kicked up enough dust to fill a canyon. She realized at once that she'd taken on an even greater challenge than trying to run the ranch while her father was laid up. But lunch had been a snap; she would eat dust for two days, if that's what it took. She was thankful that Rosa was her companion now, for the woman kept up a lively conversation as she guided the horses. Her words were a mix of Spanish and English, and at times, Suzanne had to guess at what she meant. Still, she enjoyed hearing stories of Mexico City, Rosa's hometown.

By midafternoon, even Rosa was too weary to talk, and they lapsed into silence as each woman fixed gritty eyes on the horizon.

A shout grew closer and Suzanne leaned out to peer around the back of the wagon. Mr. Parkinson was waving his hat in a circle around his head. She tapped Rosa on the shoulder and motioned for her to look back.

"Stopping for the night," Rosa interpreted, pointing to a grassy valley just ahead.

After their wagon had clattered to a halt in the pasture, Suzanne hopped down, then almost fell flat on her face. She had been sitting for so long that her legs were cramped and stiff; she could hardly walk.

She removed her hat and scratched the crown of her damp head while she squinted back toward the approaching herd. The riders had fanned out, giving the cattle more room as they moved into the far end of the valley. Her eyes scanned the group of cowboys until she spotted Luke, who was intent on keeping the yearlings in line and discouraging strays. He was holding his left arm close to his chest. She wondered if his shoulder was hurting. Well, she couldn't be worrying about him. She had her pa to think about.

Suzanne wandered to the nearest shade tree and dropped down, pressing her weary back against its trunk. They had left Morning Mountain far behind, and she found herself missing that special place that seemed to anchor her at all times. It was a comforting presence to her; as Pa said, it was a place to rest weary eyes and hearts.

Rosa waddled over and sank down in the grass, stretching her large body into a full recline. Suzanne bit her lip, trying not to laugh. She probably had the right idea, Suzanne decided, wishing she had the courage to plop down like that and think nothing of it. Then, as she spotted Mr. Parkinson cantering up, she was glad that she was seated properly against the tree.

"You ladies can rest a bit. We'll need to get water for ourselves and the herd." He looked at Rosa. "Can we eat in an hour?"

Her wide hat bobbed a nod.

"Miss Waters, you see where the stream is, don't you? Over there where the cottonwoods form a line," he said, pointing to the trees. "Help yourself to a fresh drink."

"Thank you," she murmured, dragging herself to her feet. She was even more thirsty than tired, if that were possible, for she and Rosa had drained the canteen two hours earlier.

She stumbled through the thick meadow grass to the line of trees, where a stream wound down the valley like a silver thread. She tossed her hat down and stretched out on the bank, lowering her hands into the chattering stream. She cupped her hands to scoop up the cool water, bringing it quickly to her parched lips. She slurped the water greedily, relishing its chill on her tongue.

———✦———

Luke was aching from head to toe, but the ache in his body and the grit on his tongue did not compare to the mounting frustration he suffered watching the gangly Parkinson kid make a fool of himself. He was still wet behind the ears and about as subtle as a bull.

Surely Suzanne wasn't serious about him. But if she wasn't, why was she so friendly with him? Why did she smile and flirt?

He dragged down from Smoky, trying not to grimace from the throbbing pain in his shoulder. Nobody had guessed he was injured, much less lying unconscious and close to death, only a week ago. Somehow he couldn't bring himself to ask Suzanne to keep it quiet. But he had a hunch she would anyway.

Thinking of his own health brought his worries back to what he had heard about Hank Waters on the long dusty stretch of road from Trails End. A twinge of guilt hit him and he began to walk toward the chuck wagon, parked farther up in the meadow. This was free time; most of the guys were doing as they pleased. There was no reason he couldn't have a word with Suzanne. Only there was no such thing as just a *word* with her. Each conversation seemed to end up in an argument.

He knew most of the time it was his fault. He had a bad attitude, but he was trying to change. He frowned. When had he started trying? Soon after he'd met Suzanne. He realized *why* as he spotted her walking toward the trees. Her blond hair glinted in the afternoon sunlight, and from the way she was hobbling across the meadow, he guessed she was as tired as he. Yet, she was the bravest woman he had ever known—except perhaps his mother. In many ways, Suzanne reminded him of her. Perhaps sometime he'd get around to telling her that, and he'd tell her exactly why.

Suzanne drank her fill and lay exhausted for a moment. Something moved beside her, prompting her to roll her head in the grass and look up. She saw a pair of dusty black boots. Slowly, ever so slowly, her eyes traveled from the pointed toes of the boots, up the leather chaps and silver belt—she noted the silver buckle; it appeared to be a rodeo trophy—and on to the collarless cotton shirt. Luke Thomason stood over her. He had removed the bandanna, along with his hat, and now his thick hair was damp and curling on the ends. Suzanne stared at his head, thinking most women would envy that kind of hair.

"How's the water?" he asked.

"Wonderful." She scrambled for her hat and was trying to work her stiff muscles into standing when his gloved hand touched her arm.

"Wait just a minute, please."

She stiffened, wondering what he was going to say. Well, she was in no hurry, and besides, she had been feeling pretty guilty for bawling him out so badly back at the ranch.

She turned and scanned the lush meadow, now a beehive of activity with bawling cattle, irritable shouts from weary cowboys, and the unpleasant smells associated with the beasts.

"Don't worry, I'm not going to say anything about your. . . injury. I doubt that you told them the condition your shoulder was in."

She watched his eyes drop and she knew her guess had been right.

"It's up to you if you want to abuse your body," she said. "I have enough to worry about without being a gossip or worrying about you."

"I came to speak with you about your father," he said, looking back at her.

At those words, and the gentle manner in which he spoke them, Suzanne relaxed her tense shoulders and looked away. Turning back, she stared into Luke's blue eyes as he dropped down beside her, puzzled by his change of attitude.

"Mr. Parkinson told us you had come on this drive to earn

money for your father—that he needed to see a doctor in Colorado Springs about his heart. He never mentioned a heart condition to me."

Suzanne's eyes dropped to her hands, nervously bunching the meadow grass. "We just found out the morning you left. Doc Browning came and checked him over. He said Pa's heart was beating too fast."

"If I had known. . ." his voice trailed as he stared at the western sun, a red ball of fire on the horizon.

"I guess there was nothing you could do," Suzanne replied. "It's just that I had grown to depend on you and I had no right to do that." She hesitated, then added, "I'm sorry I spoke sharply to you this morning."

"You did have a right," he said, looking thoughtful. "You saved my life. I figure you're entitled to something in return."

She tilted her head to search his face. "You've repaid the debt by helping out for a few days. And you delivered the colt! We were getting spoiled by you; that's why we hated for you to leave." Her expression changed from sadness to concern. "How's your shoulder?"

"I'm fine." His chest rose and fell as he took a deep breath and slowly released it.

His eyes drifted slowly over her face, and Suzanne felt her heart skip a beat. What did he really think of her? What was he thinking now? She liked him, even more than she wished to admit to herself. She just didn't know what to *do* about it.

"After I rode off, I felt guilty," he said. "I should have said good-bye properly, but. . ."

"You tried to make amends by leaving the ring."

"Suuu-zannne," Rosa's strong voice belted across to her, and Suzanne dragged herself upright.

"I have to get supper," she said, turning to go. Then she forced her aching muscles into a stiff run back to the chuck wagon.

Luke stared after her, ashamed of himself. He had been all wrong about their motives in helping him. It was obvious now that they hadn't been trying to trap him or force him to stay. She was still being nice to him; she was still concerned about his health. And she hadn't told on him, like some women would have done if they had felt jilted. Jilted? Why had he thought of that word? There was no courtship between them. But then. . .he would never jilt a woman like Suzanne. He only wished circumstances were different, he wished. . .

He tore his mind away from such foolish thoughts and turned to get a drink of water.

❦

Suzanne realized, guiltily, that Rosa had already heaved the chuck box from the rear of the wagon and was opening the hinged lid. Cubbyholes and drawers held cutlery, plates, and other staples. From the depths of the box, Rosa removed coffee beans and a grinder.

"I'll get the water," Suzanne offered, grabbing the enormous coffeepot.

Soon they were busily preparing the evening meal. She and Rosa had decided on bacon, beans, and biscuits, topped off with Rosa's fried apple pies. Somewhere in the background, one of the cowboys was playing a harmonica. The jaunty tune he played flowed over the camp, and slowly the cowboys relaxed after their hard day's work, smiles returning to their wind-whipped faces.

Suzanne's eyes trailed from the group back to the skillet of bacon she was frying; she loved to watch the meat sizzle, breathe the unique aroma. She lifted her eyes again, this time to the cottonwood trees where a breeze rippled the leaves. The breeze grew stronger, stretching across the valley—a cooling relief from the heat of the day.

The man playing the harmonica had launched into a lively version of "Oh! Susanna," and a tall cowboy was belting out the chorus while the others tapped their feet, clapped, and stole glances at her.

Even Luke was watching her with a rare grin.

She looked away, embarrassed, but suddenly was very glad that she had come.

Later, as the men sat around the fire, sampling her biscuits and murmuring their approval, Suzanne stole a glance at Luke.

He was watching her, she was sure of it. Yet, when she looked at him, his blue eyes skittered over her head, as though he were observing something in the distance.

Daylight gave way to darkness and the men sat around in groups, drinking coffee, discussing the next day's plans.

"Are you doing all right, Miss Waters?" Art asked, slinking up from the darkness.

She gasped and whirled, pressing her hand to her bosom. "You startled me," she exclaimed.

"I'm real sorry," he said, looking distressed.

"That's okay, Art. I'm just a bit jumpy. And I'm doing just fine. Thank you for asking."

He stood with his head tilted, staring down into her face, his arms dangling awkwardly at his sides. As Suzanne looked at him, she realized that any hope of caring for Art had vanished since she'd met Luke. The thought startled her—she and Luke had never even spoken romantically. But she knew that she couldn't settle for anything less than true love, and Art couldn't draw that from her with any amount of attention.

"Excuse me, I need to ask Rosa something," she said, smiled briefly, then sidestepped him.

She didn't want Mr. Parkinson upset with her for distracting his son. Furthermore, she was in no mood to keep up a polite charade with Art. He was beginning to wear on her nerves. For some reason, whenever Art came around, she found herself stealing a glance at Luke, trying to gauge his reaction. He didn't seem to notice Art's attention to her. Or if he did, he certainly didn't appear to care.

Everyone took turns being watchman, so the cattle were never left unattended. Suzanne's eyes followed Luke when his turn came to mount his horse and ride the perimeter.

His profile was a silhouette in the darkness, but she could see that he still favored his left side, leaning forward in the saddle, working the horse's reins with his right hand.

"Miss Waters?"

Mr. Parkinson stood over her.

"Yes, sir?"

"You and Rosa throw your bedrolls here beside the chuck wagon," he said wearily. "You'll have more privacy. I'll see that you're not disturbed."

"We'll be fine," she replied quickly.

She believed he considered her to be one more responsibility added to his load. Hating to cause him more concern, she was determined to be as helpful as possible.

After she and Rosa had cleaned up and put everything back in the chuck box, she settled down with her bedroll. From the depths of her pants pocket, she retrieved a tiny square of folded paper. She shook the dust from the paper, frowning, as she gently opened it, careful not to tear the sheet.

The verses she had copied were dim in the light of the lantern mounted on the wagon, but she knew them by heart anyway. Her eyes slipped down the list, pausing on the last one.

"I can do all things through Christ which strengtheneth me."

She thought of this cattle drive, of Luke, and finally of Pa. *God, please make him well*, she silently prayed. Then she folded the paper and nestled down in her sleeping bag, too weary to pray more.

CHAPTER 12

Suzanne felt a weight on her shoulder, pressing down, pressing harder. Someone was shaking her. Her eyes, gritty from trail dust, dragged open. Rosa's toothless smile greeted her.

She popped up on her elbow, looking around. Some of the men were already up, moving about the herd, checking the horses. She bolted from her bed and fumbled for her boots. Rosa began to motion her toward the back of the wagon. There waited a pan of water and a clean towel.

"Thanks, Rosa, you're a dear!" Suzanne smiled at her.

Suzanne turned and began splashing water onto her face. Her skin tingled from the coolness of the water, and slowly her brain began to clear. She found her mirror, whisked her hair back into a braid, then joined Rosa at the fire.

Although she had spent the night sleeping on the ground, she felt surprisingly well. She fell quickly to the task of mixing biscuits, then relieving Rosa at the big frying pan, where slabs of bacon sizzled. The smell drifted over the cool spring morning, and Suzanne quietly prayed for a good day.

After breakfast, Mr. Parkinson came up, taking the chuck box from Suzanne's hands and fitting it into the wagon for her.

"You ladies, hurry up," he said. "With luck, we'll make it into Pueblo by dark." He held himself erect, squaring his shoulders as though preparing to go to battle.

Pueblo served as a crossroads for travelers flooding into Colorado. It also provided a railhead for shipping cattle. It was a bawdy, dusty settlement nestled in a wide valley, looking rather plain to Suzanne compared to her hometown of Denver. But Suzanne and all the others on the cattle drive considered it paradise after another day beneath a blazing, merciless sun.

During lunch break tempers started flaring among the cowboys. Luke looked out of sorts. Even Art seemed rather sullen. Rosa, usually cheerful and pleasant, had lapsed into silence until the dust-layered chuck wagon lumbered into the outskirts of Pueblo. Then she blew a huge sigh and turned to give Suzanne a wide smile.

"Mr. Parkinson said to look for the Antlers Hotel," Suzanne instructed her. "That's where we'll be staying tonight."

Both women squinted into the setting sun as the wagon clattered down the narrow main street. A couple of general stores, two banks, a livery, and a narrow, two-story hotel were scattered about with a number of saloons sandwiched in between. Music drifted through the saloon's swinging doors, as women in colorful dresses beckoned cowboys inside.

Suzanne turned on the seat and glanced around the town.

"That's the only hotel I see." Suzanne pointed to the building on the comer. Trail dust gritted against her teeth as she spoke. "Yes, there's the sign, Antlers Hotel!"

Rosa carefully guided the wagon onto the side street that paralleled the hotel and stomped a boot to the brake. Suzanne leaned back in the seat, wondering if she could possibly walk after another day of sitting on the hard wagon seat.

They were just getting their feet planted solidly on the ground when Mr. Parkinson rode up.

"I'm going in to pay for your rooms," he called to them. "The others can fend for themselves. Art and I will be staying here, too, if you need anything." His eyes lingered on Suzanne.

"We'll be fine." She smiled back, wishing he would stop

worrying about her.

"In the morning, Johnny, my best cowhand, will escort you back to the ranch. The rest of us will be staying on to sell the cattle and take care of business."

"Thank you, Mr. Parkinson," Suzanne called after him, but he was already around the side of the building. "He's always in a hurry, isn't he?" she commented to Rosa.

As the women entered the hotel, Suzanne could tell from the shocked stares of those in the lobby that she and Rosa looked a mess. The desk clerk took a step backward as she and Rosa approached the counter, and he shoved the registration form across for their signatures. They must smell like cattle, too!

"You do it." Rosa handed her form to Suzanne, who signed for her.

"Second floor, last room on the right," the desk clerk quickly instructed, handing each of them a key. "Will you be wanting a tub of water? It comes with the room."

"That would be wonderful," Suzanne replied.

They hurried up the steps, trying to ignore the shocked faces of two proper women, on the arms of their husbands. On the second floor, Suzanne found her room and pointed Rosa toward hers. She unlocked the door and stepped into a small yet nicely decorated room with polished mahogany furniture. A marble-topped nightstand held a kerosene lamp beside a lush bed. She stared at the bed for a moment, taking a deep, long breath. She couldn't wait to hop in!,

Then her eyes fell to her dusty boots. Out of respect for the carpet, she reached down and removed her boots, careful not to add any more dust to the mounting pile. Depositing her overnight bag, she slipped off her woolen socks and sauntered to the window to raise the shade.

Below her, the busy street was filled with horses, wagons, and an assortment of people. She recognized two cowboys from the cattle drive. They were pushing through the bat wing doors of a saloon across the street. She pressed her face against the window, peering from right to left. Where was Luke? she wondered. Probably in the saloon already. She lowered the shade and sighed. She had hoped he wouldn't forget the lesson he had learned from his last poker game.

The knock on the door turned out to be her tub, carried by two stout men who eyed her curiously. Suzanne didn't notice their stares, as her eyes drifted longingly to the tub. The men then brought up pails of hot water. As soon as they left, she forgot about Luke, the long trail, and everything else for the next glorious hour as she soaked in the tub.

When finally Suzanne felt squeaky clean and presentable in a floral cotton she had tucked into her satchel, she left her room. She knocked on Rosa's door, planning to invite the older woman to dinner, but from the sound of the snores audible through the wooden door, Rosa had forgotten food.

Suzanne ventured cautiously down the stairs, wondering what Mr. Parkinson expected them to do about supper. She had brought the last dollar from the cookie tin, hoping it would be enough to cover her expenses until Mr. Parkinson paid her.

As she stepped into the crowded lobby and glanced around, she heard her name shouted above the murmur of voices.

Art Parkinson came, fresh from a bath and shave, dressed smartly in a topcoat over black trousers. From the looks of the crisp white shirt, she suspected his first stop in town had been the general store.

"I was on my way to your room to see if I could buy you supper," he said, beaming at her.

Suzanne hesitated. Automatically, her eyes slipped over the lobby. Luke was nowhere in sight.

"The dining room is filling up fast," he continued, "but we can still get a seat."

She smiled up into Art's angular face. She should be grateful someone wanted to escort her to the dining room.

"That's very sweet of you," she said, taking his arm.

She dragged her eyes from the lobby of strangers and walked with Art into the dining room, unaware that Luke was just entering the hotel. And now he was watching her walk away with Art.

Luke entered the opposite side of the dining room, carefully selecting a table in a far corner. He sat in back of Suzanne so he could observe her without her knowing it.

Taking a deep breath, he studied the menu that had been handed to him. He had been starved when he had arrived at the hotel, half-hoping to invite Suzanne to eat with him. Mr. Parkinson had given them a slight advance to see them to Pueblo, and he hadn't spent any of it. There was enough to buy dinner for two this evening.

How could he have forgotten about Junior? he wondered, glaring in their direction.

The young idiot hadn't stopped talking since they'd sat down. He squinted, trying to see how Suzanne was reacting, although it was hard to tell, with her back to him. And yet she was tilting her head, nodding, acting like what he was saying was the most fascinating speech she'd ever heard.

"Ready to order?"

The waiter stood by his table, waiting.

Luke looked back at the menu. Well, he had enough money for two, so he'd eat enough for two.

"I'll take the beefsteak, potatoes, and whatever else comes with it."

"Thank you, sir."

The menu was whisked from his hand. Immediately, his eyes shot back to the couple. Then, with firm resolve, he turned in his seat and concentrated on looking through the window to the busy street. He would not look their way again, he promised himself. It was a matter of pride, and he knew he could be tough enough to keep that promise.

Suzanne had listened intently as Art had given a lengthy account of his year at Harvard. He had managed to talk his way through their delicious meal. Suzanne began to wonder if all this talking was a nervous habit or if he was this loose-jawed all the time. "I would have flunked out if not for Papa pulling a few strings," he stated proudly. "One year was more than enough for me. I was born to be a rancher," he boasted.

She listened and forced a smile. From what she had observed, Art spent more time lounging on the porch than at the corral and stables. She supposed when your father owned the ranch, other things mattered—like wearing good clothes and supervising the ranch hands.

Maybe life with Art wouldn't be so bad, she told herself, recalling the satiny feel of the fine hotel soap, not the rough lye she'd had to rub on her skin for months.

". . .and I would be honored," he finished with a flourish.

Her eyes moved from his bobbing Adam's apple to his flushed face. He had obviously said something very important, but she had no idea what it had been.

"So. . .how do you feel about that, Miss Waters?" He was such a gentleman, always addressing her formally.

"Well. . ." She hesitated, wondering how to react so he wouldn't know she hadn't been listening.

"I guess I'm speaking prematurely," he rushed on. "I know you have to see to your father, but, like I said, next year when I turn twenty-one, I'd like to ask for your hand."

She gulped, wondering how she could have possibly missed his proposal. She mentally scurried to recapture her wits, knowing the importance of choosing precisely the right words.

"Art—and please call me Suzanne from now on—you understand how worried I am now, with Pa and all."

"Oh yes! I hope you don't think I'm being improper."

"No, not at all! I appreciate everything you've said, and I'm honored that you—" She broke off, swallowing. "I just think we should wait awhile longer to discuss this. But thank you." She gave him her best smile.

He was staring into her gray eyes, transfixed, blithely unaware that his size-twelve feet blocked the passage of the drunken cowboy stumbling past.

Suddenly, a crash just behind her jolted Suzanne, and she whirled to see a huge man sprawled across the adjoining table. A goblet shattered against a china plate; silver clattered to the floor.

Sputtering profanities, the man gathered his considerable bulk upright and whirled on Art, spitting fire. "You tripped me!" he roared, slamming a huge hand around Art's throat.

Suzanne stared at the hammy hand, crushing Art's Adam's apple. *Why, he could choke in seconds,* Suzanne thought and panicked.

"I . . . didn't . . ." Art choked out the words between gulps for air.

"Turn him loose," Suzanne cried. "You fell over your own feet, not his."

The man turned raging eyes to her. His companion had now joined the ruckus, snickering in the background. Suzanne glanced at Art, whose bulging eyes could pop from his face any minute.

"Well, you're a feisty one," his companion said. "I'll see to her, Buster."

The proprietor rushed up, desperate to settle the matter quietly.

"Step aside," the bully growled at him. "Me and this idiot will settle our differences outside." He yanked Art from the chair and hauled him from the dining room.

"Come on." The companion breathed whiskey into her face. "We don't want to miss the fun." He was every bit the bully his friend was, Suzanne decided, as his fingers bit into her arm.

"Stop this," she cried, looking back at the proprietor, who was trying to quiet the disrupted diners, assuring them everything was under control. There had merely been a small disagreement.

Didn't anyone care? Couldn't anyone stop these bullies?

Suddenly the ugly man who had grabbed Suzanne was shoved back and knocked flat. Luke stood over him, glaring down threateningly.

"Leave the lady alone," he warned through clenched teeth.

Suzanne gasped, looking from the man to Luke, then back again. Suddenly, she remembered Luke's sore shoulder, and the desperation she had felt for Art was nothing compared to the concern that rushed through her now.

The man was scrambling to his feet, his fists balled, when a commotion in the front of the lobby brought a dead silence to the group.

The sheriff and two of his deputies stood with guns drawn. "Buster, you and your no-good partner saddle up and ride out of town," he ordered. "Otherwise, you'll spend the night in jail. I warned you, there'd be no more fights!" The big bully loosened his hold on Art, and now Art's long legs buckled and he crumpled to the floor, gasping for breath.

"Your boyfriend needs you," Luke drawled.

"He's not my boyfriend," she hissed under her breath.

"Then you have no right leading him on the way you do."

She threw her head back, staring into Luke's face with flaming cheeks and flashing eyes. "How dare you speak to me that way!" she sputtered, forgetting that he had come to her rescue. She suddenly seethed with anger toward Luke. *How could he be so stupid?* Then she saw Art sprawled out on the floor, clutching his throat. She ran over to kneel down beside him.

"Are you all right?" she asked, smoothing Art's rumpled coat.

He was still gasping for breath, but at the sight of Suzanne leaning over him—her face flushed with concern—a bruised smile touched his purple face. He leaned against her, luxuriating in the comfort of her arms.

The crowd had begun to disperse. When Suzanne ventured a glance over her shoulder, Luke was gone.

"Uh-oh," Art muttered, and Suzanne followed his worried eyes to the direction of the stairs. His father was charging toward them, his eyes boiling with anger.

"Here are your wages," he snapped at Suzanne, shoving a wad of bills into her hand. "You and Rosa be ready to leave first thing in the morning. And Art"—he whirled on his son—"you and I have business to take care of."

Art didn't utter a sound as his father waved toward the front door, and the two marched out without a backward glance.

Suzanne had stared after them, thinking that was how it would be if she were ever foolish enough to marry Art, whose father barked out the orders and Art snapped into place.

Embarrassed and close to tears, she hurried to her room,

yanked off her clothes, and jumped in bed. Taut with nerves, her aching body lay rigid on the feather mattress for several minutes. Then, stretching her sore limbs, she told herself to forget the disaster downstairs and enjoy a comfortable bed, a luxurious room. The crisp sheets caressed her skin, and a pillow of softness cradled her head.

Still, she could not sleep.

She judged it to be midnight when finally she crept across to the window, sneaked the shade up, and peered down at the sidewalk.

Cowboys still milled about in twos and threes, talking and laughing. She didn't recognize any of the men from the ranch, and she wondered where everyone had gone. Her eyes settled on the swinging doors of the saloon across the street. She squinted down, trying to make out a familiar form in the blur of people. It was hopeless. In the smoky haze of the saloon, it would be impossible to recognize anyone.

Was Luke in there? she wondered, creeping back to bed. She closed her eyes. In her memory, she saw the look of scorn on his face, heard his scalding reproach. What troubled her even more, however, was her own behavior. She had rushed to Art's side, merely to spite Luke. She had wanted to hurt Luke—she had tried. Tears of shame filled her eyes. What had gotten into her?

Art shouldn't have let the man bully him that way, one side of her brain argued. Why, she had shown more nerve than Art. At least she had stood up to the men, while Art had done nothing to defend either of them.

How could he, when he was being choked? the other voice argued. Luke would have defended himself and her. He had come to her side even though she had been with another man. He'd been ready to fight for her, and would have, even with an injured shoulder.

She stared at the plastered ceiling, wondering exactly how Luke felt about her. As much as she wanted to believe he cared for her, she could find nothing of substance on which to pin her hopes. He probably would have come to any woman's defense. He was, after all, a gentleman, even though he could be gruff and argumentative. *Like Pa.* Was that one reason she was drawn to him?

Tears trickled down her cheeks in the darkness as the strain of the past week took its toll. Her mind jumped from concern for Pa to concern for Luke. And finally, she had one more thing to worry her. For days she'd tried to explain away her reaction to Luke. Tonight the truth had caught up with her.

I'm falling in love with him, she thought miserably, *and I might as well admit it.* It seemed hopeless, for Luke was obviously still brokenhearted over his wife; maybe he would never love another woman the way he had loved. . .G. Suzanne didn't even know her name.

She saw in her memory the wedding band with the two hearts linked together. She cried harder.

"Lord, touch his heart, please. . .and heal the broken places," she prayed.

CHAPTER 13

Luke left the hotel lobby abruptly and stood outside, breathing deeply of the night air, trying to calm his temper. He was almost as angry with Suzanne as he was with the Parkinson kid.

She would end up marrying him and living a miserable life. If money and security were that important to her, then she could have both with his blessings.

No, not his blessings.

He stared across the street to the rowdy crowd entering and leaving the saloon. He was too tired for that, and now his shoulder was killing him.

"Thomason!"

He turned to see Mr. Parkinson charging toward him, fumbling with a wad of bills. The son cowed at his side, looking thoroughly subdued.

"We can settle our own matters," the older Parkinson said tightly. "You don't need to trouble yourself."

Luke stiffened. The man was obviously mad at his son but taking it out on everyone else. He'd seen that before.

Parkinson was peeling off bills from the wad in his hand. "Here's the wages we agreed on. You're free to go."

Luke nodded, accepting the money. "Thank you, sir." He spoke with respect to the older man, but as he turned to walk away, his blue eyes slid to Art and narrowed, as his lip curled in contempt. Then, he turned and made his way to the livery.

~~~

Suzanne's return home had been uneventful. Johnny, an older cowhand with red hair and freckles, had arrived at the hotel just after daybreak to escort them. Suzanne suspected that Mr. Parkinson was trying to get her out of town as soon as possible, before she caused more trouble! Johnny had taken over the team, freeing Rosa and Suzanne to take turns napping in the bed of the wagon. They had made camp that night, then reached Trails End by the next afternoon.

Hurriedly, she had fetched Nellie and ridden away from Trails End. She was grateful for the money and relieved that she and Hank could go to Colorado Springs, but she feared she had alienated the Parkinsons.

As she topped the knoll and the log outpost came into view, she felt like bursting into tears. She hadn't realized how tense she had become the past four days. Now, seeing familiar territory brought a feeling of enormous relief. Everything looked peaceful. Only a few horses were tied at the hitching rail in front of the store.

Her eyes scanned the cabins out back of the post as she wondered about her pa. She hoped he hadn't been too grumpy with Mattie, who had kindly offered to wait on him.

She clucked to Nellie, who seemed to recognize the familiar territory as well, for she quickly responded, and they galloped across the valley in record time. Suzanne slowed Nellie up as they reached the front of the log building, then hopped off, looping the reins over the rail. She hurried toward the front door, ready to make excuses for Hank's behavior. When she pushed the door open and entered, she saw Hank reclining at the table in the rear, a coffee mug between his hands, a wide smile creasing his thin face.

Mattie stood in the kitchen door, listening intently as Hank entertained two cowboys with a tale of his rodeoing days.

As the door slammed behind Suzanne, all eyes flew to the front of the room.

"Suzanne!" Hank roared, grinning from ear to ear. "You made it back." The grin disappeared as he looked her up and down. "How did that cattle drive turn out? Did those fellows treat you all right?"

"Everything went just fine. Rosa and I tended to our business, they tended to theirs. We got to Pueblo, spent the night in a wonderful hotel, then Johnny drove Rosa and me back."

Hank scratched his chin. "Everything turned out okay, huh?"

"Just fine. How've you been?" It wasn't a lie, she told herself, she had just told her pa what he needed to hear. She leaned down to give him a big hug, forgetting the soreness in her body.

"I'm getting fat and sassy from Mattie's cooking!"

Suzanne turned to Mattie, who was coming forward to greet her, arms extended.

"I'm mighty glad to see you," Mattie said, squeezing her hand. "He's been worried and frankly so have I." Her brown eyes made a sweeping inspection of Suzanne. "You've lost a few pounds."

"I'll find them soon enough. Has he given you any trouble?" Suzanne asked, dreading to hear the answer.

"No. He's behaved himself just fine." Mattie smiled.

Suzanne saw the tenderness that touched Mattie's features as she looked at Hank. Was there something different in Hank's eyes, as well? Suzanne wondered, as he grinned at Mattie.

"I've had some mighty good meals," he said, patting his stomach.

"Doc Browning brought a doctor from St. Louis," Mattie informed Suzanne. "He agrees your father should see the doctor in Colorado Springs."

Hank fell silent, staring at the floor.

Mattie put an arm around Suzanne's shoulder. "Bet you could use some beef stew."

Suspecting Mattie might have something more to tell her, she nodded with enthusiasm. "That sounds wonderful."

Once she and Mattie had reached the privacy of the kitchen, Mattie's smile faded. The brown eyes she turned to Suzanne now held a look of concern.

"He hasn't complained, but I see him touch his chest several times a day. I'm worried."

Upon seeing her father, Suzanne had felt as though the invisible burden that weighed her down had suddenly been lifted. Now that weight returned, crushing her again.

"I can take him to Colorado Springs." She glanced toward the dining room. "We'll leave tomorrow, if possible."

Mattie was staring into the dining room, deep in thought. "I don't think he should ride a horse," she whispered.

Suzanne sank into a chair, bewildered.

"Mattie, I hadn't even thought about that. How could I be so dumb?"

Mattie hugged her. "Child, there's not a dumb bone in your body. We just forget Hank's not up to doing the usual."

Suzanne nodded sadly, hearing her father's voice merrily relating another rodeo story.

"I asked him about the wagon you brought here," Mattie continued. "He said it's still in the barn. Could you take it? That way he could stretch out in the bed if he gets tired."

Suzanne looked back at Mattie, suddenly wondering how they had managed without her.

"That's a wonderful idea."

"I'm sure you could get one of those cowboys to go along." She inclined her head toward the dining room. "You could give them a wage."

Suzanne pursed her lips, thinking it over. She hated the idea of paying someone when she and Hank might need every dollar. "Let me think about that."

"I know your pa will say he doesn't need any help," Mattie said. "And maybe you two *can* make it on your own. Wish Lilly was here so I could go." She shook her head, looking frustrated. "Listen, I have a dear friend who runs a boardinghouse there. The least I can do is let her know you're coming. She'll take good care of you."

Suzanne turned back to the woman who had become their best friend. "How can I thank you for all you've done for us?"

Mattie's eyes had strayed to Hank. "Just bring him back healthy, and that'll be thanks enough."

———⊱—⊰———

Luke stared into the campfire, trying to sort through the confused thoughts muddling his brain. As soon as Parkinson had paid him off, he had stalked to the livery, resaddled Smoky, and ridden out of Pueblo. He'd wanted to put distance between himself and everyone else, particularly Suzanne.

He had ridden for a couple of hours, letting the cool darkness wash over him, calming his frustration and anger. He had made camp late, sealed in cozy darkness with only the saunas of Smoky munching grass and a squirrel playing in the tree.

As the campfire dwindled, he found himself thinking back to his mother and the good principles she had instilled in him. His conscience was tugging at him, telling him that Hank Waters needed him. The man had been like a father to him, and he didn't know when he had enjoyed another man's company as much as he had enjoyed being with Mr. Waters.

He'd heard Johnny complaining about having to get up early and drive the women and the chuck wagon back. Apparently, Junior was staying in town with Daddy.

Luke frowned.

Did Suzanne plan to take Mr. Waters into Colorado Springs with no help?

He stood, kicked out the campfire, and reached for his bedroll. He'd sleep on it. Since he was going to Colorado Springs anyway, he just might offer to help.

———⊱—⊰———

Suzanne walked through the house, relieved to be home. She kept recalling the way Mattie had looked at her pa. Was Mattie thinking of her father as more than a friend? He had mentioned Mattie several times, as well. *They might just be a good match for each other,* Suzanne thought as she sat on her bed, yanking her boots from her weary feet. Instead of feeling a surge of joy over the idea, she was disappointed in herself to experience a twinge of jealousy.

How could she deny her father happiness in his old age? Well, knowing her father, nobody would deny him anything if he made up his mind. She stretched out on her narrow bed, then turned on her side, snuggling into the pillow.

"It's not meant for man to be alone," her mother had often told her. That was true. It would be good for her father to have a companion in his old age.

What about me? she thought wearily, wondering where Luke was by now. Halfway to Colorado Springs, no doubt.

She was almost asleep when the distant sound of hoofbeats penetrated her semiconsciousness. Her lashes parted, her eyes drifting open. Was it Pedro coming back? He had left soon after they had arrived. He'd taken good care of the horses. She had asked him to stay on while they were in Colorado Springs, but first he wanted to return to Doc's ranch for the night.

The hoofbeats were real and coming closer. She sat up in bed, wondering if Mattie had sent a cowhand to check on them.

"Suzanne," her father called, tapping softly on her bedroom door.

"Come in," she called.

He opened the door and looked at her with puzzled eyes. "Luke's riding up," he said.

CHAPTER 14

She couldn't have been more surprised. She had thrown on a housedress, brushed the tangles from her thick hair, then taken an extra moment to compose her thoughts.

Hank's voice flowed throughout the cabin, offering coffee, answering Luke's questions about his health. Suzanne took a deep breath and opened the door.

Luke sat with her father at the kitchen table, sipping the brew, munching on one of the tea cakes Rosa had packed for them. They were discussing her father's heart condition. At the sound of her steps, Luke turned in the chair and looked across the room.

Their eyes met and Suzanne caught her breath.

He needed a shave, his blue eyes looked weary and haggard, and his clothes held a layer of trail dust. Yet, she had never been so glad to see anyone in her entire life.

"Hello," she said, smiling at him.

"Hello." He nodded, preparing to stand.

"Keep your seat. Please." She sauntered across the living room to stand at the end of the table. "You must be tired."

He nodded. "What about you?"

Suddenly, *she* didn't feel tired at all. She felt as though she could run all the way to the trading post.

"I've rested." She wandered back to the coffeepot, pouring a small amount into her mug. She really had no taste for coffee at this hour, but she needed to occupy herself in some way, and maybe she needed a reason to join them at the kitchen table. Her eyes surveyed Luke's thick dark hair, waving at his neck and around his ears.

"Did you get home all right?" he asked in a casual tone, glancing at her.

"Yes, Johnny drove us back. Rosa and me," she added, then wondered why she felt compelled to explain who had accompanied them. "He insisted we get an early start."

Hank cleared his throat. "She tells me there were no problems on the drive. I'm mighty proud of her."

Suzanne's eyes flew to meet Luke's face. His expression was inscrutable. She knew the man well enough to know he would not mention the ugly scene at the hotel if she didn't want him to. For once, she was glad he was closemouthed. This was not something she wanted Hank to hear about.

"Your daughter did remarkably well under the circumstances," he said, studying the tea cake.

Under the circumstances! She cleared her throat, settling into a kitchen chair. "I assumed you were halfway to Colorado Springs by now. Or already there."

He was studying his mug, taking his time to answer. Just why had he come here? she wondered wildly, although she wasn't about to ask. She was just glad that he had.

"I've come to help you and your father get to Colorado Springs. If you want me to, that is."

That announcement seemed to startle Hank as much as it did Suzanne. "Well, that's mighty decent of you," Hank said, shifting his thin frame against the wooden chair. "We sure could use some help."

Her father's statement was equally surprising. It was totally out of character for Hank to accept help. Allowing Mattie to fuss over him was one thing; admitting that he couldn't manage a team of horses or get himself to Colorado Springs was quite another.

"I thought we'd get the wagon out of the barn, make a bed in the back," she said, glancing worriedly at her father. She hadn't even broached the subject with her father, dreading his reaction. Now the words spilled forth unchecked, and she hesitated, waiting for another objection. Hank drank his coffee in silence.

Luke looked at Hank. "What about a team? You wouldn't want to use your good horses."

Hank had the answer. "Reckon we could pay Parkinson to use some of his workhorses. He's got plenty." Hank's blue eyes drifted to Suzanne. "Since you're so friendly with them, maybe you could ride over and ask in the morning."

Suzanne's eyes shot to Luke, silently pleading.

"I'll do that," he offered. "I'm sure your daughter will have plenty to do here, preparing for the trip. When did you want to leave?"

"Tomorrow," Hank said on a deep sigh.

Suzanne stared at her father. He obviously felt worse than he had admitted, and this scared her. But with Luke sitting here in the kitchen, making plans to help them, the invisible weight on her shoulders had magically been lifted again.

Hank retired to his bedroom early, claiming to be tired. Suzanne could see he was too excited about the trip to be sleepy, but she appreciated his attempt to give them privacy.

Luke sat in the kitchen chair, staring at his empty mug, saying nothing.

"Want some more coffee?"

"No, thank you." He glanced at her.

"Tea cakes?"

"Nothing else."

He kept looking at her as though he wanted to say something. *What? The ring!* He wanted the ring back! And he was willing to see them to Colorado Springs since he was headed there anyway.

"Excuse me for a minute," she said.

She got up from her chair and went to her bedroom. She opened the drawer and withdrew the letter, recalling briefly the disappointment she had felt upon reading it.

The wedding band fell into her palm, its soft burnished gold gleaming in the lantern light. Gripping the ring tightly, she returned to the kitchen and placed it on the table before him.

"You came for this," she said.

His eyes dropped to the ring, then shot to her face. He leaned back in the chair, and she watched the grim expression he so often wore slip back over his features.

"You think I came here just to get the ring?"

She swallowed, nervously wondering if she had sounded abrupt or unkind.

"I know what it means to you," she stammered.

"How do you know that?" he asked quietly.

"Well..." Her eyes fell to the gold band lying in the center of the table, so small, yet suddenly seeming to outweigh everything in the room. Even her words lay heavy against her tongue. "I assumed..." she faltered again.

"You have a bad habit of doing that," he drawled.

She stared at him. "Doing what?"

"Assuming things."

"But the inscription on the inside," she blurted, "the hearts...*G*...*L*—" she broke off, her cheeks flaming. Her eyes flew to a darkened corner of the room. He must think she was the nosiest person he'd ever met. She'd had no right to...

"That ring doesn't belong to me." His voice cut through her puzzled thoughts.

Slowly, her eyes drifted back to him as she tried to absorb his words. *What did he just say? The ring doesn't belong to him?*

"Then who...why?"

His suntanned hand shot out, plucking up the simple band that had created such furor. He held it to the light, reading the inscription almost as though he had forgotten about it.

Suzanne stared at the ring, confused. Had he simply found it on the trail? What about the *L*? Was it possible he was lying to her?

"The ring belonged to my mother," he said at last. "Her name was Grace. The *L* is for Luke."

Suzanne sank into the chair and planted her elbows on the kitchen table.

"Luke is your father?" she asked, leaning forward, searching his face.

He nodded, saying nothing more as he casually dropped the ring into his shirt pocket. "My mother died recently."

She swallowed hard. "I'm sorry. And your father?"

"Is in Colorado Springs."

"Oh." The word fell from her throat. "You two are starting a new life there, like Pa and I have?"

A bitter laugh sliced the air, startling Suzanne. "No. Not the two of us. He started a life there long ago, when he deserted Ma and me. I'm taking the ring because she begged me to, so I could prove I was his son. Otherwise, I doubt he'd recognize me."

Suzanne's mouth fell open as her mind scrambled to take this in and provide the right response. She looked from Luke to the ring.

"You might as well know the truth," he said flatly. "I made a promise to my mother on her deathbed. I'm merely keeping that promise. Then I'll be going back to Kansas."

She stared, her mind jumbled with questions she knew better than to ask. He had already shared something very private, something that had obviously broken his heart as a young boy. She sat silent, unable to speak. Luke stood, pushing the chair back under the table.

"I can sleep in the barn," he said.

"No, you'll sleep on the couch." She got up and went to fetch a blanket and pillow. She returned, placing both on the couch. "Good night." She smiled, then turned and headed to her room.

Going back to Kansas. . . Going back to Kansas. . . The words bounced through her brain for the next hour as she tossed and turned on her bed, and the sleep she desperately needed eluded her.

⟋⟍

Their old prairie schooner was still in remarkably good shape, after being uncovered from the back of the barn and cleaned up for the trip to Colorado Springs. Suzanne had spent the morning organizing the items they would need. There had been a few tears shed in private when she'd touched the wooden box she had found on a shelf in the barn—the box they had used to pack supplies for their trip down from Denver. Suzanne recalled her mother choosing and packing the cooking utensils in this box, chatting excitedly with Suzanne about their new home. She still missed her mother desperately, but Suzanne knew she was in a better place.

The sound of Luke's horse brought her back to the task at hand. She walked out of the barn and waited for him to rein Smoky in and report the outcome of his trip to the Parkinson ranch.

"I've arranged for a team."

"Wonderful." She began to stroke Smoky's gleaming neck.

"Johnny is bringing the horses over in an hour," he continued. "We'll allow a day, even two if necessary. That will give us plenty of time to stop and rest. I can trail my horse behind the wagon."

Suzanne nodded, reaching into her pocket for the last lump of sugar. "Sorry you have to trail the wagon," she said, tucking the lump into the stallion's mouth.

She looked back at Luke. "Thank you for taking care of things," Suzanne said. "We really appreciate what you're doing. Did they mention what they're charging us for the team?"

She had vowed to be as agreeable as possible, and now both were acting as though the conversation in the kitchen had never taken place.

Suzanne tried not to think about the Parkinsons, and didn't even ask whom Luke had spoken with about the team.

"I'll pay them whatever is fair," she said.

He removed a package from his saddlebags, mumbled something about "already paid," and hurried toward the house.

———※———

Now she sat on the wagon seat beside Luke while Hank stretched comfortably on quilts and pillows in the bed of the wagon. She had begun to suspect that her father was working some secret plan, for he had become suspiciously docile. He had allowed them to wait on him and do all the planning, while he'd merely nodded agreeably to whatever had been suggested.

Suzanne recalled what Mattie had said—that he had a habit of touching his chest at intervals. She noticed this as well and suspected it was an unconscious effort to still his rapid heartbeat. Yet, he had not complained; he even seemed excited about the trip.

The metal fasteners jingled against the leather harness as the horses plodded dutifully up the road to Colorado Springs. She had prayed for good weather, and God had obliged them with a gorgeous spring day, complete with a light breeze and enough clouds to offset the sun.

Luke had left the canvas flaps open so Hank could talk freely with them from the back of the wagon, but the old man had said little. She glanced back and saw that he was dozing. Behind the wagon, Luke's horse sauntered along, looking as though he resented being hitched to the wagon.

She stole a glance at Luke. He was wearing fresh pants and a black shirt, which looked suspiciously like one she had admired at Mattie's store. She wondered how much money he had earned on the cattle drive. Clearing her throat, she forced out the words that had been nagging her since his arrival. "I want to apologize for seeming so. . .ungrateful the other night in Pueblo."

Beneath the black felt hat, his blue eyes narrowed on the road ahead.

"I'm sorry I was rude," he replied.

"You weren't," she answered slowly. "You were trying to help, and I appreciate that."

He turned and looked at her, and Suzanne saw an expression of tenderness in his eyes.

"You remind me of my mother," he said.

"I do? Tell me about her."

"She was pleasant and sweet, like you. She tried to see the best in people."

Suzanne blushed at the compliment. "And you think I'm like her? I don't know about that!"

He grinned. "You have a temper, but as far as I can tell, that's your worst trait. You're kind and forgiving, like Ma," he added.

"Did she forgive your father for leaving?"

A muscle clenched in his jaw, and Suzanne wished desperately that she hadn't asked. She didn't want to evoke unpleasant memories or turn the conversation in the wrong direction. But it was too late now, the words had already been spoken. He was opening his mouth, looking at her. He might tell her to mind her own business.

"I couldn't understand," he said quietly, "how she could keep on loving him, but she did. She said I look just like him; I probably act like him, too. I remember him being a pretty stubborn critter."

"How old were you when he left?" she asked as gently as possible.

"Twelve. My parents had worked hard, scrimping and saving to move to Colorado. They were going to homestead here. He left with the money, promising to return when he had found the right piece of property. That was the last time we saw him."

She caught her breath. "Surely there was an explanation?"

"Yep, he met another woman."

Suzanne stared at him, wishing he would elaborate, but he sank into gloomy silence. She turned her eyes toward Morning Mountain in the distance, which usually gave her a boost of courage. "My mother shared Pa's dream, as your mother did," she said, glancing at Luke. "I suppose that's natural for a woman."

His eyes slipped back to her, searching her face. She wondered what he was thinking.

"It was strange," Suzanne continued. "Ma couldn't even stay mad at her brother—despite his deception. She thought this was a beautiful place to start a new life, doing what Pa wanted to do."

"Surely your pa was less forgiving."

"Pa was mad, all right. But we were here, and it *is* a beautiful place. Maybe it was meant for us to start over. Ma read the Bible a lot, gave us verses for comfort. We might gripe about my uncle's trickery sometimes, who wouldn't? But we've managed to survive without being bitter."

"That's hard to believe," he said flatly.

"Tell me?"—she faced him—"do we seem like bitter people to you?"

He turned and looked at her; then he began to shake his head.

"No, you don't. You and your pa are the nicest people I've ever met." He turned back to the road, breathing a sigh. "I could never be that forgiving. Ma and I nearly starved. She scrubbed floors and washed dishes for people in the daytime and took in ironing in the evenings. I looked older than my years so I lied about my age to get men's work."

"Surely things got better for the two of you?"

He nodded. "I worked my way into a foreman's job at a big ranch out from Abilene. The owner, Mr. Godfrey, was in bad health, and the foreman before me had done a poor job. There were financial problems. Mr. Godfrey promised me if I'd run the ranch like it was mine, he'd pay me well. I was willing to work for less pay if he'd deed me some land. My family had never been able to own land of their own—it was always our dream."

He stopped talking, taking a tighter grip on the reins.

"You can't stop the story now," Suzanne said, touching his sleeve.

"I broke my back for two years, taking little pay, dreaming of the day I'd own my own section of land. Then his daughter decided she wanted to marry me." He shook his head slowly. "I couldn't muster up any feeling for her, and I didn't want to spend my life with a woman I couldn't love."

"I can understand that," Suzanne replied. She could scarcely believe that he was confiding such personal matters.

"I reckon you can." He grinned. "You've got the same situation with young Parkinson."

Suzanne looked down at her fingers gripped tightly in her lap. How could he guess what she was going through? It must've been written all over her on the stock drive. "I won't marry him either," she said.

"You won't? How do you know you wouldn't be happy with that rich family?" he asked.

"Because I don't love him. He isn't the type of man I'd want to spend my life with."

He was looking at her carefully. "And just what type of man do you want?"

"A man who's strong yet tender, who enjoys the things I enjoy. A man I truly love."

They were staring deeply into each other's eyes. Suddenly the wheel struck a large rock, sending them bouncing. The impact jarred the wagon, and something clattered in the back. Suzanne heard a yelp of pain from her father.

"What's going on?" Hank shouted.

Luke leaned back in the seat, tugging hard on the reins to slow the panicked horses.

Suzanne turned, peering through the parted canvas laps. "We hit a rock."

Hank was leaning out the back of the wagon, trying to calm Smoky. Glancing back over his shoulder, he beckoned to Suzanne. "I think you best get back here and let me take a turn on the seat," Hank suggested. "Luke may need my help."

The horses had finally settled down to a leisurely pace.

Suzanne swapped places with her father and stretched out on the quilts, enjoying their comfort. Her father had closed the canvas flaps, so she couldn't see the men. Still, she could hear her father's voice.

"Blue Sky people, the Utes were called, and they were the only Indians who were the real natives here. Owned a bunch of magic dogs." Hank chuckled. "Know what magic dogs are?"

"Horses, I'd guess," Luke replied.

"Horses they got from the Spanish." Hank sighed. "Reckon they had a pretty good life here in the shadow of the Peak until all us greedy white folk arrived. . ."

As Hank's words droned on, Suzanne closed her eyes, knowing she needed the sleep. But she couldn't stop thinking about what Luke had told her, and the fact that he *had* told her such personal matters. She smiled to herself. Maybe, before this trip was over, she could change his mind about going back to Kansas.

CHAPTER 15

Suzanne bent over the campfire, stirring up the stew she had brought along. Luke was rubbing down the horses, while Hank leaned back on a flat rock, smoking his pipe and studying the dying sunset.

"Pretty sight, isn't it?" he asked, his eyes fixed on the raspberry glow settling over the mountaintop.

"It's beautiful," she sighed, glancing at the breathtaking sunset. "Pa, I love it here."

Hank stared at her and suddenly his gray eyes held a sheen of tears. He looked back at the fire. "The older you get," he said slowly, "the more you look like your mother."

Suzanne's eyes flew back to him. She was pleased by his compliment because her mother had been one of the prettiest women she'd ever known. She had inherited her mother's fair skin and blond hair, but she longed for her round face and her beautiful light blue eyes, like the sky in early morning.

"You've told me I sound like her, but I'm not as pretty. I know that."

He glanced at her. "Yes, you are. You're not as delicate perhaps, but God knew what He was doing. You had to be more hardy to survive here."

Suzanne heard him speak those words and, fearing that he was thinking back to that awful blizzard that had led to her mother's death, she rushed to fill the silence.

"Tell me about when you first met her. I love hearing that story." She glanced at Luke to see if he was listening. He was feeding the horses but was still within earshot.

"Abigail was about your age when I first spotted her. I had ridden into Denver from the ranch where I was working. My boss's wife needed a bolt of cloth to make clothes for their new baby. 'Just ask Mrs. Ferguson,' I was told."

He shook his head, glancing at the clouds. "I didn't know anything about women's cloth, and I was scared to death I wouldn't find this Mrs. Ferguson. Sure enough, I didn't. She was sick that day, but her daughter was working in her place."

He looked at Suzanne, and his gray eyes began to twinkle. "Found out her daughter was named Abigail, and she was the prettiest girl I'd ever seen. I was lucky she knew as much about choosing cloth for baby clothes as her mother, maybe more."

"Ma was a wonderful seamstress." Suzanne smiled proudly. "Too bad I have none of her talent."

"Well, she had enough for both of you," he sighed. "The clothes she made for you and her. . ."

Suzanne leaned forward, wondering if he was thinking about the overloaded wagon they'd brought on their first trip out.

"If you're still worrying about making us throw out the trunk that day—we forgave you. Besides, you warned us we were packing too many dresses. And I know it was either that trunk of extra dresses or our trunk of food that had to go. Ma said she could make us more dresses."

But she never did, Suzanne thought sadly.

Hank shook his head, angrily tapping the ashes from his pipe. "It was the worst thing I ever did. If I hadn't been mad at the team and the weather and that sorry wagon wheel, I'd never have thrown out those trunks to make it on. . ."

"Pa, you threw out your trunk with the books and rodeo stuff! Will you stop being a martyr? Besides"—she leaned back, crossing her arms—"let's just dwell on the good memories. And we have plenty of those."

He looked across the dwindling fire. "I was blessed to have all those years with your mother. I still miss her, but I thank God for you. You've made us both proud."

She stared at him, suddenly at a loss for words. Her father rarely got sentimental. He looked so frail by the firelight. Suzanne wondered if his compliment was somehow an admission of his own failing health—that he might not be around long enough to say the things he really felt.

"Everything's going to be all right," she spoke softly. "I believe that, and you must believe it, too."

He nodded. "I know." He stroked his gray beard thoughtfully. "We gotta hold on, keep believing we'll get all these problems worked out."

She reached over and touched his hand. "We will work them out, Pa."

They ate quietly. The past week had begun to take its toll on Suzanne. By the time the water was hot for washing dishes, she was nodding off.

Hank and Luke seemed tired as well, and yet the silence that slipped over them was a contented one as the soft darkness sealed them into a cozy circle near the sputtering campfire.

Hank offered Suzanne the wagon bed, saying he'd spent too many nights sleeping under the stars to pass this one up. She didn't argue, and she wearily crawled into the wagon bed and was asleep in minutes.

When she rolled over the next morning and peered at the sunlight seeping through the slats of the wagon, she felt a warm joy spreading through her. Why? She sat up, wondering why she felt so happy on this particular morning.

Then, as if in answer, Luke's voice drifted to her. She heard the *pop* of the morning campfire and smelled bacon sizzling. Lifting her arms above her head, she stretched lazily. The events of the previous day and evening sifted through her mind, and she smiled to herself. Luke seemed to care for her, and he had been wonderful to Pa. He was exactly what they needed in their lives. If only...

Reaching for her hand mirror, she stared into a pair of shining gray eyes framed by a tousled mass of blond hair. She opened the lid of the trunk, searching for her brush. Underneath the pantaloons, she retrieved the brush and began to rake out the tangles. Once her hair was smooth and gleaming, she decided not to tie it back. She liked the way Luke glanced at her hair. Though he'd never said anything, she had an idea he admired it when she wore it unbound.

She dressed quickly, choosing her blue cotton. Spreading her hands over the skirt, her fingers worked at the wrinkles, trying to smooth them out. After she had done the best she could within the confines of the wagon, she emerged and glanced around.

Pa and Luke sat at the campfire as Luke cooked their breakfast. When Luke spotted her, he nodded politely and inclined his head toward the back of the wagon.

"There's a pan of water on the tailgate of the wagon," Luke said, as his eyes swept over her.

"Thank you." She smiled. "Pa, how do you feel?"

He was perched on the same rock where he had sat the night before, contentedly sipping his coffee.

"Like I could break the wildest mustang in the west!"

Luke grinned at him, and Suzanne merely shook her head as she made her way to the back of the wagon to splash water onto her face.

Just as they had done the previous evening, she and Pa prepared to say grace before eating. Suzanne noticed that Luke did not bow his head, and this made her uncomfortable. Hank seemed not to notice. Perhaps ignoring him was the best way to handle Luke's strange moods.

Luke ate his food in silence. Suzanne wondered if their prayer had brought on his dark mood. And why? she wondered. She soon gave up trying to start conversation.

After he'd shoved down his meal, Luke hurried to get the team ready to travel. Suzanne met her father's eyes across the campfire.

"Pa, what's wrong with him?" Suzanne asked under her breath.

Hank winked at her. "He's just doing some soul searching. Leave him be."

"I intend to," she snapped, hopping up from the campfire and grabbing the dishes to be washed.

⁂

Luke's mood improved once they were on the road and Hank brought up the subject of horses.

"I got a lot of dreams for that little ranch," Hank said. "There's wild horses up that canyon behind our house. The mustang I was chasing. . ." His voice droned on, and Suzanne's mind wandered. Luke, on the other hand, was mesmerized by the subject of mustangs.

She had given Pa her seat on the wagon and slipped back to tidy up the wagon bed. She knew both she and Luke were facing a challenge once they arrived in Colorado Springs. She and Pa must face the truth about his heart, whatever that was—and Luke would finally confront his father.

A stiffness settled into her shoulders, and she took a deep breath. The next few days could change all of their lives.

She reached into her trunk and pulled out the worn family Bible she had tucked in before leaving. Reverently, she turned the pages, tissue-soft from years of use. She found a comforting chapter in Psalms and began to read. Slowly, the headache that had threatened went away, and she began to relax.

At their lunch break, Suzanna was ready to engage in spirited conversation with her father, while Luke looked as though he needed some time in the bed of the wagon. Occasionally, he rubbed his forehead, as though he might have a headache.

"Wouldn't you like to grab a quick nap?" she asked, giving him a smile as she washed up the dishes.

He shook his head. "I'll catch up on my rest once I get back to Kansas."

The words struck her like a blow, and she turned quickly, scrubbing hard on the eating utensils. What had she hoped for, expected? Whatever it had been, she was obviously dreaming. Luke was determined to go back to Kansas! And why did he keep making a point of it, anyway? Nobody was going to beg him to stay, certainly not her or her pa.

Well, maybe he and his father will patch up their differences, a hopeful voice argued. But what if they did? If he stayed in Colorado Springs, she'd never see him either.

She fought against the depression creeping over her as she packed the cooking utensils beside the first-aid kit in the bed of the wagon. The joy she had felt had been snatched away by Luke's matter-of-fact statement about returning to Kansas.

Hank was putting out the fire when Suzanne came around the wagon. Their eyes met briefly before she busied herself checking to see that everything was packed. He seemed to sense the tension between her and Luke.

"What if I relieve you driving for a while?" Hank offered as Luke hitched the team to the wagon.

"No, sir. You'd better not strain yourself." He led Smoky around to the back of the wagon to tether him. "But I wouldn't mind hearing more stories about those mustangs," he called back.

That meant Luke wanted her pa to sit on the seat beside him. Well, she could take a hint! She crawled into the bed of the wagon and said nothing more to Luke. If she was not going to be seeing him again, she had to protect herself from any more heartache. The less she had to do with Luke, the better off she would be.

She closed her eyes and tried to sleep as they jostled toward their destiny.

Colorado Springs had been founded in 1871 by General William Palmer. General Palmer had envisioned Colorado Springs, situated at the base of Pikes Peak, as a resort where the dry air and high altitude would help those suffering from tuberculosis. He further intended this town to be a cultural center, with an opera house, fine dining establishments, and European-style hotels. Mattie had told her all about the town, having wintered here with her husband when they'd first come to Colorado. Then they had decided to migrate south to open the trading post.

"Old Man Palmer had no idea, when he designed the town, that the gold rush and the railroad would bring in so many roughnecks!" Mattie had laughed.

Suzanne found herself missing Mattie. If she was along, she would make them laugh, maybe give her a little advice about how to forget Luke Thomason!

As their wagon clattered down Cascade Avenue, Suzanne stared in awe at the mansions—mostly wood, with a few made of stone. Lace curtains fluttered at the windows, and some of the porches had lovely flower boxes. Someday, she vowed, their ranch house would look like a real home.

She studied the women coming and going. Wearing fancy hats and beautiful dresses, they lolled along the sidewalk, silk parasols in hand, ready to protect their delicate faces if the sun should pop out.

Suzanne shrank back in the wagon, unwilling to be reminded of how little she now owned.

The wagon pulled up before a modest building. Suzanne knew from the conversation between her pa and Luke that this was the office of Dr. Horace Crownover, the physician Doc Browning had arranged for her father to see.

She took a deep breath, forgetting fashion and lovely ladies, and she prayed Dr. Crownover would be able to help Pa.

Chapter 16

It could be worse," the doctor said, adjusting his spectacles. He was scarcely five feet tall; still, he was a commanding presence with snapping hazel eyes and a deep, confident voice. His manner was courteous yet reserved, but Suzanne sensed a razor-sharp intelligence.

She and Hank sat opposite the doctor's desk, where he was looking over the notes he had made after examining Hank.

"I'll need to do some more tests before I make any conclusions, Mr. Waters," Dr. Crownover said. "However, I believe the new medication will help you."

Hank had scooted to the edge of his seat, awaiting the doctor's report.

"Do you think I can go on ranching?" He took a deep breath, glancing at Suzanne. "Or is my condition...?"

"With medication, I believe you can go back to a fairly normal life. You may have to alter your activities somewhat."

Hank frowned at that. "What do you mean?"

The doctor hesitated. "Let's wait and see what the medication does. I'd like to start you on it right now. I have a few here." He opened the center drawer of his desk and withdrew a package. "Plan to stay in town for the next few days so we can be sure there are no adverse reactions."

"Yes, we'll be here," Suzanne answered quickly. "We'll be staying in a boardinghouse on Tejon."

"Good!" The doctor stood and extended his hand to Hank. "I'd like you to come to the office twice a day."

It was obvious from Hank's sullen expression that this suggestion did not appeal to him; however, he kept silent, allowing Suzanne to make the necessary arrangements.

Luke was waiting for them outside the doctor's office. He had been pacing back and forth on the board sidewalk. When they emerged from the building, he hurried to Suzanne's side, his blue eyes anxious.

"I think this physician will be able to help Pa," she said, smiling. "He's already started him on some medicine."

"I'm mighty relieved to hear that, Mr. Waters."

The men exchanged understanding looks. She wondered if Hank had said more about his heart to Luke than to her. She knew he had tried to be brave about this—that he didn't want to worry her.

"Doc is having a buggy and driver sent over. You coming to the boardinghouse with us?" Hank inquired of Luke. "Mattie telegraphed that friend of hers, and she's expecting us."

Luke shook his head. "No. If you want me to put the team up at the livery, I'll do that. And I reckon we could leave the wagon there, too." He turned and scanned the busy street. "I have business of my own to take care of now."

Hank put a hand on Luke's shoulder. "Is there any way we can help you, son?"

Luke shook his head. "No."

"Where will you be staying?" Suzanne asked, trying to sound casual. "In case we need you," she added, looking at Hank.

Luke shrugged. "I'm not sure. The last address I have is from the woman he lived with. I guess I'll start there."

Suzanne touched his arm. "I'll be praying for you."

He yanked his arm away. "Prayers don't help me. They didn't help Ma either. Maybe they work for you people"—his eyes blazed from Suzanne to Hank—"but not for me."

Suzanne was too shocked to respond, but Hank said, "We'll see about that, Luke."

Hank's voice had a calming effect, and now Luke dropped his head. "I shouldn't have spoken out in that way. I'm sorry."

⟨ornament⟩

Miss Martha's Boardinghouse was a two-story, white clapboard building with green shutters and a wide front porch. Rocking chairs were assembled about the porch, lending a homey atmosphere to the place.

Luke had unloaded the wagon, then hastily said good-bye. Suzanne stood in the front door, staring after him with sad eyes while Miss Martha yammered on, giving a lengthy account of her friendship with the Wileys.

"Could we get to our rooms, please?" Hank interrupted her, pressing his hand to his chest.

"Oh. Of course!"

Miss Martha was a small, thin woman with white hair and inquisitive blue eyes. She moved with remarkable speed for her sixty years as she lifted her skirts and crossed the foyer to unlock a door on the right.

"I've given you my two front bedrooms, seeing as how you have this weak heart. . ." she stated.

Hank winced at that, but Suzanne linked her arm through his and smiled up at him. "Pa, I just know Dr. Crownover is going to help you. This medicine will work. I'm confident of that."

She *did* feel a confidence in this matter. She just wished now she could stop worrying about Luke.

CHAPTER 17

Luke lingered in front of the livery, giving Smoky a lump of sugar. "That's your reward for trailing a wagon for two days. Good boy." He stroked the big stallion's neck.

He glanced up and down the busy street and told himself he had to get on with the task at hand. He swung into the saddle.

Bennett Avenue. The instructions the blacksmith had given him were easy enough to follow, allowing his mind ample opportunity to reflect on the letter Ma had saved all these years—the only letter they'd received from Pa once he'd come here. Luke had jotted the address down on a slip of paper and that was now the address he was seeking.

He turned down Bennett Avenue and glanced around. It appeared to be a respectable area, although the houses were small and close together. He slowed his horse, finding 708.

It was one of the smallest houses on the street, yet the wood looked to be in good condition, and there were lacy curtains at the front windows.

He sat on Smoky, staring at the house. The curtain fluttered; someone was watching him. He got down from the horse, aware that he must look ridiculous, staring at the house like a simpleton. Before he had made his way up the stone walkway, however, the door had opened and a young woman had stepped out, hold-ing a baby in her arms.

"Hello," he said, tipping his hat.

"Hello. Are you looking for someone?"

"Matter of fact, I am." He swallowed, suddenly finding the name difficult to speak. "Luke Thomason."

She frowned. "Who?"

He repeated the name, though he could tell by the woman's expression she had never heard of him.

"We've lived here for five years," she informed him, "but I've never heard that name. Before that, another family named Wilkinson owned the house."

Would his father have changed his name? "Don't suppose Mr. Wilkinson was from Kansas, was he?"

She quickly shook her head. "No, they came here from Tennessee."

He glanced toward the other houses. "Do you think it would be all right if I checked with your neighbors?"

She shrugged. "Sure." Then she turned and went back into the house. He could hear a key locking the door behind him as he turned to leave.

Occupants of the other houses gave him blank stares and shook their heads. Most, he learned, had only lived on the street for the past few years. One woman had offered to check with her elderly father, who was seated in the backyard. Luke had waited outside, nervously twirling his hat between his hands. She had returned, shaking her head, offering no new leads.

"He never heard of him either."

Luke had thanked her and walked back to Smoky. He climbed back in the saddle and left Bennett Avenue. He had done what he could to find the man who'd abandoned them. His eyes drifted upward, as though speaking to someone in the clouds. "I tried," he said quietly.

❦

Luke had found a cheap boardinghouse on the outskirts of town. It occurred to him that he seemed to be trying to get as far from

Suzanne as he could. And he knew why.

He'd tried to keep a wall built around his heart, but she had managed to knock that wall down with a gentleness he had not believed possible. For the first time in his life, he was a man in love. He had a better understanding of that emotion now. Real love began with friendship, admiring and respecting that person as he had Suzanne. From the beginning, he had been drawn to the delicate features, the thick blond hair, the shining gray eyes; but soon he had moved past that to learn to know the real woman underneath. Here was a woman a man could easily picture as his wife. She was kind and gentle and patient and caring . . .and still the prettiest woman he had ever known. Maybe it had something to do with the inner beauty that radiated out of those gray eyes.

He still felt bad for speaking sharply to her about that prayer business. He had reacted before he could stop himself, and now he knew why: she had struck a nerve. That's why he was so touchy. His conscience had started to jab him. . .like right now. And he didn't want to listen.

He had been lying on a lumpy cot in the small room, staring at the cracked ceiling. Now he hauled himself to his feet, reached for his hat, and headed out into the darkness. He mounted Smoky and began to ride, enjoying the feel of the crisp mountain air on his skin.

Carriages and wagons lined the boulevard leading into town. Colorado Springs was a busy place, growing, thriving. Still, his taste ran toward the quiet countryside, a place like the one where the Waters lived. There a man could feast his eyes on a green valley, the only population being his horses.

But that was their home, not his. He was on the verge of becoming attached to the ranch, as he had to the people. He had been eager to ride away before he committed himself to something.

When Amanda Godfrey had wanted to marry him, there had been no way he could imagine committing himself to a woman for life. But now, he felt certain he could do that with Suzanne; he even wanted to do that. But he was scared. He had been like his father in so many ways. "Exactly like your father," his mother had often said. Maybe he was afraid there was some dark side of his nature that would keep him from staying with a family. And he would never want to hurt anyone the way he and his ma had been hurt.

He tugged on the reins, slowing Smoky down at the corner. Down a side street, piano music and laughter drifted to him. He saw cowboys entering a saloon, and feeling lonely, he headed in that direction.

He turned Smoky in at the hitching rail and climbed down. Adjusting his hat on his head, he wondered why he'd spent the past hour thinking about Suzanne when he was so dirt-poor he had nothing on earth to offer her.

For a while, Hank had become like a father to him, but that wouldn't work either. He probably couldn't live up to the Waters' expectations of him as long as he was wrestling with these demons inside of him.

His boots thudded onto the boardwalk and hesitated before the swinging doors. A cowboy was leaving with one of the saloon girls. Both looked as if they had been at the bar too long. He almost turned away but something drew him inside.

A haze of cigar smoke hung over the saloon as Luke entered the swinging doors, pausing just inside. He was forced to blink and squint, allowing his eyes to adjust to the dim interior after leaving the sunshine outside. The room reeked of liquor and smoke, and he had an urge to bolt.

No, he was going to have a stiff drink. It had been a long time since he'd done that, but he deserved one, didn't he?

"Well, hello there."

Cheap perfume touched his senses before he turned to the young woman in the tight, green satin dress. Luke's eyes swept past the feather in her auburn hair to the uptilted face, heavily rouged.

"Hello," he replied curtly, then looked away.

He could see more clearly now, and his eyes moved past other women mingling with men around the room. Finally, his gaze settled on the mahogany bar on a side wall. He began to walk in that direction.

"That one ain't too friendly, is he?" a male voice spoke from behind him.

"Who cares?" He heard the young woman reply.

He glanced back over his shoulder and saw that she was already approaching another customer entering the saloon.

Luke elbowed up to the crowded bar, staring uninterestedly at the array of bottles and glasses reflected in the wall mirror. A rotund bartender with thick mustache and sideburns worked furiously to fill orders. Luke waited, his eyes scanning the smoky haze, when suddenly he wondered how a place like this had ever held any appeal to him.

He squinted at the woman in the green satin dress, thinking how she, too, had nothing to offer him. Nothing whatsoever.

Then the conversation of the cowhand next to him captured his attention.

"Got a real poker game going in the back room. Big Jake's cleaning out some little fancy pants."

Luke straightened, glancing through the smoke to the door at the rear. He made his way around the tables, his curiosity mounting. He had no interest in another poker game, but the description of "fancy pants" could fit the little scoundrel who'd ambushed him outside of Bordertown.

Cautiously, he entered and looked around. It was a large room with several games in progress. However, it was easy to figure out where the interest was. Several men had gathered around a table in the back. Luke headed in that direction.

Before he reached the table, one of the men left the circle, and through the opening he spotted the little weasel he had met in Bordertown—the one he felt certain had shot him.

His heart pounded as he drew closer. He wasn't sure exactly what he should do, but at the very least, he would confront him. Just then, he heard a gasp spread over the crowd.

The little man had leaped to his feet and pulled a derringer.

"You've cheated me!" he shouted.

Luke was close enough to see that the big cowboy had won all the money, and now the giant came slowly to his feet.

"Now, look here," he said. "I won fair and square. Put that gun away."

The little man was out of control. A sheen of perspiration covered his face; his beady eyes were glazed like a drunk's. Luke's eyes dropped to the table. There were no bottles or shot glasses there. He wasn't drunk; he was crazy.

"I'm gonna kill you," he said, wild-eyed. He raised the gun and took a step backward, knocking his chair over. The chair banged against the floor, and the crazy man jumped, turning his head toward the noise. In that split second, his opponent whipped out a gun and fired.

Disbelief flickered over the little man's face before he hit the table.

Luke backed against the wall and closed his eyes. He hated to see a man killed, even when that man had invited it. Luke knew if there was ever any hope of recovering his money, his last hope had died with the man. Stunned, he stumbled back to the bar as someone ran for the sheriff.

Above the roar, the bartender's voice reached him. "What'll you have?"

Luke looked from the bartender to the bottles lined up on the counter. He shook his head. "Nothing."

He stalked out of the saloon and stood on the boardwalk, breathing deeply of the fresh air. He had hoped a shot of bourbon would calm his nerves, but now it occurred to him he was looking in the wrong place for strength. He wouldn't find strength in a bottle; he'd have to reach down deep in his soul for that.

He walked stiff-legged toward Smoky. If the hour weren't so late, he would go to visit Suzanne. Saloons and everything within held no appeal to him, probably never would again.

As he walked Smoky from the noisy street, he realized it was not just the poker game, the bullet in his shoulder, and his stolen wallet that had changed him. Meeting Suzanne and Hank Waters had changed him more dramatically than anything else.

For some reason, the verse framed in their house rose up in his memory. *All things work together for good. . . .* If he'd not gotten himself shot and ended up in their valley, he never would have met them. What if he had missed knowing her, if only for a short while?

As he reached the quiet outskirts of Colorado Springs, he found himself thinking about another person: his father. What kind of woman had he found here? What kind of life had he lived all these years? And what had happened to him?

~✦~

He waited until the next day to visit Suzanne and her father, and now his spirits lifted as he spotted them seated on the front porch, rocking, listening to the little woman who stood before them, her lips moving rapidly. He saw the happy expression on Suzanne's face when he halted Smoky and swung down.

"Hello," Hank called to Luke as he approached the front porch.

"Good afternoon." Suzanne was smiling, too. He could sense that they had really forgiven him. They weren't holding a grudge about the rude words he had spoken yesterday.

Suzanne got up out of the rocker and came to stand beside him on the porch steps. "Have you found out anything?"

He nodded. "I went to the address. The people who live there never heard of him. Nor had any of the neighbors."

The disappointment was obvious on his face. No matter how hard he tried to pretend he didn't care about finding his father, it mattered more than anything to him now.

She touched his arm. "Don't give up. Someone in this town is bound to have known him."

He shrugged, unconvinced. His eyes moved on to Hank as he climbed the steps.

"Last night I saw the man who robbed me, or rather the man I suspected of robbing me."

Hank bolted out of the rocker, then pressed his chest. "You did? Where? What did you do?"

Luke sighed. "I didn't have a chance to do anything. He was killed after a poker game—accused someone of cheating." He glanced back at Suzanne. "I wasn't in the game."

Luke sank into a rocking chair; Hank followed, still gaping at him.

"That's all there is to tell," he said, looking from Hank to Suzanne. "I didn't find one man, but I found another. Guess I was too late both ways."

Suzanne frowned, following Miss Martha into the house, back to the kitchen.

"What'll you people want for supper this evening?" Miss Martha asked.

Suzanne glanced around the kitchen, her eyes lighting on a platter of chicken left from lunch. The cabbage salad that had gone with it had been tasty as well.

"Would you mind," she asked impulsively, "if I packed some of that chicken for a picnic supper? Luke is feeling low, and he probably hasn't eaten. I think a picnic would perk him up."

Miss Martha beamed. "Great idea. Take him over to the park. It's not far from here. The walk would probably calm your nerves, too, young lady. You look a bit overwrought."

She nodded. "Yes, I am."

"I'll entertain your father," Miss Martha offered quickly, smiling to herself as she bounced around the kitchen, gathering up containers. "Just leave it to me," she called over her shoulder, then began humming.

Suzanne sauntered back to the porch, wondering if Luke would like the idea. It occurred to her that her father's nerves were overwrought as well; he could use a walk and a picnic lunch. No, this time she had to think about Luke. Pa would understand.

———※———

The afternoon sunshine spilled over the small grassy park where couples strolled together and children played.

"Are you hungry?" she asked as they reached a bench and sat down.

"Not just yet."

Across from the park stood a steepled building—a church with white clapboard and stained-glass windows. He glanced away, his eyes resting on two elderly gentlemen seated at the next bench.

"Seeing that man who shot you," Suzanne said, "must have been awful."

Luke leaned back, staring up at the sky. "I felt a terrible rage come over me. Then, when I saw him get shot..." He took a deep breath. "Anyway, I just want to forget it. I learned something important last night. I don't ever care to go in a saloon again, and there won't be any more poker games."

The elderly men were getting up to leave. Their conversation drifted into the silence that had fallen between Suzanne and Luke.

"Well, enough about the war. That was a long time ago," one man was saying.

Suzanne cleared her throat. "Was your father in the war?"

"Yes. Apparently, he felt a strong responsibility to serve his country. I don't know what changed him from a loyal soldier to a coward who abandoned his family twelve years later!"

Suzanne caught her breath. It hurt her to hear him speak such bitterness, but she supposed it was good for him to talk about it, much better than keeping all the anger and hurt shoved down deep to fester in his heart. At the same time, she understood his reserve with her. At times he looked at her as though he really cared—he had told her private things about his family. Still, she was never sure when to ask questions or when to keep silent for fear of upsetting him.

"Luke, don't you have any good memories of him?" she asked in a kind, caring voice.

He closed his eyes, passing his hand over his forehead.

"Sure. He taught me how to track a squirrel, how to sit a horse, how to fish the stream down behind our cabin. Those are good memories, and that's why it took me a long time to understand how he could just ride off and never look back."

"When you find him, he may have an explanation for you."

"Oh, he'll have an explanation. The other woman. She even wrote to my mother." He glanced at Suzanne, his eyes glazed with bitterness. "That was after a short note from him. She said

Pa was living with her, that they loved each other, but he didn't have the heart to write and tell us. In her letter, she claimed she wanted to tell us so we wouldn't worry that something had happened to him when we never heard from him again."

Suzanne swallowed. "What did your mother do?"

"She wrote back immediately, asking to hear those words from him, rather than her. He never answered. She wrote a couple more times, but we never heard anything."

"Perhaps the letters didn't reach him?"

"They were never returned to us, so he got the letters, all right. I guess he just lost his head over the woman." His eyes slipped over Suzanne's features, and he thought about how pretty she was. Since he had met her, he could better understand how a man could lose his head over a woman.

"Luke, what was the woman's name? Do you remember?"

He shook his head. "I don't know what Ma did with the letters, threw them away, I guess. I never saw them again. I do remember"—he frowned—"it was a name I'd never heard before. Don't guess I've heard it since."

"What kind of name? Try to remember."

He stared into space, his eyes narrowed. "I remember; Ma saying something about a flower. The woman had the name of a flower; something unusual."

"What kind of flower? Rose? No, that's not unusual. A pretty flower? Was it a flower that grew in Kansas?"

He shook his head slowly as his eyes returned to her. "I don't know. It was a long time ago."

She tried to conceal her disappointment. *If only he could remember the woman's name!* It could be more important than his father's name, she believed, if the woman had lived here long enough to make friends. But then, they must have left town, since nobody knew his father.

She tried to suppress a sigh of frustration. There was no point in pressing him. That could only make matters worse for him.

"Well," she said, reaching for the picnic basket, "I don't know about you, but my stomach tells me it's time for supper."

"Good idea," Luke said. "Where do you want to picnic?"

"How about here?" She led the way to a private area beneath a large cottonwood.

"Perfect," he said, sinking down on the grass and removing his hat.

His dark hair tumbled about his forehead, and as his eyes began to soften, Suzanne looked at him, for the first time imagining him as a boy with tousled dark hair and glowing eyes. That would have been before his father had left. She suspected Luke had turned into a man overnight, trying to protect his mother and help put food on the table.

Luke tilted his head, looking at her. "When are you going to open that basket?" he asked teasingly.

"Right now," Suzanne said, turning her mind back to the present. She opened the basket and spread the cloth Miss Martha had thoughtfully included. Then she put out the chicken and cabbage salad, the plates and utensils.

"Oh no." She looked at Luke. "I forgot the tea."

"Doesn't matter." He smiled at her. "This is a real treat."

They ate heartily. Suzanne thought the chicken tasted even better cold. She was glad Miss Martha had packed plenty of it, for Luke kept reaching for more.

A contented silence flowed between them as they enjoyed the food and the picturesque setting. Suzanne looked up from the church across the way to the dry goods store on the corner, and on to a hardware store down the block.

"This is a nice town," she said, "but I miss our peaceful little valley and our own special mountain."

"Morning Mountain," Luke mused. "That sounds nice. Who gave the mountain that name?"

"Mattie says the first settler into the valley named it. She didn't say why, but I can guess. That mountain is beautiful in the morning. . .looking at it helps to start my day off right."

Her eyes returned to the church and she glanced at Luke. He had followed her gaze there and was solemnly studying the steeple.

"Suzanne"—he turned to her—"since we're sitting here in the shadow of the church, I need to explain something to you."

She was dabbing her lips with a linen napkin. "Go ahead."

"Well—" He broke off, folding his napkin.

"Please, go on. Say whatever you're thinking. I won't be offended."

He looked at her sadly. "Oh, I don't think it would offend you to know how much I admire you and your father. You're so strong in your faith. My mother was that way, and—believe it or not—I used to read the Bible and pray with Ma. But then. . .I got mad at God. I guess I tried to believe He didn't exist; otherwise, He'd have heard me begging Him, night after night, to bring back my father."

Now, as he spoke of God, new hope filled her heart.

"Luke"—she reached across to squeeze his hand—"you've had a very difficult time, and I don't have any answers. Sometimes things just happen, and we never understand why."

"You haven't had an easy time of it, either," he said, holding her hand, "but your heart hasn't turned hard the way mine has."

He looked at her tenderly. Suzanne saw his expression and she found herself hoping, desperately hoping, that he loved her. But would he ever admit it to himself? To her?

"Sometimes when I'm with you," he said, "I can believe that life is good, that maybe things do work out. But then. . ." His voice trailed and he dropped her hand.

Suzanne held her breath. "Luke, listen to me. Life *is* good. You can be happy again. You could start a new life here."

He shook his head. "Not here. This town is a reminder that we lost him here. I can't stay."

She bit her lip, wondering how far to go with this conversation. She wanted to plead with him to come back with them to the ranch, to let her help him heal. But Luke was his own man, and he would make his own decisions when he was ready. In the meantime, all she could do was offer him the kindness he needed in his life. And her love. When he was ready to accept it.

Should she tell him that? Wasn't it fair for him to know?

"Luke, I have to say something to you. You know I say what I think and. . ." She glanced at the church, drawing strength. "I want you to know that I love you."

Luke caught his breath. For a moment, he looked stunned by her words.

Suzanne flushed, looking away. She felt like a fool until Luke's hand cupped her chin, and ever so gently, he placed a kiss upon her lips.

When she opened her eyes, he was looking down at her with a tenderness that melted her heart.

"I love you, too, Suzanne. You're all I could ever want in a woman but. . ."

He pulled back from her, dropped his hand, and stared off in the distance.

"It's hard for me to get past today," he finally replied. "Please be patient with me. Maybe, when I can put the past behind me and figure out where I go from here. . ."

"Luke, I want you to keep looking for him."

He nodded. "Maybe I will. I don't know where that search will lead me, but somehow I don't think I can get on with my life until I find him. I promised Ma."

She nodded. "I know. You mustn't give up! You owe it to yourself—and you owe it to him."

CHAPTER 18

When Hank returned to the doctor's office the next morning for more tests, Suzanne decided to run an errand. She had spotted a library near the doctor's office, and now she was sauntering among the shelves, looking at books.

"May I help you, miss?" the librarian called helpfully.

"Yes. I'm looking for a book on flowers; specifically, the names of all kinds of flowers."

The librarian pursed her lips. "We have a new book in from a publishing house in New York." She reached up on a shelf and pulled down a thick tome. "It lists not only flowers but plants and shrubs. Would you like to check it out?"

"Yes, I would."

It was a shot in the dark, as Pa would say, but why not give it a try?

⟶⟵

Suzanne sat at the kitchen table with Miss Martha, listening as she went on about the challenges of growing roses here in the high country. When finally she stopped to catch her breath, Suzanne cleared her throat and glanced down at the open page of the library book.

There were so many different kinds of flowers. How could they possibly find the one that matched the woman's name?

"Miss Martha," Suzanne began, "I want to ask you something. You said you never heard of a man named Luke Thomason. Can you think back, fourteen years ago, to a woman who lived here—" She broke off, realizing she had no idea what to ask. "Well, we don't even know her name, but Luke remembers it was like a flower."

Miss Martha looked bewildered. "A flower? My goodness, there's Rose or Iris or. . ." Her blue eyes went blank. "That's all the names I can think of." Then she smiled warmly. "You really want to help that young man, don't you?"

Suzanne nodded. "If I read off some flowers, will you listen to the names and see if you can think of anyone you ever knew or heard of by those names?"

Suzanne could see by Miss Martha's amused expression that she believed they were not going to accomplish anything.

"I'll try," she said tolerantly.

Suzanne started at the beginning of the alphabet. Once or twice, Miss Martha interrupted her, asking her to repeat the name. Then she shook her head.

"Jasmine and. . ."

"Wait!" Miss Martha threw up her little hand. "Jasmine, that's a flower that blooms in warm climates."

Suzanne glanced at her, trying to hide her exasperation. She hoped Miss Martha wouldn't get back on the subject of which flowers were suited to Colorado's climate and which ones were not.

"I don't know," Suzanne sighed. "I never heard of it."

"Wait a minute." Miss Martha jumped out of her chair and began to pace the floor. "Tillie!" She snapped her fingers, and hurried toward the back door. "Tillie, my neighbor, owned a dress shop on Pikes Peak Avenue fourteen years ago. Every woman in town wanted a dress from Tillie's shop. Since then, Tillie got out of the business. When she stood on her feet for long periods of time—"

"Do you think," Suzanne interrupted her gently, "you've

heard your friend mention the name Jasmine?"

Miss Martha stared into space, her face perplexed. "I don't know why, but I'm associating that name with Tillie. I'll run down to her house and see what she has to say."

"May I go with you?" Suzanne asked, trailing after her.

———✦———

Tillie Ledbetter rarely ventured from her cozy frame house that sat serenely behind a picket fence. The health problem Miss Martha had referred to was apparent to Suzanne at once, for the woman's feet were so swollen she had dispensed with shoes.

Tillie was a large woman whose excessive weight had contributed to the swelling of her knees and ankles, but she chose to blame the years she had spent standing on her feet in her fashion shop.

Miss Martha first posed the question of Luke Thomason— had Tillie ever known a man here by that name?

Tillie shook her head. "No, don't recall anyone by that name."

"What about the name Jasmine?" Miss Martha prodded.

Tillie turned her large head sideways, peering at Suzanne.

"You're looking for this woman?" she inquired, frowning.

"Yes, I am. Have you ever heard the name?"

Tillie nodded her gray head slowly. "'Course I have. She was a good customer many years ago, but then. . ."

Suzanne pounced on those words, kneeling beside the chair and looking up into the woman's face. "It's very important that I find this woman. Do you know if she's still here?"

A look of disapproval sat on Tillie's face before she replied. "The top drawer of the desk there. The big black book." She looked at Martha. "I still have a list of my customers."

Suzanne quickly retrieved the book and handed it to Tillie. As the woman's arthritic fingers fumbled with the pages, Suzanne had to fight an urge to grab the book and flip through it herself. She reminded herself the woman was doing her a great favor, that she must be patient.

An eternity seemed to pass as a Big Ben clock ticked relentlessly from the hallway and Miss Martha flitted about the parlor, examining the withered leaves of an African violet.

"Needs more water, Tillie," she scolded. "Last year when I was growing—"

"Here it is. Jasmine Rogers. I haven't seen her in years." She looked at Suzanne. "There's a pen and pad on the desk so you can write down the address." She frowned again. "That's a poor section of town now. Didn't used to be so bad."

Miss Martha flew back to their sides. "Suzanne is trying to help her friend Luke find his father. The man was with this woman—well, maybe not this one."

"No, I don't think Jasmine had a man. I heard she got her heart broken years ago, and never had anything to do with men after that. But I seem to remember something. . ." The frown deepened, then she shook her head. "My memory isn't so good anymore."

"I think your memory is excellent," Suzanne said, jotting down the address. "If this should be the woman we're looking for, I'll be eternally grateful."

Tillie studied Suzanne curiously. "I don't know who this young man is, but you must think a great deal of him."

"I do," Suzanne replied, folding the paper carefully and tucking it into her pocket. "I do. . ."

Hank seemed ill and out of sorts, Suzanne thought, as they left the livery. She had insisted on leaving a note there for Luke, in case he stopped by to check on the team. Her note explained what she had learned and gave the address of Jasmine Rogers. She'd left a duplicate at home with Miss Martha in case he stopped there.

Foolishly, she had neglected to find out where he was staying. Now she was worried sick that for some reason he might decide to leave town without a good-bye.

"Daughter, you're getting too involved," Hank snapped, upon hearing her plan.

"Pa, you know you're just as anxious as I am to help Luke."

He heaved a sigh. "Do you think finding his pa will help

him? And what about you?"

Suzanne stared at him. "What do you mean?"

"He's already told us, once he settles the score with his pa, he'll be heading back for Kansas."

Suzanne bit her lip, trying not to think of that. "I know, but we have to risk losing him in order to help him."

Hank turned and stared at his daughter. "Suzanne, sometimes you amaze me." A smile softened his grim expression. "I'm proud of you. Maybe I don't tell you that often enough, but you know I am."

"I know, Pa," she replied.

She didn't like words like this, which took her back to the last days she had spent with her mother. Her mother had spoken of pride and love and...

Suzanne bit her lip. Just because her father seemed tired and out of sorts, and prone to compliment her, didn't mean he was going to die.

She stared bleakly at the streets, seeing nothing as she breathed a silent, desperate prayer.

⁓

According to the man at the livery, Luke had just missed Suzanne and her father.

"She left a note for you in case you stopped by," the burly blacksmith said, lumbering into a tiny office to retrieve the note that had seemed so important to the pretty woman.

Puzzled, Luke took the note, already worrying that she was giving him bad news about her father. Quickly, he scanned the neat handwriting, then stared into space.

Jasmine! That was her name!

Luke checked the slip of paper again, confirming the address, as the clopping of horse's hooves broke the sullen stillness in this seedy part of town. He drew rein before the cabin at the end of the street. This was it.

The wedding band was nestled deep in his pocket. He was glad Suzanne had refused to sell it. The ring would prove his identity to the man who had abandoned him. He was going to feel like a fool, seeking out a father who had run out on him years ago.

He tried not to think about it, for he might lose his nerve. He'd simply tell him who he was, show him the ring, and admit he was here only because Ma had begged him to come. Even now, he half-regretted making that promise to her. But he had, and he couldn't bring himself to back down. He'd never broken a promise to his mother when she was alive. And—he glanced idly at the clouds—he suspected she was still watching him.

He swung down from the horse and stared at the dilapidated cabin, sadly in need of paint. He glanced at the row of cabins he had passed. The others were no better.

A shutter hung crookedly against a window, covered with cheap cloth. There was no sign of life about the house. Did anyone live here? he wondered.

Well, he'd come this far, might as well knock on the door.

He tethered his horse to a sapling and crossed the small patch of yard where no grass dared grow, only weeds interspersed with pebbles and broken twigs from the lone tree at the corner. His boots resounded like a drumbeat on the rickety porch. Beneath his weight, one board shifted, and he quickly sidestepped it. The other boards were loose, warped here and there. As he hurried to the door, something scrambled under the board porch, and he wondered how many rats infested the place.

The rough wooden door looked as though it had never held a coat of paint. He knocked carelessly, not expecting anyone to respond.

Faintly, he could hear footsteps moving slowly within. His heart beat faster. What was he going to do if the door opened and he was staring into his father's face?

The steps drew nearer, approaching the door. His eyes flew back over the surroundings. No, his father was not here; he and the woman probably had stayed only a short while until. . .

The door cracked, then opened wider. He met a pair of dark eyes in a withered face. The woman did not speak; she merely stared at him. She was a pitiful-looking woman. This couldn't possibly be the woman his father had left them for.

"Excuse me." He removed his hat. "I was looking for someone, but I think I've come to the wrong place."

"Who are you looking for?" The voice was faint and labored, as though the woman had a breathing problem.

He felt more ridiculous by the minute. Still, he remembered the promise and knew he must begin his search here.

"I'm looking for a woman named Jasmine Rogers."

"She moved away." She was about to slam the door.

"Did you ever know a Luke Thomason?" he asked, thinking this was his last effort to find them.

She hesitated. Her dark eyes ran over him curiously. For a moment he thought she wasn't even going to respond. Then finally she opened her mouth to speak. He regretted coming. She was obviously too ill to be standing at the door.

"Sorry to have bothered you."

He turned to go, fitting his hat to his head again.

"Luke?" the woman called to him.

He whirled. "Yes, that was his name. Luke Thomason."

"I know. And you must be his son."

His knees were suddenly weak, as if he'd been rodeoing for the past twelve hours. Stunned, his eyes flew over her.

"I thought you were a bill collector." She sighed.

"You're Jasmine?" he asked incredulously.

"Yes. You'd better come in," she said, opening the door wider.

He stepped on the board porch, vaguely aware of the scurrying underneath. His eyes swept her, taking in every detail. She was a tall woman whose thin body was wrapped in a worn housecoat. Her feet were bare, her toes gnarled. Her skin was blue, as though she were cold, yet it was a warm spring day.

He said nothing as his mind groped with the words she had spoken. Now he tried to put meaning behind them.

"Come back to the kitchen," she said, closing the door behind him as he stepped into the front room, a cluttered living room with sagging furniture.

His eyes moved over the room, seeking a clue to the woman as he followed her into the tiny kitchen. This room was even more cluttered than the other one. Every available space on the counter was filled with canned goods, pots and pans, medicine bottles. Still, there was a pleasant aroma of something stewing in a pot on the old stove.

She motioned him to the tiny table in the center of the room. One chair was pulled back from the table. He spotted another chair against the wall and reached for it. There was no tablecloth, no flowers to grace the center as there had been in his mother's kitchen. A chipped enamel cup held something dark.

"I was having a cup of tea. I'll fix one for you."

He couldn't respond; his tongue had gone thick. This woman obviously was a link to his father, and suddenly he found himself willing to do almost anything to find him. This emotion surprised him, for he had built a wall around his heart, trying to protect it from ever feeling the awful ache he'd felt as a little boy losing the father he adored.

The woman moved slowly about her tiny kitchen, every movement an obvious effort. She dumped something into a cup, pulled a kettle from the burner, and poured steaming water into the cup. She reached for a spoon, frowning down into the liquid as she stirred. Then she handed him the cup.

He stared at her. "How did you know I was his son?" She sighed and sank into the chair, staring at him. She had probably been attractive once upon a time, he decided. Not the gentle prettiness of his mother, a coarser kind of beauty, perhaps. Her hair, like her eyes, was dark, streaked with gray, slightly balding at the crown. Her features were bold, her lips tilted downward.

"Because you look just like him."

His heart was beating faster. "Where is he?" he asked, glancing toward the back door.

She looked down at her cup for a moment, then looked back at him. "He's dead," she replied.

Luke sank back in the chair. Naturally, he had considered the fact that his father might have died by now, but somehow he was unprepared to hear that announcement spoken in such a direct manner.

"How long ago did he die?" he asked. His voice sounded scratchy; his throat felt tight.

She lifted the cup and took a sip of her tea.

Luke stared at her wrinkled lips, wishing she would hurry and speak the words, tell him what she knew so he could leave.

"He died fourteen years ago."

Luke's mouth fell open as his mind slowly began to react, counting up the years.

"Fourteen years?" he repeated, trying to recall just how long it had been. He had just turned twelve when his father had saddled up and ridden off. He was twenty-six now. "He died soon after he came here?" He spoke his thoughts aloud. "Why didn't you tell us in one of your letters?"

"I need to tell you the story," she said, her breath rasping. "The whole story." She took a deep, labored breath, releasing it slowly. "Maybe then I can die in peace."

Scarcely aware of what he was doing, he lifted the mug and took a sip of the tea. It was a strong, heady substance, racing through him, jolting some of the shock from his brain.

"When your father rode into town, I was working at one of the saloons. That's right," she said, observing the look in his eyes. "I was the very opposite of your mother, I'm sure." Her voice had grown stronger as she tilted her head back, staring at something on the ceiling. She looked at him again, and a faint smile touched her pale lips.

"It was love at first sight for me, but not for him, of course." She sighed, tilting the cup again. She closed her eyes for a moment, and Luke thought she looked ancient, though she surely would not have been much older than his father. That would make her. . .midfifties.

"I made a play for him right away. He ignored me, and every other woman, but I kept talking to him. He had just come to town, looking for land to homestead. I could tell he didn't hang out in saloons. He seemed uncomfortable. Then, as he was leaving, we heard a commotion outside. I followed him out the door."

She paused for more tea.

"A man had taken a horsewhip to a young boy out in front of the saloon. It was a pitiful sight. Don't know what the boy had done, but he didn't deserve to have a beating like that. Luke stepped in."

She stared into space, her eyes glazed as though seeing that horrible scene again. Then she shuddered. "The man pulled a gun and shot Luke. He fell facedown on the street, and the man yelled for the boy to get into the wagon. They tore out of town. The sheriff came but did nothing. Said Luke had no business interfering with a man and his family."

When she hesitated, Luke finally found his voice.

"But he didn't die then, did he? He wrote to us. . ."

"I took him to my place, had the doc with him, nursed him day and night. You see, he didn't know a soul in this town. He was shot in the abdomen, a bad shot. I fed him broth, bathed him, cared for him. The doc said he would never"—she hesitated for a moment, then looked Luke in the eye—"be able to have more children, or live like a normal person again. He was messed up bad."

Luke dropped his head, feeling all the love for his father surfacing from a remote corner of his heart.

"Luke, I never loved a man like I loved your father. I just knew I could heal his broken heart, and I didn't care about the rest. Kansas seemed faraway, and I didn't realize then how a person never stops loving someone. I thought the family he left behind would get over him. I told him he should write to you."

Luke remembered the letter—short, vague, telling them nothing, really. *Why hadn't Pa mentioned being shot? It would be just like him not to want to worry Ma.*

"My mother wrote back, but she never heard from him until—"

"Until I wrote her, saying he didn't love her anymore, that there was no point in writing to him. As for your mother's letters, I never gave them to him."

Luke glared at her, a slow rage building in him. He stood up abruptly, bumping the table and causing the tea to slosh in its cup.

"Luke, he died within three months. I had so little time with him, but—"

"You had no right," he snarled at her. "I thought the person I loved more than anyone had abandoned me. We nearly starved. And Ma believed—" He broke off, staring into space. What had she said on her deathbed?

"I don't know what happened to your father, but I never stopped loving him, and I believe he still loves me. A love like ours never dies. Please go and see him for me. . . ."

"Luke, you need to know this," Jasmine continued. Her voice had grown weak, ragged. "He called your mother's name when he was sickest, and he talked about you all the time. He said it was the reason he tried to save the boy outside the saloon—the boy was your age. He'd have given his life for you, Luke; and I think for a moment, that boy became you."

Luke swallowed hard, as the anger began to fade. He sank into the chair, staring at this woman, trying to see her through his father's eyes. She had cared for him, done her best to save his life. He supposed he should be grateful for that. Still, he couldn't forgive her for. . .

Forgive. That word stuck in his brain. He could never seem to get away from it.

"I know what I did was wrong," she continued faintly. "If you knew how I've been tormented by guilt all these years, you would know I have paid for my mistake. I know I should've written, but it became so painful I couldn't face it. What I'd done, who I'd become. Guilt is a terrible thing, maybe stronger than love, if that's possible."

She came slowly to her feet and walked unsteadily to a corner cabinet. Opening the door, she reached to the very back. He watched her with tormented eyes, still too stunned to anticipate what she might say or do next.

"Maybe you'll believe I'm telling you the truth if I give you this."

She pulled out an ordinary-looking jar, unscrewed the cap, and withdrew a small leather pouch. He stared at the pouch, his mind tumbling back to the day he had said good-bye to his father. His father had placed the pouch in a secret pocket sewn his plaid woolen shirt.

Now Luke stared at the pouch, the image of his father's strong hands etched in his memory from that day.

"Take it," she said. "It belongs to you and your mother."

Luke took the pouch and opened it. It was filled with money. He looked up at her, puzzled and confused.

"I never took a dollar out of there," she said, gripping the edge of the table as she sank slowly into the chair. "It was bad enough that I had stolen another woman's husband. Somehow I couldn't bring myself to take the money, too."

Luke didn't know what to say. He looked from the money to the woman. "I don't want it," he said at last, thrusting it across the table to her. His hand touched the tea, knocking it over. The brown liquid seeped across the table. He set the cup upright and looked around for a cloth to wipe up the mess. The woman didn't seem to notice.

"Don't be a fool," she snapped. Her dark eyes bored into his. "I've been trying to figure out how to get that money to you and your mother. I was determined to think of something, but I was running out of time..."

She had turned deathly pale. Her breathing made heavy rasps in the still kitchen as she reached for her tea.

"What's wrong with you?" Luke asked, watching her tilt the cup again.

"A lung disease. I haven't much time left." With shaking hands, she set the cup down. It made a hollow *clunk* on the wooden table, accenting the silence that filled the room. Jasmine lifted bleak, desperate eyes to Luke's face. "I don't know what kind of miracle brought you here. But I'm glad you came."

Luke stared at her, somehow pitying her, wanting to offer comfort, yet unable to do so. This woman had brought them years of pain and heartache. He didn't hate her anymore, but he was not ready to be kind.

He knew she had read the emotion on his face because she cupped her chin in her hand and closed her eyes, as though defeated.

"Please, leave now," she said, reaching over to place the pouch in his hands again.

He opened his mouth, started to speak, then fell silent, unable to find words. His mind was like a flying jenny whirling around and around, while his heart pounded and his hand tightened on the pouch. The leather was soft, warm. He looked at it, feeling the last link with his mother and father.

Abruptly, he stood, tucking the pouch in his pants pocket. Again, he tried to say something to this woman, but he could not; so he turned and walked out of the house, closing the door softly behind him.

CHAPTER 19

Suzanne paced around the waiting room of the doctor's office. Three days had passed, and she had not seen or heard from Luke. Suzanne and Hank had driven past the ramshackle address Tillie had scrawled on the paper, but upon seeing Smoky tethered out front, they decided not to intrude on the private moment. *He must've ridden fast, to beat us to the house like that,* Suzanne mused to herself. Had he found his father? Or had he found someone at that address who had sent him to another town? Why hadn't he let her know what was going on?

Her father was responding well to the medicine, and for that, she was thankful beyond words. Still, she couldn't stop thinking of Luke. She was ready to swallow her pride and try to locate him if he hadn't left town already.

She thought back to the conversation she and her father had had while James, Miss Martha's nephew, had driven them to Dr. Crownover's office in his small buggy. James was a tall, gangly young man of nineteen who vaguely reminded her of Art Parkinson, though he had more class. He worked for Miss Martha as chauffeur, errand, and delivery boy.

"I've asked everyone I've come in contact with about a Luke Thomason," Hank had blurted the name that was uppermost in their minds, though neither had spoken. "Nobody knows him; he must have left here years ago."

"And now Luke's gone, too," she had responded with uncharacteristic pessimism.

Hank had said nothing more. She knew he was disappointed, as well. How could Luke have left without telling them good-bye?

"Miss Waters."

The sound of Dr. Crownover's voice pulled her thoughts back to the waiting room of the doctor's office.

Her eyes flew to the doorway of his private office, where he now stood, wearing what she hoped was a pleased smile. "Could you step in here, please?"

"Of course."

He was going to give them his opinion on Pa's heart condition now. She wrung her hands tightly before her and followed him into the cozy room where her father sat in an armchair opposite the doctor's desk. She settled into the other armchair, giving her father a reassuring smile.

The little doctor came back around the desk and took a seat. He looked at them with keen hazel eyes that had taken on a pleasant sparkle, Suzanne noticed. He shuffled through the papers on his desk, reading something briefly, then looking back at them.

Why doesn't he hurry up and say something? Suzanne thought wildly, wondering if she and her father could contain their suspense for another moment.

Dr. Crownover cleared his throat. "I'm pleased to report that Mr. Waters' heart rate is slowing down to a normal pattern since he's been on the medication. And all the other tests indicate good health." He smiled, looking from Suzanne to Hank. "I believe you can go back to the ranch now. Just check in with me every three months. Or sooner, if there are any problems."

"You mean we can go home now?" Hank yelled, as excited as a child. "I'm going to be all right?"

"As all right as a man of your temperament can be!"

"Thank God," Hank said, dropping his head for a second.

Suzanne jumped up to hug her father. "Oh Pa, I'm so relieved. Now we can go back to teasing and arguing and living a normal life!" She laughed as tears of happiness filled her eyes. She turned to the doctor, wanting to give him a hug as well. She refrained from doing so, sensing that such a gesture would simply embarrass the shy little man.

"The fussing will be up to you two." He grinned. "I am going to require him to give up his pipe, and limit his coffee to one cup at breakfast."

Hank moaned, but Suzanne placed a hand on his shoulder. "Can he still work with his horses?"

Hank's eyes shot to Dr. Crownover.

The little man studied Hank for a moment, then grinned. "I wouldn't think of denying him that pleasure. Just be reasonable about doing anything strenuous."

A grin spread over Hank's thin face. "Thanks, Doc."

Suzanne opened her purse and withdrew the money she had earned on the cattle drive.

"We can't thank you enough, Dr. Crownover. How much do we owe you?"

The doctor shook his hand. "If you don't mind, I'd prefer to use your father as a guinea pig, so to speak."

Hank's gray brows peaked. "Beg your pardon?"

Dr. Crownover chuckled. "Don't be offended. It's simply a medical term for asking a patient to try out a new drug. You aren't the first patient to use this drug, but you are the oldest. I'd like access to use your records in my teaching and writing, if you have no objection."

"No, Doc. Don't reckon I mind if someone else could be helped."

Suzanne looked from the doctor to her father, then back again.

"You mean we don't owe you anything?" She couldn't believe it.

"You'll have to buy your own medicine when those I gave you run out," he said. "And the medicine is a bit expensive."

"We can manage," Suzanne said. "Thank you." She threw her arms around the man heedless of his awkward stance.

"You two are setting off on that long journey back all by your-selves?" Miss Martha asked incredulously.

"Suzanne and I will make it just fine," Hank replied. "Don't trouble yourself any. Now, if you can figure up our bill, we'll be on our way."

Miss Martha fidgeted with her apron strings and shook her head. "I owe Mattie a big favor, one I'd feared I'd never be able to repay. She never comes to town."

Suzanne had entered the large kitchen, where her father was drinking a glass of ice water rather than his usual coffee. Upon hearing the conversation, Suzanne walked over to Miss Martha's side.

"I don't understand. What does your owing Mattie a favor have to do with us?"

Miss Martha grinned. "Well, seeing as how you two are spe-cial friends of hers, I consider you guests in my home. I couldn't allow you to pay."

Suzanne looked from Miss Martha to her father.

"Oh no, ma'am," Hank protested. "We can't intrude on your hospitality that way."

She shook her head. "Mattie and her dear husband spent a winter here once. She became the best friend I ever had in my life. I can't count the times she insisted on cooking the evening meal when I was worn out or feeling poorly. This is the least I can do for Mattie. But"—she looked Pa over with mischievous blue eyes—"you can pay me back by showing kindness to her. She's pretty fond of you."

Hank shuffled awkwardly, tugging at the lapel of his coat.

"We're fond of Mattie, too, aren't we, Suzanne?" He looked desperately at Suzanne, trying to conceal his embarrassment.

"Of course we are. Mattie has become a good friend, too, Miss Martha. And I think Pa feels the same way."

"Well, if we can't pay you, we'd best get on our way," he said, hurrying from the kitchen.

Suzanne stared after him for a moment, then looked back at Miss Martha. "I hope you don't think he was abrupt," she said, a bit embarrassed.

Miss Martha shook her head and grinned at Suzanne. "No, I just think he and Mattie are kind of sweet on each other."

Suzanne bit her lip, trying to suppress a laugh. "Well, that's fine with me," she said, hugging Miss Martha. "Thanks for all you've done for us. When we come back in three months, it has to be understood we'll be paying guests. Otherwise. . ."

"All right, it's understood. I'll look forward to your coming. Just drop me a note in advance if that's possible, so I can have your rooms ready."

Suzanne stood in the immaculate bedroom, her eyes scanning every corner. The cherry four-poster bed and matching dresser and washstand had been a sweet taste of luxury, a reminder of the home she had left behind in Denver. Yet, she did not feel sad about returning to the ranch. With extra money the doctor and Miss Martha had refused to take, they could now buy another horse or two, and make it through summer. She was looking forward to going home.

She was saddened by the fact that Luke hadn't stopped by before he'd left for. . .wherever he had gone. But perhaps there was a reason for that. She had foolishly blurted out her love for him—and he had expressed love for her. But he had also told her, in so many words, that he was not ready to settle down.

What had he said? He had to straighten his life out first. He had asked her to be patient, but what did he expect? He knew they would be returning to the ranch soon.

Maybe he had thought it would be easier for both of them if he left without a good-bye.

She reached down to snap the lid on her trunk. She had to stop thinking about him, but even as she made that vow, an ache filled her heart, reaching to her throat. She hadn't allowed herself to cry over him. She'd been too busy being grateful about Pa. And it seemed wrong, somehow, for her to be crying when she should be so relieved, so happy that the medicine was working for Pa.

Still...

The trunk blurred before her as the tears she had fought now slipped over her lashes and down her cheeks. *I can't help thinking of him. And I can't help loving him,* she thought miserably.

There, she had admitted it again. Maybe she'd feel better.

James knocked on her door. "Are you ready, Miss Waters?" he called politely.

"Yes, I'm ready," she said, glancing around the room to be sure she hadn't forgotten something. "Come on in."

He smiled shyly as he entered, and she thought about how kind he had been to them.

"I hope you have a good year at the college."

Miss Martha had confided that her nephew was attending the prestigious college here in Colorado Springs.

"Thank you." He smiled.

She'd never get to go to college, but someday she would like for her children—

She halted her train of thought. It appeared unlikely now that she would ever marry. The only man who'd ever appealed to her had ridden out of her life forever.

"I've put your father's satchel in the buggy."

Suzanne nodded. "All right. I'm ready."

"Don't forget your letter," he said, reaching for the trunk.

Suzanne stared at him. "What letter?"

"The letter on the hall table."

Suzanne rushed past him, her skirts flying about her ankles. As soon as she spotted the envelope and saw Luke's scrawl, her heart began to hammer. She tore into the envelope and removed the brief note bearing today's date. *Today?*

> *Dear Suzanne,*
> *I came by to see you this morning, but you and your father were still at the doctor's office. I'll be back around noon. I have some business to take care of, but when I'm finished I'd like to see you back to the ranch.*
> *Love,*
> *Luke*

Suzanne reread the note as relief, then happiness, flooded through her.

"Pa, wait!" she called, running out the front door.

Luke swung down from Smoky and tied the reins to a sapling. He retraced his steps up the walk to the same cabin where only three days ago he had heard the most startling story of his entire life. He had spent these past days alone in the boarding-house when he hadn't riding over the countryside, pondering his life and his future. He had purposely stayed away from Suzanne and Hank until he had sorted through his feelings. Now he had—and he knew exactly what he wanted to do.

He stepped on the porch, avoiding the buckling board, hearing again the scampering sound underneath. He knocked on the door, then removed his hat, waiting for the slow thudding steps to eventually reach the door. Finally the door creaked open.

"Miss Rogers?"

He had been so stunned by this woman and the story she had told that he had overlooked some important details, like where his father was buried. He had found the town cemetery, however, and the tombstone marked Luke Thomason. He had stood there for a long time, making his peace.

"Hello, Luke," she said weakly. "Would you like to come in?"

"I can't stay." The words he had planned to say now hung in his throat as he twirled his hat in his hands and glanced back down the row of cheap cabins. "I went to my father's grave," he said, looking at her again. "The caretaker at the cemetery told me you've seen to its upkeep all these years. I really appreciate that."

She tilted her head and looked at him curiously. Then she smiled faintly. "I'll be put to rest beside him. I hope you don't mind."

It occurred to him he hadn't told her his mother had died.

"No, I don't mind," he said quietly. He felt sure the souls of his father and mother had been reunited. The physical aspects of life didn't seem to matter that much anymore. "Is there anything I can do before I leave?"

"Yes."

He waited, wondering what she would ask.

"You can forgive me."

His lips twitched as he tried to smile. "I couldn't have done that when I left Kansas. Along the way, I met a beautiful, kind woman. She and her father have taught me a lesson in forgiveness. And I've been doing some soul-searching myself these past days." He took a deep breath and his smile widened. "I forgive you," he said at last. "Try to find some peace now in the time you have left."

Tears streamed down the wrinkled cheeks, and for the first time the dark eyes held an expression of hope.

"Thank you, Luke. And I do hope that you and your young woman find the love that"—she paused, then continued—"your parents had for each other."

He swallowed hard. "Thank you."

———

At noon, he cantered Smoky up Tejon to Miss Martha's Boardinghouse. He spotted Hank, sitting in a rocking chair on the front porch. Luke sensed Hank's restlessness from the way the rocker was moving back and forth in swift, almost frantic, motions.

When Hank glanced toward Luke, spotting horse and rider, his face lit up. He bolted out of the rocking chair and hurried down the porch steps to greet him.

"The medicine worked," he called to Luke.

Luke swung down from his horse and shook Hank's hand. "That's real good news, Mr. Waters. I had a feeling everything was going to turn out just fine for you."

Hank nodded. "And what about you? We were anxious to hear, but we thought maybe you'd left town."

Luke looked into Hank's eyes and shook his head. "I'd never do that without coming to see you first." Luke squared his shoulders. "My father died fourteen years ago. It'll take a long time to tell the story, so we'll have plenty to talk about in the wagon." Luke took a deep breath and spoke the words he had thought about long and hard. "I'll be accompanying you home," he said.

Home, did he say? Hank grinned. "Be mighty glad to have you," he said. "And I'm anxious to hear that story."

Luke hesitated. "If you have no objection, I'll be staying on."

Hank's brawny hand fumbled absently with the breast pocket of his shirt. "Keep forgetting I've given up my pipe. Luke, that's the second dose of good news I've had. My old ticker may get out of rhythm again!" Hank stroked his chin thoughtfully. "Luke?"

Luke was looking toward the house, and Hank figured from the wistful expression on his face, he might be hankering to see Suzanne. Still, Hank wanted to speak his piece.

"Yes, sir?" Luke looked back at him.

"There's no strings attached at my ranch. I'd never let my daughter talk me out of keeping my word like that lowdown Godfrey fellow did."

Luke grinned. "Mr. Waters, I never thought of you as an eavesdropper."

"Nobody said that conversation was confidential, as I recollect."

"Well, sir, back to the subject of the ranch. What I had in mind was a partnership with you. I have some money now."

Hank looked surprised. "You don't say? Well, sure. That's something else we can jaw on in the wagon."

Luke grinned and glanced toward the house. "Where's your daughter?"

"She went out back with Miss Martha to see that flower garden one last time before we go."

"I'd like to talk with her," Luke said, shoving his hands in his pockets. He turned and walked around the side of the house, his head bent, his brow furrowed.

He spotted Suzanne in the rear of the yard, bending over a rose-bush. The funny-looking little woman had gone trotting back to the house for something, and Luke quickened his steps, seizing the opportunity.

"Hello," he called.

She whirled, and the thoughtful expression on her face turned quickly to one of radiance.

"Luke, I'm so glad to see you." She came forward and wrapped her arms around him. "Are you okay?"

Surprised and pleased, he hugged her back.

"I'm okay. More than okay." He reached down, tilting her head back. Adoring gray eyes shone up into his face. "I have a lot to tell you, but the most important thing is what I need to ask you."

She looked puzzled. He reached into his pocket and removed the gold wedding band. "I'd like to give this back again. This time, I hope you'll agree to wear it—as my wife."

Suzanne gasped. Her eyes dropped to the ring, then returned to his face. She smiled, raising her hand so that he could slip the ring on her finger.

"We'll need a ceremony to make it official," he said, looking nervous.

She smiled. "I think that can be arranged when we return to Morning Mountain."

His lips came down, brushing over hers gently. Then, as her arms went around him again, he pulled her against his chest, kissing her as he had longed to do since the day he'd met her.

When they broke apart, breathless, Luke began to chuckle. "I think we'd better plan that wedding pretty soon. Suzanne, I have so much to tell you."

"I want to hear! You have no idea how anxious I've been, how I've watched the window, hoping you'd come back."

"I'm a better man now," he said, looking with pride at this woman who had agreed to be his wife. "I have something to offer you. . ."

"You've always had something to offer me," she said, reaching up to caress his cheek. "You're all I could want in a man. There's just one thing," she said, trying to think how to broach the subject.

"Suzanne, I've made my peace with God," he said quietly.

She looked at him for a moment, saying nothing, adoring him with her eyes.

"Then there's nothing more to say," she said, linking her arm through his.

Morning Mountain

"Morning Mountain." Luke rolled the words over on his tongue. "That sounds like a great place to begin a new life."

He leaned down to kiss her cheek. "For all the mornings of our lives. . ."

Peggy Darty authored more than 30 novels before she passed away in 2011. She worked in film, researched for CBS, and taught in writing workshops around the country. She was a wife, mother, and grandmother who most recently made her home in Alabama.

A Bride's Rogue
in Roma, Texas

by Darlene Franklin

DEDICATION

This book is dedicated with many grateful thanks to Julie Jarnagin for helping me make changes to the copyedit while I was in the hospital and for allowing me to be a grandmother to her son. (Because a boy can never have too many grandmothers.)

CHAPTER 1

Roma, Texas, 1897

Salt residue marked the trail of Blanche Lamar's tears down the front of her black twill suit. "At least I didn't need to buy new clothes for the funeral." A hiccup interrupted her sobs.

Dipping a washcloth in a basin of cool water, she blotted away the evidence of tears from her face and dress. She raised her face to look in the mirror. Mama always said that a lady should present a neat appearance, no matter what.

Hollow brown eyes stared out of her pale face, whiter than usual beneath her always bright auburn hair. Her black hat would cover the chignon, hiding the riot of color that had irritated Mama so.

"Oh Mama." Blanche rubbed her eyes, but nothing stemmed the flood of tears.

A gentle knock fell on the door, and Mrs. Davenport, the pastor's wife, slipped in. "It's time." Clucking, she put her arms around Blanche's shoulders. Mama would be mortified by Blanche's puffy eyes. She sniffed the tears. . .and grief. . .inside.

"Take this, dear." Mrs. Davenport handed her a lace-edged handkerchief. "Are you ready?"

Nodding, Blanche followed her down the hall to the sanctuary. If only she had some other family member to accompany her—a father, brother, sister, aunt, grandparent—but she and Mama had been a tight family of two. Did one person constitute a family? *I'm alone.* Reverend Davenport and his wife were kind, but they couldn't tuck her in at night or tell her stories about the past. Tell her about the father Blanche had never known and now never would.

Organ music streamed through the open door of the sanctuary. "Rock of Ages." Mama loved that hymn. Blanche bit on her bottom lip against renewed tears.

"There's a good turnout. People admired your mother. You're not alone." Mrs. Davenport gestured at the sanctuary, three-quarters full of people, men and women, dressed in the same somber black as Blanche.

Except for one blot of color. A lone man, his hair nearly as red as her own, sat by himself on the back pew. His dove-gray suit glowed in the sea of black that made up the congregation. She searched her memory but couldn't place him. What was a stranger doing at her mother's funeral?

Pushing the man to the back of her mind, she took a seat on the front pew. After Mrs. Davenport sat beside her, her husband began his remarks.

Blanche struggled to pay attention to the pastor's words of comfort, about the promise of eternal life, his words of praise for her mother's good works among widows and orphans. Mrs. Davenport sang "The Old Rugged Cross," another one of Mama's favorite hymns.

At the end of the service, the pastor motioned Blanche forward. She forced herself to look down into her mother's face, prematurely white hair pulled back in a neat bun, wearing her favorite mauve silk dress, Bible placed between her hands. The mortician's blush on her cheeks looked unnatural. Mama didn't approve of cosmetics of any kind.

"Are you ready? Come, let's go," Mrs. Davenport whispered in her ear. At Blanche's nod, she cupped her elbow and led her to the church's fellowship hall. The scents of ham, beans, and potato salad greeted them, cloying her nose.

A long line of deacons and church matrons filed past

Blanche, each one with a kind word to share about her mother. Their comments fell into a predictable pattern. With every repetition of "she's in a better place now," a silent scream built in Blanche's throat.

What would Mama make of the mansion God had prepared for her? She might insist it was much too fancy, that she only needed a room or two. God would have to change her mind; no one else had ever been able to.

No one acknowledged Blanche's pain, an almost physical ache. Not that she wished her mother back, not now that she had entered a place of peace and joy. No, Blanche's grief was for herself, her loneliness, and her final loss of any ties to her past.

Ruth Fairfax, Mama's best friend, came toward the end of the line. "You know you have a home with me, as long as you need it."

Blanche's heart swelled, and once again she blinked back tears. "Thank you, Ruth."

"I'll wait until you are ready to leave, so I can take you home."

"I appreciate that." Truth was, Blanche didn't know what the future held for her. Mama left a little money, enough to keep her going for a few weeks, but not much more.

The man in the dove-gray suit came last in line. Upon a closer inspection, Blanche confirmed her first impression that she had never seen him before. What a dandy, with his three-piece suit, stiff collar and shirt studs, and curling mustache. What this man was doing at her mother's funeral, she couldn't guess.

Despite his fancy suit, the man's features settled in somber lines, his blue eyes solemn and serious. "Miss Lamar, I know we haven't met before, but first let me express my condolences on the loss of your mother."

"Umm. . .thank you." The appearance of this stranger troubled her in ways no one should have to endure at her mother's funeral.

"I know this must be a difficult time for you, but if I could have a few words with you in private either today or tomorrow, I would be most appreciative. Whatever time is convenient for you."

Blanche blinked. "I'm not in the habit of meeting gentlemen alone." She heard the asperity in her tone and chided herself for it.

"Of course not. But. . .away from all these people. Perhaps with the pastor?" The solid muscles beneath the well-fitting suit testified to his familiarity with getting his own way. Perhaps he was an attorney of some kind, with news of an unexpected will dispersing Mama's few worldly goods?

Blanche's pulse raced as another possibility occurred to her. Perhaps he knew something about her father. Perhaps Mama had broken her silence from the grave and arranged for the truth to be revealed in the event of her death. Her heart sped. "Tomorrow, here, at the same time?"

"I'll be here. Oh, and my name is Ike Gallagher." He reached into his breast pocket and handed her a card. *Ike Gallagher, purser, Lamar Industries, Ltd.*

Lamar Industries. Blanche's hopes rose another notch.

Ike Gallagher gazed across the church hall, filled with well-meaning people and tables laden with food. From his spot at the door, he had sensed at least half a dozen glances flick over him and dismiss him as not their kind.

Give them the benefit of the doubt, Captain Lamar had urged him. *They mean well.* Even if they only wanted to protect young Miss Lamar, why didn't they practice the love Christ preached? He'd rather grab a bite to eat at the saloon down the street.

Thinking of Blanche Lamar, he couldn't believe that straitlaced woman could be the offspring of Captain J.O. Lamar. Until last week, when the captain had pointed out the obituary of Cordelia Lamar, Ike didn't even know the captain had ever married. In the ten years Ike had known him, he had never mentioned one word about family.

The captain flirted with female passengers but never entertained any serious relationships. Ike attributed that to the captain's desire to avoid attachments—one of the ways they were alike.

The captain never would have revealed his secret, if not for the death of his wife. "Cordelia and me, we knew pretty quick that we weren't suited to each other. I didn't discover the news about the baby until after I had gone back to the River. And when I sent her money, she said she wouldn't accept money from me if she had to beg on the streets. I respected her wishes and stayed away. But now that she's gone...my girl. She's all alone in the world. I've got to be sure she's provided for."

After the study he'd made of Miss Blanche Marie Lamar during the funeral, Ike suspected she wouldn't be any more agreeable to Lamar's lifestyle than her mother had been all those years ago. The young lady might have only lived nineteen years, from what the captain had told Ike, but she dressed like an old maid already. He doubted she would agree to the offer he would make on behalf of the captain.

But then again...there was the set of her features, the flash in her eyes, the tilt to her chin when she'd challenged him about meeting men alone. Oh, he'd seen that tilt before, many times—when the captain wanted to make a point. Blanche Lamar might follow the rules, but she knew how to fight for what she wanted. For the sake of the captain, he would make his best effort to carry out his wishes.

Whistling, Ike flipped a coin. Heads, he'd go to the saloon. Tails, he'd go back to the hotel for the evening. Performing somersaults in the air, the quarter landed tails-up. He'd see what action he could find at the hotel. He was good at ferreting it out.

After all, Captain Lamar would expect no less.

Ike headed straight for the bar until the bartender had chased him and his companions out shortly after midnight. A few hands in Ike's suite turned into an all-night affair, leaving him about a hundred dollars richer. Pale streaks of gray relieved the black sky when the last of Ike's guests left his room. He hefted the bag of coins and cash in his hand. No matter what Miss Blanche Lamar had to say later today, he'd had a successful trip.

A quick glance at the bedside clock reminded him that only

four hours remained until his meeting with Miss Lamar. He would sleep while he could, he decided. After stripping down, he stretched out on top of the sheets, set his mind to wake up in a couple of hours, and closed his eyes.

When he awoke, he put on a fresh shirt—this one deep blue with mother-of-pearl studs. He reached for a red bow tie but decided against it. After all, they were meeting at a church; he should show proper restraint. Comb and pomade restored his hair to its usual perfection. Tugging on the lapels of his suit, he grinned at his image. Blanche Lamar didn't stand a chance against his charm.

Whistling "Oh Promise Me," he ventured down the stairs and into the bright sunshine of a summer day. With money in his pocket, time away from the river, and a pretty girl to see, he looked forward to the day. Even with her dull mourning clothes and grief-stricken face, the captain's daughter couldn't hide her beauty or the sparks that flew from her fiery hair.

Pausing by the hotel's dining room, Ike inhaled the aromas coming from the kitchen. He resisted the temptation to stop for a few minutes; Blanche didn't look like the kind of person who would take tardiness lightly. If he didn't show up at the church on time, she might decide he wasn't coming and disappear.

If that happened, he'd never hear the end of it. Thinking of that, he hastened his steps for Christ the King Church. Even when quiet and empty, the sanctuary didn't feel deserted. The air hummed with expectancy. God's house—the house where God dwells. A shiver ran down Ike's arms. He wasn't a superstitious man, but he didn't like to think of God looking over his shoulder at some of the mischief he got into. Goose bumps raced up his arms, and he shook himself. Put the same furnishings of plush pews and stained glass in a different setting, and he'd think *theater*. No need to get the whim-whams.

Shoes scuffled on the polished floor, and Ike turned to watch the approach of Blanche with the pastor. She wore the same somber black suit as at the funeral; maybe she was one of those people who thought she needed to adhere to strict rules of mourning. If anything, she looked paler than she had the previous day.

"Mr. Gallagher, I presume?" Reverend Davenport extended a hand.

Ike nodded.

"Let's retire to my study." The man, so thin he could almost have served as a model for Ichabod Crane, led the way to a room with two hardwood chairs in front of a walnut desk, surrounded by an ocean of musty-smelling books. Give Ike his purser's quarters any day, with sextant and telescope and logs. . .freedom this room didn't even afford a glimpse.

Two hard-backed chairs sat in front of a fearsome desk; no one would stay here long. The setting neither inspired confidence nor invited intimacy—something he excelled at creating, even in the dullest of back parlors. He reminded himself that this errand wasn't about him but about the captain's wishes.

He smiled to turn on the charm. "Thank you for agreeing to meet with me."

Blanche reached into her reticule and pulled out the ivory calling card he had left with her yesterday. "This says you're from Lamar Industries. Did my. . .father. . .send you?"

CHAPTER 2

Blanche held her breath for his answer.

"Captain Lamar gave me specific instructions in the event of your mother's death. As soon as I read her obituary, I headed here." A sad smile curved Mr. Gallagher's lips. "I wish we could have met under different circumstances."

Captain Lamar? Blanche snuck a glance at Mr. Gallagher. He was no more military than she was; his suit hailed more from Broadway than West Point. "Captain? He's a captain of. . .what?"

Ike tilted his head to the side, a soft chuckle escaping him. "You don't know anything about your father, do you?"

Tears sprang to her eyes as she shook her head. This stranger knew more about her father than she did.

"Your father regretted the circumstances that caused the distance between you. He's the captain of a boat."

Boat? The ocean lay scores of miles away to the south and east. How he had come to meet Mama, Blanche didn't know. Perhaps Mama had met him on a once-in-a-lifetime vacation. Maybe her father had been lost at sea, and circumstances forced Mama to return to her hometown. A dozen possibilities suggested themselves.

She turned Ike Gallagher's card over in her hand. Lamar Industries had offices in Brownsville as well as right here in Roma. The body of water connecting the two towns was no ocean, but the Rio Grande. The explanation that pushed into her mind was troubling. "A boat captain. . .on the Rio Grande? A steamboat?"

Ike smiled and nodded like a prize pupil. "J.O. Lamar was captain of the steamboat *Cordelia*. It's been traveling up and down the Rio Grande for two decades."

The *Cordelia*? He named his boat after her mother? The mother Blanche knew would never have married a riverboat captain, but only a man in love would name his boat after a woman. For a brief point in time, her parents had met, fallen in love, married, and had a child. The thought cheered her spirits.

Blanche examined Ike's words. "You said my father *was* captain? Has something happened? Is he dead?" Surely God wouldn't be so cruel, to bring her father so close only to deny her the opportunity to meet him.

"Now, Blanche. Don't make assumptions." Reverend Davenport planted his elbows on his desk and leaned forward. "Mr. Gallagher, you said you had a message for Miss Lamar from her father. May I ask what the nature of that message is?"

Blanche's stomach contracted. This was the heart of the matter.

"The captain regretted the differences that separated him from his only child."

So he did think about me.

"He respected his wife's wishes in the matter, as long as she was alive. But with her passing, he wanted to make Miss Lamar an offer." Ike turned a warm smile on Blanche again, a smile that could melt an iceberg. "You have a unique opportunity before you, Miss Lamar. The captain didn't know how you might be settled, financially. . ."

The question dangled in the air, unanswered. Her back stiffened. She and her mother had survived without her father's support for almost twenty years; she didn't need him now.

Liar.

"You will always have a home aboard the *Cordelia*. Especially since"—this time he covered his smile with a cough.—

"the boat is your inheritance."

Her heart dropped. "So my father *is* dead."

"His fondest hope was that you would spend time aboard the *Cordelia*. He felt the best way for you to get to know him was to spend time aboard his boat."

"Are you saying that Miss Lamar is the owner of the boat?" Reverend Davenport frowned. Blanche wondered what her pastor would make of today's story.

"Not exactly. Not yet." Ike stared at his hands before looking up, his eyes sparkling. "For Miss Lamar to claim her inheritance, she must travel by boat to the final stop, down in Brownsville."

I might have known—a gift with conditions attached. "My father didn't leave a letter or any kind of written instructions?"

"He left lengthy instructions in Brownsville. He hoped you would accept his invitation. His dearest wish was for you to get to know him by traveling on the boat he loved so well." Ike withdrew an envelope from inside his vest. "Here is proof of my claims. Your parents' wedding certificate. Legal papers regarding Lamar Industries. I am authorized to provide whatever proof you might require."

"Miss Lamar?" Reverend Davenport turned the request back to her, but she knew what his advice would be. *Trust the Lord. Avoid the appearance of evil.* And riverboats had an evil reputation.

Blanche allowed herself to fantasize about breaking the rules this one time. Reverend Davenport meant well, but he couldn't understand the longing in her heart for a family. He had a home for as long as he pastored Christ the King Church. His parents were respectable citizens here in town. He didn't face the necessity of finding a job. . .and a home. . .within the next month. He couldn't comprehend her hunger for a greater understanding of her parents.

"I'll have to think about it. . .pray about it. If Mr. Gallagher offered me assurance that my father is alive—"

Mr. Gallagher started forward, and she paused, giving him a chance to speak. He settled back in his chair.

"Since he hasn't, I prefer to consider my options. You understand, I am sure."

His smile faltered for a moment before returning to its full beaming splendor. "I have rooms at the Bells and Whistles hotel for the remainder of the week. Will you do me the honor of your company for dinner tomorrow evening?"

"Mr. Gallagher, you ask too much. Her mother was only laid in the ground yesterday."

"I'm afraid that's not possible. I will be at church tomorrow evening."

"Thursday night, then?"

The second rejection froze in her throat when she looked into blue eyes livened with flecks of green. What harm could one meal do? "Thursday night." She nodded. "That will help me make a decision before Friday."

Standing, Ike lifted Blanche's hand to his lips, and flame licked at nerve endings all the way to her shoulder. When he let it go, she almost expected it to be sunburn red, but it remained its usual pale color. She covered her confusion by asking one additional statement. "Mr. Gallagher, you never did confirm whether my father is dead or alive."

"All of your questions will be answered when we reach Brownsville." With a brief press of her hand, he headed for the open door. "We'll talk more about it over dinner Thursday night."

The rest of the week stumbled by for Ike. After the meeting at the church, he had indulged in a sumptuous luncheon before spending the afternoon in bed. The nature of his work required him to be a creature of the night. That evening, he lost everything he had won the day before, plus a little more. Up in his room, he turned his pockets out. He still had a few coins, enough to start another game. He never dipped into his employer's money to play and he wouldn't start now. He might be a gambler, but he was an honest man. No one ever accused him of cheating without answering for the slander.

On Wednesday, he arose from bed early enough to walk

through the town. Even though Roma was the *Cordelia*'s home port, Ike rarely spent much time exploring. Not much had changed. Prosperous as small towns went, a single bank closed its doors promptly at three in the afternoons. He caught sight of a general store, lending library, newspaper and printing office, two churches, one-room schoolhouse. A gentleman such as himself would have to special-order clothing from catalogs at the general store given the lack of a tailor or haberdasher. Even the cotton grown locally was shipped elsewhere for fabrication.

A half-dozen horses were tethered to the hitching post outside of the saloon. Glancing over the doors, Ike discovered they belonged to rough-and-tumble cowboys, not the quality of men who favored the riverboat trade. The men he had met at the hotel represented the best action in town. The place looked as boring as Blanche Lamar's life must have been to this point. His mouth twisted in a smile; she wouldn't appreciate the comparison. Even so, as long as he didn't take her to any saloons, something in her haunted expression suggested she would relish the opportunity for more excitement.

Thursday dragged by as Ike waited for dinner with Miss Lamar. He had turned in earlier than usual on Wednesday night, his companions calling it quits after he'd won a tidy sum. A smile sprang to his face as soon as he awoke late in the morning.

The maid had returned all his shirts, freshly pressed, while he was sleeping. He settled on the dove-gray suit, blue shirt, and red bow tie, almost patriotic. He speculated on Miss Lamar's attire for a minute. As pretty as she would look in spring lilac or even a soft mauve chiffon, she would wear the same black-and-white suit.

He called for the bellhop. "I am taking a lady to dinner tonight. Where can I find flowers? Or perhaps some special chocolates?" He winked.

"I will arrange for red roses and a box of chocolates." The man pocketed the coin Ike handed to him. "If I may." The man bent forward and straightened Ike's tie.

"Make those yellow roses." Red might send the wrong message. For a moment Ike felt like he had acquired a personal valet and grinned at the thought. "Thanks."

A quarter of an hour later, Ike stared at the items in his hand. He only meant to flatter Miss Lamar, to offer her some small luxuries he suspected she had seldom experienced. But would she misinterpret the gesture? He lifted the roses to his nose and sniffed. That was her problem, not his, he decided. He brought her gifts with the best of intentions.

He strolled down the street in the direction of the parsonage located next to Christ the King Church. The door opened as he climbed the steps and Reverend Davenport joined him on the porch. The pastor acted as protective as a father, a thought that tickled Ike's sense of humor given the circumstances.

"Miss Lamar will be down in a few minutes. Shall we take a seat?"

"Certainly." Ike placed the flowers and chocolate on the table between them and waited for the lecture he was certain was coming.

The pastor drew himself to his imposing height, emphasized by his thin frame. Fierce eyes regarded Ike from behind thin-rimmed glasses. "Miss Lamar has lived a sheltered life here in Roma."

"I am aware of that, sir, and here she comes. Shall we go inside?" He followed the pastor in rising and reached for the flowers and chocolates.

They settled in the pastor's study. "What assurances do you offer that you are who you say you are, and that Blanche will travel safely in your care?"

Ike shared his bona fides with the man. "As for Miss Lamar's safety, my own sister travels aboard the *Cordelia* with me. Captain Lamar took us in when we lost our parents, and we've lived there ever since."

That statement left Reverend Davenport discomposed. Ike pulled another trick from his pocket. "I am prepared to offer second berth for a companion, if you feel it is necessary, but I will warn you that space is limited."

At that statement, the pastor's shoulders relaxed, and he settled back in his chair, tapping his fingers on his desk blotter. He leaned forward and ran his right index finger through an address book, glasses perched on the end of the nose and his lips pursed in a slight scowl.

Out of the corner of his eye, Ike caught sight of Blanche. She had softened her mourning dress with a touch of gold, a locket around her throat, and her fiery hair blazed without the black boater hat. Ike relaxed.

Blanche had to clear her throat twice to get Reverend Davenport's attention. Ike stood as soon as her feet crossed the threshold to the study, his eyes lighting with pleasure at her appearance. His expression suggested he saw her as a woman, not as his employer's daughter, or a distraught orphaned daughter.

"Whom would you prefer as a traveling companion, Blanche? I'm sure Ruth would be happy to accompany you for a short trip, or perhaps you would prefer the company of a younger woman, perhaps Miss Trenton."

Miss Trenton was closer to Blanche's age than her mother's good friend by perhaps ten years, but she had spent so many years around her mother's friends that she fit right in with the older matrons. "I said nothing about a traveling companion."

"I told Reverend Davenport that we'd be happy to provide accommodations for someone to accompany you, if you feel it is prudent. But my sister is also traveling with us, and she is hoping you will share her cabin."

Blanche took courage from Ike's statement. "Then I don't think we need to bother either Miss Fairfax or Miss Trenton. *If* I decide to take the trip, I'm sure Miss Gallagher will be an adequate chaperone."

Was that admiration she spotted in Ike's eyes?

"I'll have Miss Lamar back before dark tonight, sir." Ike offered Blanche his arm, and together they walked outside, like any man escorting a woman. Blanche would have to order a glass of sweet tea as soon as they arrived at the hotel to calm the heat rushing through her senses.

Touching the tips of her fingers, he lifted them to his lips.

"Wait here for a moment, please."

He reappeared at the doorway, yellow rose in hand. "If I may?" After breaking it just below the bloom, his fingers wrapped it around her ear. "Perfect." He made it sound as if he meant *she* was perfect, not the flower, and her skin heated with embarrassment.

Moments later, she returned, and he escorted her down the street to the hotel. Temperatures had dropped a few degrees with the hint of rain in the air—a pleasant evening for a stroll.

The bellhop opened the door of the hotel for them, and Blanche's skirt swished as she entered. How much more cheerful the hotel lobby was than the parsonage, with comfortable chairs upholstered in bright colors. In this glamour, as much glamour as Roma had to offer, she felt almost dowdy.

Blanche followed Ike's suggestions for the meal. The waiter poured a glass of sweet tea for her, iced water with lemon for Ike, and left them alone. Ike leaned forward. "May I hope that your discussion with Reverend Davenport indicates you have reached a decision? I will confess that I am hoping you will join me on the *Cordelia*."

She lifted her eyes to meet his. "You said if I came today, you would tell me about my father."

"I can only repeat what I told you earlier: your father gave me instructions to invite you to travel downriver." Ike spread his hands apart on the table. "Your father did not want you to learn about him and about the river at the same time. He wanted you to form your own opinions about life aboard the *Cordelia*, unswayed by either parent's feelings. A lawyer in Brownsville has been authorized to answer all your questions and to inform you of the inheritance your father has left you."

She ran her tongue over her teeth in thought and looked out the window, watching pedestrians strolling the streets. Was she prepared to spend the rest of her life in the community that had nurtured her, without experiencing anything else? She wanted to learn about her father, but she also wanted to experience the world—a small taste, that was all. More than anything she wanted to know her father. "I greatly wish you would tell me what I want to know now." Ire rose with the words.

The waiter reappeared, bearing their food on platters.

Her ineffectual plea seemed to amuse Ike. "I am answering your questions the best way I can. As I have said before, your father felt you would come to know him best on the river. Have you ever been on the Rio Grande?"

She slowly shook her head. "I've never been more than ten miles from Roma." Her eyes peered out the window at the town's dusty street, and she wondered what it would be like to catch the daily stagecoach on a journey to somewhere else. For years she had dreamed of taking a trip, if only to the next stop on the route. She was having her wishes handed to her on a platter. Why not?

Ike laid down his silverware. "Samuel Clemens has romanticized life on the Mississippi. I've been down Old Man River a couple of times, but I prefer the Rio Grande. The 'big river' is a Texas kind of river. It's almost two thousand miles long from its headwaters in the Colorado Mountains to the Gulf of Mexico. I've seen some of that rough country, over in the Big Bend, but the steamboat traffic runs between Roma and Brownsville. It's a country all its own, business on both sides of the river mingling two countries and cultures. A meld of Mississippi Delta and wild river canyons."

"You love it." She couldn't keep surprise out of her voice.

"I guess I do. It's been my home most of my life. I can't imagine living anywhere else."

Like her father. Ike remained silent on the subject. If her father was anything like Ike Gallagher, Blanche could understand how her mother fell for his charm. She couldn't afford to make the same mistake. That was reason enough to stay in Roma: to protect her heart.

But a part of her wanted to discover if the River that her father loved so much ran through her heart as well.

Ike leaned forward, touching her little finger with his own. "Please let me fulfill your father's request."

"I. . .don't know." Stay, and be safe? Or risk everything for the chance of something better?

"I stayed behind on this boat trip. They'll be back a week from now." Reaching into his pocket, he pulled out a small packet of money. "This is to help you with any expenses you might be experiencing. If you decide you wish to join us, you can get word to me at the hotel. You can bring a companion with you, or not. I'll make arrangements for you to have a room and board in case there's a change in the *Cordelia*'s schedule. And now"—he picked up his knife and fork and sliced into a thick steak—"let's enjoy this excellent meal."

Ike kept up a well-informed patter that held Blanche's interest while not making her feel like a naive girl from a small town. The *Cordelia* had taken passengers to the Fitzsimmons-Maher heavyweight title bout held on an island downriver. They both laughed at the burial of a supposed alien in Aurora, and shook their heads at the senseless death of two spectators to a stunt involving a train wreck in Waco.

Neither one of them brought up the question of her joining them aboard the riverboat until Ike walked her back to the parsonage. "Please come. It would have meant a lot to your father—and to me also." He took her hand, kissed it, then released it slowly.

He walked away, glancing back a single time. She held her hand where he had kissed it against her cheek.

They both knew she'd sail with them. It was only a matter of time.

CHAPTER 3

Two weeks passed before Blanche took advantage of Ike's offer. She sorted through her mother's belongings, dismayed that so few items could summarize a life. As she worked, she looked for hints of her father. Surely her mother had kept some memento of the one love of her life. She must have loved him at some point. Mama would not have married a man for anything less. Perhaps she'd thought she could convince him of the error of his river ways, and her bitterness stemmed from her failure to do so.

Tucked at the bottom of the linen drawer, beneath a rose-petal sachet, Blanche found a single piece of paper folded into an envelope. "To better times. I will always love you—J.O."

Blanche drew a deep breath. A set of four gems, miniature photographs, lay beneath the envelope. A younger, happier image of her mother than she had grown up with stared at her. Not that people ever smiled in photographs, but her eyes looked brighter than Blanche had ever seen.

But she couldn't take her eyes off the man in the pictures. Even though they were in black and white, the way the light glinted on top of his hair suggested they shared the same auburn tresses. She touched her head; every time her mother had looked at Blanche, she was reminded of her failure to reform her husband. His weatherworn face was open and honest. Blanche searched his features for resemblance to her own but recognized none.

Repeating her father's inscription on the photograph—*I will always love you*—Blanche fought the tears gathering in her eyes. What had happened to the marital vows to love, honor, and protect, that had caused him to leave them alone, unprovided for? This journey was the only opportunity she would have to discover the truth.

A knock drew her attention, and Blanche opened the door to Mrs. Davenport. Steam rose from a napkin-covered plate. The pastor's wife had made sure Blanche enjoyed two hot meals a day as well as breads for breakfast every day since her mother's death. Blanche didn't know if she would have bothered eating otherwise. Her appetite had sunk as deep in the ground as her mother's coffin.

"I brought you some corn pudding and fried chicken." Mrs. Davenport replaced it for the still half-full lunch plate. "You must eat and take care of yourself."

Blanche had managed a few bites of beans and mashed potatoes but not much more. "I've been extra busy."

Mrs. Davenport took a seat. "I will stay with you while you eat tonight. I'll tell you what I used to tell my girls: you can't have dessert until you eat at least three bites of everything on your plate."

That brought a chuckle to Blanche's lips. "Mama used to tell me the same thing, especially when she served me spinach." Her nose wrinkled at the memory. She laid the photograph on the bed and took a seat next to Mrs. Davenport before dipping her fork into the corn pudding. Creamy, slightly sweet, crunchy between her teeth—perfect. Next to it lay a crisped chicken thigh. "Chicken on a weekday. You didn't have to do that."

"I know it's your favorite meal." Mrs. Davenport followed the passage of the piece of chicken to Blanche's mouth with approval. She bit through the skin with a satisfying crunch and pulled the moist meat into her mouth.

Before Blanche knew it, she had stripped the meat from the bone and eaten most of the corn pudding. A smiling Mrs. Davenport handed her a molasses cookie. "You earned it."

Blanche laughed. "Thank you, for everything. I'll miss your home-cooked meals when I leave." A sudden pang of homesickness washed over her. The Davenports were the closest thing she had to family, and Mrs. Davenport had proven herself a true friend. Blanche reminded herself she'd only be gone for a week or a little bit longer.

"Are you sure you must go? You know you have a home with us, for as long as you want one." Mrs. Davenport busied herself packing the dishes back into the picnic basket.

"I know I do. I can never repay your kindness." Mama's friends had repeated variations of the same offer since the funeral. Blanche didn't doubt their genuine concern. But she could no more refuse the opportunity to learn more about her father than she could starve herself to death. "But I've always wondered about my father. I might have grandparents. . .aunts and uncles. . ." *Brothers or sisters*, but Blanche didn't voice that thought. The implied betrayal of her mother hurt too much. "I've wanted family all my life, and now I have a chance to meet them."

"But"—Mrs. Davenport twisted her hands in her lap—"a *riverboat*, Blanche dear. It's not seemly for a young Christian woman of your standing."

Blanche lifted her chin. "I am sure I will be well chaperoned on the boat. I am only making the one trip downriver; no harm will come to me. I'm sure my father. . ." Her voice wobbled at the word. "I'm sure he wouldn't have invited me otherwise." She added a smile, meant to reassure herself as much as her friend. "I will send you a letter when we get to Brownsville. I promise I'll ask for help if I need it."

As if resigned that Blanche wouldn't change her mind, Mrs. Davenport wiped her hands on a napkin and folded it. "How can I help you prepare for the trip?"

By the end of the day, they had sorted things into four piles:

clothing and other items to give away, a small pile to throw away, and the valise that held the few items Blanche would take with her. The Davenports would hold the remaining items Blanche wouldn't take with her but wished to keep. Since the Lamars had lived in rented quarters, they had no furniture to worry about. "I hope I'll be able to send for the rest of my things soon."

"There's no hurry, dear."

Blanche had sent a message to Ike at the hotel about her decision to join the *Cordelia*, and he had responded when they returned to port. This last night of her old life, she would spend at the parsonage. Grabbing her valise, she scanned the room that had been her home, her refuge from the world, for most of her life. Reverend Davenport would bring her trunk down to the wharf later. With a final good-bye wish for the life she was leaving behind, she followed Mrs. Davenport out the door.

"Do you see her?"

Ike's sister, Effie, turned sightless eyes in his direction. Her voice stirred his own impatience. "Not yet." The *Cordelia* had made one trip downstream and back since his offer to Blanche.

More than once during the past two weeks, he wondered what decision Miss Blanche Lamar would make. Under the influence of her pastor, she might choose to stay in Prudeville, as he had dubbed the people he met at the funeral. Her unexpected message two days ago had relieved a sadness he didn't know he was experiencing.

He turned as an older man with a pilot's hat clamped on top of salt-and-pepper hair ambled next to him—Old Obie, the boat's pilot. "That's her, I'd bet my life on it." Despite his age, he still had excellent eyesight, a requirement for any riverboat pilot.

Ike spotted her when Old Obie pointed, her bright red hair showing beneath a straw boater.

"Tell me." Effie's hand grasped Ike's arm. "Is it her? What does she look like?"

Ike leaned forward, dangling his arms over the railing. "It's her indeed. Doesn't look like she's changed clothes since the funeral, unless she has identical outfits in her closet." The new hat, the only change in her attire, suggested a woman ready for new experiences. But as she drew closer, Ike discerned her facial expression. "She doesn't look altogether happy to be here."

"She's scared, Ike. She must be terribly brave, to leave everything familiar behind and try life on the river." Effie nodded her head. "It's up to us to make her feel right at home."

"She looks like she sucked on a lemon for breakfast, that's for sure." Old Obie chuckled. "But she's here. That's the important thing."

"Shall we go down and greet her?" Effie turned a brilliant smile in Ike's direction.

He took her arm. "Obie?"

"I'll wait my turn. You go ahead and welcome her aboard." He headed back to the pilothouse while Ike guided Effie to the street.

If necessary, Effie could maneuver the gangplank without the need of her cane. Even so, he knew she felt safer aboard, where she knew every inch of the boat, than on the less predictable land.

"Maybe you can give her a few pointers on her attire." Ike couldn't wait to see her in something other than her black twill suit.

"What do I know of fashion?"

"More than she does." Effie might not see color, but she had excellent taste in fit, materials, and trims for her clothing. "I have never seen her in anything other than an unrelieved black suit with a white blouse. No flounce to the sleeves or skirt. I'm hoping you can broaden her fashion sense."

"I look forward to it."

He knew the moment Blanche caught sight of them. Her chin lifted and her hesitant steps changed to more of a march. Increasing the pressure on Effie's arm, Ike increased his speed and called out, "Well met, Miss Lamar! I am pleased you decided to take us up on our offer." Without asking permission, he reached for her valise. "Miss Lamar, this is my sister, Miss Effie Gallagher. Effie, this is Miss Blanche Lamar."

"I have been so eager to meet you, Miss Lamar. My brother has told me so much about you." Effie stuck out her right hand.

Ike studied Blanche's reaction to his sister. Strangers didn't always know how to treat a blind woman. After a moment's hesitation, she met Effie's hand and shook it. "I am pleased to make your acquaintance. You are so kind to share your cabin with me."

"I'm looking forward to it. The *Cordelia* is a beautiful boat." Effie's voice conveyed a measure of pride. "It's been our home ever since our parents died when we were children."

"I don't mind. I am quite used to sharing space." In spite of her brave words, Blanche looked forlorn. Ike had considered offering the use of his cabin instead of having her share Effie's cabin, but that would mean bunking with Old Obie. That situation could create more problems than it solved.

"And it will do me good not to be alone." Blanche spoke the words softly. "Less time to dwell on my sorrow."

Brave words. Blanche was a contradiction, from red hair fiery enough to light a ballroom to black attire appropriate for a mortician's wife. "I am glad you feel that way."

Blanche smiled, and Ike decided he would do whatever he could to make her smile as often as possible. The faint lifting of her lips transformed her from a premature old maid to a lovely young woman. "I'm eager to catch my first glimpse of my father's boat. Lead the way."

CHAPTER 4

Blanche craned her neck as she walked with the Gallaghers, scanning the docks for her first glimpse of the riverboat that had stolen her father away from her. Long before she had learned about her father's business, she had daydreamed of a day trip downriver, properly chaperoned, of course. It sounded so. . .romantic. But romance and maidenly sighs didn't put food on the table, as her mother was wont to say. For all of her nineteen years she kept her feet pinned to the ground and didn't dare to dream.

For the immediate future, she would live in a fairy-tale world aboard her father's boat. Maybe she would find out she was the long-lost princess, her father the king of the Rio Grande. Her eyes wandered to Ike. If she was the princess, what role did Ike play? Sir Lancelot or court jester? With the ready smile that came to his face, he could be either.

Until she arrived in Brownsville and learned the answers about her father, she could fashion a future out of her dreams. Dreams might lead to future disappointment, but she didn't have much else to cling to for now. Except for the Lord, of course.

Mama had scoffed at Blanche's dreams, saying "God helps

those who help themselves." From an early age, Blanche learned to keep her innermost desires to herself, holding them close the way Joseph must have for all those years he spent in Pharaoh's prison.

They turned the corner to the dock, and Effie said, "There she is. Straight ahead." She spoke with so much confidence that Blanche glanced at her face again, wondering if her first impression was wrong. No, the woman's eyes remained focused on some distant sight that no one else could see, and her white cane tapped out a steady rhythm on the street.

"She's something. Whenever I catch a glimpse of her like this, I fall in love with her all over again." Ike had his arms at his waist, his suit jacket pushed behind his back by his fists.

One of Blanche's teachers had used famous steamboat races to teach math: *If a steamboat burns eight cords of wood to travel five miles per hour upstream, how much wood will it take to travel forty miles?* Miss Burton had captured Blanche's attention, as well as many of her classmates, and she had encouraged them to construct scale models of the famous steamboat, the *Robert E. Lee*, while they read *Life on the Mississippi*. All too soon Mama had heard about the project and single-handedly stopped it, much to Blanche's dismay. Now that she knew her father's history, she understood why.

From the pride and affection both the Gallaghers had used to describe the *Cordelia*, Blanche expected to see the same version of the famous floating hotels. Hundreds of passengers could travel aboard boats that had fifty or more staterooms with stained-glass ceilings and tessellated floors covered with rich carpets. Perhaps it even rose to four decks.

"There she is." Ike paused and gave Blanche her first clear look at the steamboat that had dominated her thoughts ever since her mother's death. She blinked. Painted green instead of white, a modest two decks instead of three, the gigantic stern wheel silent at the back of the boat. All in all, Blanche swallowed a bit of disappointment. Still, the paint was fresh, including curlicued gold letters announcing *Cordelia*. Crates stacked the decks. Perhaps they hauled more freight than passengers. Why would Mama object to a ship that did nothing more harmful than carry cotton and other products downriver? There was so much she didn't know.

"She may not look like much."

Mr. Gallagher read her mind.

"It's a little smaller than I expected." Blanche wrinkled her nose then held her face still. This boat represented her inheritance. She needed to learn as much as possible about its operations and all aspects of business before she made any judgments.

Effie laughed. "Don't let the *Cordelia* hear you call her an 'it.' She's a lady and expects to be greeted with respect. River and boat, both of them are demanding mistresses."

"I'll try to remember." Were river people superstitious? "Why do you say that? Is traveling downriver dangerous?"

Effie inclined her head in Ike's direction, and he shook his head. "I have lived on the river most of my life, and there's no place I'd rather live. Captain Lamar wouldn't have invited you along if he thought you were in danger."

Blanche felt like she was listening to true statements without hearing the whole truth. Fear fluttered in her stomach, although she knew no place was safe from danger. Her mother had taken sick and died in a matter of days. Fire, thunderstorms, tornados, rainstorms, floods. . .anything could happen even in a small town like Roma. The river was no different, except that she was surrounded by water and she couldn't swim. She swallowed.

"Shall we go?" Ike gestured at the *Cordelia*. "The crew has worked hard to spit and polish every inch of the ship for the captain's daughter. They're eager to meet you."

Blanche smiled. From a poor orphan to an heiress. She lifted her chin with pride and moved forward to meet her destiny.

———※———

Old Obie roused himself from his spot high above the *Cordelia*, in the pilothouse. Unable to resist, he raised the binoculars to his eyes for one more look at the young woman accompanying Ike and Effie.

Blanche Marie Lamar. Ike's description hadn't done her

justice. But how could one describe such a woman? Even in the wilting summer heat, her clothes looked as stiff as a newly pressed tablecloth, her backbone straight, the tilt of her head determined to look ahead. She wore solid black with a dull gray blouse. Her face had remained somber, with emotions of fear and excitement and hope whispering across her face as she inspected the boat from afar.

But that hair. . .as bright as red light that either delighted or warned a sailor, depending on the time of day. Old Obie would take delight in that hair, an omen that all would go well with her first trip aboard the *Cordelia*. Red sky at night, sailor's delight; red sky at morning, sailor's warning.

Obie watched her confident steps as she strode toward the boat, taking in more details of her delicate facial features, a scattering of freckles on her nose, the rakish angle of the bow under her chin, the sparkle in her brown eyes. When they reached the dock, he put away the binoculars and buzzed around the already gleaming equipment.

Let Ike and Effie introduce Blanche to the crew. He would make her acquaintance later.

As they walked the deck, Ike caught a glimpse of Old Obie's binoculars. If there was any chance Blanche would discover the romance of the river as her father hoped, sooner or later she must make her way to the pilothouse. Old Obie was just the man to teach the young lady the moods of the Rio Grande, from the present summer drought that increased difficulty in navigation to storms that pounded anyone caught in them, from the trees sweeping the riverbanks to the unexpected bridges that appeared with increasing frequency. Adjusting the pilot wheel an inch to the right or left could mean the difference between safe passage or running aground on a sandbar.

Old Obie was master of the pilothouse. Ike had learned a lot from him, but no amount of time had given him the feel for the river that Old Obie had. He was the boat's most valuable employee, the one irreplaceable member of the crew, and well the captain knew it.

The crew had loaded the cotton stored in the warehouse while Ike had absented himself. Splendid pinks, reds, and oranges painted the western sky. If Old Obie agreed, they would set sail tonight. Ike's arm tingled where it touched Blanche's. He looked forward to standing with her on the deck and watching the boat pull away from the dock, feeling the stern wheel come to life, the near deafening turning of the wheels, the water rushing beneath the boat, wind whipping through his hair.

Would the wind tease a lock from Blanche's abundance of red hair, so that it twirled and danced in front of her eyes? Or would an abundance of pins hold each lock in place? He pictured his fingers brushing those curls back against her face, running through the hair hanging loose about her shoulders. He pushed his mind away from the image. Blanche Lamar was a lady, and some images were best left between husband and wife.

The crew lined up to greet them. Everyone had dressed in uniform, as clean and sparkling as the boat. "Are you ready to meet your employees?" He held in the laugh that bubbled in his throat when he heard her suck in her breath at the words.

"Do you have any suggestions on how I should behave?" Pink tinged her cheeks. "This is a new experience for me."

"I will tell you what Ike always tells me," Effie answered for him. "It has helped me get through many difficult situations. Think like an actress and *pretend*. What would you do if you were the captain?"

Color drained from Blanche's cheeks. Effie sensed her faux pas. "That's not good advice for you. You don't know our captain. Well, pretend you're the hostess at a dinner party, or your pastor's wife speaking to the ladies' aid society."

"Just be yourself. You'll do fine." Ike took one step forward but Blanche held back.

"How do I remember all their names? I'm terrible with names," she moaned. "They only have one new name to learn, and it should be familiar—*Lamar*."

"Which is why they will love you. They'll be curious about you. Of course. Who is this mysterious daughter the captain has kept hidden all these years? But they won't ask."

"And if they do, tell one of us," Effie spoke up. "We'll set them straight."

"I'll keep that in mind and try not to be frightened away." Still, Effie's reassurance brought a smile to Blanche's face. "I'll practice with the two of you. What is your position with the crew? Ike, I know your card says 'purser.' I even looked it up in a dictionary. But I still don't quite understand."

"Paperwork and customer service." Ike wasn't ready to explain the full extent of his role on board just yet. His duties regarding passengers involved activities that would make Blanche. . .blanch. He could find some humor in the situation. He put his concerns aside and held out his hand. "Come. We will be beside you all the way. If we wait any longer, they may wonder what is wrong."

Shyly, she accepted his hand and let him lead her forward.

CHAPTER 5

Blanche put all of Effie and Ike's suggestions into practice as she followed Ike to the boat. Unlike liners that crossed the ocean, the deck lay close to the water, and she could see people lining the main deck before she stepped aboard. The crew was only a little larger than the household where her mother had worked. One white-haired lady had a soft, round face. Blanche instantly felt like she could go down to the kitchen—or was it called a galley?—for a cup of tea and conversation. Blanche relaxed.

In vain she looked for a man dressed in a captain's uniform. Her slight hope that she would find her father alive once she arrived on board, ready to greet and reassure her, was dashed. With his suit and unmistakable air of authority, Ike was clearly in control.

To Blanche's surprise, Effie took the lead in introducing the crew. The round-faced lady who had caught Blanche's attention was indeed the ship's cook, Elaine Harper.

"Tell me your favorite meal, and I'll fix it for you tomorrow night."

Blanche started to protest, but of course the cook wanted to show off for the ship's heiress.

"I should have whatever you want. We carry everything available along the Rio Grande and the Gulf Coast in our pantry."

"I'm looking forward to it." Blanche's smile came naturally. In time, she thought she could get used to this heiress position.

A young woman named Betty was the chef's help. Blanche struggled to commit the names to her memory.

Next came the engineers. Jose and Tomas worked with a brusque Scot. "I'm Harry McDonald. The engine belongs to me. Anything you want to know, come to me. If you want a hot bath, I'm your man."

Blanche almost laughed. "I'm looking forward to it." She wondered if she would remain as immaculate as the engineers did, if she spent time among the coal and steam. Her limited wardrobe had to extend to every situation she'd be facing.

The next staff member Ike introduced addressed that concern. "This is our laundress, Agatha. She also takes care of any tailoring needs that arise. I took the liberty of asking her to design new clothes for your trip downriver."

Blanche gave the woman a second look. Glasses gave her face an unfortunate pinched appearance, but her dress—she thought it was called a tea gown—was as modern, outrageous and comfortable at the same time, as anything Blanche had ever seen in the few glimpses she'd had of the catalogues in the general store. "I don't know what to say."

Agatha looked her up and down. "We'll have fun."

"My mother just died." *I will not cry.* "I want to honor her."

"You don't need to worry. Whatever we do will be tasteful but. . .more suitable for your new life aboard the *Cordelia.*"

Blanche appreciated her tact. Too fancy, not fitting well, too worn—she had heard slurs of one kind or another all her life. And she had never had clothes made for her by a professional seamstress. "That does sound like fun. However, I only expect to be here for a single trip."

The laundress bobbed her head. "Just following orders, miss."

After the head server asked her to inspect the evening's dinner service, Blanche wondered how she would fit in everything people wanted of her during a single trip downriver. So far no one had offered to preview the trip's entertainment or show her the pilothouse.

A figure hovered in the darkened room at the top of the boat, the pilothouse. He couldn't leave the wheel unattended, so she would make his acquaintance later. She didn't know whom to ask about the entertainment. Perhaps they didn't provide any, but instead only offered a means to travel downriver; she would learn.

By the time she greeted the last member of the crew, her face felt like it would crack from the constant smile. As the people filed out, Effie spoke, "You must be tired. Dinner isn't for a couple of hours, when you will meet our passengers. If you feel up to it, I have a couple of dresses for you to try."

Blanche wanted to be agreeable, but the implied criticism of her clothes made her uncomfortable. The suit was clean, serviceable, fairly new. The jabot at her neck was a new touch this year.

She swallowed against the fear crowding her throat. Money had always been at a premium in the Lamar household. Mama chose the least expensive, most durable cuts of fabric, from a similar color palette. When Blanche reached her adult stature, they began sharing their wardrobe. The annual changes to her wardrobe dwindled year by year. Mama thought the money could be better spent on other things: feeding the poor and widowed, supporting missionaries, new classrooms for Sunday school. All good, worthy causes that made Blanche feel selfish for wanting a dress with color or frills.

A soft hand touched Blanche's arm. "Let me show you to our room." As Effie led Blanche below deck, the youngest crew member, who looked like she might be a maid, relaxed. How well Blanche understood that feeling—they had passed inspection with the new boss. That gave her a feeling of power, and her back straightened. She would allow Effie to dress her up—but not too much.

※

"Come around my cabin later this evening then." Ike shook hands with Jason Spurling, a businessman checking out new markets for his products. Part of the problem for the dwindling steamboat business lay in the lack of large population centers on the route. The stops didn't offer good markets for local businesses. The other, bigger problem came with the increased presence of railroads. Not only did trains run to predictable schedules, they also kept their stations at a distance from the boat docks.

As a result, businessmen like Spurling appeared on the boat less and less often, leading to dwindling income. Hopefully, weather and river would cooperate on this trip and he could show Spurling the several opportunities offered by the *Cordelia*.

A peek in the dining room found the head waiter, Smithers, giving the tables a final polish. When Ike was a boy, the dining room was double its present size, with staff to match. According to the old-timers, like Old Obie, even those days paled in comparison to the golden days of the steamboat. He told stories of running out of food because they carried so many passengers. Ike didn't know the line between truth and wishful thinking, but he could imagine.

At the moment, silence reigned in the room, aside from kitchen noises. Where was Effie? She played the piano in the corner before each meal, popular tunes meant to encourage guests to enter and converse with each other.

Blanche must have agreed to a wardrobe makeover. He looked forward to seeing the results.

He went up to the window where Mrs. Harper passed out food. "Do you have Old Obie's tray ready?"

"Right here, sir." She hustled to the window. "Will he be joining us for dinner again soon, Mr. Ike? It's not right for him to eat by himself."

"He'll be taking meals on his own until further notice." Ike gestured for a waiter to take it up to the pilot. Elaine Harper enjoying bending the old man's ear and doing whatever she could to mother the staff. "It's best this way, so if there is something you need to discuss with him, you'll have to catch him in his cabin." He drew up his full height. "And I don't need to remind you not to discuss the situation with Miss Lamar."

She laughed and shooed him away. "I won't be giving away

any secrets. You don't have to worry about me. But speaking of Miss Lamar, she's making her entrance."

Ike glanced over his shoulder and froze for a second. He had gone through Effie's wardrobe, looking for something better than the unrelieved black and white staples of her wardrobe. Even so, the change achieved by a simple dark blue dress amazed him.

The dress was perfectly decorous, somber in color, and, from what Effie had said, a little out of date. But the dark blue instead of the black, with soft mauve touches instead of white, made all the difference. Blanche's hair lay in softly whipped layers on top of her head, and pink sparkled in her cheeks almost as if she wore rouge, something Ike extremely doubted. Her eyes sparkled, too. She lifted a handkerchief to her mouth as if to hide her shy smile.

"You'd better go rescue her before every gentleman on board approaches her." Mrs. Harper stared at him pointedly.

"I'll do that." He pulled on the cuffs of his shirt, adjusting the studs so they were aligned properly, before walking across the richly carpeted floor. A smile sprang to his lips. "Miss Blanche Lamar." He bowed deeply from the waist. "Your beauty doth bedazzle me."

"You like?" Humor laced Effie's voice.

The color in Blanche's cheeks deepened, and she tugged at the waistline of her skirt, sending it in a slight swirl.

She glanced down, and Ike's eyes followed the direction of her gaze. She was staring at the serviceable, hi-top, lace-up shoes. Even the gleaming oil of a fresh shoeshine couldn't hide the scuffed use marks on the toes. She pulled her foot back, so that the skirts hid it from view.

Ike leaned forward and whispered in her ear. "Don't worry. There are several good cobblers down in Brownsville."

She shook her head. "I never should have come, not if you have to remake me from head to toe."

Effie made a soft sound. "I need to get to the piano. I'll see you at dinner."

"We're not remaking you. Just uncovering the beauty that's

always been there. . .and what a few more dollars in the budget can make."

"I never had to go without." Her voice came out strangled.

"I didn't mean to imply otherwise. . ." He drew in a deep breath and didn't speak until Blanche's cheeks returned to a more normal color. "I only wanted to compliment you on how fine you look tonight."

The tinkling sound of piano keys interrupted their conversation, and Ike relaxed. Whatever Mrs. Lamar had taught her daughter, it didn't include how to accept a compliment. He found it refreshing compared to women who had flirtation down to an art form. Unlike those ladies, Blanche made no attempts at pretense.

When Effie shifted to a different song, Ike hummed along. Blanche tilted her head and nodded her chin in time to the music. Underneath the skirt, her feet were probably tapping. "I don't know that song, although it's a catchy tune."

"That's 'The Base Ball Song.' " He belted out a few lines, and Smithers shook his head in mild disapproval. When Ike lowered his head in mock shame, he caught sight of the blank expression on Blanche's face. "You've never been to a baseball game, have you?"

She shook her head. "Roma held a few exhibition games, and some of my friends went. But Mama. . ." She clamped her lips together.

"Mrs. Lamar suggested you had better ways to spend your money?"

Blanche shrugged her shoulders uncomfortably. "I'm afraid that the only music I know, beyond 'America' and the national anthem, are hymns. Music meant to praise God is the best music of all, don't you think?"

How to answer that? "I think God gave us everything to enjoy. As long as there are no scandalous words associated with the melody, surely music reflects praise to God." He grinned. "Even music written for a baseball game." Spotting a familiar face appear at the door, he lowered his voice. "And speaking of baseball. . .do your best to charm the gentleman who is entering the salon. He is the owner of the Brownsville Bats and is considering bringing the entire team downriver to play exhibition games at each town. It would make a big difference in our income."

CHAPTER 6

Blanche blinked her eyes. The thought of acting as hostess alarmed her. Mrs. Davenport had once shared her secret to making visitors to Christ the King church feel welcome. *People like it when you remember their names.* Blanche had memorized the passenger list and only had to associate the right faces with the names. Be polite, complimentary even. Above all, make the greetings unique to the individual.

The problem was she didn't know a thing about baseball. Maybe that's what she should say—men sometimes liked to show off their superior knowledge. In terms of looks, Mr. Ventura was short where Ike was tall, rotund instead of muscular, with a shock of thick black hair, bushy eyebrows, and a wide smile that invited the world to laugh along with him. *Open my eyes, Lord, to see what You see in this man.*

Before she had time to check her hair or adjust her shirt-waist, Mr. Ventura was in front of her, pumping Ike's hand. "*Buenas noches*, Señor Gallagher. *Dónde está el capitan?*"

Blanche held her breath. Where was the captain, indeed?

"*No está aquí.*" Ike's answer repeated the obvious: he isn't here. Switching to English, Ike said, "But this is the captain's daughter, Miss Blanche Lamar. Blanche, this is Bart Ventura, baseball owner and one of Brownsville's leading businessmen."

Mr. Ventura shook Blanche's hand, just the right firmness, leaving an impression of strength, before he released it. "*Mucho gusto encontrarle*, Señorita Lamar."

Heat tinged her cheeks. "I'm afraid I don't speak much Spanish, Señor Ventura."

"I was only saying I am very pleased to meet you."

"Likewise. Have you traveled aboard the *Cordelia* before?"

"Once or twice." Ventura slid a sideways glance at Ike. "Mr. Gallagher and I have some interests in common. But you and I, we may have some business to discuss?"

Did everyone in the Rio Grande Valley expect her to conduct business in her father's absence? Before she had even heard the terms of—she dreaded the thought—the will?

But Ike said Ventura's goodwill was important to the continued success of Lamar Industries. So she would do her best.

"That may be so. We can discuss our business as we tour the boat." *Make it personal.* "And I look forward to learning about your Bats. I have never had the privilege of attending a game."

Ventura's chuckle sent a breath across her hand that tingled her fingers. "So I am to sell *you* on the idea of the Bats traveling aboard the *Cordelia*? That is a unique sales tactic, I must say. I look forward to spending more time with you, Miss Lamar."

A reedy man dressed in what she supposed must be a tuxedo—fancier than a Sunday suit, although still in black and white. Smith, Smithson, no—*Smithers*—that was it, the head waiter, came forward. "Glad to have you back aboard, sir. Please follow me to your seat."

After that, a constant stream of passengers promenaded by Blanche. A mother with two children was traveling downriver to visit family. Those two were the only children aboard. A dozen businessmen, a half-dozen couples, a few men who looked like what Mama called "dandies," and men who lived on family money and dressed in the latest fashions, rounded out the passengers.

Blanche felt her lips curl and forced the sneer into a pleasant smile. Why, Ike himself dressed like a dandy but so far, apart from an unfortunate flare for the dramatic, had acted like a complete gentleman. Mrs. Davenport's second rule came to mind. *Be polite*; maybe they would surprise her.

Thanks to an insatiable appetite for the written word, Blanche was conversant with current news events and books, so she could carry on an intelligent conversation. All the while she smiled and made small talk, she listened to Effie playing the piano. She slipped effortlessly from one song into another. Blanche didn't recognize a single tune, but they ranged from sentimental to lively. All had her wanting to hum along.

Instead of judging, Blanche focused on associating names with faces. In the fleeting seconds between introductions, she reviewed the names of the people already seated. Of all the guests, the young men were the hardest to tell apart. Back in Roma, any one of them would have stood out. Here, they blended together in the similarity of their attire.

The ladies differed in dress and in manner. Roly-poly Mrs. Potter arrived with her thin-faced husband. The pair looked like Jack Sprat and his wife of nursery rhyme fame. They seemed like ordinary, God-fearing folk. At the opposite end of the spectrum, Mrs. Ralston was dressed in a peacock blue gown that looked as if it sported every feather and lacy frill available to the dressmaker's art. The color of her hair rivaled Blanche's, but she suspected that had more to do with a bottle than birth's generosity.

At length, Smithers rang a bell. The piano music stopped. Ike slipped his arm into the crook of Blanche's elbow. "Shall we?"

Blanche wanted to slide into an inconspicuous seat by the kitchen, perhaps, or in a corner. But Ike steered her toward the captain's table, where Mr. Ventura and the Ralstons waited. She lifted her chin and let him lead her to the table. Effie was already at her chair. All the women were seated, but the men stood behind their chairs.

"They're waiting on you to take your seat," Ike offered her whispered instructions.

"Does anyone say grace?" she whispered back, keenly aware of all eyes on her.

"Not ordinarily." Ike seemed taken aback. "Not unless we happen to have a clergyman among the passengers."

Blanche reviewed the names on the list. Not a reverend among them. "Then I will set an example." She called Smithers over. "Please hold off serving the food until I give you the signal."

Ike stood behind her chair and held it as she seated herself, then pushed her closer to the table. She tucked the glistening white napkin into her lap and spoke in her speech-class voice. "Let us take a moment to return silent thanks to the Almighty for the meal we are about to receive." Her bowed head reinforced her meaning. Thankful thoughts warred with worries that she had overstepped her position as captain's daughter at the first opportunity. She didn't know if anyone had time to return a word of thanks before she raised her head and nodded at Smithers.

Mr. and Mrs. Potter gave her an appreciative smile, Ventura was chuckling, but Ike—Ike stared at her as if he had never encountered anyone quite like her before.

⁘

"I never thought to see the like. She kept the whole salon waiting for a good three minutes while she bowed her head in a silent prayer, as pretty as you please." Ike chuckled.

Old Obie glanced at the young man, enjoying his discomfort. Although he kept his eyes fixed on the river, his ears captured every detail of Blanche's first interaction with the passengers. A smile flickered about his mouth. "How did the passengers react?"

"She's a novelty. They were all interested in her."

Old Obie peered through the window at the gathering clouds. "If the sky doesn't clear soon, we may need to shut down for the night. The weather's been dry; we run the risk of going aground when we can't see the water."

"That won't impress Mr. Ventura."

"I know. But an accident would be even worse for business." Old Obie squinted into the fading daylight. If his eyesight ever weakened, his days as a pilot were over. "So far, so good. But tell me, apart from the opening prayer, how did She handle herself?"

The *S* was a capital letter as clearly as if he had held a placard with it written down.

"Well, on the way out, she made a point of greeting everyone by name. That was a pleasant surprise. Smiles and genuine interest in everyone—she's a natural hostess. After the night in her company, Ventura was ready to sign the agreement already." He flipped a coin that rattled on the floor. "Almost."

"So she has some spunk. From what I saw, I was afraid Cordelia had driven it out of her." Old Obie took his pipe from his desk and began puffing. "Did Effie get her out of the widow weeds she arrived in?"

"She was wearing one of Effie's least favorite dresses. Dark blue, with mauve blue gores in the skirt."

"That'd look better on her than on Effie, with her coloring."

"It did." A deep sigh escaped Ike's lips.

Old Obie snapped his head around, pulling the pipe from his mouth. "Oh no. Don't repeat my mistake. If you've heard the story once, you've heard it a hundred times. Test that girl and see if she's river people before you get sweet on her. She might turn out to be a heartbreaker like her mother."

Ike didn't move. "You don't have to worry about that."

"Good." The sky darkened into night but the clouds dissipated—clear sailing ahead. Old Obie rested during the day so he could work the night hours. He didn't trust any of the other pilots to do the job. Belowdecks, the clock ticked toward nine o'clock at high summer.

Ike headed for the stairs. "I'd better warn you. She's already asking about the pilothouse. She wants to watch and learn. In fact, she seems more excited by that than most of the other functions on board."

Old Obie tamped his pipe and set it back in the bowl. "I'm ready. Let her come."

※

After a good night's rest, Blanche woke early in the morning. Breakfast would start in an hour. In the bed opposite her, Effie slept peacefully. Blanche stretched her arms and snuggled under the sheet again. If today turned out anything like yesterday, she might not have any more time to herself until she retired to bed tonight, too tired to do anything but fall asleep.

With that in mind, she slipped out of bed with her Bible. With only one day behind her, she already felt the strains and temptations that would come her way on this journey. In her deliberations, she hadn't factored in the absence of a spiritual mentor. She had never traveled more than a few miles away from the advice of Reverend Davenport. Now it would be her and the Lord alone. *Oh Lord, let me hear Your voice in the middle of the noise of this boat. Let me represent You well.* Blanche read familiar words of admonition from Colossians. "But now ye also put off all these; anger, wrath, malice, blasphemy, filthy communication out of your mouth. . . Put on therefore, as the elect of God, holy and beloved, bowels of mercies, kindness, humbleness of mind, meekness, longsuffering." *Help me to dress myself in the things that matter.*

Effie turned over in her bed. Reluctantly, Blanche put away her Bible and considered her wardrobe. Effie and Ike might insist on different clothing for the evening, but she would wear what made her comfortable in the daytime—her clean and familiar black traveling suit.

She had finished fastening her buttons when Effie yawned. "You're up early."

"Good morning. I thought I would take a turn on deck before breakfast." Blanche turned her boater over in her hands. Should she wear it? Yes, she decided. It provided some protection of her face from the sun. Without it, her skin might burn so red that it wouldn't matter if she blushed.

"Do you want company?" Effie pushed her legs over the side of the bed and reached into her chiffarobe for a dress. "I think I'll wear rose today." She felt the collars of two or three dresses before she pulled out a rose dress.

"How do you do it?"

Effie laughed. "Oh, I have my tricks. For one thing, my buttons have different shapes and textures. The buttons on this dress are round and smooth, like a pearl."

Blanche shook her head in amazement. "I have a hundred questions to ask, but I wanted to take a walk before the day gets started."

"I'll see you at breakfast then."

Should she stay and help? Effie lived on her own and dressed without assistance all the time. Blanche headed out the door.

The room was belowdecks. Effie had apologized. "Why should I have a room with a view? I can't enjoy it."

Blanche reassured her that she didn't mind. She had free run of the ship. Outside the door, the darkened interior of the hallway left her disoriented. She closed her eyes. Their room was on the left side—the *port* side, she reminded herself. She had to learn shipboard terminology. The stairs should be to her left, past a couple of rooms. Opening her eyes, she headed in that direction.

The plush carpet underneath her feet invited her to remove her shoes. Her toes wiggled, begging to be set free. She tilted her head, imagining it in different colors. Thick tapestries lined the walls. Perhaps they were intended to insulate the hall from the engine noise, but oak paneling or a beige tapestry would be better. Her imagination was running wild; instead of enjoying more luxury than she had ever seen before, she wanted to change it. Was it just the possibility that all this might be hers?

If she didn't stop staring, she wouldn't get in her stroll before breakfast. Spotting the stairs, she climbed to the deck. A cool breeze brushed her cheek. From one end men's voices raised in song, men sounding happy in their work. She looked toward the prow of the boat, where the wheel churned through the water. If she went that way, the spray would tickle her face.

Ahead of her the stairway led to the pilothouse. It was time she made Old Obie's acquaintance.

CHAPTER 7

Blanche stopped at the bottom of the stairwell, admiring the care taken with this small section of the ship. Here she found the freshly painted walls she expected below, the gleaming brass handrail without a handprint. Years of foot traffic had given the steps a bright sheen.

A sharp, somewhat woodsy scent wafted down the stairs. Blanche's nose wrinkled, striving to identify the smell. Pipe smoke, she decided, a somewhat pleasant odor. Breathing deeply to clear her lungs, she climbed the steps and waited on the top step, suddenly shy.

"Come on in," a raspy voice called. "Ike told me to expect you."

Upon entry to the room, Blanche blinked against the onslaught of sunshine. Pipe smoke thick as fog settled in the air. She coughed and waved her hands in the air.

A chuckle made its way through the haze, and a pipe tapped against an ashtray. Her eyes still stung, and she didn't dare open her mouth for fear the smoke would trigger another cough. But the chuckle had eased her fears.

"Give 'er a minute, and it will get better. If I'da known when to expect you, I'd have cleaned up ahead of time."

Blanche took a shallow breath and walked in. The air had improved. She turned around, looking at the many instruments, only a sextant one that she recognized. Her gaze fixed on the solitary figure with his back to her, facing the wheel. A weather-worn seaman's cap perched on his head, covering his hair except for a few stray waves at the back of his head the color of a rain cloud. His generous mouth looked equally ready to break into song, smile, or clamp down on the pipe still smoldering in an ashtray made out of driftwood.

Weather lines wrinkled his face. His workmanlike clothes were neat and tidy, but this man was no dandy like Ike. His eyes squinted, studying her as closely as she was studying him. Maybe her imagination was getting away from her again. He probably always looked like that, after a lifetime on the river.

"Miss Lamar." He nodded in her direction.

How should she address him? She had only heard him referred to as Old Obie. "I'm afraid I don't know your name." Heat rushed into her cheeks.

"You can call me Obie. I won't complain if 'Old' slips in there." His lips twitched. "I know my nickname. I don't mind. Figure I earned it, after a lifetime on the river."

A lifetime on the river. . . "Then you must have worked with my father. Captain Lamar."

Again that half smile as he nodded. "Ever since I started on the river. I reckon you could say I knew him about as well as anyone."

Old Obie said it with such an air of finality that the truth hit Blanche. Her father was dead. Tears sprang to her eyes. "I wish I could have known him."

Old Obie's hand reached for his pipe, but he slid it back in his pocket. "You can ask me anything you want to know."

The questions that plagued her, she wouldn't ask a total stranger. *Did he ever mention me? Why did he leave us?* "Did you know my mother?"

"I did indeed. I argued with the cap'n, telling him he had no business straying so far away from the river. I've always blamed myself for what happened. But once he laid eyes on your mother, he was a goner. For a few wild months, he convinced himself he could give up everything he ever knew for her. And he brought stars to her eyes. I was half-smitten with her myself."

"So. . .what happened?" She held her breath.

Instead of answering, he grabbed the binoculars and took a step toward the front window. When he swept the river from side to side, his shoulders hitched higher with tension. His generous mouth straightened until it stretched in a thin line. He made a minute adjustment to the wheel. Keeping his hand on the wheel, he reached for a bellpull that dropped through the floor. He tugged it once and received an answering pull. "Steady yourself. They'll be increasing speed by five knots."

Blanche's feet shifted, but she quickly regained her footing. Old Obie stood without speaking, as if he had forgotten her presence.

A bell jingled in the distance, and Blanche waited for the boat to increase speed. When it didn't, she realized that was the breakfast bell. She took a step to the stairwell. "It's time for breakfast."

Old Obie paid her no more attention than if she was a fly buzzing around his face. Repressing her disappointment over the stalled conversation, she headed to the salon.

———

"You were right." Ike's voice broke into the rhythm of the song Effie was playing.

"What's that?" Effie asked in low tones as her fingers continued to move effortlessly over the piano keys.

"She's wearing her black traveling suit again already waiting at the captain's table."

Effie held back a chuckle. "People don't dress up for breakfast."

Smithers rang a small bell, and Ike helped Effie to the captain's table. Turning in Blanche's direction she asked, "Did you enjoy your stroll?"

"Very much." A story lay behind Blanche's tone; Effie would ask about it later.

"Miss Gallagher, what a pleasure to have you playing for us before our meals."

"Thank you. I enjoy playing." Effie imagined Mrs. Ralston's appearance. People didn't understand when she said she heard colors; but she did. For instance, a song in the key of D, with two sharps, sounded yellow, where as something in D-flat could sound dark purple. Mrs. Ralston's voice felt like a garish green.

"Do you know 'I've Been Working on the Railroad'?" Mrs. Ralston asked.

Effie tilted her head. Passengers frequently had special requests, and she was happy to accommodate. "Unfortunately not. But if you sing it for me, I can probably pick it up."

Skirts rustled as Blanche stood. "Once again, we will observe a few moments of silence to return thanks for the food."

The simple invitation to return thanks pushed a key in Effie's soul. Even though she didn't make a habit of saying grace, she did turn her thoughts toward God in the silence.

Beside her, Ike shifted in his chair. His presence surprised her this morning. His work entertaining passengers kept him up half the night, and he couldn't work twenty-four hours out of twenty-four.

If she had to guess, she'd attribute his attendance to Blanche. Whether or not he admitted it, she suspected he was half-smitten with the captain's daughter, despite the warnings he had received.

"Amen." Blanche brought the moment of silence to an end.

"What plans do you have for this day?" Ike's coffee cup rattled as he lifted it from the saucer.

"So many people asked for time with me today." Blanche sounded uncertain.

"Agatha has demanded an audience this morning." Effie threw her a lifeline.

"And no one defies Dame Agatha," Ike murmured.

"Why do I need to see the seamstress?"

Ike made a sound half between cough and laugh. Blanche's terrified voice made Effie wonder if she had ever owned a dress not made by her own hands.

"It seems so wasteful to make new dresses for me until I decide whether I'm going to stay with the boat. Truly, I don't need anything new."

Ah, waste not, want not. The captain had mentioned that quality of his wife's character. How did he describe it? *She pinched pennies so tight she wore all the use out of them.*

"I insist." Ike had regained control of his voice. "Agatha is paid a salary, and the material has already been purchased."

"You won't change his mind, and Agatha is an artist with fabric. You might as well enjoy it." Effie determined to help Blanche enjoy this new experience.

"Is her name truly Dame Agatha?" Blanche steered the conversation in a new direction. "What is an English noblewoman doing onboard a riverboat?"

Effie laughed. "That's just her nickname. Because she likes to order everyone around. She probably won't give you a choice about patterns. She doesn't me." Stretching her hand out, she clutched the handle of the orange juice pitcher and poured herself a glass. "The only thing worse than enduring a session with her is missing one. She makes you feel like you've ignored a royal invitation."

Blanche didn't respond until she ate a bite of something—her oatmeal, Effie would guess. "Did she treat the captain that way?"

Good question. Blanche continued to show some spunk.

Nodding, Effie chewed on a strip of bacon. "When you're the queen of it all, everyone has to bow to your wishes. Even a riverboat captain."

"I'll just have to talk some sense into her. That's all. Pass me the biscuits, please."

Effie took the platter in both hands and handed it over. "What else are you hoping to see today?"

"I was hoping to see the engine rooms in the morning, while it is still cool."

"You can go tomorrow. They'll be happy to see you."

"And this afternoon I'm going back to visit with Old Obie."

A spoon clinked against china. Ike was adding sugar to his coffee. "Do you mind if I join you? I can always use another lesson in the ways of the river."

He was smitten, no doubt about it.

Blanche hesitated before answering. "Of course. You don't have to ask my permission." She wouldn't get rid of Ike easily, if only to help the pilot handle the inevitable questions.

Arriving late, the Ralstons took their seats at the table, and Blanche stopped talking. Out of habit, Effie picked up the slack in conversation.

Mrs. Ralston jumped in. "Is your marvelous seamstress available to fashion a dress for me? My *Ladies' Home Journal* caught up with me in Roma, and there is this absolutely marvelous dress I must have."

"I'm sure she'd be happy to—" Blanche offered.

Effie had to cut her off, "—as soon as she finishes with her current project." She was so used to acting as hostess for the *Cordelia*, she'd have to remind herself to give Blanche time to respond. Thoughts of the future troubled her. Of course the captain refused to give away his daughter's birthright, but where did that leave Effie and her brother?

"And what project is that?" The sound of crockery hitting the table pounded Effie's ears, and Mrs. Ralston screeched.

"Apologies, ma'am." Smithers appeared instantly.

Mrs. Ralston huffed. "I'll have to change my dress. *Such* a disappointment. I was hoping to wear this dress for tomorrow night's dinner performance. Will your laundress be able to get it clean before then?"

I bet she knows that our seamstress is also her laundress. Effie plastered a smile on her face, dismissing the suspicion. "Of course, ma'am."

A choking sound came from Blanche's direction, but she didn't say anything. She remained quiet, saying a word here and there, occasionally her spoon striking the plate. Effie offered her the biscuits a second time, and she accepted. "These remind me of my mother's biscuits."

The sadness in her voice reminded her that she had only recently lost her only known family. She must find it difficult to sit with people she had just met, forced into activities she had never done before and trying to be pleasant. No wonder she felt so threatened.

Whether or not she realized it, this trip was designed to test ability to adapt, to survive. Was any of the old captain in her, or was she an exact duplicate of her mother? "Then she must have been a good cook."

"She was." She pushed back unsteadily in her chair. Ike sprang to his feet to hold it for her. "If you'll excuse me." She moved away from the table at a rapid pace.

"What's wrong with her?" Mrs. Ralston spoke over the clinking of the spoon as if the accident had never happened.

"She just lost her mother." *Why did I speak? We're supposed to accommodate the passengers, not the other way around.*

<hr />

Nineteen years of living as a servant in someone else's house enabled Blanche to walk out of the dining room with every evidence of self-control. She'd spent a lifetime wearing hand-me-downs, every now and then enjoying a new dress made from leftover scraps of fabric. She glanced down at her serviceable black traveling suit. More than necessity drove her to wear it over and over again. She bought it new, with her own money, and it was both fashionable as well as practical. Her first new dress might be her last new dress, and she wanted it to last.

"Lord, help me to show Your love to Mrs. Ralston. No matter what she thinks about me." How many times had Mama prayed the same words? She had spent her life serving others without complaint, adding extra touches that spelled love. At least every member of the Winthrop family attended church, and Mama had prayed with the two littlest girls. People who didn't know the Lord needed those acts of love even more.

Blanche stumbled into the cabin and sprawled across her berth. Memories of her mother, her countless acts of love even when her words were few, crowded her mind, and her shoulders shook with sobs. She buried her face in her pillow and let the case absorb her tears. She would not appear in front of the seamstress looking like a drowned rat.

Pick yourself up, girl. No time for tears. Ma's words haunted her ears. It was all she needed, for now. She scrubbed her face and prepared to meet the dragon Agatha.

CHAPTER 8

"Is that the one you want to keep our nighttime activities a secret from?" Ralston arched his eyebrows as they watched Blanche leave the dining salon. Effie excused herself and followed behind.

Ike nodded. "She'd demand we search the ship and toss all cards to the bottom of the river—either that, or she might demand to be let out at the next stop."

"Too bad. With that hair of hers, she should know how to have a good time." Ralston's eyes lit with an appreciative gleam. He didn't know what to do with Blanche Lamar.

"You will treat her with the same respect you show my sister. More, since she's the captain's daughter."

"All right." Ralston lifted his hands in surrender. "I promise I won't bother her. That one needs someone to teach her to crack a smile."

"Don't worry. Effie's working on that."

After breakfast, Ike headed to his cabin for a few hours' sleep. When he passed Agatha's domain, his steps slowed. He had given the seamstress a detailed description of Blanche's attributes, had consulted on which colors he thought would complement her complexion, and had given a masculine impression of current fashions when asked. He appreciated a well-turned-out woman, and Blanche had the potential to put all the society matrons to shame. The captain had teased him about his knowledge of high fashion, but it suited both his personality and his job. No waist overalls or common denim for him.

The door creaked open as he passed, and Effie's cane tapped outside the door. Inhaling her breath sharply, she said, "Ike? Is that you?"

How she recognized him, he had never figured out. "What gave me away this time?"

Laughing, she shut the door behind her. "Your aftershave, of course. Detectable to my sensitive nose beneath the overlay of cinnamon toast and strong coffee. You came at the right time. From Agatha's reaction, Blanche must look amazing."

"She's already sewn a dress?" Agatha was a marvel with the sewing needle, but Blanche had been onboard for less than twenty-four hours.

"Come with me." Effie hustled down the hallway toward the stairs, her cane tapping a steady rhythm. At the stairs, she grabbed for the handrail. "She took your general comments and fashioned a dress, adjusting it according to her observations of Blanche last night, as well as the exact measurements of her traveling outfit."

She dashed into her cabin and returned with a gold hair-comb with mother-of-pearl insets in the handle. "I'm going to try my hand at arranging her hair." She tucked the comb into her reticule and left the cabin. Ike followed.

Back in the sewing room, Effie knocked before ducking her head in. "Ike is with me. May he come in?"

Agatha's agreement overrode Blanche's soft protest, and he stepped inside.

Stunning. Breathtaking. Beautiful. Regal. *Warm.* All of those words and yet none of them captured Blanche's transformation.

"Mr. Gallagher. I am so glad that you are here. I think you will agree that this dress suits Miss Lamar's position aboard the *Cordelia.*"

Words failed Ike. He could only nod.

"Miss Gallagher and I are trying to convince Miss Lamar to agree to a few dresses in jewel colors: a gold, perhaps, or sapphire or jade. Any of those would look lovely with her coloring."

Blanche didn't respond. She stood transfixed in front of the mirror, her hand held to a cheek that glowed scarlet between gloved fingers.

"Miss Lamar." Ike took her free hand and raised it to his lips. The garment Agatha had constructed was simple and modest in design, yet a world removed from Blanche's normal attire. The fitted blouse in warm beige, with vertical stripes of navy blue and ruby red, tucked in nicely at the waist of an eight-gore skirt.

"Sit down, Blanche." Effie knew how to exercise authority as well as her brother. "Let me add the finishing touch."

Blanche sat down in front of a vanity mirror, shaking her head from side to side. Effie's deft fingers pulled every pin from Blanche's head. Luxurious, thick red waves cascaded over Blanche's shoulders and down her back.

Ike settled back to watch Effie work. She had a feel for hair, insisting that each woman's head was different, telling her whether to curl, or brush, or tease.

A few minutes later Effie had sculpted Blanche's hair into a soft bun at the back, the sides held in place with the gold combs. After she tucked a few pins back into the hair, she stepped back. "That should do it."

A pale blush sprang high in Blanche's cheeks and spread down her neck. The smile in her eyes reached her lips, the smile of a woman who knew she looked good.

"You will of course wear that lovely garment when you go up to the pilothouse and let everyone on deck see you," Ike dictated. *No one more so than Old Obie.*

"But what about the dress I was wearing. . .I don't want to create extra work." Blanche offered a feeble protest.

Agatha guffawed. "I do the laundry around here. And I want you to show off my work as soon as possible. You must wear this dress to the evening meal. It is even more important that you look your best when we have additional guests." With a quick nod of her head, she turned to Ike. "Now, Mr. Gallagher. Take your leave so we can continue our work."

"Just a minute." Ike leaned close enough to Blanche to say sotto voce, "You look lovely." The heat rushing into her cheeks tickled the fringes of his mustache, and he hurried out the door before he blushed himself.

~·~

Two hours later, Blanche left Agatha's domain, worn out from a hard morning's work. No wonder Ike called her Dame Agatha. She paid no attention to anything Blanche said, as inflexible in her demands as the teacher who had drummed the multiplication tables into her head.

Blanche didn't want to offend Agatha, but she couldn't decide what bothered her more: the colors or the cut of the clothes. "Won't this dress draw attention to me?"

Agatha guffawed. "That's the point."

Effie only smiled before reassuring Blanche that the patterns they had chosen were simple, tasteful, and modest.

For the half hour remaining until the next meal, Blanche decided to retire to her cabin, but she found it hard to relax. If she laid against a pillow or leaned against a chair, she might destroy Effie's delicate handiwork with her hair. The dress wouldn't wrinkle easily, but she couldn't redo the bow by herself. When she removed the gloves, a hangnail on her left hand bothered her. She pulled at it, and a tiny pucker of blood appeared at the root. It dripped onto the perfect white of the gloves. Now what? She couldn't even keep a pair of gloves clean for two hours. Tears formed in her eyes, which made her feel even worse. She couldn't, wouldn't, cry over something as ridiculous as a drop of blood.

Effie entered the room, catching her in mid-sob. "You poor dear." She dropped onto the bed beside Blanche. "I had hoped that your dress-fitting session would lift your spirits. I always get excited when I'm getting new clothes made."

Ignoring the difference in their perspectives, Blanche pointed to the gloves before remembering Effie couldn't see her

213

gestures. "I got blood on my gloves."

"Is that all? I was afraid Agatha might have forgotten to finish a seam."

Blanche's eyes widened at the thought of walking down the hallway with her chemise showing.

"Give me the offending garment."

When Blanche handed the glove to Effie, she tossed it into the bin with other washables. "I keep several pair at all times. I'm lucky if I can wear a pair for two days."

Blanche sucked in a deep breath. "I don't know how to be fancy." She put a hand to her throat and almost ran her bloodied finger over the top button. She didn't dare. She might smear blood on the dress this time. *I'll never tear a hangnail again.* She hoped she would keep that promise. "Do you have any cures for a hangnail?"

"Don't wear gloves?" Effie smiled. "It will grow out soon enough."

"What did Agatha mean by new guests tonight?" Blanche had wondered about the comment at the time.

"We're stopping at Rio Grande City tonight. Several people usually join us for dinner and the evening's, umm, entertainment. Even more than usual this trip, because we want to impress Señor Ventura. So promise you'll wear the dress tonight. Please."

"Very well." Blanche sighed. She couldn't wait for this trip to be over so that she could go back to where she didn't face new dilemmas every few hours. "Please help me undress. I want to keep this clean until I get to dinner tonight."

After changing into a straight black skirt with a dark blue blouse that could hide dirt, she made her way to the deck. She hated being in the bowels of the ship where the air always seemed far too warm.

On deck, she closed her eyes and welcomed the fresh air. The fabrics Ike had chosen for her swam before her eyes. Such. . .color. Before her eyes had landed on the gold brocade, she thought the prettiest thing she had ever seen in her life was a triple rainbow. She had seen one only once, three years ago on her sixteenth birthday. That day, and that rainbow, had changed her life.

The pleasure she felt in the fabrics Agatha spread before her almost exceeded the pleasure of that day. As she reveled in the bold colors, she felt is if she was lusting after another god. She reminded herself that God created color.

And Ike bought it for her, for plain, practical Blanche Lamar. He said they were perfect for her coloring. A part of her wanted to gather the fabric to her bosom and hold it tight in the way she couldn't a rainbow. Another part of her wanted to throw it onto the nearest bonfire as a heathen idol.

Mist sprayed Blanche's face as she leaned over the railing. Unbuttoning the top button of her blouse, she lifted her face to enjoy the cooling drops. It brought a little relief as the sun climbed to its zenith. Raising her hand to her eyebrows to shield her eyes from the sun, she tried to gauge the time until lunch. Could she make it to engineering before the call to the dining room? No. She decided to use the time to walk about the ship instead.

A glimpse into the salon showed Smithers directing the wait staff. Mrs. Ralston came around the corner, and they nodded as they passed in the hallway.

Mrs. Potter appeared at the top of the stairs. When she spotted Blanche, she smiled. "Miss Lamar. How lovely to see you again. And I wanted to tell you how much Mr. Potter and I appreciate your quiet time for prayer at our meals. I confess, I never expected it aboard a steamboat." She chuckled. "Judge not, as the Good Book says."

Heavy footfalls ascended the stairs and Mr. Potter joined them. "She's speaking the truth. I wondered if you'd mind if I say a word or two to the Almighty out loud, before we eat? Invite some of the others to join in."

"What a wonderful idea. Thank you for suggesting it. I would have done so myself, except it seemed inappropriate somehow." She extended a hand toward the rotund gentleman. "Can I count on you for luncheon in a few minutes?"

"Of course."

Excusing herself, she walked past the deck where the staff cabins were located and stood at the top of the stairway leading into the bowels of the ship. Engines throbbed and heat blasted her in the face. Even if she dressed only in her camisole, she would still feel hot. Tomorrow morning she would leave her room early during the coolest time of day.

The bell rang, calling them to come to the salon. Rarely had a morning provided her so much entertainment. Not much of her time had been put to practical use. None of it had been spiritual, unless she counted her ruminations about rainbows and fabric colors.

But she couldn't remember the last time she had had so much fun.

CHAPTER 9

*E*s una buena noche, si?" Face ashen, Bart Ventura leaned against the railing, waiting for the gangplank to extend to the wharf at Smithville. "I know we have only been on the river for twenty-four hours, but I feel better on dry land."

Ike smiled. Any ill effects Ventura felt probably resulted from overindulging in bourbon while playing poker the night before. "Come now, a pleasant day on the river, good food, and now a night in a pleasant community. I can personally recommend Mrs. Hurley's café. The best pork ribs in all of Starr County." He glanced at the lily-white cuffs extending beyond the sleeves of his suit. "Although if we eat barbeque, I need to change clothes."

"My ballplayers like barbeque. We will try the café." Ventura turned the pearl studs of his cuff. After the walkway was extended, the two men strolled into town. "So tell me, are the ladies of the café as lovely as your sister and Miss Lamar?"

Ike's head jerked up at that statement. "So you think Miss Lamar is pretty?"

Bart's laughter rang through the air, loud enough to be heard on board the boat. "So you are thinking that way? That one has spirit underneath all the prim-and-proper manner. And you are just the man to bring it out of her. Bring her along to our game one night. We can teach her how to have a good time."

"I'd rather get honey from a beehive." Ike hoped his suntan hid the heat rushing to his cheeks.

The evening passed pleasantly. The local alcalde, Mayor Fernandez, agreed to an exhibition game by the Brownsville Bats. Later, after they returned to his cabin, Ike won a healthy amount even after he took out the boat's fifty percent cut. Despite the successful evening, he felt unsettled. After an hour of tossing and turning, he arose and cleaned his room, a task he usually left for the maid. After putting everything away, he sprawled in the most comfortable chair in the room and closed his eyes. A few minutes later, his chin nodded forward and he jerked awake.

Face it. He wouldn't get much sleep no matter what he did, so he might as well join the others for breakfast. But if he did that he'd run into Blanche and get stirred up again. No, he'd stop by the salon later to grab a cup of coffee and a bite to eat. The cook usually obliged him even when he showed close to the noon hour.

Ignoring a pounding headache and empty stomach, he stayed in his cabin going over the account books. Totaling up the income received to date, he decided this voyage would be profitable. More and more it looked like Bart Ventura would bring them repeat business. The Roma cotton gin had sent a larger than usual shipment. If they delivered the cotton within a reasonable time, that could turn into increased traffic as well.

What would Blanche think of the gambles businesses took all the time, in the hopes of making money? Expenses had outpaced income for several years. On mornings like this, he sometimes wondered if they could afford to forgo the late nights and uncertainties of gambling. Just as often, his winnings determined whether or not the *Cordelia* stayed afloat.

The grumblings in his stomach increased, and a glance out the window confirmed the late morning hour. As soon as he entered the salon, he headed for the captain's table. Elaine spooned a big portion of eggs onto a plate. Acid rose in Ike's throat. "I think I'll just have coffee this morning. And some dry toast."

"Like that, is it?" Elaine didn't say anything further. She didn't have to. She had nursed him through everything from splinters to his first hangover. Taking a sturdy ceramic mug instead of fancy china, he grabbed a biscuit with the other hand and headed for the one place where he could always find peace. He could depend on Old Obie to listen, and he hurried through the fresh air across the open deck. The worn steps to the pilot-house beckoned.

As soon as his right foot landed on the bottom step, he heard her voice. *Blanche.* His feet raced up the stairs even while a curse rose to his lips.

Dressed once again in her black traveling suit, Blanche stood at the wheel. Her hands grabbed the spokes, her right hand at two o'clock, left at ten. Her fingers curled around the wheel as if the ship would sink if she didn't hold on. Old Obie stood about a foot behind her, his head never moving although Ike knew he saw every nuance of color in the river. He grunted and pointed over Blanche's shoulder. "Do you see anything unusual about that patch of water?"

When Blanche shook her head, Old Obie handed her his binoculars. "Take a closer look." He placed his hands on the wheel while she leaned forward toward the window, adjusting the glasses.

"It looks like there's a shadow under the water. Is that possible?"

Old Obie nodded. "Yup. That's a sandbar. We have to keep the boat away from it or else we could run aground."

"And that's not a good thing."

"Not at all."

Ike hung back, enjoying the interplay between the old sailor and the young lady.

"You turn the boat."

"Oh no. I'll run us straight into it."

"No, you won't. I'll help you." Old Obie shifted position. "Here. Put your right hand next to mine."

Blanche reached out a tentative hand and placed her white hand next to Old Obie's speckled one. Slowly, Old Obie moved the wheel a fraction of an inch at a time, letting Blanche feel the shift of the boat beneath them, until they steered clear of the obstacle.

"I did it!" Blanche sounded as excited as boys at a baseball game. Ike remembered his excitement the first time Old Obie let him take the wheel. Only he didn't have Obie's feeling for the river, the instinct necessary to do a pilot's job. He served the business in other capacities.

But Blanche. . .Blanche might be a natural.

"Well done, Blanche. I'm impressed."

At the sound of Ike's voice, Blanche's right hand escaped the wheel and tucked a strand of hair behind her ear. "Ike. I didn't hear you come up the stairs." She heard the breathiness in her voice and chastised herself.

Old Obie chuckled. "Your mind was all on the river." He turned merry brown eyes on Ike. "The girl is a natural-born pilot. I insist she spend time here each day, to better learn the ways of the Big River."

Heat rushed into Blanche's cheeks at the unexpected words of praise. "Don't be ridiculous. I almost ran us aground on that sandbar back there."

"What I saw"—Ike crossed the floor and leaned against the captain's table—"was an apprentice learning from a master. The important thing is that you avoided the sandbar. You're catching on quickly."

If her cheeks weren't already burning, Ike might have blamed the color on his kind words. These two men had spoken more warmly of her abilities in a handful of days than her mother ever did. "There seems to be a lot I don't know." She turned the compliment aside.

"Different areas of expertise. If we had a quiz on Bible facts or recitation, you'd win hands down."

Laughter as big as Santa Claus issued from Old Obie. "He has you there, missy."

A smile crept onto Blanche's face. "You may be right,

although others on board might excel, like Mr. and Mrs. Potter. In fact. . ." An idea, so radical, so perfect, jumped into her mind. "We should test that theory out. What would our passengers think about a departure of music for our evening's entertainment?"

"What are you thinking of?"

"A Bible sword drill or possibly a memory contest. I'm sure the Potters would take part, and we could invite the other passengers and crew to join us." Her excitement grew as she talked. "I used to do well at things like this when I was a little girl. I won my very own Bible in my first contest." The pace of her speech increased, the words blending together, so caught up with the possibilities that it took a minute for the disbelief reflected on the two men's faces to register. Her voice trailed off.

"This is a steamboat, not a church." Ike's voice came out high-pitched.

Old Obie only shook his head. "That sounds like something Miss Cordelia might suggest. If we were transporting a revival meeting or a church convention, that might work. But people don't pay money to have a bunch of 'thou shalt nots' quoted at them."

Blanche shrank back, her shoulders slumping. Then she squared them and lifted her chin. "You're right, I shouldn't put learning the Bible in the same category as 'entertainment.' But how about a chapel service on Sundays, after breakfast? We must do that much, at least."

Grinning, Ike shook his head. "You won't give up on this, will you?"

Straightening her spine and raising herself to her full height—still nearly a foot shorter than Ike—she nodded. "I at least will spend time on Sunday worshipping Almighty God, and I will welcome anyone who wishes to join me. It would be wonderful if Effie could play some hymns for us to sing."

" 'Amazing Grace.' I always liked that song." Old Obie hummed the first few measures.

"Effie has never studied church music. . ." Ike temporized.

"I already know she plays by ear. I can sing, a little. I can teach her." Blanche relaxed.

Chuckling, Old Obie lifted the binoculars and stared over the river.

"Another sandbar? I didn't know the river was that low." Ike peered through the window.

Blanche joined them, looking in the direction where they focused their attention, scanning for whatever had them concerned. What she saw resembled a submerged tree limb, with a branch sticking above the water. But these men were the experts.

Old Obie lowered his glasses. "It's nothing. Just an old log."

I was right. Pleasure flooded Blanche's spirit. Maybe she was a natural-born pilot after all.

Old Obie returned his attention to Blanche. "It sounds like you're going to be busy. Dress fittings, pilot lessons, music lessons. You're fitting into river life just fine." He patted her on the shoulder. "The Rio Grande will grab your heart before you know it."

At that point, the dinner bell rang, and a low growl erupted in the room.

"Skipped breakfast, did you?" Old Obie spoke before he inserted an unlit pipe in his mouth. "You'd better get down to dinner."

"Why don't you join us?" Blanche had never seen Old Obie in the salon.

He waved her concern away. "I'll grab a bite after Pete—he's my relief—shows up."

Ike put his arm through the crook of Blanche's arm and led her to the stairs. She paused and looked over her shoulder. A featherlight touch landed on her shoulder.

"Don't worry about Old Obie. Elaine keeps him well fed. As Thoreau said, he hears a different drummer."

After dinner, Blanche convinced Effie to join her at the piano. "I want us to celebrate a time of worship on Sunday."

"And Ike agreed to it?" Effie's cane hesitated a fraction of a second.

Blanche tamped down a desire to remind her that she was

the captain's heir and she didn't have to ask anyone's permission. But. . . "I will simply announce that I will retire to the theater for a time of worship after breakfast on Sunday and invite anyone who wishes to join me." She reminded herself she wanted Effie's help—more than that, her friendship. Pasting a smile on her face, she stared again into Effie's sightless eyes. Forced smiles wouldn't win Effie over. Tired of seeking approval in this strange environment, Blanche decided to relax. "From the time I was a little girl, my favorite part of the service was singing hymns. I really want to include a few songs on Sunday. And you are so talented with the piano—will you help me?"

A smile wrinkled those blank-staring eyes. "I'd like that."

"What hymns do you suggest?" Blanche didn't know how much church music Effie had been exposed to.

Effie cupped her hands over the table, her fingers moving as if seeking out piano keys. "I know 'Amazing Grace,' of course. I love Christmas songs, but it's not Christmas. What else? The doxology." A smile played about her lips. "But if you sing one for me, I can probably pick it up."

Blanche bounced on her feet in time to one of her favorites by Fanny Crosby. "Can we practice right now?"

"The salon is empty now, isn't it?"

"Yes." Blanche answered the question, although Effie probably could name the order in which the passengers had left the room. She went to the piano and pulled out the bench, aligning her body perfectly with middle C. She played a few chords and hummed a few bars of "Amazing Grace," her voice a lovely alto.

"I've never heard you sing before. What a lovely voice you have. Maybe we can sing a duet." As soon as Blanche realized what she had said, heat rushed into her cheeks. "That is, people have told me I have a pleasant voice."

Effie chuckled. "I'm sure you have many talents we know nothing about. We've just met. But you must make me a promise."

"What?" Pleasure at Effie's compliment warmed her.

Effie plunked out a few chords of a melody Blanche had heard her play every night. "You must sing with me one evening."

"Why not?" Why not indeed. Her mind tumbled with possibilities as she guided Effie through a few hymns.

She couldn't remember a time she had felt happier or more at peace than the last two days. She had stayed too busy, and too happy, to spend her days in tears and recriminations.

For the first time, the possibility of living on the river no longer terrified her.

CHAPTER 10

"S hould I try to talk her out of this church service she's plan- ning?" Ike lounged against the railing in the pilothouse.

Old Obie didn't object, one of the few people he allowed the liberty of touching anything in his domain. "No need to make an enemy of the girl. She'll be your boss someday, after all." He knew the twinkle in his eyes would take the sting out of his words.

"So you think she'll stay on the river?" More than simple curiosity lay behind Ike's question.

"How do I know? She might be pulling the wool over my eyes the way her mother did to the captain." Old Obie shrugged his shoulders, pretending an indifference he didn't feel. "But I do know this. In less than one week, she's learned more about steamboats than Cordelia did in two years of marriage. Maybe we should test it, let the boat get grounded and see what she thinks about being stuck in one place for a day or two."

Ike groaned. "Don't forget the passengers. We're trying to convince Bart Ventura that we can meet our schedule and that it's safe to bring his team aboard. That's Bart Ventura's biggest concern about bringing his team aboard. Floating them down the river for exhibition games will only work if they can advertise ahead of time. The only reason he's considering the steamboat is that the railroad hasn't made it to Roma yet."

Old Obie looked down the river. Ever changing, yet constant, none of the shifting attitudes of society. "Everybody's in such a rush to get places these days. There was a time when we could relax and take life easy."

Ike pointed to the steam pouring from the smokestacks. "This from the man who adapted the design of the engine to get the boat to go a few knots faster to win a race?"

"A race is different." Old Obie waved away Ike's reaction, a smile lighting his face. "I won a pretty packet on that race." He sobered. "Of course, that was also the time when Cordelia decided she didn't like noisy engines, running fast, or gambling, and left the river for good." He stuck the unlit pipe in his mouth and chewed on the stem without lighting it.

"If I was making a bet, I'd give at least even odds that Blanche will stick." Ike placed a hand on Obie's shoulder. "She didn't have to come, but she did."

"So did Cordelia. Until she couldn't take it anymore. That just about broke the captain's heart." Old Obie turned his eyes inward to unpleasant memories of dark days.

"We'll know a lot more if. . .when. . . .no one shows up at this Sunday service she's planning." Ike straightened away from the railing. "I bet she'd enjoy a time trial. Too bad the river is too low for that."

Old Obie laughed. "She probably would. Maybe we can arrange it."

Ike tossed a coin into the air and caught it with one hand. "At least Effie is having fun. She loves learning new music. She keeps humming this one hymn, 'It Is Well with My Soul.' It was written by someone who lost his family at sea, or so she says."

The sound of a hammer raining blows against wood floated up the stairs. "What's that noise? Did something on deck need repair?"

"No." Ike stared down the stairway. He rounded the corner at the bottom of the staircase in time to find Blanche tacking a sign by the doorway leading below deck. WORSHIP SERVICE headlined the sign in bold letters. The penmanship deserved an award.

Passengers and crew alike drifted by the sign, paused, and read it.

"A church service? Here?" one of Ventura's men questioned.

Ike waited for Blanche's reaction.

"A time for believers in the Lord to gather together to worship. We won't have a sermon, just friends sharing about a Friend."

"I'll probably be sleeping before my shift in the pilothouse." Pete had arrived. "But I wish you well."

He entered the stairwell, pausing when he saw Ike. "That Miss Lamar, she's something else. A church service on any boat. Let alone this boat. Doesn't she know—"

"No." Ike's voice came out more clipped than he meant it to. "And you'd better keep it that way."

"I didn't mean any harm, Mr. Gallagher." The young man's eyes widened. "I won't say a word."

"Good." Ike joined Blanche on deck. A crowd had gathered around her. Their expressions ranged from skeptical to outright humor. Should he rescue her? No. The more he learned about her, the more he discovered surprising strength. Only today he had read in the logbook that she spent an hour observing the river in the fading twilight last night.

Today Blanche wore a brown skirt and beige blouse. The brown colors suited her coloring better than black and white, but he looked forward to seeing her in bright colors. Dame Agatha was finishing the gowns as quickly as she could, hopefully before the Sunday service. He grinned at the thought.

"I never thought I'd see the day they would hold a church service on the *Cordelia*. Doesn't the Bible have something to say about God and mammon?" Ralston's comment echoed the sentiments of others reading the sign.

Ike didn't have a clue what "mammon" meant, but he didn't like the frown it brought to Blanche's face. The lunch bell rang. "All right, let's break it up. Miss Lamar will welcome anyone who wishes to attend, and I might add that my sister will be playing the piano. And that we are in for some special music. You might find it more enjoyable than you expect."

The crowd broke up, puzzled glances alternating with outright chuckles at Ike's expense.

Ike smiled himself until he saw the hurt in Blanche's eyes. She really cared about the church service. "Don't fret yourself. They mean no harm."

"What do they find so funny? Navy ships have chaplains aboard. Why not a commercial ship?"

Since Ike didn't know how to answer her question without crushing any illusions she might still hold about him, he shrugged. "It's just not the usual thing. May I escort you to dinner, Miss Lamar?"

She nodded and accepted his arm with perfect trust. His heart twisted. How long could he continue hiding the truth from her? Could he? Should he?

The answer was no longer clear.

⌁

Blanche slipped into her cabin. Dame Agatha had delivered an emerald green dress with gold piping to her cabin, and she found herself eager to wear it. The new outfits had drawn admiring glances from passengers and crew alike—and from Ike.

If she stayed aboard the *Cordelia* much longer, she'd be as vain as Mrs. Ralston. Sunday, a day dedicated to meditating on the God worthy of all worship, couldn't come soon enough.

The passengers' reaction to the meeting struck her as peculiar. They acted like she was suggesting a preacher go to a house of ill repute. She reminded herself that Jesus said the sick needed a physician, not the healthy. Perhaps their very salvation depended on the service. With a renewed sense of purpose—and a glance in the mirror that confirmed the dress brought out highlights in her eyes and hair—she headed for the dining salon.

The Ralstons arrived a few minutes after she did. Mrs. Ralston greeted her with what appeared to be a genuine smile. Blanche kept reminding herself to *judge not, that ye be not judged.*

Over fresh endive salad, Mrs. Ralston said, "I am glad you are holding the worship service on Sunday. That is sadly lacking in many ships of this kind."

Blanche offered a silent prayer of thanks for the affirmation, and from such an unexpected source. "So can I count on your attendance this Sunday?"

"Of course. And my husband will be happy to join us. Won't you, Mr. Ralston?" She turned her glossed lips on her husband, whose mouth lifted in a half smile.

He leaned forward and refilled his water glass. "I wouldn't miss it for the world." He winked at Blanche. "I understand that we even have some musical numbers to look forward to."

Blanche opened her mouth to protest, but Effie spoke up first. "You won't have to wait that long. Blanche will sing at tonight's entertainment."

Blanche's head whipped around. Sure, they had practiced together a few times. But she still hadn't decided to go ahead with the performance—singing God's praises was one thing; entertaining the passengers was something else entirely. But she knew better than to voice that argument. "But I'm not ready."

"You'll do fine." Effie patted her hand and wiped her mouth daintily with a napkin. "And I'm sure once people hear you sing, they will be happy to attend the service on Sunday."

Backed into a corner like that, Blanche had to agree.

Ike's face broke out in a wide smile. "What is that saying, that God works in mysterious ways? I look forward to this evening with renewed anticipation. Especially if you will be wearing that fetching dress." He winked, but then his face sobered as his eyes bore into hers. Maybe he didn't believe in her abilities as much he pretended.

Her fears returned, doubled in strength. *Fear not.* The familiar command came to mind, but did it apply to her current situation? God was encouraging Joshua before he crossed the Jordan River to enter the Promised Land.

Come to think of it, Blanche was also on a river, and her own promised land, a possible future with her father, beckoned.

Maybe it applied, after all.

The waves in her stomach refused to go away. She picked at her food, although Elaine had cooked the chicken as tender, as well-flavored, as she had ever tasted. A dish of biscuits and gravy sounded good, but the *Cordelia* stayed away from such simple fare. Eating the biscuit dry brought on a coughing fit. Ike refilled her water glass and handed it to her. In a low voice, he said, "You'll do fine." His tenderness reassured her, and her stomach calmed down enough to finish her meal.

The hour between the end of the meal and the start of the performance dragged like the night before Christmas. She paced the front of the theater, pausing in front of the chair where Effie sat with perfect composure. "I want to go through the song one more time."

"If you sing it again, you'll have the fish singing along." Effie laughed. "You're ready." She wouldn't budge.

Blanche resumed pacing, humming the tune to herself. When she said the words under her breath, she forgot a phrase and panicked. She hadn't felt this nervous since the first time she had taken part in a scripture memory contest. This one performance made her as nervous as she had been when she was eight.

Mr. and Mrs. Potter arrived first, at ten minutes to the hour. The dear lady crossed the floor to Blanche's side. "I am truly looking forward to this evening. I have been praying for you."

Tears sprang to Blanche's eyes. "Thank you. That means a lot." She turned to the refreshment table. "May I get you some lemonade? Some ginger snaps?"

"Why, thank you, dear. Pour some for yourself first. You look thirsty."

Blanche groped for a glass on the shelf behind her. "I have some water, but thank you."

Bart Ventura came in, studying the newspaper he had purchased the evening before.

Blanche took her mind off her nerves. "What news of your team, Mr. Ventura?"

"The Bats? They're coming along. Coming along. You will have to come to one of their games as my guest. But I ignored another little tidbit that I thought you might find interesting."

He handed her the paper, opened to the center page.

Blanche couldn't imagine what news item the businessman thought would interest her, but she accepted the paper. "Female pilot licensed in Mississippi," the headline read. She read on with interest.

A woman named Blanche M. Leathers had taken the test to become a steamboat pilot on the Mississippi River—and passed. The article mentioned her lifetime on the River, and her years of working by her husband's side. "Mrs. Leathers is the first woman to receive a pilot's license." The paper questioned the wisdom of issuing a license to a woman because of the dangerous precedent it set.

Sympathy stirred in Blanche's heart for the woman who showed so much gumption. The possibilities suggested by her accomplishment stirred something else, something more, something that took her mind off her fear of singing in public.

By the time she finished studying the article, the room had filled. Blanche told herself not to let Ike's absence bother her. She took a seat next to Effie in the front row, folding her hands in her lap, and breathed in and out. The door opened again, and Blanche turned to spot the newcomers. Her heart sped at the sight of Ike, tall, handsome, in his suit.

At his side stood Ole Obie. Dressed in a suit that looked almost as old as Blanche, he joined the traveling company on the *Cordelia* for the first time since her arrival on board.

CHAPTER 11

The theater had filled with the faces Blanche had come to recognize from their meals together. Murmurs rippled through the crowd, and only a few people took notice of Old Obie and Ike's entrance. Old Obie chose the seat closest to the door. He whispered a few words to Ike, who made his way down the center aisle.

As Ike took his place in front of the audience, Mrs. Ralston brought her hands together. The remainder of the audience took up the applause, with a few men adding catcalls. Heat rushed to Blanche's cheeks, and she rued the fair coloring that went with her bright hair. She took a sip of water from the glass they had brought from the kitchen.

Mrs. Potter reached over and patted her hand. "You'll be fine, dear."

Ike made a dampening motion with his hands, and the noise died down. "Welcome to this evening's entertainment. I know you are looking forward to our program. Mrs. Ralston will entertain us with Helena's monologue from *Much Ado About Nothing.* Our marvelous chef will ply your taste buds with some of her marvelous petit fours. To begin the evening, my sister, Effie, will play a number of Chopin etudes. Then she will accompany Miss Blanche Lamar as she sings a variety of popular songs. And I understand that our two musical ladies have a surprise in store for us."

At the last announcement, the audience once again broke into applause.

"I have promised Miss Lamar that she will retire at a reasonable hour—"

Chuckles, mostly from the men, came at that announcement.

"So let us begin." Ike took a seat and sat back.

Although Blanche didn't recognize the etude that Effie played, her fingers made the piano sing with music that didn't need words. Blanche's heart soared with its beauty, lifting her heart in worship of God. All too soon, the melody ended.

Chef Elaine circled the room. Blanche eyed the delectable miniatures but refused one. She didn't dare chew anything before she sang, or else she might cough in midsong. Mrs. Ralston's recitation could have graced a Broadway stage. Listening to her, Blanche questioned the wisdom of her planned course of action, but she had promised God, if no one else.

As Ike stood to introduce her, Blanche took a long drink and almost spilled it on herself. With a trembling hand, she placed the glass on the tray Elaine passed in front of her.

"And now the moment we've all been waiting for. . .please welcome Miss Blanche Lamar as she serenades us."

Blanche stood to excited applause, and she saw interested smiles on most of the assembled people. At the back, Old Obie looked her in the eye and nodded. Lifting her chin, she straightened her back in perfect posture and walked to the space Ike had vacated.

She bit back the words of apology she wanted to offer. *I've never done this before, please don't expect too much.* Her one-word prayer, *Help!* would have to do. Focusing on friendly faces—her eyes swung between Old Obie and Mrs. Potter—she smiled. Effie played the introduction to "America the Beautiful," a patriotic melody as they had decided.

The next song included a more risky choice, juxtaposing

"Dixie" to "Mine Eyes Have Seen the Glory." As her voice faded away on the last line, Mrs. Potter openly cried. At the back, Old Obie wiped at his eyes. Blanche relaxed. Her fears that some might complain at her singing the "Yankee" song faded. To her, they were two sides of the same story, the pain and passion felt by both sides. Love for country, love for home, love for God—both armies shared the same feelings. She paused a beat. "God bless America."

"Amen," Mr. Potter said, and others nodded.

After the heaviness of the last song, sentimental songs took over the program. "Miss Gallagher and I agreed that we would like to sing songs by Stephen Foster. Feel free to sing along." Their voices blended as they sang parts of three songs: "Beautiful Dreamer," "Jeanie with the Light Brown Hair," and "Old Folks at Home."

When she heard people singing along, she touched Effie's shoulder to stop. "Let's all sing that last verse again." Everyone joined in singing this time, some clapping, some tapping their feet.

Now or never, Blanche decided. "I also would like to do a recitation. I'm no actress like Mrs. Ralston"—she smiled at the lady and received a smile in return—"but I have repeated this passage to myself many times since my mother's death last month. I offer them as comfort to those of you who may have lost a loved one, in recognition of the God who offers us eternal life." She closed her eyes to focus on God, as she intended, and began reciting the comforting words from the twenty-first chapter of Revelation. "And God shall wipe away all tears from their eyes; and there shall be no more death, neither sorrow, nor crying, neither shall there be any more pain: for the former things are passed away." A single tear slid down her cheek. She opened her eyes. "I miss my mother, but if she hadn't died, I might never have come aboard the *Cordelia*."

Clapping broke out, and Mrs. Ralston stood to her feet. Soon the entire audience joined in the standing ovation. As the applause died down, Ike moved forward and handed her a single, perfect rose. "Let's show our appreciation for Miss Lamar's debut performance tonight."

Applause broke out again, and she wondered if she should bow and sweep out of the theater or how she should respond. Instead she stood there, smiling and nodding. At the height of the applause, Old Obie slipped out of the salon.

As the noise died down, Ike spoke to the group a final time. "Tonight's entertainment is finished. Please finish all the trays our chef has prepared, or else her feelings will be hurt."

After his dismissal, several people came forward to congratulate Blanche individually. Mrs. Ralston made her way to the front of the line. In the same voice she used to recite her monologue, she said, "My dear, you look so lovely tonight. And your voice was even lovelier than your clothes. I, too, lost my mother at a young age." She lowered her voice. "After this evening, I look forward to the Sunday service more than ever."

"I shall look forward to it." Blanche's heart flew to the top of the ceiling.

Bart Ventura came toward the end of the line. "Miss Lamar." Appreciation shone in his dark eyes. "What depths you have. I never suspected. I must bow in appreciation." He suited his action to the words, and she laughed.

Leaning forward, he continued. "I confess, I am confused. I never expected to hear so much about God only an hour before I sit down for a game of poker. It's like your boat can't decide what kind of place it wants to be. . .church or gambling hall." He winked at her before turning to Ike. "I'll see you later."

Blanche mumbled something—she didn't know exactly what—while her mind processed everything she had seen and heard since she arrived aboard the *Cordelia*. As soon as they were alone, she turned on Ike.

"Just where will he be playing poker? In your cabin?"

⁂

Ike wanted to curse as he watched Blanche march straight-backed out of the theater. With a few careless words, Ventura had undone all the good, all the humanizing Blanche's short time on the boat had done. Lips thinned, face pale, she lost any resemblance to her larger-than-life father and had transformed back into her mother's image. She might as well have dyed her hair black.

Ike found Ventura waiting for him outside the theater. "I hope I didn't create a problem for you."

Years of experience went into the bonhomie Ike forced into his face. He didn't feel at all charitable toward Ventura at the moment. "It will be fine as soon as I soothe some ruffled feathers." He trotted down the stairs to the girls' cabin.

Effie came out and shut the door behind her. "She really didn't know." As she whispered, she moved Ike down the hall, back toward the stairwell.

"I didn't tell her. . .but I didn't lie about it either. It just never came up."

Effie shook her head. "You knew she wouldn't like it. You could have laid low for this one trip, Ike. Give her a chance to get used to life on the river first."

Ike urged Effie up the stairs and out on deck. A light breeze broke across the prow, teasing his hair. "That's just not possible. I'm good with cards, Effie. I always come out ahead. And. . .we need the money."

"Would one trip bankrupt Lamar Industries?"

"This time, it wasn't just the money. I'm trying to woo Ventura to bring his team aboard. And Ventura's a gambling man. He wouldn't even consider us if he couldn't play a friendly game."

Effie leaned over the railing. "I'm sure you're doing what you think is best. I can't imagine any other way of life. Very little frightens me, but. . ."

"It's like what happened after our parents died and the captain took us in. Only now we are adults, and we're supposed to be able to take care of ourselves." He put an arm around Effie's shoulders. "We'll be okay."

"I'll talk to her." Effie turned sightless eyes on him.

"No." He dragged out the word. "It's time for me to come clean. I probably deserve whatever criticism she offers."

Effie nodded. "Give me a few minutes with her. I'll convince her to meet you on deck."

Unable to stand the waiting, Ike paced the deck. When walking below the shadows of the smokestacks, heat and soot filled the air, the familiar hum of the engines throbbed beneath his feet. Effie loved to come up here. She called it the heart of the ship, and Ike called it his thinking space, but Blanche wouldn't look for him there. He walked on to the pallets of untreated cotton and fruit grown only in the Rio Grande Valley. The scents of summer hung heavy in the air, magnolias and citrus and burning coal. Far different from the cigar-smoke-and-brandy-filled atmosphere of his cabin after a night of poker. Housecleaning tried in vain to remove the smell, so he came on deck every now and then for a breath of fresh air.

Heels tapped on the deck behind him. " 'When I consider thy heavens, the work of thy fingers, the moon and the stars, which thou hast ordained; What is man, that thou art mindful of him? and the son of man, that thou visitest him?' " Blanche's voice floated through the air as she joined him at the rail, keeping about a foot of space between them. Ike drew in a deep breath. She didn't sound angry, but disappointed, rather.

Since he had asked for this meeting, he should initiate the discussion. But where should he start? "I didn't mean for you to find out that way."

"You didn't mean for me to find out at all," Blanche shot back. "You didn't want me to know."

At least she wasn't yelling at him, not quite. "Not right away, no." Gambling aboard a steamboat seemed as natural as a duck paddling down the river. "It's hard to explain. I'm not that good with words."

"Don't treat me like a simpleton." Her voice held a definite hard edge. "You could charm a snake out of his skin if you wanted to. At least do me the courtesy of explaining life on the river, as you will probably say."

"Very well." *I need to see her eyes.* Ike hoisted himself onto the railing so that he was facing Blanche. He tilted back a few inches but righted himself.

"Be careful."

Ike chuckled. "You'd better watch out. Or you'll worry about what happens to me."

"I don't wish you any harm, Mr. Gallagher. My concern is the harm you bring on yourself and this enterprise by playing games of chance."

Ike took a deep breath. "Lamar Industries wouldn't survive without my poker winnings. I understand that steamboats used to earn big profits before the War Between the States. But those days are long over. Things have just gotten worse and worse since I was a child."

Blanche's face looked as pale and stony as the moonlight striking the deck. "Is this steamboat all there is to Lamar Industries? Is the *Cordelia* the totality of my inheritance?"

CHAPTER 12

Ike tapped his feet against the slats beneath the railings, thinking through his answer. "I'm not at liberty to discuss details about your father's company."

She glared at him. "I have a right to know."

"Of course you do. But, remember, I'm not much older than you are. I grew up on this boat, and I always had clothes on my back and food on the table. That was all I cared about. By the time I was old enough to take part in the business, the captain had grown used to keeping it close to his chest." Ike blinked as memories flooded back. When the captain had taken him and Effie in as children, he had promised they would have a home as long as they needed one.

Those details might soften Blanche's attitude toward her father. "When our parents died, the captain stepped in. I think he missed being a father. When he took care of us, he could pretend he was looking after you." Studying her profile, he couldn't guess what thoughts ran through her mind.

"Maybe so." Face lifted to the heavens, she turned her head to the right and left, surveying the stars. "God knows the stars by name. And He knows when a sparrow falls. He showed His love for you by sending my father to you. But you don't sense His hand on your life. And that's the saddest thing of all."

"You think God used a gambling owner of a steamboat to provide for two orphans?" Ike let his skepticism show. "I should think God would have sent us to a church or something."

"Who can understand the ways of God?" Blanche continued to stare at the sky. "The point is, God knew your need and took care of you. Even if I didn't have a father." Her voice cracked. She turned to face him full-on. "When I am mistress of this vessel—if I am—all your gambling activities will cease. God has provided for me all my life without my resorting to games of chance. He will continue to do so."

You are not the only one depending on the income the Cordelia *provides.* Ike didn't voice the thought as he slipped off the railing. "I will see you in the morning." With a bow of his head, he sauntered across the deck and down the stairs to his cabin.

Blanche's gaze followed Ike until he disappeared down the stairs. Headed to tonight's poker game, no doubt.

How naive she must seem, how innocent. Back home, people held that quality in high esteem. Aboard the *Cordelia*, others laughed at her for not recognizing the obvious.

Tonight should have been a triumph. She had sung, people had laughed and cried, she had even quoted from the Bible to a good response. Even Old Obie had attended.

But all that felt like nothing compared to Bart Ventura's caustic humor. How could a Christian live in a place like this? Bear witness to the saving power of God? She should retreat to her closet and pray the night away. But she hated the thought of descending the stairs and possibly running into someone on their way to the poker game in Ike's cabin.

Lantern light blinked overhead. *Old Obie.* He would listen. As she approached the stairwell, the sign announcing the upcoming church service taunted her with her high hopes.

She climbed the steps as quietly as possible. When she entered the room, Old Obie didn't turn around. She flattened her back against the wall, seeking the words to begin.

"Do you want to take a turn at the wheel?" His voice sliced through the air.

She darted forward, freed from her inertia by the sound of his voice. "Is it safe?" She laid a tentative hand on the wheel. "It is dark out tonight. Not much moonlight."

"I'm right here. If you want to get your pilot's license, you have to know how to run the river at all times of day. So tell me, what do you need to look out for when you're piloting at night?"

Blanche scrambled to remember. "How fast the boat is going. How strong the current is. How close the banks are. What the river bottom is like along here."

Old Obie nodded with each item on the list. "Do you know any of the answers?"

Blanche thought back. "I know we were traveling twelve miles per hour this morning."

Old Obie shook his head. "You must think like a river captain. Not miles. *Knots.*"

"Why did they use the same word for bumps in thread and distance over water?"

Old Obie chuckled. "I don't know. They didn't ask me."

As he led her through the answers to her questions, he occasionally directed her to shift the wheel a fraction to the right or left. The tension that had filled her from earlier in the evening dissipated. "I could stay out here for hours."

That brought another chuckle from Old Obie. "The river is getting ahold of you, girl. Why do you think I spend so many hours up here?"

She voiced the stubborn thought that refused to go away. "I wondered if you were avoiding me."

"Now, why would I do that?"

So you wouldn't have to talk to me about my parents? Wordlessly, she shook her head.

"No, indeed. Truth is, we have a second pilot aboard, but he doesn't have the feel for the river that I do." His hazel eyes slanted sideways at her. "Like you do."

"Do you really think I could be a steamboat pilot?" The idea seemed so audacious, so impossible—so desirable. The possibility challenged her to try something few people had done.

"Absolutely. You just need to get to know the river better." He stepped away from the wheel. "I'll leave you be for a spell. You get any problems, maybe you can sing the river into submission."

She chuckled nervously. Her fingers tightened on the spokes of the wheel.

"Relax. Feel the river."

She breathed deeply, as the music director had taught her to do, in and out, and loosened her grip. Despite the cooler evening air, sweat dotted her forehead. She struggled to see the river water the same way as she could during the day. *Feel the river.*

Looking ahead, she spotted one cypress tree towering higher over the river than the ones around it. She made that her landmark. Once she passed that, she marked an outcropping of the riverbank. She passed three landmarks before Old Obie tapped her on the shoulder. "You done good, but that's long enough for now."

Blanche glanced at the sky, half-expecting the quarter moon to have reached its zenith. It had barely budged.

"You held on for fifteen minutes. That's a good spell for a beginning pilot."

The frank admiration in Old Obie's voice warmed Blanche's heart. As she let go of the wheel, she gathered her courage to mention her reason for coming to the pilothouse. "I learned something tonight."

"That you have an amazing musical gift?" Old Obie shook his head. "I'd think you knew that already."

"No. Mr. Ventura mentioned that Ike runs a poker game in his cabin."

"Yes, he does, most nights."

How could Old Obie sound so matter-of-fact about it? "I wasn't aware the *Cordelia* served as a gambling hall."

"We don't. We don't have a roulette wheel or anyone counting twenty-one."

"But card playing—"

"Is a private game among gentlemen."

"Did—my father—approve?" Was this why her mother had left?

Old Obie's fingers flexed on the wheel. "The captain of a boat does whatever is necessary to keep his customers happy and the boat running. A game of cards every now and then is one of those things."

"So he knew about it. And didn't stop it." Blanche heard the resentment in her voice. The weariness and disappointment that were kept at bay while she piloted the boat rushed back in. "I think I'll go on to bed."

"Wait a minute, girl." One hand on the wheel, Old Obie patted her shoulder with the other. "I know this is all strange for you. And you've been raised to disapprove of gambling in all its forms. And in some ways you're right. But before you think too harshly of Ike, take your time. Get to know him better before you pass judgment on him."

Judge not, that ye be not judged. Blanche didn't expect to hear the echo of God's Word coming from this unexpected source. "I'll try." She took a step in the direction of the stairs, but Old Obie stopped her again.

"I got something for you." Old Obie dug at the back of his desk and pulled out a leather-bound volume. "Here is my logbook for last summer. I thought you might like to study it. Ask me any questions you have." He winked. "Maybe you can learn from my mistakes." He patted her arm awkwardly. "It will all work out. You'll see."

His words left a warm glow, and she felt better for talking to him. "Thanks." She hugged the logbook close to her chest. "And thanks for this as well. I can't wait." Her footsteps down the stairs fell more lightly than they had when she came up.

Given Blanche's reaction to Ventura's revelation about the ongoing poker game, Ike expected her to avoid him. She surprised him by chatting with him the next morning as if they'd had no disagreement. "I haven't made it down to the engine rooms yet.

Do you have time to take me this morning?"

Once again she wore her black suit—she seemed to save her new dresses for dinner—but her hair was knotted loosely at the back of her neck rather than pulled into a tight knot on top. She looked quite fetching. He cleared his throat. "Of course."

The noise increased as they descended step by step into the bowels of the ship. He stopped before they reached the bottom, when he would have to shout to be heard. In the flickering lantern light, he looked at Blanche, a smudge of dust already marring her beautiful pale cheeks. "How much do you know about steam engines?"

"It has something to do with heating water to steam and cooling it back to water. But how does it work? How does the energy get to the wheels? I thought steamboats have wheels on both sides. Why is the wheel at the back?" She stopped to take a breath. "I have a lot of questions."

"The wheel is at the stern. It's a stern wheeler."

Her hands were making circles, punctuating each question. The more animated her voice, the brighter her cheeks grew. Her musical talents had gone without any training beyond singing at church. Old Obie said she was the most natural pilot he had ever met. And now she asked questions like a born engineer. Blanche was a lady of many talents, and the best part was that she didn't even realize it.

"I understand some of the theory, but I can only make minor repairs. McDonald is a magician with the machines. Give him a hammer, rope, and a wrench, and he can fix almost anything." After he explained the layout of the engine room, he led her to the heart of the boat.

"How much coal does it take to heat the tank?" Blanche asked. When McDonald answered, she raised her eyebrows. She probably knew the cost of coal and could calculate the expenses. "Where is the machinery manufactured? How long do they last?" She piled on questions regarding shipping costs, the benefits of steam power compared to other choices, the problems and delays.

Whatever self-righteous habits Blanche mimicked from her

mother, she showed a good head for business. If Ike presented the income from the poker games in terms of business profit and loss, she would understand their necessity.

Somehow Blanche's blouse remained pristine as they walked among the engines, even when her fingertips were coated with coal dust. The steam loosened tendrils of red hair that curled over her forehead like tiny flickers of flame. Ike didn't know any other woman, except perhaps Effie, who would be so at ease in the environment. He enjoyed their time together.

As the days passed, Ike waited for Blanche to bring up the subject of gambling, but she seemed as content to avoid it as he was. Although she didn't say another word on the subject, he gathered facts and figures to bolster his argument about the profitability of the enterprise. But she spent the week exploring the boat from stem to stern, asking for his companionship as often as not. Every now and then he caught her reading intently from a leather-bound book that looked suspiciously like one of the ship's logs.

At their last stop, among the stevedores who loaded the ship, Blanche delivered what Ike had come to consider her standard invitation. In each department, she invited the employees to attend the worship service, while making it clear attendance wasn't mandatory. Would that change if she took over running the ship? Would she want to hire a shipboard chaplain?

At Saturday evening's dinner, with Blanche wearing Dame Agatha's latest creation—a brilliant crimson that looked lovely in spite of its clash with Blanche's hair—she grew pensive. "I appreciate all the time you've put into showing me around the *Cordelia* this week. I hope I haven't taken too much time from your duties."

"Not at all." He had lost more sleep for far less pleasant reasons.

"I want to personally invite you to join us for our time of worship tomorrow." She cocked her head to one side, as if uncertain of his response. "Of course you don't have to come, but I think it may surprise you." Color crept into her cheeks. "I would appreciate it."

"I'll think about it." Until that point, Ike had planned on

skipping the morning's agenda and catching up on sleep. After her personal invitation, his curiosity overcame his hesitation. What surprise did Blanche have in store?

He decided he wanted to find out.

CHAPTER 13

Early Sunday morning, Blanche awoke refreshed, one of the few hours of the day when the tight accommodations aboard ship remained quiet. She grabbed her Bible and headed to her favorite chair at the stern of the boat, where mist from the river cooled her face.

After days of planning and preparation and worry, today was the day. None of the nervousness that had assaulted her on the day of the musicale bothered her this morning. She didn't know if there would be three or thirty people present this morning. It didn't matter. God promised to be in the midst when only two or three gathered in His name. She and the Potters made the requisite three. If no one else attended, they could rejoice in the presence of God and renew their commitment to being light and salt to the world of the *Cordelia*.

God knew each person aboard by name. He cared for each one. She dug out the list she had made, with as many names as she could remember. Digging through her memory for relevant facts, she prayed for each one, adding something beyond "God bless."

At the bottom of the list, she came to the ones she knew the best: Effie. Old Obie. Ike.

How had these three people become so precious to her in such a short time? In some ways she felt closer to them than she did to the people she had known her entire life. With so many items for prayer, she could skip breakfast altogether. But the breakfast bell rang and she decided to join them, to urge them one last time to attend the service. She looked at the sky and whispered aloud, "If there is any one thing they all need, it's Your saving grace. Oh Lord, use me. The least worthy of all Your servants." *And send them to the service*. She didn't voice that last plea, but God knew her thoughts.

Stomach growling, Blanche slipped into the dining salon behind the Ralstons. When Mr. Potter said grace over breakfast, he reminded the diners about the morning's service. Several heads nodded.

All that prayer had increased her appetite; she piled her plate high with fluffy scrambled eggs, light orange muffins, and a tall glass of fresh-squeezed orange juice. Her old choirmaster used to advise her to avoid dairy products before singing, so instead of her usual glass of milk, she drank a cup of black coffee.

Conversation flowed around her, with her making appropriate responses from time to time. After breakfast, she would change, but she hadn't decided what she should wear. Her black suit made her the most comfortable, but wearing it seemed ungrateful for all the beautiful clothes God had provided for her. Neither did she want to appear as fancy as a peacock, vying for attention with the God she hoped to glorify.

Ma would wonder why she even had a question. Effie might tell her to wear the dress that made her feel best, but she couldn't advise Blanche about whether a color was too flashy. She considered the question as she buttered a muffin.

Ike leaned in close. "A penny for your thoughts? You're not worried about the service, are you? You'll do fine."

"Not exactly." Ike would have some insight into her question. "I'm trying to decide what to wear. I want to wear one of my new dresses, but I don't want anything too—too. . ."

Chuckling, Ike dabbed at his mouth. "Just like a woman. I

didn't know you had it in you."

The muffin lodged in her mouth. Had she become one of those women who thought about nothing more than what she should wear, in one short week?

He straightened his lips, holding his humor in check. "You would look stunning in any of the dresses. I can't advise what is better for church, but I can tell you the difference between day wear and evening wear. I'm fairly sure that day wear would be acceptable for church."

"That sounds reasonable." She swallowed the last crumbs of her muffin with coffee. "So, which is which?" Heat wormed its way onto her cheeks. "They all seem pretty fancy to me."

"Maybe after breakfast? We can ask Effie's opinion as well, about the style if not the color. Unless you want to put the choice up to a vote by the breakfast crowd?"

A hint of a smile blooming, Blanche shook her head. A couple of forkfuls of egg remained on her plate, but she felt full. "I'm ready whenever you are."

The brief explanation of current styles left Blanche befuddled; the differences between the day and evening seemed blurred, but Ike could tell at a glance. Under his guidance, she decided on the beige dress that she had worn on her first day on board. With her hair, she reverted to her old style, pulling it into a tight knot on the top of her head. She didn't want any strands falling into her eyes at an inopportune moment. Effie changed into a dress much like the one Blanche had donned. "Are you ready?"

Effie patted her hair. "Yes." They made their way to the theater, where they had held the musicale earlier in the week.

"I can't tell you how much I appreciate your playing for us this morning. I can't imagine worshipping God without music—or singing without a piano. We tried it a few times when our church pianist was ill, but we always sounded like a single bird trying to fill a canyon with sound. Not good at all."

"It's my pleasure." Effie waved aside her thanks. "Besides, I figure it doesn't hurt to add a few good deeds to my account with God."

Effie smiled when she made that statement, but Blanche's heart faltered. Did her friend think a right relationship with God could be earned? She prayed that truth, and so much more, would become clear throughout the course of the morning.

Blanche paused at the entrance to the room and lit the first lantern. Early morning sunlight streamed through windows, throwing the room into dazzle and shadow. Squinting, she decided the sunshine was too bright.

"How does it look?" Tapping with her cane, Effie made her way around the chairs to the piano.

"Too bright." Blanche adjusted blinds over the windows. "That's better. We need to be able to read." Even as she said the words, she realized the cruelty of the comment to someone like Effie. "Do you read Braille?"

Effie nodded. "I learned how, but I haven't had much opportunity to practice. We don't keep many books aboard."

An obvious question shocked Blanche in its simplicity. "Do you have a copy of the Bible in Braille?"

"No, although I read one once, at a school for the blind."

Blanche glanced at the well-worn volume she held in the palm of her hands, with favorite verses marked and notes from Reverend Davenport's sermons written down, smudges on the pages where she had memorized verses and passages. She had prized the Bible ever since she received it at the end of second grade. Once again she felt the rightness of her presence aboard the *Cordelia*. How they hear without a preacher, indeed. As soon as the *Cordelia* arrived at their destination, she would seek a way to obtain a copy of the Bible in Braille for Effie.

"I really liked the verses you read at the musicale. About heaven, and about the wonderful things that happen after death. I like to think of my parents being in a place like that."

Blanche glanced around the room—some setup was still needed—but decided the opportunity to speak to Effie mattered more. "If you died today, do you think you'd go to heaven?"

Effie's shoulders lifted almost imperceptibly. "I hope so. I'm a pretty good person. I figure the good outweighs the bad in the balance scales."

Blanche closed the distance between them and put a single light hand on Effie's shoulder. "The Bible says that not one of us is good enough. God demands perfection, and no one is perfect."

Effie frowned, and her foot tapped the floor. "Then why does the Bible talk about heaven, if none of us is good enough to go there?"

"Because God made another way. Jesus, God's Son, lived the perfect life none of us can. Then He offered Himself to God as a sacrifice for our sins. Remember those scales you talked about? All our sins—yours, mine, everybody else's—all sit on one side. Jesus' death on the other. They balance perfectly. All we have to do is believe it."

Effie tilted her head to one side as if considering what Blanche had said. The Potters came in, and the mood was broken. Blanche prayed that the seed planted in Effie's soul would find fertile soil.

"I'll set the chairs up in rows, shall I?" Mr. Potter suited his action to his words, setting up five rows of chairs. Blanche hoped they would need that many. As he worked, he whistled a few bars of "Blessed Assurance." That reminded Blanche. . .

"Have you ever heard of Fanny Crosby?"

"No. Should I have?" Effie ran her hands lightly over the keyboard, seeking out chords.

"Maybe not. But she writes hymns. And she's blind. She composed the melody Mr. Potter is whistling."

Effie cocked her head and her hands began strumming the keys. "What a lovely melody. What are the words?"

God put that hymn into Mr. Potter's mind. Smiling, Blanche said, " 'Blessed assurance—Jesus is mine.' Just like we were talking about."

"You'll have to teach me the rest of the song."

As Blanche agreed that she would, a figure appeared at the door. Timid Mary, who worked in the kitchen with Elaine and rarely said two words. "Is this where you're holding the church service, Miss Lamar?"

"Why, yes it is." Blanche crossed the room and shook her hand. "Where would you like to sit?"

Mary took a seat in the back row. Blanche suspected she would feel uncomfortable any place close to the front, although in this venue, it didn't matter, at least not to her. As soon as Mary settled in, three stevedores came in. Blanche hoped her face didn't betray her surprise. Somehow she hadn't expected the grizzled, rough-spoken men who made the docks of the Rio Grande their home to attend church. *Thank You, Lord.*

So many people entered over the next five minutes that Blanche couldn't greet each one individually. Out of the corner of her eye she spotted Mrs. Potter helping people find seats. If they had pews, they'd be applying the "SOS" rule—"slide over some."

Ike stood a few paces down the hall, watching people enter the theater. Almost as many people had shown up for the service as had for the musicale. He peeked through the door to see the crowded room while Blanche greeted Mrs. Ralston. Blanche played the part of affable hostess perfectly.

He entered. "You need more chairs."

"You came." Blanche turned a smile on him that he would swear had little to do with church and everything to do with his being a man.

"I wouldn't miss this for the world." He winked at her. "I'll be right back." In the dining room, he grabbed a couple of chairs. Soon they had a sixth row set up against the back wall.

"Thank you." Blanche glanced at the clock. "It's time to start."

"You'll do fine." He repeated his reassurance. He settled back in his chair to watch her go to work. She made her way to the front of the room, stopping to say a few words here and there. At the end of the front row, she paused long enough to square her shoulders then made her way to the podium placed on the stage area.

She moved with a natural grace, one that even her ugly black suits couldn't hide, and which the day dress she had chosen made evident. As soon as her foot reached the top step, silence fell across the room. The tap of her heels on the wooden floor reverberated in the stillness. At first she directed her gaze to the floor—probably praying, Ike realized—then raised her face with a radiant smile.

"Thank you all for joining us here today. We have come together to worship the Lord of lords, the Lord of all. He is the Lord of everything, even the Rio Grande." She took a minute or two describing some things she had observed during her time on board that taught her more about God.

"Miss Effie Gallagher has kindly agreed to accompany us as we sing. I have written down the words to the songs." So saying, she turned around an easel that had a sheet of paper with the words of a poem of some kind written on it. "Please join me in singing a song that praises the God of all creation, 'All Creatures of Our God and King.'"

The song marched along, carrying Ike and the others with it. When the last word finished echoing through the room, Blanche looked straight at Ike and smiled. "I'm not going to be doing all the talking this morning. We don't have a preacher; we're just believers in the Lord Jesus who want to worship. So I'm going to ask for your participation. First of all, I'd like to hear about any of God's 'creatures' you have known and loved. Maybe you had a special pet, or maybe there was a stubborn mule, or maybe a fish you caught in the river. We want to hear about them."

From his seat at the back, Ike saw bent heads and heard whispers circulating among the audience. They needed someone to break the ice. Would she welcome his support? Deciding she would, he raised his hand.

CHAPTER 14

Yes, Mr. Gallagher?"

A frisson of satisfaction skipped down Ike's spine at the relief in Blanche's voice. Standing, he turned around to face the audience. "We used to have a cat. I wanted a dog, but Mama would only let us have a cat. After our parents died, Effie carried that cat with her everywhere."

At the piano, Effie nodded her head, a smile playing about her lips. "His name was Blackie."

"When Captain Lamar took us in, he said they'd never had a cat on the ship. Blackie sniffed his ankles and rubbed around his legs, the way cats do, and the captain grew stiffer than a piece of cloth soaked in salt water. I knew how sad Effie would be if she didn't get to keep Blackie, but I didn't know what we were going to do."

Blanche leaned forward to listen, as if eager to hear what her father had done.

"When the captain showed up again the next day, he said they had discovered mice aboard the *Cordelia* and a good mouser would be a welcome addition. If Blackie's owners would join him on board, of course. And so the captain took in two orphans and a cat."

Blanche's smile widened, and Ike thought back to her comments that God was watching over them even back then.

Ike shook his head. "There weren't any mice, of course. Or if there were, Blackie got rid of the evidence."

Blanche cleared her throat. "That's a beautiful story. It sounds like God was taking care of you and your cat. So tell me. What happened to Blackie?"

"He lived to a ripe old age." Effie's fingers tapped out the tune to "Three Blind Mice." She smiled. "He slept on my bed every night."

"Let's keep the *Cordelia* mouse-free." Blanche smiled. "Perhaps we'll get another cat, as a mascot. Thank you for telling us about Blackie, Mr. Gallagher. Does anyone else have a story to share?"

Ahead of Ike, a small hand shot into the air. Before Blanche could call on him, the young child said, "I have a dog. He's almost as big as me."

"Why, then, he must be a big fellow."

The boy straightened in his seat, lifting himself to his full height. "Yes, ma'am, he is. My papa says he eats as much as a horse."

The audience laughed while the child's mother shushed him. "What is his name?"

Other stories followed. Even Ventura added a humorous anecdote about a stubborn mule he had encountered.

"The Bible says that God gave Adam dominion over animals. I have read about men who go into cages with lions." Blanche shivered. "I wouldn't dare do that, but I think about that verse when I read the stories. Let's take a moment to thank God for His creatures." She closed her eyes and brought her hands together. "Thank You, heavenly Father, for the gift You have given to us in the animals that share this earth with us. Amen."

The service continued in the same vein. They sang a hymn and Blanche asked an everyday question that she managed to tie back to God or the Bible. After people shared anecdotes, they prayed. Everyone present had told at least one story by the time the hour ended.

Ike never expected the meeting to pass so quickly or so pleasantly. If anyone had come expecting a lecture on the Ten Commandments, he left disappointed. As promised, Blanche steered the conversation in praise of the God she worshipped, one she portrayed as involved in everyday life. The possibility comforted Ike and scared him at the same time.

After the final prayer, he slipped up to the front to wait with Effie at the piano. Blanche joined Mr. and Mrs. Potter at the door in greeting their guests as they left. Over the babble of conversation, Ike heard good comments. He lounged against the wall, a smile playing around his lips. "Who would have thought it."

He had spoken mostly to himself, but Effie responded. "She truly believes in all this, you know. And she reads that Bible of hers every day."

"Whatever else, she's a natural showman. She'll do well at the helm of Lamar Industries, if she's willing to bend some of her principles."

Effie chuckled. "Good luck with that."

The room slowly emptied, and with a start, Ike realized it was almost lunchtime.

"Duty calls," Effie said. "I'd better get down to the salon and begin playing." She caught up with Blanche, murmured a few words, and then departed.

"Where do you want these chairs, Miss Lamar?" Mr. Potter held one in each hand.

"Those came from the dining room." Ike took two more. "The rest of them stay here."

"Mrs. Potter and I will put the other chairs in a circle around the walls, shall we?" Blanche looked at Ike as if seeking his approval.

He nodded. "That will be perfect."

"Thank you for your help."

The way she smiled, with that pretty color in her cheeks, was enough to turn a man's head. "It's my job." Whistling the tune to "Three Blind Mice," he held the door open for Mr. Potter and walked toward the salon.

The aromas of roast chicken and stuffing filled his nostrils before he reached his destination. Was this what people looked forward to on Sundays—church, a good meal, and maybe a nap?

If all church services were like the one this morning, the practice no longer seemed so odd.

⸻⁂⸻

"It went well, didn't it?" Blanche looked around the restored theater, empty of their congregation.

"God was with you, dear." Mrs. Potter sank into a chair with a grateful *oomph*. "People enjoyed themselves."

Blanche frowned at that comment. "It wasn't meant as entertainment."

"Of course not." Mrs. Potter patted the seat next to her, and Blanche accepted the implied invitation. "You worshiped the Lord with your whole heart. People were touched and maybe thought about God in a new way. I think it was just right."

The luncheon bell rang. "I believe Elaine has roast chicken on the menu today." Blanche's mouth watered at the thought. "Let's not keep the company waiting."

Over the food-laden tables, Blanche glanced around the room, making a mental checklist of who had attended the service and who hadn't. Several passengers had stayed away, perhaps taking advantage of the extra time to sleep. Mr. Ventura's presence had provided the biggest surprise.

Ike had come.

Old Obie hadn't.

The handful of crew members absent from the service were involved with keeping the ship running. Everyone should have an opportunity to attend. She would speak with Ike about rotating shifts to make that possible. She nodded, pleased with the decision. Would Old Obie come in that case? She didn't have a clue.

"What's going on in that pretty little head of yours?" Ike dabbed his mustache with his napkin.

He just called me pretty. "I was thinking about ways to make it possible for everyone to attend the worship service, at least on alternate weeks."

"I should have known." He shook his head. "I would venture a guess that not everyone will come, but after the turnout this morning, I'm not so sure."

"Yes." Unable to help herself, she asked, "What did you think of the service?"

His blue eyes darkened, as if calculating the answer to her question. "It wasn't what I expected. I guess I was expecting more hellfire and brimstone."

"While hell is as real as heaven, I prefer to remember that God loved us enough to send His Son to die for us."

He nodded but didn't comment. She was probably hoping for too much to expect him to do a complete about-face after one service that didn't even include a clear presentation of the Gospel.

"What changes do you have in mind for the schedule?" His fingers drummed the table.

"Nothing major. I realize that some men must work on Sundays, to keep the boat running." What would Ike say to docking on Sundays? She thought she knew and suppressed a smile. "But can they alternate weekends so that everyone has an opportunity to attend a Sunday service, if they want to?"

A smile curled Ike's lips. "For someone who has only committed to one trip downriver, you want to make a lot of changes. Or have you decided to make the *Cordelia* your home?"

Blanche jerked back at that. "I—no, not yet." She dredged out a smile. "How about a onetime change? For next Sunday?"

Ike's smile grew wider. "We can do that, sure." He winked. "And hope it becomes a permanent change."

Does Ike want me to stay? Blanche wished she had a fan to cool her face. *I shouldn't care what he thinks of me.* Mama had warned her often enough to beware of men with sweet words and wicked ways.

Then again, Mama didn't approve of anyone—including Blanche. Nothing she ever did was good enough for her mother. Mama would be shocked and disappointed at Blanche's decisions since her death. Her shoulders drooped. "Please make the arrangements for next Sunday, then."

Her appetite disappeared. The lemon squeezed into the sweet tea turned sour in her mouth. She forced down the last couple of bites of mashed potatoes and excused herself from the table.

At the top of the stairs, she hesitated. Did she want to walk the deck, or should she head to her cabin? The light breeze rippling across the water called to her, but she decided against open air. After the morning's excitement, she felt the need for solitude and quiet, time to consider her life, like self-reflection in preparation for the Lord's Supper. A pang of homesickness for Christ the King Church struck her. She missed the sonorous organ that accompanied the hymns, Reverend Davenport's sometimes dry but always challenging sermons, the loving fellowship that surrounded her at all times. In her cabin, she disrobed and stretched out on her berth. One by one she pulled up events from the past week for review.

<hr>

"Poor dear." Effie put a finger to her lips and gently closed the door behind her. "She must be tuckered out. Out like a light on her bed."

"That sounds like a good idea." Ike didn't bother hiding his yawn. "I think I'll do the same."

Effie laughed. "You've had a time of it. I've seen more of you this week than I usually do in a month. Before you rest, though, come with me on deck." She felt her way to a deck chair and settled down, arranging her skirt so that it flounced prettily. An umbrella protected her from the heat of the midday sun.

Ike took the seat next to her and spread his legs in front of him. With the umbrella shading his face and his stomach full, hymns from the morning lulled him to an almost doze. Closing his eyes, he said, "Go ahead and tell me what's on your mind before I fall asleep."

"That's not necessary." Effie's light chuckle tickled his ears as she pulled a light blanket over his form. "Rest while you can. Maybe hidden away up here people will leave you alone." Soft footfalls receded in the distance, and he relaxed into a light doze. *Just a few minutes.*

The next thing Ike knew, the aromas of the evening meal

awakened him from the best sleep he'd had in a week. For a brief moment, he kept his eyes closed. An elusive image had imprinted itself on his mind during a dream, of a lovely maiden with fiery hair and a spirit to match, dressed in the improbable colors of a peacock. But the memory proved elusive, disappearing as soon as he opened his eyes.

He swung his legs over the side of the chair and rotated his shoulders and neck, working out the kinks from sleeping upright. He glanced at his suit, glad it wasn't much creased from his unexpected outdoor nap.

He glanced up at the pilothouse. If he went right up, he had enough time before supper to tell Old Obie about the morning's service as promised. Tugging at the lapels of his jacket and whistling through his teeth, he bounded up the steps with renewed enthusiasm.

"You're a cheerful soul today." As usual, Old Obie didn't turn, but kept his eyes fixed on the river ahead.

"I had a most refreshing nap, thanks to Effie." Ike joined Old Obie at the window. The pilot made a minute adjustment to the wheel. Ike strained forward, scanning the water for a hint that had caused Old Obie's reaction. Giving up, he shrugged. "I don't know how you do it. I never see whatever you see."

"That Blanche girl. She sees a lot of them." In spite of the matter-of-fact voice, pride showed through Old Obie's words. "She's a natural."

Ike turned his back on the river so that he faced his friend and mentor. "Do you think it will make a difference? That she'll stay? She'll never be a pilot."

"Don't see why not. Not since they made that woman a pilot over on the Mississippi."

Ike had his doubts, but he didn't argue them. "She's got a lot of tricks up her sleeve. You should have seen her this morning." As he described the service, he realized how much he had come to admire her. "Sometimes she seems like a nervous cat, ready to run away at the first sign of trouble. Then she gets up in front of everybody like she's been doing it all her life."

Old Obie looked at Ike out of the corner of his eyes for

a second before he turned his attention to the river. "She's got courage. And backbone. The backbone comes straight from her mother, but the courage. . .maybe her father had something to do with that. At least I like to think so."

The longer Blanche spent on the river, the more of her father's qualities she displayed. Ike grinned, and Old Obie looked at him, teeth bared in a matching smile.

CHAPTER 15

Blanche woke up, stretched out on top of the covers of her bed. She stared at the ceiling of the cramped cabin. "What am I doing here?"

"You're awake. Good. I was beginning to think I would need to wake you up so you wouldn't miss dinner."

Blanche glanced at the only chair in the room, where Effie sat working a pair of knitting needles. She raised up on her elbows. "Is it that late?" Rubbing her eyes, she stood and went to the wardrobe. She'd wear her black traveling suit, a penance for the insights she had during her earlier time of reflection.

Reaching the end of the row, Effie paused in her knitting. "I don't mean to pry, but I've been told I'm a good listener." She turned the row and started moving the needles again.

Blanche watched her flying fingers. "Do you ever drop a stitch?"

"Of course." Effie's laughter tickled Blanche's ears. "But that's true for everyone who knits. And then I go back to find my mistake and fix it. Once I had to start over again from the beginning."

Give me words. "That's like what happens when a person becomes a Christian."

Effie's face scrunched while she recounted the stitches on her needle. "I don't understand."

"Everyone makes mistakes and breaks God's laws. Jesus died for those sins. When we ask God to forgive us, He takes away all of those mistakes. He makes us into new people."

"I've never thought of it that way." Effie continued down the row then tucked the knitting into her bag. "When we were little, before our parents died, Ike and I used to go to Sunday school. One day our teacher asked us if we wanted to ask Jesus into our hearts. I didn't know what she meant, but I knew I loved Jesus and so I prayed with her." A smile played on her lips. "I haven't thought of that for a long time."

Blanche's heart sped and she threw her arms around Effie's shoulders. "That means we are sisters in the Lord." And what about Ike? The question dangled in Blanche's mind but she didn't voice it.

Blanche felt Effie's smile without seeing it. "I always wanted a sister." Effie returned the hug before stepping away. "I'd better get down to the salon. It's almost time for dinner." With a whisper of fabric, she left the cabin.

Blanche wanted to call her back, but God would give her another opening. As children, Effie and Ike had heard the Gospel. But when their parents died, they no longer received regular religious instruction.

Blanche would double her prayers for the captain—her father. When he took the children in, they stopped attending church. Righteous anger sang along her nerves. How could he? Charging out of the room, she headed for the pilothouse.

Her route took her past shining brass fixtures, and Blanche caught sight of her reflection. Lines marred her forehead and lips, her slitted eyes looked stormy dark. Even the hair that escaped her bun looked like flames of fire ready to devour anything that got in her path.

She stared at her image, the resemblance to her mother obvious. Nothing about that angry face spoke of God's love. No wonder her father had run away. Flushed and sickened, Blanche bolted to the railing and leaned over the side. Her stomach heaved, and she opened her mouth. Nothing came up, but acid burned the back of her throat.

Oh Lord, forgive me. A fresh breeze blew across the bow, and she breathed deeply of the clean, cool scent. Closing her eyes, she recalled the morning's service, voices raised in songs of praise to the Lord. Overhead a bird called. She followed its flight to a tree branch on the opposite bank, and she thought whimsically of the two languages spoken on either side of this great river, but how the birds only spoke one language and God understood all of them. "All creatures of our God and king." The hymn from the morning bubbled up in her throat and burst out. Starting as barely more than a whisper, it grew until she sang with full voice, unmindful of anyone else who might be on deck.

When her voice trailed away, a solitary clap of hands welcomed the end. Heat rising in her cheeks, she checked her reflection in the brass again. The angry lines that bothered her earlier were gone, replaced with color and life and, yes, joy. God extended His grace to her even when she was her most ungracious. She turned to greet her audience.

❦

Renewing his applause, Obie stepped out of the shadow of the stairwell. "You sing with all your heart." He could also have said she sang well, with the voice of an angel. But the color in her cheeks told him he had chosen the right words.

"Thank you." She regained her composure. "I don't believe I've ever seen you anywhere except the pilothouse." Putting her hand over her mouth, she gasped. "Except for the musicale the other night."

His lips widened in a broad grin. "I'll let the assistant pilot hold the wheel for a few hours, until full-dark. Walk with me?"

When she agreed, he took her arm and walked to the bow of the boat, used mostly by the crew. "Ike tells me the service went well this morning."

"It wasn't much. We shared testimonies and songs. No

preaching."

"Sometimes the only Bible people read is your life. And a lot of people are watching you, weighing your actions." He patted her arm.

Blanche stiffened. Silence accompanied them as they walked a few more feet.

"They did the same thing to your mother, of course." When they reached the stairwell, he leaned against the side rail, remaining in the open air instead of the confined space on the steps.

Obie couldn't read her expression. Did she think he was comparing her to her mother? He hadn't thought much of Cordelia's "Bible."

"Am I...very much like her?"

He took off his pilot's hat and twisted it back and forth in his hand while he considered his answer. "Yes. And no. You could probably say the same of most children and their parents, I suppose." He pointed his finger at Blanche. "The captain would be pleased that she didn't manage to snuff all the life out of you. You love your God, that's clear enough, but there seems to be more to your faith than a list of dos and don'ts."

A joyful smile followed Blanche's flinch. "That means a lot to me. Jesus lives in me. He's a part of everything I do and say."

"I know." Obie winked. "You might even convince an old reprobate like me to listen one of these days."

A smile spread across her face. "I would like that, very much."

"I'm sure you would." He took her right hand in his and patted it. "I don't want to give you the wrong idea about your mother. The captain adored her. He just couldn't live with her." An old longing swept over Obie.

"You were sweet on my mother, weren't you?"

The pilot needed to do a better job of masking the longing. "Some might say so. But she only ever had eyes for Captain Jedidiah Lamar, his highfalutin manners and snake-oil charm, not an old river rat like me." He shook his head. "You see things more clearly than Cordelia ever did. You keep that quality, girl."

Impulsively, she hugged him. Heat slammed into his cheeks

and he plopped his hat back on his head. "Thank you kindly." He let go of her hand and walked into the darkness of the stairwell.

It had been quite a day.

———✦———

After sunset, Ike waited in his cabin for his poker cronies to show up. Bart Ventura arrived first, followed by Ralston. Ike poured drinks for the three of them while they waited to see if anyone else would join them. No one did.

"It looks like it's just us tonight." Ike gestured for his guests to sit down and slit open a new pack of cards, a weekly ritual. The cards Bart provided featured the logo of the Brownsville Bats—a black bat wrapping its wings around a Louisville slugger. Mr. and Mrs. Ventura provided the inspiration for the king and queen, and the manager served as the jack. VENTURA MARKET was blazoned beneath the logo. "I like these." He gestured with the pack in his hand before shuffling them.

"We'll give a deck to everyone who attends the games we're setting up. Might draw business for both of us." Ventura winked. "Unless Miss Lamar shakes things up more than she already has."

Ike fanned the cards on the table and continued shuffling. "The captain made sure that won't happen."

Ralston slanted his eyes in Ike's direction. "Does she know we've continued our friendly game?"

He shrugged. "Not as far as I know. And I intend to keep it that way as long as possible." After shuffling the cards twice more, he tossed them to the other men, one at a time around the table. "This may be her only trip downriver."

Ventura and Ralston exchanged a look. "She'll be back." Ventura spoke with Latin assurance. "We can see it, even if you can't."

His words disturbed Ike, and he stroked his ear in an unexpected tell when he turned his cards over. Ralston arched an eyebrow and grinned. *I might as well toss my cards on the table.* As expected, he played a mediocre hand.

Ralston bent his head in Ventura's direction. "That's our

secret to winning. Keep talking about Miss Lamar."

Chuckling, Ventura nodded. "Maybe he'll be convicted, and he'll stop taking our money."

Taking a sip of whiskey, Ike swished it around his mouth, bringing calm back to his spirit. "That's not going to happen." He leaned back in his chair, a complete picture of peace. "We *welcome* your contributions to our coffers."

From there on, the game turned serious. Perhaps Ike could blame his lack of luck on one glass of whiskey too many, but he suspected it had more to do with the thoughts swirling through his mind about Blanche.

Ventura lost more than Ike did. Over the course of the trip, he had easily lost a thousand dollars. More money disappeared into his baseball team. He ran a profitable business, but how much of his apparent prosperity was smoke and mirrors? A flicker of guilt washed over Ike, but he shook it off. Ventura's financial well-being wasn't his responsibility. The *Cordelia*'s future was.

Ike's guests left a little early, which suited him fine. Not yet sleepy, he sat by the porthole, studying the reflection of the moon on the water. He fancied Blanche staring at the same view, except the girls' cabin lacked portholes. The only people definitely awake this hour were the engineer on the evening shift and Old Obie. As a child, Ike used to explore the decks till all hours of the night. He knew every inch of the ship; he could probably rebuild it from memory.

Until Blanche, the only other person he had ever seen with the same passion for the *Cordelia* was the captain.

He closed his eyes. Why did Blanche keep cropping up in his every thought? Shrugging out of his suit coat and removing his bow tie, he slipped out of his room. This late at night, he risked comfort, hoping the night air would cool his troubled emotions.

He made his way through the bowels of the ship, nodding at the engineer from a distance, allowing the sweat to build up and roll down his back. He skipped the deck with the passenger rooms. As disheveled as he was, he had no desire to run into anyone. A stop at the salon netted him a sugar cookie with a cup of cool water. After two more glasses slaked his thirst, he returned to the hall, opening the door to the theater. Flicking on a gas lamp, he walked the perimeter, his mind placing the passengers in their appropriate seats. Almost everyone on board had attended the worship service. More than attended, they actively participated and enjoyed the experience. The support surprised him. Blanche Lamar's simple trip down the Rio Grande was going to change life aboard the *Cordelia* in ways no one had imagined when the captain first proposed his plan.

One long stride brought him to the stage, and he walked to the spot where Blanche had presided over the gathering with such skill. She didn't use any fancy tricks or powerful oratory, only sweet sincerity and genuine kindness shining from her eyes. No one could resist. Him least of all, even if he didn't understand all this talk about a Savior. He didn't understand, but he wanted to believe, at least as far as Blanche was concerned.

Blanche. He couldn't afford to like her. Lamar Industries might not survive with her running the business. Tired of worrying about her, he jumped off the stage and scurried up the steps to the deck.

His long legs ate up the deck as he paced back and forth. Long ago, Effie memorized the number of steps from one spot to another until she could walk about without the aid of a cane. Ike did the same thing, adjusting the number of steps as his legs grew longer.

If only the *Cordelia* was a bigger boat, he wouldn't pass over the same spots time and again, listening to the same creaks. His shoe might miss the nail he had hammered down more times than he could count, although it always came loose again.

The moon sank low, and the sky lightened a smidgeon. Below the railing, the river rippled invisibly around the prow of the ship, and the wheel churned slowly. When the visibility decreased, Old Obie kept the speed down. He had every inch of the river memorized, the same way Ike knew the decks of the ship, but the river constantly changed. Even in the darkest reaches of the night, Old Obie could tell something was wrong within half a foot.

The light in the pilothouse testified to Old Obie's presence, and he would welcome Ike's company. As tempting as the idea sounded, Ike needed to puzzle out this problem on his own. When the captain turned everyday affairs over to Ike, he vowed to lessen his worries. That meant Ike kept some things to himself. Railroads began to make their presence felt even down here in the Rio Grande Valley, and business profits had dropped every year under his management.

Ike didn't know how long the *Cordelia* could stay in business. If he really cared for Blanche, he would make sure she had a miserable trip and never wanted to come back.

That shouldn't be a problem. All he had to do was tell her he ran a nightly gambling hall that kept them in business.

She'd run back to Roma in a second and retreat into the shell of the woman she could become.

He didn't know which loss would bring more grief—the loss of the *Cordelia* or the departure of Blanche Lamar.

Whichever way things turned out, he'd let down his captain.

CHAPTER 16

Blanche straightened in her chair and stretched her arms, rolling up the map of the river Old Obie had given to her and slipping it into a case. As she read the logs, she marked down every spot where he mentioned obstructions and other warning signs to study. When not studying the maps, she stared at the river as it sped by, so that she could identify the potential problems she knew were there.

Now that she had finished reading the logs, she would indulge in one of her favorite activities: heading to the pilothouse and steering the boat under Old Obie's watchful eye. Even though she hadn't reached a decision about whether she would stay on the river or return to Roma for good, she had developed a passion for earning her pilot's license. The study was not only fun, it also made dull subjects like math and science important in a way that her teacher never managed.

Five new dresses hung in her closet. Colors and stylish cuts, which seemed inappropriate and prideful in her mother's domain, were perfectly acceptable in this setting. God's flowers of every shade and shape filled the earth all year long. Why would He prefer His people to dress in uniform black and white? She would enjoy the dresses Madame Agatha had made for her, even if she only brought them out for special occasions when she returned to Roma.

Today she donned her persimmon-colored dress, a shade of red her mother would have insisted clashed with her hair. But the color made her feel alive, like the first rays of daylight awakening the earth. She thought Old Obie would approve.

Realizing she had dawdled a little too long over her attire, she hurried to the pilothouse. She dabbed at the unladylike sheen of sweat on her forehead with a handkerchief and headed in.

The soft scent of rose water alerted Obie to Blanche's presence. "I was wondering when you would come."

"I apologize." Her voice was hushed, less confident than usual. "I spent so much time studying the maps that I rushed to get here."

Satin whispered against the wall, and Obie turned around, a smile spreading across his face. "Dame Agatha has done well. You look lovely, my dear."

Red a shade between her hair and dress flooded Blanche's cheeks. "Thank you, kind sir." She dipped in a curtsy and giggled.

"You are most welcome." He waved his hand, inviting her to turn around. She pirouetted for his approval, shaking a little as she completed the turn. In that moment, she looked so much like her mother that Obie's heart constricted. "Your mother would have looked lovely in that dress. I saw her in a red dress one time. Then she hung it at the back of the closet."

Blanche dropped to the soles of her feet. "I never saw her in red, not even at Christmas."

"I'm not surprised, but that's unfortunate. Bold colors brought out her coloring, made her beautiful, but she was more comfortable in the background." He glanced at Blanche's feet. "Perhaps Ike can do something in the matter of new shoes."

Blanche sneaked the toes of her boots under her skirts. "These are perfectly serviceable."

Obie laughed out loud. "You sounded just like Cordelia."

Blanche kept her gaze on the floor.

"That's not a bad thing." He gentled his voice. "But you are not her. To use words that Cordelia herself might use, God created you, a separate and beautiful young woman. He welcomes your laughter. In heaven, Cordelia would want you to be happy." In a low voice almost more to himself than to her, he said, "The captain wanted her to be happy, but he couldn't do it. They loved each other but made each other miserable." He lifted Blanche's chin with one gnarly finger. "Never doubt that your parents loved each other, and their child."

Tears welled up in her eyes. "My mother loved me?" Her voice broke as she said the words.

"Never doubt it."

It felt like the most natural thing in the world to take her in his arms and rest her head on his shoulder, comforting her as she cried.

~*~

Ike searched the boat to inform Blanche of his dinner plans in the town of La Joya with Bart Ventura. As expected, he found her in the pilothouse.

He wanted to pinch himself at the transformation. Could the woman wearing the persimmon-colored dress in midafternoon be the same woman he first saw at the funeral a few short weeks ago? She, who always wore black and white, until that first cream-colored dress Dame Agatha had made for her sight unseen?

Neither one of them paid attention to his arrival.

"What's coming up in the next mile of the river?" Old Obie lounged at the side, ready to step in if she made an error. Given the fact he still hovered behind Ike on the rare occasions he took the wheel, the pilot was offering Blanche a tremendous compliment. Did she know?

She laughed, a lighthearted sound that Ike would love to hear every day. Her happiness mattered more than a compliment. He leaned against the wall, watching them chat.

"There should be a sandbar right up there, to the left of the poplar tree." She leaned forward, as Ike had seen Old Obie do time and time again. "I see the shadow. Over there." She raised a draped arm, her delicate hand pointing a single finger.

The pilot nodded. "So how do you correct?"

"If it was spring, runoff would raise the river level and I wouldn't have to worry." She drew in her features as if running through options in her head. "The water goes down in summer, but we've had several afternoon showers. I'm not sure."

"Look at the shadow again. Use your eyes."

Blanche tilted her head. "I think the boat can pass over it."

Old Obie didn't speak.

"But—I'll ask them to slow the engines?"

Old Obie remained silent, and Ike laughed. The two of them turned and stared at him.

"That's a favorite trick of Obie's. He's testing your confidence." Ike came forward. "Which means you are correct."

Shaking his head, Old Obie smiled. "Don't go telling her all my secrets."

Blanche laid her hand on the bell she used for alerting the engine room to slow down. Both men nodded, and she pulled it. She tilted her head, her ears peeking out beneath her halo of hair, as if seeking the telltale sounds of the bottom of the boat scraping the riverbed. The prow glided forward, past the danger zone, and Blanche's grip on the wheel relaxed.

"Well done." Ike brought his hands together in a single clap. "Not only will you be one of the few women with a pilot's license, but you will also earn it the fastest if you keep things up at this rate."

The grin on Blanche's face was more little boy than young woman.

"She still needs hours on the river." Old Obie was a little stingier with his praise. "She's had just enough experience to be cocky and think she knows it all."

"I could never do that." Blanche shook her head.

"Not on purpose, no. But you might look for what you expect to be there and not see what is different."

"That takes a lifetime." She acknowledged his experience.

"My father was lucky to have you."

Old Obie cast an amused glance at Ike, and he stifled a laugh. "We put in a lot of years together." The pilot nodded.

"Don't let him fool you. You're his prize pupil, and he knows it." Ike changed his plans for the night. "I know how we can celebrate. We are stopping in La Joya tonight. Why don't you come with me? Meet the customers who use the boat for shipping, and then go out to dinner? There's a wonderful restaurant that serves the best steaks on the Rio Grande."

Blanche kept her eyes trained on the river, avoiding his gaze. In a flat voice, she asked, "Will Mr. Ventura join us? I thought you introduced him to town officials at each stop."

Ike arched an eyebrow. "So you were paying attention."

"Of course. Every place we have stopped has agreed to exhibition games. You've done a good bit of business for Lamar Industries." She glanced over her shoulder, the expression in her brown eyes an enigma. "I will come with you, if Effie will consent to host dinner for the evening."

"She will." Ike grinned. "She has before. I will suggest that Mr. Ventura visit the town council on his own this time. We'll be in Brownsville before we know it. I'd like to do something special before we reach the end of the line." He came forward and leaned against the window, so that he could see Blanche from the front. "You look like a vision in that dress. You will light up the restaurant."

Blanche's hand went to her throat, and she looked at the ruffled cuffs at the end of her sleeves. "I. . .will think about it."

"I will meet you at your cabin then, about fifteen minutes after we dock. Until then." He nodded his head and withdrew.

Whistling, Ike debated whether or not to return to his cabin. During this time of day, he often rested for a few hours. But today thoughts of his upcoming dinner with Blanche filled his mind, and he knew he wouldn't sleep. Effie would say he should lie down, rest his body if not his mind. He'd rather sweat out his uncertainty than lie in bed and dwell on it.

While Ike dawdled at the top of the stairs, Ventura climbed from below deck. "What's on your mind?"

Ike rolled his shoulders and balled his fingers into a fist. "This is one of those rare occasions when I wish I lived on land. A long ride on horseback sounds perfect, or perhaps an hour toiling the soil."

Ventura threw back his head and laughed. "I can see you on the back of a horse, but turning the sod like a farmer? That would make the headline on towns all up and down the river."

"You may be right." Ike unclenched his fists and turned sideways, imitating the swing of a bat. "Perhaps a friendly game of baseball with your Bats."

"It's physical exercise you're wanting. . ." Ventura rubbed his chin, considering. "I might be able to accommodate you. Perhaps a sparring bout, between you and me? With a friendly wager on the outcome? My man could keep the score."

"Where?" The idea held appeal. Channel his energy into quick jabs. Punch his feelings into line. "We don't have a gymnasium on board."

"The theater is large enough. And we are unlikely to be disturbed there at this time of day." Ventura pulled out a pocket watch. "What say you? I'll go get my man."

"Easy money, Ventura. Easy money. I have ten years on you, man. Shall I spot you a point or two?"

"Not necessary." Ventura grinned. "You don't know everything about me. Fifteen minutes?"

"I'll see you there."

"And you can bring a second, if you wish."

"Duel at dawn?"

Ike trotted down the stairs. In his cabin, he rustled through his clothing. His stylish wardrobe filled him with pride, but he had precious little suitable for a boxing match. He settled for the clothes he wore when helping the stevedores loading and unloading—worn slacks, a shirt with loose buttonholes and a few paint splashes on the sleeves. What else? A pair of leather gloves might protect his hands. Slipping them into his pocket, he went to the theater.

Ventura danced around the floor, his feet shifting and arms darting with an invisible partner. As the door shut behind Ike, he looked up. "Where's your second?"

"I didn't bring one." Ike said. "You won't last more than five minutes."

"How much do you want to bet?" Ventura grinned.

"Oh, I don't know. One dollar a point? Five?"

"Five. Let's keep it interesting." Ventura handed his pocket watch to his man. "Terms. One point for every hit landed. Punches only allowed above the waist. Two five-minute bouts, a third if we are tied. Agreed?"

"Agreed. Are you sure you don't want me to spot you a point or two?"

"No chance."

After Ventura's second moved the chairs to the perimeter walls, he met Ike in the middle, where they knocked their knuckles together.

"Shall we separate six paces before we come out swinging?" Ike couldn't get over how much this felt like a duel.

"A yard should be plenty." Ventura backed up a few feet. Both of them waited for a signal from his second. At his nod, Ventura darted forward, swinging his right fist. Ike shifted, but the blow glanced off his chin.

"One point!" Ventura danced back. Ike threw right, left, right, but Ventura dodged all of them.

Ike's estimation of his opponent rose a notch or two. Ventura was tougher than he looked.

"We grow them strong in Old Mexico. Like a bantam rooster. Small and tough." Ventura grinned as he darted forward and swung his left hand toward Ike's chest. Ike avoided the blow.

As they continued to dance around each other, feinting, avoiding, darting forward, Ike worked up a sweat. This room would smell like the engine room. He'd have to give special instructions to the cleaning crew tomorrow.

"Five minutes," the second called. "Halt."

The first period ended with Ventura ahead two points to one. Ventura tossed a towel to Ike. In the absence of a bucket of cold water, he accepted it and wiped at the sweat pouring from his face and neck and down his arms.

"Take your places."

Ike copied Ventura's stance, holding his elbows in close, protecting his vulnerable chest. This time he landed the first blow on Ventura. "Even."

Ventura circled Ike, moving him to the left, his weak side. "Not for long." He darted in and landed his right fist beneath Ike's protective block with his left arm.

Ike resisted the urge to jump back and protect the injured area. He would smart tomorrow. Instead, he channeled his aggravation into vigilance and landed a second punch before time was called again. Ike took his seat, swiped at his face with the now-damp towel, and wished he had a cold drink.

"What is going on in here?"

Ike's head snapped up and his gaze collided with the astonished glare of Blanche Lamar. "We're. . .letting off steam."

"You're fighting! I heard you all the way at the end of the hall." She took a step into the room, glanced at Ventura, but crossed to Ike. "You're hurt." Her finger pointed to his chin. "I'll get some cold water."

"In Mr. Gallagher's defense, I'm the one who suggested this." Ventura stood up. "Nurse him later. We're not done yet. The next man who lands a hit wins."

"This is a game?" Blanche looked as mystified as women always had since they watched boys fight in the schoolyard.

"It's not so much a game as a way—"

Ike hastened to interrupt. "I felt the need of exercise, and my choices on board are limited. Ventura came up with this suggestion. Now, if you will excuse me. . ." He stood and crossed the distance to Ventura in one long stride. His hands lashed out, left, right, left, and all three landed.

CHAPTER 17

Ike raised his arms in the universal signal of victory. Gasping, Blanche stepped in Ventura's direction to make sure he was uninjured.

"Well done! We'll settle things later." Ventura accepted his man's towel and buried his face in its folds. Swinging the towel around his neck, he smiled as if he hadn't lost the bout. "Good day, Gallagher. Miss Lamar. I will see you later." A tune whistling between his teeth, he walked out the door, happy with the world.

Blanche counted to ten once, then twice. "Was that really necessary?"

"Of course not." The corner of Ike's mouth lifted in a half smile. "But it was fun."

"Grown men, fighting like two boys in the schoolyard." She shook her head. "I thought the two of you were friends."

"Have you ever heard of boxing?"

Blanche shook her head.

"It's a kind of organized fight. With rules."

"You still were hurt. Your chin is already turning color." She peered at it, questioning whether what she saw was a bruise or his whiskers. Her fingers stretched out to check before she pulled back, embarrassed by her close examination of the man.

He touched his side and winced. "I didn't expect you to leave the pilothouse so early."

Old Obie had sent her out early with strict instructions to rest and fix her hair for the evening, but she wouldn't give Ike the satisfaction of telling him so. "I was just taking a break before we come to La Joya. I was on my way to my cabin when I heard all the commotion in here." She drew a deep breath. "Since it appears you will live, I will go on ahead."

"I'll see you this evening then." Ike grabbed a towel and walked her to the door. "Looking like a gentleman, I promise you."

Blanche watched his back as he walked away. Damp patches darkened his shirt where it stuck to his skin. Dressed in these clothes, he looked more like farmers she had seen working around Roma, and less like the suave man of the world. They transformed him into a real man with muscles, one who sweated when he worked—strong enough to defend his family. She turned away, heat spreading into her cheeks and down her arms. So, he was a man, like any other man. A man who had invited her to dinner at a restaurant.

Confused by her feelings, she slowed her steps, seeking direction. She should go to her cabin, grab her Bible, and ask God to clear her momentary muddle. What she did instead was return to the pilothouse.

"Back so soon?" Old Obie gestured her forward. "It's just as well. We are almost at La Joya."

"I thought so. I want to watch you pull up to the dock."

"Maybe you want to do it yourself?" The corners of Old Obie's hazel eyes crinkled as he patted the wheel.

"I would like that." Learning something new would take her mind off Ike. Old Obie did an amazing job of explaining how to pilot the sternwheeler. As long as he stayed by her side, she'd be willing to risk it. She stared into the depths of the water, as dark and murky as Ike's brown eyes.

". . .but the river is deep enough here to get close to the wharf. No ferry needed."

"A ferry?" she said stupidly.

"To move the cargo to the town." He tilted his head toward his shoulder. "You haven't been listening. Something is on your mind. What is it? You can tell me."

Blanche shifted from one foot to another. His listening ear had drawn her to the pilothouse in the first place, but she found it difficult to put her feelings into words. "I ran into Ike." Her voice sounded strangled.

"It is a small ship." His measured tones invited her to explain further.

She wouldn't mention the fight she had seen between Ike and Ventura. "He had changed clothes. I have never seen him dressed in anything except his suit before."

"I think I understand. It was like you were seeing him for the first time."

"Yes." The word came out as a whisper. "He was injured."

"There was an accident?" Old Obie stiffened at the wheel, knees flexed as if he was prepared to spring into action.

"It was no accident. He and Mr. Ventura engaged in fisticuffs—on purpose." Her voice grew stronger as her indignation asserted itself.

The older man laughed. "I would guess that you haven't spent much time around men."

Blanche shook her head.

"When you were at school, did you ever see two boys get into a fight?"

She nodded.

"And afterward they were best friends?"

Her face tightened in concentration. "That was so strange."

"Boys—men—are like that. They take pleasure in physical challenges." His eyes crinkled, waves lapping in the hazel of his eyes.

"I believe you." She shook her head. "Although it still seems strange." Ike's image floated in her memory again. What she had seen bothered her far more than memories of childish playground tussles.

The mirth in Old Obie's eyes altered, transformed into

concern. "If you want the opinion of an old river rat like me, I'll give it to you."

You're like the father I never knew. The thought sent more uncertainty swirling through her. In this arena, she trusted Old Obie more than she would Reverend Davenport. Her pastor was a good Christian man, but she couldn't imagine him raising his hands in a fight between friends. "I'm listening."

"Life in Roma hasn't prepared you for life aboard a steamboat, and you haven't met many men like Ike. But people are people, and Ike Gallagher is like a son to me. He's a good man. The captain trusted him. He earned his position in the crew." Coughing, Old Obie wiped his sleeve against his mouth, closed his eyes, and sagged against the wheel. He opened his eyes, drew a deep breath, and clasped the wheel with both hands.

"I've kept you from your rest time today." Blanche backed away.

He pulled in his lips, pain creasing his face. "I get to rest all night, as soon as we arrive at La Joya. You go on and get ready. I'll be fine." The lines on his face argued against the strength he projected in his voice.

Blanche promised herself she would check on him when she returned. On impulse, she threw her arms around his shoulders, stooped from carrying the weight of the world. "I like to think my father was a lot like you."

"That's right kind of you, Blanche." He wiped at moist eyes. "Now, go on, before tears blind me and I can't see to pilot the boat." He wiped his hands on his shirt and clasped the wheel with both hands.

Blanche paused at the head of the stairs, glancing at him over her shoulder. Her own eyes filled, and she hurried down to the main deck. Today, emotions she had rarely felt scraped against each other. She'd have to ask God to protect her heart tonight, or else she might break down and do something foolish.

⟨※⟩

Ike stared at his wardrobe, full of the latest in men's fashions in a variety of fabrics and colors, with tasteful accessories. Fewer choices would make his decision easier. He hadn't missed the gleam of appreciation in Blanche's eyes when she saw him after the match with Ventura. But dressing in workday clothes felt like an insult. In fact, the restaurant where he planned to go required a suit jacket. Without a jacket and tie, he would not be admitted.

He settled on wearing a suit coat without a vest, neither black nor white, but pale gray. He rejected the dark blue shirt, hesitated over pale blue, and reluctantly picked out the white with his usual bow tie. His hand hovered over his pocket watch. *Take it,* he decided, and tucked it into the front pocket of his black slacks.

Did Blanche spend half as much time as he did worrying what to wear? He shook his head. It didn't matter. Even a potato sack couldn't hide her figure or her beautiful face, the sparkle in her eyes when she was excited.

Face it. You're smitten. He shook his head. The feelings would pass. They had to. Blanche Lamar would no more settle for a gambler like him than he would become a Sunday pew sitter, although that possibility no longer seemed as impossible as it once had.

"I'm ready."

At Blanche's soft voice, Ike turned around. Her hair was swept up in a style that spoke of Effie's flawless hands, held in place by a white comb. Black leather toes peeked from beneath the hem of her dress. A few simple changes made her even more beautiful than she was before, if that were possible.

A slow, warm smile spread across his face. If she was a different sort of woman, he might have whistled. Instead, he let his admiration linger for a moment. Then he swept his hat from his head and bowed before extending his hand to take her arm. "I will be the envy of every man in La Joya tonight."

She ducked her head, sending the feather attached to the comb aflutter, shining against the vivid color of her hair. "I doubt that." She raised her head. A brief glimmer in her eyes suggested she appreciated the trouble he had taken with his appearance. One gloved hand reached toward his chin but stopped short of touching him. "Is it sore?"

"I'll live." Ike led Blanche down the wharf, the heels of her shoes clicking on the wood of the wharf. He had held many women's arms before, but never had one felt so fragile, never had the desire to protect one surged so strong in him. "I have hired a carriage to meet us at the wharf."

Her head swiveled, her nose twitching as she breathed, eyes widening as she took in the appearance of the town ahead. She could have been someone just released from prison, seeing home with new eyes.

She caught the expression on his face and laughed. "I've never been so far from home before."

Home. Roma was her home, not the *Cordelia.* Ike pushed the thought out of his mind. "How does it compare?"

They reached the end of the wharf where their carriage awaited them. The livery had outdone themselves, sending a sparkling white carriage with matching horses to pull it.

He offered his hand to help her step up for a ride designed to impress Blanche, but she looked down the street instead. "How far is the restaurant? I would like to walk if possible. It's such a lovely evening."

"And you haven't been able to walk far in any direction for over a week. I understand the feeling. Yes, we can walk." Stifling his disappointment, Ike explained the situation to the driver.

"She is the señorita?" The driver's mustache quivered beneath his smile.

Ike nodded. "She has a yen to take a walk."

He nodded. "Keep her happy, that one. You are a fortunate man to have such a lovely lady on your arm."

Ike's grin widened. "I intend to do everything I can to keep her happy." He gave the driver some money for his trouble. The smile stayed on his face as he walked back to Blanche.

"The restaurant is this way." Ike felt like he was ten feet tall as he walked with Blanche at his side. Block by block, they turned heads. Men followed their progress with envy, women with interest.

Blanche remained oblivious of the attention, instead

sweeping her head from side to side, as if memorizing the route.

"Is it so very different from Roma?" Ike asked.

She stopped their progress, studying a church on the opposite corner. A statue of the Virgin Mary out front dominated the buildings around it. Squinting, Ike read the sign: La Iglesia de la Virgen de Guadalupe.

"In some ways it resembles Roma," Blanche said. "I wonder if that's the largest church in town."

Ike looked at the adobe structure, gleaming white. He shrugged. "I honestly don't know."

"Of course not." She said the words half under her breath, but he could hear the disappointment.

They resumed walking. Every few feet she'd stop and stare in the front window of a building. After each stop, her pace increased, until she was nearly skipping down the street.

"You're having fun."

"Of course." Blanche spread her arms, taking in the street. "If I close my eyes and just breathe in the air, it would seem like I'm back home in Roma." She inhaled deeply. "Sawdust and horses. Honeysuckle and pine. Baked bread and chilies." Opening her eyes, she scuffed the dirt underfoot with the toe of her shoe. "I even like having the ground under my feet."

Some of Ike's good humor seeped away with her outburst. Was she so homesick for Roma so soon? "I feel the same way when I have to be away from the *Cordelia* for more than an overnight stay. The mist of the water on my face, the smoothness of the floorboards and railing, Elaine's good cooking."

Something across the street caught her attention. Instead of responding to his comments, she pointed across the street. "Look! There's a mercantile. Do we have time to stop?"

Ike fingered the watch in his pocket but didn't pull it out. He wanted to keep this evening carefree, not worried about the clock. "Let's." His sister had taught him how much women enjoyed shopping.

"Oh, thank you." Blanche stepped down from the boardwalk in the direction of the store.

"Of course." Ike trailed behind, curious about which section of the store would attract her first. Her choices would reveal a lot about her.

Once through the door, again she breathed deeply. Ike followed her example, his mind sorting through the odors— licorice, pickles, tobacco.

Blanche's swift run through the store surprised him. She bypassed the baubles that had caught the attention of a pair of young girls who were chattering over the counter. She also strode past the sewing supplies, Effie's favorite section.

A bookshelf distracted her for a moment. Her fingers ran along the spines of the books. Shaking her head, she turned to him. "Do you know if there is a bookstore in Brownsville?"

"Ventura will know."

"They probably won't have what I'm looking for in stock." She backtracked to the sewing area and picked up a pincushion. "If I order something, can it be delivered directly to the boat?"

"Of course." Did that mean she was committed to stay long enough to receive a package? Ike's hopes resurrected.

Blanche lifted a box of stationery to her nose. "Rose-scented. Very nice." She paid for it and they left the store.

"You're going to write some letters." He almost made it a question.

"I have special plans for this stationery." She didn't elaborate. "I'll get started as soon as we get back to the boat tonight."

Her hint of a promise of future plans concerning the boat lifted his spirits. So did getting back on board the *Cordelia*.

Land was fun to visit, but he wouldn't want to live there.

CHAPTER 18

"D id Ike buy you roses?" Effie asked when Blanche entered
the cabin. She had stayed up to chat with Blanche after
her dinner with Ike. What fun these days had been, sharing her
cabin as if Blanche were her sister.

"You're still awake!" A sigh accompanied the *whoosh* of the
chair cushion. "Is he in the habit of giving girls flowers?"

"Only a special few." A smile played around Effie's lips. "He
did give you flowers, I can tell."

"No flowers, just a lovely dinner and conversation."

Effie sniffed the air, detecting a light floral scent. "I thought
I smelled them."

"If you're smelling roses, it's from a box of stationery that I
bought."

"Oh, I almost wish I could write a letter, if it meant I could
enjoy that scent every time I opened the box."

Blanche handed Effie a sheet of the paper. "Here. Keep this.
Perhaps you would like to place it in your bureau drawer, like a
sachet."

Effie brought the sheet to her nose and sighed as she breathed
it in. "I'll put it under my pillow, so that I can enjoy it as I fall

asleep." She tucked the stationery into her bed and pulled out her knitting. "Will you be coming to bed soon?"

"Not for a few minutes. I have some notes I want to write." The tip of a pen scratched against paper while Effie worked on an intricate shawl. An hour passed before they called it quits for the night. Blanche continued her project for all the following day. After breakfast the second morning, she set down her pen at last. "Done."

"I won't ask what has kept you so busy these last two days." Effie changed yarn colors for her shawl. "You have given me pleasure, filling our room with the scent of your stationery while you've been writing so busily."

"You make the perfect roommate. I could wrap all your Christmas presents right in front of you, and you wouldn't know what they were."

"Don't be so sure about that. I've fooled a lot of people that way." Effie laughed. "I can tell a lot by the sounds something makes, or the scent. And the feel, of course. I used to drive Ike crazy, when I could guess and he couldn't."

"So what do you think I've been doing?"

"Writing something, of course. But what you've been writing, or to whom, I don't know. I would guess you have written letters, and to more than one person. You've opened several envelopes."

"You are good at this guessing game." Blanche didn't explain any more, and Effie didn't press.

"Are you looking forward to arriving in Brownsville? We should be there tomorrow or the day after at the latest."

A small silence formed around the word *Brownsville*. "I am hoping to have my questions answered."

Effie switched back to the original yarn color. "What if you don't like the answers?"

"God promises a good future, plans to prosper me and not to harm me. Not necessarily wealth, but whatever answers I find are ones that will help me."

"I wish I had your faith."

"My pastor used to say it wasn't the amount of faith that a

person has—the Bible talks about faith as small as a mustard seed—but the object of our faith. God is big, even if my faith is small."

Effie shook her head. Such thinking went against everything she understood about religion. "God seemed big to me when I was a little girl. Then my parents died, and I realized even He couldn't make everything right."

"But He brought Old Obie into your lives about that time, didn't He? I know losing your parents when you were so little must have been terrible. But God still took care of you." The pleading tone in Blanche's voice got Effie's attention.

Effie stuck her tongue between her lips, a habit she had when she was concentrating on something, and counted the number of stitches in the row. "Didn't drop a one. I always check after I have to change yarn." She turned her sightless eyes in Blanche's direction. "I only know that sometimes the answers God gives aren't the ones I want. And I hope you're not disappointed with what you learn."

Blanche caught her breath. "I can't say I won't be disappointed. But if I am, know this. The problem is with me. God is good, all the time."

Effie's half smile returned. "I know that's what you believe." She tucked the yarn away. "Are you ready to leave?"

Blanche dropped several envelopes into a bag. "Now I am."

Rising early the next morning, Blanche donned her black suit to better blend into the lingering nighttime shadows, and made her way around the ship she had come to know as well as the hallways and rooms of her childhood home. First she headed for the salon, where she went to each table and left envelopes addressed to their guests.

Finding the right words to thank each passenger for their business had come fairly easily. She tucked a couple of envelopes into the waiting muffin baskets, trusting that the kitchen staff would discover them in the process of serving breakfast. Elaine was already at work, but aside from nodding good morning, she stayed at the back of the kitchen, preparing bread and other baked goods for the day.

Next Blanche headed to the crew's quarters. A special envelope went to Dame Agatha, who would shake her double chins in severe disappointment if she spotted her prize customer in her "dowdy country clothes," as she had described Blanche's suit. The transformation the lady's needle had wrought in Blanche still confounded her, changing her in ways she still didn't understand. About half the crew remained abed, and Blanche slipped notes for everyone under their cabin doors. She added Effie's letter to Ike's, trusting he would read it to her. She brought that envelope to her nose, hoping the stationery would hold the scent a long time.

Last of all, Blanche headed for the pilothouse, where Old Obie stood on watch. She couldn't leave it at his cabin, since she didn't know which cabin was his. As for letting Ike deliver the note, she decided to keep it between the two of them.

The bow of the boat parted liquid gold as they slid into sunrise. If she could capture it, she would make a fortune that no amount of money could buy. She waited on deck, watching the water turn from black to gold to bloodred. *Red,* the color of blood. The color of joy. She'd felt such joy on the excursion to La Joya with Ike. Then she reminded herself that he was an unbeliever. Someone she could never marry. She placed her hand over her heart as if she could protect herself from the unwanted emotions flooding through her. She feared it was already too late.

She touched the remaining letter in her pocket. Effie had laughed when she asked for Old Obie's full name. "That's a closely guarded secret. You'll have to ask him yourself." Humming a few bars of "When Morning Gilds the Skies," Blanche mounted the stairs.

Sunshine outlined Old Obie's form in fiery reds. "My songbird is up early this morning." He turned, and Blanche saw he was holding a cup in his hand.

"Coffee."

He laughed. "Do you want some?" He dug out a coffee mug and poured from a pot that would look right at a campfire.

She sipped it and sighed. "Perfect." She enjoyed coffee first thing in the morning, before the day became too warm. Drinking deeply, she studied the river. To the left she spotted a submerged log. Maps indicated a sandbar on the right, but the water level would carry them over it without a problem. "How do you adjust for the sun on the water?"

"I slow down and look out the side windows instead. Fog is worse. More than one morning, I've had to stop the engines until visibility improved." He tapped the wheel. "A good pilot is never afraid to stop if necessary. Don't let an anxious owner push you to do something that is unsafe."

"You sound like I will actually get to pilot the boat one day."

"Of course you will. I have no doubt."

She finished her coffee and set the mug down. Taking care that her fingers were clean, she pulled out the envelope. "This is for you. I would have addressed it, but I don't know your full name."

"A letter." He didn't offer his name. "I haven't had one of these in a long time. Should I open it now?"

Suddenly shy, she shook her head. "It's not much. Just something to remember me by."

He turned his complete attention on her, piercing her with his gaze. "I won't ever forget you. It's not possible. And I still hope you will choose to make your home on the river, so I won't need something to remind me. But, I will treasure this." He gestured with the letter. "As I would treasure anything that you give to me."

———✦———

Ike dressed slowly, as if delay on his part could prevent the coming revelations from the captain's lawyer. He read the few lines of Blanche's letter to him again. The balanced message, poised between a polite letter of appreciation and a personal note to a friend, betrayed more than she intended to, he suspected. He lifted the paper to his nose and breathed in. Every time he passed a rosebush, he would remember this letter.

Oh Blanche. Would she feel the same way after she talked to

the lawyer, only a few hours from now?

Bringing the letter to his lips and placing Effie's letter in his suit pocket, he headed for breakfast. He treasured these hours of uncluttered friendship, hoping against hope that she wouldn't reject him once she knew the truth. When he glanced up at the pilothouse, Old Obie waved for him to come.

The click of heels behind him announced Blanche's arrival. "Do we have a scheduled time with the lawyer?"

Ike noted, with amusement, that Blanche had returned to the security of her black traveling suit for this business appointment. "Not exactly. We didn't know when we would arrive. But they are expecting us sometime this week."

They rode in the carriage to the offices of Cox, Carver, and Chavez in relative silence. Ike knew the answers to most of the questions Blanche had held at bay since they left Roma. Neither one of them indulged in idle speculation as the carriage drove them to the office on East Washington Street, adjacent to Washington Park.

"That must be their office." Blanche pointed to the modest storefront office. "Mr. Carver was my father's lawyer?"

Ike nodded. He circled the carriage and helped her down. Her smattering of freckles stood out darker than usual on her skin, color having fled her face. He didn't have any words to reassure her. He offered her his arm and led her inside.

A young man Ike had never met before sat at the front desk. He half-rose from his chair. "May I help you?"

Something resembling panic filled Blanche's eyes. Ike took a step forward. "Blanche Lamar and Ike Gallagher, here to see Mr. Carver."

The man's nose quivered. "Do you have an appointment?"

"No." Blanche backed up a step.

"He is expecting us this week." Ike moved forward. "Why don't you let him know we're here? We can wait." He escorted Blanche to a chair.

The young clerk frowned. "That's not possible."

Before Ike could retort, Blanche spoke. "Pardon me, what is your name?"

Her request erased the unpleasant young man's frown. "I am Walter Brown, ma'am."

Blanche glanced at Ike. "Mr. Brown, we'd like to make an appointment. Is there an opening with Mr. Carver this afternoon?"

"That is what I was attempting to explain." Brown glared at Ike. "Mr. Carver has business out of town today. He will return next week. May I schedule an appointment for you?" Leaning forward, he unbent a little. "Can Mr. Cox assist you? He is available today."

Blanche looked at Ike, her eyes sending a silent plea, but Ike didn't care to discuss the situation with someone reading the file for the first time. Struggling to make his voice pleasant, he said, "We don't expect to be in Brownsville that long. Is there any possibility that Mr. Carver will return earlier than next week?"

Brown scanned the calendar in front of him. "His court case is scheduled to last through this week. There is always the possibility it will end early, but we do not expect it." He offered an apologetic smile. "And it could also, unfortunately, last longer."

Ike nodded. "Then let us make an appointment for Friday afternoon, and hope he returns earlier than expected."

Brown held the pen in his hand for a moment before making a note on the appointment book. "Two o'clock on Friday afternoon, Mr. Gallagher and Miss Lamar to meet with Mr. Carver." He copied the information onto a calling card and handed it to Blanche. "I cannot guarantee that Mr. Carver will have returned."

"We understand." Blanche glanced at the card before tucking it into her reticule. "Thank you, Mr. Brown. You have been most kind."

"It's my pleasure, Miss Lamar."

The sun beat down on their heads as they exited the building. As instructed, the carriage had left to return in an hour. Blanche clasped her reticule. The courage she had demonstrated only minutes earlier had disappeared, and she looked anxious for their ride.

"Mr. Brown would not object if we want to wait inside until the carriage returns. Or we could walk a couple of blocks in that direction." Ike pointed to the right, toward the center of town they had passed a short time earlier. "We could find a bakery or a mercantile."

"A walk sounds pleasant." Blanche accepted his arm at her elbow and shifted her reticule to her other hand. "I would love to go shopping again, but I shouldn't spend any more money. God promised to provide for my needs, but knickknacks don't fall into that category."

The look of longing that filled her face told him all he needed to know about the absence of nonessential items from her childhood. He wished he could buy her an entire cabinet full of curios from every town in the river and more beside.

"The letters were a wonderful idea." The words she had written to him had seared themselves in his brain. *Dear Ike. . .friendship. . .support. . .you have made me feel special.* She had even copied a Bible verse, something about God loving him. "Creative. Personal. Everyone is talking about them." He smiled.

"You didn't mention the low cost." Blanche's smile let him know she meant no offense. "Thank you. I learned a lot about giving from my mother. We never had much money, but we always had enough to give away."

"I felt the same way, growing up on the *Cordelia*. We always had what we needed, and we knew the captain loved us. Those are things money can't buy."

"Just like God's love." She nodded. "He was there for you, even back then."

CHAPTER 19

"This isn't the quality of cotton we have come to expect from Roma." The owner of the textile factory, a Mr. Draper, shook his head over the pallets that had been delivered from the decks of the *Cordelia*.

Blanche stood uncertainly by the carriage. She didn't know how to respond. In the past, her only business consisted of dealing with school supplies and food from the local mercantile in Roma. But from the time she had spent reviewing the accounts for Lamar Industries, she knew delivery of cotton played a big role in continued profitability. Was this kind of complaint common?

The chief stevedore shrugged. "I just load it and unload it, boss."

"And I'm telling you, this isn't what I ordered." Draper's voice grew agitated.

This disagreement was going around in circles, and she took a step forward. "Do you have a copy of the order you placed?"

"What's that?" Mr. Draper switched his gaze to her. "Who are you?"

"I am Blanche Lamar. Captain Lamar was my father. I'm

sure there's been some misunderstanding. The order might clear it up."

Mr. Draper looked at Ike out of the corner of his eye, who nodded. Blanche stepped on her irritation. How long had Ike been handling business for her father?

"I have a copy in my office." Mr. Draper headed for the small adobe building at the back of the property. "This way."

Ike held a chair for her while Mr. Draper rustled through his file drawer. He laid a sheet of paper in front of her. "This is what I ordered."

The handwriting was legible, but that didn't make the meaning any clearer. She'd guess it referred to the weight and quality of the raw cotton. Did she have to understand the cotton business to operate a profitable steamboat operation?

Ike zeroed in on the heart of the problem. "You requested six bundles. We delivered the requested half dozen. Any problems you have with the product, you need to take up with the farmer."

"And if I refuse delivery?"

Were all business owners this belligerent?

"That is acceptable, as long as you pay for the return shipment."

Panic rose in her throat. She thanked God for Ike's presence and calm demeanor. She didn't know if she could speak.

The two men continued arranging the details while she tried to relax. She clasped her hands in her lap, tapping her fingers against her palm, settled her back against the chair, and let a smile play on her face. A lemon drop might renew the moisture inside her mouth. They could stop at the mercantile for some penny candy. She could afford that much. Visions of hard candy ran through her mind while she ran her tongue around the inside of her cheek. From the posture of both Ike and Mr. Draper, she guessed they had engaged in this duel of words many times before.

I still have so much to learn.

Including the information the lawyer would convey. As his associate had predicted, Mr. Carver didn't return early. With the completion of today's business, the *Cordelia* was ready to return to Roma. They couldn't justify spending an additional three days in Brownsville so she could talk with the lawyer.

Ike shook Mr. Draper's hand, and he turned to her. "Is that acceptable to you, Blanche?"

She hadn't followed all the steps of the negotiation. "Th– that's fine."

"Good. Then we'll be on our way." They left the office by one of the many side streets in Brownsville. All roads led to the river eventually, at least they did in Roma. Follow the flow of traffic, follow the smells, follow the birds, and she would find the wharves.

"How do you want to spend your last night on land?" Ike had relaxed, perhaps glad that the business had finished.

The words sounded a gong in her heart. Was this her last time in Brownsville? She didn't dare risk another trip down the river. One time had already turned her whole world upside down.

She also didn't know if she wanted to settle in Roma; she had changed from the person she was. The meeting with the lawyer should have provided some direction, but for some reason God hadn't allowed that to happen.

"What are you thinking?" Ike nudged her shoulder. "You went somewhere faraway."

Blanche brought her thoughts back to the presence of Ike at her side, the community of Brownsville out before them. "You don't have to keep me company. Did you already have plans?"

"Nothing, except this." He reached into his pocket and flashed three tickets before her. "Ventura has invited us to join the Brownsville Bats for a baseball game."

The carriage returned for them, and Effie sat next to the driver. "Have you told Blanche yet?" Her smile was as warm as the white cotton dress with gay red stripes she wore.

"Just now." Blanche realized Ike's clothes matched Effie's, thin red pinstripes in his shirt and a red bow tie. "Someone should have told me to wear red."

"You noticed." Ike's lips lifted in a lopsided smile. "The team's colors are red and white."

Blanche glanced at her black suit and decided that it would cover a multitude of sins, with all the dust and spills possible at a baseball diamond.

"You have been to games before." Blanche made it a statement, not a question.

"As often as possible." Effie's light laughter rippled through the air. "You're wondering why a blind woman wants to go to a baseball game."

"The thought did cross my mind." Blanche accepted Ike's arm as he assisted her into the carriage.

"The ballpark, please," Ike said to the driver. The horse moved at a slow trot.

"There must be more to baseball than watching men running around the bases."

"Oh my, yes. A bag of peanuts and a box of Cracker Jack."

"Cracker Jack? What is that?"

"A delicious snack that Elaine would never allow in her kitchen." Ike rubbed his stomach in anticipation. "Caramel corn with peanuts. There is something to be said for the pleasures of childhood."

"I can't wait to taste it."

"And hot dogs and pretzels and—"

"Stop! You're giving me a stomachache."

"Do you mind if we walk the rest of the way?" Effie glanced over her shoulder. "I enjoy a chance to stretch my legs. We'll take a carriage back after the game."

Blanche nodded. Soon the three of them were walking down the street, Ike's hand tucked through the crook of Blanche's elbow. He made her feel protected, special. Tonight he was offering her another new experience. "Effie, what do you think of baseball?"

"I love it. I hope you enjoy it. Have you ever played?"

Blanche paused in her steps. "What, me, play baseball? No." Shock showed in her voice. "Girls don't play baseball. Do they?"

"Maybe in the schoolyard. Even I have played catch." Effie kicked a pinecone and caught it with her hand. "They tell me I caught nearly as many balls as the girls who can see." Pushing her hands out, she said, "Here, catch."

The pinecone brushed the ends of Blanche's fingers before

dropping to the ground. She giggled.

"I guess you won't be catching any fly balls today." Ike smacked his fist into his palm. "I'll have to catch one for you."

"Fly ball?" The image of a ball with tiny white wings brought a smile to Blanche's face.

"Let's get to our seats. I'll explain it all to you."

Their "seats" turned out to be bleachers. Blanche tucked her skirt beneath her, hoping to avoid soiling the fabric.

Peanut shells crunched beneath their feet. "Ah. The sound of peanuts." Effie lifted the hem of her skirt and settled down next to Blanche.

"What do you want to eat? Hot dogs, Cracker Jack, peanuts? Candy?" Leaning in close, he whispered, "Beer?"

"Ike!" A giggle accompanied Effie's reprimand.

"I take that as a no."

Blanche considered. "I don't know. They all sound good. Except beer, of course."

"I'll get one for each of us, together with Dr Pepper." Ike left a handkerchief to mark his place, on Blanche's right. "I'll be right back."

"Is he always like this before a game?" Blanche watched him half-run down to a vendor carrying a box full of snacks supported by a shoulder harness.

"Turn back into a little boy all over again? Yes. I think it does him good."

Blanche leaned forward to see Ike's retreating back. He encountered the vendor, the pitch of his head suggesting laughter, filling his arms with food. "He's buying enough to feed everyone here."

Effie laughed. "He does that on purpose. He sneaks it back on ship and then skips breakfast for a day or two. I think Elaine knows his secret, but she lets him get away with it."

Blanche had brought sweets home from a friend's house once or twice, but Mother had never caught on.

Impossible. In the short time Blanche had shared Effie's cabin, she knew one or two of the places she kept special treats, and could guess at others. Mother must have known most of

Blanche's secrets, but she had pretended otherwise. The thought warmed her down to her toes. Mother had allowed her the small piece of childhood.

Ike returned with his arms laden with food. "Here's a bag of peanuts for you, and one for Effie, and one for me."

Removing a peanut, Blanche squeezed the shell. It crushed beneath her fingers, popping the nut onto the floor. The shattered shell clung to her skirt. She tried to pick it off.

"Just brush it underfoot." Ike handed her another nut. "We get to make all the mess we want to here at the game." He snapped a shell in half and dropped two peanuts into his hand before he dropped his shells onto the floor. Lifting his foot, he ground them into powder.

Blanche gingerly brushed off her skirt. She succeeded in getting the second nut. "It's salty."

"They roast and salt them before bagging them." Ike popped another one in his mouth. "The game is starting." Ike pointed to the field, where nine men had taken positions. The men tossed balls—at least Blanche assumed they were balls. It was hard to tell, as quickly as they sailed through the air. One man stood on a mound in the middle of the diamond, throwing to a man crouched behind a bag. They all wore matching outfits, white with the words "Brownsville Bats" emblazoned in red over a cartoon bat holding a baseball bat. Ike's hat sported the same ridiculous picture.

Munching on their snacks, they talked and laughed while the team continued throwing balls. Everyone ignored what was happening on the field. Eventually they cleared the field and a brass band marched out.

"Ah, now we're about to start."

Mr. Ventura walked in front of the band. Spreading his arms like Blanche imagined a circus ringmaster might, he said, "Ladies and gentlemen, please rise for the national anthem." Seconds later they were singing "The Star-Spangled Banner."

As soon as they finished singing, the Bats returned to the field, joined by a man swinging a bat. On the first pitch, his bat connected with the ball.

"Leadoff home run. Not looking good." Ike popped a piece of caramel corn in his mouth.

Effie patted Blanche's hand. "Do you understand any of this?"

"Honestly?" Blanche shook her head. "No."

"I'll explain it to you." Ike's chest seemed to expand as he began explaining the system of hits, balls, strikes, and runs that made the difference between winning and losing.

"So they can make a run two ways. They either hit the ball over the fence into the crowd, where anyone can get hurt." She pretended offense. A couple of balls had felt like they whizzed by her ears. "Or they can hit the ball and run to the base and try to make it around all four bases."

Ike opened his mouth, as if ready to explain more. Shaking his head, he said, "There are foul balls and strikes and steals and. . .but that's it in a nutshell."

"And the Bats are winning. They have seven runs, and the Hurricanes only have six."

"It's a good thing that the Bats have the last at bat." Effie popped a peppermint candy into her mouth. "The game is too close to pick a winner yet."

The game ended with the Bats winning by a final score of nine to six. Smiles wreathed Ike and Effie's faces, and Blanche felt sure she looked the same. "Come, let's congratulate Ventura on the win." Ike offered his arm, and Blanche accepted it.

"Are all the games this exciting?" Blanche heard the breathless sound of her voice, as if she had been the one running the bases instead of the teams.

"Some more, some less. Sometimes the pitchers keep the batters off base. That's exciting, in a different sort of way."

The three of them wormed their way through the crowd that was going in the opposite direction, surging toward the gates. Blanche was glad for Ike's presence. Without him, the noise and the bustle might have paralyzed her.

"Ventura was successful in arranging games in all the towns between here and Roma?"

"They're looking forward to it."

"So am I." *If I'm here.* Depending on what the absent lawyer had to tell her, she had to find work, soon. The trip on the *Cordelia* had been enough adventure to satisfy her for two lifetimes.

"There he is." Ike pointed to the spot where Ventura stood in front of the Bats' bench. Instead of the smile Blanche expected, a frown creased his face as he spoke with a young lad. He looked vaguely familiar; about the time they reached Ventura, Blanche placed him as one of the young stevedores who had helped unload the boat upon their arrival.

Ventura caught sight of them and gestured for them to draw close. "Jim-boy thought he might catch you here at the game. There's been an accident."

CHAPTER 20

W hat happened?" Ike asked sharply.

"Has someone been injured?" Blanche asked at the same time.

Ventura nodded to young Jim-boy. "We was loading the cotton back on board, sir. Mr. Draper sent it back. I wondered about that, but he had all the proper paperwork so I thought it was all right."

"He didn't waste any time." Ike grimaced. "But yes, that's fine. What happened?"

"Since you wasn't there, I went to ask the cap'n, sir. He came down on deck, and the crane slipped and knocked into him. Knocked him clean out."

"The *captain?*" A glance at Blanche reminded Ike of another reality. Her skin paled beneath the light sunburn, and her breath came out in short gasps.

Ike couldn't afford that distraction now. He had to find out the extent of the injuries. "Have you sent for a doctor?"

"He's on board already. And I came to find you, straightaway."

"The *captain?*" Blanche's eyes went wide. "Captain Lamar—

my father—has been on the ship the whole time?" She turned agonizing eyes in his direction.

Worry warred with guilt. "I'll explain it to you later. Right now, we have to get back to the boat."

Blanche whirled, turning her anger on Effie. "You must have known."

Effie's mouth worked, but she couldn't seem to find words to respond either. "Let's get back to the ship. I'll explain while Ike sees to things."

"Don't bother." Blanche's voice was cold. "I want to meet my father." She headed toward the exit, Ike hurrying after her. When he caught up with her, she stopped, tears streaming down her cheeks. "I don't know the quickest way back."

"We'll walk. The crowd would only delay a carriage, even if we could find one. Come with us. We all want to get back as quickly as possible."

After Effie offered a few more details that Jim-boy had supplied, they walked in silence. Ike was torn between worry about the captain, injured and unconscious, and what it could mean to Blanche.

The plan for father and daughter to get to know each other before making Blanche aware of their connection didn't allow for illness. What if something interfered, denying them the opportunity? All the preaching against gambling didn't stir Ike's soul, but that single deceit weighed on his conscience.

Ike weaved his way through the streets without thought, trusting his instincts to lead his feet aright. When the *Cordelia* came into view, Blanche sped up. He matched her step for step, wanting to get there first, to ease the discovery for her.

She pressed forward, leaving him a little breathless when he swept past her on the gangway. "Where is the captain? How is he?"

"Mr. Gallagher, I presume?" A small man, with a bushy salt-and-pepper mustache and no-nonsense cut of a suit coat, greeted him. "John Foster. I'm the doctor they called in."

Blanche placed herself between Ike and the doctor. With a glare at Ike, she said, "How is Captain Lamar?" Only a slight waver in her voice betrayed her overwhelming emotions.

Dr. Foster glanced at Ike, which only fueled Blanche's anger. "Doctor, this is the captain's daughter, Blanche Lamar."

"I see." The man turned to Blanche apologetically. "I was given to understand there was no family to notify."

Notify. The word hung between them with horrifying import.

"Is he—" Ike left the question unfinished.

Dr. Foster flinched, as if he realized what his words had implied. "Oh no. Nothing like that. He's had a nasty bump to his head, but he regained consciousness while I was with him, and was alert to his surroundings. That's a good sign." He smiled reassuringly at Blanche while explaining the signs they should watch for: disorientation, problems with eyesight, fever—the usual. "The most important thing is to keep him quiet for a few days, give his body a chance to heal. I hear he can be stubborn. Can you keep him to his bed?"

"I'll make sure he doesn't move," Ike said.

"Will you be back, to check on him?" Blanche asked.

"Of course. I'll come by morning and evening. If problems arise, feel free to call for me in between times." Shifting his black bag to his other hand and nodding at Blanche, Dr. Foster walked down the wharf.

Tapping her right foot, Blanche turned the full force of her glare on Ike and Effie. "Are you ready to introduce me to my father?"

❧

So close. Blanche had been on the boat with her father for more than a week, and no one told her. Every time the facts repeated themselves in her mind, her anger increased. They had no right, no right at all, to keep the truth from her.

She wanted to scream in frustration, but their discussion with the doctor had already brought curious glances from the crew. Lowering her voice, she said, "Where is he? *Who* is he?"

Effie looked resigned, but Ike looked almost—sheepish. An air of uncertainty clung to the usually cocky purser.

"Come this way." Effie walked toward the bow of the ship,

past the pilothouse. Blanche glanced up. Old Obie's replacement was there. The pilot must have known about the deception as well. No wonder her mother had warned her against steamboats. People she had trusted had turned out to be nothing more than thieves and liars.

"This way." Effie headed toward the cramped stairs at the end of the boat. "His quarters are nothing special. He said Ike needed the captain's cabin more; all he wanted was a place to lay his head. That's just the kind of person he is."

Effie's voice trailed away as they circled down the stairs, ending up in the bowels of the ship, hot and steamy and dark except for a few lamps down the hall. She stopped in front of a dingy black door, no different in appearance from the three before, and hesitated. "This isn't how he wanted you to find out. Please. . .think kindly on him. Listen to what he has to say."

The door swung open, and Elaine the cook came out, carrying an empty tray. "Mr. Gallagher. I'm so glad you're back. I was just bringing some of tonight's supper, like always."

"Thank you, Elaine." Ike placed a hand on the doorknob. "Let me go in first, explain what happened."

"That I found out my father has been hiding from me? Go ahead, warn him. That's more than anyone did for me." Reeling from the shock, Blanche knew she sounded bitter.

Ike offered an apologetic smile before slipping around the door. The wait felt like an eternity, but it couldn't have been more than five minutes before he reappeared. "He's expecting you."

"Do you want me—"

Blanche forestalled Effie's question. "No, I want to be alone with him." When neither one moved, she added, "I can find my way back." Turning her back on them, she opened the door and paused. What would she discover inside? Her heart welled up in a single-word prayer. *Help.*

For a room awash in lantern light, Blanche had a hard time making out the figure on the bed. Ginger-and-gray hair she had only ever seen in tufts beneath a hat. . .

"Cordelia. You've come back."

Old Obie's voice welcomed her into his cabin.

CHAPTER 21

B lanche's heart skipped beats. *It can't be.* Thump, thump. *Of course.* Thump, thump. *I always knew.*

"You." She reached his side in three quick steps, took a seat on a plain, straight-backed chair, and took his hands in hers.

"Can you forgive me, girl?" Old Obie's eyes searched hers.

"*You're* my father." Wonder filled Blanche's voice. She couldn't answer him. Not yet. "But my father's name is J.O. Lamar."

"Jedidiah Obadiah Lamar. My mama and pa were good, God-fearing folk." Old Obie chuckled. "But I've been Old Obie for more years than I can count."

Blanche noticed the envelope she had written to Old Obie tucked under the edge of his lamp. No wonder Effie wouldn't tell her his real name. Doing so would have revealed their closely guarded precious secret.

Old Obie followed the direction of her gaze. "I've memorized your letter, word for word. In it, you said I'd become like a father to you." He looked away, down the length of the bed, to where he kicked at his covers. "I hope learning I'm your father for real isn't too big of a disappointment."

Blanche stared at her feet. "I meant what I said." She forced herself to meet his eyes. "But I can't connect the man who was teaching me all about life on the river with a father who would lie to me. Deny our relationship."

"My dear girl."

Blanche gritted her teeth. She wasn't his girl, dear or otherwise.

"I have never denied you. I had no way of knowing what Cordelia had told you about me. I hoped, you see, that if you liked Old Obie the pilot, you might be able to like Captain J.O. Lamar, your father." He locked his fingers together and stretched his arms in front of him. "I guess I got what I deserved, not telling you up front."

Blanche studied the light and shadows on his face. She had dreamed of meeting her father all of her life, and now that she had, she didn't know what to think. The man before her was complex, contradictory, charming, and irresponsible, all at the same time. "I don't know how I feel about things. Not yet." She leaned forward and took his right hand. "But I do know I care about you, whether I call you Old Obie or. . .Father." With her other hand, she brushed his hair away from his eyes. "I think a part of me knew as soon as I saw your hair. I just didn't want to admit it."

"A halo of fire around your head." Old Obie reached up and pulled down a tendril from her hair. "I was ridiculously pleased that a part of you took after me, and worried that you would make the connection." His eyes drifted shut.

"I've tired you too much." Worry thundered through Blanche.

Old Obie opened his eyes a slit. "I like having you here. I have a lot to tell you—" his eyelids fluttered shut again—"as soon as I sleep a little while."

"Don't worry. I won't go anywhere, as long as you want me here." She had spoken to herself more than to him, but he squeezed her fingers. They sat there, hand in hand, while he drifted back to sleep.

Should I let him sleep? Blanche had some idea that people knocked unconscious should stay awake. But the doctor hadn't said anything, and her—father—was clearly alive. His head thrashing back and forth, he muttered unintelligible words.

At last she had learned the truth about her father. Part of her oscillated between fear and disbelief. But the biggest part of her rejoiced, head over heels happy to learn Old Obie was her father.

The way he was thrashing about couldn't be good for him. Blanche thought of fractious infants she had cared for on occasion. Singing while she rocked them helped. She couldn't rock her father but she could sing. She began with Christmas carols.

At the end of "Away in a Manger" mumbled words continued to stream from his lips. After "Joy to the World," his words had changed to an occasional groan. They died away to soft snores when she finished the final verse of "Silent Night."

Advent onboard ship might not resemble the Christmas traditions she had grown up with, but how would they celebrate the birth of the Lord Jesus? And what brought her to thinking so far ahead? She wouldn't be on the *Cordelia* in December. Would she?

The answer depended on the man lying beside her. She tapped her fingers against his palm, sending up a confused prayer. Thanksgiving and prayers for his salvation warred with anger and questions about why God let things work out this way.

<hr />

"They're both sound asleep." Effie closed the door quietly behind her. "I would take over so she could go to our cabin, but she is sleeping so peacefully I hate to disturb her."

"She'll wake up with a crick in her neck." Ike spoke from experience, from the times he had fallen asleep in his chair after a particularly long night.

"And joy in her heart. We should have told her a long time ago." Effie sighed. "I'll bring something down from the dining room in case she gets hungry later."

"Good idea. I'll be here, waiting." Keeping watch by the door for the night seemed like the least he could do. The two of them had tangled his heart and soul. He had no illusions. If Old Obie died, Blanche would leave the *Cordelia* at the next town.

He banged his head against the hallway wall just as Effie reappeared. Her steps sped up. "Is everything all right?"

"As far as I know."

She whisked open the door, and Ike followed behind. Blanche's halo of red hair was splayed across the coverlet on the bed, her hand still entwined with Old Obie's. He was going to check for a pulse, but he saw the coverlet rise and fall. "They look peaceful."

Effie lifted her fingers to her lips and opened the door. "I'll be out in a moment," he whispered. Bending over, he listened for Old Obie's breathing. It was even, relaxed—none of the signs the doctor had warned him about. His eyes strayed to Blanche. Faint blue lines showed in her neck and on the back of her hands. From this new angle, she was even more beautiful.

He pushed himself up and left the room before he got any more notions about Blanche.

He left the room, to find Effie waiting in the hall, a plate in her hand. She handed him a thick roast beef sandwich with a slab of apple pie. "You didn't eat much supper."

"This would be even better with a glass of milk." Ike's smile showed in his voice.

"Like this?" Effie brought her right hand out from behind her back. "As long as we can share it. I brought a couple of cookies for myself."

Ike leaned against the wall and took a bite. Thick, juicy. He devoured the rest in short order.

"I wish we had told her a long time ago." Effie nibbled on her cookie. "I wanted to. Her faith in God is so real. I wonder what this will do to her. I've been thinking about the decision I made myself, so many years ago."

The juice in the sandwich turned to dust in Ike's mouth. "Are you a Christian now?"

"I guess. . .I always have been, according to Blanche. I hope she can forgive me for not telling her." Shaking her head, she yawned.

"Go get some sleep. There is no reason for us all to lose a good night's rest."

Effie's face crumpled and she set down the glass. "He's been a father to me, too."

Ike gathered her next to him and let his tears join hers. After the sobs stopped, he held her in a loose embrace. "Old Obie will be okay. He has to be." He flashed back to the day their parents had been injured, when they were waiting for news. He had said the same thing back then, but their parents still had died.

"No one lives forever, Ike." Pushing her hands against his chest, Effie put distance between them. "I will go to my cabin, although I doubt if I'll sleep. You will let me know if anything changes?"

"Of course. Let me walk you back." After Effie turned in, Ike continued to the dining salon and grabbed a chair. Furniture was preferable to sitting on the floor. He unbuttoned the top few buttons on his shirt, removed his jacket, tossed it on his bed on the way past, and headed back to Old Obie's cabin.

When he arrived back at the door to Old Obie's cabin, he heard soft murmurs from inside. Part of him wanted to open the door, to sit with the man who had been like a father to him for most of his life, to offer and receive strength. But that would be selfish. Father and daughter needed time alone together, time that might be limited.

Leaning his head against the hallway wall, Ike could hear the tone of the conversation, every now and then a word discernible. Several times he thought he heard "Cordelia," although he didn't know if they were discussing the boat or Blanche's mother. Laughter followed tears.

Their conversation was none of his business, but he couldn't shut his ears so he wouldn't hear. When the chair proved no more comfortable than the floor would have been, Ike gave up his vigil and went up to the deck. He rolled up the arms of his shirt and let the evening breeze cool his arms and neck.

With Old Obie ill, responsibility for the *Cordelia* fell on Ike. They couldn't afford to stay in Brownsville for too long. Every day the boat remained in port, they lost money. Old Obie would tell him to go, to take care of business, not to let sentimentality overrule business sense. But even if he was willing to leave Old Obie in Brownsville, the loss of their primary pilot would hamper their progress. Once they left Brownsville, they might not return for three weeks.

A lot could happen in three weeks. Staring at the waterline reminded him that life streamed by like the boat rippling down the river. The moon's reflection drew Ike's gaze to the sky. He opened his mouth to howl, but instead he said, "Oh, God. Help us."

God. If God controlled man's life from birth to death, then Ike was talking to the right person. He had never doubted God's existence; God just never seemed relevant to his everyday life.

"From what Blanche says, You're not too pleased with the way I've lived my life. But I'm not asking for me. I'm asking for Old Obie. He gave us a home when we needed one. And I'm asking for Blanche. And I know You must care about her. She certainly brags on You all the time. So please make our stubborn old captain better."

He remained on deck awhile longer, staring up at the sky, unsure what he was expecting. For God to thunder back an answer? For Old Obie to jump out of bed and run upstairs?

Nothing happened. Wind ruffled through his shirt, bringing some comfort. After an hour, he returned to his station by the door. The pillow he used as a headrest muffled the murmurings still emanating from the cabin. With a calmer spirit than an hour earlier, he fell into a light sleep.

"It was love at first sight." Obie drew out precious memories that he should have shared with Blanche as soon as they met. "On both sides." He dipped his spoon into the soup they had found when they awakened.

"What made you fall in love with Mother?" It was obvious that Blanche hungered for every detail he could provide.

"She was so beautiful, with that halo of dark hair and long, slender fingers that I wanted to kiss one at a time. Her brown eyes revealed the warmth she hid behind her severe exterior." He sighed. "She was as beautiful on the inside as on the outside. I learned that as we spent our days together. One long, amazing week in Roma."

Blanche chewed her sandwich, eyes wide.

"You are probably wondering why she fell in love with me." Obie shrugged, and the blanket slid down his chest. "I don't know. I had never met anyone like her before, but I like to think it was more than that."

Blanche's eyes misted over. "I can think of some qualities she might have loved."

"And what might those be?" With each spoonful of soup, he felt stronger. "She didn't tell you much about me, did she?"

Blanche shook her head. "But I know what I've seen for myself. You are kind and generous, and you know how to bring out the best in people." She took a deep breath. "I never thought I could pilot a boat, but you made it easy for me to learn." She averted her gaze, picking at her food.

"You have a knack for it."

The conversation continued between them, flowing gently. Obie told her about his family, all of them dead. "I'm sorry. I know you were hoping to find family."

She told him about some of her best childhood memories. So far they had avoided the topic that had driven a loving couple apart. He knew she would bring it up eventually.

After she chased the last crumb of the piecrust from her plate, Blanche cleared her throat, and he knew what was coming.

"You say your parents were church people. They gave you two biblical names."

"They made sure I knew about it. Jedidiah was another name for King Solomon. And Obadiah was a book in the Bible. It was so short they made me memorize it once upon a time."

"Can you still remember it?"

"Bits and pieces. I remember something about fire. . ." Obie closed his eyes, searching old memories. Then he looked at her. " 'And the house of Jacob shall be a fire, and the house of Joseph a flame, and the house of Esau for stubble, and they shall kindle in them, and devour them.' I dreamed about all that fire." He chuckled.

"Do you believe in God? In the Bible?"

Obie didn't have a problem answering that question. "Of course. Only a fool doesn't believe in God."

"But have you asked Jesus to be your Savior?"

There. She'd asked the question. It hung between them.

Now Obie hesitated. "I always intended to. But I figured I had plenty of time. I wanted to enjoy my life first. Then I drove your mother away, the best woman to walk God's green earth." He closed his eyes to block the pain. "It's too late for an old sinner like me."

CHAPTER 22

Blanche couldn't speak for a moment. Tears clogged her throat. She sipped her tea to moisten her mouth, all the while shaking her head. "It's never too late. Not as long as you are alive and breathing."

"Figured you'd say that." He set aside his pie, only half-eaten. "But I know what I know. I've spent a lifetime saying no to God, I'm not going to be a hypocrite and ask Him to save me now."

A tear rolled down Blanche's cheek, and she turned her head so he wouldn't see.

"Ah, sweetheart, don't feel bad for me. Having you in my life is more of a blessing than I had any right to expect. I've had a good life, and meeting you, why, that's the frosting on the cake."

Blanche couldn't stop her tears. "I'll pray that you see the truth."

He patted her hand. "And now, if you don't mind, it's late at night for this old man. I want to rest." He closed his eyes. Blanche waited, praying, while her father slipped into sleep. When he began gently snoring, she planted a kiss on his forehead. At peace, she decided to set the half-eaten tray of food outside the cabin and try to sleep. When she opened the door, she found Ike in a chair, his head slammed back against a pillow, arms crossed. Whiskers darkened his cheeks. With his shirt unbuttoned at the neck, no suit jacket, and sleeves rolled up, he looked almost. . .heroic.

She wanted to hold on to her anger for not telling her the truth about her father, but how could she when he guarded the door like a knight of old? Laying the tray on the floor, she found an extra blanket and tucked it around Ike's shoulders. Back inside her father's room, she fell asleep as soon as she closed her eyes.

⁂

When Ike woke up in the morning, someone had covered him with a blanket. Blanche? What a homey, motherly touch. He shrugged off the good feeling that gave him. He didn't need a mother.

The breakfast bell sounded as he pulled out his pocket watch. Everyone would want an update on Old Obie's condition. He knocked on the door, and when no one answered, he turned the doorknob and entered. Blanche's hair was splayed across the white coverlet. He forced his gaze away from the display and watched Old Obie's chest rise and fall. His mouth hung open, and his breath rasped a little. His color concerned Ike; he'd check on him again after breakfast and see if anything had changed.

He allowed himself to look at Blanche again. With the blanket she had given to him, he returned the favor, easing it across her back. His fingers tingled where they skimmed her neck.

The bell sounded again, and he jerked his hand away. He had dallied long enough. Smithers arched an eyebrow when Ike strolled into the dining room, but no one else commented on his late arrival. The headwaiter brought him a plate piled high with all kinds of good food; Elaine must have poured her worries into her cooking.

"How is he?" Effie's drawn face showed the aftereffects of a sleepless night.

"I'm not sure." Ike grimaced. He brought a cup of coffee to

his lips, swallowing the scalding liquid down without a qualm. "Give me a few minutes to eat, and I'll tell the crew. Then I want you to come with me, to check on him."

"Why? What's wrong?"

People turned in their direction at the sound of her raised voice, and she lowered her head. "What happened?"

"I didn't like the way he looked." Ike forced himself to take a few bites and then stood.

The room fell silent.

"Captain Lamar survived the night. As far as I can tell, he spent the night comfortably. He was still asleep when I came downstairs," Ike announced.

Question marks formed on the faces circled around him. He held up a hand. "That's all I know. At this point, I am uncertain when we will leave Brownsville. Until then, continue your regular work schedule."

As the workers filed out, Ike sought out Smithers. "Go ahead about your duties. I'll take care of my dishes."

Smithers nodded and withdrew.

Ike stopped by the serving window. "If you prepare a tray for the captain and Miss Lamar, I'll take the food to them."

"The poor dears." Elaine whisked around, creating a masterpiece of appearance and taste.

Effie waited with Ike while Elaine put the platter together. As she finished, the door burst open.

Blanche stopped as soon as she spotted them. "Come quick. He's taken a turn for the worse."

CHAPTER 23

I ke leapt to his feet, Effie at his elbow. "Is he—" He stopped shy of the dreaded word.

"No." The word exploded from Blanche's mouth. "But he sounds like he's having trouble breathing." Tears pooled in her eyes. "He sounds like Mother did before she died."

Effie let out a strangled cry.

"I'll send for the doctor." With the call to action, Ike felt an icy calm descend on him. "You stay here and grab a bite to eat while Effie goes with the captain."

"But—"

"Five minutes one way or the other isn't going to matter. And if anything at all happens, I'll send someone right away."

When Blanche repeated her protest, Effie stood her ground. "This would be a good time for that prayer you're so fond of."

"Prayer isn't a genie's bottle that you can use to demand whatever you want." Blanche looked sick to her stomach as she stared at the pile of fluffy eggs in front of her. She dug her fork in and brought it to her mouth. "Go on," Ike urged.

Effie headed in the direction of Old Obie's cabin, her white cane tapping the way down the familiar route of the corridor. Ike ran down the gangway to find a porter on the wharves.

"I need to get a message to Dr. Foster. Do you know where his office is?"

The man nodded, and Ike gave him enough money to take a cab. "Ask him to come as quickly as possible. Captain Lamar has taken a turn for the worse."

With that business taken care of, he raced back to the *Cordelia*. He headed for the stairs. He met with Blanche as she was leaving the dining room. "I've sent someone to fetch the doctor and bring him right back."

"Good." She had bitten her lips until red beaded on her flesh. She moved so quickly that he had to hustle to catch up. If she had the freedom of movement of men's trousers, she would have traipsed down the stairs two at a time. As it was, her feet sped down the stairs with the lightness of ballet slippers. His feet hammered the steps loud enough to wake anyone still attempting to sleep.

A handful of the crew had gathered outside the door, keeping a silent vigil. "Mr. Gallagher. Miss Lamar," the head engineer addressed them. "I thought we would stay here, in case you needed help."

Blanche cleared her throat. "That's a kindly thought, Mr. MacDonald. One of you should remain on deck and bring the doctor down when he arrives."

"I'll go up." One of the waiters disappeared in the direction of the stairwell.

Ike opened the door and motioned for Blanche to enter first.

"I bet that's them now." Effie looked up as she heard them enter the room.

Old Obie lay on a pile of pillows that failed in its purpose of easing his breathing. He burst into a fit of coughing.

"Papa." Blanche dashed forward. "You should be sleeping."

"Don't have time to sleep. There are things that need saying." Old Obie speared Ike with his gaze. "I'll have a minute with you then I want to be alone with my daughter." Renewed coughing made Ike wonder how he could speak. "Sorry, Blanche, but I need you to go out for just a few minutes."

Effie took Blanche by the elbow and led her out. As the door closed behind them, the color drained from Old Obie's face, and he collapsed against the pillow in a coughing fit. Ike darted to his side.

Old Obie waved him back. "I'm not long for this world."

"Don't be foolish. Dr. Foster will be here in a few minutes. He'll fix you up with a snap of his fingers."

The captain frowned at him. "Don't lie to me, young man. You can fool a lot of other people, but not me. Now, listen up."

He coughed again, and helplessness burned through Ike. Wordlessly, he handed him a clean handkerchief. When the captain used it to swipe his mouth, it came away filled with phlegm.

"There are two things I've done right in my life. Maybe three. One was taking you and Effie in when you were children. You think it was an act of kindness, but I'm the one who was blessed with two children who brought me so much joy."

Ike swallowed past the lump in his throat and coughed. "Let's call us even then. You've given us far more than we could ever repay."

Old Obie patted his hand, his fingers barely tapping his skin. "You're a good man. The son I never had." He dropped his hand. "Then there's the *Cordelia*. She's a good ship, and I'm proud of her time on the river." A slight tinge of color came back into his cheeks. "And now there's Blanche. I'm a proud old cuss, and I'm prouder of her than anything else." A sigh brought on another fit of coughing. "But now that's another burden on my conscience. I hoped for more time with her, but such is not to be. I need you to promise me something."

"Anything. You just need to ask." Ike dredged a smile from the depths of his grief. "And if it's for Blanche, you don't have to ask."

This time, Old Obie's cough came out as a watery laugh. "Like that, is it? I figured as much. And you have my blessing, you know that, don't you?"

Relieved, Ike nodded.

"She won't want your help, you know. She'll fight you. But

I figure that with her moral backbone and your business sense, you stand a good chance of keeping the *Cordelia* in business for a while longer. That's the only legacy I have to leave her, and I want it to last as long as possible."

"Your legacy is much more than that."

"I'm counting on you to tell her my story." Old Obie struggled back to a sitting position, cleared his mouth another time with the handkerchief, and smoothed the coverlet across his legs. "Now, go out there and send my girl in."

"Yes, sir." Ike laid a hand on Old Obie's shoulder. "I'll do everything in my power."

"I'm counting on it."

<hr />

Blanche jumped to her feet as soon as Ike opened the door. She placed her hand on the doorknob, but Ike stood in her way.

"He loves you, you know. Don't be too hard on him for not telling you the truth earlier."

Blanche's mind blanked, and she blinked her eyes. "I know that." She paused at the entrance. "Send in the doctor as soon as he gets here."

"Of course."

She brushed past Ike in the tight confines of the entrance and closed the door.

"My girl." Old Obie had combed his hair, and a smile wreathed his face. "You don't know what joy you have brought to my life. I wish we could have had more time together."

"And we will." He looked so much better that she could almost believe it. Until he coughed again, a cough that drew from the soles of his feet.

"Maybe we will. But just in case. . ." Coughs racked his chest.

Blanche couldn't hide her dismay. "The doctor should be here any time."

"Then let me talk before he gets here. First thing is, I know you have your doubts about Ike. But you need to give him a chance. He's a good man." His failing strength punctuated his words. "I wouldn't speak so plain, if I had more time. But I'd like to see you settled, and I don't know a better man than Ike Gallagher."

Ike. "He may be as good as you say, but he's not a Christian." The words brought tears to her eyes. *And neither are you.* "And I can't be interested in anyone who isn't a Christian."

"And that's the other thing." He glanced away, revealing deep lines at the corners of his eyes. "I've been thinking about what you said. You told me it's never too late. Do you have any reason for thinking that way, besides wishing it was so?"

The heaviness in Blanche's heart lifted. "Oh Papa." A smile, bright enough to light the dark cabin, burst on her face. "You don't know how long I've wanted to hear you say that." She realized she had betrayed herself, in the best possible way, of course. "Yes, Papa. I've always known God is my heavenly Father, but now He has given me back my earthly father. If nothing else told me God loves both of us—that does." Even if she could stem the tears flooding her eyes, she wouldn't. They were happy tears, tears of rejoicing and love.

"Ah, darlin'." Tears glistened in his eyes. "Of course God loves you. It's me I'm wondering about."

"But our meeting again was God's gift to you, as well as me. But your question. All kinds of people came to our church and gave testimonies of the lives they lived before the Lord saved them. They did some awful things. But they claimed the promise that God will save everyone who calls upon His name."

Papa shook his head. "I don't want to disillusion you, but I've heard some of those stories, too. The same men went straight from church to the nearest saloon and bellied up to the bar and ordered a round of whiskey."

Lord, give me the right words. "I'm so sorry to hear that. Not entirely surprised. Some of the men said they slid back into their old ways, two, three, even half a dozen times, before they stayed on the straight and narrow."

A glance at her father's face told her that he didn't entirely believe it, but she went on. "Then there's the stories in the Bible. The man who was crucified next to Jesus was a thief and a murderer, sentenced to death—and Jesus promised, 'Today shalt thou be with me in paradise.' He's the only one I know of who became a Christian right at the end, but there are others who did all kinds of bad things. Both Moses and King David killed a man, Paul hunted down Christians, Peter denied the Lord." She paused long enough to draw a deep breath.

"Add another talent to the list of things I'm discovering about you. You're a preacher."

A woman preacher? She laughed at the thought. "I guess Jesus said it best. 'They that be whole need not a physician, but they that are sick.'"

"That makes sense. I haven't gone near a doctor in years. Why pay out good money when you're feeling okay and listen to him tell you how you ought to change your ways if you want to stay well?" He coughed again. "I guess that's how I've treated God."

"Think about how quick the doctor came when Ike called him yesterday. God doesn't even have to run. He's standing at the door to your heart, knocking. Waiting for you to let Him in."

"Is it really as simple as that?"

"It is." Blanche suspected her eyes were shining, between excitement and tears. " 'For whosoever shall call upon the name of the Lord shall be saved.'"

Blanche's heart leapt, certain her mother rejoiced with her as Jedidiah Obadiah Lamar at last returned to the God he had spurned for so long.

Ike paced up and down the hallway. What was taking the doctor so long? Every turn or two he paused by the door, listening to the soft murmurs of conversation. However short their time together was, Ike was glad to the soles of his feet that Old Obie and Blanche had found each other.

As still as Ike was nervous, Effie sat in the chair Ike had slept in, plying her knitting needles. Only an occasional tremor in her shoulders hinted at her distress. Her needles stopped clicking, and Ike stopped his pacing. "He's here."

Running to the bottom of the steps, Ike saw the doctor taking the stairs at a good clip. "You made it."

"I was setting a broken leg when the messenger came in. What has happened?"

Effie turned those uncomfortable, sightless eyes in his direction. "It's his breathing. He's coughing. It sounds like his lungs."

A frown creased the doctor's face. "I'm sorry to hear that." Pausing at the door, he inclined his ear to listen. "Who's in there with him?"

"Blanche. His daughter."

"Why don't you wait with her while I examine the captain." After knocking, he opened the door, Ike following behind.

Blanche held Old Obie's hand, softly singing "Amazing Grace." The old man's eyes were closed, a smile on his face, a harsh rattling sound emanating from his chest chasing it away every now and then.

She stopped abruptly in midverse. "Dr. Foster, I'm so glad you're here."

Old Obie's eyes flew open. "Back here to disturb a sick man, doctor?"

"Come with me." Ike put an arm around Blanche's shoulders as if it was the most natural thing in the world and led her out of the cabin. She collapsed against his chest, so that he supported her weight. Every instinct in him wanted to shield her from this pain. She felt as fragile as a butterfly's wing in his arms.

Effie stood outside the door, her knitting returned to its bag. "I could use a cup of tea about now."

"Coffee for me." Blanche took the seat that Effie had abandoned. "I need all my wits about me."

"Come with us."

People usually obeyed when Effie used that no-nonsense voice, but Blanche remained seated. "I want to be here when the doctor comes out."

"You heard what the lady said. Do you mind asking Elaine to send down coffee and muffins?" He wasn't hungry, but he hoped he could get Blanche to eat something.

Effie gathered her skirts and straightened her back. "We'll fix up a tray. I'll be back in a few minutes. I hope to see Old Obie after the doctor leaves." Her voice came close to breaking.

Neither Blanche nor Ike spoke as her soft footfalls headed up the steps.

"I've been selfish, keeping him all to myself." Blanche spoke in a low voice. "He's like a father to both of you."

"No, I understand. And so does Effie. We're already provided for. I'm sure he wants to do the same for you."

"Yes." She took a shaky breath. "God will provide for me, but I've stopped guessing what form that will take."

CHAPTER 24

Ike leaned against the wall opposite Blanche, his eyes trained on the floor, his ears straining for every sound coming through the door. Within a few minutes, Effie returned. She set a food-laden tray on the floor and joined Ike at the wall. The next time the door cracked, Blanche jumped to her feet and Ike and Effie took a step forward.

The somber expression on the doctor's face told Ike everything he needed to know even before he shook his head. "There is nothing I can do. Keep him comfortable. I've left some laudanum, but I doubt he'll take it. Says he can't afford to waste whatever time he has left."

Effie shuffled forward. "Can I go in to see him?"

"Of course."

Blanche trailed behind the doctor while Effie went into the cabin. Ike looked at Effie, then at Blanche. Which one?

"Stay with Effie. I'll be all right," Blanche called over her shoulder. "She needs you now more than ever." Accepting the doctor's arm, she disappeared from view.

When Ike opened the door, Effie sat next to Old Obie on the bed, holding him in a sitting position, her head leaning on his shoulder. ". . .made her happy." A small laugh escaped through her tears.

"Mind if I join you?"

Effie's head tilted in the direction of his voice. "Come in."

He took the seat beside the bed, the same one Blanche had occupied through the night.

"You know where the papers are?" Old Obie's voice held a small bit of his old strength.

Ike knew what papers he meant. "Yes."

Old Obie nodded. "I've made some changes, though. You'll have to see Carver to learn what's up."

"Don't talk like that." Effie raised her head from his shoulder. "You and Blanche have years ahead of you."

"We don't know, do we?"

Something had changed. Old Obie's voice didn't sound so much stronger as more resolved. "Now that I've made things right with God, I'm ready to go, if it's my time. I don't want you feeling bad on my account."

Made things right with God? The words tripped in Ike's mind.

"Don't look so shocked, son." A ghost of Old Obie's smile returned. "I never doubted the truth of the Gospel. And this little accident has shown me that I need God after all. If you're as smart as I think you are, you won't wait as long as I did to recognize the fact." A fit of coughing interrupted any further talk.

"Take the laudanum. It will ease your cough." Ike picked up the bottle from the nightstand.

Old Obie shook his head. "It'll put me to sleep." He winked. "I want to enjoy every minute I have left."

Refusing Elaine's insistence that she take a short rest in her cabin, Blanche balanced a tray with a bowl of chicken and dumplings on her arms. "It's his favorite comfort food. Maybe I can convince him to take a few bites."

The savory smell teased Blanche's nostrils, and her stomach grumbled. Maybe if she ate a bite, she would encourage her father to eat as well. When she entered the cabin, he was chatting with Ike and Effie as if it was an ordinary day.

"Come in. We were just talking about the day Ike jumped into the river from the deck. Scared us all half to death, he did."

"I got wet, that was all." Ike shrugged. "At least I knew how to swim."

"It was the middle of the winter. And you caught a cold." Her father's voice held a teasing note.

"And here I thought you were proud of my little escapade."

Ike's laughter sounded more forced than her father's.

"Elaine sent food for all of us." Propping the door open, Blanche set down a tray filled with chicken and dumplings, chicken salad sandwiches, tea, and cookies, and then took the seat Ike offered. "Now, eat up. Your cook scares me. I don't want to report that you refused her food." She lifted half the sandwich to her mouth and took a bite. While she chewed, she dipped the soup spoon into the bowl and extracted a single dumpling. Eyes twinkling, Old Obie opened his mouth. He seemed to have trouble chewing, so for the next spoonful, she offered broth only. That went down more easily. By the time they finished, she had eaten half a sandwich and most of the broth in the bowl was gone.

"That's enough." Old Obie settled back against the pillow. A little bit of color had returned to his face, and Blanche allowed a small beacon of hope to arise in her heart. Then she reminded herself what the doctor had said: a day, two at the most, more likely less.

Ike disappeared through the door and returned with an extra chair. Effie shifted from the bed to the chair, smoothing the spot where she had sat. Blanche's fingers itched to smooth the hair back from her father's brow, to offer the comfort Effie did, but Old Obie was as much Effie's father as he was hers. Ike took a seat on a weathered sea chest, his long legs folded in front of him.

Effie and Ike kept up the reminiscences. . .escapades that Effie shared in equal measure with her brother. . .while her father added an occasional grunt or comment. The longer they talked, the less he contributed, his eyes closing for brief spells in between coughs. A westerly sun burned through the porthole when his eyes sought out Blanche. She knelt on the floor beside his bed. "What do you want, Papa?"

Across the bed from her, Ike's eyebrows lifted and he smiled at the word.

"I want to hear you sing. Some of those hymns you're so fond of." The words that only a day ago might have sounded like a reproach now rang with bell-like clarity in her ears. "Sing Christmas carols. Those are my favorites."

"Mine, too." Blanche cleared her throat then in a low voice began "Silent Night." Effie's hands moved across her lap as if she was playing along on the piano. Blanche jumbled some of the verses together, but no one seemed to care. Her father's breathing eased.

As the last note faded, he opened his eyes. Struggling to a seated position so that he could see all three of them, he speared each of them with his gaze in turn. "I don't want you to feel bad for me. I am ready to go. God, in His mercy, reunited me with my daughter and restored me to Himself. You are my family. Take care of each other."

The speech sapped his energy, and he collapsed back on the pillow. "Stay with me. Please." The words came out as a whisper.

"You don't have to ask." Blanche pressed his hand. "Do you want me to sing some more?"

At her father's nod, she held his hand and sang as the songs occurred to her, from Christmas carols to Stephen Foster ballads to gospel songs. His breathing rasped, and slowed down. While she sang "Lead, Kindly Light," his fingers relaxed in her grip.

Silence descended, no one moving. Blanche locked eyes with Ike, and he pushed himself up from his sitting position. He leaned over the bed, placed his hand over her father's nose and mouth, and then felt at the side of his neck for a pulse. Shaking his head, he said, "He's gone."

Effie sobbed, tears falling from eyes that peered not into their faces but into their souls. Tears clustered in Blanche's eyes, but she didn't cry. Her mouth dried. She couldn't speak or cry.

How could God take both of her parents from her in such a short time? Wordlessly, she stood to her feet.

Ike pulled her close to his side, his chest heaving with grief. "It's time you rested."

Blanche found her voice. "Join me, Effie."

"But someone needs to... I need to—"

"I'll take care of it." Ike helped his sister to her feet. With his arms supporting both women, they left the cabin.

Blanche had had to handle all the details of her mother's death by herself. She tried to dredge up gratitude for Ike's strong presence, but all she felt was grief.

***

"Ashes to ashes, dust to dust." The pastor of the local community church spoke the familiar words.

Ike knew the pastor from other funerals. Old Obie wasn't the first person to die aboard the *Cordelia*, and his funeral wasn't the first one he had arranged. Because of his parents' deaths, Ike had experienced death from a young age. But aside from his mother and father, whom he had loved with a child's simplicity and intensity, he had never lost someone he loved until now.

He opened his mind, etching every detail of the funeral on his memory. A good-sized congregation, including all the *Cordelia*'s crew and many local businessmen, attended. Others might have come in after Ike took his seat at the front with Effie and Blanche. She had insisted that they join her as members of Old Obie's immediate family.

The pastor adjusted his glasses on his nose and glanced at the notes he had made. Blanche stared straight ahead, while Effie held a handkerchief to her eyes. The preacher cleared his throat. "In addition to being a well-respected businessman of the river trade, Captain Lamar was blessed to find his long-lost daughter in the last few weeks of his life."

At those words, Blanche's reserve broke, and a single tear rolled down her cheek. Ike ached to place his arm around her shoulders, but this wasn't the time or the place for such familiarity.

The pastor continued. "He is survived by his daughter,

Blanche Lamar, and by his two adopted children, Isaac and Effie Gallagher."

Blanche had also insisted on their inclusion in the obituary.

"In recent days, Captain Lamar made peace with God. Even as we gather here to mourn his passing, he is in the place where God has wiped all tears from his eyes. If he were here, he would urge you not to mourn as those without hope. He would challenge you to find that same hope, of eternal life, that he at last embraced."

The words fell like a snake's venom and sank teeth into Ike's soul. The preacher's comments might bring comfort to others, but not to him. The Old Obie he had known and loved wasn't a religious man. And Ike resented the implication that he must become a Christian himself to honor the man who had been like a father to him. He closed his mind to the remainder of the sermon, only cuing back in when music emanated from the piano. Standing, he helped both women to their feet and walked behind them to the front where the casket lay.

Blanche trembled, and he tightened his hold on her, to make sure she didn't buckle at the knees. Effie's hand formed a fist.

Blanche noticed the movement as well. "He looks good. He's dressed in a navy blue suit, a handkerchief tucked in the pocket. They slicked his hair away from his face. I wish he had his cap on." Her voice cracked.

Feet shuffled behind them. "I'm sure he looks fine." Effie relaxed her hand. "Let's go."

In the basement, people streamed by. Everyone shared a memory of Old Obie's laughter, his sense of humor, a trip down the river, his solid business sense. After the first few, Ike gritted his teeth, wishing the well-wishers would leave them alone. How Blanche kept her composure, he didn't know. This scene must remind her of the loss of her mother, only a few weeks ago.

One man lingered at the end of the line, waiting to speak with them—Carver, the lawyer. At length he approached and acknowledged Ike with a nod. After expressing his condolences, he mentioned that he was handling the captain's final affairs. "Shall I join you aboard the *Cordelia* to go over the terms of the will, or do you want to come to my office?"

"The *Cordelia*—" Blanche began.

"Let's meet at your office," Ike interposed. He didn't want the crew speculating about the future until he heard from the lawyer. "The sooner, the better. We have already delayed our departure."

The lawyer shot him a sharp glance, and Ike wondered again how the future would change. What would he do, and where would he go, if he could no longer call the *Cordelia* home? More importantly, what would Effie do?

The lawyer turned his attention to Blanche. "Would tomorrow afternoon suit you?"

Blanche blinked. "But tomorrow is Sunday." She looked from Ike to the lawyer. "Do you normally do business on the Lord's Day, Mr. Carver?"

His eyebrows rose. "I thought you would prefer to take care of things before Monday."

Blanche glanced at Ike, and he nodded. "That would be best. Perhaps we can meet later this afternoon?"

They arranged to meet at half past two.

Ike didn't have much of an appetite, which was just as well as guests continued interrupting them to speak another kind word. Blanche ate even less than he did, mostly sipping sweet tea. Effie stared straight ahead without saying a word. Within half an hour, Blanche was yawning. Perhaps the last few days had caught up with her. Ike sought out the pastor. "This has been a difficult day for my sister and Miss Lamar. Is there a room where they can withdraw for a short time?"

The pastor led them next door to the parsonage. His wife invited the ladies to retire to one of the guest rooms before offering Ike a comfortable seat in the front parlor. The next thing he knew, the pastor was gently shaking his shoulder. "I hate to bother you, but you mentioned an appointment this afternoon?"

The grandfather clock rang two bells. Blanche came down the hall, looking somewhat refreshed from her brief rest. A smile had returned to Effie's face. "Thank you for giving us refuge. It has been a difficult few days."

"Churches have always offered sanctuary." The pastor's smile offered understanding. "We could do no less. I have hitched up my carriage, and I will take you to your appointment."

A couple of minutes before the half hour, they pulled up in front of a single-story building that housed three of the city's law offices. Ike assisted first Effie, then Blanche, out of the carriage.

"I'll wait out here," their host said. "It's a long walk back to the wharves."

———❖———

"Thank you." Blanche managed to get the word out. She took short breaths between biting on her lower lip to keep panic from setting in full force. She had lived a lifetime since Ike had walked into Christ the King Church at her mother's funeral and turned her life upside down. In reality, only a month had passed.

God, give me strength and wisdom. She had already completed her first quest, finding her father. She had also found an unexpected family in Ike and Effie. However, her desire for a relationship with her father had been cut short. Soon she would know what provisions he had made for her in his will, if anything.

What if he'd left her penniless? Fighting the urge to pant, she accepted Ike's arm and walked up the steps to the office to learn her future.

CHAPTER 25

Blanche was surprised when Mr. Carver met them at the door himself. "Please pardon the informality. My clerk doesn't work on Saturdays. Would you care for a cup of coffee? A glass of cool water?" He gestured to a sideboard that held glasses and cups, together with a pitcher of cream and a sugar bowl. Blanche would have preferred tea, but she accepted a glass of water to keep her mouth moistened. As much coffee as she had drunk in the past few days, she was afraid she'd turn into a coffee bean if she drank more.

Only Ike was brave enough to take more coffee. Effie declined anything to drink. A few minutes later, they had taken their seats in Mr. Carver's office.

The lawyer turned his gaze on each of them in turn, a trick Blanche recognized from singing in public—make a connection with the members of the audience. The simple gesture helped her relax, prepared to hear what he had to say.

"I have had dealings with Mr. Gallagher in the past, and I have had the pleasure of meeting Miss Gallagher before. I looked forward to making your acquaintance, Miss Lamar, but I am sorry it is under these circumstances." He paused, took off his glasses, and wiped at his eyes.

Putting his glasses back on, he assumed a serious expression and opened a file in front of him. "Captain Lamar has always kept his affairs in good order. He came to me on Thursday instructing me to draw up a new will."

Effie let out a soft moan.

"So he came here on the day he had the accident." Ike spoke the words that were on all their minds.

"Yes."

Ike frowned. "So which will is in effect? The one he had previously drawn up or the one with changes?"

That's right, Ike knew the terms of the old will. The lawyer's announcement must be as unsettling for the brother and sister as for her.

"The new will is in effect. The captain always waited while we drew up whatever document he needed and had it witnessed. He didn't like to wait on the fortunes of the river for his legal matters."

Ike sat back straight in the chair, eyes intent on the lawyer, but he didn't speak.

"He said he had recently had a change in family circumstances. He was delighted to have you in his life again, Miss Lamar, and wanted to be sure you were provided for."

The tears Blanche had held at bay for the morning welled up and tumbled out. *This isn't the time or place. What must this lawyer think of me?* But no amount of self-criticism stopped her tears. She pressed the handkerchief she had tucked into her pocket to her eyes. No one spoke. Effie placed a hand on Blanche's arm while Ike rested his hand on her shoulder.

She drew in a shaky breath. Wordlessly, Ike handed her a fresh handkerchief. Nodding, she gave the others a smile. "I believe I'm ready to go on."

"Are you sure you don't want to come back another time?" Mr. Carver leaned back in his chair, not rushing her, open to whatever happened.

"No. I'm ready to listen. We can't make any plans until we know where we stand." She wiped the last of the traces of tears from her face and crumpled the handkerchief in her lap. She focused on the diploma behind the lawyer's head, testifying to the successful completion of his college studies at the University of Texas.

"I assume that the captain added his daughter to the will. How significant were the other changes?" Ike asked about the heart of the matter.

At Ike's query, the lawyer spread his hands. "Captain Lamar brought in the most recent financial information from Lamar Industries. The *Cordelia*, while still showing a profit, no longer brings in the money that it did when he first set sail. He wanted to be fair to everyone concerned."

Blanche's blood pounded in her ears. She didn't want any provision her father made for her to put others in jeopardy.

Ike nodded, but his face gave away none of his emotions.

"He left token amounts to all the employees who had worked for him for a minimum of a year. He also requested that every effort be made to retain any employees who choose to stay with the boat."

"Of course."

"He regretted that he didn't have more cash for the three of you. Most of his capital was tied up in the business. Of his cash, he left half to his daughter and the other fifty percent to be split between Isaac and Effie Gallagher." He named the amount. "It's not much, but the captain hoped it would help ease the transition."

Blanche sat back. Not much, perhaps. She wouldn't be rich. But it would provide a living, more than she had from her mother. "And the boat?" Her father's pride and joy.

A smile played around the lawyer's lips. "Here, Captain Lamar's wishes were a trifle unusual." He looked straight at Blanche. "The boat belongs to you, Miss Lamar. It was your father's wish that you study for a pilot's license. I questioned that direction, but he informed me that a lady pilot on the Mississippi recently accomplished the feat." His smile widened a fraction. "But the ownership comes with one important stipulation." He turned his attention to include Ike. "Miss

Lamar owns the *Cordelia* provided she leaves the running of day-to-day operations in Mr. Gallagher's hands, with a salary commensurate with his position. If this is a problem for either one of you, the *Cordelia* will be sold and the profit divided among the three of you."

Ike threw his head back and laughed. "The old salt."

Tilting her head, Blanche glanced at Ike. "Is this arrangement acceptable to you? It sounds like you will be doing the majority of the work while I control the money."

Ike shifted in the chair. "What about my sister?"

"Yes, what about me?" Effie spoke for the first time.

"She should have a salary for her work. She acts as hostess and she arranges entertainment." Blanche sounded like an owner already.

Ike opened his mouth about the entertainment then closed it. Blanche wouldn't welcome his comments.

"Oh, that's not necessary. The *Cordelia* has always been my home."

"It still will be your home, but that doesn't mean you should work for free." Blanche smiled. "No argument."

"You're sounding like the captain already." Ike put encouragement in his tone.

"Captain Blanche Lamar." Blanche's face lit up more than at any point all week. "I like the sound of that." Then she grew serious again, worry darkening her eyes to walnut brown. "But I do have one concern. I know you host games of chance for passengers in your room. I am willing to enter into this partnership only if you agree to end all gambling activity."

Ike ground his fists together, keeping a smile on his face. If he hesitated too long, she wouldn't believe anything he said. "I promise not to do anything that will bring trouble to the *Cordelia* or bring disgrace on the Lamar name."

Tiny wrinkles tented between her eyebrows. Ike held his breath. His promise didn't quite match her request. He admired Blanche with all his heart, but he couldn't work under the conditions she wanted to lay down. He extended his hand. "Are we partners?"

"Yes." A thin smile took away some of the wariness in her eyes. "We will work out the details as we go." She stared at his hand for a moment before accepting it. Her handshake was surprisingly firm, but nothing about Blanche shocked him anymore.

No one spoke much after that. Blanche spoke in monosyllables at the evening meal. The crew remained quiet, so still that Ike could hear the teapot whistling in the kitchen.

Blanche struggled to her feet to address the group. "I'm sure you have questions about the future. I don't have any answers for you tonight. I appreciate your patience while we figure things out." She placed a trembling hand on Ike's shoulder. "I am going to bed and hopefully sleep. Take things slow tomorrow. But first thing Monday morning, we'll get together and make plans for the trip back to Roma."

Old Obie's death had accomplished one important thing: Blanche would remain aboard the *Cordelia* for the foreseeable future. Whether the business would survive, he wouldn't risk a bet. His desire to take action, to get away from this city of death and mourning, to return to the business of riding the river and making money, chafed against Blanche's desire to spend an extra day in Brownsville—a Sunday, at that.

After a quiet evening—Ike couldn't name the last Saturday night he hadn't spent playing cards—he slept soundly, awakening shortly before breakfast. After a good night's rest, he had a better perspective on Blanche's day of forced inactivity. After all, she hadn't demanded everyone attend a worship service, and she hadn't said *he* couldn't work. His initiative should please her. He shook his head. No. She'd be happier if he sought out a church for Sunday morning worship.

Blanche didn't come to breakfast. Ike considered taking a tray to her cabin but decided against it. The earlier he left, the sooner he could finish his business in town. After sending a message to Ventura to meet him for lunch, he took the list of items that customers upriver needed and headed to the warehouse district. The greater the margin between what the cost of the purchase and the amount he was authorized to spend, the more profit Lamar Industries would make. He enjoyed the challenge of the hunt.

First up: fabrics. A seamstress in Roma had a specific request for silk taffeta. He knew the best sources.

Greg Palmer, a portly man, greeted him at the door. "Mr. Gallagher, I didn't know if we would see you on this trip. We were saddened to learn of Captain Lamar's passing."

After accepting the condolences, Ike waited while Palmer disappeared into the bowels of the warehouse to bring out the requested materials. Ike took advantage of the break to walk up and down the aisles, studying the variety of colors and textures and shine. He found himself measuring each bolt against how they would appear on Blanche. Materials that were practical, yet beautiful. Vibrant colors, but not ones that would shout out loud. She would look good even if she only had dark calicos in her wardrobe. Classy and classic, in other words.

He forced himself to walk the aisles a second time, thinking in terms of the shop owners along the river route. This warehouse carried everything needed for a well-dressed lady's wardrobe, from fabrics from around the world to sewing notions. To purchase other items requested by merchants in Roma, he would have to make several more stops.

The warehouse manager wheeled the bolts of materials to the center table. Ike examined them, looking for those minute imperfections that could bring about a reduced price. A water stain appeared on a tiny section of mustard-colored silk. *Perfect.* He haggled with the manager until they arrived at a price that was more than Ike wanted to pay, but less than he expected to.

"Thank you for doing business with Lamar Industries." Ike made arrangements for delivery of the materials. After he doffed his hat in a salute, he headed to the next warehouse.

Several hours later, Ike left the final warehouse, dust dirtying the light gray of his suit and grinding into the creases on his hands. Sweat had welded his hat to his head. Levi's would make more sense, but then he'd reduce himself to the level of the working man. Dressing as a man of means served to keep prices at a profitable level. He would enter the day's purchases in the account books this afternoon.

As he walked back in the direction of the *Cordelia,* a thought struck him. Perhaps Blanche would have preferred to shop with them. But Old Obie had left daily operations up to him, and shopping fell into that category, didn't it?

When he turned onto the wharf leading to the steamboat, the deck lacked its usual bustle. The Lady *Cordelia* looked sad, almost dead, lacking signs of life. Part of him hoped Blanche would be waiting for him at the railing, and he felt strangely empty at her absence.

Ike resisted the urge to wipe his grimy palms on his already dirtied suit. He would change, leave his clothes for Agatha, and head to the captain's quarters to update the books. Sunday's slower pace usually brought him pleasure, but today loneliness and grief weighed him down. The prospect of Sunday afternoons gathered around the kitchen table, replete with food his wife had prepared, their children gamboling around the table legs—that held appeal. Children with curly, flame-red hair and the captain's hazel eyes.

The *Cordelia'*s accounts should distract him from thoughts of marriage and family. He wished he could hand Blanche a fortune, not a business on the brink of failure.

Tomorrow Blanche was expecting a full accounting of the state of affairs with Lamar Industries. While entering the days' purchases, he realized no one had noted the goods delivered from upriver. He pawed through the papers on the desk and found everything except the receipt for the cotton. Chewing the end of his pencil, he studied the room, searching for spots where the receipts could have fallen. He poked around a few places but didn't find it.

Without a record of their largest delivery, the trip registered as a loss. Old Obie's death couldn't be considered a business expense, but that led to another question. Where did he keep track of his personal expenses?

So much needed to be done, starting with sorting through the things in Old Obie's cabin. He kept a room in Roma, but Ike couldn't do anything about that until they returned downriver. If possible, he would like to hire another pilot. Old Obie didn't entirely trust Pete at the helm, so Ike wouldn't either. The problem was, the best pilots were already employed or had retired.

Ike had promised Old Obie that he would make sure Blanche was provided for, and to help her obtain her pilot's license.

He had no idea how he would keep either promise.

CHAPTER 26

The hours on Sunday passed pleasantly. Blanche remained secluded in her cabin, refreshing body and soul. With her remaining sheets of stationery, she decided to record her short time with her father. Words spilled on page after page until she had filled front and back of each sheet. She wrote in the margin to finish the last sentence. Thoughts crowded to the front of her mind, wanting to find their way on paper. If there was time on Monday, she would buy more, or perhaps even a journal. She could think of so many things she wanted to say, things about her mother, even new things she had learned about herself.

Tears stained and blurred portions of almost every page, but by the end, her tears had dried.

The more she wrote, the more she realized how little she knew about her father. Despite her immersion in life aboard the *Cordelia* for the past two weeks, she remained so ignorant. She'd have to depend on Ike. Her father's insistence on his continued employment made total sense.

Blanche awoke on Monday morning refreshed, ready to make some preliminary decisions about her future. Her black suit needed laundering, so she set it aside for Dame Agatha. Instead, she reached for the deep purple dress her father had adored.

Effie turned over in her berth with a groan. "Would you like me to bring something back for you?" Blanche asked.

Effie flopped onto her back and yawned. "Maybe some toast and tea. I'm not all that hungry."

"I'll bring some." With honey and butter and jam and maybe some bananas and orange juice—anything to tempt Effie's taste buds. "I plan to meet with Ike about the business later this morning. I'd appreciate it if you could be there."

Effie's eyelids fluttered as if she were trying to see something through the curtain of her blindness. "I know very little about the business side of things. I wouldn't be any help."

Effie might not know dollars and cents, but she had her fingers on the pulse of the ship and crew. She would ask her opinion at a later time.

After a brief spell in front of the mirror, arranging her hair in a loose knot on top of her head, Blanche inched the door open. Smithers stood outside, his hand raised, ready to knock. "So you are joining us for breakfast." He sounded pleased.

"Yes."

"I will let Elaine know." He bowed and headed for the staircase.

Blanche followed. The floor undulated with minute dimensions, suggesting a wind was rustling the river beneath them. The first breakfast bell sounded, so she had time before beginning the day. She headed to the main deck. Wind whipped around the floorboards, whistling past the empty spaces where cargo had waited on the trip downriver. Voices called from the wharf, and she glanced at stevedores toting pallets to the ship. Somehow, business was continuing as usual.

The wind teased her hair out of the loose knot, but she was glad for the cooling breeze, not going downstairs until the final warning bell sounded. As she walked through the open door to the salon—quiet, without Effie's usual piano music—wide smiles broke out on several faces. A few brave souls applauded, but a frown from Smithers brought that to an end. Instead, he came forward to escort her to the captain's table. "It is good to see you this morning, Miss Lamar. We are most distressed about the captain's death."

Ike rose to his feet, and his smile helped ease the core of cold at her heart. When Elaine brought the food to the pass, everyone paused, waiting for the grace Blanche had instituted. If she tried to pray out loud, she doubted her voice would carry across the room.

Smithers—*Smithers?*—led in a simple, but effective prayer. The waiters brought out heaping platters. Elaine made a rare trip from the kitchen. "If there is anything special you wish to eat, just tell me and I will cook it for you."

Blanche shook her head, but Ike touched her arm. "Let her. She wants to help."

Blanche couldn't eat all the food already served, but she scrambled to think of something not on the table. "Maybe…some fried bananas? No, warm applesauce with cinnamon."

"Yes, Miss Lamar. I will get right to it." The cook's smile was as good as a bear hug.

No one had treated Blanche with such tender care in her entire life, not even after her mother died. She waited, expecting tears to well up and spill out of her eyes. But they didn't. Instead, tender gratitude held sway, filling her heart with peace. She'd like tea with cream and sugar. British-style, Mother used to call it. "Elaine?"

The cook appeared at the window in an instant. "Yes?"

"I would like to have a cup of hot tea. Do you have a cozy?"

"Yes, ma'am. Right away."

Soon Blanche heard a teakettle whistling merrily and her insides warmed. She'd know she was truly better when the ice-cold spot at the center of her heart melted. For now she couldn't seem to get warm. Grits, that might be good. She shook her head. She had already given Elaine plenty of extra work.

Ike offered her the basket of biscuits first, and she took one. They both reached for the gravy boat at the same time. He pulled his hand away, gesturing for her to take it first.

"I've never seen you take gravy on your biscuits." He spooned eggs onto his plate.

"It sounds good this morning."

Elaine appeared with a teapot encased in a crocheted cozy and poured Blanche's cup mostly full. "Do you want more?"

Blanche shook her head. "That's perfect." She handed the gravy boat to Ike and added a spoon of sugar to the tea, then enough cream to fill the cup.

After she ate her biscuit, her hunger returned, and she ate bacon and eggs. When she had finished, she could almost see her reflection. Her mother used to say that. The memory brought a smile to her lips.

Ike smiled back. "You were hungry."

Blanche stared at her empty plate. "I feel like I haven't eaten for a week."

"You haven't done more than pick at your food since the accident." Ike brought the cup of coffee to his lips. "I speak for everyone here when I say I'm glad your appetite has returned."

Blanche finished a dish of warm applesauce, then she settled back in her seat with a sigh.

"You know Effie better than I do. What will tempt her?" Blanche surveyed the choices.

"Biscuits." Ike wrapped the hot bread in a napkin inside the basket before adding butter and honey. "With sweet tea. I'll carry it for you." Together they headed down the stairs.

———※———

After delivering breakfast to Effie, Ike and Blanche returned to the salon. Logs and account books filled his arms; Blanche had to open the door. She brought pens and pencils, including a red one. Add "sensible and resourceful" to the list of qualities that described Blanche. His boss. He shook his head at the thought.

She poured herself a cup of coffee from the sideboard and added a dollop of cream. "I can't seem to stay warm this morning."

Summer heat bothered Ike as usual, but he nodded. "Do you want me to fetch a wrap from your cabin?"

"No, I'll be all right." She drank about half a cup, topped it off, and sat down at the table, keeping the cup away from the papers. "I was good with sums at school. I hope that will help."

Ike wondered if she intended to keep the account books now that she was the owner. Did that fall under daily operations? Or owner's prerogative? He wasn't ready to explain the special entertainment income.

He cocked his head at Blanche. "You've had a lot thrown at you at once. Where do you want to start?"

She picked up the coffee cup and blew across the top before taking a sip. "I want to know everything." She set the cup to the side. "But today, we need to decide our next actions. Are we ready to return to Roma? Roma *is* the *Cordelia*'s home port, isn't it?"

"No, we're not ready. And yes, Roma is our home port." Ike hesitated then decided to mention what was on his mind. "Your father kept a room at the hotel in Roma. You'll want to go through his things when we get there. Or you may wish to keep the room, for yourself."

A lost look brushed across her face. "That sounds like a good idea. I don't have a place I can call home anymore."

"Yes, you do." Ike laid his hand on top of hers, where her trembling fingers held the red pencil. "The *Cordelia*, for as long as you want to stay."

"So I'm like Mrs. Noah, my home afloat on a sea of water. At least I don't have to take care of any animals." She brushed a stray curl behind her ear. "Only my ark won't come to rest on a mountaintop anytime soon."

"There are worse places."

She removed her hand from his and pointed to the stacks by Ike. "I recognize the captain's logs, but what are the other books?"

"Accounts. Sums, as you called them. Income and expenses listed. Details of salaries. All the information needed to run Lamar Industries."

She nodded. "I will want to study those, I'm sure. But what do we need to do before we can leave? We already have cargo on deck. Are we expecting more? Or do you go from business to business, asking?"

"We could carry more cargo, but it's not too bad. I've posted notices in the hotels for passengers to contact us about a ride upriver."

Blanche nodded. "Do we have definite dates for the baseball trip with Mr. Ventura's team?"

Ike shrugged. "River travel is never that precise. The towns are expecting us, but they will announce the game after we arrive in town." He drummed the table with his fingers. "The main thing we are lacking is a pilot."

"What about Pete? I know my father did most of the work himself, but I always thought that was because he loved his work."

"He did." Ike nodded. "But he didn't completely trust the *Cordelia* with anyone else. Pete is an adequate pilot, but he doesn't have the feel for the river that Old Obie had. That you have, for that matter."

"Do you think I should apply for my pilot's license? Like my father suggested?"

The corners of Ike's lips quirked upward. "Absolutely. But we need someone to help us in the meantime."

Her eyes dancing, she challenged him. "Didn't I hear that you're a pilot yourself?"

He shook his head. "I'd be willing to take over for a few hours, in an emergency, but I'm less experienced than Pete. I don't want to risk our future with my hands on the wheel."

"Then what are our options?" She hit on the crux of the problem.

"I have a few ideas, but I have to warn you, there are reasons why none of the men I have in mind are on the river at the moment."

She grimaced. "Let's talk it over together."

"If we can coax him out of retirement, I'd like to get Captain Pettigrew. He helped teach Old Obie way back when."

Blanche absorbed that bit of news. "So he must be elderly by now."

"He quit the river about ten years ago when he decided to give up the fight against the railroads. I haven't seen him for a couple of years, but the last time I laid eyes on him, he was hale of body and sound of mind."

"And if he's not interested or available?" She left the question dangling.

"The others are either as old as Pettigrew or men who have lost the battle with booze." Ike didn't blunt the truth.

Her face paled, and she took a single swallow. "It's cooled off."

Standing, Ike reached for the coffeepot and refilled her cup. Satisfactory steam rose from the surface, and she gripped it gratefully. She closed her eyes, and her lips moved in silent words. When she opened them, determination shone from within. "Do you think Captain Pettigrew will be home this afternoon?"

That's my girl. Ike nodded. "So, you want to come with me?"

"Of course."

The first luncheon bell rang. "I'll put these away."

Blanche tugged the account book toward her. "I want to study this one. Unless there are some figures you need to enter?"

"Not today." He wondered how long it would be before she began raising uncomfortable questions. If he was lucky, not on this trip. She'd be too busy studying the books, if he had anything to say about it.

CHAPTER 27

B lanche inched the door to her cabin open, in case Effie
was asleep. She needn't have bothered. Her roommate was
buttoning up a pretty apricot-colored dress, with square buttons.
"Good morning, Blanche. Thank you for the breakfast."

"Elaine fixed a feast, with more to come." Pleasant aromas
promised chili and corn bread for the noon meal.

"When Elaine is upset, she cooks. The captain said he always
knew when something was on her mind." Tears filled Effie's eyes.
"I promised myself I wasn't going to cry again."

"Oh Effie." Blanche threw her arms around her friend's
shoulders. "I've cried enough tears to make the Rio Grande
flood its banks, if they had fallen in the river. No one expects you
to have a smile on your face."

"Maybe not." She poured water into the bowl on her dressing table and dampened a washcloth. She dabbed it at her face,
neck, hands, and then added a small amount of lotion below
each ear. Blanche imitated her actions. Amazing how such a
small gesture could offer so much refreshment.

"Are you ready?" Blanche gently encouraged her.

Effie nodded. Blanche laid down the account book and

handed Effie her white cane. Arm in arm, they headed to the dining salon. Blanche explained about plans she had made with Ike to visit with Captain Pettigrew that afternoon.

"Captain Pettigrew." Effie smiled. "I remember him. He was funny. I loved listening to him exchange stories with Old Obie while I played with his cats."

"Would you like to come with us? I bet he still has cats."

Effie stopped midstep. "No. I feel close to the captain as long as I'm aboard the *Cordelia*."

"I understand." And Blanche did. She had never seen her father any place other than on board the *Cordelia*. She had a hard time imagining him in any other setting.

"You don't think I'm being silly?"

"Not at all." Whatever time Effie needed to grieve, Blanche would allow. She didn't want her friend's life turned upside down the way her own had been since her mother's death. Her first nineteen years in Roma, even the fellowship at Christ the King Community Church, seemed like they happened to another girl.

The earlier chill continued to cling to Blanche, and she would have welcomed a brisk walk, but Ike had arranged for a carriage. As they trundled past the wharves and the downtown district, toward the residential district, she recognized the wisdom. "Is he expecting us?"

"I sent a messenger to arrange the meeting."

"Thank you." Ike did so many things so efficiently.

Blanche studied the streets as they rode, noting the presence of more palm trees than she had seen upriver, with an occasional seagull diving for a morsel of food as they rode by. "Is the ocean close by?"

"Not far."

An impulse seized Blanche. "I want to see it. Can we go, after we meet with Captain Pettigrew?"

Ike twisted in his seat to face her more directly. "You've never been to the ocean? Of course not. I should have taken you before."

Her face turned downward, hoping to hide the heat in her

cheeks. "As long as I am this close, I ought to see it. Don't you think so?"

"Absolutely. And here we are."

The house had to belong to someone who had spent his life on the water. Maybe she formed that impression from the narrow walk that circled the roof. What had she heard it called, a widow's walk? For the whalers' wives who waited at home? "Have you ever read *Moby Dick*?"

"That's the story about the crazy man who went after the whale, right? Great stuff. I'm surprised you read it, though. Didn't your mother think it was too harsh for your delicate mind?"

Laughter bubbled out of Blanche. "She didn't know everything I read. My reward for finishing my schoolwork early was to read, and my teacher kept me supplied in books. I fell in love with the idea of steamboats when I read Mark Twain's books."

"He got a lot of it right. Things have changed since his time, though." Ike helped her out of the carriage and opened the gate in the white picket fence. Flowers edged the length of the walkway, and rosebushes hugged the house. If her father was a different kind of man. . .if her mother were a different sort of woman. . .she might have grown up in a house like this. Blanche shook away the thought. Wishing couldn't change the past.

A man with a blue sailor's cap on his head and dressed in white came out on the front porch. She thought she had seen him at the funeral, but she wasn't sure. He waved them forward.

"Mr. Gallagher, Miss Lamar. I am honored that you would call on me in your time of grief." He came forward with an affable smile on his face.

"We appreciate you seeing us on such short notice." Blanche's nod felt stiff.

"I can guess what you came here to see me about." He flashed white teeth at her. "But first let me introduce you to my wife."

A kindly looking woman, a little plump, with a happy expression on her face, appeared at the front door at that moment, bearing a tray. "Do you mind if we take our refreshment on the porch?"

"That sounds lovely."

No one mentioned business as they made introductions and shared in sweet tea and pinwheel cookies. Blanche made an effort to finish the cookies Mrs. Pettigrew pressed on her. The affection between husband and wife was evident, a man comfortable in his retirement. She wondered if any inducement could convince him to leave the comforts of home to return to life on the river.

After they emptied the pitcher of tea and Mrs. Pettigrew disappeared inside, Captain Pettigrew grew serious. "As I said, I can guess why you're here. You need a pilot."

Beside her, Ike stirred but stayed silent. Perhaps he wanted her to approach Captain Pettigrew about the position. "From what I've heard, you're the best man for the job." She looked at him directly, refusing to drop her gaze.

"You're Obie's daughter, all right." Captain Pettigrew wiped at his eyes. "My wife stood by me all the years I spent on the river. I promised her before God that I would spend the last years of our lives at home."

"Are you a Christian?" Blanche couldn't keep the surprise out of her voice.

"Amen, sister." He winked at Ike. "Not all river men are heathen."

That statement sent heat rushing to Blanche's cheeks. She sipped her tea to give herself a moment to regain her composure. For once, Ike remained silent. He seemed to be enjoying her disquiet.

"We are not asking you to come out of retirement—not permanently." Blanche took a deep breath. "In fact, I am interested in securing a pilot's license for myself. My father"—she still stumbled over the word—"felt I had an aptitude for it. And I have to confess, the idea intrigues me."

"But a woman pilot?" Captain Pettigrew left the question dangling.

Ike cleared his throat. "A woman on the Mississippi recently qualified as a riverboat pilot. Our Blanche plans to follow in her steps."

"Obie was a good judge of talent." Captain Pettigrew looked

across the expanse of lawn. Standing, he went to the open door to the house and called for his wife. They conferred briefly in low voices then came out hand in hand.

"Is there room on your boat for my wife to travel with us?"

"Of course." Blanche smiled in relief.

"We have about an hour before the carriage will return." Ike held the gate open for Blanche to pass through. "You can see the ocean from here. We can spend a few minutes on the beach."

Blanche stood on tiptoe. "I can't see it."

"You can smell it, though." He took a deep breath. "All that salty air."

"Is that what it is?" Her nose wrinkled. "It reminded me of fish."

"That, too."

Palm fronds reached out to brush against them as they walked down the street, narrowing to a footpath about a hundred yards from the Pettigrews' house. Seagulls flew an elaborate dance overhead, demanding a tribute from the two intruders.

"Is that the ocean I hear?"

Ike stopped to listen. Ripple and swish. Not the roar of water tripping over rocks, such as he had experienced on a memorable trip to the headwaters of the Rio Grande, but the gentle wash of waves on sand. "Yes."

The boardwalk stopped about thirty yards shy of the high-water mark. Blanche dipped a tentative toe into the sand, and her shoe sunk in the soft surface. Giggling, she pulled back. "Do I dare walk forward?"

"If you do, sand will cover your shoes. Anytime we went to the beach, we came home with sand in every possible crevice. Dame Agatha complained she couldn't get the sand out for two washings." The memory brought a smile to his face. "If you want to skirt the grass here, it shouldn't be bad. There's another board-walk in that direction."

Blanche glanced at the sand, then at Ike. "I'd like that." She kept turning to look at the ocean, mesmerized by the undulating waves. "I don't think I would ever get tired of watching the water. Each time the waves wash over the beach, they draw pictures in the sand."

The rather fanciful description suited the beach. "It's peaceful." Ahead of them, a family had spread out a blanket where gulls squatted, begging for leftovers. The father held a pair of binoculars to his eyes, and the mother glanced at a book between admonitions to their children. The young ones were busy filling a pail with sand. Pail-shaped mounds defined the outline of a sand castle. Ike pointed it out.

"Oh, that looks like fun."

"Another time, perhaps."

"If I come back."

They needed to return to the Pettigrews' house to meet the carriage on time, but Ike hated for Blanche's time at the beach to end. The wave came up and washed away part of the castle.

"Oh dear." Blanche laughed. "That must be what the Lord meant when He talked about a house built on sand and a house built on rock. The house built on sand would be washed away."

"Temporary as sand, as eternal as the waves." Ike stood behind Blanche, and she leaned ever so briefly against his chest. He resisted the urge to put his arms around her and pull her closer.

Sighing, she said, "It's time to go back, isn't it?"

He nodded, and they turned in the direction of town.

The driver held a slip of paper in his hand and offered it to Ike after he assisted Blanche into the carriage. Ike read the message and nodded. Good. Today was turning into a lucky day, after the difficult times last week.

"What's that?" Faint pink appeared on Blanche's face. Ike hoped she wouldn't suffer from sunburn after their short time on the beach.

"Business." He smiled and patted her hand. "Nothing you need to worry your pretty head about."

She opened her mouth as if to protest then closed it without speaking. "Thank you for this lovely afternoon. I've been able to forget, for a few minutes, that I have lost both father and mother. God's reminder that life goes on and I won't be sad forever."

Leaning back against the seat, she closed her eyes. When her head fell against his shoulder, he adjusted her wrap and let her rest. He sought to nap but stayed locked awake.

As soon as they finished supper, Blanche and Effie excused themselves. Blanche took the account book with her. "I hope you don't mind."

"I regret anything that takes you away from me." Eventually he would have to list the day's business in the books, but it could wait. "Until tomorrow then?"

She smiled, and the two women left.

Ike retired to his cabin and set up things, setting out the bottle of whiskey he had managed to purchase before Old Obie's death and opening a packet of cards. After full dark fell, he returned to the main deck and greeted Bart Ventura as he came down the wharf with a couple of business associates whom Ike had met.

"I've told my friends this is the best game in town. I'm glad you could accommodate us."

"Glad to oblige." He didn't host games in port very often—if he wanted a game, he sought one out on land—but he wouldn't refuse Ventura's request. They would discuss some business tonight, now that Ike had final details about the return trip to Roma.

The evening passed the midnight hour, with Ike stone-cold sober but his guests feeling the effects of multiple shots of whiskey, when a sharp knock rapped at the door. Ventura swept the cards off the table in a practiced gesture, and the men removed their markers. Only whiskey glasses remained as telltale signs of the night's activities.

"Who is it?" Ike spoke through the closed door.

"Police. Open the door or we'll break it down."

A swift glance at the table confirmed all signs of the game had disappeared. Half a dozen officers stood at the entrance, pistols in hand. With one hand pulling the door closed, he stood inches in front of the first officer.

"What can I do for the officers of the law?" Ike turned on his most convincing smile, the one smile that made women swoon and men agree to harebrained schemes. More than once, Old Obie had remarked that he was glad Ike was a reasonably honest man.

"Open that door." The officer—a captain, Ike guessed by his uniform—shoved a piece of paper in his face. "Here's the warrant."

"Certainly." Ike tried the door, pretending it was locked. "Silly me." He took his time fishing his key out of his pocket. Heavy breathing and the smell of sweat identified the cops as men on the hunt.

The door opened to three men sitting around the table, cigars burning in ashtrays, which helped to mask the scent of whiskey. The drink, and the glasses, had disappeared, and all money had been put away. Ike allowed himself to relax. "How may I assist you this evening, Captain? As you can see, some friends of mine have gathered to offer their advice in this time of transition. You must have heard that our captain, J.O. Lamar, died last week."

"The police have an exhaustive history of this boat, Mr. Gallagher." He speared Ike with his glance while the officers pawed through his belongings. Ike bit his tongue to keep from asking what they were searching for.

"Here it is." One of the officers, a black-haired man who sounded like a Cajun from nearby Louisiana held up a decanter.

The police captain—Ike had determined his name was Mason—opened the decanter and sniffed. He tipped it and let a drop drip on his finger, which he licked. "You have been serving whiskey."

"What's going on?" A feminine voice pierced through the crowd of men. Wrapped in a dressing gown that covered her from neck to toe, Blanche appeared in the doorway like an avenging angel.

CHAPTER 28

The clamor of half a dozen feet stomping down the stairs and hallway had awakened Blanche from a sound sleep. Worried about some emergency on board—a problem with the engine? A sandbar?—she had pulled on the dressing gown that covered her completely and followed the noise down the hall.

The hubbub centered in Ike's cabin. Policemen crawled through his belongings like ants covering an ant hill, together with several men she had never met—and Bart Ventura. She almost coughed on the miasma of cigar smoke and sweat-soaked bodies and something else she couldn't identify.

"Nothing you need to concern yourself with, ma'am."

Blanche wished she had taken the time to dress. It was hard to exert authority while wearing bedclothes. "Let me be the judge of that. You are?"

"Captain Benedict Mason, ma'am. There is no need to be alarmed. I'll have one of my officers escort you back to your cabin."

When a dark-haired officer laid his hand on her arm, she shook him off. "If there is a problem with the boat, I want to know. I am the new owner."

Too late she caught Ike's frantic gestures.

Captain Mason's eyebrows rose. "You are?"

"Blanche Lamar. Captain Lamar's daughter."

The man's eyes darkened. "Were you aware that your—Mr. Gallagher was selling illegal whiskey to customers?"

Blanche looked at the decanter in the captain's hands. Whiskey must have been the odor she couldn't identify.

Ike pushed his way forward. "Captain, there is no need to distress Miss Lamar."

"No, I want to hear your answer." She wouldn't let Ike send her away.

"I brought a bottle to ease my friend in his time of grief. No money has changed hands." Mr. Ventura joined their circle.

Blanche reeled as the revelations poked more holes in her innocence in the ways of the world. "We don't have a license to sell liquor."

"No, you don't, which is why we were concerned when we received word about this evening's gathering." Captain Mason had toned down his belligerence.

A cry from one of the officers announced his discovery of a stack of money. He handed it to Captain Mason. His belligerence returned in full force. "If no money exchanged hands, why does this paper say 'IOU'?"

Gambling.

Mr. Ventura and Ike exchanged a long look. Ike gave an almost imperceptible shrug of his shoulders before speaking. "We were playing a friendly game of chance. I, um, wrote out the IOU until I can bring him the rest of the money. And that's not against the law." He cast an apologetic look in Blanche's direction.

The policeman shifting through Ike's trunk straightened. A shake of his head indicated he had found nothing.

The lines on Captain Mason's face deepened into a scowl. He turned on Blanche. "I'm surprised that a lady such as yourself would allow drinking and gambling aboard your boat."

Blanche slammed her mouth shut, jarring her teeth.

During the course of their conversation, two strangers had slipped through the door. Mr. Ventura stuck his right hand out and clasped Captain Mason's palm. "I wish we had met under different circumstances, but I trust there is no lasting ill will."

Did Blanche imagine it, or did he slip a bill to the captain?

"No." The word lacked the captain's earlier anger. "But the next time I board this boat, I trust I won't find any illegal refreshments?"

"No, you won't." Blanche took control. "I guarantee it." She decided to take it one step further. "And Mr. Ventura, I believe it's best if you make your future travel plans with a different company."

"Now, wait a minute—" Ike barreled forward. "Bart, don't pay any attention to her."

"Do we have an understanding, Mr. Ventura?" Blanche extended her hand the way he had earlier.

He bowed over her hand, all of his earlier charm evident. "We will not be seeing each other again." Straightening, he shook Ike's hand. "It's been a pleasure." He wasted no time walking out the door.

Captain Mason bowed over Blanche's hand. "I wish you the best on this new venture." He nodded in Ike's direction. "Mr. Gallagher."

"Captain Mason."

They could have been two men about to walk six paces and duel at dawn. Ike walked him to the door and watched his departure. "They're gone." Grabbing a shot glass in his hand, he raised his arm as if he was going to throw it. Instead he placed it on a clear spot on his dresser. "Do you have any idea what you've just done?'

"Do you remember your promise?" she shot back.

"Ventura's one of our best customers. We have no way to make up for losing his business." Ike stalked the room. "There's a reason why the captain left me in charge of day-to-day operations. We *need* his business." He tossed things in his chest, not bothering to fold his clothes.

His actions reminded Blanche that she was alone with Ike in his cabin, wearing only her dressing gown. "This isn't over. We will discuss it"—she glanced at the clock in the corner—"in a few hours." Keeping her eyes dry and her back straight, she whirled around and headed back to her cabin.

Effie sat in the rocking chair, knitting needles clacking in the silence. "What happened?"

Effie would have to know sooner or later. "Police raided the boat." The words came out in clipped syllables. "They accused Ike of selling liquor without a license."

"Ike would never do that." Effie didn't appear in the least bit upset.

"There was liquor." Blanche still thought she might be physically ill. The smells in that room had overwhelmed her senses. Dry heaves shook her shoulders now. After a couple of unproductive bouts, she poured water into a basin and splashed her face.

"Ike doesn't drink. Maybe a glass every now and then. But he does provide refreshment for his guests."

Effie couldn't understand the effect of such simple words on Blanche. Her mother, her pastor, her church, were all teetotalers. Her background taught her a single drink always led to drunkenness. But that bothered her less than gambling—an activity she had expressly prohibited. "His marks. Isn't that the word they use? They were playing poker."

At those words, Effie's knitting needles stopped clacking. "I was afraid he would continue."

"He promised." Blanche choked on the words. "I thought I could trust him."

"Oh Blanche." Effie folded the yarn back into the bag. "Come here." She patted the berth next to her chair.

"I can't sleep." Blanche plopped down on the pillow and unbuttoned her dressing gown. Even if she couldn't rest, she could be cool.

"You can trust Ike to do everything he considers in the best interest of the *Cordelia* and Lamar Industries and you."

"But he promised not to—"

"He promised not to do anything that would get you into trouble. Not the same thing." Effie lifted a single finger. "The police raid will weigh heavily on his conscience."

"He twisted my words." Blanche rang her hands. "You'll have to teach me how to knit. It might relax me." When she picked up a ball of yarn, it rolled across the floor. That brought a giggle to her lips. "Maybe that's not a good idea. I never was all that good with thread and needle." The giggle turned weepy. She lay on the bed without climbing under the covers.

"There's nothing more we can do about it until tomorrow morning." Effie patted Blanche's shoulder before she climbed back into bed. "I'm praying about it."

Lately prayer felt like a wasted effort. Was prayer going to make up for the difference between Ike's promise and his betrayal? She had prayed and prayed and still had no clue what she should do for her future. Had she traded the sure friendship of the people of Roma for the passing regard of Effie and Ike? She never should have left home. She should have known nothing good would ever come of living on a steamboat.

If she had never boarded the *Cordelia*, she never would have met her father.

Once Effie's breathing had settled into a steady pattern, Blanche took her place in the rocking chair and stared at the door. Staying or leaving, she had to decide.

❦

Ike didn't bother cleaning his cabin. He cleared off his bed and lay down. Guilt-plagued dreams that had police locking him in jail while he was awash in a river of whiskey troubled his sleep. After tossing and turning for a couple of hours, he awoke, his head splitting, leg sore where it dangled over the side of the bed.

The whiskey decanter stood on his table, taunting him, inviting him to drink a shot, to take the edge off the terrible day ahead. He had done what he must to protect Blanche's inheritance. That's why the captain had made him the director of daily operations. Wasn't it?

Ike had never used alcohol as a crutch and he wouldn't start now. No amount of alcohol or coffee would answer the central problem: would Blanche decide to direct Carver to sell the

Cordelia and split the profits? Would his actions deprive himself and his sister of both a means of support and their home?

Whatever the day might hold, he would greet it with his usual savoir faire. A single glance in the mirror revealed dark stubble on his chin that made him look more sinister than daring, and dark circles emphasized the harshness of the night. Nothing could remove the dark circles, but he would allow himself the luxury of a hot shave. While he waited for the water to heat, he checked the suit that Dame Agatha had returned to him yesterday, freshly pressed. His hand wandered over his tie rack, settling on his red tie. Red always made him feel better.

Once he had his basin of hot water, he sudsed soap with his shaving brush and lathered his face. The bristles fell into the basin, and the brace of aftershave woke up his skin. He added pomade to his hair. Now he could face the day. With a tip of the hat he pretended he was wearing, he left the cabin with a swagger.

Soft piano music filtered from the salon as Ike approached. Effie must be doing better. The melodies flowed from one of Old Obie's favorites into another. Sentiment washed over Ike, causing a hitch in his step. When Effie began a new melody, Ike began whistling "Yankee Doodle Went to Town." The hand-clapping, happy song brimmed with the captain's larger-than-life personality. She must be doing better.

Taking courage from his sister's music, Ike pushed through the door. The room seemed empty, with only the crew and no passengers. Blanche wasn't at her usual seat at the captain's table. Relieved, he took another step into the room before he spotted the head of red hair at the long table with the rest of the crew. She talked and laughed as if nothing out of the ordinary had happened only a few hours earlier.

Two could play at that game. With a warm smile and a practiced air, he swept into the room. "Good morning, everyone."

Blanche's shoulders stiffened before she twisted in her seat. "Good morning, Mr. Gallagher."

Mr. Gallagher. That didn't sound friendly, not friendly at all. Ike headed for the opposite end of the table, but Blanche waved him back. "There's a seat across from me. We have some matters to discuss."

How did she sound so chipper? Ike took the seat she had indicated. Smithers poured a cup of coffee before he had a chance to say no. "I'll take a glass of milk as well."

Effie stopped playing and took the seat next to Ike. Blanche said grace over the meal. Conversation flowed around the three of them, sparing Ike the necessity of saying anything.

Under the cover of laughter, Effie's voice intruded on his thoughts. "How are you this morning?"

She knows. Of course she did. She knew everything that happened onboard. "I've had better nights." He kept a smile on his face for Blanche's benefit in case she happened to glance in his direction.

After the crew members finished eating, Blanche stood to her feet. "I want to thank all of you for your patience and support through all that has happened in the past week. I'm sure some of you expected to be back in Roma by now."

A couple of the crew looked at each other and nodded.

"Captain Bruce Pettigrew has agreed to pilot the *Cordelia* until we make permanent arrangements. I'm sure you will make him as welcome as you have made me." She brought her hands together, and the others joined in clapping.

The salon emptied after she dismissed the crew. Ike tried to slip away, but Blanche motioned for him to stay. Effie remained as well. Elaine withdrew to the sink with the breakfast dishes. Blanche poured herself a fresh cup of coffee. "Let's change tables." She led them to a back corner, away from both the kitchen and the salon door.

"You're going ahead with the return to Roma." Ike decided to be direct. "So that means I'm coming with you."

"I have to get back to Roma. So do most of the crew. This is the most reasonable way to do it." Blanche's lips thinned, but her voice remained steady. "It will be a straight trip, no stops at any of the towns, and we're not carrying passengers. I trust that will limit your temptations of the games of chance you insist on playing."

"We'll lose money." He blurted the words out.

"Nevertheless, that is my decision."

Ike could swear she had tears in her eyes to match the wobble in her voice.

"I would rather be broke than be a stumbling block to others and take food out of the mouths of their families."

Ike didn't have a response to that. He hadn't left anyone penniless that he knew of. As far as he was concerned, that was their responsibility, not his.

Effie ran her fingers along the table, humming to herself, the way she did when she was thinking. "I have an idea about how we might increase profits."

Blanche widened her eyes and leaned forward. "Tell us."

Effie shook her head. "I need to think it through. I'll have something for you tomorrow."

"I'll look forward to it." Blanche settled back. "I'll be spending as much time as possible with Captain Pettigrew, once he arrives."

Ike started to speak, but she swept on. "In case I decide to stay, I will prepare to qualify as a pilot. I also want to look at the ship's accounts. Let's meet again tonight. In your cabin. It's too public in here."

"Is there anything you need me to do today?" He was prepared to crawl on the floor if she asked.

Blanche's mouth screwed in concentration. "Go through the captain's clothing. If there is anything that you can use, take it. Or if there are any personal mementos, set them aside to ask me. Effie, I need you to do the same thing."

At her dismissal, they each went their separate ways. He and Effie had a roof over their heads for a few more days. Ike felt light-headed with relief, a prisoner granted a stay of execution.

CHAPTER 29

"You'll do well." Like Old Obie, Captain Pettigrew kept a light hand on the wheel and a sharp eye on the river. "Obadiah was right. You have a feel for the river."

Blanche glanced up from the compass she was studying. After the grueling session he had put her through, she didn't expect the compliment. "Truly?"

"Miss Lamar." The captain was painfully polite. "I have trained many pilots in my day. You already know as much as that wood-headed Ike Gallagher, even though he's spent a lifetime on the river." He tapped the wheel. "I refer of course to his ability to pilot the boat. He is an excellent businessman. You couldn't have a better partner."

Those words brought a cough to Blanche's lips. "That remains to be seen. This is all so new to me."

"The Bible says that when we are weak, that's when Christ shows His strength in us. He doesn't want a know-it-all. He wants men and women who will depend on Him for everything."

Blanche tried the compass one more time. For a second, she thought she had figured it out. Then her arm quivered and the needle turned before she had determined the direction. "My mother said the same thing. But everything that's happened since her death has tested me in ways I never experienced before."

"God puts us in new circumstances to test us. You don't have to know all the answers. You just need to know who to ask."

The sextant clattered as Blanche picked it up. Captain Pettigrew turned his attention on her for a second. "Call it a night. Tomorrow is another day."

Blanche rolled her shoulders, stretching her muscles. "That sounds wise." She stowed the compass and sextant. "I'll see you midmorning, then. I have more material to cover with Ike and Effie." With a last glance at the river, she headed down the stairs as Ike was coming on deck. He looked impossibly handsome in his gray suit and natty red bow tie. A grin crossed his face when he spotted her.

"Blanche." He sprinted across the deck to join her. "I've gone through Old Obie's things, found a few things that might fit me. But I also found this." He held up a slender book. "His personal ledger." He gestured for Blanche to walk with him. On this return trip, the deck was only half loaded with cargo. They had a lot of space to walk.

"I hope you don't mind, but I looked at it. I was looking for clues about where Old Obie did his personal banking. His business account is with a bank in Brownsville, but he kept his personal account in Roma." He paused and opened the book to the front flap, which held a small bankbook.

Blanche's interest stirred at the idea of an account in Roma. Perhaps there was a little money to help tide all of them over until they found other paths in their lives.

"The thing is." Ike withdrew the bankbook and slid his finger between the first two pages. "There are two names on the account."

Not Ike, or he wouldn't be so surprised. Surely not. . .another wife? Bile rose in Blanche's throat.

"The first name is, of course, Jedidiah Obadiah Lamar. The second name. . .is Cordelia Adams Lamar."

Cordelia? "My mother?" Blanche wondered if her face paled as much as the patches of light wood beneath the places where pallets of cargo usually waited.

Ike nodded. "Regular deposits, but no withdrawals that I see." He placed the book in Blanche's hands.

Blanche read the lists of credits and debits, deposits, but no withdrawals. She wobbled on her feet.

Ike led her to a stack of crates, the right height for her to sit on. Adjusting her skirts around her, she held the book out to Ike with trembling hands. "I had no idea he'd been sending money all along."

"It appears so, yes."

"Will the surprises never end?" Blanche looked over the side of the boat without seeing anything on the riverbank. "Every time I think I have things figured out, I learn something new. My mother never did anything with this money. We lived on her income. I'm sure of it." Neither had sorting her mother's belongings revealed any hidden stashes of money.

"He always loved you, Blanche. And he continued to provide for your mother as well. He was an honorable man."

"So I'm learning." Blanche estimated the total amount of money withdrawn over the five-year span. Over five hundred dollars. "I wonder if there are earlier ledgers." Drawing a shaky breath, she added, "Thanks for showing this to me. Of course I'll split it among the three of us."

Ike just shook his head. The dinner bell sounded. "Ready?" At her nod, he extended his arm.

Music Blanche didn't recognize floated through the salon door.

"Effie's been in there most of the afternoon." Ike opened the door for Blanche. "She used to do that when she was upset. She said playing the piano helped her to feel better."

"I thought she was doing better." Blanche took a step in the direction of the piano then thought better of it. "It comes in waves, though. For all of us." The words brought renewed grief over her, for the father who had provided for his daughter, sight unseen.

At their entrance, Effie turned around and smiled. "Look who's here."

She stepped away from the piano bench and touched the back of each chair as she moved toward the center of the long table. "It's nice when we can all eat together, isn't it?"

Whatever emotions she had processed while playing the piano, Effie seemed in good spirits now. "I made good progress this afternoon." Her voice held a hint of breathless excitement. "How has your day gone?"

"Interesting." Blanche left it at that. She wanted to tease Effie's secret from her, but she doubted she would succeed. Instead, she'd enjoy this meal without all the worries and secrets and uncertainties that had dominated the past few days. At least she would try.

❦

Ike awoke on Wednesday morning with two things on his mind: curiosity about Effie's plan—and a determination to make things right with Blanche.

Effie only stayed in the dining salon long enough to wolf down a soft-boiled egg and a couple of slices of toast before she excused herself. "Come ahead to the theater when you are ready."

Her departure left Blanche and Ike in a cocoon. Around them, the crew laughed and chattered. He broke a strawberry muffin in half and buttered it. After he took a bite, butter chased the tasty crumbs down his throat. Clearing his throat, he leaned forward. "I need to ask your forgiveness for what I did the other night."

Her eyes flashed. "You mean, the. . ."

He nodded. "For everything. I still disagree with your decision, but I was wrong to go ahead when you believed I would stop." Now came the last part, the hardest part. "I promise it won't happen again."

Hope flickered in her eyes then disappeared. *She doesn't believe me.* Why should she? Ike would earn her trust day by day, week by week, by behaving in an honorable manner. If she let him have that long.

Warmth just shy of trust shone in her eyes. "Thank you for saying that to me. I know it was difficult for you. 'I'm sorry' is always hard to say, so thank you."

The chatter flowing around them slowed, and they ceased their personal conversation. Blanche drank a cup of coffee with evident relish. "Are you ready to learn what Effie has for us? She seems very excited."

As they neared the theater, more of the unknown music piped through the open door. Effie repeated the same section several times, and Ike wondered if she was trying to commit it to memory.

Blanche approached Effie. "I like that song. What are the words? Or are there words?" She hummed the melody Effie had been playing.

"There are." Effie's smile widened. "Let me explain what I have in mind." She swiveled around the piano bench, her face alight with enthusiasm. "I've had the most marvelous idea. Blanche, you are committed to stopping the gambling; and Ike, you're worried about how to make up the difference in income."

Ike and Blanche exchanged an uneasy glance. "I've promised I won't do it again."

"But you are still worried." Blanche laid a gentle hand on his arm. "I know you have the best intentions, but I just can't allow it. What do you have in mind, Effie?"

"Instead of offering gambling to a handful of guests, why not invite the people of Roma to come to dinner and a play aboard the boat, the nights that we are in town? Elaine thrives on cooking for banquets. We can easily fit one hundred fifty people in here. If we hold four performances in a weekend—we could do five or even six if we gave performances on Sunday as well, but I know you would object—we could make quite a bit of money."

Blanche looked at Ike, neither one of them having any idea how to respond. "And the music?"

"An idea I have for the first show. A musicale, about Noah and the ark. Perfect for a boat setting." Her laughter delighted his ears.

Intrigued, Ike said, "Sing the words."

Effie ran through several songs. One recorded Noah's argument with God. "Build me an ark of gopher wood. But God, what is this rain You're talking about? Build me an ark." Another reminded Ike of the children's song about Old MacDonald's farm, one that imitated the animal sounds. A piano solo echoed rain pounding on the wood of the boat, the roof, the walls, the surface of the river.

"I didn't know you were so talented." Blanche clapped her hands together. "I love it, but I don't have any experience with plays—not unless you count nativity plays at church. Do either of you? Would we have to hire actors? Or do any members of the crew have unexpected talents?"

Effie waved her concerns away. "You and Ike would play the title roles. You might not have heard him sing, Blanche, but my brother has a good voice."

Ike shut his mouth. "I didn't volunteer."

"I'm your sister." Effie wasn't concerned. "I've drafted you. We could hold auditions for the other parts; and I wondered if Captain Pettigrew would be willing to do God's voice in the play."

"He certainly has a lovely, deep voice." Blanche leaned forward. "But I told you. I don't know a thing about theater."

"You'll learn. I wondered if we could prepare the play for a premiere when we arrive in Roma. I know that's only a few days away, but I believe we can do it if we start right away."

"With a small cast, we could offer the performance at other towns on the river route." Blanche looked thoughtful. Her eyes were completely serious as she turned to Ike. "How do you feel about playing Noah?" She held up a hand. "I'm not criticizing you. But such a play has spiritual implications." She let out a self-deprecating laugh. "If you don't believe the truth, can you at least act well enough to convince everyone else?"

The words Effie had spoken echoed in his head. "Build me an ark of gopher wood, Noah. But God. . ." Ike was stuck in the "but God" phase. "I can try. You will have to be the judge of how effective I am."

"Then will you announce auditions at luncheon today? For anyone who is interested to come to the theater after dinner tonight? And I'll need your help, Blanche, in writing the scripts

I've written in my head."

"Yes."

Effie's crazy idea gave both women purpose for the day. He consulted with them about set construction. His sister's requests for simple animal pens would provide a pleasant diversion of his other duties. "I'll determine ticket prices. Is that acceptable?"

"It sounds like a good idea," Blanche said, and Ike left them to writing the script.

Blanche's nerves tripled as she climbed the steps to the pilothouse. Effie's idea, which seemed so brilliant in the indoor theater, faded as she walked into the light of day. She and Effie agreed Captain Pettigrew would be perfect for God's voice, but she hated to ask even more from him.

"You've neglected me today, Miss Lamar." His voice teased her as she entered.

She edged into the room.

"What is it?" The man seemed to have eyes in the back of his head, much like her father had. Maybe she would acquire the same skill, in time.

"Effie has come up with a wonderful idea to make money for the boat. Dinner and a play, a musicale, based on the story of Noah."

From the side, she saw the captain's left eyebrow rise high. "A play, hmm. Interesting idea. Aboard a steamboat—maybe churn a few miles up and down the river—could be an attractive proposition."

"We would like for you to take part in the play, Captain." She held her breath.

"Me? I have no theater experience."

"You wouldn't even appear on stage. We just want to take advantage of your marvelous bass voice." Blanche smiled and used her most persuasive voice. "You see, God and Noah have an argument when God tells Noah to build an ark."

Captain Pettigrew threw his head back and laughed. "That would have been quite an argument. Who's playing Noah?"

Blanche hesitated. "Effie, um, suggested Ike."

"Ike." The captain stared straight ahead at the river. "If he plays the part of a man of faith—especially one who was willing to argue with God about it—he might think about what it means to him personally. I like it, a lot." He winked at Blanche. "Where do I show up?"

"Ike suggested we hold the rehearsals for your scenes together up here. The performances will be given Thursday, Friday, and Saturday, after we arrive in Roma."

With the major roles covered, Blanche wondered who else would be interested in participating. Effie said they could use everyone who expressed interest. They needed neighbors, Noah's three sons and their wives, even animals. If no one showed up, the four of them would have to manage.

They needn't have worried. Every member of the crew came through the theater at some point. Either they auditioned, or they sat in the audience and applauded. Smithers proved the surprise of the evening, handling some of the humorous dialogue with a skill unexpected of him. Blanche thought he would be perfect for the role of the officious mayor who refused to listen to Noah's warnings. Even Dame Agatha offered to create costumes from scraps of leftover material.

At the end of the evening, Effie faced the group. "Thank you all for coming this evening. We will announce the cast at breakfast in the morning. We'll also schedule rehearsals around your work schedules and plan for the entire cast to join together in the evenings."

Blanche stood next. "I know this is extra work for all of you. Thank you so much for coming out! We have a lot of work ahead of us in the next few days, but I believe the people of Roma will enjoy our production. And now, I will pray and ask God's blessing on us as we seek to communicate His eternal truth."

Peace permeated the corners of the room after her amen.

God was doing something unexpected, something unexpected indeed.

Chapter 30

T he bow shall be in the cloud; and I will look upon it, that
I may remember the everlasting covenant between God
and every living creature of all flesh that is upon the earth."

Even though Captain Pettigrew repeated the familiar words
offstage, Blanche felt as though God Himself was speaking the
words of eternal promise. A solemn hush fell over the theater
until one brave soul clapped, and then the room rang with applause. The actors who had played the townspeople, including
Smithers, walked onto the stage and took a bow. Next the actors
who played Shem, Ham, and Japheth, Noah's sons, and their
wives, entered to louder applause. Last of all Ike took her hand
and swept her onto the stage. The audience stood to their feet,
clapping. "Encore!" someone shouted.

They had debated whether Captain Pettigrew should also
take a bow; but he had demurred, saying he didn't want to de-
tract from the holiness of God's covenant. In the end his argument won out, although he was mentioned in the credits of the
programs they had distributed among the audience.

As the cries for an encore continued, Effie played the introduction to "Build Me a Boat." The chorus and cast joined

Blanche and Ike in singing it one more time.

When the applause at last died down, Blanche took her place at the front of room. Although her stomach roiled with butterflies, she focused on first one smiling face then another. Toward the back, she saw the Davenports from Christ the King Community Church. Their facial expressions remained neutral, and Blanche's insides tensed. Once she passed on to the next smiling face, her nerves settled. "Let's offer another round of applause for the composer of tonight's musicale, Miss Effie Gallagher."

Effie stiffened at the piano.

"Take a bow, Effie."

Effie swung around on her piano stool and stood, shock and surprise on her face. When the audience noticed the cane by her right hand, applause grew louder. She bowed and sat back down.

"We will have a repeat performance tomorrow evening and twice on Saturday. Please tell your friends and family." Nods and whispered conversations encouraged Blanche that they would spread the word. After her dismissal, she resisted the temptation to slip out the side door, but instead remained at the front. A few people pushed forward, including the Davenports. The expressions on their faces told her nothing, and she struggled to focus on the person in front of her.

"We'll be back Saturday afternoon, with our children," a matron dressed in a suit in a colorful blue with gray piping gushed. "We wanted to check it out first. It gave me several things to think about. It's not always easy to trust God."

Blanche thought back to the day when Effie had asked, "What will you do when God doesn't seem to come through for you?" Noah might have wondered the same thing, fearing if he would ever get to leave the ark.

The Davenports were next to last in line. Mrs. Davenport embraced her briefly before stepping back.

"I must confess I was surprised when I heard about this performance," Reverend Davenport's voice rumbled.

"I told him, there must be some mistake. Cordelia's daughter wouldn't be involved with anything so worldly."

The joy drained from Blanche.

"I was pleasantly surprised that there were a few redeeming qualities in the play. I will not speak against it." Reverend Davenport nodded his head as if his lack of condemnation should please Blanche, but her heart ached for more.

"Miss Gallagher did an excellent job in capturing the spirit of the biblical account." Captain Pettigrew entered from the wings, now that the audience had wandered out. "I had misgivings myself, until I read the script."

The man behind the Davenports—dressed in a somber dark suit but with a welcoming smile—stepped forward. "I have to agree. 'Build Me a Boat.' Pa-rum-pa-pa-pum." He hummed the melody. "I believe I'll be singing that tune the next time I have to hammer something together. My compliments to Miss Gallagher." He bent in her direction then took her hand and kissed it. Effie giggled.

"I am Ronald Sanders. Former gentleman of the stage and now a preacher for the Lord." He sounded more like an actor than a preacher like Reverend Davenport. "I have often despaired that God could use anything from my former life, but you have shown me differently."

Blanche looked from Sanders to the Davenports to Captain Pettigrew. The differences of opinions didn't help clarify the decision she must make.

Mr. Sanders said it had helped him. Despite his old-fashioned hairstyle, bushy eyebrows, and long sideburns, kindness shone from his eyes, the love and joy of Christ. "I'm glad our little play helped you, Mr. Sanders. Are you pastoring a church in Roma?" She didn't think she had met him before, but she didn't know much about the churches of Roma outside of her home fellowship.

Reverend Davenport's frown indicated he hadn't either, and Mr. Sanders confirmed that by shaking his head. "God told me to come to Roma, that someone here needed my help." He winked at her. "Now I am wondering if that person might be you, Miss Lamar. Do you have need of a chaplain? Or perhaps a theater director?"

Mrs. Davenport drew back. "You must have a lot to do.

Come see us, if we can help you with anything." She embraced Blanche one last time and left without a backward look.

Blanche wanted to run after them, to chase that expression of disapproval from their faces. But nothing she did now could undo their disappointment in the play.

Blanche shook aside the distraction. "Mr. Sanders, I'd love to discuss your ideas with you. Tomorrow morning? Say, at eleven o'clock?"

"I'll be here, eleven on the dot. It's been a pleasure." With a sweeping bow, he took his departure.

"Don't worry about anything Reverend Davenport has to say. That play of my sister's gave me plenty to think about. It's a different kind of sermon. One that settles on a listener's ear easier than sitting in a church listening to someone drone on in a monotone."

He mimicked Reverend Davenport's tone so perfectly that Blanche couldn't quite stifle her giggle. "It's not that bad." She wouldn't admit how often she had to fight a desire to nap about halfway through his sermons.

"Whatever else Mr. Sanders might be, I doubt he ever speaks in a monotone."

"No, I doubt that." Ike's words had helped restore her good humor. "This idea of Effie's seems to be working. Do you think people downriver would like to see the play?"

"Positively. Does that mean—?"

She nodded. "We'll make one more trip to Brownsville and back."

~⋘~

Ike woke early on Sunday morning. Amazing how much more sleep he was getting since he stopped gambling. If he had any intentions of continuing on the sly, he couldn't have. Either Blanche or Effie stopped by every night, checking on him.

Life aboard the *Cordelia* ran to a different rhythm now— prayers at meals, Sunday services, a midweek Bible study as well. Blanche had even provided a multivolumed Braille Bible that Effie spent hours reading. The latest volume remained propped open on a corner table in the dining salon. Musicales, plays, and recitations had taken the place of gambling for entertainment. In the week since they had left Roma, they had performed "Build a Boat, Noah" to sold-out crowds every night and enthusiastic requests for a repeat performance when next they came to town. In fact, they made as much money through the plays as he had expected from sponsoring the Bats' exhibition baseball games.

Then again, their expenses had increased; they were paying two additional salaries, for Captain Pettigrew and Mr. Sanders. In addition to serving as ship's chaplain, Sanders took over the role of Noah in the play. The reprieve gave Ike additional time to drum up shipping business.

All in all, business was faring better than he'd feared, but not as well as they needed. On this Sunday morning, he decided to check out the worship service. He chose one of his darker gray suits with a white shirt. Not his favorite, but he thought Blanche would approve.

As he reached the head of the stairs, he encountered Captain Pettigrew headed in the same direction. "Good morning. I thought you gave these Sunday services a miss." Pettigrew had made no work Sundays a condition of his employment, and Blanche had gladly complied.

"I don't have anything better to do." He noticed the Bible in the captain's hand. He hadn't given it a thought. "Go on ahead. I'll join you in a moment." He peeled away from Pettigrew and headed for Old Obie's cabin.

One of the surprises that had come from sorting through Old Obie's things was the discovery of a worn Bible among his possessions. Ike intended to give it to Blanche; he'd do it after the morning service. A glance at the clock told him he'd miss the first few minutes of the service. He'd bet—not that Blanche would allow him to bet—that she would be happy to see him, late or not.

Music streamed through the open door. One of the young maids scurried down the hall ahead of him and headed into the theater. Had a church service ever been held in a stranger location? Half the congregation was dressed for work, ready to return to the business of the day once the final amen sounded. Most of the passengers attended—that would please Blanche. For the most part, they had dressed in their Sunday best. Theater backdrops remained on the stage. Plush chairs rather than padded pews formed rows for the congregation. Ike slipped onto the last available seat, next to one of the single male passengers, Robert Albertson. Someone he would have recruited for a hand of poker, and here he was attending church.

When they finished the hymn they were singing, Blanche glanced at Ike and smiled. "Next we will sing 'Blessed Be the Tie That Binds.' In my short time aboard the *Cordelia*, I have met many wonderful Christians. The tie that binds us together is indeed a blessing."

Albertson held a hymnal where Ike could see. Hymnals? Where had they come from? No one kept him informed of developments in this Christian business, but things appeared to be going well.

With the presence of Sanders, Ike expected to endure an hour-long sermon. He kept his remarks short, directing their attention to the biblical account of Noah. Even though Ike didn't know much about the Bible, he did know Genesis was the first book. He found the sixth chapter without much trouble.

As Sanders read the verses like the Shakespearean actor he had once been, Ike remembered another reason why he hadn't read the Bible all that often. Full of *thees* and *thous* and *shalts* and verbs ending with *eth*. He preferred plain speaking. A glance around indicated a few others felt the same way.

Then Sanders set down his Bible and began speaking. Preaching, Ike supposed you could call it, but it was neither like the rantings he had heard from some tent evangelists nor the monotone of preachers like Davenport. Nor was it melodramatic posing—what Ike might have expected. No, Sanders spoke as he might to a table of close friends. Humming, he started in on a few words of "Build Me a Boat, Noah." He began clapping; Effie joined him, then Blanche, then Ike as well as everyone else in the back row. Soon everyone was clapping and singing. The place rang with enthusiasm and felt nothing like any church service Ike had ever attended.

Sanders cut them off. He spoke the words of the song. " 'Build Me a boat, Noah.' But Noah didn't have any idea what a boat was. It had never rained before. But God gave him a blueprint, and Noah started building. And *building*."

He laughed. "Now, I know people lived longer in those days than they do today, but even back then, a hundred years was a long time. And that's how long it took Noah to build the ark. A hundred years."

Sanders kept going through the story, singing different parts of the music, pointing out how time after time it wasn't easy for Noah to trust God. "And how about all those months they lived on the boat? With all those animals?" He chuckled. "I've only lived on a boat for one week and my feet are already itching for dry land. I can't imagine what it was like for Noah."

Laughter rippled around the room.

Sanders made it clear that Noah had plenty of reasons to doubt and complain. But he trusted God, no matter how bad everything got. His reward? Rescuing all of his family, not to mention all mankind.

Nothing that had ever happened to Ike could compare to what happened to Noah. The light shining from Blanche's face made sense to him in a way it never had before. Nothing he had ever done, or could ever do, would bring that expression to her face. He couldn't compete with her faith—but could he share it?

He found himself fidgeting in his chair and biting his lip. Not because he was bored—but because he wasn't. He wanted to put his fingers in his ears, to stop the words cascading down his eardrums to his heart. Surveying the theater for needed improvements helped pass the time. The sound of shuffling feet, Effie moving to the piano, broke into his attention and he noticed everyone around him was bowing their heads. Sanders finished his final prayer with a loud "amen," not a moment too soon.

Ike stood with the others and slipped through the door, unnoticed. The always-moving, unpredictable but at least familiar, river would restore him to balance.

Blanche hoped to greet Ike, but he disappeared before she could reach him. Something in his face tugged at her heart, as if he was taking a good look at his soul for the first time. But he left before she had made her way past the first row. With a final glance at the door, she approached the preacher. "That was an excellent sermon, Reverend Sanders. When I think about what Noah had to face, and the comparatively minor problems I have encountered, I am put to shame."

"We all feel that way. He's an example, a demonstration of what faith in God looks like." He gestured with his hands then clapped them together. "I'll stop before I start preaching again."

The people around them laughed. Blanche said good-bye to the gathering and went in search of Ike. No sign of him lingered in the hallway or the dining salon. Her footsteps led to his cabin, but she left without knocking. If he was there, she didn't want to disturb him. She headed on deck. He might be up in the pilothouse, or perhaps in what she had come to call his thinking spot. Only one silhouette appeared in the pilothouse, so she headed for the prow of the ship.

She took two, three, half a dozen steps in his direction, her shoes making soft clipping sounds on the floor. His shoulders stiffened but he didn't turn around.

When only a yard separated them, she stopped. "Ike?"

He kept his gaze on the sky. "Looks like we're in for a bad storm. What happens if we have a Noah-sized rain?"

CHAPTER 31

Gray clouds scudded across the sky, whipped into a frenzy by lightning striking the earth to the east. "It looks bad." Blanche heard the thread of fear in her voice. "What are storms like on the river?"

"The boat will rock a little bit. If it gets bad, we can stop forward progress and drop an anchor."

"Is that what my father would have done?"

She felt the shrug through his suit jacket. "Probably not. But he had a lifetime of experience on the river. And he did shut down the engines once or twice."

An overnight stop now would mean a day's delay in their arrival in Brownsville. Three more meals. Another day's expenses. The time she had spent pouring over the account books had revealed how close to the bone the boat ran. "Captain Pettigrew is a good pilot. We'll continue running unless he decides it is dangerous. I'll ask him to take over at the helm after dinner. Before, if the weather deteriorates."

"Wise course." The corner of Ike's lips lifted in a smirk. "Why not go full steam ahead and trust God to keep us all safe?"

His eyes expressionless, she couldn't tell if he was serious or joking. "Trusting God doesn't mean being foolish."

"I don't know. From what Sanders said today, it sounds like it was pretty foolish for Noah to build that boat."

A definite challenge. "That was different. God spoke to Noah directly."

"So God doesn't speak to you today?"

Blanche bit her lip. *Give me wisdom. And patience.* "Not in the same way. We have the Bible." A bit of humor wouldn't hurt. "And I have never read in the Bible about steamboats or the Rio Grande River or even the great state of Texas."

"Touché." He smiled that strange half grin again. "Would you like for me to quiz you on the pilot's test after we eat?" Captain Pettigrew had agreed to work a maximum of three months; she dedicated time each day to earning her license before he left.

Blanche gave thought to the safety of her cabin, but life as the owner didn't allow for self-indulgence, at least not on a day with a looming thunderstorm. "Yes." A single drop of rain fell on her face. "Perhaps I can take the wheel for a few minutes before the weather gets too bad." She laughed nervously. "I have to learn how to manage the boat in all kinds of circumstances."

Three hours later, she debated the wisdom of that decision. Pete was more than happy to let her take his shift at the helm. Since Ike was a licensed pilot, although he seldom worked in that role, he could supervise Blanche. She stood on a crate, an adaptation her father had recommended to make up for her short stature. The additional height didn't make up for the cascading rain. She found herself trying to look between raindrops—an impossible task. "I'm afraid I'm going to miss changes in the river."

"Want to quit?" Ike lifted an eyebrow.

"Captain Pettigrew said he would come up if he felt it got too bad." She took a shaky breath. "But if this isn't bad, I don't know what is."

"Your faith in God isn't up to the task?"

Leave God out of it. Squinting, she didn't respond.

Ike put his hands on her shoulders and rubbed her sore muscles. "Relax. Look at the whole tree, not the leaves."

"I'll try."

After that, Ike remained quiet. Blanche's shoulders kept rising, tensing her entire body until a soft touch of his hand reminded her to relax. Even so, her muscles would feel sore in the morning. She'd resort to willow bark tea and soak in hot water. Rain lashed against the front window, giving both sky and river a rippled effect. The sun disappeared from view, melding white sky to gray horizon that gradually darkened to the same shade.

After half an hour by the hourglass, the pattern of the rain changed, and she called for an increase of power. The *Cordelia* plowed her way through the spot, and Blanche called for a return to normal speed.

"Well done." Ike clapped twice. "Old Obie was right, you know. You have a real feel for the river."

She rolled her shoulders. "Thank you."

After that, she felt more comfortable as she made small adjustments in direction or power. The dinner bell sounded.

"Do you want me to call Captain Pettigrew when I go to dinner?"

Blanche stared out the window, debating how much time remained before the sky turned a blinding black. "I can wait until after he eats."

When the captain arrived after dinner, Blanche accepted his hand in getting down from the crate. Her legs trembled more than she liked, but she felt exhilarated.

"You go get a bite to eat, warm up some." Captain Pettigrew stood behind the wheel as if the rain didn't bother him in the least. "Do you want to keep watch with me tonight?"

Blanche blinked. "That sounds good. I've only been here one other night."

"I'll see you later then." He crammed his captain's hat on his head and nodded, turning his full attention out the front window.

"How do you feel?" Ike welcomed her to the dining salon.

"Tired enough to sleep for a week." She thought about it a bit more. "And excited enough to stay awake until Christmas morning."

That earned a laugh. "I know the feeling."

The smell of chicken soup drew Blanche like a magnet. Ike brought out two steaming bowls with a plate of crusty rolls. Elaine came to the window. "What can I get you to drink?"

Blanche was about to ask for a glass of cold milk, but then thought about the long night ahead of her. "Better make that black coffee. I want to stay awake and alert tonight."

She breathed in the steam from the soup. "It smells wonderful." She spooned it quickly and cleaned the bottom of the bowl with a roll.

When she finished her first bowl, he exchanged it for a fresh serving. Ashamed by the speed with which she ate a single bowl of soup, ordinarily enough for an entire meal, heat slammed into her cheeks. She ate the second with more ladylike decorum.

Ike studied her with undisguised humor. "Do you want to rest before you go back to the pilothouse?"

Blanche considered. "I'm afraid that if I lie down, I won't get up again before morning." She poured another cup of coffee, her third, and drained it before wrapping a couple of rolls in a napkin. "I'll chew on these if I get sleepy."

"Do you want me to come with you?" Hands square on the table, eyes level with hers, Ike gave no hint of his preference.

She should leave him alone and let the Holy Spirit do His work. "That's not necessary. I'm just there to watch, and Captain Pettigrew will answer any questions that I have."

Ike started to object, but Blanche raised a hand. "If it's a question about the *Cordelia* that only you can answer, we'll get you right away. Or if possible, I'll ask you tomorrow. Take the rest of the day off. And thank you for all the ways you've helped me today."

Smiling, he held on to her hands. Then he leaned forward and kissed her briefly on the cheek. He withdrew, sketched a wave, and walked toward the staircase leading to the cabin level.

Blanche stared after him, her hand cupping her cheek where he had kissed it. *Oh Ike.* Her prayers for him doubled, but it seemed as if the overcast sky held her thoughts earthbound.

Once she joined Captain Pettigrew in the pilothouse, she focused on the worsening weather. Thunderstorms had never bothered Blanche. Before now. Before she was on the water. Before each strike of lightning felt like it would break the glass and knock them down. Before the wind rocked the room at the top of the boat in a constant seesaw.

"Should we stop the engines?" She had to shout to make herself heard.

He shook his head. "That would create more problems than it would solve. It's better if we run with the wind and steer clear of any problems with the river." He flashed white teeth at her in a blast of lightning. "And pray with your eyes open."

"I'm already doing that." She hadn't stopped praying since she arrived on deck. Crossing the few feet from the indoor stairway to the door to the pilothouse had left her soaked to her unmentionables. If she hadn't memorized the route from previous trips, she doubted she could have found the door. Rain pounded her skin, causing her to close her eyes against the onslaught.

Wind whistled overhead, rattling the ceiling and windows. "Will the glass break?"

"It might." Pettigrew pulled the bell, alerting the engine room to a slight change in speed. "Can't worry about that now."

Blanche spared a thought for the danger broken glass would pose. But she was here to learn, not to tremble in fear. "Why did you tell them to decrease speed?"

"Wind is pushing us along. We need less steam to keep the boat moving at the same speed." He tugged the wheel one spoke to the right. "If we were going in the other direction, we'd increase power instead."

Lightning crashed and thunder sounded immediately. A lack of power wasn't the problem on this evening.

A Bride's Rogue in Roma, Texas

In the wake of that spontaneous, spectacular kiss, Ike stumbled on the first step. He straightened himself, but he couldn't do anything about the silly grin on his face. He had kissed women before, several of them, but none of them made him feel like that innocent caress of Blanche's cheek. He lifted his foot to take the second step when the boat rolled underneath him. The storm had risen another notch. He skipped down the steps two at a time to reach the bottom as quickly as possible.

At the bottom step, the boat lurched again, throwing him to the floor. Down the corridor, Effie opened the door to the girls' cabin. "Is everyone okay?"

Ike stood and dusted himself off. "It's just me."

A frown creased Effie's face. "I thought I heard something fall down. The rocking motion is tossing things around my cabin. I've put a few things in my dresser drawers."

"It's pitching badly." This time when the boat swung, he braced himself against the wall. "Anything broken?"

"Not yet. Isn't Blanche with you?"

"Captain Pettigrew asked her to stay with him during the storm. She wants to learn how to pilot the boat in all kinds of weather."

"Oh." Effie's shoulders slumped. "I might as well go to bed. If the wind doesn't toss me out of my berth." For a moment, she reminded him of the little girl who was scared of staying alone for the first six months they lived aboard the boat.

"Would you like me to stay with you for a while?"

"Would you mind?" Her words offered an out, but she was already opening the door to let him in.

Her bag of knitting sat tucked under her chair. "I tried working on the sweater, but after I jabbed myself once and lost stitches twice, I decided I better put it away."

"And on the desk, is that the Bible Blanche got for you?"

"Yes. I was reading the story of Noah again. And it was a little frightening, with the storm tonight."

Thunder rumbled through the deckboards overhead, and she shrank away.

"Stop reading before you give yourself nightmares."

"If that happens, I'll come running to my big brother."

Thunder, or perhaps waves, shook the cabin, and Effie trembled. Ike planted himself behind Effie and placed his arms around her shoulders. "Shh, I've got you."

Her shivering continued. After the next crash of thunder subsided, she asked, "Ike, would you pray? For our safety?"

Her simple request yanked him back by fifteen years. Their mother lay dying in another room, and she asked him to pray. When God didn't answer that prayer, he had stopped praying.

"For you, Effie, anything." At church, people bowed their heads and closed their eyes when they prayed, but Ike felt more natural speaking with his eyes open. He looked at the ceiling, where thunder crashed and the boat shook.

"God. According to the Bible, it'll never rain for forty days and nights again. I guess I should thank You for that. But even shorter storms can turn deadly, and You didn't say anything about them. So I ask You first of all for the lives of the people on this boat."

"Amen," Effie whispered.

"And I suppose I should ask You for anybody else crazy enough to be on this river tonight. Or on the riverbanks, if it floods.

"Then I guess my mind rushes to things. Does that make me selfish? I don't care, not a lot. We need to deliver our cargo safely to make a profit. We need to make a profit for us not to run a gambling game. And You want us to work for our food, right? Well, if we lose the cargo, that's going to be hard. So I ask that things won't get broken or wash overboard."

Effie reached up and patted his hand, as if reassuring him that his prayer was acceptable.

"And I pray for Captain Pettigrew and Blanche. Effie, too. I know she's scared. So I ask that You will take away that fear."

He paused. "I guess I can't think of anything else. So, how do I say good-bye? I guess, amen."

"Amen," Effie echoed, a sob breaking the word.

Ike's arms tightened around her. "What's the matter?"

"You prayed." Tears moistened his shirtsleeves. "Oh Ike, are you ready to trust God with your life?"

Ike didn't move or speak. "I think I am. Who would have believed it?"

"Me. God. Blanche. Mr. Sanders. Lots of people." She laughed through her tears. "No time like the present to ask Him to save you."

He couldn't fight it any longer. He and God had been waging war ever since he first saw Blanche at Christ the King Church, and God had won. He stifled the desire to fold his hands and bow his head. Now if ever he wanted to face God like a man. Raising his face to heaven and lifting empty hands to accept God's gift, he reopened his dialogue with God.

"God, I know I'm a sinner. I never pretended to be anything else. Not the worst, but I'm not a good person either, and besides, I hear that doesn't matter to You. You sent Your Son to die for me. Will You forgive me for all the things I've done wrong, please?"

He squeezed Effie's shoulder. "Is there anything else I should say?"

"God sees your heart. There are no perfect words."

"Well then, I guess that's it. Again. So. . .amen."

Thunder crashed again, and Effie laughed. Ike joined her.

"I guess that's God's answer."

"What, a big no?"

"No, silly. Amen! Exclamation point!"

A big grin split Ike's face to the breaking point. "Exclamation point! I like that." He jumped to his feet.

"Careful, now." Effie's tears had stopped, her fears at bay. "I don't know if that prayer will protect you from sheer foolishness."

The ship pitched, slamming him against the wall. The loudest crack of the night sent shudders through the ship. The nightstand tilted, throwing the lantern off. Ike caught it with his hands, heart in his mouth. *Fire.* He blew it out, the sudden darkness disorienting him. A sharp *crack* ripped through the air.

"Effie."

"I know. You have to go."

"I have to find out what happened."

He took a lantern in his hands and doused each lamp as he went down the hallway. He knocked on the doors. "Anyone hurt? Turn out the lights." His heart urged him to get up to the pilothouse, to Blanche, but the danger of fire couldn't be overlooked.

God, if ever we needed help, it's now.

CHAPTER 32

Lightning shimmered off the water and raced to the boat. Shivering, Blanche couldn't manage much of a prayer beyond *I'm scared, God.* The fear didn't go away, but she gained control of it, trusting God to look over the boat and all its inhabitants. Short breaths interspersed with quick glances out the window. The boat headed straight into the heart of the storm. Lightning traveled through water, didn't it? That meant she was more in danger from the storm on the boat than on land.

When Blanche was a little girl, a tornado had ripped through Roma. Wind whipped sand in the air as they rushed to the storm cellar. Belowground she could hear but not see the wind devastating the town.

Tonight she could both see and hear the wind. The mixture of wind and water could turn over this sturdy boat as easy as a house made of matchsticks.

Lightning struck so close that it blinded her. The boat heaved to one side, sending her into the wheel. Captain Pettigrew groaned, and she heard the sound of him hitting the floor. Hearing replaced sight as thunder crashed and a loud *crack* suggested something had broken.

Grasping the wheel, she pulled herself upright and sight returned. Miraculously, the windows remained intact; and the boat appeared headed on a straight course. She turned, expecting Pettigrew to take charge of the wheel.

He lay slumped against the captain's table, blood seeping from his forehead, his eyes closed. "Captain! Captain!" Panic laced her voice.

A moan greeted her cry. *He's alive.*

The need to keep her eyes on the river battled with the need to attend to the man lying on the floor. Deciding she'd have to chance it, she knelt down. "Captain?"

His eyes fluttered open. "Can't. . .move. . .my arm. You have to pilot the boat."

"Me?" Blanche's stomach flipped. Piloting the boat on a calm sunny day was one thing. A night when storm filled the skies was another matter indeed. "I haven't even taken the test yet."

"Noah didn't need a test when God called him to pilot the ark."

With a pleading eye on Captain Pettigrew, Blanche dragged the crate behind the wheel.

"Keep your eye sharp out there. Don't worry about me." He grunted, a cry of pain, and Blanche jerked her head to keep from turning around to see what had happened.

"It's my job to pray while you man the helm. Remember what I told you. Keep to the middle of the river. If the wind dies down, slow the engines."

Unwilling to trust her voice, she nodded. *I'm not ready for this.* "You need medical attention."

Pettigrew chuckled. "Have you hired a doctor recently? Ike will know who takes care of minor injuries while you're on the river. But you can't leave the wheel and I can't get down there on my own power." Another chuckle. "Besides, I'll be right here if you need to ask me a question." The words stopped, and his breathing rasped.

Lightning flashed again, farther away this time. *Praise God.* The captain cupped his right arm with his left, his face twisted in pain, his eyes closed. The thunder drowned out his breathing.

God, why this? Why tonight, before I'm ready? She channeled her fear into angry questions that helped strengthen her shivering limbs. *You gave Noah one hundred years. I haven't even had a month. Is this all some kind of punishment? Or maybe You're testing me, to see if I'm worthy?*

Her internal argument with God continued unabated while she kept her eyes fixed out the window, when the crate fishtailed beneath her and she had to climb off and reset it behind the wheel again. In between flashes of lightning, she snuck glances at Captain Pettigrew. Despite his brave words, he was in no condition to answer her questions. Had the wind lessened? Was it time to decrease the speed? Not yet.

Blanche needed to get a message to Pete and Ike, but she couldn't leave. They hadn't considered this possibility when they planned the schedule.

I suppose You planned that, too, God.

Where was Ike? She hadn't asked him to come to the bridge tonight, but she missed the security of his presence. *God, send him here tonight.*

She thought she heard the stairs creaking, but when no one came into the pilothouse, she decided it was only the deck shifting in the wind.

So I guess it's just You and me tonight, God.

Another clap of thunder followed, as if God was saying *I'm right here.* What had Reverend Sanders said about Noah's argument with God? That you have to believe in God to argue with Him? She looked at the clouds racing alongside the boat, the lightning striking on the Mexican side of the river. "You are here. Right here with me."

Her grip on the wheel remained strong and steady, but her heart stopped racing as fast as the boat. God was here. She could trust Him.

Ike stood still in the center of the hallway, gauging the motion of the boat. She rocked a little as it might at sea, but nothing felt broken beyond repair. Up until now, he had stayed busy taking care of passengers. People ran in and out of cabins, screaming questions and fighting small fires.

The storm had decreased in power, and he finished his inspection of the cabins. Next he would check the communal areas. In the kitchen he ran into Elaine, her round face gray by lantern light. "I turned off the ovens. It'll be a cold breakfast in the morning."

Ike nodded. "Smart move." Elaine was a veteran of storms on the river. After the kitchen, he toured the theater. Aside from a few repairs to stage props, the room remained undamaged.

When he put his foot on the staircase leading to the main deck, wind carrying raindrops whistled down the hole. Frowning, he considered going back to his room for a rain slicker. *No.* Someone might interrupt him with another problem. He wanted to check on Blanche and Captain Pettigrew, to reassure himself that the storm had left them unscathed. He hadn't hurried before now because the boat continued to run smoothly.

As he crossed the deck, lightning revealed pieces of a broken crate and other items scattered across the deck. In the pilothouse, a slight, feminine figure stood at the helm. Dark and rain descended again, and he couldn't see where Pettigrew was located.

What the fool was the man doing allowing Blanche to take the helm in weather like this? Keeping the lantern aloft so he could spot obstacles underfoot, he ran up the stairs.

Turning the corner into the room, he almost stumbled over Pettigrew's prone body. For a quick, frightening moment, he wondered if the man had died. Then the captain's chest heaved and a moan came from between his lips.

"Ike?"

Blanche turned her face, white in the bright flash of lightning, a hint of lines at her eyes suggesting she had peered into the heart of the darkness of the sky. He also thought he saw a hint of excitement.

It's the Lord. What would Blanche think if he said that? She might faint alongside Pettigrew, and what a mess that would make of things. "What happened?"

"Captain Pettigrew fell and broke his arm. Since someone had to stay at the helm. . ." She risked a quick glance at Ike then returned her attention to the front window. "I had to take over."

"She's doing a fine job of it, too." A weak voice spoke from the floor.

"You're awake." Blanche shifted her feet beneath her. "I was getting worried about you. Ike, is there someone in the crew who sets bones and such?"

"One of the valets."

"Good. Get him to look after Captain Pettigrew."

Ike hesitated. He had come to offer them his help and support, and she was sending him away?

"Unless you want to take the helm?" She didn't turn around.

"Not him. You. You're doing a good job," Pettigrew said.

"Old Obie would be proud." Ike draped Pettigrew's good arm over his shoulder and helped him to his feet. His right arm dangled at his side, the elbow jutting out at an odd angle.

Ike speared Blanche with his eyes. "I don't like leaving you here alone."

"I'm not alone." Her voice shook the slightest bit.

Ike glanced around the pilothouse. *Who?*

"God." She answered his unasked question. "God reminded me that He is always with me."

Of course. A smile came to his face. He couldn't wait to tell her about his decision, but now wasn't the time. He took her words to his heart.

"Now go. Send Pete up here once you leave the captain with the valet."

Lightning flashed in the distance, accenting her words. "The storm is moving away. I'll be fine."

Ike and Pettigrew had already taken a step down the stairs. She was wrong about one thing; he would come back himself rather than send relief. Until the crisis had passed, he wanted to stay by her side. In good times and bad. The two of them had a lot to talk about.

⁓

Somewhere, in the long stretches of the night, Blanche's argument with God turned to praise. With each shift of the wheel, each tug of the bell pull to the engine room, she felt His presence stronger and stronger. Every time lightning illuminated the sky, she remembered lessons her father had taught her. If she could get through this storm without harm to vessel or personnel, she could pass the pilot test with ease.

Lightning flashed to her far left, and she held her breath while she counted under her breath. One Mississippi, two Mississippi. . . She got as far as ten Mississippi before thunder followed. The storm was falling behind them. She pulled the bell to slow the engines.

Ike was sweet, the way he didn't want to leave her to face the big bad storm alone. He hadn't even teased her when she said God was with her. Was it possible? No. God had given them one miracle in bringing her through this storm. She couldn't expect Ike to change his soul-deep beliefs after such a short time.

She jerked her mind back from the subject, rejecting the distraction. What she needed was a cup of coffee. Weariness warred with her stamina. When Captain Pettigrew and Ike were in the room, she could carry on a conversation. Of course she could talk with God, but it wasn't the same.

Sing. That worked in the past when she needed help focusing. She envisioned the hymnal from Christ the King church. Starting with the front piece, she sang the doxology. "Praise Father, Son, and Holy Ghost." Also inside the front cover she envisioned the Apostles' Creed and the Nicene Creed. She scrunched her eyes in concentration then forced them open to keep her eyes on the river.

The first hymn, "Holy, Holy, Holy," repeated the cry of the angels in front of the emerald throne from Revelation. She sang through hymns of praise, sometimes singing one verse, sometimes all of them, humming when she couldn't remember the words. With each song, the time between lightning and thunder grew further apart. By the time she got to "Praise to the Lord, the Almighty!" she realized she hadn't seen any lightning for a few minutes, and she caught a glimpse of the moon as the wind blew the clouds away.

Praise the Lord. They had survived.

CHAPTER 33

The back of Ike's eyes felt like sandpaper, but his heart was as soft as cotton. The night had ended and the storm had passed. He and Blanche planned to walk the ship from stem to stern, to determine what damages the *Cordelia* had sustained. Elaine had changed her mind and relit the oven for a hot breakfast. Never had grits, crisp bacon, and orange juice tasted so good skipping down his throat.

"We should get going." Blanche wore her old, sensible black traveling suit, but Ike didn't blame her. He had donned Levi's himself. Water, mud, splinters—he suspected they would find all of that, and more, from what the watery moonlight revealed last night.

"We have time to finish another cup of coffee." Ike poured them each a fresh cup and grabbed a couple of peach muffins for good measure. "I asked Effie to join us."

Blanche blinked. "I thought you would want to check everything right away." She made no effort to leave the table.

"I do, but I have something I need to tell you first. And here's Effie." The door opened and Effie took a seat at the table. "I have coffee and muffins for us to celebrate."

Blanche stirred cream into her coffee. "What are we celebrating? Surviving the storm?"

"That's part of it." Effie nudged Ike in the side. "Tell her."

Blanche set the spoon back on the napkin. "What is it?"

Ike couldn't keep the scowl on his face, and a smile broke out. "Effie asked me to pray during the storm."

"And he did."

A smile as brilliant as sunshine lit Blanche's face. "That's wonderful. Amazing!" She grabbed one of the muffins and split it open.

Another nudge poked him in the ribs.

"And then I realized—with Effie's help, of course"—he patted her hand—"if I believed in God enough to think He'd care about us in the middle of a storm, and if I believed He had enough power to do something about it. . .then I must believe the rest of it, too."

Blanche slowly spread butter on her muffin that melted into the surface while her smile grew even bigger. "You mean. . ."

"I asked Jesus to be my Savior. I've joined the good guys, or I guess, God made me one."

The butter knife slipped from Blanche's hand and clanged against the plate as she clapped her hands. Her cheeks grew fever pink, and her breath came in little gasps. She swallowed a couple of times and drank from her water glass. When she finally spoke, her voice came out in a whisper. "Praise God. Oh, praise God." Tears sparkled in her eyes. "I doubted God." Her laugh came out as a hiccup. "You seemed, well, different, last night, and I wondered if something had happened."

"But you didn't think I would ever change my mind?" Ike didn't blame her. "I didn't think so, either."

This time the tears slid from her eyes down her cheeks. "I told God He had performed one miracle already, helping me pilot the boat. I didn't want to be greedy and expect two miracles in one night. But He was, He is always, gracious and compassionate and giving. He gives more than we can ask or think."

Standing, Blanche put an arm around Effie and then Ike. "I had no idea why God brought me to this boat. I felt so alone.

But when Effie came back to the Lord, He gave me a sister. . ." She squeezed Effie's shoulder as she said the words. "And then a father." She sniffed back a tear. "And now a brother."

Ike forced a smile as his heart sank. Her *brother*?

"The family of God," Effie said.

"Adopted by the Father and coheirs with Christ. This *does* call for a celebration." She sat back down and ate the muffin in tiny bites. "Do you have a Bible?"

"I found a Bible in Old Obie's cabin. I thought I could borrow it, if you don't mind."

Blanche nodded. "That's a good idea. Effie and I are studying the Bible together at night, some basic information new believers need to know. Do you want to join us?"

"An instruction course in how to be a Christian?"

"Nothing that fancy." Blanche laughed. "But a lot of people get bogged down if they start in Genesis and try to read through the Bible. Or maybe you should meet with Mr. Sanders."

"Or both?" He grinned.

"Good idea."

They finished the muffins and polished off the pitcher of coffee. Effie stacked their plates and headed for the kitchen. "What do you think about holding a service this evening, thanking God for bringing us safely through the storm?"

"Of course." Blanche giggled. "And Ike, you'll even want to come."

"Amen." Ike used his best actor's voice. With a chuckle, he said, "Can you believe it?"

"I'll get together with Reverend Sanders then." Effie stood. "And I have some ideas for a new play that I want to think about."

"My little sister." Ike shook his head. "You are amazing." He offered his arm to Blanche. "Shall we?"

Blanche leaned on his arm as they walked out of the dining salon. "I want to check on Captain Pettigrew first. And we need to come up with a schedule to pilot the boat until we arrive in Brownsville." She paused, her hand on his arm holding him back. "Do you think I'm ready to take the test for my pilot's license?"

Ike threw back his head and laughed. "I'd say anybody who

brought the boat through that storm already passed the real test. You're more than ready."

"I want to arrange for it as soon as possible then. Captain Pettigrew can't work until his arm heals. We're back where we were before we hired him. We need another pilot."

"We'll have to stop at night until we take care of that." Ike nodded. "I've thought of that. It's a good thing we're only a couple of days away from the mouth of the river."

The sling on Pettigrew's arm couldn't hide his pain. "I'm sorry to leave you in a lurch."

"And I feel terrible about your broken arm." Blanche took the chair next to the berth.

"Don't worry about that." With his good arm, Pettigrew waved away her concern. "God will work it all out."

"For both of us." After they said their good-byes, Ike and Blanche stopped by each cabin. The furniture had been tossed about, but nothing had broken except a few cracked lanterns, and no one was injured.

Ike made a mental list of needed repairs below deck. "I've seen a lot worse damage in other storms."

He glanced at Blanche, and they spoke at the same time. "God."

Next they headed for the main deck. Fresh cedar scent washed through the air, carrying a refreshing after-rain smell. Blanche drew a deep breath. "I bet the earth smelled like this after the flood."

"And required a lot more cleanup." Ike took her hand and led her toward the cargo hold. A mixed mess greeted them. Most of the heavy crates, tied in place with heavy rope, hadn't budged, but the wind had moved some of the empty pallets. Water stained heavy burlap sacks of flour, sugar, and cornmeal.

"Can we salvage the flour?" Wheat flour didn't grow easily in Texas. Of the different consumables, it was worth the most money.

"I. . .doubt it." She lowered her face and closed her eyes as if in prayer.

Ike also sent up a silent prayer. He supposed God could listen to more than one prayer at a time. Add that question to the list of things he didn't know.

Opening her eyes, Blanche took a resolute step forward. "We'll get someone up here to get a count. Let's see what other damage we're faced with."

A couple of the smaller crates had broken open, but the straw packing had protected most of it. "The foreman can check the number of crates, but it doesn't look like we've lost much. I think the foodstuff is the worst of it." Grimacing, he shrugged his shoulders. "It could be worse." A night or two of cards with Ventura and his friends would make up the difference.

"Thinking about the gambling you gave up?"

Could she read his mind? "I wish I could say no. I don't have a handle on this faith thing."

"None of us do. Even Paul said, 'Not as though I had already attained, either were already perfect.' And Paul had more faith than anyone else in the entire New Testament." She gave a shaky laugh. "So what if we don't have hot bread for a few days? And besides, the plays are bringing in more money than we expected." Turning, she looked Ike straight in the eyes. "Being a Christian doesn't mean everything is easy. But it does mean God is with us through everything that happens."

Ike thought about that. No one could call Blanche's life easy, but her faith in God grew stronger with each challenge. "It will be interesting to hear what everyone has to say at the service tonight. I'm sure we'll hear some tall tales."

~❖~

Blanche enjoyed listening to the testimonies. More than any time since she had arrived aboard the *Cordelia*, she felt at ease with the members of her crew.

The stories varied from childhood memories of running to her father's lap when she was a little girl—a surprising revelation from the imposing Dame Agatha—to playing baseball during a rainstorm when lightning hit the field—an equally surprising revelation by Smithers.

After everyone who wanted to had shared—only one extremely shy server and a couple of the gruffer stevedores demurred—Ike rose to his feet. "I had a life-changing experience during this storm."

He glanced at Blanche, and she nodded, smiling to encourage him to go forward. He looked handsome as always, dressed in his beige linen suit, a gold brocade vest, and an olive green shirt. Perfect match with his bright blue eyes. Yesterday she had called him her brother, but if she was honest with herself, the feelings growing in heart differed from those for a brother.

"When the storm started last night, I prayed for the first time in a long time. I'm not sure why." Shrugging a single shoulder, he flashed that amazing grin. "Those of you who have been with us on the river for a while know we have these storms from time to time. And I haven't prayed before. But yesterday I did.

"And then I realized that if I trusted God enough to ask Him to save us from the storm, I could trust Him with the rest of my life. And so I did. I asked Jesus to be my Savior."

"Praise the Lawd," Reverend Sanders called out. Around the circle, several people clapped and others added a quiet "amen." Some of the engineers and stevedores exchanged covert looks, probably wondering how life aboard the *Cordelia* would change.

"And I guess. . .that's all." He bowed to another burst of spontaneous applause and sat down.

"I'll share next." Effie rose to her feet with a quiet rustle of fabric. "When the storm kept raging and it became clear we wouldn't get much sleep last night, I made my way to the dining salon. When I felt bad when I was a little girl, I played the piano. I still do." She walked in the direction of the piano. "So last night, I remembered a hymn I heard at a revival service about a year ago." She sat on the stool and began to sing "It Is Well with my Soul." When she reached the chorus, Blanche added the echoing "It is well" in the alto voice, to Effie's strong soprano. Her heart beat strong. *It is well with my soul.* They sang all three verses, ending with the resounding excitement of "Haste the day when my faith shall be sight." They'd have to teach Ike one of the men's parts and sing it at their next Sunday service.

After the resounding amen at the end of the hymn, Effie turned around on the piano stool. "I knew it was a special song as soon as I heard it, but the story is even better. Horatio Spafford had already suffered the loss of a son and of a fortune when his four daughters died in a shipwreck. Only his wife survived. When he said 'when sorrows like sea billows roll,' he was speaking the literal truth." Lowering her head, she dabbed at her eyes. "I have to confess I couldn't have said 'it is well with my soul' or written such beautiful music after I lost my parents, or after Captain Lamar died. But this man did. So last night, while the thunder continued crashing and crates rattled around overhead, I sang Mr. Spafford's song. It is well with my soul, because God is always with me. In the worst storm or on the hottest summer day. In the dining salon or aboard Noah's ark." Twirling the piano seat back to the correct position, Effie made her way back to the congregation.

The crew turned their attention to Blanche. This part of her inheritance still caught her in unexpected ways. Nothing in her life had prepared her to lead a company, but she enjoyed it more than she thought she would.

The closest thing in her past was singing in front of an audience, but it didn't feel the same. The people waiting before her were both employees and her new family, people to whom she was bound by cords of responsibility, concern, and affection. She looked around the room, engaging each pair of eyes for a brief second before moving on. "After everything that's been said, I don't have much to add. I love that hymn. It is well with my soul. I didn't know if I would ever feel that way again after my mother died. I was scared when I first arrived onboard. I didn't know anyone. Even worse, I didn't know if I could trust anyone. But God." To her surprise, tears clogged her throat, and she coughed to clear her throat.

"But God had other plans." Blanche reviewed some of the highlights of her time aboard the *Cordelia*. She found something to say about everyone, although Ike dominated her thoughts.

"Now I hope to become an official pilot. For as long as God permits us to make a living, I look forward to life aboard the *Cordelia*." She sat down amidst enthusiastic applause, and realized she had announced a decision that she wasn't consciously aware she had reached.

Everything was well with her soul, aboard the steamboat *Cordelia*.

God was good.

CHAPTER 34

One month later

Blanche sat next to Effie at the piano, making a stab at noting the melodies from the new musical on music graph paper.

"Dum, de-dum, dum," Blanche hummed. "Sorry this is taking me so long."

"I'm thrilled someone can write it down." Effie's hand riffled over the keyboard. "I don't think anyone has come up with Braille for music yet."

Blanche giggled. "I'm picturing someone trying to read Braille music and play the piano at the same time."

"That might be hard." Effie repeated the first line again. "I'm glad Mr. Sanders suggested the story of the Israelites crossing the Jordan River and the fall of Jericho for this musical."

"He's preparing a list of all the stories that take place on a river or the sea. We won't run out of ideas for a while."

"Moses in the bulrushes—"

"Jesus calming the storm—"

"Paul's shipwreck—"

"But the walls of Jericho is an exciting story to start with. I can't believe I'm going to be Rahab." Blanche draped a pillowcase across her face like a veil and giggled.

"With Ike as Salmon." Effie kept a straight face. "Rahab's future husband."

Blanche cheeks heated, and she was thankful Effie couldn't see her face. There were times when Effie's blindness was a blessing. "And I can't believe Dame Agatha has offered to make all the costumes we need, so everyone who wants to can march around Jericho."

She wanted to hug herself. God had blessed their showboat drama program so that their financial problems had disappeared for the moment. "We're not getting anything done this way. Go on."

They had already finished the marching song, with the chorus they repeated seven times. This song occurred earlier in the story, when the spies told Rahab about the one true God. Effie had written a haunting melody with memorable harmonies, but Blanche struggled to get them on paper. Half an hour later, she had managed the three voices. "I'll work on the piano part later. If we run out of other things to do."

The first lunch bell rang. "That's all we'll get to today. I'm going to be in the pilothouse this afternoon." Work filled Blanche's days from morning to night, and she loved every minute of it.

Outside the theater door, the thrum of footfalls raced down the hall. Blanche frowned. "Who is making all that noise? There aren't any children onboard this trip."

"Give me a minute to clean up. Then we can go see."

Blanche wanted to go remind—whoever it was—that crew didn't run in the halls. But she wouldn't run out on her friend. Minutes ticked by, the halls grew quiet, and the last warning bell rang.

"I'm ready to go now. Sorry it took me so long today." Even with those words, Effie leisurely stacked papers on top of the piano and took up her cane. If they didn't get to the salon soon, they would delay the meal for everyone else.

Blanche matched Effie's speed as they made their way down the hall to the dining salon. The aroma of saucy beans greeted her nose. She loved beans and corn bread for lunch. Her stomach growled.

Through the door—closed, not propped open the way

Blanche had instructed—she heard low murmurs, as if the room was crowded. "I'm afraid we're really late."

"I don't think Elaine will mind." Effie's voice held a hint of laughter as Blanche swung the door open.

"Surprise!"

Every member of the crew not on duty stood in a loose circle around the room. Someone had draped a banner reading "Congratulations, Captain Lamar!" in gigantic red letters across the kitchen window.

"You—you. . ." Blanche stammered.

Ike stepped forward. "I ran into Mr. Roberts from the Board of Examiners when we were in Brownsville the last time, and he told me the news."

Smithers exited the kitchen, bearing a shining silver platter with a thin envelope. Elaine and one of her assistants followed, balancing a cake between them. A single white candle burned brightly in the center.

"Here is your mail, Captain." Smithers smiled. He *smiled*. With the envelope between two thin fingers, he extended it to Blanche.

Two dozen pairs of eyes trained on her. What if. . . Blanche couldn't stand waiting any longer. Grasping the letter opener, she slit the end of the envelope and pulled out a thin sheet of paper. "It's from the Board of Examiners." Blanche read the return address.

"What does it say?" Effie's smile told her she had known about the celebration.

"We are pleased to inform you. . .you are now qualified to pilot a boat on any of the waterways in the state of Texas." The letter dropped from Blanche's hand, her arms, her legs, her shoulders trembling beyond her control. "I'm a pilot." Her voice came out as a squeak.

The room rang with applause.

"Ahoy, Captain."

"Aye, aye, Captain!"

Different calls erupted across the room.

Elaine had positioned the cake on the table. "Blow out the

candle." She gestured to the fantastic concoction of flowery frosting and "Captain Lamar" written in blue and red letters. "I know it's not your birthday, but it seemed right."

Heat rushing into her cheeks, Blanche leaned over the center of the table and blew. As nervous as she was, she didn't know if she could expel enough breath to blow out the flame. It flickered and went out.

With a sparkle in his eye, Ike handed her a knife. "Go ahead and cut the cake."

With the knife as long as her forearm, Blanche cut a two-inch corner piece. "You take the first piece." Ike took over with the server.

Each crew member stopped by to say a few words, so Blanche ate the cake very slowly.

"Well done, Miss Lamar." Dame Agatha came about midway through the line. "I have asked Mr. Gallagher to buy some material to make you a captain's uniform."

"Why, thank you, D—Agatha."

Some of the crew ate quickly then slipped out. Others came when they left. "Sorry I couldn't be here earlier," McDonald said. "I stayed downstairs so Jose and Tomas could be here at the start. Congratulations, Captain!"

"Thank you for coming." Tears came into her eyes. Her crew had done so much to make this day special.

She eventually finished that first piece of cake and eyed a second piece. Ike slid a corner piece onto a plate and handed it to her. "I saved this piece for you."

One of the younger maids approached, and Blanche asked Ike to set it aside for later.

Alice, the maid, approached. "I just wanted to say, ma'am, how very pleased and proud we all are of your passing your pilot's test. I can't believe as how they let a woman do that. It makes me think maybe someday women will be able to do anything they want to. Maybe even vote." The timid girl's eyes blazed.

"Who knows what the future holds?" Blanche hugged the girl. "Whatever dreams God gives you, pursue them with all your heart."

Elaine disappeared to the back of the kitchen, and Blanche glanced at the clock. When had it grown so late? Soon the dinner bell would ring. "I hate to say it, but. . ."

". . . We have a show to put on tonight. Don't worry. Several of the crew members are in the theater getting everything ready. You should rest."

"I'm supposed to be in the pilothouse!" Blanche's hand flew to her mouth.

Ike and Effie laughed. "We've been anchored at the wharf for the past two hours. Pete decided he should rest, since he knows we'll want to leave as soon as we clear out from tonight's performance. He sends his congratulations, by the way."

"I'm a pilot." She whispered the words. Butterflies fluttered in her stomach, and she had no room for the second piece of cake. "Save it for me, Elaine. I'll eat it later."

"I'm going to rest until supper." Effie headed for the door. "Are you coming with me?"

Blanche circled, taking in the banner, the remains of the cake sitting on the table, with the single white candle in the middle. She picked up the letter from the board and raised it to her lips. "Not this afternoon. I'll take a turn around the deck."

"May I join you?" Ike held his hands behind his back.

"Of course." They walked toward the door.

"Congratulations. Again. I am so proud of you." With a flash of his hands, he brought a single red rose from behind his back. "For you."

"How beautiful." She brought the rose to her nose as he opened the door. "But how did you. . . When did you. . ."

"I dashed into town as soon as we received the mail and begged the rose from someone with a rosebush in her front yard." His eyes darkened to the midnight blue. "I told her it was for a special occasion for a special woman."

How should she respond to that? "Thank you."

They promenaded around the perimeter until they reached the prow. The boat split the water, causing small waves to stream backward.

"I can't ever decide what I like better. Watching the water

spill over the stern wheel or watching the prow split the river." Blanche kept the rose close to her nose. The velvety soft petals brushed against her cheeks.

"Isn't there a verse that warns against looking at what lies behind?" Ike picked up a small piece of wood and tossed it over the side. "But I know this: I am looking forward to the future."

"That's good. So am I."

"So you should, Captain Lamar."

They didn't speak for a few minutes. Blanche felt long fingers wrap her free hand in his, and she turned to look at Ike.

"I can't predict the future, but one thing I know for sure." Ike spoke in a low, warm voice. "I love you, Blanche Marie Lamar, and I can't imagine a future without you."

Blanche's gaze slowly traveled from the spot where their hands joined, to his shoulders, to his strong chin, at last allowing herself to gaze into his clear blue eyes. She reached a hesitant hand to caress his cheek. "Oh Ike."

"I know that I have a lot to learn, to be ready to be the kind of husband God wants me to be."

"Ike—"

"Let me finish." He took a deep breath. "All I can ask you for now is if you are willing to wait for me, until I *am* that man, and I feel qualified to ask you to share my life." His eyes stayed as sharply focused, but had turned to a lighter shade of blue, more like the color of fragile china.

"Ike. Oh Ike." She leaned forward and kissed him on the lips then stepped back, shocked at her boldness. "I don't expect perfection."

Ike stepped forward, closing the gap between them. "Then?"

"I will gladly wait." She blinked through the happy tears. "As long as you don't take too long."

This time Ike leaned in and sealed her promise with a kiss.

⇥⇤

Christmas Sunday, 1894

Blanche had never worn such a fancy gown, although Dame

Agatha insisted the lack of puffed sleeves made it plain. The skirt fell in unbroken folds of winter white brocade. White tulle trailed from her veil down her back. The hairdresser Dame Agatha had recruited from Roma was weaving strings of pearls as well as orange blossoms into the soft curls on top of her head. Blanche could never have managed such an elaborate coiffure on her own.

The red roses of her bouquet were a different matter. Blanche had approached the same lady who provided the rose from her garden and asked for a posy. She had agreed and fashioned a beautiful bouquet.

"I don't often mind being blind, but I wish I could see you in your dress." Effie herself looked beautiful in her Christmassy dark green dress.

When planning the wedding, they had debated whether Effie should play the piano—her preference—or be her maid of honor—what Blanche wanted. When the Davenports heard about the impending nuptials, Mrs. Davenport graciously offered to play the piano for the wedding. Reverend Davenport and Mr. Sanders would both officiate.

"I will tell Mrs. Davenport to start Lohengrin's 'Bridal Chorus'." Agatha dipped in what could have passed as a curtsy. "You are truly beautiful."

Ike and Blanche had given brief consideration to holding the wedding at Christ the King Church but decided the best place for the wedding was aboard the *Cordelia*. She had dressed in Dame Agatha's room, since the laundry was on the same deck as the theater. Various members of the crew had decorated the theater like a chapel; half the town of Roma was invited.

Even now Ike was making his way into the theater. A thrill ran up Blanche's spine as she considered him waiting for her, dressed in a black tuxedo. After his salvation, he had devoured the Bible, reading all the way through it twice, and had become as committed to following the Lord as he had pushed Him away earlier. So when Ike asked for her hand at Thanksgiving, Blanche had gladly accepted.

Captain Pettigrew appeared at the door. "Is the bride ready?"

Blanche blinked away the happy tears. She imagined Old Obie watching from heaven.

"Yes." She accepted his arm.

"You are breathtaking, my dear. And so are you, Miss Effie."

Music streamed through the open doors of the salon. Effie had decided not to use her cane since she knew the boat like the back of her hand. She took half a dozen steps, turned at the entrance to the salon, and walked through.

At the first chords of the "Wedding Chorus," Captain Pettigrew drew Blanche gently forward. When she crossed the threshold, Ike filled her vision. He smiled, and her face widened in answer.

When she reached her groom, the "Wedding Chorus" ended, and Effie began singing. "When peace like a river attendeth my way..."

It is well; it is well with my soul.

Award-winning author and speaker Darlene Franklin recently returned to cowboy country—Oklahoma. The move
was prompted by her desire to be close to her son's family; her
daughter Jolene has preceded her into glory.

Darlene loves music, needlework, reading, and reality TV.
Talia, a Lynx point Siamese cat, proudly claims Darlene as her
person. Darlene has published several titles with Barbour Publishing.

To learn more about Darlene and her work, check out her
blog at http://darlenefranklinwrites.blogspot.com/

Valiant Heart

by Sally Laity

VALIANT HEART

By Sally Laity

The first time I laid eyes on you
    I thought you were like all the others. . .
Helpless, weepy, and a lot less bright than you should be.
    How wrong I was.
For what I perceived to be
    A stubborn streak turned out to be the opposite. . .
Fortitude. Backbone.
    A spirit of adventure.
Yet despite those admirable traits,
    What struck me most about you
Were things entirely different. . .
    Qualities I could not even name, at first.
Trust. Hope. Striving onward for what is right.
    I see now that faith is something
Which stretches beyond Sunday
    to all the days of one's life.
And character comes from deep within. . .

    As intangible and enduring as a valiant heart.

CHAPTER 1

Missouri
May 1848

Amanda Shelby stared out the window of her second-story room in the Bradford Hotel. Scattered showers had dotted the dirt streets of Independence with puddles—glossy brown mirrors that reflected the puffy clouds and blue expanse of the ever-changing spring sky above.

And everywhere were people. Young and old, whole families of them, eager and waiting to start out on the trail to the rich, fertile valleys and hills of Oregon. They had all but emptied the mercantile and hardware stores of goods until new shipments arrived, and then those, too, would be snatched up before they had time to gather dust on the shelves. The process would repeat itself over and over throughout the spring as numerous companies of travelers gathered to begin the westward trek over mountains and plains to establish new homes before the onset of winter.

As she gazed wistfully at the bustling scene below, the iron-rimmed wheels of a pair of Conestogas splashed through the puddles, rumbling toward the growing encampment near the spring on the outskirts of town. Two small boys leaned precariously out of the bowed canvas top of the second wagon, their eyes round with excitement. At the sight of a garishly dressed woman in red satin and a feather boa, in front of the Bluebird Saloon, they elbowed each other, then darted back inside the confines of their arched haven.

Amanda released a sigh and steeled her heart against a twinge of sadness. Only a few short weeks ago, Pa had driven her and Sarah Jane in their own prairie schooner over the quay and up the steep grade to Independence Square, their hearts full of hopes and plans for the trip overland to the Far West. But that seemed so long ago, almost like a dream. Nothing could alter the grim reality that Pa now occupied a fresh grave on a lonely hillside a mere stone's throw away. The cruel twist of fate had brought a swift end to the visions of their wondrous new life. Now the world felt bleak and empty, and Amanda had no idea what she and Sarah would do.

Almost as if the last thought had been an audible summons, her seventeen-year-old younger sister breezed into the room, wheat-gold curls slightly tangled by the breeze. The triumphant smile that lit her guileless face looked a little out of place against the shadows beneath her eyes. Amanda had been more than aware of Sarah's tossing and turning each night during the past few weeks—and her soft crying. But during her waking hours the younger girl flitted about in a near frenzy of activity, as if trying to keep too busy to dwell on their losses.

Sarah draped her woolen shawl over the back of a chair and held out her tote. "There were only three bottles of sarsaparilla left in the whole town! I nearly had to fend off a mob to get one of them!" Then she sobered, concern drawing her fine brows together above shimmering eyes of clearest blue. "Something wrong, Mandy?"

"Just thinking a little too much." Amanda silently regarded her sibling, who was the very picture of what she herself had always wished to be—willowy and graceful as Mama, with delicate features and a face that never failed to turn heads. But alas, that particular dream had been in vain. Amanda had conceded long ago that it was only fair that one of them resembled the plainer, sturdier Shelby side of the family, and she was the only other one there was. Twisting an errant strand of light auburn hair absently between her thumb and forefinger, she backed away from the muslin-curtained window and sank to a chair, smoothing the skirt of her somber brown cotton dress.

Sarah set down her booty on the small round table next to the door, then crossed the room and gave Amanda a hug. "As Mama always said, death is as much a part of life as birth is." She made a wry grimace, and when she spoke again, her tone sounded tart. "Maybe we should be used to it by now, after losing everyone dearest to us this past year."

Yes, everyone. Shaking off the tormenting reminder that her own losses went beyond mere beloved family members—to the death of her most cherished dream as well—Amanda quickly snuffed the thoughts that could so easily consume her in bitterness. "I'll never ever be used to it."

The younger girl smiled gently and gave Amanda's shoulder a comforting squeeze. "No, I don't suppose I will either, to be truthful. But at least we can think on what Pa said just before he passed on, about not wanting us to wear black and drown in mournful tears. He felt his time had come, and he had peace about where he was going. And he's with Mama now. Her and the baby. As for us, well, I think we owe it to him to heed his words and keep alive his dream of starting over."

"Whatever you say." Pressing her lips tightly together before she voiced a thought about the senselessness of life, Amanda heard a growing noise outside. She stood and returned to the window to see a handful of rowdy boys wrestling in the soggy dirt on the street below. Not far from them, two shaggily dressed buffalo hunters with clenched fists were in a heated debate of their own, their gruff voices spewing bursts of profanity to which no one paid the slightest heed.

From the corner of her eye, Amanda could see her sister filling two tall glasses.

Sarah offered one to her as she stepped to her side. "What's all the commotion?"

"Another fight. I'm looking forward to some peace and quiet when that train finally pulls out."

"So am I. Surely the spring grasses along the route are green and tall enough for the animals to graze on by now."

Several minutes of silence lapsed as they sipped their drinks and surveyed the harried activity that seemed never to cease. Independence, far from being a sleepy little hamlet, was second only to St. Louis as a river port. The hotel proprietor had assured them that the height of each spring season was the same—the whole town overrun with river men, steamship captains, hunters and trappers, traders, teamsters, and hordes of emigrants, the latter all fighting over the scant grazing for their thousands of horses, mules, and oxen. Even on the Lord's Day, constant movement and voices of the transients filled the air.

"What do you think will become of us?"

Amanda caught her breath. She had been wondering the very same thing herself. Staying at the hotel indefinitely was not even a remote possibility. The expense of lodging and meals was putting a serious drain on their funds and would soon make it necessary for them both to seek employment. The home and possessions that had been sold before leaving the verdant green woods of northeastern Pennsylvania now seemed not only part of some other world, but another life as well.

Unbidden memories of sailing the Great Lakes to Chicago, then boarding a steamboat to St. Louis and securing their outfit for going west, were as real in her mind as if they had occurred yesterday. Who would have imagined all of that would come to naught, all Pa's plans to relocate in Oregon Territory and use his woodcrafting talents to provide for the three of them. Now it was left to Amanda and her sister to make their own life somewhere. Somehow.

Sarah Jane stepped away from the window and moved to the dark pine four-poster abutting one wall of the room. She picked up her guitar from where it leaned against the headboard. After absently twisting the tuning pegs and adjusting the pitch, she sat down on the quilted counterpane and strummed a soft chord, then another, and a dreamy smile curved her lips.

Amanda groaned inwardly. Strumming always led to singing, and for all Sarah's innocent sincerity and melodious speaking voice, she was blissfully unaware of the fact she could not carry a tune. "I, um, think I'll go for a walk and get the cobwebs out of my head," Amanda blurted. She grabbed her gloves and warm shawl from the armoire and made a swift exit on the first few hummed notes.

Outside, the soles of Amanda's hightop shoes made hollow sounds on the board sidewalk, the rhythmic echoes blending with the voices and footfalls of others as she threaded her way through the throng, dodging loose chickens and the occasional small farm animal in her path. False fronts on the assorted wooden buildings lining both sides of the street gave the illusion they were more impressive than they actually were. After passing the bank and the barber, the wheelwright and gunsmith, she finally stopped at the last smithy's shop on the street.

The owner, a stocky, muscular man in his midforties, glanced up from the red-hot horseshoe he was plucking from the fire with a pair of long tongs. "Afternoon, miss." He nudged the beak of his black working cap higher, exposing a band of light skin on his soot-streaked forehead.

"Good afternoon, Mr. Plummer. No one has purchased the prairie schooner as yet?"

" 'Fraid not. Folks what need 'em, already has 'em by the time they get to town, unless they arranged ahead of time for one of the wagonwrights to build 'em one." He set the glowing shoe down on the anvil and raised a muscled arm to administer a few whacks with his hammer.

Amanda's ears rang with each blow, and she sighed as she gazed at the big wagon Pa had bought, now parked alongside the enterprise. Such a waste, brand spanking new, and complete with foodstuffs and tools sufficient for the journey west, plus three braces of mules being housed in the livery. Surely someone should have been interested in it by this time. It galled her to think she might end up having to sell the entire outfit to that shrewd Mr. Cavanaugh, the owner of the mercantile, after all. The offer he had made for it was shockingly low—despite the ridiculous prices he charged for things in his store. The knowledge that her and her sister's loss would be very profitable to that scoundrel was a bitter pill to swallow. Amanda could just picture his smug expression of triumph if she were forced by circumstance to acquiesce. "Well, I'll check back with you tomorrow," she said, turning to leave. "Perhaps someone will still come along and want it."

"Could be. I did have a couple of people askin' after the goods." He cocked a bushy eyebrow in question.

Amanda shook her head. "No. We wouldn't want to sell things off that way except as a last resort. Certainly a full wagon would be of much more value to a latecomer, don't you think? We've been careful to leave everything intact so the entire outfit would be available for a quick sale."

" 'S'pose there's always that possibility, but time's runnin' out, miss, till the next train starts gatherin'.'"

"I'm aware of that. But still. . ."

He sniffed and wiped his bulbous nose with a large kerchief, then returned the cloth to his back pocket. "Well, don't worry, I won't do nothin' without your say-so. I'm keepin' an eye on it for ya."

"Thank you, Mr. Plummer. My sister and I truly appreciate all your trouble. Good day."

With a heavy heart and at a much slower pace, she strolled toward the hotel. Slanting rays of the sun at Amanda's back elongated her shadow as it flowed gracefully over the walk ahead, making her appear several inches taller than her five-foot height—and nearly as slender as Sarah. She lifted her chin.

Several hours later, kneeling at her bedside, Amanda did her best to ignore the outside racket while she formulated her heavenly petitions. When the cool breath of night rustled the curtain on the partially open bedroom window and raised gooseflesh, she rose and climbed into the warm bed.

"Your prayers took longer than usual," Sarah said.

"I have a lot on my mind," Amanda confessed.

All at once her sister's seemingly blithe acceptance of their fate irked her. Blinking back stinging tears, she raised up on one elbow to face the younger girl, unable to bite back the angry words that insisted upon tumbling out of her mouth. "Aren't you the least concerned that we're completely alone in the world now—

and have only a pittance to get us by for heaven knows how long? It took everything Pa could scrape together after paying off those debts that—that—" Amanda fought to keep from choking on the name, "*Morris Jamison* dumped on him, you know, to finance this venture. And when our money is gone, I haven't the slightest idea what we're going to do."

"I never said I wasn't concerned," Sarah said quietly.

Chagrined at the sight of the moisture glistening in her sister's eyes, Amanda berated herself for her hasty words and reached over to hug Sarah. "I know. I'm sorry, Sissy. I shouldn't have said that."

"The Reverend O'Neill told us we have to trust God for the strength we need to go on. And the more I think about it, the more I agree. We can't spend the rest of our lives moping around, however tempting that might be. Pa did that after Mama died, and look what it did to him. Working day and night, not sleeping, barely eating. . ."

"Yes, you're right."

"It's no wonder his malaria came back again—only this time he wasn't strong enough to fight it off. Even if we still have days when we're so sad we can't think straight, we have to keep living. And whatever pit of trouble we're in now, we have to climb out of it ourselves, no matter what." She folded her arms over her bosom. "So I'm going to apply myself to finding a husband—one handsome and rich—so I can get as much as I can out of life."

Amanda blinked, aghast. "And how do you plan to do that, exactly. . .if you don't mind my asking. No one has bought that stupid wagon yet, and we really need the money."

Sarah's quiet, even breaths made the only sound in the room for several seconds. "Things work out for the best, don't they? I figure the wagon didn't sell because we need it."

"I beg your pardon?" Amanda sat up in bed, the covers clutched in her hands as she stared through the dim light in her sister's direction.

"We need it. You and I. We're going to go west ourselves, the two of us."

CHAPTER 2

Amanda's mouth fell open at her sister's statement. "That has got to be the most—" She fluttered a hand in speechless futility. "I'm surprised that even you could say such a dumb thing!"

Sarah Jane flinched and lowered her gaze.

Amanda knew her younger sister considered her pessimistic and staid, a stick-in-the-mud person, one who rarely gave the girl credit for having a sensible thought in her little blond head. But with both Pa and Mama gone and no one else left to them in this world, the crushing weight of responsibility Amanda felt made it almost impossible to temper her words. It was high time Sarah started acting more like the young woman she was than the little girl she still wished to be.

"It isn't dumb," Sarah said evenly. "Surely you can see this town is not a fit place for two unchaperoned girls. We left Pennsylvania to begin a new life out west, didn't we? Well, now that we've started in that direction, I think we should keep going."

Amanda could scarcely breathe. She stared toward the parted curtain panels, where the glow from outside cast silver outlines on the roofs across the street and glazed the edges of the furniture in the hotel room. She released a despondent huff and flopped back down on her pillow. "I just don't know. I truly don't."

Sarah, the contours of her slight body shrouded in blue-violet shadows and blankets, remained silent for a long moment as her tapered finger tapped the counterpane. "I picked some spring flowers today and took them out to Pa's grave. And something inside of me made me start singing—you know how he always loved my singing."

An inner smile struggled for release, but Amanda managed to contain it as her sister went on.

"Anyway, when my song was done, I asked him what we should do, where we should go. He always did give the best advice. And it came to me—as if Pa had said it himself—the wagon is bought and paid for. It has everything we need to go west just like we would have if he hadn't passed on. The least we can do is to try to see that dream of his through. He would want us to. We owe it to him."

Amanda didn't respond for several moments as her sister's preposterous notion warred in her mind. She gave a shaky sigh. "Know what really scares me?"

"Hm?"

"You could be right. I don't see any other choice for us at the moment. No matter where we go, we're going to be alone. We've got no one to go back to, and I sure don't want to settle in a place like this, full of ruffians and drifters." She paused again in deep thought. "If we did go west the way Pa wanted—and I'm not altogether sure we should, mind you—maybe it would feel like a part of him would be with us." She paused. "We might just find a good new life for ourselves. Those new woodworking tools of his could provide the resources we need for a while. Maybe even enable us to open a shop of our own in Oregon."

"What kind of shop?"

Unexpectedly, with the decision to go not actually settled yet, a feasible possibility came to mind. "If there's one worthwhile thing Maddie managed to teach us, it was how to use a needle. Think about it. More flocks of people are heading west all the time. And they'll all be in need of clothes. They'll have their hands so full trying to clear land and build homes before the onset of winter there won't be much time for less needful things, like sewing."

"Yes!" A growing excitement colored Sarah's breathless voice. "That's a grand idea. Truly grand! And we wouldn't have to wait to settle somewhere before we got started. We could buy some bolts of dry goods right here in Independence, then one of us could ride in back and sew bonnets and aprons and baby things while the other drove."

"Maybe. It's just a thought." Amanda, feeling the first flickers of doubt after her initial enthusiasm, needed time to ponder the idea before making a definite commitment that would alter their lives forever. Then she tossed caution to the wind. "I'll get in touch with the wagon master and make the arrangements to go with the train as planned."

Sarah Jane's teeth glistened like pearls in her wide grin, and Amanda couldn't help wondering what sort of unpredictable hopes and dreams were taking shape in her sister's imaginings. It would be one huge chore keeping the flighty girl in check during a long westward journey.

Nevertheless, in that brief instant, Amanda felt a tiny bit of Sarah's optimism course through her being, accompanied by an uncharacteristic surge of adventure. Maybe for once in her life Sarah was actually right. Heading west would be far better than letting sadness and grief defeat them...and besides, if they really put their minds to it, perhaps they truly could make a good life out there. A small smile tugged at her lips as she relaxed and closed her eyes, sloughing off the guilt from not having sought God's guidance in the matter.

⸺⸱⸺

Early the next morning, the crowing of the rooster out back awakened Amanda. The curtain of night had barely begun to lift, spreading a band of thin light outward from the eastern sky. She checked over her shoulder to see Sarah still in deep slumber. It was an opportune time to talk things over with the Lord.

Reaching for her flannel wrap, Amanda slipped her arms into it and tied the belt snugly, then knelt beside the bed. *Dear heavenly Father,* she prayed silently, desperately, *I don't really know what to pray. Nothing has happened the way we expected it to since we three came to Independence. And now with Pa gone, Sarah and I have nowhere to turn. We can't go back to the home we used to know, and it's a fact this town is not a fit place for us to settle. We've decided to see to Pa's wish and go west.*

She paused to gather her thoughts. *In truth, I don't know how we'll manage this long journey alone, since neither of us is used to doing for ourselves. Back home we had Maddie to cook and keep things nice while we girls wiled away our time in what I admit now were frivolous pursuits. But we're strong and healthy, and we can learn. I know that for certain. Please go with us on our way. Grant us wisdom and courage, and stay close to us in the weeks ahead.*

When there were no words left inside, she rose and crawled back into the warm bed again for a few more minutes of sleep, thankful for the blankets that chased away the chill of the early hour. She would have liked to have more inner peace over her decision, but perhaps that would come in time. Pa always said a person's steps were ordered by the Lord, and circumstances had all but forced this plan upon them. Surely it had to be God's will. Determined, she pressed her lips together and closed her heavy eyelids as peace settled over her like a quilt of down.

A short time later, Amanda awoke again to full morning brightness. She dressed in her best navy worsted dress, confident that the tailored fit and fashionable sleeves made her look older than her twenty years. After twisting her long hair into a neat figure-eight coil at the nape of her neck, she added her Sunday bonnet, tying a stylish bow just beneath her chin.

"You look divine," Sarah Jane gushed. "Ever so grown-up and important."

"I'm trying very hard to convince myself I feel important," she confessed. "Let's go have breakfast, and then I'll try to locate the man Pa made the arrangements with."

At Martha's Eatery, a bustling restaurant popular with trail guides and mountain men alike, Seth Holloway shoved the empty plate away and leaned back in the chair, unfolding his cramped legs. He glanced across the table at rusty-haired Red Hanfield, his partner and longtime friend. "I had word that the O'Bradys pulled into town this morning. That's the last family we've been waiting for. I'll see they have all their supplies so we can head out day after tomorrow. You ride point with the first wagons this time, and I'll follow along with the cow column."

"Yep, just make sure you don't ride last in line," his wiry pal quipped. "Wastes a lot of time high-steppin' them cow pies." His coppery mustache twitched in barely suppressed humor.

"I get the picture," Seth grated. Picking up his coffee mug, he drained the last bit in one gulp, then set it back down.

"Ready for a refill?" At his elbow, good-natured Martha Griffith, owner and chief cook, poured a fresh cup.

"I do thank you, ma'am," Seth said, grinning up at her with admiration. No matter the time of day, the perky woman always sported a crisp, spotless apron over her calico dress, and the ruffle on her cap was always neatly starched over her salt-and-pepper bun. The two serving girls who worked for her were similarly attired. "You never let a man run dry."

"No sense in it a'tall, when the pot's always on! I like to make sure my regulars always come back."

"As if anybody else in town cooks as good as you," Red piped up.

Martha's pink cheeks dimpled with a smile as she filled his cup also. "Mighty kind words for a busy woman. I knew there was a reason I always like to see you two comin' in off the prairie." With a cheery dip of her head, she continued making the rounds with the coffeepot.

Seth observed her efficient movements absently as he slowly drank the hot liquid, his mind recounting endless last-minute details that needed his attention before the wagon train departed Independence two days hence.

On the edge of his vision he noticed a dark-clad figure approaching the table he and his pal occupied. He looked up when the rather small, smartly dressed young woman stopped beside them. Her classic features were composed in a businesslike expression, but it was her eyes that drew his like a magnet. Large and luminous, an unmistakable sadness lurked within their clear green depths.

"I beg your pardon?" she said softly.

"Miss?"

"I'm looking for Mr. Holloway."

They both rose at once. "That's me," Seth said, mentally noting some nicely rounded curves, neat, nearly auburn hair beneath a prim bonnet, a tempting but unsmiling mouth. "Seth Holloway. This is my partner, Red Hanfield. What might I do for you?" Noticing that her hands, gloved in white kid, trembled slightly despite her confident demeanor, he returned his gaze to her eyes, caught again by the cheerlessness accented by the fringe of long lashes.

She moistened her lips. "My name is Amanda Shelby. My father—"

Seth recognized the name at once. "Oh, of course. I heard of your unfortunate loss, Miss Shelby. You have my deepest sympathy. We'll refund the fee he paid right away, if you'll just let me know where to bring it."

"That won't be necessary."

Seth frowned in confusion. "We can't keep—"

She regarded him steadily. "Well, you see, that's why I've come. My sister and I will be leaving with the rest of the group, just as planned. So the registration money our father paid you is rightfully yours."

Red Hanfield choked on the gulp of coffee he had just taken. One side of his mustache hiked upward in a comical expression of uncertainty as he sat back down.

Seth had trouble finding his own voice. Aware that patrons at the nearby tables were gawking at them, he finally managed to link a few words together. "Surely you're joking, Miss Shelby."

"No, I am quite serious. We will be ready to leave with the other wagons."

Searching for just the right reply, Seth kneaded his jaw, then met her relentless gaze. "Look, miss. I don't mean to be rude, but whatever your intentions were before you came here, you're gonna have to forget them. There's no way we can let you and your sister make the journey. In fact"—he reached for the inside pocket of his leather jacket and withdrew a thick packet, from which he pulled out several bank notes. He pressed them into her hand— "here. This is the cash your father paid for the trip. Take my advice and go back to wherever it is you came from."

He could tell just by looking at her—rooted in that spot without a change in her countenance, other than the obvious set of her teeth—that his words had not dissuaded her one bit.

"I cannot take this," she said flatly. Placing the funds intact on the table beside him, she held her ground. "My sister and I are quite set on this. We will be going west. Good day, Mr. Holloway. Mr. Hanfield." Turning on her heel, she headed for the door.

Seth cast an incredulous look at Red, who made no effort to hide his amusement. Then he snatched up the bank notes and used them to punctuate his words in his friend's face. "Thanks for backing me up, buddy!" With a huff of disgust, he started after Amanda Shelby.

He caught up with her three doors down, in front of the Bluebird Saloon, where raucous piano music from inside the swinging doors tinkled around them, creating an absurd carnival atmosphere for any intended serious conversation. Frowning, he tapped her shoulder.

She stopped and turned, and her eyes flared wider. Instantly, a soft vulnerability in her features disappeared behind a facade of purposeful determination. "Oh, it's you."

"Who'd you expect?" he spat, instantly regretting his harsh tone. "Look, take the—" Conscious of the intense interest of a growing number of passersby, Seth knew better than to wag a handful of cash out in the open, and instead slid the bank notes back within the confines of his jacket pocket. Then he grabbed Amanda Shelby's elbow, ignoring the mortification that glared at him from her narrowed eyes, and steered her to an unoccupied spot a short distance away. There he turned her to face himself. "Please, Miss Shelby. I've been called blunt at times and have probably hurt a few feelings in my day, so if I'm hurting yours I'm sorry. But you don't seem to understand. The journey west is grueling, even for tough, experienced folks, and some of the hardiest souls won't survive it, let alone a couple of gals like you and your sister."

"I don't believe that."

"Do you know how to shoot?"

"No, but—"

"Can you change a wheel? The trail rattles the best wagon to shambles."

"No."

"How about repairing a harness?"

The last thing he was prepared for was the sheen of tears that glazed her eyes before she lowered them in defeat. It nearly melted his resolve altogether. But she blinked quickly and brushed the imprint of his grip from her dark blue sleeve before raising her gaze to his.

"But. . .we have to go," came her small voice.

There ought to be a law against a gal crying, for what it did to a man inside, Seth thought fleetingly. He hardened himself against the sight of her whisking a stray tear from her cheek as he mustered up all his reason. "Look, if there was some way we could let you come, any way at all, we would. I mean that. But it's out of the question. Even if by some stretch of the imagination you could make the trip—and you can't, take my word for it—at best, you'd slow us down. You're too much of a risk. Now, I'm taking you back to your hotel, and when we get there I'm giving you back your father's registration fee. That's my final word on the subject."

Her shoulders sagged in hopelessness, and her despair cinched itself around the middle of Seth's stomach. But he had to hold firm. It was the only thing to do, and all for the best. In time she'd see it, too. He watched her turn and walk mutely toward the Bradford.

Seth accompanied her without speaking. When they reached the hotel, he escorted her inside, then once more pressed the money her father had paid him weeks ago into her palms.

She didn't even look at him.

He cleared his throat. "Again, my deepest sympathy to you

and your sister in your loss. I wish you well. Good day, Miss Shelby."

Seth felt like a heel as he strode away from her and called himself every choice name he could think of. But the entire scheme was insane. Any fool could see that. There was no way on earth two very young—not to mention unattached—females could endure the hardships that faced the emigrants on the Oregon Trail. All the overlanders started out with grandiose visions and optimism. . .but the entire route was littered with discarded furniture and household possessions, carcasses of dead horses and oxen, and worse yet, graves of every imaginable size. As if the trek weren't rough enough over rugged mountains and endless blazing prairie and desert, there were plenty enough other threats—wild animals, bizarre weather, Indians, disease—to instill fear in the stoutest heart. It took everything a person had, not to mention an unquenchable, unbeatable spirit, to make that journey.

It took a much more valiant heart than Amanda Shelby possessed. . .but that didn't make Seth feel any less like a cowardly snake for being the one to shatter her dreams.

CHAPTER 3

Amanda trudged wretchedly up the enclosed staircase to the second floor. Earlier this morning she had managed to acquire at least a portion of peace after kneeling before the Lord in prayer. Now a scant few hours later the grand plans were in ashes. Hopeless. And simply because of that insufferable, overbearing Mr. Holloway with his long, rugged face and squinty eyes and morbid words. How was she going to break the news to Sarah after all their high hopes?

Reaching their room, Amanda drew a deep breath to fortify herself. Why, oh, why had life taken such a sad turn? Why did Pa have to die and leave them stranded way out here so far from everything they knew? Wasn't it heartbreaking enough that death had claimed Mama and the tiny baby her frail body had not been strong enough to bring into the world, without heaven's laying claim to Pa as well? And that, on top of—

No! her mind railed. *You cannot think about him. Not now. Not ever.*

Well, whatever the reasons the little family had been dealt such dreadful blows, Mama would have been the first to remind her girls that God's ways are often beyond understanding, and one should accept troubles just the same as good fortune. But that, Amanda reflected with a sigh, was truly hard to do. She straightened her shoulders and reached for the latch.

Sarah Jane looked up from writing in her journal and sprang to her feet, her face a portrait of bright expectation as Amanda entered the room. "Well? How did your meeting with the wagon master go? Tell me everything!"

"Not as well as we hoped," Amanda fudged. Then, seeing her sister's crestfallen expression, she decided to come right out with the truth. "Mr. Holloway refuses to allow us to accompany the rest of the wagon train."

"You can't mean that!"

She nodded. "He returned the money Pa paid him and practically ordered me—and you—to go *'back where we came from,'* as he put it. I'm really sorry." Untying her bonnet, Amanda slid it off, not caring as it slipped from her fingers to the floor. The urge to give it a swift kick under the bed was hard to resist. . .but it wouldn't solve anything, and someone would only have to retrieve the thing. Instead, she flopped onto the quilted coverlet and lay staring up at the dismal ceiling.

"I don't believe it!"

"Believe it, Sissy. There was no reasoning with that obnoxious, opinionated, bullheaded man. He didn't give me a chance to explain our plight."

"How. . .perfectly horrid!" Sarah declared. "Forbidding people their destiny." With a toss of her golden curls, she flounced over to where she'd been putting her innermost thoughts down on paper and tore the half-written page out of the journal, crumpling it in her hand. An oppressive silence hovered in the room as Sarah plopped grimly back onto the chair, arms crossed in front of her, staring at the opposite wall. Her exhaled breaths came out in a succession of audible exclamation points.

Amanda finally broke the stillness. "Well, this isn't getting us anywhere. I'm going downstairs for the noon meal, and while I eat I'll think about groveling at Mr. Cavanaugh's feet to persuade him to take that wagon off our hands. Much as I hate the prospect, it's the only sensible solution left to us. At least it'll give us money to live on until we make other plans."

Sarah shrugged. "Whatever you say. I'm not hungry. In fact, I may never be hungry again. Think I'll wander on over to the mercantile and browse through the fabrics and jewelry. It doesn't cost anything just to look. And afterward I may go visit Nancy Thatcher at the bakery until she closes up."

Seated in the dining room moments later, Amanda heard scarcely a word of the cheerful chatter bantered about the rectangular pine table by other hotel guests during the meal. Her thoughts were occupied back at Martha's Eatery, upon the most infuriating man she had ever had the occasion to meet.

Seth Holloway certainly seemed taken up with his own importance, she concluded, swallowing a spoonful of beef stew. Not even allowing her an opportunity to explain the reasoning behind the decision she and Sarah had made. Who did he think he was—ruler of the world? Humph. Some king he would make, in buckskins, with a face that looked in need of a good shave, unruly dark brown hair and hooded, deep-set brown eyes that had a sneaky quality to them. Even that low voice of his rasped in her memory as the conversation mentally took place again. *Go back where you came from.* It would serve the beast right if the sky clouded over and it rained for days and days, making the trail impassible for a month. Or better yet, forever. Then he'd have to give everyone's money back, leaving him flat broke.

As she bit into some warm corn bread, a glance out the window revealed the object of her scathing thoughts passing by with his partner and several other men, obviously from the wagon encampment. He wasn't exactly smiling—in fact, Amanda had serious doubts the man ever broke into a smile at all. But he did appear pleasantly cheerful and walked with long, confident strides.

What she wouldn't do to take him down a peg. He had no right to refuse her and Sarah's inclusion with the rest of the overlanders, no right at all. If only she'd become acquainted with some of the migrating families there might have been someone to stand up for them and demand they be permitted to join the company. But when Pa had come down with chills and fever it made folks leery of coming too close, so Amanda had moved the wagon to a spot some distance from the encampment. And after he expired, she and Sarah had mostly kept to themselves in the hotel. It was too late to try to make a friend now. Much too late.

"Mr. Randolph," Seth said, resting a hand on the lantern-faced man's shoulder as he, Red, and two other emigrant leaders walked toward the hardware store. "I'm calling a meeting around the campfire this evening after supper. I want all the men to be present. Think you can handle that?"

The older man stroked his close-cropped beard and gave a nod of agreement. "No problem at all, Mr. Holloway. We're all pretty anxious to leave, after sittin' around for nigh on three weeks."

The heavyset man on the end snorted. "That's an understatement—it's been four weeks for us. It's getting harder and harder to keep a handle on all the loose young'uns. Even the womenfolk are antsy."

"We understand, Mr. Thornton," Red chimed in. "But your waitin's about over, an' now we need to go over the rules we expect folks to abide by for a smooth crossin'."

He nodded. "We'll be there. Count on it."

"Soon as we get back to the wagons we'll spread the word," Randolph said, glancing to the others.

"Good." Seth touched the brim of his hat as they reached the store. "See you then, gentlemen." He turned to Red as the other men entered the establishment. "Guess I'd better start getting my own gear together."

"Me, too. Say, did you manage to smooth that little gal's feathers—about heading west?"

"Fortunately, yes. Took some convincing, though." He shook his head with a droll smirk. "Can't imagine a girl being fool enough to think she—and a sister who I know is even younger than she is—could make a journey like that all by themselves. But at least they're off our hands. I gave their pa's money back. That's the end of it, far as I'm concerned."

Amanda hesitated outside the mercantile for as long as she could, dreading the inevitable. Then, knowing the task would never get any easier, she slipped inside as two chattering women exited. She didn't see Sarah Jane in the store, but spied Mr. Cavanaugh across the cluttered room, chewing on a fat cigar while he spoke with another customer beside the pickle barrel. Amanda stopped near the display of fabrics and fingered a bolt of violet watered silk as she eyed the proprietor with disdain, taking in the waistcoat that strained across his protruding belly, the shiny bald circle atop his head.

His gaze flicked her way and a snide quirk twisted his thick mouth. He excused himself and approached Amanda in self-assured calm. "Well, well. Had a feeling I'd be seeing you sooner or later, Miss Shelby."

She dipped her head slightly. "Mr. Cavanaugh."

"Come to accept my offer, did you?"

"Well, I—"

"'Course, I haveta tell you, the stuff's not worth as much to me now, with the train about to leave. I'll have to lower the price some. You understand, I'm sure. I'm still doin' you a favor. Least I can do, under the circumstances."

Amanda stiffened. The man was actually gloating! All so certain that she'd hand over what amounted to the entirety of her and Sarah's worldly possessions for next to nothing! And she had no doubts whatsoever that the moment he got hold of all those supplies he'd take advantage of some other poor souls— turning her misfortune into an indecent profit for himself. She felt her spirit grow ice-solid. The sudden reply that popped out of her mouth surprised even her. "I didn't come about the wagon. I'd like to arrange a trade. My father's tools for some dry goods."

"Hm." He rubbed his chin in dubious thought. "I s'pose that could be done—"

"Fine. I'll bring them to you shortly, then, and choose some yardage."

"What about the rest? The outfit. The supplies?"

She offered a cool smile. "We're only discussing Pa's tools,

Mr. Cavanaugh. I'm afraid our wagon isn't for sale after all. We do thank you, however, for your. . .*generous* offer. Good day." Gathering a fold of her skirt in one gloved hand, Amanda whirled and fled before she changed her mind.

She fairly flew back to the hotel and up the contained staircase to her rented room. A depressing heaviness settled over her. Her own pride had just caused her to act prematurely—and make a decision that could end up being far more foolish than anything Sarah had ever conceived. What was that verse Pa had quoted so often? "Pride goeth before a fall"? Well, if she and Sarah were in for a big fall now, it would be all her fault.

Letting herself in, Amanda released a shaky breath of relief to discover her sister had not yet returned. At least there'd be time to reason things out, to pray. Instead of coming from the mercantile with cash in hand for the two of them to live on until they decided what to do, she had just thrown their one chance away. She sank to her knees in yet another frantic prayer.

Dear Lord, I've really done it this time. Slammed a door You left standing wide open for us. . .and all because of my silly pride. But Mr. Cavanaugh wasn't being fair to Sarah and me. He just wasn't. You must want us to go west. You must. She paused, rolling her eyes heavenward as if expecting to see the answer inscribed bright and clear on the ceiling. Finding none, she closed her eyes once more. *So we need You to help us now. I know You will see us through.*

Trusting that to be sufficient, Amanda picked up Pa's Bible and took a seat in the overstuffed chair near the window. When her sister's light step sounded outside the door a short time later, she looked up from the Psalms and met the younger girl's curious eyes with a smile.

"I take it you were successful," Sarah Jane said airily. "We have funds to tide us over for a while, until we can find some kind of employment."

"No, I'm afraid not."

"No?" The younger girl removed her shawl and draped it on the nearest chair. "You did go to see Mr. Cavanaugh."

"Yes—" Amanda felt her face growing warm, and looked away. "But I could not let that brute *steal* our things. He wanted to give me less than before. *Less!* Can you imagine? I couldn't bring myself to let him cheat us like that. I just couldn't."

Sarah crossed the room and knelt at her feet, eyes troubled and imploring. "But. . .what will we do now, Mandy, when our money runs out?"

Giving her sister's hand a pat where it rested on her own atop the Bible in her lap, Amanda shrugged nonchalantly. "You said it last night. We're going west, just as we decided."

"But the wagon master said—"

"I know what he said. But I've been thinking about it, and we're going anyway. . .just not with him."

"I don't understand."

"We'll wait until the others have all gone. Then, later on that day or the next, we'll follow behind them. No one will be the wiser."

"Do you think we can do such a thing? Truly?"

"Of course. We belong to the Lord, you and I. God will take care of us. He has to—after all, He promised, didn't He?"

"I. . .suppose."

Amanda forced herself to relax and appear calm and assured. It wouldn't do for Sarah to know how doubtful her older, wiser sister actually felt in the hidden reaches of her heart. Journey across half a continent. Alone.

CHAPTER 4

Amanda got barely a wink of sleep all night. One minute she was convinced she'd made the only decision that had any merit, but the next, the absurdity of considering such a monumental undertaking assaulted her. She couldn't even pray. Despite numerous attempts, the words refused to come out right. It seemed folly to expect the Lord to bless their venture, when the wagon master himself pointed out how lacking she and Sarah were in many of the basic and necessary travel skills.

Heaven only knew exactly what they might encounter ahead. Swollen rivers, swift and deep from spring rains, trouble with the wagon, possible injuries to herself or Sarah. And what about wild animals that freely roamed the open country? Or Indians? Amanda's stomach knotted just imagining the two of them alone in the wilderness, no one knowing or caring where they were. But on the other hand, she reminded herself, the Bible did say that God was all-knowing, so nothing would take Him by surprise. The Almighty, in His omnipotent wisdom, had surely known that Pa would pass on to his eternal reward and leave them to fend for themselves. The Lord must have a place for them out west. He would be with them. He would take away all their fears.

Grasping that conviction, she closed her heavy eyelids and finally dozed off.

A pair of distant gunshots echoed a few hours later, awakening Amanda with a start. Sarah, next to her in bed, was still breathing in the slow, regular pattern of deep slumber. Amanda, her head aching from the lack of sleep, raised the coverlet and slid out of bed, then padded to the window.

The first pale streaks of dawn were beginning to stain the dark sky in the east. Turning her head in the opposite direction, Amanda spotted the golden lantern glow rising from the conglomeration of wagons amassed in the rocky-outcropped meadow near the spring on the edge of town. Everyone had anxiously awaited those signal shots over several unbearably long weeks. She could imagine the people milling about, hitching teams, readying their wagons. What suppressed excitement there must be, what cheerful chatter, bright hope, and sheer happiness. Last-minute preparations before setting out for a new life.

She heaved a sigh. What she would give to be part of that exhilarated throng about to depart for Oregon.

Brisk morning air ruffled over Amanda's bare arms, and she shivered. Hugging herself, she retreated to the warm sanctuary of the bed while her plan reaffirmed itself. No telling how long it would take that whole wagon train along with the vast herd of cattle and livestock to depart Independence. But once a sufficient span of time passed to allow the emigrants to put some distance between themselves and the town, she and Sarah would leave, too.

That settled, Amanda again relaxed, and her eyes fluttered closed.

"Mandy?"

Sarah's voice seemed fuzzy and far away, but the gentle hand shaking Amanda's shoulder felt very real. She raised her lashes. How could it be this bright already? Only a minute ago it was still dark.

"We'll miss breakfast if we don't hurry."

She bolted upright, noting that her sister was fully dressed.

"Oh! I must have overslept! Sorry."

"I left water in the basin for you."

"Thanks." Amanda rose and dashed across the room to wash up. The cool liquid she splashed on her face felt refreshing, and she was surprisingly rested after that last unexpected snatch of sleep. After blotting her hands and face on a towel, she shimmied out of her night shift and into her chemise, then reached for the sturdy burgundy calico dress laid out the evening before.

Sarah moved up behind her and helped with the buttons. "Are we, you know...still going?"

Amanda peered over her shoulder. Her sister's brow bore uncharacteristic lines of worry. "Of course. Why wouldn't we?"

"I just wanted to make sure."

"But we'd best not let anyone know. If we so much as let a single word slip, good-intentioned people are sure to stop us. We'll bide our time, wait until we can leave unnoticed."

"Right." Finished with the buttons, Sarah nibbled her bottom lip with unconcealed excitement. "I've packed our things."

"Splendid!" Amanda smiled and sat down to pull on her stockings, then jammed her feet into her hightop shoes and used the buttonhook to fasten them. After some quick strokes with the brush she tied her long hair at the nape of her neck with a black velvet ribbon and stood up. "Do I look presentable?"

Sarah nodded.

"Well, what are we waiting for?" Sputtering into a giggle, she hugged her younger sibling. Arm in arm, they headed downstairs to the dining room, reaching it even as a handful of other patrons were taking their leave.

Mrs. Clark, the middle-aged widow who provided hearty meals at the Bradford Hotel, greeted them as they entered the now-empty room. Her apple-dumpling cheeks rounded with her smile. "We wondered where you two were this morning," she said pleasantly, a hand on her wide hip.

"Everything smells luscious," Amanda said, averting her attention from the gray-haired cook to the long table. She resisted the impulse to offer an explanation for their tardiness.

"You missed all the goin's on," the older woman announced.

"The train pulled out first thing this morning."

"Oh, really?" Feigning nonchalance, Amanda exchanged a cursory glance with Sarah. "It certainly seems like a perfect day to begin a journey."

"Yep, that it does. Pity you two couldn't be among them. Well, set yourselves down in one of them clean spots, and I'll bring you some flapjacks and eggs right quick."

The remainder of the morning seemed interminable to Amanda and Sarah as they peered constantly out the window, checking the immense, distant trace of dust stirred up by wagons and cattle. Finally they gathered their belongings and stole down to the livery to tuck their bags unobtrusively into the wagon.

The two of them heaved down the heavy chest containing their father's woodworking equipment and lugged it to Cavanaugh's Mercantile. Amanda had to bite her tongue at the pathetic sum the storekeeper offered for the finely crafted tools, but there was no recourse but to accept. She and Sarah ignored his questions as they casually perused the bolts of material he had on hand and chose several different kinds they thought would prove most useful for their new enterprise.

In midafternoon, on the pretense of wanting to get current with all their affairs, Amanda settled their hotel bill, and the girls checked their room one last time to be sure they hadn't forgotten anything. No doubt they'd miss the comfort of that big four-poster soon enough, Amanda surmised. But she eagerly anticipated some solitude after the constant racket of this rowdy frontier town.

"There's no sign of dust above the trail now," Sarah Jane mused, closing the window. "Do you think it's time?"

Amanda subdued the butterflies fluttering about in her stomach and gave a solemn nod. "It's now or never. But first we must say good-bye to Pa. It's only right."

With the emigrant train gone from Independence, the diminished noise level outside seemed all the more apparent in the stillness of the grassy knoll just beyond the simple white church on the far edge of the settlement. Amanda and Sarah treaded softly over the spongy ground.

A soft, fresh breeze whispered among the scattered wooden crosses bearing the names and life years of the dear departed. It gently billowed the girls' skirts as they stood gazing down at the forlorn rectangle of mounded earth beneath which Pa lay awaiting the heavenly trumpet call.

Amanda felt a lump forming in her throat, but swallowed hard and sank to her knees to place a bouquet of wildflowers on the grave. It took every ounce of strength she could muster to force a smile. "Pa, Sarah and I've come to say good-bye now," she said, her voice wavering slightly. She drew a deep breath. "We're setting off for Oregon, just like you planned, so this will be the last time we can visit you. Tell Mama. . .we send our love. Farewell."

Beside her, Sarah Jane sniffed and brushed tears from her cheeks. "We'll keep you and Ma in our hearts. . .until we're all together again. We—we love you. Good-bye. . .for now." After a few moments of silence they met each other's eyes and stood. "We'll have an early supper, then head over to the livery and watch for Mr. Plummer to go have his," Amanda announced.

The blacksmith was busy shoeing one of a pair of workhorses when they peeked around the edge of the doorway after their meal. But finally he exited his shop and walked over to Martha's Eatery. The door of the restaurant closed behind him.

"That is it." Amanda led the way around back of the livery, where they sneaked inside. Ever grateful that Pa had made her practice hitching up the mules and driving them, she located the required equipment belonging to them and followed her father's instructions to the letter. Then she went to Mr. Plummer's makeshift desk and left a packet containing sufficient funds to cover the expenses incurred from boarding and feeding the animals, along with a short note of thanks for his kindness.

Everything finally in readiness, they climbed aboard. Amanda released the brake, clucked her tongue, and slapped the traces against the backs of the mules. The heavy wagon lurched into motion, its huge wheels crunching over the gravelly dirt.

Without Pa, the cumbersome vehicle felt huge. Immense. And

the mules seemed less than enthusiastic about having to work after weeks of being penned up and lazy. But Amanda gritted her teeth and held on, steering them around the sheltering grove of trees behind the livery and then guiding them in an arc that would soon intersect the trail to Oregon Territory.

Sarah leaned to peer around the arched canvas top at the busy river port they were leaving behind. "I don't think anyone even noticed us drive off. Oh, this is so exciting, Mandy! We're actually doing it. . .heading west, just like Pa dreamed. I can't wait to start writing about it in my journal. I'm going to put down every single thing that happens along the way!" Gripping the edge of the hard wooden seat, she filled her lungs and smiled, staring into the distance.

A person would have to be blind to miss the sparkle in the younger girl's wondrous blue eyes, Amanda conceded. If it weren't for the sobering knowledge that she herself was now in control of both their destinies, she might have shared some of her sibling's lilting optimism. But right now her hands were full. Returning her attention to the long trail stretching beyond the horizon, she put her full concentration on the hard job ahead.

The road west, impossible to miss, already bore deep ruts from vast hoards of wagons that had made the journey in previous years. Amanda filled her gaze with the absolutely breathtaking landscape all around them. Groves of budding trees dotted the gently rolling ground, itself a wondrous carpet of long, silky grasses. Myriad flowers speckled the spring green in a rainbow of glorious hues. Surely in such a delightful season of new life, nothing could spoil their adventure. To make certain, Amanda lofted yet another fervent prayer heavenward, beseeching the Lord to bless and protect them on the journey.

"I wonder when we'll reach Oregon," Sarah mused.

"Papa expected it to take months. But according to that guidebook he purchased back home, it's a fairly pleasant drive, even if it is rather long."

"Why would Mr. Holloway try to scare us off, then?"

At the mention of the wagon master's name, Amanda

tightened her lips, forcing aside an exaggerated mental picture of his obnoxious smirk and insinuating eyes. "He's just a pompous beast, is all. But he isn't going to stop us now, Sissy. And neither is anybody else. We are on our way west!"

And Seth Holloway will never even know it.

CHAPTER 5

Guiding the team over the gently rolling northwesterly trail that ambled along the Kansas River, Amanda drank in the breathtaking wooded ridges lining either side of the serene valley. Springs and patches of timber interspersed a tranquil landscape much more vast and open than the familiar dense forests and winding, irregular hills of northeastern Pennsylvania. Already she found the spaciousness refreshing, the immense sky overhead magnificent. "Space to breathe," Pa had called it, and now Amanda knew why. She loved being able to see so far in every direction, and swallowed a pang of sadness that he wasn't there to enjoy it, too.

"I'm getting thirsty," Sarah said, drawing her out of her musings.

"We'll stop at that little grove ahead. It looks like a good place to make camp."

The sun had already sunk beneath the horizon, its slanting rays painting the western sky vibrant rose and violet. Amanda halted the mules, then hopped down and began unhitching them.

"I'll gather wood before it gets too dark," Sarah offered, and bustled off out of sight.

———✦———

Sarah Jane found an abundance of deadfall among the trees and quickly gathered a generous armful. On her way back to the wagon she saw that Amanda had hobbled the mules and was now freshening up at the riverside. Sarah grabbed a towel. "How far do you suppose we've come?" she asked, joining her sister.

Amanda shook excess water from her hands before drying them and her face. "Our late start only gave us a couple hours of travel time. We'd better get up early tomorrow if we ever hope to see Oregon."

After a quick light meal of bread and cheese, they returned to the wagon to dress in their night shifts.

Sarah watched her older sister brushing out her long, auburn hair with the usual regulated strokes, then gave her own curls a few dutiful brushes. "Think I'll write for a little while before I blow out the lantern."

"Just don't be long. We need to be on the road at first light." With a yawn, Amanda slid into her side of the mattress and almost instantly fell asleep.

Sarah retrieved her journal and moved closer to the glow of the lantern.

> *Dear Diary,*
>
> *Today is the most glorious day of my entire life! Amanda and I set off on our adventure to find our destiny. I thought it would seem a little lonesome, traveling by ourselves, but instead it feels more like we have sprouted wings and are completely free. We can make our own rules, which surely must be one of the most wonderful benefits of all.*
>
> *You cannot imagine how beautiful this wondrous countryside has been so far. It's as if some grand and heroic knight of old rode through the vast stretches of the land and carved out the most lovely of routes westward, full of sparkling rivers and fragrant spring flowers. Somehow it would not surprise me to discover he is still here, mounted*

upon his swift steed just beyond our sight as he looks
after travelers on this road to Oregon, keeping them
always from harm.

Smiling to herself, Sarah closed the book and hugged it. Imagine if it were true, and some handsome champion were just around the next bend in the trail, ever watchful of the weary pilgrims on their way to a new life. How wonderful to know there was nothing to fear. As glorious as it was to be free now and on their own, a tiny part of her had felt a little afraid of what lay ahead. But since heading west without Pa had been largely her idea in the first place, she'd squelched those feelings and concentrated on the mild weather and the lovely scenery instead. She leaned over and blew out the lamp, then crawled into bed.

The faraway howl of a wolf pierced the night stillness. Sarah's eyes flew open as a second howl answered from much nearer. Nervously she pulled the blankets over her head and snuggled closer to her sister's slumbering form. But not until the vision of a stalwart man astride a glorious golden horse drifted into her thoughts was she able to relax as she imagined him patrolling the grounds around them. A peacefulness settled upon her, and her eyelids fluttered closed.

Morning arrived all too quickly. When Sarah felt behind her, Amanda's side of the bed was empty. She gathered the topmost blanket around her shoulders and went to peer out of the wagon into the semidarkness.

Amanda was fully clothed and kneeling before a feeble fire she was coaxing to life.

"You're up early," Sarah called. "It's not even light yet."

"Thought we'd better not waste any of this morning if we expect to ever get anywhere."

"Of course. I'll wash up and get dressed."

Her older sister nodded and set a pot of water over the flames to boil. By the time Sarah got back, Amanda was stirring a thick mixture of mush.

"I wonder if it's supposed to be this hard to stir," she commented as Sarah handed her two tin bowls. Then with a shrug she ladled out a sticky gob for each of them, and they took seats on a fallen log. Amanda bowed her head. "We thank you, heavenly Father, for this new day and for the food you've provided. We ask your blessing and continued presence on our journey. In Jesus' name, amen."

"Amen," Sarah whispered, then smiled. "It smells good." She spooned some of the gooey substance to her mouth, struck by the unusual taste—or lack of same—as she slowly chewed.

Amanda, beside her, spit hers out. "Blah. This is horrid."

"What did you put into it?"

She shrugged. "Just cornmeal, flour, and water."

"Not even salt?"

Amanda shook her head. "I didn't know it needed any. Maddie's mush always tasted just fine."

"I think she used a bit of sugar, too. And maybe it didn't need flour."

"Well, how was I to know?" Amanda huffed.

"Sorry." Sarah bit her lip at her sister's uncharacteristic outburst. "I'm sure if we just sprinkle some salt in it now, it'll help," she said hopefully, and went to get some at the wagon. "Anyway, I'm more thirsty than hungry. That coffee should be about finished, shouldn't it?"

Amanda's glum face brightened. "I'll pour us some." But when Sarah returned with the salt box, an irregular black stain in the dirt steamed next to the fire.

"Thank your lucky stars you didn't even taste it," Amanda said miserably. "We'll just have some water instead." She offered one of the two cups she held.

"I'm not that fond of coffee anyway," Sarah assured her, taking it. "As a rule, I'd much prefer tea." She bent over and sprinkled a pinch of salt into the pot of mush, then reached for the wooden spoon. But the mixture had hardened, and now the spoon stuck fast, right in the middle. It would not even budge. Sarah fought hard to restrain a giggle as Amanda groaned.

"We are going to starve to death, do you realize that?" her sister groused. "This breakfast wasn't even fit for pigs. And look at this pot. The mush is hard as a rock." With a grimace she tossed the container, spoon and all, into the weeds.

"Well, no matter," Sarah said brightly. "We can have more of that two-day-old bread Nancy from the bakery was going to tear up for the birds. And there's lots of cheese in the cornmeal barrel."

While her older sister put the collars on the mules and hitched them to the wagon after the meager breakfast, Sarah traipsed happily from the grove with another armload of dried wood, which she put in back. Then the two of them climbed aboard. Glancing backward shortly after they drove off, Sarah saw a small coyote prance tentatively up to the castaway pot of mush. He put his snout into it, then scampered away. She almost laughed out loud as she settled back onto the seat. It would make a funny entry in her diary, one she'd have to keep secret.

⟶⟵

Amanda hoped they would cover a decent stretch of ground before nightfall. So far there had been no trace of the wagon train ahead. She couldn't help wondering how many miles' advantage the emigrants had. But before any thought of Mr. Holloway could intrude, she glanced at Sarah, who was removing some light blue thread and a crochet hook from her sewing bag.

"Thought I'd work on a baby cap," her sister said, nimbly forming the first few loops of a chain stitch.

"Good idea. During our nooning today I'll cut out some aprons. We should be able to work by firelight in the evenings. By the time we reach Oregon we could have a fair number of things made for our store."

Sarah smiled and went on crocheting as they left their first camp behind. Before them lay even grander spring displays amid the trees and swells of the greening landscape, and the cheery songs of bobolinks echoed across the meadows.

The first narrow stretch of the Blue River to be crossed presented no difficulty, and after fording it they stopped for dinner and a rest. Amanda figured it was probably too much to hope the entire trip would pass as smoothly and effortlessly as these first days, but in any case, it was better to dwell in the moment. No sense borrowing trouble.

Another long day of lumbering onward began a set routine as the girls divided chores related to making camp each evening and breaking it the next morning. Good as her word, Sarah took over the cooking, so Amanda no longer dreaded noonings and suppertimes. The throat-closing splendor of green swells star-dusted with tiny frail blossoms and great spillings of mountain pink, larkspur, and other more vivid wildflowers continued to fill them with awe.

"The train must have spent a night here," Amanda stated, hopping down from the wagon one evening. They had stopped near a solitary elm with a trunk three feet thick. The tree towered over the headwaters of a little creek. "There've been lots of cook fires here recently."

Sarah placed a hand on her hip. "Yes, and they didn't leave much wood, you'll notice." Tightening her lips, she walked some distance away to find enough to make supper.

The middle of the following day they passed the fork where the Santa Fe Trail split off in a more southwesterly route, a land-mark Amanda regarded in silence, brushing off the solemn re-minder she and Sarah were in the middle of nowhere.

⟶⟶

"What's that up ahead?" Sarah asked one afternoon, looking up from a flannel baby blanket she was hemming.

"Must be the ferry over the Kansas River." Amanda had been assessing the questionable-looking scows at the edge of the wide, swiftly running water ever since she'd first glimpsed them. And the nearer they came, the less optimistic she felt—especially con-sidering the two somewhat disheveled, black-haired characters in buckskin breeches and rumpled calico shirts who were manning the contraptions. She would have rather faced another cozy little stream like others they had driven through.

"They're Indians!" Sarah murmured. "Unsavory ones like we saw loitering around Independence. Is this the only spot we can cross?"

Amanda shrugged. "It's part of the trail. The rest of the train must have crossed here."

"Well, I don't like the way those two are snickering and leering at us."

Amanda took note of the more-than-interested glances the swarthy pair aimed at them while muttering comments behind their bony hands. The fine hairs on her arms prickled, and her heartbeat increased. Glancing nervously upstream and down, she saw no fordable sites and wished as never before that they were in the company of other travelers. She swallowed and sent a quick prayer heavenward, pretending a confidence that was far from her true feelings as she drew up to the edge of the steep bank and stopped the team.

"Good day."

One of the unkempt men approached. A lecherous smile curved one end of his mouth. "No more wagons?" Beady dark eyes peered around the schooner, searching the distance before exchanging a wordless look with his chum.

The second one's lips slid into a knowing grin. He stepped nearer, hungrily eyeing Sarah up and down.

Amanda's skin crawled. She barely subdued a blush as Sarah's hand latched on to hers.

The motley louts whispered something. Then, black eyes glinting with devilment, the taller one took hold of the wagon to hoist himself up.

"It's all right, Pa," Amanda said over her shoulder. "We've reached the ferry."

The man paused.

Amanda quelled her sister's questioning expression with a stern look, then returned her attention to the Indians. "He's feeling poorly. Came down with a fever early this morning." The calmness in her voice amazed even her.

"Fever?" Dark fingers instantly released their grip on the wagon. He leapt backward.

The other, with some hesitance, thrust out his palm. "Five dollar for wagon. Two more for mules. One for passengers."

Amanda was fairly sure the price was outrageous, but wasn't

about to make an issue of it. She smiled politely and turned to Sarah. "Go inside, Sissy, and get the money from Pa, will you?" As the younger girl complied, Amanda prayed all the more fervently for the Lord's help and protection.

When Sarah returned, Amanda forced herself to remain casual as she placed the fee in the dark hand.

He motioned the two of them inside the rig, and the girls watched out the back while a rope that had been looped around a tree was attached to the wagon. The taller Indian led the team forward toward the boat, while the other used the rope to help slow the schooner's descent down the bank. When everything was finally positioned on the ferry, the men used poles and paddles to propel the scow across the fast current. On the other side, the larger of the dark-skinned pair drove the team through deep sands leading up the northern bank and a short ways beyond. Halting the mules, he nodded to Amanda and jumped off, then loped back to join his cohort on the return across the river.

With the greatest relief, Amanda drew what seemed like her first real breath since the entire process had begun. She emerged from the confines of the wagon bed and moved to the seat.

Sarah, inches behind, grabbed her in a hug. "I'm so glad they believed you. I was never so frightened in my whole life."

"Me neither." Returning the embrace, Amanda gathered her shattered emotions together and allowed herself a moment to stop shaking. Then she clucked her tongue to start the mules and put as many miles between them and the Kansas River as they could before stopping for the night.

After a supper of bacon and fried mush, Sarah refilled their coffee mugs. "I'm too tired to sew tonight," she said on a yawn.

"It's been a long day." Amanda looked dejectedly down at her hands, growing tender from the constant rubbing of the traces against her soft flesh.

"I think there are some of Pa's work gloves in the back," Sarah offered. "They might make the driving easier."

Amanda only stared.

"Or shall I take a turn tomorrow?"

"Actually, that's more what I had in mind, if you must know," Amanda admitted.

"Well, that's fair. You shouldn't have to do it all."

~⊷~

After the nooning stop, Amanda took the reins again, more relaxed after Sarah's turn driving than she would have thought possible. The rhythmic, soothing clopping of the hooves and the jangle of the harness now brought a misty half-consciousness, and she lost herself in memories of their old life, of family times.

Very few people enjoyed such a privileged existence as she and Sarah had once known. But that was before their father's partner—bile rose in Amanda's throat—her own betrothed, had swindled Pa and absconded with all the cash from the land investments, leaving him alone to face creditors and wronged clients. Amanda felt partly responsible for her pa's death, though she had never voiced the dire thought. Morris had fooled them all. Only through her father's grit and hard work, plus the sale of the grand house and most of their worldly possessions, had all the monies been repaid. The three of them were able to set out for Oregon with their heads high.

Even if we would have preferred to stay home, Amanda mused caustically, immediately cutting off thought of the dastardly blackguard whom she had foolishly trusted enough to promise her heart. Well, at least he was out of her life. She was twenty now—old enough to know better than to trust any man's sweet words, ever again. She would remain forever a spinster, one whose sole responsibility in life was to look out for her beautiful younger sister—and she would do that to the very best of her ability. Firm in that resolve, her gaze rose idly into the hazy distance.

A jolt of alarm seized her.

A sullen, angry mass of clouds churned across the faraway horizon.

"Uh-oh. Looks like we might be in for some rain."

Her sister looked up. "Well, a shower shouldn't bother us. The wagon, after all, does have a double-canvas top."

Amanda could only hope the younger girl was right. But

eyeing the irregular black cloud bank crawling toward them from the west, she had a niggling fear it was no mere spring shower heading their way.

She urged the team faster as the pleasant breeze began to turn strong and cold.

All too soon the first jagged bolts of lightning forked the slate-gray sky in the distance. Amanda strained to hear the low growl of thunder, then nudged Sarah. "We'd better stop for today. We'll have an early supper."

At the nearest likely spot, they made camp in the fading light, then draped India-rubber tarps over the bedding and the barrels of supplies. Amanda tied the drawstring closure tight on their haven, and the girls wrapped in shawls and sat down in the eerie darkness, hoping the mules would fare all right.

Soon enough, a strong gust of wind rattled the wagon. The arched top shuddered. A mule brayed.

Amanda drew her lips inward as tentative raindrops spattered the canvas. Maybe Sarah was right, it was just a shower after all. But relief vanished almost as quickly as it had come.

The gentle patter turned sinister. With each second, the pounding overhead grew more deafening. The torrent roared over the heavy bowed top, pouring down the sides of the wagon and splashing onto the ground.

A bright flash of lightning glowed through the sodden fabric like daylight for a split second. An earth-shattering boom of thunder rent the night.

Sarah's scream was drowned out by another blast. Amanda huddled close to her, cringing with every flash and crash. Rain began to drip through the cover overhead, trickling down onto the tarpaulins.

"I'm c–cold," Sarah said, shivering as she inched nearer.

Thunder boomed again.

"This has to end sometime," Amanda assured her as an icy drop spattered her nose and rolled off her chin. She hugged herself and tucked her chin deeper into her shawl, pressing close to her sister.

The elements crashed around them for what seemed like

forever. Then, ever so gradually, almost imperceptibly, the thunder began to lessen in degree. The spaces between lightning bolts grew longer. Amanda eased out from under the heavy tarp and went to peer through the closure to see how the trail was faring. She gawked in dismay when a bright flash revealed they were surrounded by a sea of water and mud. The wagon ruts were not even visible.

A small part of her harbored the wish they had the comforting company of the other emigrants, but she was not ready to concede that the know-it-all Mr. Holloway had been right. Surely this wasn't the first bad storm that faced an overlander on the westward trek. If others had made it through, so would she and Sarah Jane.

"If I weren't so cold, I could at least play my guitar," Sarah groused. "It would pass the time."

Amanda silently thanked the Lord for the cold. It was bad enough being soggy and chilled without adding the headache of Sarah's toneless singing. Soon would come the blessedness of sleep, when they would be less aware of how miserable they were. Heaven only knew how long the rain would last. It had to stop sometime. It had to.

CHAPTER 6

S teaming! We're steaming!"

"What?" Amanda opened her eyes, momentarily blinded by bright sunshine. How had they slept so late?

"Look at everything, Mandy," Sarah insisted.

With a yawn and a stretch, Amanda lifted the drenched tarp and sat up. Fragile wisps of mist floated upward in the confining interior of the wagon bed from the scattered tarpaulins and blankets. Rising, she untied the drawstring and leaned out.

The sodden earth sparkled in newly washed glory. Beside them, the rushing stream and a thousand puddles reflected the last puffs of cloud and the blue sky. And Sarah was right. The whole wagon was steaming in the warmth of the brilliant sun. So were the hobbled mules, unharmed and grazing contentedly nearby.

"See if any of that last wood you gathered is still dry," Amanda said. "We'll have hot tea to go with our breakfast. While the water heats, we'll open the sides and set things out to dry."

Sarah stripped down to her drawers and chemise, then rooted through the piles of damp supplies to find the wood she'd wrapped in blankets. "It's not wet at all, Sissy."

Within an hour, the bushes in the surrounding area sported a colorful array of blankets, linens, and articles of clothing, and the soft spring breeze wafted over them while the girls sipped mugs of tea. The temperature warmed considerably, inching higher and higher, the opposite extreme from the previous day.

Alas, the soggy rutted road ahead looked less than hopeful. The ground remained spongy to the foot, much too soft for travel. Amanda knew they'd be stuck here for at least a couple of days, but if nothing else, they'd have ample time to sew.

In the middle of the third lazy afternoon, Sarah laid aside the sunbonnet she'd finished and stretched a kink out of her spine with a sigh. "Know what I'd love right now?"

"What?" Amanda recognized that particular spark in her sister's eyes.

"I would absolutely adore a bath."

"You're kidding, right?"

"Not at all. I'm dying to wash my hair."

"But the stream is still swift and muddy from the rain."

"I know, but we can stay near the edge, can't we? And we can rinse off with rainwater from the barrel. Wouldn't you just love to be clean again—all of you, instead of just washing up?"

"That water was freezing cold when we did our clothes. And besides, we're out in the open."

"So? We haven't seen a living soul since we crossed the river on the ferry. And anyway, we can leave our drawers on."

Amanda searched all around and beyond, as far as she could see. There truly wasn't anyone in sight. For all intent and purpose, they were the only two people in this part of the world. And she had to admit, she did feel grubby. What harm would there be in taking a quick dip, so long as they stayed in shallow water? "Well, I suppose we could try it."

"Oh good!" Sarah all but tore out of her shirtwaist and skirt and undid her hair ribbon. Grabbing a cake of rose-scented soap and a towel, she dashed, shrieking, into the rushing water.

Amanda, not far behind, gasped when she stepped into the frigid flow. This was going to be the quickest bath in history. But once she was completely wet, the water didn't seem quite so cold, and the sunshine blazing down on them felt incredibly warm. A sudden splash drenched her.

Sarah giggled.

Turning, Amanda met her sister's playful grin. "So that's how it's going to be, eh?" Leaning down, she skimmed the surface of the water with her palm, directing an arc of water at the younger girl. It cascaded down her face, and over her shoulders.

"Enough, enough! I'm sorry!" Hand upraised in a gesture of defeat, Sarah acquiesced and began wetting her hair.

Amanda followed suit. But seeing her sister bent over at the waist with her behind in the air as she rinsed her long hair was too much to resist.

A little shove, and in Sarah went, headfirst. She came up sputtering, ready to reciprocate.

Instead, she froze, eyes wide.

Amanda whirled.

In the distance, a small band of Indian braves on ponies rode straight for them.

Her mouth went dry. "Back to the wagon! Hurry!" Though what security the two of them would find there, she could only question.

After they clambered up into the back, they seized blankets and wrapped themselves up, then perched fearfully on the seat.

Any remaining doubts Amanda may have had regarding the lunacy of this westward venture now vanished. Everyone knew the sad fate that had met Narcissa Whitman and her doctor husband, Marcus, last November. Missionaries to the Cayuse Indians of the Far Northwest, they had been brutally massacred in their mission home by the very tribe with whom they had labored faithfully for several years.

Now Amanda's dreadful realization that she and her younger sister would soon join Ma and Pa in the hereafter dropped with a thud. She prayed the end would be swift, if not merciful. *Please, Lord, help us to be brave.*

Sarah Jane's expression was no less fearful, but she hiked her chin. "Well, if I'm about to die, I at least want to go happy." She darted into the wagon bed and returned with her guitar.

Mouth agape, Amanda could not respond.

The Indians were almost upon them now. Their skulls were

shaved but for a thick strip of dark hair running from front to back that was roached into an upstanding comb. Naked, except for leather clothes worn about their loins, they also sported vermillion face paint applied in lurid rings about their eyes.

As if completely oblivious to the approaching uninvited audience, Sarah Jane strummed a few chords of introduction, then sang at the top of her lungs:

"Oh, don't you remember sweet Betsy from Pike,
Who crossed the wide prairies with her lover Ike,
With two yoke of cattle and one spotted hog,
A tall shanghai rooster, and an old yaller dog?

"Sing too-ral-i, oo-ral-i, oo-ral-i-ay,
Sing too-ral-i, oo-ral-i, oo-ral-i-ay.

"They swam the wide rivers and crossed the tall peaks,
And camped on the prairie for weeks upon weeks. . ."

The young braves reined in their pinto ponies and sat motionless atop them, staring dumbfounded as Sarah completely destroyed the tune of the comical song.

Amanda didn't know whether to laugh or cry as her sister continued belting out verse upon endless verse:

"They soon reached the desert, where Betsy gave out,
And down in the sand she lay rolling about;
While he in great terror looked on in surprise,
Saying, Betsy, get up, you'll get sand in your eyes.

"Sing too-ral-i, oo-ral-i, oo-ral-i-ay,
Sing too-ral-i, oo-ral-i, oo-ral-i-ay."

Still moving nothing but their dark eyes, the Indians passed curiously astonished looks among themselves. They maintained a safe distance as Sarah launched into another four stanzas.

"...Long Ike and sweet Betsy got married of course,
But Ike, getting jealous, obtained a divorce;
And Betsy, well satisfied, said with a shout,
Good-bye, you big lummox, I'm glad you backed out.

"Sing too-ral-i, oo-ral-i, oo-ral-i-ay..."

Amanda, not entirely recognizing some of the ridiculous lyrics, wondered inanely if her younger sibling had penned some of them herself. She was almost relieved when the final phrase ended. Moments of heavy silence ensued. Even the Indian ponies stood as if frozen, except for the occasional flick of a tail.

Amanda had to force herself to replenish her lungs.

"I suppose I should sing a hymn, too, as my last song." Sarah Jane drew a fortifying breath:

"I'm just a poor wayfaring stranger,
While trav'ling through this world of woe,
Yet there's no sickness, toil or danger
In that bright world to which I go.

"I'm going home to see my father,
I'm going there no more to roam,
I'm only going over Jordan,
I'm only going over home.

"I know dark clouds will gather round me,
I know my way is rough and steep.
Yet beauteous fields lie just before me,
Where God's redeemed their vigils keep..."

As the last note of the fifth stanza died away, Sarah moistened her lips and stood the guitar in the wagon bed, then bravely raised her chin.

Amanda herself had yet to move. She could feel her heart throbbing, her pulse pounding in her ears. Now, awaiting her own most certain demise, she could only wonder what form of torture the two of them faced. How sad that someone so young and pretty as Sarah would meet such a tragic fate, would never find the dashing husband she dreamed of most of her life. If only Amanda could wake up and find this whole foolish idea had been only a dream. Independence could probably have used some good seamstresses. . .there were far worse places for the two of them to live.

After an eternal moment, the brave in the center gave an almost imperceptible signal, and en masse, the band turned their mounts and galloped away. Without even looking back, they crested the top of a near rise and vanished from sight. "D–do you think they'll come back, Mandy?" Sarah asked in a small voice.

Amanda, as befuddled as her sister, merely shrugged.

A ridiculous phrase of off-key singing burst from behind the hill. Then a howl of laughter.

Sarah loosened her soggy blanket and stood. "Humph. They don't even know good music when they hear it!"

At this, Amanda, too, exploded into a giggle, then laughed hysterically until tears coursed down her cheeks. Though her sister joined halfheartedly, it was easy to see she didn't quite see the humor of the moment. Amanda suddenly realized the Indians had thought her sibling was possessed by some strange spirit. . .one they were hesitant to anger. It made her laugh all the harder.

Finally regaining control of her shattered nerves, she turned to Sarah. "Well, Sissy, we can thank the Good Lord for His protection this day. We could easily have made our entrance through the pearly gates."

Sarah paused in the process of stripping off her wet under-things. "I suppose you're right. God definitely is looking after us." But she leaned out, peering in the direction the Indians had taken, just to be sure.

CHAPTER 7

"How's it look up ahead?" Seth asked, riding alongside Red's chestnut gelding in the late afternoon.

"Well, coulda been worse." His friend's copper mustache spread with his grin. "I'd say we've wasted time aplenty. Cy an' T. J. scouted far as the river, an' say the Big Blue's still pretty high from the rain. Trail's hardening up, though. Reckon the worst of the storm passed behind us."

Seth nodded. "Yep, but we have other things to consider, pal. While I was collecting some strays, a bit ago, I spotted a handful of Kanza braves in the distance. Before they get ideas about helping themselves to the livestock, we need to double the guards till we move out of here tomorrow. Pass the word."

"Right, boss."

With a dry smile at his partner's lighthearted formality, Seth waved and headed back toward the rear of the wagon train. The heavy rainfall had necessitated a few precious days' wait for the ground to firm up again, but as Red declared, things could have been worse. Nevertheless, it was the Big Blue they had to worry about most. Always a crotchety river even at the best of times, when it was flowing high, the current was incredibly strong and swift.

Skirting a cluster of cows grazing directly in his path, Seth navigated around them and rode to the crest of the knoll. He took out his spyglass and peered toward the rise where he'd glimpsed the Indians. There was no sign of them at the moment, but no telling where they'd gotten to. He moved the glass and searched what he could see of the undulating landscape.

Just as he was about to inhale a breath of relief, the telescope picked up some movement. He blinked and looked again. No. It couldn't be. He'd counted all the wagons on his way to talk to Red. How could there be a straggler? And several miles behind them, yet! He reined in for a better view.

His heart sank at the sight of two very feminine forms in skirts and bonnets fussing about the winding, silvery ribbon that made up a narrow section of the stream. He had a very strong inclination exactly who'd be fool enough to travel alone in this sometimes-hostile country. "Of all the harebrained—"

Seth took off his hat and rubbed his forehead on his sleeve before replacing it. Another look confirmed his worst fears, and angrily he slumped back into the saddle. It would serve that empty-headed female right if he simply let her and her sister keep on the way they were until they came face-to-face with that cantankerous river—see what they'd do about crossing those treacherous waters without a ferry. They'd discover soon enough how idiotic they were to set out by themselves. If they had a lick of sense they'd turn around now and return to Independence. Maybe the next train out would take them under supervision, but he wanted nothing to do with them.

Red would never believe this. In fact, Seth had half a mind not to even mention the Shelby sisters to his partner. The last thing the company needed was to be slowed down by two girls who didn't have the sense the Almighty gave a fencepost.

But even as he enumerated in his mind the reasons why he should continue on as if he hadn't seen them, the possibility that those wandering Indian braves might find them easy pickings cut across his resolve. A full train wasn't likely to be attacked, but a single wagon out in the open with two vulnerable young women aboard might be another story entirely. No telling what gruesome fate would befall the Shelby girls then.

Seth realized that the next train that happened along would blame him for whatever misfortune befell the pair and spread the word that he couldn't look out for folks under his care. He'd never lost a family to Indians yet. Cholera and dysentery, yes, accidents and drownings. But even when the odd wagon rumbled apart on the rough trail, he'd always managed to find folks willing to lend a hand to the unfortunates. Emulating his idol, the famous trail guide Thomas Fitzpatrick, Seth was trying to earn a reputation for taking people all the way to their destination—and he wasn't about to let all his hard work be ruined by the likes of Amanda Shelby.

That decided, he ground his teeth and nudged his dapple-gray mount, Sagebrush, into a canter. He'd try one more lecture first, and in the unlikely event Miss Shelby still wouldn't take his advice, he'd figure out what to do then.

~⚜~

Amanda washed up the dishes from their early supper of the usual beans and biscuits while Sarah retired to the wagon to record the events of the day in her journal. Tomorrow they would leave this restful campsite. Ahead, miles of rolling prairie in all its green glory stretched to the sky.

This had been their most pleasant stay so far, and restful, thanks to the torrential rain that had brought the journey to a halt. Of course, there had been the encounter with those half-naked Indian braves. Amanda would thank the Lord till her dying day that He'd kept them from harm. She still had qualms regarding further unknown dangers. But as long as the land remained so open, with its gently rolling hills and long prairie grasses, she and Sarah would fare well enough. Amanda couldn't help wondering, though, what lay beyond the horizon.

Standing to shake the excess water off the plates, she lifted her gaze far away to the west, then frowned. It had to be her imagination, the lone rider like a speck of black against the ocean of undulating green. And coming this way! A tingle of alarm skittered up her spine. Was this what they'd be facing every live-long day of this journey? Strange men everywhere they turned? Tomorrow when they stopped for their noon meal, she would get out Pa's rifle and figure out how to use it. Amanda had seen him load and fire it often enough. Surely it couldn't be so hard to master. After all, with Sarah being as fetching and winsome as she was, there might be dozens of occasions when some overly interested man might need to be convinced he should be on his way.

That decided, she sloshed the heavy frying pan in the stream and then wiped it dry while she prayed again for protection. *What time I am afraid, I will trust in Thee.* The precious promise her parents had often quoted drifted to mind, bringing with it the assurance that God was still in control. An unexplainable calm began to soothe her jangled nerves. The cookery and utensils had been stowed away and the campfire doused by the time the rider was near enough for the horse's hoofbeats to be heard. The man looked vaguely familiar, which struck Amanda as curious, since they had gotten to know only a few people during their stay at the hotel. But when he pushed back the brim of his dark hat, revealing his long-faced scowl, her heart sank. The wagon master! For an instant she entertained thoughts of trying to hide, but it was too late. She inhaled a deep breath and assumed an air of indifference as he rode up.

"What do you think you are doing?" he demanded.

Amanda, sitting on a crate, placed the apron she'd been stitching on her lap and looked up. "And good day to you, Mr. Holloway," she returned sarcastically.

"You heard me." The wagon master's brown eyes sizzled with fury as he glared at her from atop his mount, his granite expression hard and rigid as his posture.

"Why, I believe it's quite evident to anyone who can see."

"Yes, well, this has gone far enough. Turn this rig around tomorrow. Won't take you any longer to get back to town than it did to get this far."

Amanda smiled thinly. "Thank you. That's quite the brilliant deduction." She rose casually and started toward the wagon to put her sewing away.

Leather creaked as he shifted position in the saddle. "So you do have some sense after all."

"I beg your pardon?" She paused and turned, arching her brows.

"You're finally giving up on this brainless notion of yours to head west."

Brainless! Amanda felt growing rage at the crass remark. Only her good breeding enabled her to restrain her tongue as she stared without blinking at the domineering, cantankerous man. "Not at all. My sister and I are getting along just fine. . . not that it's any concern of yours, I might add."

"Is everything all right, Sissy?" Sarah Jane called, leaning to peer from the confines of the wagon.

"Perfectly. Mr. Holloway came to wish us well. And now he's leaving."

"In a dog's age I am," he bellowed. "Now, see here—"

"Really, sir, whatever your purpose in forsaking your own duties to come here, you've said your piece. However, it does not change anything. So I would like you to. . .how did you put it? *'Go back where you came from,'* wasn't it?"

A muscle worked in his jaw. He dismounted and reached to grab Amanda's arm, but she shied away. He rolled his eyes. "Look, Miss Shelby," he began, his patronizing tone an obvious ploy to get her to listen. "I know I sounded a mite blunt when I first rode in. I apologize. It was no way to speak to a lady. But I can't seem to get through to you what you need to hear."

"Oh? And what might that be?" She crossed her arms in supreme disinterest.

He filled his lungs and let the breath out all at once. When he spoke, his voice was much kinder, almost pleasant. "I must admit, I was surprised when I looked back and saw you coming. I wouldn't have thought you'd make it this far."

Amanda, with an inward smile of satisfaction, had to remind herself not to gloat.

"But I have to tell you," he went on, his voice taking on a more ominous quality. "This is the easy part. When folks start out for Oregon they think the whole trail's gonna be like this. But it's not. Far from it. There's hardship coming up. Real hardship. First off, there's a mighty river just ahead. It's running high and fast now from that rain, and there's no ferry to make the crossing easy. We'll have to float every wagon over it and hope none of them gets swept away in the current. After that will come the mountains. There'll be places so steep we'll have to haul the wagons up one at a time with ropes and chains, then let them down on the other side. 'Course, a whole passel of them'll rattle apart long before they ever make it that far. And don't forget the watering holes we'll come to that aren't fit to drink. Folks and animals weak with thirst will drink anyway. And every one of them will get sick and die."

Amanda tapped her foot impatiently. Anything to keep from revealing that his dire predictions were beginning to get through to her.

"And that doesn't even take Indians into consideration," he continued. "Or the rattlesnakes, the cholera, and even the weather. You may think you've seen wind and lightning since that little storm we just had. But that was a spring shower compared to what we'll face once we hit the high country. We could get pounded with hail. It could even snow on us before we're through the passes, and the lot of us could freeze to death. Think about it. You've got a younger sister to be responsible for. Is that how you want her to end up?"

Amanda swallowed hard. What he was telling her was the complete opposite of what Pa had read in the guidebook he'd bought. Yet something in the wagon master's face seemed honest. Trustworthy. He'd been over this route before, and he should know more than the books reported. But still— "Well, the Lord has been with Sarah and me up till now, and the Bible says He'll take care of His own always," she reasoned.

Mr. Holloway's demeanor hardened. "I'd say that's a mite presumptuous, myself. Expecting Almighty God to come to your rescue when you don't use the sense He gave you."

Amanda broke eye contact and lowered her gaze to the gritty ground. She took a few steps away, thinking over his words. If she hadn't been enduring the railings of her own conscience along that same line, she'd have been livid. She could not deny that the Lord had already spared them from impending doom twice—and they'd barely begun the journey. Perhaps this was the last chance He was giving them to turn around.

But to what? an inner voice harped.

She stopped and turned. "I want to thank you for coming, Mr. Holloway. I know you mean well. But I'm afraid Sarah and I have to keep going west. We don't have anyplace else to go. If we die along the way, then it's God's will. But we're still going to try."

He slowly shook his head.

"We don't expect you to understand or to feel concern over us. You gave Pa's money back, and we don't have the right to count on you to look after us. We'll just keep on by ourselves. We'll be all right. Now, I'm sure your duties are calling you back to the train. I wish you good day."

He didn't respond for several moments, just stared. Then his expression flattened, along with his tone. "Well, now, that's where we differ. About the last thing I can do is leave the two of you here alone." He hesitated again, a look of resignation settling over his sun-bronzed features. "The train will camp by Alcove Spring tonight so we can start getting everyone across the Big Blue tomorrow. Pack up in the morning and come join up. Travel with the company."

"But—"

"Do it." Without further comment, he swung up into his saddle and galloped away.

Amanda wanted more than anything to ignore Seth Holloway. But for some unexplainable reason, she could not will herself to do so. Nor could she restrain her eyes from gazing after him.

CHAPTER 8

He's quite handsome, don't you think?" Sarah asked, emerging from the wagon to lounge on the seat, her journal in hand. "In an outdoors sort of way, I mean."

"Hm?" Dragging her gaze from the departing horseman, Amanda turned.

"The wagon master. He's handsome, I said. Not at all the way I pictured him from things you told me."

Amanda barely suppressed a smirk.

"Well, not that he appeals to me, of course," Sarah amended. "I fully intend to find someone much more refined, myself. But in general, Mr. Holloway seems to have a certain. . .charm."

Charm! Amanda thought incredulously. *That's the last attribute I'd assign to Seth Holloway.* "I didn't pay him that much mind," she finally said.

Sarah gave a dreamy sigh. "The man I'm looking for must be head and shoulders taller than anyone I've ever met, and stronger, with gorgeous thick hair, expressive eyes and lips, and a voice that sings across the strings of my heart. And he'll be rich, of course. I refuse to settle for less."

The raspy voice alone would eliminate Mr. Holloway, Amanda decided, but didn't bother answering. After all, his eyes were too

471

dark to be very expressive anyway, and his lips had yet to reflect anything but his anger and irritation. She wondered absently if he ever bothered to smile.

"Are we going to do what he asked?"

"You mean *ordered*, don't you?"

"Well, are we?"

Amanda met her sister's questioning face as Mr. Holloway's blunt accusation about presuming upon God came to mind. Loath as she was to admit it, his remark did have merit. "Well, at—at first I didn't plan to," she hedged, "but already in the few days we've been on the trail, God has had to rescue us twice. We really shouldn't expect Him to come to our aid every time we encounter any sort of peril."

Sarah did not respond.

"The fact is," Amanda went on, "the wagon master is right. Sooner or later we're going to face some serious difficulties we won't be able to handle on our own. With the other emigrants there'd be someone who could help us. Folks look out for each other. I'm afraid if we don't join the train it could be to our folly."

"I see what you mean." Sarah glanced westward momentarily, in the direction their visitor had taken. Then she sat, opened her diary and began writing once more, a fanciful smile curving her lips.

Amanda saw that Seth Holloway was no longer within sight. Reaching into the wagon, she retrieved her sewing and returned to the crate she'd occupied earlier. If the man had not appeared at their campsite out of the blue, she'd never have guessed the other wagons were within such close proximity. They, too, must have had to wait out the horrific rain. Oh well, she concluded, knotting the last stitches in the apron she'd been making, if she and Sarah were actually hoping to meet up with them in the near future, it would be wise to turn in soon so they could get an early start. She bit off the remaining thread. After making swift work of attending to all the evening chores, Amanda hurried to the wagon, where she discovered Sarah already asleep in bed. She shed her cotton dress and tugged on her night shift, then took her place beside the younger girl on the hard mattress. But her mind remained far too active to relinquish consciousness easily. In the stillness broken only by the uneven cadence of the night creatures, she analyzed Mr. Holloway's unexpected visit.

Something about the man disturbed her in a way she had never experienced before. It wasn't so much his domineering manner, or even his patronizing attitude toward her and her sister—those she could understand. But when he'd realized they were determined to make the trip with or without the benefit of company, he'd mellowed. For a few seconds he'd even seemed. . .kind. And she preferred him the other way. Sarah was right. Seth Holloway did possess a certain rugged, outdoors look that some might consider handsome. But aware that the man had proclaimed her brainless and foolhardy, Amanda saw no reason to concern herself with such inane fantasies as trying to convince him otherwise. With a sigh, she fluffed her pillow and settled down on its plumpness.

Seth, on the last watch of the night, poured the dregs of the coffee into his mug, then drank it slowly as he walked the outside perimeter of the circled wagons. Spying Red keeping a lookout on the westward side, he joined him. "All's quiet, eh?"

His friend nodded. "Ain't seen hide nor hair of them Injuns or any other creatures lurkin' about."

"Me neither." Seth tossed the dregs from the mug into the bushes. He would have preferred not to have had an encounter with the Shelbys, much less have to talk about it, but it needed to be aired. His partner would also be affected by their joining up with the train. He cleared his throat. "There's something I might as well tell you."

Red looked up, his brow furrowed. "You happened on some other trouble?"

Seth shrugged. "Not exactly. Well, maybe. I, uh, spotted the Shelby sisters trailing us some ways back."

"What?" His partner's jaw went slack, his expression tinged with a combination of humor and disbelief.

"You got it. Fool females took it upon themselves to set out after us. I tried to persuade them to turn around while they still could, but it was no good. Trying to get through to that older one's like butting up against a stone wall." He grimaced and shook his head. "Stubbornest gal I ever did come across."

"Hm. Worse than that sister-in-law of yours is, eh? The one who soured you on marriage, I mean."

Seth didn't dignify the comment with anything but a glower. The mere thought of his younger brother being linked up with that conniving, sharp-tongued Eliza always made him angry. Red snickered, then rubbed his jaw in thought. "Well, if they made it this far on their own, I s'pose they have as much a shot at goin' west as anybody else."

"Maybe. At least on the easy end of things," Seth grated. "Figure if we're gonna end up playing nursemaid, we might as well have them within reach. I told them to join up with us this evening. Who knows, they might get their fill when they stare the Big Blue in the face."

Neither spoke for several seconds.

"Guess I'll head on back to my end," Seth said with resignation. "Folks'll soon be up and cooking breakfast before those cockamamie Sunday services they insist on having."

"Strange comment, if you don't mind me sayin' so—'specially comin' from the grandson of a circuit-ridin' preacher."

Seth branded him with a glare. "See you later."

"Sure. Could be an interestin' day."

Ignoring his partner's chuckle, Seth strode away.

<hr />

When Amanda came within sight of the train of emigrants, the next evening, the first thing she noticed was the warm glow of lantern light that crowned the circle of wagons like a halo. It bolstered her spirits, as did the happy music drifting from the encampment from fiddles and harmonicas. Drawing nearer, Amanda heard soft laughter and the sound of children and barking dogs.

"I think I'm going to like being with the others," Sarah said happily.

Before Amanda could answer, her eyes locked on to Seth

Holloway's where he leaned against the nearest rig with his hands in his pockets as if waiting for the two of them to arrive.

His expression unreadable, he shoved his hands into his pockets and walked toward them. "Pull up over there," he instructed with a slight jerk of his head.

Amanda nodded, guiding the team to an empty space in the formation. As she did so, a threesome of men approached. "Evenin', ladies," a solid-chested older man said, thumbing his hat. "Name's Randolph. Nelson Randolph. This here's Ben Martin and Zeke Sparks," he said, tipping his head to the left and right to indicate a rawboned man in his early thirties and a narrow-faced one with a long nose and prominent ears. "We'll help get you into place."

"Why, thank you." Amanda accepted his proffered hand as she climbed down. "I'm Amanda Shelby."

"And I'm Sarah, her sister."

"Glad to make your acquaintance," Mr. Randolph said, reaching to help Sarah also. "We'll be neighbors of yours along the way, so you'll soon get to know us an' some of the others in this mob."

"An' which ones ya should keep an eye out for," Ben Martin said with a good-natured wink. He nudged his lanky pal in the ribs.

In a matter of moments the mules had been unhitched and the wagon rolled into the open slot, its tongue beneath the back of the wagon ahead of it.

"When you gals get settled in," Mr. Randolph said, "make yourselves to home. Mosey in by the big fire and introduce yourselves, if you want to. Folks generally do most of their visitin' in camp. Or just sit an' listen to the music, if you druther. With it bein' Sunday, folks seem to like hymns best."

Amanda smiled. "We'll do that. Thanks for your help."

As the men left, she glanced around self-consciously at the several curious but friendly faces turned their way and returned a few smiles. No one was familiar, but then Amanda hadn't actually met more than one or two emigrants back in Independence before Pa had taken sick. The only person to whom she'd spoken was Mr. Holloway, and he was nowhere to be seen. "Well," she said, turning to Sarah, "we're here."

"Yes." The younger girl's gaze swept across the open circle, where a few couples were blending their voices in song. Clusters of children frolicked everywhere.

Amanda recognized her sister's peculiar smile and its accompanying blush immediately. Habitually checking to see which young man in particular had caught Sarah's eye, she noticed a gangly youth who extracted himself from a group of others and sauntered toward them.

"Evening, ladies," he said, grinning broadly on his approach. He doffed his hat in an elaborate gesture, revealing curly brown hair, then plunked it back on, blue eyes sparkling as his attention settled on Sarah. "I'm Alvin Rivers. Delighted to welcome you to camp."

Amanda noted the young man's clothing seemed of finer cut and quality than that of the men they'd met earlier.

"Why, thank you, Mr. Rivers," Sarah gushed. "My name is Sarah Shelby, and this is my older sister, Amanda."

Amanda cringed.

Alvin gave her a respectful nod, then switched back to Sarah again. "Anything I might do to help you get settled in for the night? Check your wheels? Grease the hubs?"

"Grease the hubs?" the younger girl echoed in puzzlement.

"Right. We do it most every night, miss. With the bucket of grease hanging back by the axle."

Both girls followed his gesture.

Amanda hadn't missed his surprise at Sarah's question. She had a vague recollection of Pa mentioning something about that chore, but she'd neglected to do anything about it up until now. How fortunate that Mr. Holloway wasn't around to witness her stupidity. "Thank you, Mr. Rivers," she said. "Sarah and I would be most grateful to have you tend to greasing the hubs this evening." *While I watch to see how it's done!*

"Glad to, miss." He tipped his hat and started toward the back of the wagon, with them in his wake. "Where do you two hail from?" he asked casually over his shoulder.

"Pennsylvania," Sarah answered. "Tunkhannock. And you?"

"Baltimore, Maryland. My aunt and uncle are looking to buy some prime land in the Oregon Territory where there's room to spread out. Too many people were bottled up in the little valley we lived in back east." He took down the grease bucket and set to work.

"Excuse me, miss," Amanda heard someone say. She turned to see a pleasant-faced grandmotherly woman smiling at her, accenting deep laugh creases on either side of her smile. "Since it's late, and all, I thought you and your sister might like some stew. We've finished up, but there's plenty left in the pot. Name's Minnie Randolph. Husband and me are three wagons down." She pointed in that direction.

"Why, thank you, Mrs. Randolph. You're most kind. I'm Amanda, and she's Sarah. Shelby."

"Glad to know you. When we heard you two were coming, I figured you'd be tired by the time you got here. And don't worry about a thing, you hear? A lot of folks're gonna be keeping an eye out for you gals on this trip. We didn't get to know your pa, but he seemed a decent sort the little time we saw him readyin' for the journey. Downright shame he had to pass on so suddenlike." Obviously noting the distress the reminder had caused, she quickly cleared her throat. "You just come right on down as soon as you're ready."

Amanda nodded her thanks. She turned back to Sarah, catching the end of something Alvin Rivers was saying as he finished the last wheel.

"...so you wouldn't mind if I come by of an evening and show you around?" His voice cracked on the last word.

"That would be very nice," Sarah answered.

And once all the other eligible young men in the group catch a glimpse of my fair and lissome sister, you'll have to stand in line, Amanda couldn't help thinking.

"Sarah," she called. "We've been offered some supper. Let's go wash up."

Her sister gave a nod of assent, then turned to Alvin. "Thanks for helping out with the wagon. Perhaps I'll see you tomorrow."

"Yes, miss," he said, hanging the bucket back on its hook. He took a large kerchief from a back pocket and wiped his hands. "Tomorrow." The grin he flashed at her broadened to include Amanda. "Miss Shelby."

Amanda nodded. She bit back a giggle as he moved backward, almost stumbling over a rock in his path before he turned and strode away. Then, aware of someone else's scrutiny, she glanced curiously around. Part of her expected to find Seth Holloway's critical gaze fixed on her, ready to find fault, but it wasn't the wagon master after all.

Two wagons ahead, a tall, somber man stared unabashedly. He held a fussing little girl in his arms. Another small child, a boy a year or so older, clung to his knees. He patted the tow-head and said something Amanda couldn't hear, then bent and scooped him up. He placed the two tots inside his wagon and climbed in after them.

"I'm ready," Sarah Jane said, coming to her side.

"Hm? Oh. I'll be just a minute." Accepting the dampened cloth her sister held out, Amanda scrubbed her own face and hands, then brushed her hair and retied the ribbon. "Best we not keep Mrs. Randolph waiting." Shaking some trail dirt from the hem of her skirt, she fluffed it out again, and the two went to join the kind older woman.

After enduring even those few days of their own inadequate cooking, their neighbor's hearty stew tasted like a feast fit for royalty. Amanda relished every drop, mopping the last speck from her bowl with the light biscuits, even as steady, sad crying carried from the next wagon. It caught at her heart.

"Would you like more?" the gray-haired woman asked, interrupting Amanda's musings.

"Oh no, we've had plenty, thank you." Amanda placed a hand on the older woman's forearm. "It was truly delicious."

"I'm afraid we don't share your gift for cooking," Sarah confessed. "All I've managed so far is some pretty ordinary beans with biscuits or corn bread."

"Well, cookin's more skill than gift, I'd say. There'll be plenty of time on this trip for both of you to pick up some of the basics of makin' meals on the trail. I'd be more'n happy to pass on what I know at some of the noonings and suppertimes."

"Why, that's very kind of you." Amanda fought sudden and unexpected tears at the woman's generosity. Up until this past sad year, she hadn't been one given to displaying her emotions, and she sincerely hoped this was not becoming a habit. She must merely be overly tired. She smiled and got up. "We'll just wash up our dishes and bring them back." She nodded at Sarah, and the two hurried to the spring with the soiled things.

The beauty of Alcove Spring was not lost on either one. They gazed in rapt delight at the pure, cold water that gushed from a ledge of rocks and cascaded ten feet down into a basin. Quickly finished with their chore, they left the idyllic spot.

Mrs. Randolph graciously inclined her bonneted head on their return. "I know this has been a long day, so I won't keep you. Tomorrow I'll introduce you to some of the folks around. Meanwhile, don't waste time worryin' about anything. We'll all take real good care of you two."

A wave of reassurance washed over Amanda, and she couldn't help wondering if everyone in the train would be so kind and thoughtful. She lifted a hand in parting and took her leave. "Thanks again. Good evening."

Passing the next wagon, Amanda once more met the brooding eyes of the lanky man sitting inside as he cuddled his two forlorn children. She gave a polite nod and continued on. Tomorrow she'd ask Mrs. Randolph about those little ones.

CHAPTER 9

At the wakeup signal the next morning, the girls expectantly threw on their clothes. From all around the camp, a curious assortment of whistles, snorts, shouts, and cracks of bullwhackers' whips filled the air as the company came to life. Women put coffee on to boil and started the bacon to sizzle over crackling fires, while the men went to gather their oxen or mules and hitch them up. Sleepy-eyed children yawned and stretched, then hustled to wash, dress, and tend to chores before the order came for the wagons to roll.

"Sure is a busy place," Sarah commented, measuring tea leaves into the tin coffeepot.

Amanda only nodded. "I'd best round up the mules while you see to that. We'll have to do like everyone else now." She stepped over the wagon tongue and hurried toward the animals.

Hardly had the company finished breakfast when the first outfit set off for the river. The girls stashed their things and boarded their schooner, waiting to take their place in line.

A movement on the edge of Amanda's vision brought a brief glimpse of Seth Holloway riding herd on the cattle. She did not allow her gaze to linger. Concentration was needed to maintain a proper distance between her mules and the wagon ahead.

"This is all so exciting," Sarah Jane gushed. "I never realized before how dead our camps were. All this organized bustle and activity. . ." Her words trailed off as she swiveled on the seat to look around the edge of the wagon.

"I liked the quiet," Amanda mused. Cutting a glance toward Sarah, she found her too occupied in observing the surroundings to have heard. Amanda tightened her hold on the reins.

Soon enough, she glimpsed the belt of sycamores, oaks, and elms lining the banks of the awe-inspiring Big Blue, the sight and sound of which became more and more unnerving the nearer they got. She reined to a stop.

The long, slow process of crossing had already begun. A number of wagons dotted the opposite shore, and several more now inched across the swiftly flowing water at an upstream angle. Amanda noticed that some outfits drove right into the Blue, while others, at the river's edge, had men grunting and straining to remove the wheels so the beds could be elevated on wooden blocks. Still others were being hitched to double teams. Sarah jumped down without a word and walked ahead, where a handful of women stood watching the men at work.

Amanda's gaze returned to the brave souls traversing the roiling water, and her heartbeat increased. She tried to study the way the drivers retained control against the force of the current, knowing soon enough she would face that same challenge.

Sounds came from farther downstream, from bawling and balking cattle whose bobbing heads kept time with their sporadic movements. Several swing in wide-eyed frenzy to return to the riverbank, and a few of them lost their footing, only to be swept away by the rushing water. Amanda held her breath as outriders ignored those and quickly set to persuading the rest to continue on. She easily picked out Seth Holloway. With the determined set of his jaw and distinctive rigid posture, he stood out from the others. Watching him, she couldn't help but admire his mettle and strength.

"You'll be next, miss."

The low voice startled Amanda. She swallowed and obeyed the signal to pull up to the edge of the water. Sarah Jane climbed to the seat and clutched the edges, her knuckles white, as their schooner, somewhat lighter in weight than the more cumbersome Conestoga wagons, was checked over for the crossing.

Mr. Randolph stepped near, astutely reading the apprehension Amanda knew must be evident in her expression. "Don't worry, little gal. Just keep a firm hold on your animals. They're strong swimmers, an' I'll be right behind you, keepin' an eye out." With a grin of encouragement, he turned and strode to his own rig, parked off to one side so she could precede him.

Amanda tried to smile, but failed miserably as the men coaxed the skittish mules down the slippery bank and into the dark current that whooshed by unimpeded as it swirled over the animals' shoulders. They hee-hawed in protest, but began their unhappy swim.

The wagon bed rocked fore and aft, jouncing uncertainly on the choppy waves, and cold wetness splashed over the wooden sides to slosh about Amanda's feet. She couldn't have spoken if her life depended on it, but sent a frantic prayer aloft and held on for dear life.

The churning water surrounding them now seemed wide as an ocean. Hoping her own inexperience would not hinder the mules from following the rig ahead at a similar angle, Amanda clutched the reins, watching anxiously as the animals labored toward the opposite shore. Sarah, huddled beside her, kept her eyes closed the whole time. Amanda only hoped her sister was adding fervent prayers to her own.

An eternity later, forelegs and hind legs gained footing on the other bank, where men armed with strong ropes and other teams lent a hand and ushered the mules up to dry ground. It took all Amanda's stamina not to collapse in relief.

Moments later, the Randolph wagon followed and pulled alongside. A grin of satisfaction spread across the lined face of the older man, but his wife's was devoid of color. "Land sakes," she murmured. "Thank the good Lord we made that one!"

⟞⟝

As soon as Amanda had parked the wagon out of the way of the last remaining rigs and got down to unhitch the team, Sarah

Jane climbed into the back and settled down with her journal:

> *Dear Diary,*
>
> *I cannot even describe how good it feels to have come to the end of this busiest and most frightening day! Poor Mandy shook like a leaf when we had finally made it across the Big Blue—a curious name for a river flowing with such brown water! But when word reached us to make camp, both of us could have jumped for joy. Everyone else seemed grateful, too, since so many hours of light had been given to the effort of getting the entire assemblage to the westward side.*
>
> *Now it is oddly peaceful. The animals graze contentedly on the shining grass, while the setting sun haloes the slim trees with a border of hazy gold. Most of the songbirds whose sweet trills lighten our journey have returned to their nests, and the twilight air is filled with the pungent smell of wood smoke. I wonder what tomorrow will bring.*

"That was some mighty fine driving you did earlier."

At the sound of Alvin Rivers' voice outside, Sarah quickly closed her book, set it down, and exited the wagon.

The young man's freckled face bore a grin from ear to ear at her sister, but his gaze immediately sought Sarah's. "If I hadn't had my own hands full helping out my aunt and uncle, I'd have gladly taken the reins for you."

Sarah saw Amanda smile her thanks.

"Mandy's almost as strong as Pa," she blurted.

Rolling her eyes, Amanda shook her head and began getting into the wagon. "I'll see if there's enough dry wood and kindling to make a cook fire."

"Anyway," Alvin went on, "I'll see that the hubs get a good greasing after all that water."

"Why, how very sweet." Sarah tied her apron ties more snugly about her waist, then got out the cookpot while Alvin tended to the wheels. She returned to the fire Amanda was laying.

They both looked up at the sound of footsteps.

"No use botherin' with viddles tonight," Mrs. Randolph said. "One of our neighbors shot a fine pair of rabbits while the rest of us were comin' over the water. I'm just about to fry one of them right now, and you gals are more than welcome to join us. There's wild honey for the biscuits, too, thanks to him."

Coming after the trying day, the invitation was more than welcome. "We'd be delighted," Sarah said.

"If we can contribute something," Amanda quickly added. "Potatoes and carrots, at least? And may we watch?"

The older woman's bonnet dipped with her nod. "Don't mind if you do. Come anytime."

"Thanks ever so much. We'll be there soon as we put these things back inside." Amanda flashed a grin of relief at Sarah.

<hr>

At the close of the delicious meal, the girls made fast work of washing the dishes. When Alvin and some of his friends came by to claim Sarah for a walk, Amanda chose to linger over a second cup of coffee with their kind neighbor.

Twilight was deepening, and the cacophony of music made by the night creatures began to fill the air. . .pleasant sounds against the intermittent crying coming from the next wagon. Mrs. Randolph heaved a sigh. "Poor little thing starts up every night about this time."

Amanda dragged her gaze back to her hostess. "Where's her mama?" she couldn't help asking.

"That's a sorry tale." The older woman paused in raising her cup to her lips and slowly wagged her head. "While we were camped at Independence, the child's mother—scarcely more than a kid herself—was cavorting with her brood out in one of the fields, gathering wildflowers, racing to see who could pick the most. Running toward a real purty bunch of flowers, she turned to look over her shoulder at the little ones, and tripped over a root. Hit her head on a jagged rock, she did. Prit' near bled to death on the spot."

"How awful."

"Somebody went and fetched the doc right quick. But by the time he came, it was too late. Little gal was so weak she never even come to. She was in the family way, too, which didn't help matters." Mrs. Randolph gazed toward the motherless children.

A raft of sad memories flooded Amanda's mind, and her eyes swam with tears. She quickly blinked them away.

"Had ourselves our first funeral before we even left town," the older woman continued. "And now those precious babes are without a mother's love." Then, as if suddenly recalling that hadn't been the only death among the families gathering to migrate west this spring, she blanched. Her hand flew to her throat. "Mercy me. I'm as sorry as sorry can be, child. You losin' your own pa, too. I should be more careful to think before I talk."

Amanda reached to pat her gnarled hand. "It's all right. Truly. I've accepted Pa's passing on. We both have. And at least we're grown. What must those poor darlings be going through?" Her curiosity once again drew her stare toward the sobbing child—and met the somber gaze of the widowed father.

Amanda quickly averted her eyes, focusing on the half-empty cup in her hands. She gulped some of the lukewarm coffee. "What are the children's names, Mrs. Randolph? Perhaps there's something Sarah or I could do to help."

She nodded thoughtfully. "You know, there just might be, now that you mention it. The little girl's Bethany, as I recall. The boy, now. . . Hmm." Frowning, she folded her arms over her generous bosom and tapped an index finger against her mouth. "Thomas, maybe. No, Timothy, Goes by the nickname Tad."

"And the father?" Amanda prompted, aware of a rising flush at her boldness.

The older woman seemed not to notice. "Name's Jared Hill. Seems a decent sort, leastwise from what we've gotten to know of him since we been on the trail. He's a mite standoffish."

Jared Hill. It suited him, Amanda decided—or did from a distance. She had yet to see him close up. The important thing was that the poor man had his hands full, and anyone with a sense of Christian duty should be more than willing to help in whatever small way she could.

By the time Amanda finished her coffee and made her way back to her own wagon, Bethany's sobs had ceased. She surmised that the children had been tucked in for the night. Mr. Hill, however, remained outside, kneeling in the circle of firelight, checking a section of harness. He looked up as Amanda neared.

She felt it only polite to smile. "Good evening."

"Evening, miss." Putting the traces aside, he rose, straightening his long limbs to tower a head above her. The eyes beneath his sandy hair appeared dark in the dim glow, their color indistinct, but a pronounced downward turn at the outer corners gave evidence of his grief.

Amanda stopped. "I—I couldn't help hearing your little girl cry."

He shrugged in resignation.

"So sorry to hear of your loss." Taking a step forward, she reached out her hand. "I'm Amanda Shelby, your new neighbor."

"Hill," he replied, shaking her hand. "Jared Hill. I'll do my best to see Bethy doesn't disturb you anymore."

"No!" Amanda gasped. "Please don't think—" Flustered that he'd mistaken her remark as criticism, she started over. "I—I only wanted to offer help. My sister Sarah's especially good with children. If there's anything we can do, please don't hesitate to ask."

His fingers raked through the tousled strands of his hair. "Well, thanks. Don't see as I need help, though. Or pity. We'll get by." One side of his mouth turned upward in the barest hint of a smile, softening his narrow face.

Amanda nodded. "Oh. But— Well, I just wanted to offer, that's all. Good night." At his nod of dismissal, she walked briskly away. . .trying not to feel utterly humiliated.

CHAPTER 10

"You'd be surprised what an interesting life Alvin has led," Sarah Jane declared as the wagon rumbled onward the following morning, the harness jangling in time with the clopping of the mules. "His great passion is art. Last year his aunt and uncle took him to Europe to art museums in Spain, Italy, France, and England, just to view the work of the great masters. He even showed me some of his own drawings. He's got wonderful talent."

"Oh, really?"

"Um-hmm. He's working on a book of sketches of the various terrain and landmarks along the trail. He's planning to try to interest a publisher in putting together a project of that sort for other folks thinking of heading west. Someday Alvin hopes to become a real artist. Maybe paint portraits, or—"

Her sister's sigh indicated she was only half-listening.

Sarah paused and turned her head, a ringlet falling forward on her shoulder with the movement. She flicked it back. "You're awfully quiet this morning. Something wrong?"

Staring at her for a few seconds, Amanda finally spoke. "It's that man and the two young children, in the wagon behind the Randolphs."

"What about them?"

"The mother died accidentally back in Independence. The kids—especially the daughter—have taken it real hard."

At the sad news, Sarah's mouth gaped in dismay. "How very tragic. That would account for the crying I've heard from time to time. How old are those little ones?" She peered ahead, in the direction of their wagon.

"The boy, Tad, looks to be about four. Bethany must be three, or nearly so."

"Maybe we could help out somehow."

Amanda gave a soft huff. "That's what I thought, too. Only their father as much as told me to mind my own business."

Recalling her own first experience in the valley of the shadow of death, Sarah could easily identify with other people's sorrow. "Well, I'm sure he must not have meant to put you off so rudely. He might just be hurting, too. Remember how we felt when Mama died?"

Her elder sibling momentarily appeared lost in the sad memory of their own wrenching loss. "We knew our lives would never be the same. Nor had we expected to stand before another open grave so soon." she added with a pang of near bitterness.

"Maybe I'll make a doll for the little girl and take it by. She needs to be around women."

"I think that's a splendid idea." Amanda visibly relaxed. Sarah lifted her gaze to the countryside, making mental notes she would enter into her diary later. There were considerably fewer trees since they'd crossed the river, no forests filled with glorious red-budded maples, no thickly wooded groves like those in the East, which seemed like nap on earth's carpet. Now she saw only the occasional solitary tree standing alone to face the elements.

The grasses, too, were taller, growing to a height of six or eight feet in the moist areas. The land itself was more open, allowing the wagons to spread out. some of them even traveling side by side as they meandered westward along the Little Blue River, a calm glistening ribbon of satin accented by the floral beauty of spring. Most of the womenfolk and youngsters had taken to walking now, in deference to the hard, springless wagon seats. Sarah often walked with them herself, taking part in the cheerful chatting as they gathered wood or colorful bouquets of wildflowers to pass the miles.

"Does Alvin Rivers have any other family?" Amanda asked, reverting to the previous topic.

"Not since he was quite young. His relatives have been raising him. He's pretty happy, though. Apparently they have a lot of money."

Her sister quirked a brow at her.

"Well, Alvin can't help that," Sarah said, her prickles up. "It isn't as if he lords it over anyone. He's just had advantages a lot of other young people have never enjoyed. Anyway," she added, lifting her chin, "we were quite comfortable ourselves not too long ago, if you recall."

"True."

"So maybe you shouldn't judge someone you don't even know."

Amanda flushed. "Yes, Mother," she said wryly.

"Well, if I'm going to make little Bethany a new doll, I'd best get to work." Sarah Jane swung her legs over the seat and retreated into the back, where she began rooting through the sewing supplies.

~⚹~

After a quiet supper of beans and fried mush, Amanda took the dirty dishes over to the river and knelt to wash them. The drowsy sultriness of the spring evening was crowned by the tranquil richness of a glorious sunset, which spread deepening violet shadows everywhere. She filled her lungs with the perfumes emitted by blue lupine and other flowers.

Splashing sounds from nearby ceased. Not twenty feet away, a man rose to his feet behind a curve in the riverbank that had concealed him from view. Stripped to the waist, he stood motionless for several seconds, his skin glistening like purest gold. When he pulled on his shirt, it clung to his muscular contours in a few enticingly damp places. Amanda caught herself staring.

So did he.

Her cheeks flamed.

Seth Holloway held her gaze, his expression altering not a whit as he fastened the last shirt button. He bent and retrieved his wide-brimmed hat, then nodded ever so slightly before plunking it on his wet head.

Amanda tried to quell the flush of heat in her face. Why hadn't she looked away, for pity's sake? She busied herself scrubbing the heavy iron frying pan in the flowing water with added vigor.

"Miss Shelby."

The sloshing water had covered the sound of his approaching footsteps. Amanda nearly lost her balance as she jerked her head to peer up at him. "Mr. Holloway. . ." She wondered what else to say, but needn't have been concerned. He was already striding away without a backward glance.

Thank heaven.

After returning to her rig, Amanda did her best to dismiss the mental picture of the wagon master from her mind. Had she been Sarah, she conjectured with a smile, she'd have flown right to her journal to pen flowery phrases of the magnificent vision Seth Holloway had made against the vibrant sky. But she wasn't Sarah. . .and anyway, a spinster shouldn't dwell on such nonsense.

With new resolve, she gathered her sewing and sat on a crate outside to enjoy the pleasant music and banter of camp as she hemmed the ties of another apron. It was quite gratifying to see the stock for the future store accumulating. Besides the half-dozen other aprons she had completed herself, Sarah had finished quite a pile of calico bonnets and flannel baby blankets. But with the younger girl's evenings so often taken up by Alvin Rivers and other young people, Amanda knew her own items would soon outnumber her sister's. Sarah had never lacked for friends. Amanda released a resigned breath.

A tall shadow fell across her work, blocking the glow from the big center fire. "Excuse me, miss?"

Startled, Amanda looked up to see that the low voice belonged to Jared Hill. "Yes?"

He removed the hat from his sandy hair and cleared his

throat, then shifted his weight from one foot to the other, as if working up courage to speak. "I came to apologize. Had no call to be short with you when you asked after my kids. I know you meant well."

"Oh. Well, thank you. I took no offense, Mr. Hill." The statement wasn't quite true, but after Sarah's comments had put the whole thing into perspective, Amanda felt better about it and had been able to make allowances for the widower.

He nodded. "Well, I said my piece, I won't keep you from your chore." Offering a faint smile, he turned and walked away.

Amanda's spirit was lighter as she watched him go back to his own wagon. She had no intentions of forcing herself on the man's children, but it was nice to know that if she did have occasion to befriend them their father wouldn't shoo her away.

Seth laid his hat on a rock, then spread out his bedroll and climbed in between the blankets, resting his head on his saddle. Face up, he clasped his hands behind his neck and stared idly at the myriad stars speckling the midnight sky. It reminded him of something. He searched his memory and grimaced...the Shelby girl had been wearing navy calico. That had to be it. He rolled over onto his side.

Truth was—and he'd be the last to admit it even to Red— it completely astounded him that those two young women had actually made it across the Big Blue on their own. Or rather, Amanda Shelby had done it on her own. Who would have expected a female of her tender age to have such pluck! A low chuckle rumbled from deep inside him.

On the other hand, he reasoned, that river was but one of numerous obstacles the train would face. There'd be plenty more opportunities for her to give up and turn back for Missouri. Yep, for all her faith that God would see her through, Seth knew they had to be merely brave words. Most people he'd met only put on that religious act to go along with their Sunday go-to-meeting duds. Come Monday morning, they all reverted back to their normal selves. She wouldn't be any different.

'Course, when he'd been a tadpole, Seth had possessed quite the religious bent himself, much to his chagrin. His grandfather had seen to that. But after Gramps passed on, and Seth had grown up enough to see a few too many prime examples of church folk, he had wised up.

Too bad his brother Andrew hadn't been so perceptive, letting the wool be pulled over his eyes that way by that beautiful but scheming Eliza. Once a female had a man where she wanted him, she went in for the kill. Seth winced. That would be the day he would fall for any woman's goody ways or holy-sounding words. He was bright enough to see right through people, thanks to her.

Far in the distance, the lonely howl of a wolf carried on the wind. Seth raised his head to see the men on the night watch add wood and buffalo chips to the fires. He lay back down.

Enough time wasted thinking about women. There wasn't one of them worth the time of day.

But his mind refused to keep in line with his intentions. Seth found himself grinning. He had pretty near scared the prim Miss Shelby out of her skin, earlier. She'd all but toppled right into the little Blue—and he could just imagine the sight she'd have made, all sputtering and flustered, water streaming off that long hair, her dress clinging to those fetching curves of hers...

Quickly reining in his wayward thoughts, Seth deliberately forced aside the vision of troubled green eyes that had a way of lingering in his mind as if he had no say in the matter. It was beginning to aggravate him how that at times he found himself comparing the variegated greens of the prairie grasses to the shade of those eyes. He'd best start keeping some distance between that gal and himself and concentrate on doing what he was hired to do—get these folks out west. Once he dumped them all off on that side of the world, he'd have no more cause to cross paths with that Shelby girl. End of problem. He squeezed his eyelids closed. . .but sleep was a long time coming.

CHAPTER 11

Wood, water, and grass were plentiful along the friendly Little, Blue, and so were flies and mosquitoes. Several evenings in a row, the wagons stopped to park alongside one another on its shady banks instead of drawing into the customary circle. A big, common fire continued to draw forth fiddles, harmonicas, flutes, and lithe feet of emigrants eager to lose the weary monotony of travel in dancing and music. The menfolk, after tending to needed wagon repairs, would loll about and smoke their pipes, and the women would ignore the pesky insects long enough to visit and swap life stories.

During noon stops, Minnie Randolph had introduced Amanda to many of the other travelers. Added to the younger set she'd been meeting through Sarah and Alvin, Amanda now felt more a part of the company.

"I'll tell ye," Ma Phelps, a tall, rawboned woman, was saying as Amanda carried her sewing over by the great fire. "I've yet to find a better way to make johnnycakes."

A wave of murmured assents made the rounds, followed by a "Hello, Amanda-girl."

Amanda smiled and took a seat on the blanket that frail little Rosalie Bertram patted with her multi-veined hand. The woman kept right on subject. "Hazel Withers just gave me a recipe for the most mouth-waterin' dried-apple pies t'other day. Y'all need to try it." Her nod loosened one of the skimpy braids in her graying coronet and her nimble fingers quickly repositioned the hairpins.

Thin, weak-eyed Jennie Thornton squinted through her gold-rimmed spectacles at a nearby wagon as another muffled birthing scream contrasted sharply with the happy music. She exchanged knowing nods with the other women, then picked up the conversation again. "I'm still hankerin' for some of that buffalo steak the outriders rave about. Ain't even seen one o' them critters yet."

"We'll come across them soon enough, from what I hear," Mrs. Randolph said confidently. "Then there'll be meat to spare and enough to make jerky, to boot."

During a lull in the music, a soft slap sounded from the wagon confines, followed by a tiny cry. "Ohhh, that be our first young'un born on the trip," Ma Phelps breathed. "Shore hope the little angel makes it."

Several seconds of silent contemplation followed. Then the fiddles broke into another tune, and laughing couples linked elbows for the next jig.

Amanda felt a cool gust of wind. Pulling her shawl more closely about her shoulders, she noticed gathering clouds.

"Another shower's likely," Mrs. Randolph said. "Guess I'll go make sure everything's closed up nice and tight."

"Me, too." Amanda folded her project and went to shake out tarps and cover supplies in the wagon.

Sarah Jane came soon afterward. "Whew!" she breathed airily. "Sure is breezy out there. I hope it's just another nice rain like we had last night. I might be able to finish that doll for the little Hill girl. There's only the dress left to do." Reaching for the blue calico and the shears, she moved nearer to the lantern.

Amanda nodded. "It's turning out really cute. Where'd you get the hair?"

With a slightly embarrassed grin, Sarah flinched. "That old shawl of mine. . .the brown one. It was getting rather worn, so I pulled a thread and unraveled the bottom row."

"Bethany is sure to love her."

"You're not mad at me for being wasteful?"

"Heavens, no. It was very unselfish—and industrious of you." Amanda picked up the small muslin figure and examined it more closely, from the tiny embroidered face to the ingenious woolen braids. It was sure to make one sad little girl perk up.

"I couldn't think of anything to give the boy," Sarah said.

"Well, I can!" Amanda jumped up. "Didn't Pa bring along that slingshot Johnny Parker gave him for luck?"

"Now that you mention it, yes, I think so. It's probably in with the wagon tools."

Amanda untied the canvas opening and went to dig through the tools in the jockey box. "It's here!" she exclaimed upon returning. "It brought us luck after all!"

Sarah Jane giggled. "Now, should I make the dress with full sleeves, or fitted? And it needs an apron, don't you think—which, by odd coincidence, just happens to be your specialty."

~☙~

A few nights later, Mrs. Randolph again extended an invitation for supper. Sarah tucked the newly completed dolly deep into her pocket and handed the slingshot to Amanda to do the same, in case the opportunity arose to present the gifts. "What if they don't like them?" she asked, voicing her worst fear.

Amanda looked askance at her. "How could they not?"

"I don't know. I'm just wondering if we did right, is all. It really isn't interfering—is it?" Nervously she nibbled her lip, trying to recall when she'd last spent time with children.

"Don't be a goose. You're trying to befriend a lonely little girl, that's all."

"And her brother. And I'm not used to little boys. What if he doesn't like me?"

"Really, Sarah," Amanda sighed. "He doesn't have to like you, just the slingshot. He probably doesn't own one yet."

"You're right. I'm being silly. If they don't like me, I just won't bother them." *Ever again,* she added silently.

Coming up on the Randolph wagon, the tantalizing smells of crispy fresh fish and amazingly light biscuits greeted them. Sarah swallowed the lump in her throat and drew a calming breath.

"Oh, you're here," Mrs. Randolph said warmly, accepting with a nod of thanks the cheese and the tin of peaches they'd brought along. "Sit right down. Everything's ready. Nelson? You say grace, will ya?"

He gave a gruff nod, settling his husky frame on one of the crates by their cook fire. "Almighty God, we thank You for the traveling mercies and for the food You provide us every day. Bless it now, we pray, and make us fit by it. Amen."

Raising her head, Mrs. Randolph whisked away an annoying fly. "I swear, such pests," she remarked, forking a portion of fish onto a plate and handing it to her husband. She passed the next serving to Amanda. "Hear tell somebody up front has come down with the fever."

The older man nodded gravely. "And once we come to the bad water spots, there'll be lots more of it."

A shudder went through Sarah. "What'll they do? The sick folks, I mean."

"Pull off by themselves, I 'spect," he answered. "Wait it out. See how they fare. Won't stop the rest of the train."

"It won't?" Amanda asked, obviously shocked. "That's hardly Christian."

"Mebbe. But it's what we all voted, back in Independence— and the only way to keep other folks from catchin' it. If they live, the next train along'll pick 'em up."

But what if they don't live? Sarah looked from one troubled face to the next. Things had gone so smoothly up until this point, she'd actually believed the whole trip would continue on in the same pleasant fashion. Now she felt a deep foreboding that this was just the beginning of woes to come. Who knew how many of this company would be called home to their eternal reward before ever reaching the western shores? Accepting the food Mrs. Randolph held out, she settled back in thought.

"We'll wash everything up, Mrs. Randolph," she heard

Amanda say sometime later. Looking down at the plate in her own lap, Sarah noticed it was empty—yet she couldn't remember eating. Brushing crumbs from her skirt, she stood and helped her sister gather the soiled dishes, then walked woodenly beside her to the stream. "Mandy? Do you think we'll really make it out west? Truly?"

"All we can do is try," came her sister's honest answer. "We do our best, same as everybody else. . .and trust God, same as everybody else. In the end it's up to Him."

Sarah pondered the words in silence. "I—I haven't been keeping up with my prayers," she admitted at long last, regretting her laxness. "The days seem so busy. There's so little chance to find quiet times for prayer. I haven't touched Pa's Bible—haven't opened it once since Independence."

She felt an encouraging pat on her forearm. "Fortunately, the Lord's faithfulness isn't dependent on ours, Sissy, or we'd really be up a crick. It's never too late to get back to reading the scriptures or talking to the Lord. He's always there."

"Good. I'm going to start praying and reading the Bible again tonight."

"And I'm going to be more faithful myself," Amanda replied. "Lots of nights I've been tired and skipped my prayers. That has got to stop. Right now."

New hope dawned in Sarah Jane as they finished the dishes and returned to the Randolphs'. No one could be sure about the future, that was true. But at least she would keep her hand in that of the One who, as the Bible said, knew the end from the beginning.

The train had stopped early for the night because of the onset of sickness. In the remaining daylight, Sarah peered expectantly at the next wagon. It was empty. But she caught Jared Hill on the edge of her vision, strolling along the river, a child's hand in each of his. "Mandy?" She nodded in the direction of the threesome. "Shall we go see them now?"

"Now or never, I suppose."

They took their leave and headed toward the water. Sarah Jane, slightly less at ease in the presence of a man easily ten years older than herself, had to muster all her courage, when the tall widower glanced their way and stopped. "Good evening," she said politely. "I'm Sarah Jane Shelby."

"Miss Shelby," he answered with a nod, a look of surprise on his narrow face. "Jared Hill." Releasing Bethany's hand, he took the brim of his hat between his thumb and forefinger and dipped it slightly as he met Amanda's eye. "Miss."

"And who have we here?" Sarah added cheerily, more than glad to switch her attention to the little ones. She bent down to smile at the somber little girl.

Huge blue eyes grew even wider in the delicate face beneath fine blond hair. The child pressed closer to her father's leg.

"She's Bethy," her brother announced with four-year-old importance. "Her real name's Bethany. I'm Tad."

Sarah Jane beamed at the towhead, liking him at once, especially the sprinkling of freckles across his nose. "And you must be the big brother."

"Yep."

"Well, I'm very glad to meet you. I have a sister, too. Right here. This is my big sister. Amanda." She gestured behind herself as she spoke.

"Aw, I saw her lots of times. She comes to the Randolphs."

"That's 'cause they're our friends," Sarah replied. "Do you have friends in the train?"

He shrugged. "Mama used to let me play with Sammy and Pete sometimes. They're over thataway." He pointed down the line. Then his bright expression faded. "We. . .we don't have a ma anymore."

Sarah noted the catch in his voice. "Oh, how sad," she murmured. "I know just how you feel. Our ma and pa live up in heaven with Jesus, too. And you know what?" she added brightly. "I'll bet our mas are friends already."

"Think so?"

She nodded. "And they'd probably like us to be friends, too. What do you say?"

"I danno." Tad sought his father's approval. "I guess."

"Good." Expelling a breath of relief, Sarah stood and

motioned to Amanda. "We found something in our wagon you might like—that is" —she looked anxiously to Mr. Hill, feeling her color heightening—"if your pa says you can have it."

Tentatively, Amanda held out the slingshot.

The lad's mouth dropped open. "Oh boy! Can I keep it, Pa? Can I? Can I?"

No one could have resisted the pleading in that impish face, least of all his father. Nor could Sarah miss the depth of love that softened Jared Hill's demeanor as he gazed down at his young son. It warmed her heart. "Sure. I'll teach you how to use it, so you can do it right."

"Thank you! Thank you!" Tad said, awed by his new treasure.

Sarah touched his shoulder. "You're most welcome. Friends, remember?"

"Friends," he parroted.

Noting the way Bethany seemed drawn to the conversation, Sarah next knelt by her. "Would you be our friend, too, honey?"

The little girl pressed her heart-shaped lips together in mute silence, clutching her father's hand all the harder.

"It's all right," Sarah assured her. "Sometimes it takes a while to make a real friend. But my sister and I made something for you." Retrieving the dolly from her pocket, she offered it to Bethany.

The child stared longingly. Then, after glancing up and receiving her father's nod of approval, she slowly reached out and took it, hugging it for all it was worth.

Sarah Jane smiled. "She'll be a real true friend, you'll see. Pretty soon we'll come by and see you again, to make sure she's been minding her manners. Would you like that? My sister might even tell you a story. She knows lots of them."

A tiny smile curved her lips upward at the corners.

"Thank you, miss," Mr. Hill said with sincere gratitude. "Thank you both."

Completely charmed by the man's offspring, Sarah lifted her gaze to his and would have responded, but Amanda beat her to it.

"People like to help each other, Mr. Hill," her sister said

kindly. "It's what neighbors are for. Do have a pleasant evening." With a smile at the children, she took Sarah's hand and started for their prairie schooner.

Sarah's backward glance revealed the tender sight of a father sweeping his two little ones up into his arms.

No crying issued from the Hill wagon that night.

CHAPTER 12

Three more families fell prey to sickness the next day. Then two more. The number of wagons in the train began to dwindle as those afflicted dropped out of the column while the rest continued on—a concept the girls found utterly appalling. Even though other brave Good Samaritans willingly stayed behind to look after the sick—or worse, dig needed graves, the fate of the unfortunates weighed heavily on Amanda's mind. *Oh Lord,* she prayed fervently, *be with them. Please, take care of them. Bring them back to us.*

Weeks passed in tedious sameness as the wagon train rumbled through Nebraska in an upward slope of terrain so gradual the travelers were unaware they were going uphill until the bullwhackers' whips cracked more frequently and oxen and mules strained against the harness.

Amanda often watched her sister silently observing the world around them and knew she was memorizing scenes, sounds, and sensations to record the minute they stopped for the noon meal or evening camp. From the various passages the younger girl had already related to her, Amanda knew entries in Sarah's journal chronicled how the grass along the route now grew shorter, the trail sandier, and the weather more changeable, and the way a day could dawn in mild and colorful splendor—only to cloud over and turn cold, pelting the travelers with rain or even hail. But with spring's fragile beauty lingering into early summer, the younger girl's spirits—along with everyone else's—remained high. Especially considering the plentiful elk and antelope to provide respite from the daily fare of smoked or salted meats.

On one of the meal stops along the arid plain between the Platte River and the low hillsides lining the valley, Amanda watched Sarah scribbling furiously in her diary. "Does it help much?" she teased.

Sarah stopped writing and crimped her lips together. Then she smiled. "Well, not that I'm likely to ever forget the way the wagon wheels screech in protest with every turn lately or the huge clouds of dust they throw up into our faces. But I thought I'd jot it down for posterity anyway. At least we can breathe through our handkerchiefs or apron hems. I'll be glad to see the end of this section."

Amanda had to giggle.

One afternoon, lulled into a state of half-awareness by the clopping of the animals, Amanda was brought rudely back to the present by an ear-shattering crack. Horrified, she watched as the wagon ahead tipped crazily, then crashed to the ground over its splintered rear wheel. She struggled to maintain control of her own startled mules, then steered cautiously around the disabled outfit so she wouldn't be in the way of the men who would immediately assist in replacing the wheel.

"That's the second one today," Sarah Jane whispered.

Amanda nodded. "The dryness of the air is making the wood shrink. I wonder when our turn will come."

"Alvin says that when he finishes helping his uncle tonight, he and his friend Jason will soak our wheels in the river."

Despite the comforting news, Amanda's unrest persisted. So many, many miles lay ahead. Could she have been wrong to presume the Lord wanted her and Sarah to go west after all? Pa had often teased her about her stubborn streak. What if she had placed her own will above God's? The two of them might make the entire trip—only to meet with unhappiness and misfortune in the Oregon Territory! She couldn't help recalling the incident in the Bible where the Israelites demanded meat in the wilderness rather than the manna God so graciously provided. He granted their request, but sent leanness to their souls.

"Let's teach the kids some songs tonight."

"Hm?" Amanda swallowed, forcing aside her disquiet.

"I said," Sarah Jane repeated, "Bethany and Tad might like to learn some songs."

With her mind occupied by more serious concerns, Amanda merely shrugged. "Sure."

"Good. Tonight when we go to see them, I'll take my guitar." Reaching around for the instrument, Sarah unwrapped the sheet shrouding it, plucked a few strings, then adjusted the tuning pegs. "What with all my sewing and visiting, it's been ages since I practiced. I wonder which tunes they might particularly like." Her face scrunched in thought as she strummed a chord.

The slightly flat tones brought a smile to Amanda. So did the realization of how the children had grown to welcome their visits. It seemed a fair exchange when Mr. Hill offered to look after repairs on both wagons while she or Sarah sometimes both took the little ones for walks along the rocky outcroppings on the hills or near the shallow river.

But when this evening finally came, Amanda's pensive mood knew the further aggravation of a dull headache, precluding even the enjoyment of the usual camp music. She left the visiting and singing to her sister and strolled somewhat apart from the train.

The night breeze rustled the dry grasses beneath the huge dome of starry sky as she walked, and nightly cricket sounds blended with the familiar lowing of the cattle. Amanda sank to her knees and clasped her hands. *Dear Father,* began her silent plea. To her frustration, no further words would come. She loosened her shawl and lay back, losing herself in the display of the twinkling host so high above her. . .almost wishing she had never left Independence.

"Isn't that the Shelby gal?" Red asked, with a jut of his chin toward the open prairie beyond the camp perimeter.

Seth followed his friend's gesture as if it was news to him. . .as if he hadn't seen Amanda's slender form depart, hadn't observed nearly her every step. "Probably. Just like her to go off by herself as if there isn't a wolf or rattler for miles."

"Want me to go bring her back?"

"Naw." Rubbing a hand across the bridge of his nose, Seth let out a slow breath. "I'll just keep an eye on her from here."

"Don't appear as if you're the only one. I've noticed a certain widower's a lot less sorrowful lately, since her an' her sister have been ridin' herd on those little ones of his. I s'pose it would solve more'n a few problems if he hitched up with one of 'em."

Seth huffed. "No never mind to me." But the confirmation of a niggling suspicion sank slowly to the pit of his stomach.

⚬⚬⚬

"This a private party?"

Amanda bolted upright with a start. "Not at all, Mr. Hill. I was just looking for some quiet."

He sank down a few feet away, propping an elbow on one bent knee and followed her gaze to the starry heavens. "Does get pretty noisy some nights."

Neither spoke for several seconds.

"Don't you think it's time you quit being so formal?" he finally asked. "We're not strangers anymore."

Amanda regarded him in the twinkling light. "No, we aren't strangers."

"Friends, then?"

"I guess so."

"Then it's Jared. And Amanda—unless you say otherwise." She shook her head, then looked away. Everyone needed friends. There was no reason to keep always to herself. But she wasn't silly enough to expect—or even desire—anything more than friendship again. Once was enough. And anyway, she assured herself resolutely, Jared Hill couldn't possibly be putting more into this relationship than there was. It was far too soon for him to even be thinking about replacing his dear late wife. Amanda relaxed and began idly plucking at the stiff grass. Another span of silent seconds passed.

Jared raked his fingers through his hair. "Helped two young fellows take your wheels down to soak in the river a while ago. Should keep you going a ways now."

She smiled. "I don't know how we'd make it but for the kindness of folks on the train. Thanks."

"Least I can do after what you and Sarah have done for my boy and girl." He filled his lungs, quietly releasing the breath through his nostrils.

"They really miss their mama."

Jared didn't respond immediately, but Amanda felt his gaze switch to her. "Well, guess I'll head back." Standing up, he offered a hand.

She grinned and placed hers inside his more calloused one, and he raised her effortlessly to her feet. They walked in companionable silence back to camp.

~❖~

The crossing of the shallow but fierce, mile-wide south fork of the Platte went without mishap. Advised about the threat of quicksand, no one ignored the order to water all animals beforehand to prevent them from stopping in the middle of the chocolate-colored river.

But Amanda would never forget the terror that seized her some miles later, poised on the brink of Windlass Hill. She and Sarah Jane gaped down the steep grade, watching the harried descent of other wagons. Even with the back wheels chained to prevent them from turning, and with dozens of men tugging on ropes to slow the downward progress, gravity sucked mercilessly at the rigs skidding and sliding to the bottom. To the girls' horror, midway down the slope, one outfit broke free of restraint. Amid screams of onlookers, it teetered and toppled over the side, careening end over end till it came to rest, a shattered heap of rubble. For a moment of stunned silence, no one so much as breathed.

"That does it," Jared Hill announced, climbing up to the seat and taking the reins from Amanda. "No way I'm gonna let the two of you try this one." A jerk of his head ordered the girls out to walk with the other women. "See that my kids keep out of the way, will you?" He wrapped the traces firmly around his hands and eased the mules forward, already applying pressure to the brake. Neither girl could bear to watch their schooner's descent to the reaches below.

When the nerve-racking day came to a merciful end with the arrival of the last wagon in Ash Hollow, the cool, bountiful meadow at the base of Windlass Hill seemed a glorious oasis. The very air was fragrant with the mingled perfume of the wild rose and scents of other flowers and shrubs in the underwood of majestic ash and dwarf cedar trees.

"Why, there's actual shade!" Sarah Jane cried, as she and her small group reached the bottom of the hill. Taking Bethany and Tad by the hand, she bolted ahead of Amanda and Mrs. Randolph, with the children in her wake. Under the green canopy of a huge ash, she swooped the little girl up and swung her around. Tad ran circles around them both.

Mrs. Randolph joined in with their gleeful laughter. "I declare! It's the Garden of Eden, that's what it is." Joining Sarah, she kicked off her worn boots and wiggled her plump toes in the silky grass, her expression almost dreamlike.

Amanda's gaze drifted to the center of the meadow, where prattling little streams merged together in a translucent pond, sparkling now in the late afternoon sun. She hadn't realized how thirsty she had been. The last truly decent water had been long since past. Glancing around, she spotted her wagon parked beside Jared Hill's and hurried over to get a pitcher.

Her neighbor was tightening the straps on his rig's canvas top when she approached. "Some place, huh?" he said pleasantly. "Almost feels like we deserve it after a day like today."

Amanda laughed lightly and clambered aboard her schooner.

Jared's low voice carried easily through the bowed fabric. "Wagon master says we're stopping here for a day or two. Plenty of folks have a whole bunch of new repairs to see to. And most everyone will pitch in to help the Morrises salvage what they can from their wreck."

"That was truly a horror," Amanda said, emerging with the coveted pitcher in hand. "On the way down the hill, at least half a dozen ladies speculated on which of them could best make room for the family, bless their hearts. And I couldn't be more grateful for a day of rest. Tomorrow's Sunday anyway, isn't it?"

"Come to think of it, you're right."

"Pa! Pa!" two young voices called out above their scampering footsteps. They made a beeline for him and flung their arms around his long legs.

Gratified at the sweet display of affection, Amanda averted her gaze and hopped to the ground.

Sarah Jane stepped beside her at the spring. "Alvin's aunt has invited me to supper. Do you mind, Mandy?"

"Of course not. Just don't stay out late."

"Yes, Mother." With a wry grimace, her sister joined her curly-haired escort.

Oh well, Amanda decided, watching the pair walk away, *I've been wishing for solitude lately. This should provide a nice quiet night of sewing.*

Or praying, her mind added. What she needed above all was to know inner peace again. There had to be some way to find it.

CHAPTER 13

The summer sun warmed the faithful flock gathered in the meadow for Sunday service on a curious collection of wooden chairs, crates, blankets, and the odd fallen log. The breeze rustling the leaves in the glen was gloriously free of the mosquitoes that had plagued the encampment late last evening. Now the voices blended in harmony with the fiddle and harmonica.

Amanda had known "Abide with Me" most of her life but had never paid close attention to the words. But as Sarah had pointed out a week ago, it must have been a lot of folks' favorite, the way it got requested almost every Sunday. Going into the second verse, Amanda listened even as she sang:

> "Swift to its close ebbs out life's little day;
> Earth's joys grow dim, its glories pass away;
> Change and decay in all around I see;
> O Thou who changest not, abide with me."

Certainly this trip had brought about drastic changes. Amanda surmised that other folks' dreams of a new life had probably been every bit as grand as hers. Yet despite the fact that many of them had already lost friends and loved ones to sickness or accident, they found strength to continue on. Lonely, saddened, they somehow remained hopeful. It had to be of tremendous comfort to know that the Lord stayed ever constant. She observed the peaceful countenances of some of the folks within her range of sight and went on to the third stanza:

> "I fear no foe, with Thee at hand to bless;
> Ills have no weight, and tears no bitterness.
> Where is death's sting? Where, grave, thy
> victory?
> I triumph still, if Thou abide with me."

When Amanda saw a woman blot tears on her apron as she sang, her own eyes stung, rendering her unable to voice the lyrics herself. She finally managed to regain her composure for the final lines:

> "Heaven's morning breaks, and earth's vain
> shadows flee;
> In life, in death, O Lord, abide with me."

Never again would that hymn carry so little meaning. Amanda realized for the first time that it had not been her own strength that had held her together after the loss of her parents. It had been the Lord all along. His strength, His faithfulness— and those, without a doubt, loving answers to her mama and papa's faithful prayers. Humbly she bowed her head and breathed a prayer of gratitude.

She opened her eyes to see the jug-eared man most folks had started calling "Deacon Franklin" rise from his seat and move to the vacant spot the fiddler left behind at the close of the song.

"Folks," he began. "As you've figured out by now, I'm not much of a preacher. But like I said before, I love the Lord, and I love His Word. Thought I'd read a favorite verse that has been a real blessing to me for a lot of years. It's in Romans, the eighth chapter, verse twenty-eight." He opened his worn Bible to the page his finger had held at the ready. " 'And we know that all things work together for good to them that love God, to them who are the called according to his purpose.' "

Looking up from his text, he scanned the rapt faces before him and smiled gently. "There's hardly a one of us who hasn't at some time or other questioned the Lord's doings. Especially these last hard weeks, as we've all of us watched helplessly at the hardships that came to folks who were once part of this travelin' family of ours."

Bonneted heads nodded, and murmurs circulated in the ranks.

"But in spite of all that comes by," the leader continued, "whether sickness, or death, or accident, I know we can still trust God. There's no lack of people in this world who don't give Him any part of their lives a'tall. Can't help wonderin' what gets them through the hard times, or where they turn for help. There'd be none to find if we just threw up our hands and turned our backs on the One who made us, the One who is workin' out His purposes through all the circumstances of our lives. Yes, I said *all*," he injected without a pause. "There's not one among us who's here by chance."

Amanda's ears perked up.

"It doesn't make a lick of difference what made us choose to make this trip," the speaker said with a firm nod. "What does count is that the God who brought us here will never let us down. Think about that today and tomorrow—and all the tomorrows yet to come. Trust your well-being to the Lord and keep a good hold on His strong hand. And whatever effort you've been givin' to complainin' about hills or rivers or dust or mud, spend instead in thankin' God for takin' you through it. If you see somebody beside you startin' to sag, bolster him up with a kind words or better yet, lend a hand. This journey is gonna take all of us pullin' together, helpin' one another along."

Deacon Franklin rocked back onto his heels and tucked his Bible under one arm, and a twinkle in his eye accompanied his smile. "Well, that's all I have to say this morning. Be sure and enjoy this nice purty restin' spot the Good Lord put here just for us, right enough! Now, let's close in prayer."

A new calmness began to flow through Amanda's being as she closed her eyes. The words hadn't come from behind a proper pulpit. The speaker was not in reality a man called to be a preacher to the masses, and the speech hadn't even been what one might term a sermon. Yet her spirit felt strangely comforted and encouraged. She almost felt like dancing.

~~⁂~~

Behind the furrowed gray trunk of a swamp ash, Seth flicked a crumpled leaf through his fingers and headed for the cook wagon. No sense having Red catch him listening in on a sermon, that's for sure! It wasn't worth the endless mocking that was certain to follow.

It beat all, though, how this bunch seemed to handle the misfortunes and tragedies that struck so relentlessly now. Unlike some of the travelers he'd taken west in previous years, these folks even seemed sincere in believing what that farmer told them. Took it right to heart. Of course, Grandpa had been that way, too, he remembered. Never once doubting the Good Book or the Lord above. Seth could still picture the shock of white hair above the aged face, could still see the piercing eyes that seemed to see clear into a person's soul. The old man's voice contained a gravelly quality, as if preaching had used it up somewhere along the way. But those long arms of his, which could spread so wide to make a point, had felt mighty warm and strong wrapped around a young boy's shoulders.

An unbidden memory came to the fore of times he and Drew had ridden double on old Lulabelle while Gramps took them along on a preaching trip. He'd sit the two of them right in the front row, where one look could still their squirming through the longest sermon. Seth smiled, knowing if he thought back far enough, he'd have to admit there was a time he thought of becoming a circuit-riding preacher himself! Wouldn't Red get a kick out of that!

Seth emitted a ragged breath. A lot of years had passed since then. He'd ended up on a far different path. . .but a very small part of him was starting to hunger for the kind of sincere faith he'd known as a young lad.

———✦———

"Sarah?" Alvin extended a hand as they left the service. "Will you come for a walk with the rest of us? Aunt Harriet wants me to pick her some currants and chokecherries."

She smiled, but shook her head, mildly disappointed. "Can't. I promised Bethany I'd help her make a flower crown."

"You could do that later."

Sarah felt compelled to refuse. "I wouldn't want to disappoint her, Alvin. She's only a little girl, and I—"

"—sure spend a lot of time with kids that aren't even related to you," he finished. "You used to be more fun."

Ignoring the critical note in her friend's usually jovial tone, Sarah just nodded. "I still like to have fun, Alvin. But sometimes there are other things that need doing. Anyway, it's hard to resist a pair of big blue eyes."

"Exactly." A rakish gleam lit the hazel depths of Alvin's. "Won't I ever get to finish that sketch I started of you?"

"Sure you will. We'll have plenty of time together, you'll see. Now, I really must go. Thanks for the invitation, though."

"Right." The edge of his lip took on a strange curl before he turned and strode away.

Almost wishing she'd accepted, Sarah stared after him. She felt Amanda step to her side.

"It's really sweet of you to turn down an afternoon's frolic just to keep a little girl happy."

"I promised," Sarah Jane said simply.

"I know. I'm very proud of you."

"Really?"

A blush tinted her sister's cheeks. "Well, it's just— You know. When we first spoke of coming west, I was afraid you'd get in one pickle after another. But you're changing by the day."

Sarah cocked her head back and forth. "I imagine it's called growing up."

"I suppose. Just wanted you to know, I like the change."

"Thanks, Sissy. And while we're at it, I'd like to say I'm sorry for not being more help sewing, cooking, driving. . .I've let you down. That's going to change, too."

When the company again took up the journey, a new, lighter mood prevailed. . .until the nine-year old Thornton boy, riding the tongue of his family's wagon on a dare, plunged under the wheels shortly after departing Ash Hollow. An unexpected funeral took place that noon. The little body was laid to rest in a grave dug right beneath the rutted trail. The wagons to follow would pack the earth hard again, too hard for wolves to ravage.

And another new baby came into the world that night.

"'The Lord giveth, and the Lord taketh away,'" Mrs. Randolph muttered as Amanda poured a cup of coffee for them both outside the schooner. "My old heart goes out to Jennie. He was their only boy, you know. The others are girls. He'd have been a big help when they got settled in Oregon."

Sipping her own coffee, Amanda could barely swallow.

"Say, these are right fine apple fritters your Sarah made."

"She's been—well, we've been practicing."

"And it shows."

"Thanks to you."

The older woman sloughed off the compliment. "Pshaw. You'd have picked up all the cookin' you needed in time anyway."

"Even if that's true," Amanda said, patting her friend's arm, "you surely made it much easier for us. We both appreciate it." She paused with a smile. "I don't know if I'm going to want to part with you when we get to the California Trail and you and Mr. Randolph head off to go be with your sons. What did you say their names were?"

"Nelson Junior an' Charlie," the older woman said proudly. "Don't mind admittin', though, if I had my druthers I'd still be back home in our Allegheny Mountains. At my age, thought of sittin' in my rockin' chair in front of a cracklin' fire was soundin' mighty pleasurable. But when Nelson, the oldest, got the notion to go see what lay beyond the hills, he up and took our other'n and they lit out. Ended up in northern California—far as they could get—then convinced their pa an' me to come, too. One of 'em might even come to meet us partway."

Amanda smiled. "Well, it'll truly be a whole new life for you then—without having to start from scratch, like most of us. You might even arrive to discover they've built you a nice little cabin, fireplace and all, complete with a rocker."

"If not, I brung my own along," she admitted with chagrin. "Didn't want to take a chance. It was my own ma's. Our two boys got rocked on it, so did our girl. 'Course, little Rosie wasn't with us too long. . ." Blinking away a sudden sheen in her faded blue eyes, she looked Amanda up and down, then tapped a crooked finger against her bottom lip in thought. "You'd make our Charlie a pretty fair wife, if you don't mind my sayin' so."

Amanda, having raised her mug for another sip, swallowed too quickly and choked instead.

"There, there," her neighbor crooned, thumping her on the back. "Just take a deep breath, now. You'll be right as rain." Barely stopping, she resumed the conversation where she'd left off. "Nelson Junior took himself a wife out west. Found her in Sacramento. Name's Cora. But our Charlie's still loose."

Amanda had to giggle.

Barely stopping for breath, Mrs. Randolph rambled on. "'Course, I know you an' Sarah Jane have high hopes of openin' a store an' all—which sounds fine. Real fine. I think folks will need new clothes, just like you said." Handing Amanda her empty mug, she ambled to her feet. "Well, I'd best be gettin' back. But store or no store, give some thought to my Charlie, would you? Don't mind tellin' you, a body could do worse havin' you for a daughter-in-law."

At this, Amanda couldn't resist hugging her. "Or you for a mother-in-law. Thanks for coming by."

CHAPTER 14

For three more weeks, the train continued along the sandy banks of the North Platte. A mile or two off to the left and right, two lines of sand hills, often broken into wild forms, flanked the valley beneath the enormous sky. But before and behind, the plain was level and monotonous as far as the eye could see.

"Nights are growing colder now," Sarah read to Amanda from her open journal; Tired of walking, she had hopped aboard for a short rest. "Even though it's still the dead of summer, the temperature continues to drop as we go higher. Soon we'll glimpse the peaks of the Laramie Mountains, I'm told, their frosted caps sparkling diamond-white against crystal blue sky." Amanda smiled to herself. Her sibling had always possessed a gift for writing, and the abundant wonders of the trail brought that talent to the fore. More and more often she would look up after finishing a paragraph, obviously eager to share her latest entry—whether it chronicled the pesky sand flies that replaced the mosquitoes everyone found such a torment during the nights at Ash Hollow, the thunderous sound of a buffalo herd on the move, the delicate appeal of grazing antelope, or how the landscape was becoming more brown than green and was empty now of timber, sage, and even dry grass.

And Amanda couldn't help noting a vast improvement in the younger girl's vocabulary as the miles passed. Sarah's association with artist Alvin Rivers revealed itself in new, eloquent words and phrases she now used in her diary. She did not share all of her innermost thoughts concerning Alvin, but had no qualms about revealing passages about special times she spent with the Hill children.

But best of all, in Amanda's estimation, had been her sister's written accounts of the various landmarks whose unique formations had come into view while still a whole day's travel away. Sarah painted word pictures. . .visions of glorious rainbow hues cast over the towering shapes by the ever-changing play of sunlight between dawn and dusk. She likened the mounds of stone to castles and ships and slumbering animals. Amanda felt those images would remain forever in her mind.

She truly appreciated the diversions in the tiresome journey. More than once she had caught herself straining for a glimpse of the wagon master and that gray horse of his, then would quickly chide herself for such foolishness. Having Sarah's daily narratives to concentrate on kept her wandering thoughts in line.

Not long after the snow-patched Laramie Mountains appeared on the far horizon, cheers and whistles came from the front of the company. Sarah, walking beside the wagon, jumped onto the slow-moving vehicle, then craned her neck to see around the outfits ahead. "Mandy! It's Fort Laramie! And I'm just covered with trail dust. I do wish we had time to freshen up." She grabbed the hairbrush from a basket beneath the seat and tugged it through her curls, then removed her apron and fluffed out her skirt. "Do I look all right? I hear we'll be able to replace the flour and other supplies."

"If there's any to be had after everyone else restocks, of course," Amanda reminded her. "No doubt it'll cost us dearly."

"Well, whatever the price, we'll have to bear it. We've still a long, long way to go." She paused. "Oh! Look at the sparkly river—and all the Indian shelters everywhere!"

Amanda nodded, her gaze lost in the sharp contrast between

the Black Hills, thick with cedar, and the area's red sandstone. Speckled with sage, the sparse grass was turning yellow. She flicked the reins to keep pace with the others, urging the mules up the steep bank leading to the entrance of the fort, where huge double doors had been raised to permit the train to enter.

"Not as impressive as I expected," Sarah murmured, nearing the cracked, decrepit adobe walls. But exhaling a deep breath, she waved to the sentry perched in the blockhouse erected above the gateway as they pulled inside, where Indians in buffalo robes stared down at the new arrivals from perches on the rampart. After stopping the team, Amanda glanced around the interior. Long, low buildings stretched out in a large circle, forming the walls around a great open area crowded with Indians and traders. Among the horde strolled lean, rough-looking frontiersmen, their long rifles at the ready for any sign of trouble. The noise and bustle of the bargaining reminded Amanda of Independence. Within moments, Alvin Rivers came to offer a hand to Sarah, then to Amanda. "Word has it we're to rest here for two whole days. Mind if your sister and I explore a bit?"

Amanda smiled as she stepped to the ground and arranged her skirt. "Not at all. I'll likely do some of that myself, once I've tended the animals." That evening, the replenished emigrants joined forces and shared their bounty with some of the fort folk. The men quickly assembled makeshift banquet tables from wagon boards propped up on barrels, and the women filled them end to end with heaping platters of roast hen, antelope, buffalo steak, fried fish, and all manner of vegetables and breads, followed by a delectable assortment of berry pies, tarts, and jelly cakes.

Much laughter and banter passed to and fro as everyone caught up with the latest news from back East. Word regarding conditions of the trail ahead brought raised brows and shakes of the head, then expressions of resignation and determination.

When at last every appetite was sated, an even grander celebration began. Double the usual number of instruments broke forth in song, aided by clapping hands and stomping feet, which drew the more energetic souls to frolic.

"You should go have some fun with the other young folks,

Amanda," Mrs. Randolph said, gesturing after them. "Leave the cleanin' up to us old fogies."

"I'd rather not. Really," Amanda assured her friend. "I prefer to be useful." But a small part of her wished she still felt as young as Sarah and her friends. In an effort to tamp down the wistful longing, she began humming along with the happy tune while she worked.

"Land sakes," Mrs. Randolph exclaimed, putting leftover bread and biscuits into a sack. "I'm full near to burstin'!"

"Me, too," Ma Phelps chimed in. "I might never take another bite of food as long as I live. Or at least till tomorrow." She guffawed at her own levity.

Amanda had to grin as she gathered some half-empty tins and scooped the remaining portions of the pies into them. She licked berry juice from her sticky index finger and glanced around for another chore.

Disassembling tables with some of the other men a few yards away, Jared Hill looked up and caught her gaze with a smile. "Care to go for another stroll with me and the kids?" he asked.

Spending time with the little family had become a commonplace activity by now. She shrugged a shoulder and nodded.

A sudden movement in the shadows between two of the warehouses revealed Seth Holloway as he spun on the heel of his boot and stalked away.

⸻⸺⸻

"Oh Alvin," Sarah breathed, flipping through his sketchbook as they sat on crates outside his uncle's wagon, somewhat apart from the noise. "These are truly wonderful." She studied a sketch of a vast buffalo herd, then one of a valley filled with the animals' whitened bones and skulls, before turning to the more pleasing views of Chimney Rock and the majestic Courthouse Rock. "I was certain nothing could be more beautiful than your drawing of Devil's Gate, but this. . ." She leaned closer to examine his most recent landscape, Fort Laramie and the Laramie River, with the Black Hills as a backdrop. She ran her fingers lightly over one of the bastions.

"What about these?" he asked tentatively, taking down a second drawing pad and holding it out.

Sarah observed the peculiar gleam in the young man's blue eyes as she took the proffered book from him and opened it. The warmth of a blush rose in her face. Page after page presented renditions of her. All were very good...and almost too flattering. She swallowed. "But I never posed for these."

"You didn't have to. Everywhere I look, I see you. Don't you know that by now?" Taking the sketches from her unresisting fingers, he stood and drew her to her feet, encircling her with his long arms.

He had been a perfect gentlemen over the hundreds of miles the train had traveled, almost always sharing her company with other young people. Now, Sarah's heart raced erratically as she felt Alvin's breath feather her neck. "Please, don't—" she whispered.

But his head moved closer, until his lips brushed hers. "You're so beautiful, sweet Sarah. I could spend my whole life drawing you, painting you. You could become famous right along with me."

Though the last was said in a jesting tone, his previous remarks had been anything but so. Uncomfortable, she drew away. Mixed emotions—confusing emotions—rushed through her being. "But we're friends.. Neither of us knows for sure where our paths will lead at the end of this trip."

Alvin's expression did not alter a whit. "It's afterward I'm thinking about, Sarah. You, me, the two of us. Forever. I won't be a pauper when we reach Oregon, you know, unlike most folks. I'll have a lot to offer...and I want you to think about that." He took one of her hands in his and pressed it to his lips.

Sarah searched his eyes, afraid to utter the question closest to her innermost longings. How could she ask something so deeply intimate as whether or not he ever wanted children?

She didn't know him well enough yet—and she wasn't sure she truly wanted more than friendship from him...now or ever.

Gently she pulled her fingers from his grasp."I—I—" But words failed her. She turned and ran blindly for the wagon.

———❖———

"Sure is a pleasant evening," Jared said.

Amanda, walking by his side, could only agree as she drank in the star-dusted night sky, the warm lantern glow from the many rooms and buildings of the fort. She smiled after Bethany and Tad, who were skipping ahead of them. "Everyone's so happy to have their barrels refilled. And to rest, I might add."

He nodded, and his gaze returned to his children. "They're a lot happier, too. Thanks to you. . .and your sister."

Something in Jared's tone sounded an alarm in Amanda. She moistened her lips. "Well, the whole train was eager to lend a hand—" she began.

"But no one did, except you."

Amanda felt an inward shiver and drew her shawl tighter around her shoulders.

"They're almost their old selves, now," he went on. "The way they used to be."

Determined to keep the conversation casual, Amanda responded only generally. "It's nice to see them smiling."

"I sure don't have to tell you they think a lot of you, Amanda. And so do—"

"I think we should head back now, Jared. don't you?" she blurted."Bethy! Tad! Time to go." Grabbing them one by one in a hug as they ran to her, Amanda turned them around and pointed them toward the clustered wagons. "March."

"Like soldiers?" Tad asked. "Yes, sir!" Immediately he straightened to his full height and puffed out his chest. "Hup, two, three, four. . .hup, two, three, four."

A giggling Bethany did her best to mimic her older brother's longer strides. The effect was enchantingly comical.

Grateful for the lightened mood. Amanda picked up the pace to discourage further conversation. This night she would be spending more time than usual at her prayers.

———❖———

"Ah! Some real, actual rest. At long last." Red yawned and straightened his legs as he leaned against the wheel of the supply wagon and crossed his arms. "Let somebody else do the lookin' out, for a change." He tugged his hat over his eyes.

In no mood to make small talk, Seth only grimaced. The rowdy music was giving him a headache. Above the camp smells he could detect rain coming. And he detested wasting travel time when early snow could close the mountain passes.

His pal plucked the hat away and leaned his head to peer at him. "Boy, you sure do have a burr under your saddle."

"Why do you say that?"

"Oh, nothin'. 'Cept, you ain't said a word for the last three hundred miles or so, that's all."

"Nothing to say."

Red nodded, a lopsided smirk pulling his mustache off-kilter.

"Look. Do me a favor, will you?" Seth rasped. "If you want to talk about trail hazards or the trip in general or the storm that's coming, go ahead. We'll plan accordingly. Otherwise, clamp those jaws of yours shut and give me some peace."

"Right, boss. Will do." With a mock salute, Red replaced his hat over his eyes and nose and resumed his relaxed pose.

A pair of pregnant minutes ticked by.

The hat fell to Red's lap. "Er, get the letter that was waitin' for you?"

Seth slanted him a glare.

"I just asked. None of my business, I know. Even if it was wrote by a woman. Same last name as yours, I noticed."

Releasing a lungful of air all at once, Seth lurched to his feet, whacking dust off the seat of his britches.

Red jumped up, too, and grabbed Seth's sleeve. "Hey, buddy, I ain't pryin'."

"Oh really?"

"Sure. Your brother's got the same last name, too. Figure it must be from her. That wife of his."

"So?"

"So nothin'. Figure you know what you're doin'." He rubbed his mouth. "Just hope you're not foolin' around with—"

Seth's fist sent his partner sprawling backward in the dust.

Immediately he regretted the hasty act and leaned over to help Red up. "Sorry. I didn't mean that. And I'm not."

Kneading his jaw and working it back and forth, Red shrugged and gave a nod. "Didn't really think you were." He smirked again. "You really hated that woman Andrew married, didn't you?"

"Hated her?" Seth looked him straight in the eye. "On the contrary, pal. I was in love with her, but she refused me." Turning, he left Red gaping after him as he walked away.

CHAPTER 15

Ten exhausting days after leaving Fort Laramie, the wagon train labored up and down the slopes of the Black Hills, where sweet-scented herbs and pungent sage permeated the air. Mountain cherry, currants, and tangles of wild roses lay against brushstrokes of blue flax, larkspur, and tulips. Game was prevalent, and solitary buffalo bulls roamed the ravines of terrain so rough it tested even the most recent wagon repairs, to say nothing of the most rested soul. Trudging a little off to one side while Sarah Jane took a turn driving, Amanda observed for the first time how rickety most of the rigs appeared. Even their own prairie schooner, once so new and sleek against the more clumsy Conestogas, showed the same deterioration. Hardly a wheel in the company was without a wedge or two hammered between it and the rim to fill gaps in the shrinking wood. Canvas tops above the rattling, creaking wagons were stained with grease and dust and bore patches or gaping holes from hail and wind. Animals that had begun the journey hale and hearty now appeared jaded and bony. . .and ahead lay even rougher country. So many, many miles yet to cover.

"Mandy?" Sarah barely paused. "What do you think of Alvin?"

"He's quite nice-looking," Amanda fudged, then ventured further. "He has very gentlemanly manners, shows definite artistic talent, and will be quite rich someday, from what you've told me."

"Yes. That's true. All of it."

"Why do you ask?" With sadness Amanda skirted a child's rocking horse that had been discarded by someone up ahead.

"I was just wondering."

"Has he...I mean, has he done something...ungentlemanly?"

Sarah shook her head. "No. But he's beginning to care. For me." Her voice vibrated with the jouncing of the seat.

The news did not come as much of a surprise, considering all the time the two had spent in each other's company. Glancing at her sister, Amanda expected to see a hint of excitement—even happiness—in her expression, yet Sarah seemed glum. Amanda could only pray that her sibling's trust in men would not be shattered as her own had been. "What about you, Sissy?"

Sarah's gaze drifted away, and she smiled. "He does meet a lot of the qualifications I set out when we first started this journey, doesn't he? He is rich. He is quite handsome."

"But?"

The smile wilted.

"I couldn't help but notice you seemed to be avoiding him, at Fort Laramie, while you spent more time with Bethany and Tad."

"I...needed time. To think."

Amanda could see her sister's unrest. "Tonight at camp we'll pray about things. Together, like we used to. Would you like that?"

Sarah only nodded.

———※———

After Amanda fell asleep, Sarah Jane eased off the pallet. The sudden absence of its comforting warmth became even more apparent as the chill of night crept around her. Shivering, she shook out an extra blanket and wrapped it about herself, lit a small candle, and opened her journal.

Dear Diary,

It's been days and days since last I visited with you. The rest at Fort Laramie did wonders for both people and animals. A hard rain made the river too swift to cross, so our departure was delayed an extra day. The upper crossing of the North Platte, however, was without mishap, thanks to the Mormon ferry. . .eight dugout canoes with logs laid across the tops—an effective, if flimsy, method of transport.

Now, heading into the mountains, the land is bleak and barren. Things that appear green in the distance turn out to be only dry sand and rock, sprinkled with stunted clumps of sage and greasewood.

It makes me sad whenever we pass castoff treasures along the trails but folks are trying to ease the burden on the animals lumbering so earnestly in this upward climb. We've been examining our own meager stores, wondering what we might be able to do without, should our mules begin to falter.

I pray we all make it through this rough section of country, so full of ravines and treacherous slopes. Progress sometimes slows to a point that tempers flare at the least provocation, and the men remain on their guard for rattlesnakes and other wild animals.

Tapping her pencil against her chin in thought, Sarah frowned. Then, after a short pause, she continued writing.

Alvin has expressed a desire for some kind of commitment from me, but I've managed to put him off, suggesting we remain friends for a while longer. I always thought wealth was important, along with one's outward appearance. . . But now such things seem trivial. Especially in the face of true loss and real struggle, like poor

> *Bethy and Tad endure every day. I feel a lit-*
> *tle guilty about hiding behind those little ones,*
> *though, while I try to decipher my true feelings*
> *regarding Alvin. Mr. Hill seems greatly ap-*
> *preciative of any thoughtfulness shown to his*
> *children. He's quite a sensitive man—and ever*
> *so much more mature than Alvin. I—*

She stopped writing and nibbled at her lip, trying to put her feelings on paper. Then she erased the last word.

Two of the hard days following the ferrying of the river were made all the more loathsome by scummy water, alkali springs, choking dust, and the putrid stench of animal carcasses lying in gruesome little pools of poisonous water. Then came a hideous stretch of deformed rock strata that tore relentlessly at hooves, boots, and wheels.

Finally, to everyone's relief, the valley of the Sweetwater River came in sight, with its easier grades, fine water, and grass to be enjoyed for more than a week's travel. Cheers again rang out when the huge bulk of Independence Rock loomed on the distant horizon.

"We'll be there to celebrate July Fourth, Mandy," Sarah Jane exclaimed. "Right on time."

Amanda nodded. No one appreciated rest days more than she. Of all the recent tortures—steaming marshes, odorous sulphur springs, and the like—most horrendous had been the huge crawling crickets that crunched sickeningly beneath wheels and boots for a seemingly endless stretch of miles. Each day took increased effort to remain optimistic for Sarah's sake, while inwardly her feelings were anything but pleasant. Surmising that other women appeared to have things so much easier than she, with men to drive the wagons and look after repairs and animals, Amanda gritted her teeth, fighting feelings of jealousy and self-pity.

". . .so I said to him—" Sarah stepped closer to the wagon.

"You're not even listening to me, are you?"

"Hm?"

"Oh, never mind. Do you feel all right, Mandy? You look flushed."

"I'm fine. Fine!" At her own uncharacteristic outburst, Amanda watched the scenery blur behind a curtain of tears.

"No, you're not. You're not fine at all."

Even Sarah's voice sounded faint, sort of fuzzy as she scrambled aboard. "You need to go lie down in back. I'll take over."

You can't. I'm the oldest. The one in charge. But the words wouldn't come out. In a wave of dizziness, Amanda relinquished the reins without a fuss and nearly toppled off the seat. She crawled back to the pallet. The rumble and rattle of the wheels made her head pound and pound. . .

Voices. Everywhere. Loud and laughing. Noise. Too much noise. And it was hot, so hot. . .or cold. How could one shiver so much when it was hot? Why couldn't the world just stop and be still? There had to be quiet somewhere. Where was Oregon? All a body really needed was peace and quiet, a place to rest. To sleep.

~◦~

"Do you think she'll be all right?" Sarah looked anxiously to Mrs. Randolph, hating the waver in her own voice as she peered down again at Amanda's flushed face. At least her sister had stopped thrashing about and now appeared to be sleeping peacefully.

"Right as rain, soon enough," came the soothing reply. "Poor child's plumb exhausted, that's what. She's been workin' herself near to death, always doin', doin', never takin' time to be young."

"It's my fault," Sarah moaned miserably. "I've let her carry the whole load this entire journey. Now I'm being punished. What if—"

"Don't even think such nonsense," the older woman chided. She removed the wet cloth from Amanda's brow and rinsed it out in cool water before replacing it again. "Your sister's a person who takes responsibility serious, is all. She likes makin' it easy for you, seein' you having fun with the others. It makes her happy."

The truth of the statement only made Sarah feel worse. "And I was only too glad to run off and leave everything to her—even after declaring I'd help out more. I hate myself."

"Now, now." Mrs. Randolph patted Sarah's arm. "These days of rest here at Independence Rock will do her a world of good, you'll see. And when we're on the road again, she'll perk right up, wantin' to take over. See if she don't."

"I hope you're right. Mandy's all I've got left in this world. I'm sure not about to give her up!"

"Well, I'll be bringin' some broth by in a little while. See if you can get her to take some." With a nod, their kindly neighbor took her leave.

Sarah took Amanda's limp hand in hers and softly massaged it, praying she would open her eyes, be herself again. . .her dear strong Mandy, who was everything she wished to be herself. Confident, independent, capable. . . A rush of tears threatened to spill over, until a shuffling at the rear of the wagon brought her emotions back in check.

A voice cleared, and a familiar face peered through the back opening. "How's the patient?"

"Doing better, Mr. Holloway," Sarah answered. "Resting comfortably now."

He nodded and his expression appeared to relax. "Well, if you need anything, let me know."

"Thank you. That's very kind. I will."

More visitors came by throughout the day, one by one. Jared Hill, Alvin, Ma Pruett, all of them speaking in quiet voices.

Even Bethany tapped gently on the side of the wagon, her smudged face scrunched with concern. "I brought Miss Amanda some flowers," she whispered, clutching a raggedy bouquet in her hands. The stems were too short to put in water.

Sarah accepted the offering with a gracious smile. "Thank you, sweetheart. She'll just love them when she wakes up."

"Papa said I can't stay, so I'd best go now."

Sending her off with a hug, Sarah felt comforted and hopeful. Maybe she and Mandy had a family after all, one given to them by God. She bowed her head in a prayer of thanks.

"So I missed the whole celebration," Amanda said in amazement as the train meandered past the spectacular slash in the granite mountains known as Devil's Gate, heading toward Split Rock and the much-anticipated Ice Slough folks were eager to see, still a few days hence.

At the reins, her sister nodded. "Fireworks, gunshots, the raising of the flag, everything! I'd have thought the racket would have disturbed you."

"I never heard it. Any of it! Sorry I was such a bother."

"You weren't. You earned that rest—I'm just sorry you had to get sick to get it!"

"Well, I'm better now. Did you get to climb the rock, at least?"

Sarah's smile held a hint of guilt. "Actually, when I saw you were doing all right, I did go up with some of the others while Mrs. Randolph stayed with you. Alvin took a pot of axle grease along and wrote his name and mine together for all the world to see. Do you believe that?" She giggled. "When he went with Jason to catch the view from the far side, I added a few other names to the list. By the time we left to come back down, the list read, 'Jason and Alvin and Sarah Jane and Amanda and Mary Katharine, Bethany, and Tad.' Alvin never noticed."

Amanda couldn't help laughing. She adjusted her shawl over her warm coat as they rode in mountain air crisp with pine and the sweet perfume of wildflowers. Tomorrow she would either walk or drive to spare the mules, but today it did feel good to ride—even on the hard, springless seat. She just wished she hadn't missed the festivities at Independence Rock.

"You sure had a lot of visitors while you were sick."

"Oh?"

Sarah guided the team around a fallen log. "Mrs. Randolph, of course, was a godsend. She was the one who knew it wasn't cholera, just exhaustion, and was a great encouragement to me. She made you that good broth."

"Sounds just like her. She's a dear."

"And then Jared Hill came, and Alvin, and Ma Pruett. Bethy

picked the sweetest flowers and brought them to you. Even the wagon master checked on you."

Amanda's heart tripped over itself. "Mr. Holloway?"

"Mm-hmm. Told me to let him know if we needed anything. I know you think he's domineering and stodgy, but I found him to be rather. . .nice."

"Well, I suppose everyone has his good points," Amanda hedged. The man probably kept tabs on everyone in his train. Yes, that had to be it. Of course, chances were he'd come to see if the problem was cholera, even yet hoping to force her and Sarah to stay behind!

But, on the other hand, there was no harm in allowing a tiny part of her to dream he truly cared. . .as long as she didn't voice the thought aloud. No one needed to know such a seemingly inconsequential gesture would be locked inside the treasure house of her heart forever. After all, someone destined for spinsterhood could probably use a few secret dreams to look back on in later lonely years. Pretending to adjust her bonnet during an elaborate stretch, Amanda turned to see if the wagon master was anywhere within sight.

~⚬~

Seth nudged his mount over a knoll, keeping an eye on the straggling cattle that plodded in the wake of the wagon train. Not many head had been lost up to this point. Not many travelers, either, considering how quickly and effectively an outbreak of cholera could wipe out an entire company. They'd been pretty lucky so far.

He'd noticed Amanda Shelby was up and about, too, after wearing herself out. Not that he cared, particularly, but someone with her spirit deserved a quick recovery, and he was glad the Almighty saw fit to give her one.

Strange, how he'd started attributing occasional circumstances to God's hand of late. Gramps would like that. Could he be smiling down from the pearly gates now? Next thing, Seth would find himself going back to praying on a regular basis, dusting off the little black Bible he'd kept out of Gramps's possessions.

Wouldn't that be something. He smirked, hardly bothered by the fact that the concept no longer seemed so unthinkable. He must be getting old.

Shifting in his saddle, Seth felt the letter he'd gotten at the fort crinkle in the pocket of his trousers. He compressed his lips. So Liza wanted him back. The gall of that woman! After worming her way into his younger brother's life for no other reason than to spite Seth, she'd seen the error of her ways and wanted to call it quits. As if he'd go behind Drew's back like that! He grimaced and shook his head.

Time to get rid of that fool thing before Red came across it. Removing the papers from his pocket, Seth tore them to shreds and let the wind scatter the pieces far and wide.

Women. There sure was a shortage of truly honest and decent ones. Ones with real spirit who could bring out the best in a man, make him want to settle down.

When a certain feminine face and form drifted across his consciousness, Seth wasn't quite so quick to squelch the green-eyed vision. . .even though he figured he had a lot of good years left to boss trails while he saved up for that thoroughbred horse ranch he'd always dreamed of.

Urging Sagebrush after a cow that was too far off the trail, Seth spotted a familiar-looking cloth item on the ground and swung down to pick it up.

CHAPTER 16

Just before going over the sloping shoulder of the mountains, the girls paused for a last glance backward in the sagescented morning, memorizing a scene they were unlikely ever to see again. The shining Sweetwater River, after its tempestuous roar through Devil's Gate, meandered lazily beneath a lucid aquamarine sky. Independence Rock looked like a slumbering turtle in the vast expanse of dry sage, and on the eastern horizon, misty hills discreetly hid their cache of new graves.

The trail ascending into the Rockies was lined with crusted snowbanks soiled with mud, twigs, and animal tracks. The route grew increasingly rough and rugged, some portions necessitating the use of chains and double teams to drag wagons one at a time up the steep grades. The temperature, too, reached new extremes. In the pleasant sunshine, rivulets of melted ice would trickle downhill to water sporadic patches of green starred with brilliant yellow flowers and clumped with iris. But at night, folks shivered around the insufficient sagebrush fires, longing for some of the spare blankets only recently discarded.

Hard days later they crested the summit, where massive clouds churned threateningly across the curved sky. Early snow dusted the range to the north. Sarah hunkered down into the turned-up collar of her coat and frowned at her sister as Amanda drove onward. "Isn't this where we're supposed to cross the Great Divide?" she hollered above the howling wind. "Somehow, I expected to see a dramatic gorge, or something spectacular—but it's only a grassy meadow!" She perused the wide, bumpy plain between two solid walls of impassible mountains.

"My thoughts exactly." Amanda grinned as a gust flailed her scarf. Then she sobered. "They say Dr. Marcus Whitman knelt with a flag and a Bible and prayed over the West on his first trip through this pass; before he ever set up the mission where he and his wife ministered to the Cayuse Indians."

Sarah pondered the tragic end of the courageous missionaries a moment before turning to a cheerier thought. "Well, at least the place isn't as rough and rugged as the route we had to take to get here. But I still would have expected some unforgettable landmark to indicate the crossing of the *Great Divide!*"

Amanda nodded in agreement.

The train rolled steadily through South Pass, then began the downward grade to the west. They paused at a spring for an icy ceremonial toast from the westward-flowing water, then continued down to camp beneath the willows at Little Sandy Creek.

After supper, Sarah Jane left Amanda working on sewing projects and headed toward the Hill wagon.

Bethany and Tad came running the minute they saw her.

"Look at the pretty flowers I picked, Miss Sarah," Bethany said, proudly displaying the colorful wildflowers in her hand.

"And I found a real nice stone." Tad held out his open palm. "Pa says I can keep it, too."

Sarah smiled. "That's nice. I'm happy for both of you." Their father laid aside the worn harness he was examining and stood. "Mind keeping an eye on my pair while I go talk to your sister?" he asked.

Meeting his gaze, Sarah felt the color heighten in her cheeks. "Not at all. I'll take the children for a walk."

"Thanks. Much obliged." With that, he strode away.

Sarah wondered what he and Amanda would be discussing, then filled her lungs and exhaled. A person could have all kinds of things to talk about on an extended journey like this one. Maybe he was weary of having to look after their wagon in addition to his. Maybe he needed some mending done.

"Will you tell us a story, Miss Sarah?" Bethy's huge blue eyes rounded as she gazed raptly up at her.

"A scary one," Tad chimed in. "With dragons and sailing ships and—"

His sister pouted. "No. One with princesses and castles."

Sarah Jane wrapped an arm around each of them and gave a light squeeze. "Tell you what. I'll tell you my very favorite Bible story, about Naaman the leper and his little slave girl."

"Oh goody!" Bethany clapped. "I like that one, too!"

<hr>

Sewing the hem in a flannel baby gown, Amanda looked up as Jared came toward her. "Good evening," she said politely.

He removed his hat and inclined his head, then without waiting for an invitation, lowered himself to a corner of the blanket. His posture remained rigid. "Where is everybody?" she asked lightly, gazing hopefully past him for his brood.

"The kids, you mean? Sarah took them for a walk."

Amanda gave an understanding nod. Something was in the air, she could feel it. Taking up her sewing again, her fingers trembled unaccountably, and she pricked her finger.

He appeared nervous, too, fiddling with the brim of his hat, not quite meeting her gaze. "Amanda, I have something to ask you," he began.

Now she was more than a little uneasy. "Something wrong with one of the children?" she asked, trying to steer the conversation in a safe direction.

"No, no. Nothing like that. Nothing like that at all."

"Oh, well, have we been making pests of ourselves, then? Sarah and I? Taking up too much of their time?"

He let out a slow breath. "This has nothing to do with Tad or Beth. Well, actually it does, sort of."

"I don't understand." Alarm bells were clanging in earnest inside Amanda's head. *Please, please, don't let it be what I think it is,* she prayed silently even as her heart began to throb with dread. Laying aside her project, she expended the enormous amount of effort required to look directly at him.

"This'll probably come as a shock, but I want you to hear me out. Don't say a word till I'm done."

"But—"

Jared's straight brows dipped slightly, silencing her. He cleared his throat and looked around. Then his eyes met hers. "I don't have to tell you how hard it's been on my kids—and me— losing their mother."

"I understand, but—"

This time a pleading look cut her off. "I came pretty near to changing my mind about heading west, when she died. But there was nothing to go back to."

Feeling a shiver course through her, Amanda held her hands out to the warmth of the fire a few feet away.

"Gave more thought to dropping out when it seemed the trip was gonna be too hard on the young'uns. But then you and your sister stepped in." He shrugged. "Now they're normal kids again. Happy, enthusiastic about living out west. And you know what? So am I."

"Jared—"

"Not till I'm done, remember? I might never have enough gumption to bring this up again."

Amanda clamped her lips together.

"What I'm trying to say is, the kids and I would be mighty pleased if you were to go with us to wherever we settle. It's not right for them to grow up without a ma. I'd marry you, of course, make no mistake about that. And I'd be good to you, Amanda. Real good. I think the world of you, and so do my little ones."

Her mouth parted, whether in shock or dismay, she really wasn't sure. But her heart truly went out to Jared Hill. No one had to tell her he was a kind man, a sensitive and caring father. And she felt instinctively that he'd make a wonderful husband, too. . .if a woman were so inclined.

He tipped his head self-consciously. "Oh, I know I'm not

much to look at. You could do lots better than me, that's for sure."

Amanda reached over with her hand and covered one of his, stilling its assault on the poor hat. "You, Jared Hill, are one of the nicest, most decent men I have ever met in my entire life. And you've done twice as much for us as we've ever done for you."

He smiled wryly. "Pretty sure I hear a but coming."

"Not for the reason you think," she admitted, then rattled off the first thing that came to her head. "It isn't you. It's me. I already have my future all planned out. . .and it doesn't include marriage—to anyone. There are things I want to do, on my own. And there's Sarah to consider. I'm the only family she has."

"But your sister's welcome to come with us, too," he insisted. "We'd both look after her until she found someone she wanted to spend her life with. You wouldn't have to worry about her at all."

Amanda hesitated.

Jared filled the silence. "Well, it'd be enough if you'd just think on it. Would you do that? Who knows, maybe by the time we go the rest of the way to Oregon you might change your mind."

"I wouldn't count on it," she answered in what she sincerely hoped was a kind tone. "It's not fair for you to get your hopes up too high."

"Then I won't. But just know the offer stands. I'll not beat you over the head with it. It's up to you."

"Thank you, Jared. I really mean that. It's the kindest, nicest offer I've had in my life."

He grinned, a touch of embarrassment tugging it off center. "I might have figured you'd had others."

"Only one. One too many," she confessed bitterly.

His expression softened into one of understanding. "Must have been a dimwit to let a fine woman like you slip away." His face grew solemn and he cleared his throat once more, then ambled to his feet. "Well, I'd be obliged if you just gave the matter some thought. It's all I ask."

Amanda got up also. "I will. Truly. But—"

"I know." With a cockeyed smile, Jared turned and went back in the direction of his wagon.

A host of conflicting emotions made her watch after him until he was out of sight.

That night, when the majority of folks gathered around the campfire for a hymn sing, Amanda remained behind. Taking down the empty wooden pail outside her wagon, she glanced toward the gathering. Hardships of the journey showed on everyone, clothing ragged and worn hung loosely on the thinner forms, but the faces aglow with the golden light of the big fire looked peaceful. It was no surprise to hear "Abide with Me" issue forth soon after the singing began. Smiling, she drew away and strolled the short distance to the stream.

The quiet, gurgling brook had been pretty in the fading light of day, but now in the growing darkness it surpassed its former beauty as the ripples spilled over rocks in the streambed, catching remnants of firelight in shining ribbons of silver and gold. Amanda set down the bucket. Stooping near the edge, she trailed her fingers in the cold current, then licked her fingertips, enjoying the sweetness of pure water after so many bitter and cloudy springs.

"Nice crisp evening," a low voice said quietly.

Amanda sprang to her feet.

Several yards away, the wagon master stood after filling and capping his canteen. He thumbed the brim of his hat in a polite gesture.

"Mr. Holloway." She returned her attention to the creek as, to her dismay, the rate of her pulse increased.

"You don't cotton to singing'?"

Her hands slid into her coat pockets in an effort to remain casual. "Normally I would. Just not tonight."

From the corner of her eye, she saw him nod slightly. "I was glad to see you back on your feet so soon after being sick."

Slowly raising her lashes, she peered toward him. Warmth coursed through her, almost making the cool, fall evening feel more like a midsummer night. She swallowed. "I heard you'd come by. Thank you for the concern."

His dark eyes were completely lost in the shadow of his hat brim, but Amanda could feel the intensity of his fixed gaze. "I like to make sure my company stays healthy."

Amanda didn't respond.

"You've been kind of a surprise—or rather, amazement—to me," the man went on. "Never thought you'd stick out the hardships of the trip."

"I hope you didn't lose any bets over it," she blurted, immediately hating herself.

But he chuckled.

Amanda felt compelled to smooth over the hasty remark. "We're thankful God has brought us this far."

With a soft huff, he started toward her. "You're really serious about giving the Almighty all the credit, even though you're the one doing all the work?"

Sensing that he was baiting her, Amanda frowned. It seemed immensely important for the wagon master to understand her simple logic, her simple faith. "He gives us strength to do it."

"I suppose," Closer now, he picked up the pail and dipped it into the stream, filling it to the brim, then set it next to her on the grass.

Her surprise over the act of kindness almost clouded over the realization that he hadn't made light of her convictions this time.

Mr. Holloway continued to stare. "Oh." He reached into an inside pocket of his buckskin jacket and drew out a calico bonnet. "I believe this belongs to you."

"Y—yes," she gasped. "It does. I lost it a few days ago." Taking the article from him, her fingers brushed his calloused hand, and a maddening blush flamed her face. It intensified with the awareness that the cloth retained the heat of his body. She knew better than to trust her voice. "Thank you," she could only whisper.

He nearly smiled. "Wouldn't want you coming down with something else, now, would we?" he teased.

Amanda's lips parted in disbelief at this glimpse of yet another aspect of his personality. He was far more complex than she'd given him credit for. . .and perhaps, far more *fascinating*. Realizing the dangerous turn her imaginings were taking, Amanda became aware that she was gawking at the man and clamped her mouth closed.

"Well, I wouldn't stay out here too long, Miss Shelby. Night brings out all kinds of thirsty animals." He bent to pick up the water bucket, then motioned with his head for her to walk beside him.

"Do you—?" Both of them spoke at once.

Having paused at the same time as well, they smiled. He gestured for her to go first.

Amanda only shook her head. "Never mind." In an attempt to prolong the conversation she was on the verge of making some inane query regarding the trail. She was more curious as to what he had to say.

"I. . .don't suppose you like horses."

Completely taken by surprise, she turned her gaze fully on him. "I—they're beautiful creatures. I've never had one of my own, of course, but who wouldn't think they're wonderful animals?"

He showed no visible reaction. They had reached her wagon. Setting the pail up on the schooner within her easy reach, he then assisted her up as well.

Conscious of the touch of his hands on her waist, Amanda had to remember to breathe as he lightly set her down. "Thank you, Mr. Holloway," she managed as, with a half smile, he walked away.

Inside the warmer confines of the bowed top, Amanda fought a peculiar assortment of giddy, fluttery sensations she had never before experienced. Left over from her bout with sickness, she rationalized. That was it. Surely her imaginings were getting the best of her. It was time to calm down.

When at last she had regained her composure, she thought again of the unexpected marriage proposal—more than likely the cause of all this confusion—and knelt in the honey-colored lantern light.

Dear heavenly Father, I thank You for the opportunity to come to

You in prayer. You've been so merciful to Sarah and me over the many miles we've traveled. You've looked after us, kept us from harm, and given us so many blessings, so many friends.

Surely You know of this new predicament I face. A proposal— after all the time I've spent convincing myself never to trust a man again, much less expect one to look upon me with favor. I don't think I've given Mr. Hill the slightest indication of my desiring to replace his dear dead wife. Nor have his actions toward me, to be truthful. More than likely he's thinking of his children, trying to do what's best for them.

She paused and sighed. *But I couldn't imagine committing myself to another man unless I truly, truly loved him. And the affection I feel for Jared is not of that nature. In fact, I—*

Refusing even to finish the stunning thought trying to come to life within her heart, Amanda steeled herself against it and returned to her petition with renewed urgency. *Please give me wisdom to make the right choice. Help me to do Your will, to do what's best. In Jesus' name, amen.*

Not exactly at peace, Amanda draped her coat over one of the barrels and slid into the warm quilts and blankets on the pallet.

But it was not Jared Hill's face that remained in her thoughts.

CHAPTER 17

While they camped at Little Sandy, a vote was taken to bypass Fort Bridger and navigate the shorter route to Bear Valley known as Sublett's Cutoff. The idea of saving eighty-five miles—even at the price of heading straight out into a grassless desert tableland—seemed of more import than the difficulties they knew would have to be faced. Every available water container was filled to the brim in the clear cool river before leaving, and the men cut a supply of long grass for the animals.

The thought of seven days' less travel appealed to Amanda, whatever the hardships. Considering all she and Sarah Jane had endured up to this point, she had no qualms about trusting the Lord to take them through a dry march as well.

The memory of Seth Holloway's unexpected kindness last evening had kept her awake long into the night, try as she might to slough it off as mere good-neighbor courtesy. The man was an enigma. Though usually displaying a hard, domineering side of his character, he also possessed a caring, thoughtful side. The latter caused Amanda the most unrest and was hardest to ignore.

And there was Jared Hill's proposal to consider. The more she thought about it, the more convinced she became that the needs of the motherless children were uppermost in the widower's mind. After all, a remote homestead in sparsely settled territory demanded the combined efforts of a man and a woman to provide a nurturing environment for little ones. And she truly loved Bethany and Tad as if they were her own younger brother and sister. . .yet—

"Mandy?" Sarah asked, keeping pace with the plodding mules. "Would you like me to drive? You look tired."

Amanda shook her head. "I'm fine, really. It was just kind of a short night." She paused, debating whether or not to seek her younger sister's advice. But who else was there to ask? "Sissy. . .what do you think of Mr. Hill?"

Sarah turned her head so abruptly she stumbled on the uneven terrain. "Why?"

"He. . .he's asked me to marry him." Amanda watched the color drain from her sister's face.

"D–do you love him?" she asked, her words barely audible over the hoof falls and the rattle and creak of the wagon.

Amanda averted her gaze to the countryside, still amazingly pleasant for all the dire predictions of what lay ahead. "I like and respect him very much. It would be hard to find a more decent man." Hearing no reply, she glanced at her sibling again.

Sarah moistened her lips. "Does he . . .love you?"

A ragged breath emptied Amanda's lungs. She tipped her head in thought. "We both love the children. I think that's what's most important to him at the moment."

"They are dear, aren't they? Truly dear." A wistful smile played over Sarah's lips.

Amanda thought she detected a mistiness in her sister's eyes before Sarah quickly cut a glance to the earth. But the tear her sibling brushed away while trying to hide the action was not imagined. "Are you all right, Sissy?"

Sarah merely nodded. But she did not speak another word for hours.

※

Crossing the crucible of sand speckled with prickly creosote and mesquite shrubs, the temperature climbed with the merciless sun. The bone-weary emigrants decided to rest during the day under the meager shade of canvas or wagon and journey at night, to spare the animals. But at least half a dozen beasts perished anyway, dropping right where they stood in the extreme scorching temperatures. People began abandoning wagons and doubling what remained of their teams.

Days later, the sight of the Green River on the far western side couldn't have been more welcome. The animals practically stampeded toward the swift, deep water. When everyone's thirst had been sated, the necessary preparations began for transporting the company across the formidable river. Some people by now routinely unpacked their heavy wagons and floated their stores over the water on rafts, then had to repack everything once the empty wagons reached the other side.

Amanda, having successfully forded numerous rivers, decided to chance this one as well. She tied down everything and inched the team into the Green after one of the other rigs.

The mules balked at the force of the flow, but started toward the opposite bank, making slow but steady progress.

Partway across, a front wheel struck something and buckled. The wagon pitched sharply to the left.

With Sarah's scream still ringing in her ears, Amanda plunged headlong into the frigid mountain flow. The roiling water whisked her away, hiding any view of her sister or the wagon.

Helpless against the force of the current, she made a futile attempt to swim, but the weight of her sodden skirts pulled her under, tangling about her legs, and her shoes felt as heavy as anvils. With the icy river roaring over her head and shoulders, Amanda fought desperately to keep her face above the surface, but each time she gasped for air she swallowed more water. She had to try to make it to shallower water, but no amount of thrashing with her arms could overcome the force of the relentless current. And the cold mercilessly sapped her strength. *I'm going to drown!* The sick realization clenched her heart. What would become of poor Sarah! *Dear God,* she prayed desperately, *take care of her. Don't let anything happen to her.*

Suddenly something snagged her around the shoulders. Cut off her air.

Amanda writhed frantically to get free.

"Don't fight me!"

As the command penetrated her numbed mind, Amanda became aware of a strong arm encircling her. Exhausted, she gave in, aware only of a man's labored breathing as he attempted to get them both to shore.

Coughing water from her lungs, Amanda clung to her rescuer. She blinked to clear her vision, then raised her lashes and discovered that the masculine body pressed to hers was the wagon master's! The two of them were being pulled toward the bank by a rope.

When Amanda's feet grazed the sandy bottom, she was scooped up and carried to dry land. Still coughing as Seth Holloway set her down and she loosed her death grip from his neck, she shivered uncontrollably in the wind.

His partner quickly wrapped the blanket from behind his saddle around her, while Mr. Holloway, enshrouded in his own, mounted his horse. Then she was lifted again into the wagon master's arms, and he started back toward the crossing site.

Deep shudders racked Amanda as the horse plodded along. She relived the ordeal as if it were a dream that hadn't ended yet—and she wondered if she would ever again in her life feel warm enough. Gathering the pitiful remnants of her remaining energy, she tried to speak over her violent shivers as they jounced along. Nothing would come out. "S–Sarah," she finally managed between chatters of her teeth.

"The others are probably looking after her."

"Y–you s–saved my life. Th–thank you."

An angry *whoosh* deflated his chest. "You almost got us both killed!" he ranted. "You had no business driving that wagon across by yourself. But you're bound and determined to prove me wrong." With another furious huff he shook his head. "I swear, you've been nothing but trouble from the first time I saw you!"

Utterly crushed by the attack, Amanda felt welling tears, but she had no time to respond. They had arrived at camp.

"Mandy!" Sarah ran up and yanked her to the ground in a bone-crushing hug. "Thank heaven you're all right!"

"Poor thing's near froze to death," she heard Mrs. Randolph say as another blanket was thrown about her. "Bring her over by the fire. Give a hustle, now. We have some good strong coffee on to help warm her up."

Amanda allowed them to lead her to the blazing campfire. Glancing over her shoulder, she saw Seth Holloway headed in the opposite direction. But she was far too spent to give further thought to her reluctant rescuer or his insulting tongue lashing.

Shielded from view by a wall of blankets and concerned women, Sarah Jane stripped Amanda's sodden clothing from her stiff, shivering frame. Then layers of dry covers and quilts wrapped her from head to toe, providing the first measure of real warmth she'd felt since being drawn from the frigid river.

Much sooner than she would have expected, the ministrations of her sister and the kind older woman who'd become such a friend to them began thawing her out. With her stiff fingers wrapped around a hot mug, Amanda drained the last drop of coffee, then asked the question foremost in her mind. "When can I go lie down in the wagon?"

Sarah paled. "That's the bad news. But the men were able to salvage most of our things, and Mr. Hill is trying to fashion a cart for us from what's left of the schooner. When it tipped, he and another man came to help me. They saved the mules, too. Poor things were scared silly, braying their heads off."

"But don't you worry none, darlin'," Mrs. Randolph said gently. "You and Sarah Jane can sleep under our rig every night. We'll look after you."

Still stunned by the dire fate of the prairie schooner, Amanda drew little comfort from her neighbor's offer. Her expression must have been transparent, for Sarah Jane swiftly took command of the conversation, saying more all at once than she'd said for days. "Your heroic rescue was the talk of the camp, Mandy," she announced much too brightly.

Amanda just stared at her.

Her sister nodded. "Everyone gasped when that wheel

snapped and you were flung into the river. Mr. Holloway had already crossed with the herd and was riding along the bank when you fell in. You should have seen him!" Sarah's eyes grew large. "He yelled something to that Mr. Hanfield and charged after you. Honestly, if ever a real true knight existed, that man fits the bill. It was almost...romantic." A smile gave emphasis to her airy sigh.

But Amanda felt tears gathering inside her soul. All she wanted was to be alone so she could cry her heart out. And she knew it had nothing to do with her harrowing experience.

~⁂~

Having merged from the cutoff onto the rugged hills of the main trail once more, Amanda truly appreciated the way the much smaller cart handled. It wasn't exactly as stylish as something back East, but considering the poor shape of the materials used to make it, it rolled over the high ridges and through the pine forests as well—if not better—than many of the heavy wagons. Best of all, hitched to only four mules rather than six, it gave the animals an easier lot, too. Amanda could rotate them. And Jared Hill had thoughtfully made a canvas cover, which provided at least some shelter, in a pinch.

She had not seen Mr. Holloway since the incident at the Green River. Nor did she intend to see or speak to him for the remainder of the journey. Sarah, too, she noticed, had reverted to that oddly quiet way she'd acquired of late. She rarely spent time with Alvin or his friends, and even her moments with Bethany and Tad seemed weighted by her countenance.

Jared Hill had insisted the girls drive in front of him so he could keep an eye on their tentative conveyance, so the children normally walked beside either her or Sarah Jane, whichever one of them was afoot. Their endless chatter kept Amanda's mind occupied—another of life's blessings—while yet another ten, twenty, fifty miles ticked by. Would this tedious journey never end! Points of interest they passed along the way no longer held the slightest appeal, not even the amazing springs where the water tasted like soda.

Lost in moody depression, one afternoon, Amanda thought she imagined a cry in the distance. She peered ahead at a tiny cloud of dust that appeared to be coming toward them.

The shout came again.

"Gold!"

And again. *"Gold!"*

Much clearer now. Folks up front hollered it back to the rest and halted their teams.

Upon reaching the company, the galloping rider skidded his mount to a stop. "There's gold in California!" he yelled for all to hear, panting between breaths. "At Sutter's Mill, on the American River. Enough for all! I'm ridin' east to fetch my brothers." With that, he spurred his lathered horse and sped on.

A moment of silent shock swiftly evolved into an excited murmur, then erupted to hoots and howls.

"Well, I, for one, am headin' to Californy," one man bellowed. "Soon as we pass the fort!" Waving his hat, he kicked up his heels and jumped aboard his outfit, clucking his team to motion.

"Me, too," another hollered.

A virtual shouting match broke out down the line, between folks bound and determined to grab this chance to get rich, and others who declared they were continuing to Oregon despite what could turn out to be a rumor started by some practical joker.

Just listening to the melee, Amanda and Sarah exchanged questioning frowns.

Then Mr. Holloway cantered by, one hand raised, on his way to the front of the line. "Let's not get all het up, folks," he said a number of times. "Stay calm. Whether there's gold or not, there's plenty of time for you and your animals to rest up at the fort while you think the matter through. Then if you decide to turn off on the California Trail when we come to it, at least you'll have a better chance of getting there in one piece."

But there was no slowing down some of the determined travelers. Breaking off from the rest of the train, those wagons pulled ahead, anxious to set out on fortune's path.

A much smaller group made camp that night.

Amanda felt exposed as she and Sarah were forced to sleep out in the open. Listening to plaintiff yips and howls of coyotes and wolves, the rustlings in the sagebrush that could be any number of wild things, she rolled up in her blanket like a mummy and lay awake waiting for utter exhaustion to claim her.

All she wanted was to get somewhere. *Anywhere.* Never to go another mile again. Someplace where she never had to set eyes on Seth Holloway as long as she lived. As they had for the past several nights, burning tears slid out from behind her closed eyes and into her hair.

CHAPTER 18

From a distance of five miles the whitewashed fur-trading post of Fort Hall was visible, occupying half an acre of sagebrush plain alongside the shining Snake River. The breeze played over the red flag on the pole, ruffling the initials of the Hudson's Bay Company. But this time upon approaching a fort, the mood of the company was a peculiar mixture of excitement and subdued resignation.

Amanda gave no more than a cursory glance to the five-foot wall surrounding the two-story bastion or the hewn-log buildings inside. Word had it there was no meat, flour, or rice to be had. Only a small supply of coffee and sugar—and that at fifty cents a pint. Nevertheless, two days of rest would be appreciated. "Look, Pa!" she heard Tad shout. "A cannon! A real cannon!"

But before the lad could skip off to the piece of artillery parked in the courtyard, his father reined him in. "Slow down, son. That's nothing to fool with."

The boy groaned in disappointment.

Jared tousled the towhead's hair on his approach to Amanda and Sarah. "If you two would look after the young'uns, I'd like to go hunting with the other men. See if I can replenish our stores."

Amanda nodded. "Go on. I'll see to your oxen."

With a grateful smile at her and Sarah, he retrieved his rifle and walked toward the loose horses among the animals that had trailed the company. Amanda thought she caught a wistful longing in her sister's expression as he left.

"I'm hungry, Miss Sarah," Bethany implored.

Her brother perked up. "Me, too."

"Well, let's see what we can scrape together," Amanda heard her say, "while Sissy takes care of the animals."

———✦———

That night, the camp was anything but quiet. News of the gold strike had the whole place abuzz, precluding the customary music and dancing while folks made plans for the remainder of the journey. Amanda and Sarah sipped coffee by their evening fire until Jared tucked his little ones into bed.

Moments after he came to join them, the Randolphs paid a visit as well. Beaming from ear to ear, the older couple had stranger in tow. It took Amanda only one look to guess the young man was their son. He bore an uncanny resemblance to his father, already possessing similar body structure and bearing, and the same pear-shaped face. But one striking difference stood out—he had the brightest red hair Amanda had ever seen.

"We'd like you all to meet our Charlie," Minnie Randolph said proudly, her small blue eyes aglow as they rested on him. "He's just come over from California to meet his pa an' me. Charlie, this is Amanda—the sweetest little gal a body could know—and her sister, Sarah Jane, and Jared Hill, our neighbor." She indicated each in turn.

Amanda blushed at the emphasis of her name.

"Howdy," he managed, fair sunburned skin turning an even deeper hue up to his hairline as he nodded to her, then Sarah. He shook hands with Jared, who had risen to his feet.

"How'd you find the desert trail?" Jared asked.

"Not much good a person can say about that," the young man admitted candidly. "But I figured my folks would do all right with me to help out."

"Would any of you care for some coffee?" Amanda asked,

regaining her composure as Sarah spread out an extra blanket.

"Don't mind if we do," the elder Mr. Randolph said, kneading his bearded jaw. He assisted his wife, then settled his solid bulk between her and their son as they accepted the proffered refreshment.

"Mm. Tastes mighty good," the old man commented. "Near as good as Minnie's, if I do say so."

His spouse beamed in agreement. "Reason we come by," she said, centering her attention on Amanda, "is to invite you an' your sister to come to California with us when we take the cutoff."

Aware of the woman's son on the fringe of her vision, Amanda blanched. "We—"

She held up a gnarled hand. "I know, the store an' all. But seems like the Good Lord's layin' a real good chance at your feet. You won't know a soul when you get to Oregon, and more'n likely, folks who've suffered the hot sands and dry waste of the desert will be needin' clothes as much as anybody else. Might be, you could even happen across a few nuggets of gold to help get you started. We'll be passin' nigh Sutter's Fort on the way to our new place, a handful of miles farther."

"I've been considering heading off on that fork myself," Jared announced out of the blue before Amanda had opportunity to reply. "I was gonna make you and Sarah Jane the same offer."

Sarah, raising her mug to her lips, halted midway and lowered it to her lap instead.

Amanda had never once considered branching off the main trail and settling in California. Her sights had been fixed on Oregon since before leaving Independence. She looked to Sarah for a response and found her sister's expression unreadable as the younger girl stared at Alvin Rivers's wagon.

"My other offer still stands, too," Jared told Amanda quietly when the others began talking among themselves.

It was all too much to take in at once. Amanda felt torn in two. Either route had definite merit as well as dreaded pitfalls. But she wasn't exactly up to committing her entire future in marriage just yet, either. Looking to her sibling once more, her gaze drifted above Sarah's shoulder and happened upon Seth Holloway, exiting the fort's general store with his partner. That same instant, his attention flicked her way. He tipped his head slightly in Amanda's direction and said something to Mr. Hanfield. They both laughed.

Amanda set her jaw. *One good thing about the Lord*, she reasoned, *He always provides a way of escape, just as He promised in First Corinthians.* With a glance encompassing the Randolphs,- Jared Hill, and her sister, she hiked her chin. "We'll do it. We'll go to California!"

─────※─────

"You're not serious!" Alvin snapped his sketchpad closed in the only true display of his temper Sarah had ever witnessed. His charcoal pencil and blending stick fell unheeded to the sandy ground outside the fort, where he'd been working on a new landscape.

"I'm afraid I am," she replied, shielding her eyes from the bright sun. "When the wagon train leaves this fort tomorrow morning, Mandy and I have decided to take the California Trail with the Randolphs, Mr. Hill, and whoever else will be splitting off from the company."

"But why would you do a fool thing like that?" Not to be put off, he sidled up to her, his fingertips lightly grazing up and down her forearm. "For—gold? I'm already in line for a considerable fortune, you know. I'm not about to waste weeks and months grubbing through a bunch of rocks and mud for a few paltry nuggets."

"I never suggested you should."

His movements halted. "I see." The light that dawned in his head was almost visible in his eyes and lent them a steely glitter. "So this is good-bye, then. Fare thee well and all that."

Sarah nodded, brushing aside a loose tendril the fall breeze whisked over her face. "I thought I'd tell you now, while there's still time to talk. But please don't think ill of me, Alvin. I'll always remember you. I'll think back with pleasure on the happy times we shared on this journey. And I truly hope one day you'll find someone who'll fulfill all your dreams. She'll be a very fortunate person."

"Indeed."A smirk lifted a corner of his mouth. "I thought I already had."

"No." Slowly shaking her head, Sarah smiled thinly. "There was only room in your heart for me. My dream is to be part of a family. . .the bigger the better. To bear children and watch them grow and have children of their own. Even if I were poor and had to scratch for my existence I could never settle for less than that."

He raked long fingers through his wiry curls and shook his head. Then, reaching for both her hands, he pulled her into a warm hug, his heart beating against hers for several seconds until finally he eased her to arm's length. "I'll tell you one thing, Sarah Jane Shelby. If it were a few years down the line and I'd already been to the places I plan to see, I just might be tempted to *settle for* a piece of that dream of yours. But not right now."

She smiled sadly.

Alvin paused and searched her face as though committing it to memory. Then he raised her chin with the edge of an index finger and lightly brushed her lips with his. "Well, do be happy, little friend. Any young lady who happens across my path in the future is sure going to have a lot to measure up to. Who knows, perhaps one day we'll meet again, and you'll be able to show me your brood of little ones."

Fighting tears, Sarah could only attempt to smile as she took his hand and squeezed it in mute silence. Then she turned away and walked slowly back to the gate.

~·~

Amanda braced her heart against even a twinge of regret the next day as the cutoff to California loomed ever nearer. Ignoring an inner sense of guilt over not having prayed about her rash decision, she purposefully closed her mind to scenery and everyday matters and focused on the future, on the blessed time when she would no longer be forced to suffer the unbearable presence of wagon master Holloway. She determined not to even announce her change in plan to the man. Likely he would be relieved anyway that she and Sarah would no longer be his responsibility. And Amanda had no desire to provide another opportunity for him to gloat. Nor would she permit her gaze to seek him out during nooning stops or evening camps. Whatever strange fascination she might have felt toward the man, it was time it died a quick, natural death. So decided, she ceased the solitary evening walks she had previously enjoyed and expended the supreme effort required to center her attention within the three- or four-yard circumference around her person. After all, she had mules to tend, meals to cook and clean up. It would do well to get used to being with the lesser number of travelers who would be turning off at the split tomorrow.

That night at the campfire, Deacon Franklin prayed for those who on the morrow would part company with the remainder of the Oregon Trail travelers. Reflecting on his thoughtful words afterward, Amanda finally willed herself to sleep. Morning dawned in grayness, and Amanda drew perverse pleasure that it matched her mood. After what seemed an interminable length of time to dispose of breakfast and early chores, the signal finally sounded to roll.

"This is it," Sarah breathed, her excitement barely concealed. With Bethany on one side of her and Tad on the other, she waved to their father and began walking at a brisk pace.

Amanda mustered all her resolve. Tonight, camped on at new trail, her heart would sing a victory song. She was sure of it. Refusing to acknowledge the silly tear that teetered over her lower lashes and plopped onto her hand, she clucked the team forward.

~⁂~

Riding at the rear end of the column, Seth watched the company dwindle as, one by one, wagons turned off onto the California Trail, taking along several head of cattle that they had cut out of the herd earlier this morning. Granted, some folks retained sense enough to continue on to Oregon Territory, but out of the nearly thirty families who had begun this journey at

Independence three months ago, it appeared only a handful would stay with the original plan.

Oh well, he mused, it would make the job easier on him, Red, and the scouts. There were some pretty rugged mountains yet to be crossed. He shook his head. The hardships on this route were nothing compared to what lay ahead of those gold-crazy fools. His friend, Thomas Fitzpatrick, had related some amazing tales of overlanders he had bossed across that frying pan.

Only three wagons had yet to come to the branch. Seth watched the Randolphs turn off. He'd known from the onset their destination was to be northern California. He'd found Nelson Randolph a decent man, one who had acquired respect from a lot of the folks during this journey. Having a son come to meet them with the foresight to trail a string of extra mules and water, Seth figured the old couple would make out okay—provided the heat didn't do them in.

Nearby, a bony heifer meandered away from the fringe. Seth nudged his mount in that direction and brought the wanderer back in line.

He glanced ahead once more, and his heart lurched. The Shelby cart had veered onto the southerly trail toward the Raft River—with that widower, Hill, right behind!

A battle raged as Seth fought the irrational desire to chase after Amanda and spare her from the horrific dangers of that route. After all, he had somewhat enjoyed playing rescuer once. But on the other hand, he reminded himself, she was no longer his responsibility now—wasn't that what he'd wanted all along?

He shifted grimly in the saddle and watched the rickety cart growing smaller in the distance. Once Amanda crossed the river, she would be on her way to an entirely different world.

Leaving his own profoundly empty.

Chapter 19

Sarah Jane studied her sister as Amanda walked with the children along the blistered sagebrush trail. For days, ever since they had foregone their original plan and taken the California branch, Amanda had been moody and quiet. She seemed to be doing her best to be cheerful around Bethy and Tad and polite to Jared and the Randolphs. . .but she had changed drastically after her near drowning.

Before the incident Amanda had been her normal, jovial self most of the time. Even inwardly happy, as if she had come to terms with the shameful way Pa's dastardly partner had humiliated them all, before thoughts of heading west ever came up. For some time, now, there'd been nary a shred of the bitterness only Sarah could discern in her sibling's eyes. That close brush with death had disturbed Amanda far more deeply than she let on. With a deep sigh, Sarah sent a prayer aloft that God would bring her sister through this hard time.

That night she waited until Amanda's even breathing indicated sleep, then lit a candle and opened her journal to the next page.

> *Dear Diary,*
> *In my worst imaginings, I never would have*

*dreamed a more sterile, desolate region than is all
around us on this California Trail. After crossing
the river, we descended upon a landscape consisting
entirely of burnt rocks and cinders. High, blackened
cliffs towered above our camp the first night.*

*We found surprisingly good grass and water
when we reached the Humboldt River, whose
benefits we enjoyed for nearly two weeks—but one
day it disappeared into a most distressing alkali
swamp, and we left it behind to make our way
across a vast sea of hot sand.*

*The sun beats down upon us mercilessly,
sucking the very moisture from our bodies, while
the wagon wheels churn up an unbearable cloud of
dust. It coats man and beast alike from head to foot,
filling our nostrils and burning our eyes. How I
yearn to see another glorious waterfall like those we
passed after departing Fort Hall.*

A snore drifted her way from the confines of the Randolph
wagon. Sarah peeked around to see if the sound had roused any
of the others, then resumed her writing.

*We should reach the mountains tomorrow. We've
been looking at them for the past two days as they
sat on the horizon like a mirage. Hopefully there
will be water there—and grass for our poor, weary
animals. Mandy and I both long to see the end of
this journey.*

A cool gust of night wind caused Sarah to shiver. Marveling at the vacillating desert temperatures, she tucked the journal
away and snuggled deep into her covers.

~~~※~~~

It was a delightful treat to camp beside a stream again, to have
actual shade and lush grasses. For one whole day, the company

rested, bathed, and washed clothing in readiness for the trek up the rugged mountain trail.

Amanda had never enjoyed a bath so much—even such a cold one. After the tortures of the desert, she was beginning to feel her spirit come to life again. It seemed the passing of miles helped ease the ache in her heart as well, but she knew it would take some time before it dissipated completely. . .if ever. Surely the worst of the journey must be over. Traipsing back toward the cart with some wet laundry draped over her arm, she saw Jared staring her way as he leaned against the trunk of a tree. "Jared," she said pleasantly.

"Amanda." He tossed a handful of pebbles aside that he'd been rolling around in his hand. "Mind if we talk a spell? Your sister's got the kids."

"Not at all." But a trickle of uneasiness crept along her spine. She carefully laid the clothes on the grass.

Jared sank to the ground and brushed a spot smooth for her, then offered a hand. "Give any more thought to the offer I made a while back?" he asked, his long face becoming serious as he came right to the point.

She chewed the inside corner of her lip and nodded.

"And?" he prompted.

Turning to him, Amanda let out a nervous breath. Loath as she was to hurt the man, leading him on would be ten times worse. "I cannot accept it," she said softly. "I'm truly sorry."

Jared stared at her for a timeless moment, then expelled a resigned breath as he looked off into the distance. "Figured as much."

"Somehow, I knew you might," she replied, "but I also knew you probably wouldn't understand my reasons."

He plucked a handful of grass and let the breeze take a few blades. "Mind if I ask what they are?"

"One of them, you might be surprised to hear, is love." At his perplexed expression, she went on. "I've grown to love you a lot, on this journey, Jared. . .but it isn't the right sort of love to build a life on."

"Sure about that?"

She nodded. "I told you once that I had no plans ever to marry, and that's truer now than the day I said it. You're an incredible, wonderful man. You deserve a wife who will love you with all her heart. . .and it wouldn't be fair for me to stand in her way."

Jared slowly filled his lungs, obviously mulling her words over in his mind. Averting his gaze once more, he cocked his head back and forth. "Well, I only asked you to consider it. I'll do my best to accept your decision. Even if I don't agree."

"One day you will," Amanda said with a smile. "You'll see."

———◆———

"It'd be a shame not to share some of these apple fritters," Amanda remarked, "after hoarding the last of our dried apples so long. "She gathered several and wrapped them in a cloth.

Sarah tried to ignore a peculiar awkwardness within as her sister left her and Jared and crossed the small wagon circle toward the Randolphs, seated around their own evening fire. "You've gotten to be a mighty fine cook, Sarah Jane," the widower said, popping the final bite of his own fritter into his mouth. "You and Amanda both." He refilled his mug from the coffeepot and relaxed against the wheel of his Conestoga.

More than a little aware of Jared's presence and close proximity, the scant width of a blanket from her, Sarah Jane tried not to blush as her eyes met his. She wished she had courage enough to lose herself in their sad blue depths, but quickly looked away instead. "I think Sissy and I are more surprised than anyone! You would not believe the awful fare we had to choke down when we first started out on the trail. Of course," she rambled on in her nervousness, "we had a pretty good teacher in Mrs. Randolph. She's taught us a lot."

"Fine woman."

"Yes. A great friend. Mandy thinks the absolute world of her and her husband after all they've done for us. That's probably the main reason she wanted to share our dessert with them tonight."

He nodded, idly taking another gulp of the strong brew.

"Mr. Hill—"

"Jared," he corrected. "Fits better."

Sarah swallowed. "I know," she said breathlessly. "It's just that— Well— You're so much older than the boys I've been around all my life."

He gave her a pained look.

She wanted to crawl into a hole. "I—I don't mean you're old. Not at all."

A chuckle rumbled from deep inside his chest.

Drawing a huge breath to calm herself, Sarah tried again. "What I mean is, you're different. Not like any man I've ever met before. That's what I was trying to say."

"Thanks. I think." A strange grin curved one side of his mouth. "A pity your sister doesn't share those sentiments."

"What do you mean? She admires you a lot."

"Right." His sarcasm was evident.

"Truly."

"Just not enough to marry me, is all."

Certain she was dreaming, Sarah's heart skipped a beat. "Mandy told you that?" She cast a disbelieving look toward the Randolph wagon and held her breath, waiting for his reply.

"Yep. Well, no use bothering a young gal like you with my troubles, is there?" Dumping out the remains of his coffee, Jared got up and brushed off his backside, then stepped over the tongue of his wagon, exiting the circle.

Nibbling her lip, Sarah flicked a cautious glance around to make sure no one was paying them any mind. Then she gathered every ounce of gumption she possessed and rose to follow him, not even sure what she'd say. "I'm not exactly a child, you know," she blurted, flushing scarlet at being so brazen. What on earth would he think of her?

Jared, about to take a stride, stopped mid-motion and turned.

Sarah's pulse began to throb. She could barely hear over the rush in her ears. "Just because Mandy's the oldest, that doesn't mean she's the smartest. I—"

A small incredulous smile crept across the widower's mouth. He didn't move, didn't interrupt. His countenance softened considerably as he gazed down at her.

Sarah felt her insides quiver. She couldn't hold back shuddering breath. Amanda would certainly call her to task for such boldness—but there were so few occasions to be alone with Jared Hill. And now to take a chance she never would have considered had Amanda accepted his proposal. But with her sister's rejection, he could easily turn off the trail at the next branch—and neither of them would ever see him again. Sarah pressed onward, hoping her voice and her shaking legs wouldn't fail her. "I. . .wouldn't have refused you." There. She'd said it, even if the utterance had been barely audible. Now she waited—almost prayed—for the world to open up and swallow her. She would positively die if he made light of her declaration.

He stared for a heartbeat. That merest hint of a smile reappeared as his even brows rose a notch. "Sarah. . .if you're—" He stopped, kneaded his temples, then began again. "A beautiful young girl like you—"

"Woman," she corrected bravely. *Desperately.*

"But I'm old enough—"

"To need someone who loves you," she whispered, unable to stop now without baring her soul. "And loves Bethy and Tad, too. And can't bear even the thought of having to say good-bye when we get to the end of—wherever it is we're going."

"You mean that?" he asked, appearing utterly astonished. "You'd actually settle for me? With that face of yours you could have your choice of a thousand young bucks!" He wagged his head in wonder even as undeniable hope rose in his eyes.

"My heart has already made its choice."

Jared searched her face for a moment, as if still uncertain whether to believe this was really happening. Then ever so gently, he reached toward her.

Sarah melted into his arms, barely able to hold back tears of profoundest relief as she felt his strong heart keeping pace with hers.

"I never thought for a moment I could have you," he said softly, cradling the back of her head in his palm as he rocked her in his embrace. "I figured, I mean, with you being young, you deserve somebody just starting out in life, same as you. Your sister didn't seem as taken up with fellows her age."

"Does that mean you might grow to love me, too, someday?"

His embrace tightened as he hugged her closer. "It means I won't have to go on fighting the feelings I've had for you since the first time I saw you with my young'uns. When I was sure I'd never have this chance."

Sarah turned her face up to his with a slightly teary smile. "Life's filled with chances, isn't it?"

"It is at that, Sarah Jane. It is at that." And Jared's lips at last claimed hers.

~~~~~

Seth stared up at the midnight sky. It seemed as if every star that had ever been created was out tonight, each of them representing one of the countless ways he'd been a fool. If he lived to be a hundred he would never forget the sight of Amanda's cart turning off the trail.

Or the anguish in her eyes on that day at the river.

He turned in his bedroll, seeking comfort in the stillness while Red was on watch. What had possessed him that he'd railed at her after she'd nearly drowned? Thinking back on the event, he realized those had been the last words he'd spoken, no, bellowed, to her. After that, she'd given him a wide berth. And he sure didn't blame her.

But Amanda should have known he'd reacted out of anger. Anger at the Green for wrecking her wagon, nearly wiping out everything she owned in this world. And maybe foremost, anger at the fact that Widower Hill was paying her so much attention.

But there was one thing she couldn't have known. He had only now come to where he could admit it himself. He loved her. *Loved her.*

He'd set ridiculous standards after Liza dumped him. They had him scrutinizing a woman against some insane checklist. Truthful? Check. Reliable? Check. Sensitive? He deflated his lungs in exasperation. What were all those traits anyway, compared to spunk, an unquenchable spirit, or a valiant heart?

Come to think of it, Seth realized, there was nothing he

didn't like about Amanda Shelby. Including her faith. In its utter simplicity, it took him back to his own roots, when his deepest desire was to do justly, love mercy, and walk humbly with his God, as the Old Testament said. Since he'd turned his back on the Lord, his life had been nothing but a sham. Amanda, not Liza, was the example of true Christianity. . .and much too good for the likes of him. Maybe it was for the best that she ended up with someone else. After all, he'd practically pushed her into Jared Hill's arms himself!

Seth waited for the pain of that thought to subside.

It would take some time before the emptiness would go away, though. And inside, he knew where he had to go for the strength to live the rest of his life without her. Easing out of his blankets, he knelt beneath the stars and sought forgiveness from the God of his youth.

CHAPTER 20

April 1849

D o I look all right, Sissy? Oh, I'm still so thin."
Standing in the Randolphs' spare bedroom, which she and her sister had shared through the winter months, Amanda had to fight tears as she fluffed out Sarah's veil. Throughout the long trek over the Oregon Trail she had envisioned life with the two of them together, running a store. . .for several years, at least, if not forever. But God's plans had proven to be vastly different from hers. She would content herself with the few months that dream had been reality.

"He'll be rendered speechless," Amanda finally murmured, mustering a smile. Her fingertips lightly touched a cluster of seed pearls and alabaster sequins adorning the fitted lace bodice. "You've done a beautiful job on your gown. Maddie would be pleased to see how those years of stitching and samplers paid off."

Sarah covered Amanda's hand with hers. "I only wish I weren't moving away. Won't you please reconsider closing the shop and coming with us to Mount Shasta?" she pleaded. "Jared always said you were more than welcome. And you know how Bethy and Tad became enamored of you while they stayed here and Jared went off to find a place of our own."

With a stoic smile, Amanda met the younger girl's shimmering eyes in the oval cheval glass. "Not just yet. It's so convenient here on the farm, with Sacramento only a few miles away. You know how busy we've been, what with that tide of newcomers pouring west. Mr. Randolph doesn't seem to mind my using the wagon to drive to town and back every day—and besides, you need some time to be alone with that new little family of yours. You're a bride, remember?"

"I. . .sometimes feel a little guilty about that," Sarah confessed quietly. "After all, he did ask you first." Taking a fold of the lacy skirt in hand, she stepped away from the mirror and sat on the multihued counterpane draping the four-poster.

Amanda eased gently onto the rocker, so as not to crush the cerulean taffeta gown she wore. "Well, it's time to put those feelings to rest. You and I both know I never loved him in that way. And *I* could hardly miss seeing that *you* did."

A light pink tinted her sister's delicate cheekbones.

Increasingly conscious that soon enough the buckboard would bring Jared and his children, Amanda was determined to keep the mood light. . .the last sweet moments before Sarah's wedding ceremony would bring the younger girl's old life to an end and embark her upon the new. "It'll be ever so exciting," she gushed. "I wonder what your house looks like. I'm surprised Jared was able to finish it so quickly."

"Probably not quite as grand as this one, I'd venture. He wouldn't even give me a hint in his letters—and no doubt the little ones have been sworn to secrecy, too. I only hope the curtains I've sewn will fit the windows. It'll be nice having those braided rugs Mrs. Randolph taught me how to make, though, and the pretty needlepoint pillows you've done. But no matter what, I'm determined to like it—and to be the best wife and stepmother in the world. Perhaps one day the Lord will see fit to bless me with a child of my own."

Amanda felt tears welling deep inside. Tomorrow the shop in town would seem unbearably quiet and empty without Sarah's bubbliness. Happy as she was for her sister, it was difficult to dismiss the waves of sad reality that insisted upon washing over her.

The sound of approaching wagon wheels drifted from the lane leading into the rolling section of land.

Sarah sprang to her feet. "He's here!" she whispered breathlessly, and moved to peer out the window.

"Don't let him see you," Amanda teased. "I'll go downstairs and find out if everything's ready."

There was a soft rap on the door. Mrs. Randolph opened it and peeked around the jamb. "It'll be just a few minutes, my dears." Her glance fell upon the bride, and her eyes misted over. She stepped inside the room. "Oh now, just look at my sweet Sarah. Almost too purty to look at, I swear. I couldn't be prouder of you if I was your own ma."

Sarah Jane flew into the older woman's arms. "Don't you dare make me cry. I'll spoil your pretty new dress."

"Pshaw!" Mrs. Randolph clucked her tongue. "Don't pay me no mind, even if some of my mountain of happiness spills out of these old eyes." She switched her attention to Amanda, slowly assessing her from head to toe. "And my other sweet gal. Never were spring flowers as purty as the two of you."

Barely containing her own emotions, Amanda joined the huge hug.

Mrs. Randolph's bosom rose and fell as she tightened the embrace, then stepped back. "I'd imagine everybody's in the right spot by now. I'll go tell Cora to start the organ. Nelson Junior never told us his wife could play."

As the first reedy notes drifted to their ears, Amanda moved to the top landing. Her eyes grew wide at the breathtaking transformation of the staircase and parlor. While she and Sarah had been fussing with curls and gowns, masses of brilliant orange poppies and blue lupine had been gathered to fill garlands, vases, and centerpieces to near overflowing. Here and there, tall tapers lent a golden aura of candlelight to the lovely scene. Taking one of the nosegays of spring beauties that Mrs. Randolph had thoughtfully left on the hall table, Amanda slowly started down, aware that all eyes in the house were upon her.

Hair slicked back and in his Sunday best, Charlie Randolph met her at the bottom landing and offered an arm, then escorted her toward the fireplace, where Jared Hill, in a crisp new shirt and black suit, waited with the minister. Bethany and Tad, seated off to one side with Mrs. Randolph, waved and smothered giggles.

Amanda took her place, then watched Jared flick his attention toward the top of the stairs to his bride. His expression of awe almost shattered her fragile composure. It was all she could do to hold herself together as Mr. Randolph escorted Sarah Jane to the side of her husband-to-be.

Lost in remembrances of all that had transpired to bring this moment about, Amanda witnessed the simple ceremony as if it were a dream. . .a blur of loving looks, tender smiles and murmured vows, the breathless kiss. Soft laughter at the end brought her back to reality. She blinked away threatening tears and fortified herself to extend her best wishes to the newlyweds. "Much happiness," she managed to whisper as she hugged Sarah.

Returning the embrace, her sister kissed Amanda's cheek. "Oh Mandy. . .I never knew there could be so much happiness as I feel right at this moment."

Amanda moved into Jared's open arms next. "I always wanted a brother," she told him. "I'm so glad Sarah chose you. May God bless you both."

He gave a light squeeze. "I'll take care of her for you. I promise."

"I'm sure you will. Be happy. God bless you both."

He nodded. "When you come to visit, the kids will sing you a whole raft of new songs, I'll wager. They begged me to make sure she brings her guitar home with us."

Amanda's lips parted. "You really like her music?"

"Well, sure! Can't carry a tune in a bucket, myself, but Sarah's pretty voice pleasures me."

Amanda had to laugh. After a lavish celebration of Mrs. Randolph's grandest fare, everyone went outside to see the newlyweds off.

Daylight was fading into a watercolor glory of muted rose and mauve as the setting sun gilded the edges of slender clouds low on the western horizon. A perfect end to a perfect day, Amanda decided. She bent to kiss Bethany and Tad, then their father swept them up into the wagon bed.

Sarah Jane threw her arms around Amanda once more, and they hugged hard for a long silent moment. Amanda knew instinctively that her sister was no more able to utter a word than she. Finally they eased apart with a teary smile. "Be happy," Amanda whispered again as Jared came to whisk his bride away.

Waving after them, watching until the wagon was but a speck in the distance, Amanda's heart was filled to bursting. She had never known such happiness.

Or such sadness.

———※———

Amanda plucked her shawl from a hook by the door and tossed it about her shoulders, then grabbed the parcel containing the men's shirts she'd finished the night before. "Good-bye, Mrs. Randolph," she called out. "I'm going now."

"Take care on the road," came the older woman's answer from the backyard, where she was beating rugs on a clothesline.

Amanda drove the wagon at a leisurely pace toward the teeming settlement of Sacramento, whose level of noise and activity seemed to increase constantly. Every day brought more and more newcomers to replace those who had pulled up stakes and moved on to the next gold field. New businesses sprang up overnight in the very structures abandoned only days before. And an amazing number of lonesome, homesick men appeared at Amanda's shop on the pretext of needing a button sewed on or a tear mended. She never imagined she'd receive so many proposals! But after having her heart shattered two times already, marriage was the last thing on her mind. Inhaling the heady scent of the spring flowers adorning the greening countryside, Amanda wondered if there were as many farther north, where Sarah had gone two weeks past. Perhaps one day soon, after the newlyweds had settled in, it might be fun to take the stage and visit. After all, the store was hers, and she could close it up whenever she took a fancy. Smiling at the thought, Amanda felt considerably more cheerful.

Dear Lord, her heart prayed. *Please watch after my dear Sarah Jane. I'm lost without my sister, my best friend, my confidant. I miss her so, yet I would never begrudge her this happiness. It still humbles me to think back on the indescribable journey You kept us through. Deserts, swamps, horrific storms, torturous mountains—to say nothing of how easily I might have drowned that day...*

As happened so often despite all her best efforts to the contrary, the memory of Seth Holloway intruded. Amanda had never so much as spoken his name aloud since the incident at the Green River...but a small, secret part of her couldn't help wondering what had become of the man. "Oh, what does it matter?" she hissed. The farm horse twitched an ear her way. Chagrined, Amanda returned her attention to the road.

Guiding the gelding along the bustling dirt streets of town, she took pride coming into view of the painted sign above her own enterprise. *Apparel and Alterations,* grand forest green letters proclaimed, then in much finer print, *A. J. Shelby, Proprietor.* She turned alongside and drove around to park in back of the small square building Mr. Randolph and Charlie had fitted with shelves and counters months ago.

Using the rear entrance, Amanda hung her floral-trimmed bonnet on a peg, then went through the swinging half doors to the salesroom. There she slid the shirred curtains apart on the front window and turned the Open sign out...duties she would perform every day, save Sundays, for the rest of her life. It was her lot, and what she had planned—or, nearly so, anyway. She would get used to the solitude. To help matters, she would look for a room to rent this afternoon as well, so it would no longer be necessary to burden the kind Randolphs or tie up their wagon. Thus decided, she began tidying the simple shop in readiness for the day's business.

After eating a bite at noon, Amanda walked several doors down the street to Mrs. Patterson's boardinghouse and put a deposit on a room that only that day had been vacated by a former tenant. Then, returning to her own shop, she tackled the ledgers.

The bell above the entrance interrupted the chore. Amanda set her quill aside and peered toward the dark figure silhouetted against the bright daylight. "How may I—?"

He removed his hat.

"W–why, Mr. Holloway!" Amanda gasped, rising to her feet.

Seth watched the blood drain from her face. He had been similarly shocked himself when, moments ago, he'd exited the Crown Hotel a few doors beyond the boardinghouse and glimpsed Amanda as she strolled to a clothing store up the street. He'd have recognized her anywhere, even with that long hair of hers tucked ever so primly into her bonnet.

He gave a perfunctory nod and settled for a simple greeting. "Good day," emerged on his second try.

"W—what are you doing here? I mean, you're the last person I ever—" Amanda's expression was one of utter confusion as she stood still, her mouth agape.

Another nod. Seth suddenly realized his hand was crushing his good hat and eased his grip. Lost in those glorious green eyes, he couldn't recall a word of the great speech he'd worked out so carefully in his head through the Oregon winter. He cleared his throat. "You're well?" *Great beginning, idiot!*

"Yes. . .fine. . .and you?"

"Not bad. Your sister, she's well?" It was all he could do not to roll his eyes at this inane conversation.

She nodded, then blinked quite suddenly and shook her head as if to clear it. "What are you doing in Sacramento?"

No point beating around the bush, when the truth was so much easier to get out. He shored up his insides. "Looking for you, actually."

"I—I don't understand," she said, her fine eyebrows arching higher. "Why would you—?"

Seth raked his fingers through his hair. "Sorry, I never asked if you were busy, Miss Sh—I mean—are you? I won't take much of your time."

She frowned, still perplexed. "I'm not busy just now."

"Good." A tiny flicker of hope coursed through him. He breathed a quick prayer that the Lord would loosen his tongue. "I must have asked at a hundred gold camps if anyone had seen you or knew of you. I was just about to give up, when you appeared out of the blue, just down the street."

Her expression remained fixed.

"I've been wanting very much to apologize," he went on, "for the callous things I said that day at the river. They were rude and completely uncalled for."

Amanda moved nearer the swinging doors and sank slowly to one of the chairs occupying either side of them. "Really, Mr. Holloway, the incident has long since been forgotten, I assure you."

"Not by me, it hasn't." He paused. "Do you mind if I sit down?"

"Oh. Not at all." She indicated the other chair.

Noticing the absence of a wedding band during her gesture, Seth thought it odd, but figured her preferences were none of his business. Obviously Hill must be an addlebrain, unconcerned about letting the world know she was taken. "As I was saying, I came to tell you how sorry I am. My partner seemed to take singular pleasure in pointing out what a cad I was—which is true. It's gnawed at me ever since."

"Well, pray, suffer no more, then. I accept your apology." A tiny smile softened her face, revealing a touch of her old feisty spirit. He didn't realize how much he'd missed it. Missed her.

"Splendid." Swallowing, Seth stood to his feet. "Then I won't keep you from your work any longer. Thank you for hearing me out. I wish you well."

"And you," she whispered.

Watching him cross to the door, Amanda rose, still in shock over his sudden appearance. "Mr. Holloway?" He paused, his hand on the latch, and turned.

"Since you've come so far, and all. . .might I offer you some tea?" At her rash invitation, Amanda felt her knees wobble as she rose. The whole thing seemed unreal, dreamlike.

"That would be. . .kind. Yes, thank you."

She waved toward the chair again. "I'll be only a moment. I had some brewing in the back room." Hastening there, she filled two cups and returned. By sheer determination she willed her hand not to tremble as she gave one of the cups to him. There was certainly no reason to be nervous.

"Thank you."

"I don't see any familiar faces in town," she said, noting the presence of circles under his dark eyes, a day or two's growth of beard. And his boots were dusty. He really must have been traveling. For some unaccountable reason, she thought that was sweet. Touching. She felt her face growing warm. He couldn't be the ogre she had painted him after all. His gaze, wandering about the premises, returned to her. "This your place?"

She nodded, gathering herself. "Didn't you see the sign?"

"I wasn't paying much attention."

"Oh. Well, it was Sarah's and mine, until she left."

"Left?" He raised the tea to his mouth.

"Moved, actually. To Mount Shasta, after she and Jared married."

He swallowed too quickly and choked, and some of the scalding brew spilled over on his hand. The cup crashed to the floor and shattered in a thousand pieces as russet spokes of tea stained the plank floor. He knelt to collect the shards. "How clumsy. Sorry."

Amanda was more concerned about him. "But you've burned yourself. Let me look at it." Before he could argue, she knelt beside him and took his work-roughened hand in hers. Gently she unraveled the clenched fingers, turning them this way and that to assess the reddened skin. "It's not"—she raised her lashes, finding his face mere inches from her own—"not too bad." The last words were barely audible.

She released her hold even as her face turned every bit as scarlet as his burn. Why had she been so impetuous? This man somehow managed to bring out the absolute worst in her—and had since the first time their paths had crossed a summer ago. She'd never been more humiliated. . .unless she counted those half-dozen other times she'd been in his presence. She tried to regather her dignity while easing graciously back onto her chair seat.

He sputtered into a laugh. Then roared.

Hiking her chin, Amanda turned her back. Perhaps he wasn't the gentleman she'd thought she'd glimpsed mere moments ago. "I'll thank you not to make fun of me."

"Oh, I'd never make fun of you, Amanda," he said in all sincerity. "I promise you that."

It was the first time he had ever called her by her given name. And it sounded so—different, in that raspy voice of his. Her heart hammered erratically against her ribs as she turned and shyly met his gaze.

He wasn't laughing now...but a strange almost-smile caught at her, stealing her breath. "You truly came all this way just to see me?" she asked in wonder.

"Mostly. I'm trying to acquire some good horseflesh for my new venture, so I answer every advertisement I come across. But in my travels, I've been looking for you." He reached to brush a few stray hairs from her temple as his intense gaze focused on her eyes. "Everywhere."

Her mouth went dry. "That's—that's really—" Unable to think straight, she moistened her lips.

"I thought I could forget you, Amanda Shelby," he continued. "Tried my hardest to. Drove Red crazy with my mutterings. That day I saw you turn off the trail, I figured you would be marrying that widower. Even when I saw you today, I thought you'd become his wife by now." His face blanched. "Or someone else's. Are you promised to anyone?"

She shook her head, wondering where this was all leading, fearing the hope that it could go anywhere at all. And did she want it to?

"Good." He appeared visibly relieved. "Then I might as well go for broke. If I were to stay on at the hotel here for a while—" He swallowed nervously. "What I mean is, would you be opposed to being courted? By me?"

Amanda felt suddenly light-headed and took hold of a spindle of the chair to steady herself. "Aren't you forgetting the matter of my being—how did you put it—brainless and foolhardy, wasn't it?"

Seth had the grace to smile, though it was tinged with more than a little guilt. "I deserve that. I've been unbearably thoughtless to you. But I know now that I was way off course, Amanda. After you drove off the trail and out of my life, I had to face up to the way I'd mistreated you—and forsaken the Lord. I finally sought His forgiveness and then knew that to have true peace I needed to seek yours as well. I'm no longer the man you met in Independence. I've changed. Because of you. I'm asking for a chance to undo that bad impression I made on you. . .if you'll allow me to."

Looking at him, Amanda could see how vulnerable he was. There had been a considerable amount of ill feeling between them, but thinking back, she could recall sensing almost from the onset of the journey west that he was trustworthy and honest. He affected her in ways she'd never before experienced, stirred chords within her soul as no man she had ever known. And she felt profound inner peace about his offer, because for longer than she cared to admit, she had been in love with Seth Holloway.

All things considered, she had only one choice. . .to be honest in return. "I would be truly honored, Seth, to have you court me."

His vulnerability evaporated, leaving a fragile hopefulness in its place. He expelled a ragged breath and drew her close, close to the beating of his heart. "I promise you, Amanda, you will never be sorry."

Raising her lashes, Amanda tipped her head back, needing to glimpse again the intensity of the love he made no effort to disguise. Seeing it, she smiled.

Seth held her gaze for a heartbeat, then slowly lowered his head, until his lips were barely a breath from hers. Then with tenderest reverence, he kissed her.

Amanda felt her heart sing and wanted the moment to last forever. But all too soon he eased away.

"I've wanted to do that for a long time," he murmured huskily.

"And I wished for a long time that you had." The remark came in all honesty.

He wrapped his arms about her just as the bell above the door tinkled, announcing a customer.

Seth took a step back, and a comical spark of mischief glinted in his dark eyes. "Well, thank you kindly, miss," he said with a mock bow. "That's mighty friendly service, I must say. I'll be by later for that new shirt." With that, he exited, whistling.

Amanda smiled after him. *Yes, come back later, my love. I'll be here waiting.*

Sally Laity has written both historical and contemporary novels, including a coauthored series for Tyndale House, nine Heartsong romances, and twelve Barbour novellas. She considers it a joy to know that the Lord can touch other hearts through her stories. Her favorite pastimes include quilting for her church's Prayer Quilt Ministry and scrapbooking. She makes her home in the beautiful Tehachapi Mountains of Southern California with her husband of over fifty years and enjoys being a grandma and a great-grandma.

Lessons in Love

by Nancy Lavo

DEDICATION

To Debra and Louis, precious friends and wonderful role models of courage and strength. And in loving memory of Casey, their daughter, a seven-year-old freckle-faced spirit whose too-short life inspired so many.

What glorious reunion heaven will be!

CHAPTER 1

Danger.

Frissons of energy, like icy fingers, shot up Luke's spine. Every nerve in his body was on alert. Life on the fringes gave a man a sixth sense about danger, and right now that sense was screaming life and death.

Luke scanned the area. Though in the deepening shadows of twilight it appeared he was alone, the feeling of imminent danger intensified. He nudged his horse through the swaying grasses toward the copse of trees fifty yards ahead, slowing as he reached the perimeter. Without a sound he dismounted, pulled his rifle from his saddle, and crept through the tangle of mesquite to the other side. At the sound of voices, he froze.

"Is he dead?"

"How would I know? Check his pockets. See how much he's carrying."

Not ten feet from where Luke stood, two men, their backs to him, crouched over a third man lying motionless on the ground. Luke stepped out from the trees and cocked his rifle. "Move away from him."

They whirled around to face Luke. The first man, scarecrow-thin and clad in tattered butternuts, pulled a pistol and fired.

Luke was faster. He fired, felling the gunman. His stunned companion didn't appear to suffer from an overabundance of loyalty, and without a backward glance he sprinted to his horse, scrambled into the saddle, and galloped off.

Luke stepped over the body of his would-be assailant to kneel at the side of the unconscious victim. He was a large man, probably in his late forties. His cotton shirt was torn and dirty, but dry. No sign of a gunshot wound. Luke's gently probing fingers located an egg-sized lump on the back of his head. Not fatal, but sure to bring on a headache like a mule kick.

The man stirred, blinking twice in an effort to focus. "What—?" He stiffened at the sight of Luke.

"I won't hurt you."

"Two men," he gasped. "Ambush."

Luke laid a calming hand on the agitated man's chest. "They won't bother you now."

Unconvinced, he pushed Luke's hand away and struggled to a sitting position, his glance falling on the body beside him. His eyes darted back to Luke. "Where's the other one?"

"Rode off."

The man relaxed then and lowered himself to the ground. He closed his eyes to digest the information. After a long silence, he reopened them, leveling his gaze on Luke. "You saved my life."

Luke shrugged.

"Not many folks around here would stick their necks out like that." He shook his head, wincing as the bump on his head met the hard ground. "These are sad times for Texas. Since the war, we've been overrun with thieves. Bad enough the carpetbaggers are stealing us blind, but when our own turn on us. . ." His voice drifted off.

The man pushed himself back up and squinted at Luke, studying him in the falling shadows. "I don't know you." The statement wasn't unfriendly, merely curious. "New to the area or just passing through?"

Luke didn't have a good answer so he shrugged again.

His reticence didn't slow the other man down. "We could use a man like you around here. Somebody good with a gun to stand for law and order. My neighbors and I got us a ranchers' association. We'd pay top dollar for your services. We'd make it worth your while to settle here."

Luke wondered if that offer would stand in the light of day. "Not looking to stay."

The man considered him a moment before speaking. "I understand. If you ever change your mind, you look me up at the Double-L Ranch." He extended a beefy hand. "I'm Jed Crandall."

"Jed." Luke nodded his acknowledgment. "I'm Luke."

<hr />

Despair was not an option.

How many times had she told herself those very words? Despair was not an option when war broke out and claimed the lives of her older brothers. Despair was not an option when she lost her parents to grief and her family home to fire. Deborah had stood fast in the face of each crisis, knowing her younger brother depended on her to be strong.

Deborah raised her grime-streaked face to the horizon—to her future—and swallowed hard. Despair might not be an option, but it was surely a temptation.

"Is that it?" an excited voice squeaked from the wagon. "Is that our new home?"

Somehow, *home* seemed too fine a word for the primitive log structure. *Shanty. Shack. Hovel.* Deborah thought those would be more accurate descriptions of the desolate site.

Her brother released a long, contented sigh. "It's the Promised Land. Just like you said."

Deborah stared into her brother's freckled face. Was he serious? His front-toothless grin assured her he was. The depthless imagination and optimism of a seven-year-old boy was staggering. She found herself smiling back at him, in spite of serious misgivings.

"Shall we go on then? Shall we inspect our new home?"

Case whooped his response, and Deborah urged the team of oxen into motion. They passed through a broken gate in the ramshackle split-rail fence and entered the yard of packed dirt and tall clumps of bright green weeds. She led the creaking wagon up the dusty rutted road to the house and halted the team in front of the porch.

The house did not improve on closer inspection.

"Can we go in?" Case asked. "Can I see where I'm going to sleep?"

"In a minute, dearest. Let me catch my breath."

Deborah loosened her heavy black bonnet and pulled it off her head, leaving it to dangle by the ribbons. A cooling gentle spring breeze whispered across her forehead and stirred the tendrils of hair on her neck. She removed a dusty linen handkerchief from her pocket and swiped at the sheen of perspiration at her hairline.

Now that they were finally here, her first order of business would be to peel off a few heavy layers of clothes. That and a bath. And not just a quick sponge bath at the bank of a creek, but a full sink-down-to-your-neck bath, the kind she hadn't enjoyed since they left Louisiana.

"Have you caught it yet? Your breath, I mean?"

Deborah turned to her impatient brother and chuckled. "I have. Are you ready to go in?" Not that the answer wasn't written across his impish face.

He scooted to the wagon's edge where she caught him under the arms and carefully lifted him down. He staggered before finding his balance. Once stabilized, he slowly made his way across the hard-packed dirt to the plank porch. His awkward gait made progress slow, but his wide smile never faltered.

The scarred wooden door of the house was slightly ajar. Though she knew the house was theirs, Deborah felt uneasy about entering. Her brother suffered no such qualms. He pushed open the door and stepped inside, his sister at his heels. "Welcome home," he called brightly.

They paused just inside the door to allow their eyes to adjust to the shadowy interior. Case found his voice first. "It doesn't look much like the Promised Land, does it?"

Deborah couldn't decide whether to laugh or cry. Case was correct. Their dream house wasn't a dream. It was a nightmare.

They were standing in a hall, some seven feet wide, which ran the length of the house, front to back. Square openings in the mud-chinked walls on the left and right led into rooms. But it was not the length of the hall, or the size of the rooms that held Deborah's attention. It was the filth.

The hallway was littered with dried leaves, broken furniture, tin cans, and heaven only knew what else. Deborah shuddered as something small and furry darted out from behind a pile of refuse and scurried down the hall in the opposite direction.

"Maybe it's better in there," Case suggested, pointing to the room on the right.

Slowly and somewhat reluctantly, they picked their way through the trash to the opening and stood there, studying the first room. No improvement. This room, obviously the kitchen, was also a disaster. A large cast-iron stove stood along the far wall. Two tall windows flanked the stove, but the thick film on the panes of glass prevented light from pouring in. Toward the center of the room was a wooden table and two chairs. Two more chairs, each missing a leg and part of the back, were lying in a heap beside the table. Trash was scattered everywhere. More leaves, fragments of pottery and paper, and empty cans covered the floor and tabletop.

They crossed the hall to the room on the left and found more of the same. Leaves and twigs carpeted the floor. Skeletal remains of furniture lay in dusty heaps. Ashes and charred remnants of logs clogged the opening of the large smoke-blackened stone fireplace on the far wall.

Deborah was so stunned by the degree of deterioration, she had forgotten her brother's presence until she heard him squeal.

"Look, Debs. A loft." He pointed to the second-story room opening onto the area where they stood. He eyed the rickety ladder longingly. "I'll bet that's where the beds are. Do you suppose I can sleep up there?"

The hopeful look in his eyes almost broke her heart. "I'm sorry, Case. You could fall. You're not strong enough to climb a ladder."

Tears shimmered in his eyes as he nodded.

His stoic capitulation was harder for Deborah than if he had ranted and raved. She hated the unfairness of it all. She hated to deprive him of the adventure he sought, and yet his welfare was hers to protect. She took his small hand in hers and gave it a squeeze. "What do you say, we make you a nice bed down here?"

He mustered a brave smile. "Okay, Debs."

They found two more rooms, much smaller than the first, coming off the hall at the back of the house. The room behind the kitchen, with its steeply sloped ceiling, must have been used for storage. Crude shelves lined the walls, and several wooden crates were stacked haphazardly beneath them.

Across from there, beneath the loft, was a narrow room, empty except for a lumpy straw mattress pushed against the wall and a brightly woven blanket folded neatly on top.

Deborah fought back a rush of hot tears. Plans for this house and the future she and her brother would build here had fueled her dreams for months. The dismal reality of the place made her doubt the wisdom of dragging themselves away from comfort and familiarity to an uncertain future in Texas.

Case's hand trembled slightly within hers, a sure sign he was tiring. "Come, dearest," she said. "Let's find a place to sit for a while." As the room where they currently stood was by far the cleanest in the house, they sat on the straw pallet. For a moment, they were silent.

"It doesn't look like a very happy place, does it?" Case asked at last.

His dispirited observation plucked at her heartstrings. Case had the rare gift of seeing the brightest side of everything. She could count on one hand the number of times he'd given in to negativity. This time she could only blame herself. She'd spent the entire journey telling him how great their new life in Texas would be. The reality of the house didn't match the "Promised Land" she'd described.

"I think we should pray." Even as she made the suggestion, Deborah went to her knees.

"Okay," came Case's unenthusiastic reply as he obediently knelt beside her.

"The Bible tells us God gives us a garment of praise for a

spirit of heaviness. Let's praise God for all the good things He's provided for us since we left Louisiana."

"You start." Obviously, Case was not convinced.

"Well, hmmm." Deborah bowed her head and closed her eyes as she searched for something positive to say. "Heavenly Father, we acknowledge You as the source of every good thing. I thank You for. . .for the good weather You granted us for the journey."

She paused, waiting for Case to chime in. Silence.

She cleared her throat. "Yes, well, I'm also very thankful for the adequate provisions we enjoyed."

Case shifted beside her. "Especially Aunt Mimi's tea cakes."

Deborah bit back a smile. "Thank You for the dependable wagon and team."

"And thank You for Aunt Mimi's bonbons."

Deborah took a deep breath to speak her next words, which truly stretched her faith. It would take all of Case's imagination and optimism. "We thank You for supplying all our needs with this house."

More silence. Evidently Case's imagination and optimism didn't extend quite that far. Maybe a little prompting would help. "Thank You for the strong door."

"Thank You for the beeyoutiful loft and ladder."

Deborah ignored the painful compression of her heart. "And the cookstove."

"And the Indian."

"And the—" Deborah's eyes snapped open as she swiveled to stare at her brother. "The what?"

"The Indian," he repeated calmly. "The big one standing right there."

CHAPTER 2

The woman moved fast. In a flurry of shawls and skirts she scrambled to her feet and swept the boy behind her. She raised fear-filled eyes to him and spoke with admirable defiance for one who trembled visibly. "Do not touch me."

There was a gruesome thought—touching that strangely lumpy and head-to-toe dirty woman. Luke lifted his hands slowly, palms out. "No, ma'am."

Not a chance. He wouldn't risk touching her with a stick. She could be anywhere from age fifteen to fifty-five for all he could tell since a thick layer of grime on her face obscured her features. Except for her eyes. Pupils dilated with fear glowed from luminous pools of green, the rich color of summer grass. She blinked as he spoke.

His answer appeared to surprise her, whether because it was delivered in perfect English or the fact that he had no intention of molesting her he couldn't be sure.

"Y–y–you must leave," she commanded while maintaining her wobbly warrior stance in front of the boy. "You don't belong here."

He folded his arms across his chest and lifted a brow. "And you do?"

Again she looked startled, and this time more than a little annoyed. She straightened and thrust out her grimy chin. "I most certainly do. This is my home."

"This place belongs to Cyrus Marbury."

The child, slender and pale with wide green eyes like the woman's, managed to peer around her wide skirts to ask, "Do you know my uncle Cyrus?"

Luke crouched down to meet the little fellow eye to eye. "Very well. I helped him build this place."

The child tugged her skirts. "You see, Deborah. He's not a bad Indian. He's friends with Uncle Cyrus."

"*If* he were friends with Cyrus, then he would certainly know Uncle Cyrus went west and left the house to my father."

"Went west—?"

"Indeed he has, and if you were any friend at all— What are you laughing at?"

Luke threw back his head and howled. "The old coot. I can't believe he really did it."

When she was angry she seemed to forget to be wary. He could hear her foot tapping impatiently beneath the skirts. "Yes, yes, I'm sure it's all very amusing, but the fact remains, the house is mine, and you don't belong here."

"Your father's," Luke corrected. Ordinarily Luke wasn't one to argue, but for some reason, he enjoyed watching the green-eyed woman get riled. "The house belongs to your father. Is he here?"

The child popped around again. "Papa is in heaven. With Jesus."

"Hush." She pushed the child behind her before raising her dirty face to Luke. "I want you to go. Now."

"Fine." Luke took a step toward her and could swear he saw her blanch beneath the layer of dirt. He lifted his hands to placate her. "My blanket," he said by way of explanation. "Behind you. On the bed."

"Oh." She sidestepped him, dragging the boy behind her, to give him a wide berth.

Luke could feel her eyes on his back as he scooped up the

folded blanket and tucked it under his arm. He said nothing as he turned and walked from the room. He was at the back door when he heard the child call out, "Come back for a visit, won't you?"

Luke could hear the woman scolding the boy in hushed, furious tones and heard the childish voice ring out in protest, "But I *liked* him."

Luke smiled as he exited the house.

His horse, a large paint mare, nickered as he entered the darkened lean-to that served as a stall. "Time to go, old girl."

Luke tossed the worn leather saddle over her back and cinched it. He slid his rifle, which he'd left leaning against the inside wall, into the holster before swinging into the saddle and riding across the yard and out through the broken gate without looking back.

He replayed the short encounter as he rode away. The last thirty minutes had been a novelty for Luke. Not the part about being thrown out. Rejection was as familiar to him as breathing. The unusual part was that someone wanted to see him again. Of course, that someone was a child, too young to know that Indians, more specifically half-breeds, were not fit companions. Still it was a nice feeling to be wanted.

No one wanted Luke. Occasionally someone like Crandall came along, someone with a need who appreciated Luke's skill with a gun. But with the exception of the small boy back there, no one had ever wanted Luke for Luke.

Except maybe Cyrus.

Ten years ago, Cyrus had saved his life. He had taken in Luke, a starving fifteen-year-old boy, and provided him with food to eat and a place to sleep. It didn't seem to bother Cyrus that Luke was a half-breed.

The thought of Cyrus brought a smile to Luke's face. Cyrus had always been a loner, not by necessity as Luke was, but by choice. He was a quiet, gentle man who preferred the wide-open spaces and sounds of nature to the noisy confines of a settlement. Yet he had welcomed a sullen teenager with open arms.

Luke reined in his horse and swiveled in the saddle to look

back at the house. He and Cyrus had built that house, log by log. For months they'd labored together in an odd kind of companionship that didn't require many words. For Luke it had been a comfortable time, though he couldn't have said which he liked more—the acceptance of another human being, or having a full stomach and warm bed.

But Luke hadn't stayed. The restlessness within him, like an itch that needed to be scratched, kept him moving. Cyrus understood. He'd let the boy go, to find whatever it was he sought, with the knowledge that a warm bed and hot meal always awaited him.

It had been several years since Luke had been back the last time. Evidently the tide of settlers from the East was enough of a threat to Cyrus's solitude for him to continue west. Luke hoped he'd find the peace he needed. He'd miss Cyrus.

Luke kicked up the horse and rode on, away from the memories of Cyrus and the only home he'd ever known. A home that now housed Cyrus's people.

They'd never make it, the lumpy woman and lame boy. Texas was a wild place. Life was hard, luxuries few. He'd give them a week before they'd had enough and packed up their wagon and headed back for wherever they'd come from.

Good riddance. It wasn't as if they were his problem.

Luke rode another few yards before his conscience stopped him. The memory of a half-starved kid wandering up to a campfire and his warm reception by Cyrus clung like a burr in his mind. He hadn't been Cyrus's problem, yet Cyrus had clothed him and fed him.

Could Luke do any less for Cyrus's people?

Luke sighed. At times like this he hated the strong sense of justice that reared up in him. He didn't know where it came from, only that it forever had him stepping into fights that weren't his or sticking his nose in other people's business to right wrongs that weren't any of his concern.

Cyrus had said it was honor. Luke thought it was crazy. Still, he knew better than to resist it. He knew from experience it'd plague him till he finally acted.

Luke sighed again. He'd have to take care of Cyrus's folks.

He was no fool. He knew the woman didn't like him. She'd never willingly accept his help. There seemed to be a lot of pride lurking beneath all that dirt. Pride and fear. Any assistance from him would have to be anonymous.

Their biggest need would be protection. The twosome would be easy prey for anybody looking for trouble. The sorry state of Cyrus's house was evidence that drifters had been using the place as home. They might take exception to the new owners.

Even as the thought surfaced, Luke grimaced. He'd been in such an all-fired hurry to leave he hadn't thought to ask if they had a gun to defend themselves. Not that it would do them much good. He could almost smile at the picture of the woman pointing a shaky gun at an intruder.

Resolved to carry out what he knew to be a thankless mission, Luke redirected his horse, heading southeast toward the small tree-covered rise he and Cyrus had called home over the months it took them to build the main house. They'd nailed a few rough boards together to provide basic shelter. It'd been years since Luke had thought about the shack, but if it still stood, it would be perfect for his needs. It was far enough from the house they'd never know he was there, and protection enough to keep out the rain should they be lucky enough to get some.

Minutes later he topped the rise. For a long moment he scoured the landscape, looking for signs of the shack. Finally he caught a glimpse of a weathered gray board from behind a stand of mesquites and he rode over to investigate.

Even standing just two feet in front of the building, he'd never have noticed it had he not known it was there. Thick vines entangled with other vegetation completely covered the small wooden structure. This was perfect. His presence would go undetected.

Luke dismounted and walked to where he knew the door was located. With the knife he wore in a sheath tied to his thigh, he cut through the weeds and vines and pulled them off, discarding them in a pile. Then he pried off the boards he and Cyrus had nailed over the door to keep out varmints. Finally he could push open the door and step inside. Inside the shack, the air was cool and stale. Threads of light sifted through the tiny cracks between the boards and shone on the thin layer of dust blanketing the room.

He left the door open, allowing the breeze to cleanse the air. The single room wasn't fancy, but no worse than many of the places Luke had stayed over the years. Besides, it wasn't as if he'd be here very long. In a week he'd be back on the road, seeking answers to ease the restlessness within him.

Chapter 3

By nightfall Deborah was dead on her feet. She ached in places she didn't realize she had. But with that ache came a tired sense of accomplishment.

She'd unloaded the bulk of the load from the wagon, unhitched the team, and settled them and the milk cow for the night, and prepared a meager dinner for Case and herself from a can of beans and leftover biscuits. Sadly, she didn't have the energy left to pump and heat water for a bath, so the much-awaited soak would have to wait till tomorrow.

Her brother didn't share her exhaustion. "What do you think, Debs? Did I do a good job?" His freckled face beamed up at her with the question. "Didn't I make it cozy for you?"

"Dearest," she said with a tired smile, "you've made it very cozy. Just like home." Truthfully only a bear could feel at home amidst such squalor, but she'd never say so to Case. His natural good humor rebounded nicely from this morning's low ebb, and he was obviously proud of his effort to make the place more homey. While she unloaded their belongings, he had cleared a path down the hall and into the kitchen using the broom they brought with them.

Over dinner, he confessed to Deborah he hadn't gotten as far as he would have liked, but he'd spent a great deal of time with a lovely nest of baby mice he'd found in the hall. A nest that he promised his horrified sister he would relocate outside first thing in the morning.

Case pulled his chair closer to hers and sat beside her as he surveyed the room. "It *is* the 'Promised Land,'" he said, slipping his hand into hers, "just like you said it would be."

Deborah winced. The "Promised Land." From the stories her father told of a grand house with every luxury, she envisioned something much different than a rustic log home with puncheon floors. She supposed having a water pump in the house was a great convenience, but at the moment, she couldn't muster up much enthusiasm.

"It's late, Case. Let's have prayer, then get on to bed. Tomorrow will be another busy day." She knelt, slowly and painfully, onto the scuffed plank floor. Case joined her. "Heavenly Father, we thank You for our safe journey. We thank You for this house. Keep us safe tonight, we pray. In Jesus' name, Amen."

"Amen." Case struggled to his feet, picked up the pewter candlestick from the kitchen table, and limped across the room and down the hall to the small room at the back of the house where Deborah and he had decided they would sleep until they could clean up the larger room with the fireplace.

Earlier in the day, Deborah had dragged in the mattress and made it up with fresh sheets. Case placed the candle on the wooden crate they'd converted to a nightstand and climbed onto the bed and snuggled in. Deborah pulled the covers up tightly under his chin.

"Aren't you coming to bed, Debs?"

Deborah shook her head. "Not just yet. I thought I'd check to be sure the house is locked up tight before I get in." She pressed a kiss to his forehead and stood up to leave.

"I wonder where our Indian is tonight. Do you think he has a warm bed to sleep in?"

Our Indian. Deborah shivered at the thought. If she lived to be hundred, she'd never be so frightened as she had been this morning when that giant savage had appeared in the room.

Mercy! What a monster. He'd looked big and mean with his broad shoulders and piercing dark eyes, and as far as she was concerned, she hoped they never saw his face again.

"I'm sure he's fine, Case. Now go to sleep." She took the candle with her, its flickering light casting eerie shadows in the cluttered hall. She thought she saw something move just inches from her hem and she screeched.

"What is it, Debs?" Case called from his bed.

She forced herself to take a deep breath and speak calmly. "It's nothing, dearest. Go to sleep."

Deborah clasped a hand over her hammering heart. She needed to get ahold of herself. There was nothing in the hall, just as there had been no one watching her all day. It was just a case of nerves. She'd been jumpy since they met the Indian. He would be long gone by now. She had nothing to fear.

Still, she checked the latch on the back door for about the fiftieth time since she'd bolted it this afternoon. Secure. Just as it had been the other forty-nine times.

With her skirt clutched in one hand and the candlestick in the other, Deborah moved carefully down the hall to check the front door. She hadn't been able to latch it. The hinges of the door were so badly bent, the door wouldn't close completely, so she had to be satisfied with bracing it shut with her Sheraton trunk. She had placed several glass jars on top of the trunk so that if someone tried to move it during the night, the jars would fall and alert her to the intruder.

Satisfied that all was as it should be, Deborah returned to the bedroom. Soft snoring indicated Case was already asleep. She smiled into the darkness. At least one of them was enjoying their adventure.

She rested the candle on the crate and reached up to remove her dress. Her tired fingers stumbled over the buttons. Finally she finished the last of the long column of tiny shell buttons and slipped out of the black wool dress, letting it drop in a heap on the floor. Beneath it was a second dress, this one of heavy cotton twill, which she also unbuttoned and removed, adding it to the stack. Beneath the second dress was a blouse of lightweight cotton with tiny puffed sleeves and a gray skirt. Once out of the third outfit, Deborah removed the two layers of heavy petticoats and finally the pair of pants that had belonged to her eldest brother. The discarded clothing on the floor made an impressive mountain.

She sighed as cool night air brushed across her skin. Wearing only a light muslin chemise, she felt as though she could finally draw a full breath, her first one in weeks.

The idea of wearing the layers of clothing as a disguise was her Aunt Mimi's. Aunt Mimi was convinced that a young woman and child could not make the trip from Louisiana to Texas without attracting unwanted attention. The only way Deborah could reassure her aunt of their safety was to agree to disguise her youth by wearing layers of clothing, the top layer being heavy, black mourning clothes.

The disguise had worked wonderfully. All those clothes were hot and cumbersome, but she knew of no better way to avoid notice than to look the part of a frumpy widow. The fistful of ashes she'd scrubbed into her face and hair probably didn't hurt. Even that sharp-eyed Indian saw nothing but a dirty, shapeless hag.

She probably didn't need to keep wearing all those clothes once they'd arrived here, but seeing the Indian made her afraid to shed the bulky disguise. She still had the oddest feeling that he watched her throughout the day. Impossible, of course, she'd seen him ride away, but she couldn't shake the feeling her activities were being observed.

More nerves. She'd let the stress of the journey and need to protect her brother make her overwrought. Deborah bent to blow out the candle then crawled into bed beside her brother. She lay there listening to his rhythmic breathing and waited for sleep to claim her.

"Good morning, Debs. Are you awake yet? I'm awfully hungry."

Deborah's eyes shot open to meet those of her brother just inches from her face. "I'll be up in a minute."

Deborah closed scratchy lids over tired eyes. She'd slept little and fitfully through the night. Each sound had had her wide-awake and wondering if someone had broken in. Just as she would finally drift off to sleep, another noise would jolt her awake.

She forced herself to crawl out of the warm bed, shivering in the early morning chill, and donned the black wool mourning dress. Without the layers of clothing beneath it, Aunt Mimi's cast-off dress sagged and bagged unbecomingly. But Deborah found she wasn't quite ready to discard the disguise completely. Just in case.

She pinned up her long hair and wrapped it in a cotton turban as she'd seen servants do. It was difficult to do without a mirror and a goodly quantity of hair straggled from beneath the red calico headdress.

Deborah opened the back door slowly and carefully scanned the yard before going to the lean-to to milk the cow. The milking done, she handed the cow several fistfuls of hay, then carried the bucket of warm milk inside.

For breakfast, she and Case had the rest of the leftover biscuits topped with some of Aunt Mimi's peach preserves and a cup of frothy milk.

"As soon as we're finished, can I take the mouses outside, Debs?" her brother asked between mouthfuls.

She looked into his hopeful face and smiled. "Yes, you may take the mice outside, but you must promise me to be very careful. If you see anyone, I want you to hurry back inside. You must wear a warm coat to keep from being chilled, and you must wear my leather gloves to protect you from bites."

"Oh no," Case said with a solemn shake of his head. "These mouses don't bite. They like me."

"I'm sure that's true, dearest, but you must wear the gloves. And hurry back inside, just as soon as you have them settled."

Case gobbled the last of his breakfast and hopped up from the table to hobble out to his beloved creatures. Deborah lingered at the table only a moment more before picking up the dishes and carrying them over to the tub to be washed.

First on her agenda for the morning was to clean the kitchen. She stood in the center of the room, hands on hips, and tried to decide which part of this impossible mess she should tackle first. Her eyes lit on the stove. She'd been afraid to light it last night, fearful that the thick layer of grease might ignite and burn down the house. She'd have to clean it before she could use it. Since growing boys needed more than cold beans, she might as well get that done first.

Before she could scrub it, she'd have to empty the overflowing ashes. She scooped them out and placed them in several of the large tin cans she found on the floor.

That accomplished, Deborah pushed up the sleeves of her dress, pumped a bucket full of cold water, and with a stiff brush and a bar of lye soap, she set to work. The accumulation of grease clung stubbornly to the stove. It took three changes of water and several hours of backbreaking work before the stove was clean.

By then, Case had come in to join her. "Oh Deborah, you should have seen the baby mouses. They were so cute."

"Mice," Deborah corrected automatically.

"They were pink and wiggly. Their little eyes weren't even open yet. I wanted to pick one up, but I remembered what you said about worrying the mama if I touched the baby, so I carried the whole nest of rags very carefully and put it out under a bush by the fence post, just like you said."

"Thank you, Case. I know they're happier outside."

Case nodded. "The mama twitched her whiskers at me. I think I saw her smile."

Deborah kissed him on the tip of his freckled nose. "I'm sure she did."

Case looked around the room. "I'm ready to help you clean. What can I do?"

"How about getting out your McGuffey reader? We have some lessons to catch up on."

Case wrinkled up his nose. "Aw, Debs, can't I help you instead? I could sweep some more."

How could she resist such a heartfelt plea delivered so sweetly? "You can clean today, but tomorrow it's back to the books. And remember, I don't want you to get overtired."

Case launched himself into her arms and pressed a great

smacking kiss on her cheek. "Thank you." He limped over to the broom propped against the wall and began sweeping so enthusiastically that he raised a cloud of dust in the air.

"Let's see if you can get some of that in the dustbin, dearest, and not all in our nostrils."

Case giggled with delight but did manage to calm his efforts enough to corral the dirt.

By suppertime the kitchen was much improved. The stove gleamed in the corner. The table and two chairs were washed, and glowed under a fresh coat of beeswax. The floor, though still scuffed, was free of dirt and trash.

"What's for supper, Debs?"

Supper! She'd been so busy scrubbing and cleaning, she'd forgotten about food. If she was going to prepare something hot, she'd have to light the stove, and she hadn't cut any wood. She glanced toward the still-dirty windows. Even through the grime it was plain the sun was already sinking in the sky. Too late to go out to chop wood, she'd have to make do with twigs or any branches she could find lying around the yard.

She took her shawl from its hook in the hall, and wrapped it around her shoulders before stepping out the back door onto the porch. The first thing that caught her eye was a large stack of wood lined up along the outer wall of the lean-to. She stopped to stare at the pile. Funny, she hadn't noticed it before.

The wood was split into large pieces, the kind that would work well in the fireplace, but a bit too big for the stove. Still, it was a blessing. Instead of having to scour the countryside for twigs, she had only to split the cut wood into smaller pieces to fit the stove. Deborah went back into the house for an ax and her cowhide gloves. Thirty minutes later she carried a nice bundle of split wood into the house and stacked it by the stove.

She regarded the fragrant pile of freshly cut wood with satisfaction. It should hold them till tomorrow evening, when she'd have to chop again. Deborah set the wood in the stove and lit it before beginning preparations for dinner.

Following a dinner of ham and biscuits, she heated several pots of water and filled a basin on the kitchen table for a bath. It wasn't a sink-down-to-your-neck soak, but she was too weary to fetch the heavy tin bathtub out of the wagon.

After Case was scrubbed clean and tucked into bed, Deborah peeled off her clothes and washed her hair and skin with a bar of sweet-smelling soap. It was the first time she'd felt clean in weeks. She still hadn't hung the mirror she'd brought from Louisiana and didn't know how she looked, but she felt much better.

That night, after checking the barricade at the front door and the latch on the back door, Deborah fell into bed, certain she'd be asleep in seconds. Hours later, still awake and alert to every sound in the strange house, she wondered if a body ever grew accustomed to functioning with only a few hours' sleep.

⟨⟩

The next day progressed in much the same manner. Deborah and Case were up with the sun and worked till nightfall, trying to make their log home habitable. Progress was slow but steady. Deborah still had her doubts about the wisdom of having left Louisiana, but they were fading as their new house took shape.

It was early evening and the chores were done when Deborah slipped on her shawl and stepped outside to chop another day's supply of wood. To her surprise, stacked on the far end of the woodpile, was a large pile of wood cut just the right size for the stove.

Twice she rubbed her eyes with fisted hands to be certain she wasn't seeing things. Had she been so tired last night that she hadn't noticed the smaller wood pieces? Was she so tired tonight that she was imagining the whole thing?

She approached the mysterious woodpile warily, looking from side to side in the yard to be certain she was alone before scooping up an armload and scurrying back into the house, bolting the door behind her.

She fought back a sense of panic and the hideous notion that someone had been watching them. Nonsense. She was tired, that's all. Surely tonight she'd get some sleep.

CHAPTER 4

S urely tonight I'll get some sleep," Luke said, stretching wearily in the saddle. He rubbed sleep-gritty eyes with his gloved hands. The first glimmering rays of dawn lanced across the wide Texas sky, signaling him he could head back to the shack to grab a couple of hours of sleep before he needed to get back on patrol.

His horse, familiar with the route she'd trod several times a day for the last week, needed no direction. She walked to the grassy patch on the far side of the rise and stopped. Luke dismounted and tied her loosely so that she might graze. He pulled his rifle from its sheath, then trudged up the short hill to the shack and his pallet.

Too tired to pull off his boots, Luke flopped down on the blanket and was out in minutes.

He awoke several hours later to the jeering calls of a mockingbird. For a moment he lay there, uncertain where he was. Seven days of short snatches of sleep, an hour here, two hours there, were beginning to take their toll. His thinking seemed continuously foggy, his senses dulled, his reflexes slowed.

Lack of sleep coupled with a meager diet of dried beef strips and underripe berries for a solid week left Luke feeling mean as a rattler. It was only the knowledge that his nursemaid vigil was up today that kept him sane.

He folded his blanket, a deeply ingrained habit of tidiness held over from his days with Cyrus, and laid it in the corner. He'd be back to collect it and seal up the shack after he made sure Lumpy and the boy were loaded up and on their way.

Rifle resting on his shoulder, Luke strode down the slope toward his horse with considerably more enthusiasm than he'd moved with in days. With the departure of the greenhorns, Luke's duty to Cyrus was fulfilled, freeing him to follow his own pursuits.

His week spent guarding Cyrus's people had left him plenty of time to think about his life, to plan his future. And if he hadn't been too tired to string two thoughts together, he'd have done just that. As it was, he resolved nothing. He was no closer to quieting that nagging voice of discontent than he had ever been.

His horse, still saddled from the evening's ride, stood patiently munching the tender shoots of grass. He stroked her nose and she nuzzled his arm. "Tour of duty is just about up, old girl. Soon, it'll be just the two of us again."

Luke climbed into the saddle and swung the horse around to head back to the main house. The sun's position in the sky told him it was close to noon. Cyrus's people should be packed and ready to leave.

They had grit for city people, Luke thought as he rode across the open field. They didn't belong here in Texas, couldn't have survived the hardships, but somehow he admired them for trying.

From what he'd observed, they were industrious people. Though Lumpy mostly kept indoors, he could tell by the growing pile of trash she'd hauled out that she'd been busy straightening the place up. Shame she'd done all that hard work for nothing. Maybe he should stick around a day or two and enjoy the fruits of her labor.

Luke approached the house from the rear. Since Lumpy had washed the windows day before yesterday, he couldn't ride up in front undetected.

Just as he suspected, the yard at the back of the house was

clear. The wagon and oxen were gone. He didn't bother to peek into the lean-to on his way past it, but he knew the milk cow would be gone as well.

A smile, his first in a week, stretched across his face. He slid off his horse, looped the reins around a post by the lean-to and stepped confidently onto the back porch. He pushed open the back door and walked inside, nearly colliding with Lumpy.

A piercing scream rent the air.

———⋇———

Deborah woke up tired, achy, and generally out of sorts after another night of fitful sleep. She'd washed her hair last evening, but had been too exhausted to sit in front of the stove to dry it before she went to bed. Now it curled in wild rebellion. She fought the curling mass for several minutes, trying to confine it in a nice, respectable knot on her head, but it refused to co-operate. Finally in exasperation she gave up and pulled it off her face with a length of blue ribbon, allowing the hair to wave down her back.

She eyed the folded black wool dress on the bedroom floor with disdain. She'd worn it every day for a week now, scrubbed in it, chopped wood in it, perspired in it. It was too filthy to con-template wearing it again. It was probably too filthy to use as a rag. It wouldn't surprise Deborah if the dress got up and walked around on its own.

The weather was too warm for wool anyway, she thought as she pulled her long-sleeved cotton dress from the nail where she'd hung it. She pulled the dress over her head and buttoned it, enjoying the comfortable fit after a week of wearing a sack. The cheerful cornflower-blue color gave her low spirits a lift. Since she didn't have the luxury of ruining any more clothes, she tied a full-length apron over the dress before going to the kitchen to start breakfast.

"What are we going to do today?" Case asked around a mouthful of biscuit.

"First thing this morning I'd like to find a nice place for the cow to graze since we've used up the little bit of hay we found in the lean-to. Then I'm going to harness up the team, and drive the wagon around to the front. I'm determined to get the tub in the house today, and since it won't fit through the back door, I'll have to bring it in through the front."

"Can I drive the team?" Case asked hopefully.

"No indeed. They're too much for you to handle. You could be hurt." At his crestfallen expression she added, "Maybe you'd like to help me find a nice grassy spot for Ruth."

Case lowered his eyes, but not before she read the hurt in them. "Okay."

Deborah felt guilty all morning. She felt guilty as they led Ruth, the cow, to a nice patch of tender green grass just outside the split-rail fence, she felt guilty as she harnessed the oxen and drove the wagon around to the front of the house. Though he never complained, she felt guilty every time she looked at her brother.

"Whoa." Deborah pulled the team to a halt. She secured the reins, then jumped down from the seat. "Shall we go have a bite to eat before I unload the tub?"

Case's eyes brightened at the mention of food. "That sounds great. I'm hungry."

She lifted him down and they walked in the front door together. "Why don't you sit at the table, and I'll fix us something tasty."

Case headed into the kitchen, while Deborah continued down the shadowed hall to the storeroom. She wasn't two feet from the back door when it swung open and a man stepped inside. Deborah screamed.

⟝⟞

"What are *you* doing here?" both shouted at once.

"I *live* here."

"Not anymore." The Indian pointed toward the door. "You're supposed to be leaving."

At that moment, Deborah was madder than she was tired. And that was saying something. "Who says?"

The Indian moved closer and thumped his broad chest. "I says."

Drawn by the noise, Case limped into the hall. "Oh Deborah," he cried in delight. "He's back. Our Indian has come back. Can he stay to dinner?"

"No, he can't stay to dinner," she snapped, her eyes never straying from the Indian's. "He's leaving."

The Indian advanced. "*I'm* not leaving. *You* are!"

Deborah's eyes shot wide at his close proximity. "Do not touch me!"

The Indian rolled his eyes in response. "Are we back to that again?"

Case wedged between the combatants. "Why does he say we're leaving? Where are we going?"

"Home," Luke said.

"Nowhere," Deborah said.

Case's head swiveled to study the Indian first, then his sister. "I don't want to go home," he said in a very small voice.

The marked contrast between his statement and the shouting got everyone's attention. Deborah placed a comforting hand on his slender shoulder, all the while staring down the dark-eyed man. "Don't worry, dearest. We're not going anywhere. This is our home now."

"This place isn't fit for a woman and child alone." In frustration, Luke clamped a large hand around her forearm. "You aren't safe."

She glared at the offending hand before shaking it off. "We were plenty safe until you arrived, you. . .you molester."

Mild disgust registered on his face. "Lady, is that all you ever think about?"

"Her name is not *Lady*," Case corrected him. "It's *Deborah*. And I'm Case. What's your name?"

"Luke."

Case's eyes glowed with delight. "Luke's a Bible name. Luke was a friend of Jesus. Are you a friend of Jesus?"

Deborah didn't like the turn of conversation to personal matters. At any moment, her brother would be inviting the man to stay. "Luke is a savage, dear."

Case studied the man for a second, taking in his clean-shaven face and neatly trimmed hair beneath a cowboy hat, his cotton shirt, and brown canvas pants, then shook his head. "Can't be. He ain't wearing war paint."

"*Isn't* wearing war paint."

"That's right, he isn't wearing war paint—or feathers neither."

"That's lovely, dearest." Deborah placed a quelling hand on her brother's shoulder and attempted to turn him back toward the kitchen. "Why don't you go sit down and wait for me?"

"Do you like hot biscuits with Aunt Mimi's peach preserves?" Case called over his shoulder as he was being bustled away. "That's what we're having for dinner. Debs always makes plenty. Can you stay?"

"No, he can't—"

"I can stay."

Deborah's mouth clapped shut. At the moment, she could have cheerfully wrung her tenderhearted brother's neck for inviting the man to stay. She was so angry, she was certain steam must be pouring from her ears.

And how dare that Indian accept the invitation when he knew very well he was unwelcome?

She resisted the urge to stomp her feet in frustration. The invitation had been extended and accepted. She might as well make the best of it. She'd serve up the meal in record time and hustle the savage out the door and bolt it behind him.

"How nice," she gritted out between teeth clenched in what she knew would never pass as a smile. "Won't you come in and sit down?"

She led the way down the dark hall and into the kitchen. She heard the Indian gasp, and whirled to face him. "What is it?"

He was staring at her as though he'd seen a ghost. For a split second, she thought his jaw went slack. He recovered quickly. "Nothing, ma'am."

The sudden appraising look on his face did odd things to her stomach. She wasn't wearing her protective layers of clothing today, and it appeared he noticed and appreciated the difference. Deborah lowered her eyes away from his pointed gaze and smoothed her skirts self-consciously. "I'll have your dinner ready in a minute."

"You can sit in my chair," Case offered. "I'll sit on the floor."

Luke glanced at the table, noting the arrangement of the two chairs. Without saying a word, he turned and left the room. He came back with a wooden crate from the storage room. He carried it to the table and sat it on end. "Try this," he said, patting the slatted seat.

Case sat, gingerly at first until he was sure of his balance. Then a wide grin split his face. "Look, Debs, my friend Luke made me a chair."

She supposed she should appreciate his kindness to her brother, but in her present mood she couldn't get past the ungracious thought that two chairs had been plenty before he intruded.

She scooped a dozen biscuits onto a platter and carried it to the table. She gathered plates and utensils from the stack in the corner and placed them on the table. Lastly, she carried the glass jar of preserves over and took her seat across from Luke.

"Case, would you ask the Lord's blessing?"

Case extended a hand to both her and the Indian. Luke looked at it, then back at Case.

"Take it," Case prompted. "We always hold hands when we pray."

Slowly, as though the concept was foreign to him, Luke took the small pale hand within his own large bronze one. Deborah was careful to keep her free hand tucked in her lap. She had no intention of holding Luke's hand.

Case was grinning from ear to ear. "Dear God, thank You for our dinner, especially Aunt Mimi's preserves. And thank You for our wonderful new Indian friend. In Jesus' name I pray. Amen."

Luke seemed to be as reluctant to release Case's hand as he had initially been to take it. He considered the clasped hands for a moment before opening his to free Case.

"Would you care for a biscuit?" Deborah handed the platter to Luke. He took two and held the plate while Case selected one for himself.

Deborah was half-disappointed Luke didn't wolf his food like an animal. Instead, he ate with all the polish of a well-bred gentleman. A hungry well-bred gentleman. As much as she wanted to dislike him, it was difficult to harbor malice toward someone who obviously enjoyed her cooking as much as he did. It was downright flattering to see the look of undisguised ecstasy on his face as he savored each bite. So intent upon eating, she doubted he noticed she refilled the platter of biscuits once, his cup of milk twice.

Finally, long after she and Case had eaten their fill, Luke seemed satisfied. He pulled the napkin from his collar and laid it beside his empty plate. He raised dark eyes to hers. "Thank you, ma'am. That was delicious."

She didn't mean to smile at him. She certainly didn't like the man, but she felt the corners of her mouth turn up as she said, "You're welcome."

He pushed back in his chair and cleared his throat. "We need to talk."

The feeling of camaraderie, of shared pleasure, evaporated as quickly as it had appeared. "Case, would you please go and begin your lessons? I'll be with you in just a moment"—she turned to face Luke to finish her sentence—"as soon as Luke leaves."

Case obediently rose from the table, carrying his dishes. He deposited them in the washtub before making his way slowly across the room. At the door, he paused and turned around to say, "Thanks for coming, Luke. I hope you'll be back real soon," before exiting the room.

As he left, the smile on Deborah's face faded. She sat forward in her chair, her back ramrod straight, her hands folded on the table. "What is it you'd like to discuss?"

Luke straightened, matching both her position and tone. "You can't stay here. It isn't safe."

"So you said."

She could see the mounting frustration in his stove-black eyes. "Ma'am, I'm looking at your best interests. Cyrus would say the same thing if he were here. Go home to your family."

"Cyrus is not here. And we cannot go back."

"They don't want you? Turned you and the boy out?"

What an odd remark. And made with such depth of feeling, such pained compassion, as if he could somehow understand their plight. Which of course he could not.

"We were not turned out," she snipped. "They did not want us to leave." Deborah unbent enough to repeat her aunt's hurtful words. "They thought we were crazy to leave."

"I'd have to agree with them."

For a minute Deborah wasn't sure the quietly spoken words were his, or simply the refrain of doubt that played in her mind. His pointed look assured her he did indeed speak them.

A week of backbreaking work and little sleep left her feeling close to the edge of her endurance. At his matter-of-fact denouncement of her plans, the dam of her pent-up emotions burst.

"Is it crazy to want the best for Case?" she demanded, her volume increasing with each word. "Is a normal life without pity too much to ask? Am I crazy to know there is something better here—something more—and to be willing to risk all to find out?"

He stared at her for a moment. Through her angry haze, she could see her questions struck a chord deep within him. "No," he said at last. "That's not crazy."

It felt so good to hear someone say it. To agree that her plan wasn't crazy. Her shoulders relaxed slightly, and she swept the hot tears from her face. Deborah took a deep breath and released a long, ragged sigh. "I'm staying."

"Then so am I."

CHAPTER 5

He was crazy.

Luke lay on the lumpy pile of straw serving as his bed, looking up at the early morning sky through narrow cracks in the roof of the lean-to. He wondered how in the world he'd gotten himself into this. Was it more of that honor Cyrus had talked about years ago? Luke snorted. If so, he could do with a little less honor right about now.

A full night's uninterrupted sleep gave him a clear enough perspective to see that he'd gone about this whole thing all wrong. He was man enough to admit his mistakes. He'd been wrong to assume Cyrus's people would leave. His assumption was based on what he thought he knew of Lumpy. . .Deborah. He could see now he'd grossly underestimated the lady.

Luke folded his hands behind his head and grinned. What an understatement. If it weren't for her soft voice and wide green eyes, he'd never have believed the fiery beauty he met yesterday was one and the same as timid Lumpy. Beneath the shawls and dirt, Lumpy. . .Deborah was a pleasing combination of creamy skin and graceful curves.

He'd underestimated her looks just as he'd underestimated

her spirit. She might look soft and womanly, but she had plenty of grit and determination.

He'd been wrong to judge her at face value. He knew from painful experience how much he hated it when people took one look at him and rejected him because of his Indian heritage.

He'd been crazy to expect she couldn't last a week. She had conviction written all over that pretty face of hers. No doubt about it, the little lady dug her heels deep into Texas soil.

A rustling outside snagged his attention. Intruders. Luke cursed his stupidity. He'd been so wrapped up in his thoughts he'd let his guard slip. Careless men didn't live to be old men.

Silently, quickly, Luke rolled to his side and pulled his rifle from beneath the blanket. He raised the gun, lined up the door in his sights, and slid his finger over the trigger guard. Every cell in his body was on alert.

"Hello in there!" Case's head peered around the corner. "Are you awake yet, Luke?"

Luke's heart hammered with the guilty realization he could have shot the child. He lowered the rifle, but not fast enough to escape the boy's notice.

"Say, what a fine-looking gun," he said, hobbling into the lean-to. "Can I see it?"

Aware of what an overanxious trigger finger might have wrought, Luke's hands were none too steady as he extended the gun, now uncocked, toward the boy.

Case blew out a long, admiring breath. "I'll bet you've killed a lot of outlaws with it, huh?" He bent slightly, squinting to examine the gun in the shadows. "I don't see any notches. Haven't you notched it to keep up a count? Have you got a name for it? Can you teach me to shoot it?"

As Luke listened to the rapid-fire questions, he had an uncomfortable memory of his own youth, when he had been full of questions and there had been no one to answer them.

"It's a Sharps rifle, Case. Buffalo gun. It's not notched because I'm not proud of killing any man. Killing isn't sport. Killing's for food or self-defense. As for teaching you to shoot it, I'm afraid not. It's a sight bigger than you are. Probably weighs as much as you."

It unsettled Luke to see the sparkle in Case's eyes dim. He deliberately softened his voice. "Maybe when you grow some I can teach you."

The child launched himself at Luke, throwing his skinny arms around his neck and squeezing tightly. Caught unawares and unsure how to proceed, Luke left his arms at his sides.

He'd never been embraced before. Not in his entire life. Once or twice Cyrus had clapped him on the back, but this bear hug was different. Luke felt a strange warmth seep through his limbs. There was such a feeling of acceptance in the embrace of a child.

Before he could fully come to terms with the hug, it was over. As Case drew back, the feeling of belonging dissipated.

"I like you, Luke. I'm glad God sent you to us." Case clapped a hand over his mouth and giggled. "Oops, I almost forgot. I was supposed to call you to breakfast. We'd better hurry or Debs will be mad."

"Debs" didn't look any too pleased when Luke arrived in the kitchen minutes later, though whether her displeasure stemmed from their tardiness or his presence, he wasn't sure.

"Good morning, ma'am."

She didn't look up from her work at the stove. "Good morning. You two sit down so we can eat before the food gets cold."

Luke didn't need to be asked twice. His reluctant hostess set out quite a spread.

Deborah carried a plate stacked high with steaming hotcakes to the table.

"Johnny cakes!" Case cried. "My favorite."

Deborah took her place at the table. "Would you ask the blessing, Case?"

This time Luke was ready for the strange ritual. He extended his hand to Case, accepting the small, smooth hand in his own. He darted a look at Deborah, gauging whether she wanted to take one of his hands as well, but she kept her free hand under the table and her eyes down.

"Lord God, we thank You for this special breakfast, and our new friend. In Jesus' name. Amen."

Since he was not feeling hunger as acutely this morning,

Luke could eat at a more leisurely pace and study his surroundings as well. He hardly recognized the kitchen as the same room he'd seen a week ago. The once-neglected room now shone with Deborah's labors. Fact was, he didn't ever remember it looking quite this nice when he and Cyrus lived here. Must be the woman's touch that made everything look warm and inviting.

He stole a glance at Deborah. She looked better today. If he wasn't mistaken, the dark circles under her eyes looked less pronounced. Her hair, which he'd been stunned yesterday to realize was not a dull graying brown, but a rich brown with glints of red, was pulled back off her face in a tight knot. It was scraped back so severely, it looked as though it might be painful. Maybe that was the reason she didn't smile much.

He took a big bite of the hotcakes as he recalled the transformation of her face when she smiled yesterday. She was a pretty enough woman when she frowned, but when she smiled, the combination of straight white teeth and an answering sparkle in her eyes nearly knocked him off his chair. Maybe it was best she was a solemn sort of woman.

"Guess what, Debs? Luke said he'd teach me to shoot his gun."

Luke glanced up to catch her reaction to Case's announcement. It didn't take a genius to see she wasn't pleased with the news. Her face squinched up as it had yesterday when Case had invited Luke to stay for dinner. Luke took a deep gulp of milk to wash down his breakfast and replaced his cup on the table, waiting for the explosion.

"He did, did he?" Deborah calmly wiped her mouth with her napkin, then laid it beside her plate. "Case, if you're finished with your breakfast, I'd like you to run along and work on your lessons. I'll check them when you're done."

"Aw, Debs." Case's stricken face suddenly brightened. "Can Luke do my lessons with me? He can check 'em when I'm done so you won't have to."

"Lessons?" Luke shook his head while lifting a hand in protest. "No."

"No," Deborah said firmly. "Luke will be staying with me. There are some things he and I need to discuss."

Case shrugged. "Okay." He collected his dishes and carried them to the sink. "Thanks for breakfast, Debs. See ya later, Luke." He gave a little wave and limped out.

The temper she dampened in front of her brother surged to the fore. "How dare you!" she hissed.

She must have read the look of complete bewilderment on his face because she went on to elaborate, "How dare you try to draw my brother into your violent lifestyle?"

Violent lifestyle? Draw him in? Brother? Luke was tempted to look from left to right to see whom she was addressing.

He said the first thing that came to mind. "Case is your brother?" The thought never occurred to Luke. He figured Case to be her son. Of course, she was young, but he wasn't too good at judging age. And she was real good at camouflage.

"Of course he's my brother," she snapped. "And don't try to change the subject. Whatever possessed you to mention guns to him?"

Luke didn't figure the truth would be too palatable, seeing as how the whole gun business wouldn't have come up if he hadn't drawn on the kid. Silence seemed like his safest bet.

She waited, her fingertips tapping on the table. "Have you nothing to say for yourself?"

She was itching for a fight. He could see it in her flashing green eyes. He wasn't about to give her one. "The boy saw my gun, and naturally he was curious. He asked questions and I answered them as best I could."

"There will be no guns in my house." She thumped her finger on the table for emphasis. "There will be no talk of guns in my house. Do you understand?"

Luke's gaze never wavered from hers. He understood plenty. She was crazy. Folks didn't live off by themselves in Texas, unarmed.

"And there's something else you need to understand. You don't belong here. Your presence in this house is completely unsuitable."

"Because I have a gun?"

"Yes. No. Well, not completely." She was the one to break eye contact. "It's because you're. . .well, you're a man."

Luke thought for a moment. "Does this have anything to do with that touching stuff you keep talking about?"

She blushed strawberry red. "Yes."

Luke considered her for a long time before shaking his head. "Ma'am, is that all you ever think of?"

"It's not just that," she said defensively. "Surely you can see that you are different from us."

He shouldn't have been disappointed with her comment, but he was. "Because I'm a half-breed, you mean."

"No, I don't mean that," she said with a dismissive wave of her hand. "May I ask you a question?"

"Why not?"

"Do you have a home? Permanent ties to anyone?"

"No."

She nodded. "Just as I thought. You are a wanderer, coming and going as you see fit. To a child of seven, your life is an exciting adventure. You are free, with no responsibility to tie you down. I mean no criticism to you when I say I want more for Case. I want him to have a normal life."

Deborah got up and started to clear the dishes from the table. "I'm sure you've noticed Case is not like other children. He's been lame from birth—his left foot is misshapen and his leg oddly turned. In addition, he has a weak constitution. He is often ill and tires easily. Since we lost our parents, I have been responsible for him."

"I thought you said you had people."

"We have an aunt, Aunt Mimi, my mother's sister, back in Louisiana."

"Ah, the aunt with the peach preserves."

Deborah returned to her chair, looking around to be certain Case could not hear. "We lived with her for a time, but I couldn't bear it. She's a good woman, very kind to take us in, but she could not abide Case's infirmity. She was embarrassed by it, and while she tried not to show it, she often slighted Case. She kept him hidden, refusing to allow him to play with other children his age or even to attend church. Case was unaware of her feelings, but

I believed that should we have stayed with her, eventually her careless cruelty would damage Case. He's so full of life and spirit; I couldn't bear to see them crushed.

"Several months ago, we received a letter from Cyrus telling us he was leaving his land and home in Texas to move out West. The letter was addressed to my father. I guess Cyrus hadn't received the news of his death. When I read the letter, I believed it to be a direct answer to my prayers.

"It was difficult to persuade my aunt to let us go. When at last she relented, Case and I traveled here to Texas to begin a new life. A normal life." As they locked eyes he noted hers glowed with the fire of pure determination. "And I've already invested too much in establishing our new life to allow your influence to ruin it."

Luke understood her position. Now it was time to establish his. "Place needs work," he said. "Barn needs work, too."

Deborah frowned. "Once we've had a chance to settle in, I plan to hire a man to come do some of the repairs."

"I'm your man."

His offer obviously took her by surprise. "I hardly think—" she sputtered.

"You said yourself you needed to hire someone. Who better than me? I know the place, heck, I built the place. And I've got the time. Since I've got a clear understanding of your feelings on touching, seems a shame to let good labor go to waste."

She looked at him hard, as if somehow she could see past his flesh to his innermost thoughts. "I don't understand you, Luke. You're young and healthy. Why aren't you working to make a place for yourself? Why waste your time with Case and me? You have nothing to gain."

Luke didn't think he'd go into the honor bit. He didn't have a real good handle on it himself. "A long time ago, Cyrus looked after me. He had nothing to gain. I owe him. I figure you and the boy are payback," he said simply.

"That's a lovely sentiment, but completely ridiculous. I release you from any debt you feel you owe to my uncle."

He folded his arms across his chest. "Can't."

"There's nothing I can say to dissuade you?"

The pained expression on her face brought a grin to his. "No, ma'am."

She sighed in resignation. "Well, then, you're hired. You can take your meals with us and live out in the lean-to. You'll have the Sabbath off."

"Seems fair."

"Let me reiterate. You are to stay away from Case. If at any time I feel your influence on him becomes a stumbling block to his normal life, I will insist you leave, debt or not. Have I made myself clear?"

"Completely."

"Then we have a deal."

He couldn't resist one last jab. He extended his hand to her. "Shall we shake on it?" At her horrified expression, he chuckled. "Didn't think so."

Chapter 6

S he'd made a mistake, Deborah thought as she swept wide arcs with the broom across the grayed plank porch. Allowing Luke to stay on, to serve as handyman, was an error in her normally good judgment.

Not that she could complain about his work. For the week since she'd hired him, he'd put in a full day every day. He toiled tirelessly from sunup to sundown, breaking only for the noon meal.

From her current vantage point, she could admire the fruits of his hard work. The front door now hung squarely on its frame. The split-rail fence encircling the house was repaired and the gate restored to usefulness. From the hammering sounds coming from behind the house, it sounded as though he'd moved on to the barn.

She could not fault his work or his behavior. As she'd requested, Luke gave her and Case a wide berth. The only time she saw him was during meals.

Case wasn't satisfied with such short visits and often gravitated toward the place where Luke was working, but even then Deborah observed Luke did nothing to encourage the child.

Yet, in spite of his exemplary work and behavior, Luke made

her uneasy. For one thing, he moved too quietly. It was just plain unnatural for a big man like him to be able to walk without making a sound. Several times he'd come up behind her unseen and frightened the daylights out of her. He didn't seem to do it purposefully; it appeared to be a habit he'd developed. An Indian thing, she guessed. Still, she didn't like it.

And she didn't like the way he looked at her. She couldn't put her finger on why exactly it disturbed her, but it was unnerving. Not that he treated her with anything less than respect, but his dark, brooding eyes seemed always to be measuring her, studying her. If he were a suitor, she supposed she would have been flattered by his undivided attention, but as he was only the hired man, the direct, searching gazes unsettled her.

On the positive side, she'd slept better since he'd arrived. The knowledge that the front door now bolted securely and that Luke slept in the lean-to just outside the back door allowed her to relax enough so when her head hit the pillow each night, she fell into a deep, untroubled sleep.

Still, she'd be glad when he finished up the work and moved on.

———※———

"I could help you with that, ya know."

Luke didn't look up from the board he was measuring. "No."

"I could carry boards for you," the squeaky voice persisted. "I'm pretty strong."

"No, thanks."

"Maybe I could just sit here and watch you," Case said hopefully. "I won't talk or anything. And if you get thirsty, I could get you a drink."

Luke's patience had worn thin. "Don't you have something else to do?" he snarled. "Lessons? Chores?"

Unfazed, Case took a wobbly step forward and raised his freckled face to Luke's. "You don't like me, do you?"

Luke's head snapped up. Too stunned to speak, he stared at the child. He felt the force of the softly spoken words like a sharp blow to the gut. There was no reproach in the innocently direct question, no anger in the words. And for some reason, that made them all the more painful.

He didn't dislike the boy, though he could see where the child had gotten the idea. He hadn't had time for him. Whenever possible, he'd avoided him.

Not that it had been easy. From morning till night, the kid was underfoot.

A smile pulled at the corner of Luke's mouth when he remembered the way Case had pestered him while he'd repaired the fence. And talked constantly. Could he help? Had Luke noticed that weed leaves had jagged edges? Did he have any brothers? Why was the sun so hot?

Case's requests to be allowed to help were interspersed with chatter about his life and family. Luke had paid only slight attention to the child. He'd given his word to Deborah not to influence Case, and he would honor it.

"It's okay if you don't like me," Case reassured him, laying a small white hand on top of Luke's dark one and nodding with patient understanding. "I understand." He flashed a brave smile. "I'm different. Crippled. Lots of people don't like cripples." His wide-eyed gaze locked with Luke's. "I'm not mad or anything. I still like you a lot."

Luke's throat constricted painfully as he looked into those earnest green eyes and saw the resignation and wisdom of a child too old for his seven years. It wasn't difficult to picture the condemning looks Case had faced or to hear the jeering calls. Cripples and half-breeds had that in common.

The amazing thing was that instead of becoming hardened and withdrawn from the rejection, Case had somehow remained unspoiled, rising above his circumstances.

"Why?" Luke asked. "Why aren't you mad? You have every right to be."

Case shook his head in the slow understanding way of a parent to a child. "I'm not angry because of my friend Jesus. He says I'm so special to Him that I don't have to feel bad about other people not liking me."

This guy Jesus came up a lot in conversations with the kid. Must be somebody from back home. No matter. Ol' Jesus might like little Case, it was hard not to like the kid, but even Jesus wouldn't like a part Indian.

"I bet Jesus doesn't think half-breeds are special." Luke spoke the words without thinking.

Case's face grew solemn. "Oh no, you're wrong, Luke. Jesus loves you, I'm sure of it. Half-breeds can't be any worse than Samaritans, and I know Jesus loves Samaritans."

Luke had to chuckle at the boy's confidence. Likely misplaced, but somehow just hearing Case say it lifted Luke's heart. "Think you could bring me that board over there? The one leaning against the first stall?"

Case's eyes lit up like a lantern in the dead of night. "You mean it? I can help?"

Luke reached over and ruffled the boy's silky curls. "You bet. Now get busy. We've got lots of work to do."

<hr />

Deborah pushed open the front door and stepped inside the house. The pot of soup she'd put on to cook earlier smelled wonderful. She entered the kitchen and leaned the broom against the wall. She lifted the lid on the bubbling pot and stirred twice. After checking the pan of corn bread in the oven, Deborah walked to the back door to call Case and Luke for lunch.

As always, the transition from the shadowy hall to the bright Texas sun was blinding, and Deborah blinked several times to adjust her vision. When it cleared, the first thing that met her eyes was Luke—naked to the waist—standing just outside the door of the barn, nailing a board in place. For a fascinated instant, she watched his powerful shoulder muscles ripple beneath bronze skin as he held the board in place with one hand and swung the hammer with the other.

Having had two older brothers, she was not completely ignorant of the male physique, but to see it displayed so prominently. . . . Of course, being a savage he was probably unaware that appearing in such a state of undress was completely unacceptable. It was up to her to set him straight.

Even as she deliberated over the best way to instruct him,

another sight met her eyes, this one more astonishing than the first. Case limped out from the shadows of the barn dragging a three-foot section of board behind him. And, like Luke, Case was naked from the waist up.

"Case," she shouted as she strode purposefully across the dirt yard. "Case, what are you doing?"

Case paused to look up toward her, his pale face flushed, his green eyes bright with delight. "I'm working, Debs. Luke said I could." If possible, the smile on his face widened. "Luke said he needed me."

"Oh, he did, did he?" She flicked a stormy glance at Luke before kneeling in front of her brother and taking his thin shoulders in her hands. "Case, dearest, where is your shirt? You'll catch your death out here."

Case frowned. "Debs, sometimes men need to work without their shirts. Hard work makes us powerful warm. Besides," he added angelically, "I didn't want to get my shirt all dirty and make more washing for you."

She kissed the tip of his nose. "I thank you for your consideration, but I must insist you fetch your shirt and put it on immediately."

Case looked from Deborah to Luke and back to Deborah. "Aww, Debs."

She hardened her heart against the pleading in his voice. "No, sir," she said firmly. "Shirt now. And then you hurry on inside and wash up for lunch."

The announcement of food didn't earn its usual squeal of delight. "Okay, Deborah." He retrieved his shirt from the post where he'd hung it, pulled it on, and began to button it up as he headed for the house. "Aren't you two coming?" he called back over his shoulder.

"In a minute, dearest. Luke and I have something to discuss."

The instant her brother was out of earshot, she whirled on Luke. "How dare you? How could—?" she broke off and turned her back on him. "Would you please have the decency to put on your shirt?"

She gave him a moment before turning to face him once

again. By then he'd buttoned the first three buttons, obscuring the sight of his broad bronze chest that was making it difficult for Deborah to think.

"What is the meaning of recruiting my brother to do your work?" she demanded.

"I was helping you give the boy a normal life."

"You were—" She slammed her hands on her hips and advanced on Luke. "Do not presume to excuse your actions."

Luke hitched up the brim of his hat a fraction. "No, ma'am. No excuses. I was doing the very thing you told me about. Giving the boy a normal life. What could be more normal than having chores to do around the house?"

"Case *has* chores."

"Case has women's work. Chores like collecting sticks and dusting furniture are fine for a young child, but a boy of seven needs to be learning men's work."

"Case is not a typical boy of seven. He's. . .he's—"

"He's crippled, ma'am, not to put too fine a point on it. But are you gonna let his having a bad leg cripple his whole life?"

"How dare you insinuate such a thing! You don't know what you are talking about."

"I know that when he grows to manhood he's gonna need to be able to repair a barn or a fence. Dusting tables isn't going to prepare him to live independently or raise a family."

"Raise a family?" she repeated, her voice trailing off to an awed whisper. "Case raising a family?"

"Why not? I've seen plenty of men make a good life for themselves and their families without the use of an arm or leg."

In all the years she'd been responsible for Case, she'd never once considered his growing up to be a man, a man with a family of his own. It made sense of course; she'd have seen it for herself if she'd looked out that far into the future. Deborah chewed her lip. If that was true, then perhaps Case would benefit from additional training. She wouldn't want to hold him back.

Her eyes hardened. But if that man, that Indian, thought he was going to decide what was best for her little brother, he had another think coming.

"I will concede that *perhaps* my brother could use a broader range of skills; however, in your ill-advised attempt to help me provide him with a normal life, you have exposed him to danger."

Luke cocked an ominous brow.

"Case has a delicate constitution, always has. He tires easily and is highly susceptible to colds. He is never subjected to either early morning or late night air, and I'm very careful to restrict his physical activities to a minimum. It's my responsibility to prevent him from overexerting himself."

"No wonder the boy's frail. You've weakened him with all that cosseting."

"I've protected him."

"I'm sure you believe that—"

"What makes you the expert?" Deborah scarcely recognized the screaming voice as her own. "Have you ever been completely responsible for someone you love?"

Luke opened his mouth, then closed it.

Complete silence marked the abrupt end to their shouting match.

Luke's dark eyes looked blacker than ever. Cold. Shuttered. "No," he said at last, "never."

Her anger evaporated with his hopeless syllables. He continued to tower over her, tall and fierce, yet at that moment, she wasn't frightened for herself. She was frightened for him.

CHAPTER 7

The April sun shone warm and bright on Luke's face as he led the ox across the yard.

"Hey, Luke, I'm almost as tall as you," Case chirped from his perch on the ox's back.

The kid had been hinting around that he'd like to ride since they walked out to the barn after breakfast. Luke couldn't see any harm in it, and it meant an awful lot to the boy. Fact was, it would be good for Case to build up his strength, besides giving him a working knowledge of handling an animal.

Luke had settled the boy securely behind the ox's bony neck and looped a thick leather strap around Case's waist and tied it to the ox's harness. No way the kid was in any danger.

Still, Luke shot several nervous glances toward the house as they plodded along. He didn't figure Deborah would take to the sight too kindly.

Case, however, was in raptures.

"Look, Luke," he squealed. "I'm controlling him. I really am. You can let go of the lead. I won't let him run off."

Luke grinned. The ox, Esau they called him, wouldn't run off if they set fire to his tail. Wasn't in his nature. He was so mild-mannered you could let him loose in the house.

Didn't seem right to remind Case of the facts. He was having too fine a time.

Luke looked Case square in the eye. "You think you can hold him?" he asked in a tone that suggested a hint of doubt. "Esau's a pretty big fella."

Case's eyes widened. "I can do it, Luke," he answered gravely. "I can hold him."

Luke paused, as if considering the idea for a moment, then made a show of handing Case the lead. "He's all yours."

Case accepted the leather strap with a solemn nod and gripped it tightly with both hands. Esau, unconcerned about the change in command, continued his course at the same lumbering, deliberate pace.

Once they'd reached the spot Luke had marked off for the kitchen garden, he stepped into Esau's path and the ox stopped.

"I did it!" Case cried. "I rode by myself. Did you see, Luke? Esau stopped, just like I wanted him to."

Luke bit back a smile. "Fine handling of the animal. If we can get Deborah to come around to the idea, I'll teach you to ride my horse."

Case's eyes looked ready to pop from his head. "Do you mean it? You'd let me ride Horse?"

Luke nodded as he untied the strap from Case's waist and leaned forward to pick him up. Case wrapped his skinny white arms around Luke's neck and squeezed hard as Luke lifted him off Esau's back.

"You're the greatest, Luke," Case whispered into his ear. "I'll bet there's nothing you can't do."

Seems like Luke'd get accustomed to the boy's hugs, seeing as how he was getting them regularly, but Luke doubted he ever would. There was something so sweet in the spontaneous embraces. They were quick, no more than a second or two, but for those brief moments, Luke felt a part of something he'd been standing outside of his whole life.

Luke lowered Case to the ground, pausing a second for him to stabilize before releasing him. Never still for a minute, Case fluttered around Luke while he attached the old iron plow to Esau's harness, jabbering about every little thing that flitted into his imaginative mind.

Did Luke hear that rustling under that cluster of weeds? Did Luke think it was a critter or a snake? Did Luke know that Debs hated snakes above everything? Didn't Luke think that weed had the prettiest leaves?

By the time Luke was ready to plow, Case was drooping. The combination of the excitement from the ride and all the chattering had worn the kid out. Luke had seen the signs before, Case's already pale little face grew paler still, and his limp was more pronounced.

"Tell you what. Why don't you sit down over there?" Luke said, pointing to a spot well out of his way, some fifteen feet from where he'd be plowing. "Soon as Esau and I get this ground plowed up, you and I can practice some whittling."

"Whittling? With a knife?"

Something about the kid's obvious delight in the smallest things touched Luke's heart. "Yes, with a knife. But you've got to promise to sit still till then—otherwise the deal's off."

Case limped as quickly as he could carry his exhausted body and dropped obediently onto the spot Luke indicated. "I'll be still. I won't even say a word."

Luke coughed to cover his laugh. The way he figured it, if the kid didn't talk, he'd probably explode.

The ground was hard and packed from too little rain. Standing behind the ox and plow, his gloved hands gripping the iron handles, Luke pierced the rock-hard soil with the blade of the plow, and he and Esau began the slow, difficult work of plowing. It was a small plot of land, not more than a tenth of an acre, but it was several hours of arduous labor before he pulled Esau to a halt and looked over the freshly turned earth with satisfaction. True to his word, Case remained silent the entire time. Luke thought he'd fallen asleep he was so still, but a glance over his shoulder indicated the child watched his slow progress with eagle-eyed attention. Luke knew he shouldn't be surprised. The kid was interested in everything.

Luke pulled his hat off and mopped the sweat from his face with his sleeve. "You ready for some whittling?" he asked as he approached Case.

Case's head bobbed. "You bet I am."

Luke was relieved to see the return of some color to Case's freckled face. He pulled his knife from its sheath on his thigh and sat down beside the boy.

Case's eyes gleamed as bright as the shining blade. "Are you gonna let me hold it?"

Luke nodded. Case immediately reached for the knife, but Luke held it away.

"Before you use a tool, any tool, you need to understand it. A knife can be a mighty dangerous thing, and a man needs to respect it."

Case's eyes were glued to Luke's face as he absorbed every word.

Luke shifted to pull a flint from his pocket. "First thing we need to do is sharpen the blade." While he spoke Luke drew the long blade across the flint in slow, measured sweeps. "A sharp blade works best. And it's safer."

He carefully placed the knife in Case's hand and showed him how to hold it. The knife handle was large for Case's small fingers, but he was so determined, he stretched his fingers around it and satisfied Luke that his grip was steady. After they talked a few more minutes about safety, Luke pulled a short, fat stick from his back pocket, and they set to work.

Deborah balanced the basket of wet laundry on her hip so she could open the back door and step outside. Laundry was not one of her favorite tasks, but at this moment, with the washing behind her, she could reflect on her morning's work with pleasure. She had only to hang the clothes on the line Luke had strung up for her between several posts and let the sun do the drying.

She heaved a wistful sigh. If only the sun would do the ironing.

From beneath the covered back porch, she could see the rectangle of earth Luke had been plowing up for her kitchen garden. The slight breeze carried on it the pungent scent of freshly turned soil.

The dirt looked fertile, not the dark black earth of Louisiana, but the rich reddish brown she'd come to associate with Texas. She'd brought seeds from home in anticipation of having her own garden. She couldn't wait to begin harvesting the fresh vegetables. Combined with the few staples she'd need from the general store, she and Case would be pretty much self-sufficient.

She knew getting in a garden would be her number-one priority after she got herself and her brother settled in. However, she'd never dreamed it wouldn't be her hard labor that brought the garden into being. What a blessing to have Luke to do the backbreaking digging.

Luke a blessing? Deborah could almost laugh at the thought. When she'd first seen him several weeks ago, she'd thought the grim-faced Indian was a demon from hell. And, for a time, her opinion of him went steadily downhill from there.

Slowly, her opinion had begun to change. She wouldn't go so far as to say she liked Luke, but she had come to respect him. He was clean, hardworking, and reliable. He seemed to know his way around a ranch and had been invaluable in helping her set the place to rights.

He was even good with Case. In spite of his size, he was patient and gentle with her little brother. Not that she appreciated any of his impertinent suggestions on how she should be raising him, but Luke did seem to have a great deal of insight into boys.

And Case adored him. Deborah put down her basket and stepped to the end of the porch to look out toward the place where Case and Luke now sat with their backs to the house. She couldn't imagine a more unlikely pair than the two of them, a small, frail boy who chattered incessantly and a tall, proud Indian who rarely spoke.

Yet, she marveled, somehow they'd bonded. Since that

unfortunate scene in the barnyard when they'd had words over her brother, Luke and Case had become inseparable. Not that Luke had any choice in the matter. Case spent every spare moment at the Indian's side, dogging his steps like a persistent gnat.

The thought should bother her, but somehow it didn't. After all, Luke understood clearly her objective to give her brother a normal life and supported her in it.

There had been no more talk of guns or weapons. Luke had obviously seen the error of his ways. Deborah need not fear that Luke would somehow foist his violent ways onto her brother.

Case's clear laughter rang out in the quiet of the late morning and brought a grin to her face. Never a morose child, Case had seemed to blossom with his association with Luke. She might as well admit it, Luke was a blessing.

She heard Case laugh and an answering chuckle from Luke. Drawn by the merriment, Deborah left her basket on the porch to join them.

While she'd never master Luke's skill of silent motion, she congratulated herself that she did come up on them undetected, though if she were honest she'd admit it was probably because her brother's chatter masked any noise she'd made.

"What are you two doing?" she asked brightly.

Case swiveled around, a long-bladed knife clasped in his hand. "Oh, hi, Debs. I didn't hear you come up." He pointed the knife, as an extension of his arm, toward the garden plot. "Luke finished your garden."

"W-w-what is that?" she squeaked. She wasn't sure how she was able to speak, as she was certain her heart had ceased to beat.

Case pointed the knife toward her, the vicious-looking blade glinting in the sunlight. "It's Luke's knife. Isn't it great?"

She couldn't answer. No air would come from her lungs. She couldn't breathe. She simply stared.

Her brother, rightly interpreting her silence, said, "Don't worry, Debs. It's real sharp."

Dark spots suddenly blurred her vision. She blinked twice to clear them, but they multiplied. Her limbs went from lead to water, and she started to fall.

———❖———

"Deborah? Debs, are you okay?"

Deborah blinked, trying to focus her strangely blurred vision. Two deeply concerned faces loomed over hers. "What's going on? Where am I?"

"You fainted, Debs," Case crowed in awed appreciation as only a young boy could. "You woulda hit the ground, too, if Luke hadn't caught you. Boy, did he move fast. Scooped you up in mid-fall like you were a feather or something. He carried you into the house and laid you on the bed so you could rest." Case frowned. "Are you tired, Debs?"

Fainted? For years her mother despaired over the fact Deborah couldn't fall into a swoon as all gently bred young women did. Now, all of a sudden, she fainted?

Images flooded back to her. Case and Luke laughing. Case wielding a huge, sharp knife. *Luke's* huge, sharp knife.

She sat up abruptly, causing the room to spin. She locked her elbows, ignoring the dizziness as she said, "Case, dearest, would you go get started on your lessons? Luke and I have something to discuss."

Case shrugged. "Okay, if you want me to. Seems like you two always have something to discuss."

She waited until he'd disappeared around the corner before unloading on Luke. "What were you thinking?" she hissed in a venomous whisper, mindful that her brother was nearby.

Luke looked bewildered.

She was too angry to elaborate, so she repeated, "Just what were you thinking?"

After a long silent moment, Luke's frown eased, the confusion on his face clearing. "Oh, I get it. It's about that touching thing, isn't it? You're mad because I carried you into the house."

The only sound she could make sounded amazingly like that of a teapot reaching a boiling point.

Luke apparently took the hissing squeal as affirmation. "I didn't want to leave you lying in the dirt." An unexpected grin pulled at the corner of his mouth. "Besides, I didn't think I'd be setting too good of an example for the boy by dragging you by the hair."

He thought this was funny? He instructed her precious brother in the ways of violence, nearly killed her with fright, and then laughed about it?

"Get out," she growled. When he opened his mouth to protest, she pointed to the door and screamed, "Get out!"

CHAPTER 8

Bible time was Luke's favorite part of the day. After dinner, when the dishes were cleaned and everyone was washed up, they'd gather in the warmth of the kitchen. Deborah would light the lamp against the growing darkness, then go to the trunk and get out the big black leather-bound book.

Once settled in her chair, her full skirts arranged just so, she'd open the book, flipping the thick yellow-white pages until she found her place, then she'd begin to read. With her fine, strong voice, Deborah had made the stories come alive.

Sometimes she would read of people and places Luke had never heard of, like the Israelites and the Promised Land. Sometimes she would read poetry that made his heart ache, but always she read of a mighty, all-powerful God who loved and protected His people.

For the fleeting minutes of Bible time, the great yawning hole within Luke—the grinding hunger of his spirit—would quiet. Bible time gave him a taste of real peace. He figured that peace would be the thing he missed the most when he left.

Tonight would be his last time to share in Bible time. Deborah had announced over dinner that Luke was to be gone in the morning. Little Case had cried and pleaded till Luke figured there couldn't be a drop of water left in the boy, but to no avail. Deborah would not be moved.

Luke had to go.

Luke tried to explain what they'd been doing with the knife, tried to tell her a boy needed to learn how to handle a knife to lead a normal life, but she wasn't having any part of his explanation.

Deborah equated knives with guns and guns with violence and she would tolerate no violence. Seemed she lost her brothers to the violence of war and she was still grieving for them. She figured if guns and knives were prohibited, there'd be no more war. No more senseless killing.

So Luke, with his gun and knife, would be gone in the morning.

He wouldn't go far. He owed it to Cyrus to look after his kin, and he vowed to do it, even if it meant living up in the hilltop shack and riding patrol. Deborah would never be the wiser.

Luke put the last of the dishes in the tub of soapy water. "Your turn to dry tonight, kid."

Case limped over, more slowly than usual, to stand beside Luke. "I'm gonna miss you when you're gone, Luke."

Luke dried his hand on his pants then mussed the boy's hair. "I'm sure you are. Who'll help you wash the dishes?"

The attempt at levity fell flat. Case lifted a mournful face to Luke's and shook his head. "Oh no. It's not just the dishes," he said earnestly. "It's you I'll miss. You're my best friend. I l-like you."

Luke crouched low to meet Case at eye level. "I like you, too."

***

Something wakened Deborah early in the morning. She lay still in the pitch-black room, waiting to hear a repeat of whatever it was that woke her. Nothing. The house was silent.

She relaxed into her pillow, now too wide awake to drop off to sleep. Fact was, she'd slept only fitfully all night.

The whole evening, actually, the whole day had been a disaster, she reflected. One minute she was standing on the back porch, counting Luke as one of her blessings, next minute she was flat on her back, convinced he was a demon from the pit. Now, when she was feeling more rational, she admitted that Luke probably fell somewhere in between the two extremes.

After she'd had some time to cool off, to regroup her scattered thoughts after her scare, she could see that perhaps she'd overreacted. She had observed Luke enough to know he would never do anything to hurt her brother.

Sure, handing a knife with an eight-inch blade to a seven-year-old was sheer idiocy, but from what Case told her when she'd calmed down enough to listen, Luke had exercised extreme caution throughout the entire "lesson." Furthermore, the intent of learning about knives, according to Case, was not to use it as a weapon, but rather as a tool with which to whittle. He'd wanted to whittle Deborah a present.

Deborah frowned up at the darkened ceiling as her conscience bombarded her with guilt. She felt guilty for making Case cry. She felt guilty for overreacting. She felt guilty for sending Luke away.

She even felt guilty for depriving Luke of their company. Though she'd always considered him a loner, she sensed he relished their companionship. It was especially evident during family Bible time. She doubted he'd ever admit it, but she could clearly see the pleasure in his face as she opened the Scriptures and began to read.

Her mother had often said Deborah possessed a very soothing voice, pleasant to listen to, but there was more to what she witnessed on Luke's face than a reaction to her oratory skills. He was enthralled with the stories. He hung on every word. Unlike herself or Case who had heard the Old Testament stories time and again, it was obvious they were completely new to Luke.

Lately, she'd begun to read a bit farther each night, though her brother began to fidget, just because she knew Luke enjoyed it. The truth was, his appreciation of the Bible stories enhanced her appreciation of them. It was as if she was seeing them with new eyes.

But not anymore. She'd sent him away.

She rolled onto her side, facing the door. Still, she tried to reassure herself, she'd done the right thing. Luke was a menace. He had no concept of the protection a young boy needed. They would be better off without him.

She flopped onto her back and sighed. Her mind might think getting rid of Luke was a good idea, but her heart didn't agree.

Case had been so crushed over her pronouncement, she wondered if he'd ever forgive her. It nearly broke her heart to hear him quietly sobbing until he fell asleep.

At least now he was finally resting peacefully. She rolled over to check on him. He wasn't there. She felt the sheets where he'd been lying. They were cool to the touch.

Deborah sat bolt upright in the bed, her mind racing in a dozen different directions. In the whirlwind of frightening thoughts, one thing was clear. Her brother was gone.

Fueled by blinding fear, she sprang off the mattress and raced into the hall. "Case?" she called. "Case?"

Nothing. The house was silent. She was alone.

As she hurried down the pitch-black hall, she noticed a thin, silvery shaft of light filtering in from the back. The door was ajar, and light from the full moon seeped in through the crack.

Her heart was pounding so hard, she could hardly think. Case must be outside. Had he run away?

She pulled the door open without making a sound and stepped onto the back porch. Moonlight cast eerie shadows across the yard. The place looked threatening, hostile. And Case was out there.

Deborah paused to pray. "O God," she whispered. "Help me find him. Please keep him safe."

She heard a slight sound, a voice coming from the lean-to. Moving silently, she made her way to the door of the lean-to and peeked in.

Case, his nightgown-clad body illuminated by moonlight, stood at the foot of the pallet where Luke slept.

"Luke?" Case said in a loud whisper. "Luke, are you awake?"

Luke grumbled something, then sat up with a start. "Case? What are you doing in here?"

"I couldn't sleep. I needed to talk to you." A belated thought seemed to occur to him. "I didn't wake you up, did I? I don't want to bother you."

Luke gave a deep, throaty chuckle. "Not much, kid. You know I always like to talk to you."

Case pulled something from behind his back and thrust it toward Luke. "I brought you something. A going-away present."

"That's awful nice, Case, but I don't need anything."

Case took a step closer and pressed the parcel into Luke's hands. "It's my Bible. My very own Bible. It used to belong to my father, and when he died, Deborah gave it to me. I want you to have it."

"Aww, Case—"

"A man ought to have his own Bible. Maybe when you read it, you'll think of me."

"Come here." Luke directed Case toward his pallet and moved to the side to make a place for him. He patted the blanket. "Sit down."

Case obediently limped across the dirt floor and sat.

Luke held up the Bible. "This is the nicest present I've ever received. But I can't accept it."

"Why not?"

"First of all, your father meant for you to have it. One day you'll read to your children from it. Second of all, it'd be a waste to give it to me. I can't read."

Deborah hoped Case's sharp intake of breath masked her own. "I didn't know that," Case said. "You never let on you couldn't read."

Luke shrugged. "I didn't want you to know. You always said you thought I could do everything." Deborah watched the proud man drop his head to confess, "I didn't want to disappoint you."

Case threw his arms around Luke and held him tight. "You could never disappoint me, Luke." After a second or two, he pulled himself away to say, "I wasn't completely honest with you earlier tonight."

"Oh?"

Case nodded. "Remember when I told you I liked you?"

Luke nodded.

"It wasn't exactly the truth. The truth is, I love you, Luke."

This time Deborah watched Luke take the initiative. He spread his arms wide and when Case moved into them, Luke wrapped him tight. "I love you, too, Case," he whispered against the child's hair. "I love you, too."

CHAPTER 9

No regrets.

If he'd had it to do all over again, he'd have done the same thing.

Luke moved methodically through the small lean-to, gathering up his few possessions and stuffing them into his worn leather saddlebag. It didn't take him long to pack. A man without roots didn't accumulate things to tie him down.

His gaze swept the room, making certain he left nothing behind. Satisfied, he tucked his bedroll under his arm, tossed his saddlebag over his shoulder, and extinguished the lamp.

The door creaked as he pushed it open and stepped out into the yard. It was still dark as he silently made his way to the barn. He didn't want to risk waiting around for sunrise before leaving. He didn't think he could take the good-byes.

His mare nickered softly as he approached her stall. He reached out to stroke her head. "Looks like it's just you and me again, Horse. You ready to hit the trail?"

"I'd rather you didn't."

Luke whirled around to find Deborah standing in the door of the barn. She was dressed in her nightclothes, a gown and wrapper, her hair hanging in a long braid over her shoulder.

"What are you doing up?" he asked.

"Waiting for you." She walked toward him, hugging her arms to her chest. "I wanted to talk to you."

"Shoot."

"I wanted to ask you to stay."

Afraid she'd be able to read the relief in his expression, Luke turned back to his horse. "Why?" he asked, reaching for his saddle.

She closed the gap between them. "Because I don't want you to go."

He looked at her from over his shoulder. "Why?"

"You're not going to make this easy for me, are you?"

He turned to give her his full attention. "Last I heard, you said you wanted me out of here at first light. Are you telling me I heard wrong?"

She hung her head. "I'm telling you I made a mistake."

He had to lean toward her to catch her whispered words. "I want you to stay, Luke. Case needs you. We need you."

Luke was certain he'd never heard more beautiful words in his life. They needed him. Still, the woman had made his last twelve hours a living hell. No way he was letting her off easy. He kept his expression and tone grim. "Why the change?"

Her eyes downcast, she said, "After I had time to cool off, I realized you would never do anything to harm Case. You've been really good for him." Her voice trailed off to almost nothing, "You were right when you said—"

"Do you mind repeating that?"

Confused by the interruption, she lifted her gaze to meet his. "Repeat what?"

He couldn't suppress a grin any longer. "The part about me being right."

She caught a glimpse of his smile and realized he'd been teasing her. She gave him a playful shove. "Wretch."

Luke's eyes shot wide with amazement. She'd touched him. First time ever.

She must have seen his astonishment because she beat a hasty retreat. She took three steps backward, nearly falling into a stall in her hurry. She cleared her throat. "So, will you stay?"

He nodded. "I'll stay."

A wide smile of relief lit her face. "I'm glad."

For a moment they stood facing each other in awkward silence. Finally she broke it saying, "How about some coffee?"

"Sounds good. I'll drop my stuff back in the lean-to, and I'll meet you in the kitchen."

Deborah scurried off to start the coffee.

"What do you think about that?" Luke asked his horse. "She says they need me and want me to stay."

He picked up his saddlebag and bedroll and headed out of the barn. "Doesn't that beat all," he marveled to himself. "They want me to stay."

At the same instant Luke was entering the house from the back door, a sleepy-eyed Case stepped out of his bedroom and into the hall. "Luke!"

Case made a hobbling run and threw himself into Luke's arms. "You're back!" Suddenly his little face fell and he whispered, "Does Debs know?"

Luke nodded and whispered back. "Yup. She's decided I can stay."

"Yippee!" Case gave Luke a quick squeeze, then wriggled out of his arms to find his sister. Luke rounded the corner in time to see him launch himself at Deborah, nearly knocking her off her feet. "Oh Debs, you're the best."

Luke and Deborah spoke very little over coffee. Words didn't seem necessary. By some unspoken agreement, yesterday would be forgotten, and they would return to the way things had been. After two cups, Luke went off to chop some wood and milk the cow while Deborah fixed breakfast.

By the time the sun was up and breakfast was on the table, an air of celebration seemed to have settled over the threesome. Luke and Deborah unbent enough to exchange more than one-syllable words, and Case chattered nonstop about anything and everything. After lingering at the table much longer than usual, Deborah said reluctantly, "It's time to start your lessons, Case."

"Aww, Debs."

Luke rose to carry his plates to the washtub. He needed to

get on to work. He wanted to put in a low fence around the kitchen garden.

"Luke, I'd like you to join us for lessons today."

Both Case and Luke turned to stare at Deborah.

"But—"

She raised a slim hand to silence Luke's protest. "I must insist. Case's concentration has not been at all satisfactory, and I believe that with your presence, he might be induced to put forth more effort."

"But—"

She was already out of her chair and carrying off dirty plates. "Help me clear off the dishes, and we'll use the table for lessons. Case, would you please get me two slates and two pieces of chalk?"

Case shuffled from the room.

Luke was feeling like a cornered rabbit. "Listen, Deborah, I don't think—"

"Trust me, Luke." He recognized the look of determination in her cool green eyes as she raised them to his. "It'll be good for Case. And who knows," she added with a flip of her head as she turned to walk to the washtub, "you might even learn something."

He ought to tell her. Just get it over with and tell her straight that he was ignorant. Never spent a day in school in his life. He opened his mouth, but he couldn't get the confession past his constricted throat.

He knew for a fact his shameful secret would be out the minute she pulled out a book and asked him to read, but still he didn't speak. He didn't have any learning, but he had his pride. He'd hold on to it for as long as he could.

"I found the slates, Debs." Case held up one in each hand as he reentered the kitchen. He limped over to the table and placed one in front of Luke. "You can use the one that Debs used when she was in school."

Luke eyed the small rectangle with a mixture of horror and dread. "Thanks."

"Will you both please be seated." Deborah stood at the end

of the table, with Case seated on one side of her and Luke on the other. "First thing we'll work on is the alphabet—that is the letters that make up words."

Case tipped his freckled face up to hers, "But Debs, I already—"

"Case," she said sharply. "Please do not interrupt."

Luke had never heard her use that tone with the boy before.

"I'm sorry," Case said.

She flashed him a smile before saying, "I will make an *A* on your slates. You will trace over it several times in order to see how the letter is formed, and then you will make a row of *A*s on your own."

She took Case's slate, wrote something at the top, then handed it back to him. "You may begin."

Case went to work.

She picked up Luke's slate and chalk, made a mark on it, and handed it back to him. "Trace the letter with the chalk several times to get used to the shape." She lightly traced over it as a demonstration before handing him the chalk. "Now, you try."

Luke glanced from Case back to his own slate. This didn't look too tough.

He scooped up the chalk, clutching it in his hand like a dagger, and pressed it to the slate.

"May I make a suggestion? I think it would be easier if you held it like this." She positioned the chalk correctly in her hand for him to see.

It wasn't so easy as it looked. Luke fumbled with the chalk, trying to copy Deborah's grip, and ended up dropping it. It rolled off the table and onto his lap. His face burned. He'd never felt like such a clod in his life.

"I'm sorry," Deborah said gently. "Holding such a small piece of chalk in your big hand must be extremely awkward. Let me see if I can help." She moved a chair over beside him and sat down. "Give me your hand, please."

He gave her his hand.

She smiled. "It's a piece of chalk, not a rattlesnake. Relax, Luke."

He blew out a long breath, rolled his shoulders, and forced

the tense muscles in his hands to loosen.

"That's better." She swiveled his hand so the palm faced down. Carefully, she inserted the chalk between his fingers, stopping to bend the knuckles slightly or position a finger just so. "Good, now let's trace the letter together."

With her hand over his to guide it, they followed the outline of the *A*.

"Good. Now you try it."

She watched as slowly, painstakingly, his chalk traced the letter. The wobbly, nerve-racking journey around the one-inch *A* was the most arduous work Luke had ever performed. By the time he picked the chalk up from the slate at the end of the letter, a thin sheen of perspiration had sprung up along his brow.

"Excellent. Go ahead and trace it a few more times, then when you're ready, you can make your own *A*s below it."

Deborah walked back to the washtub to wash dishes. Luke rolled his shoulders again and shook out his cramped hand. He took a deep breath and traced over the letter again and again.

He looked up, mopping his brow with his shirtsleeve, to see how little Case was faring under this torture. His jaw dropped. The kid had already made two neat lines of *A*s and hadn't even broken a sweat.

Not one to be whipped by a scrawny seven-year-old, Luke bent his attention back to his own slate. Slowly he made the two lines for the sides, then added a crossbar. He sat back to assess his efforts.

Not too good. It didn't look much like the letter Deborah had made. In fact, if he was honest he'd admit the *A* he drew looked like a tent listing after a heavy storm. He furrowed his brows and tried again.

By the time Deborah took pity on Luke and dismissed him, he'd made a creditable row of *A*s, a rather disreputable row of *B*s, and a fine row of *C*s. In addition to forming the letters on his slate, he could also make the sounds associated with each letter.

Not bad for a first day's work.

Luke was still marveling over his good fortune while he hammered fence posts around the garden plot. He'd had a whole morning of learning, and the subject of his ignorance hadn't come up once.

At first he figured maybe Deborah didn't know he hadn't had any teaching, that she just wanted him to work alongside Case to keep him company. But when he bobbled the chalk and she had to teach him how to hold it properly, he knew she'd seen the truth—he was as dumb as one of these fence posts.

Still, she didn't say anything. As far as he could tell, Deborah didn't think it was a bit strange to be teaching a grown man his alphabet.

Luke raised the sledgehammer high over his head and brought it down on the post with a satisfying *thud*. He couldn't remember ever being happier. His heart felt as light as a cloud.

This morning was easily the best of his life. To be told he was wanted *and* get some teaching all in one day. It was how he always figured Christmas ought to feel.

Even better than the feelings, which he knew wouldn't last, was the fact that he was gonna be able to read. After all these years, he'd despaired of ever learning.

Of course, until a few days ago, reading wasn't a priority. The only time he'd needed to read was when he was transacting business, and he got around that problem by trading with a select few men he knew to be honest.

It wasn't until he'd heard Deborah read stories from the Bible that he'd begun to hunger for the ability to read. He wanted to be able to open that big black book and read it for himself. Imagine having access to that strange peace the Bible afforded him anytime he chose.

⟶✦⟵

Luke lay on his pallet, his arms folded behind his head, looking up through the cracks in the ceiling of the lean-to at the starlit sky. The still night was full of noise, crickets chirping, owls hooting, and the occasional howl of a coyote.

Deborah and the kid had finally settled in; he'd heard her rattle the bolt on the back door one last time as she always did before she went to bed. He smiled into the dark. She surely did worry.

Luke was bone tired, the good kind of ache that came from a full day of hard work. He'd finished the fence more quickly than he'd anticipated. His head had been so full of plans that he didn't even notice he'd been working.

He closed his eyes and tried to imagine the shapes of the three letters he'd learned today. *A*, *B*, *C*. Nothing to it. The way things were going, he'd have this reading business licked in no time. Next time he was in town, he was gonna buy himself a big black Bible of his own.

He smiled into the darkness. With a Bible and the mysterious peace it afforded, Luke's wandering days would finally be over. Funny, that elusive thing he'd been seeking his whole life had been hidden between the pages of a book.

As he drifted off, he reminded himself to ask Deborah just how many letters were in the alphabet.

CHAPTER 10

"Twenty-six!"

Deborah nodded, biting back a smile at Luke's obvious chagrin. "At least that's how many there were at last count."

Luke's dark skin paled. "They're not adding *more* letters, are they?"

She laughed. "No. I'm teasing. The alphabet is set at twenty-six letters."

"Twenty-six letters, each makes at least two sounds. . . ."

She could see where his grumbling calculations were leading. "It'll go faster than you think," she reassured him.

"Some letters hardly get used at all," Case added. "Don't worry, Luke. You can do it."

Luke shot a quick grin at Case then handed the chalk to Deborah. "*A, B, C*—what's next?"

"*D.*" She drew one on the top of the slate. "Give me your hand." She positioned the chalk in his long fingers and guided his hand as they traced the letter. "You make a straight line down, then go back to the top and make an arc that connects at the bottom."

His hand was not quite so stiff beneath hers as it had been

yesterday. His movements were slow and deliberate, but noticeably more relaxed.

"Good," she said, withdrawing her hand. "Now you trace it by yourself. When you think you've got it, make a line of *D*s below it."

Her brother peeked over his slate, watching Luke's halting progress like a proud parent. She'd spoken to Case last night when they were alone. She explained she'd overheard their conversation and knew Luke couldn't read. When she told him of her plans to teach Luke, Case agreed to do whatever he could to help, even if it meant the supreme sacrifice of "relearning" the letters he'd mastered two years ago.

She noted Case hadn't made a single mark on his own slate. She hated to scold him, but it was necessary to keep up the pretense. "Get to work, Case. I'd like to see some *D*s."

He smiled at her, then bent over his slate.

Her students occupied, Deborah settled back in her chair to do the mending. Case's pants were torn at the knee, and the cuff of one of Luke's shirts was frayed. She pulled a spool of brown thread from her sewing basket and threaded her needle.

Every few stitches she'd glance up to see how her students were progressing. It was hard not to admire the determination she saw shining in Luke's dark eyes. It had to be humbling for a proud man to sit hunched over a child's slate, struggling to learn the alphabet, but Luke hadn't let that stop him.

Lips pursed and brows locked in concentration, he worked the elementary exercises with the same diligent care she'd seen him use in everything he undertook.

At that moment, Luke raised his slate to her to display the neat line of wobbly *D*s. He was proud of his misshapen little letters, though she could see he tried to conceal his pride behind his customary unreadable countenance.

"Excellent, Luke. Very nice indeed." The gleam of pleasure her slight praise brought to his eyes touched her heart. "I believe you're ready to go on to the next letter. The letter *E*."

After she'd gotten him started on *E*s, she returned to her mending. Her brother's pants finished, she rooted through her basket to find the right shade of thread to repair Luke's shirt. It needed red, not the bright red of an apple, but the rich, muted red of a barn. She hadn't failed to notice he looked particularly handsome wearing the color; it seemed to enhance his skin tone and raven black hair.

She pulled out several possibilities and laid them against the sleeve to choose the closest match. She marveled over the quality of the shirt. The fine weave of the fabric and tiny perfect stitches indicated this was no homespun garment, but a costly one.

She surreptitiously raised her eyes from her work to watch Luke labor over the straight line of *E*s. It occurred to her that he was very much a mystery.

He appeared to be a drifter, with no aspirations to better himself, yet she'd never known a man with a stronger work ethic or a more rigidly defined sense of honor. He couldn't read or write, but she'd witnessed his uncanny skills with numbers when he helped Case with his arithmetic yesterday. He appeared to have little interest in money, yet his few possessions were of the highest quality.

He kept himself from them, preferring to remain aloof, yet she'd seen the delight in his eyes when Case followed him around, and there was no mistaking the genuine emotion in his voice the night he told Case he loved him.

Who was this man, Luke, who had somehow become a part of their little family? Deborah was determined to find out.

<hr />

One week later, the threesome was again gathered around the table after the breakfast dishes had been removed to do their lessons. Deborah had come to look forward to "school," as they'd begun to call it. Fact was, it had become her favorite part of the day. Through the enforced confinement of the "classroom" they'd developed a comfortable camaraderie that banished any loneliness she'd felt being so far from home and family.

Luke lifted his slate, with a completed row of *U*s, for her approval. "How's this?"

"Very nice," she said. "And now I have a surprise for you."

"You're going to tell me that the bit about twenty-six letters was all a joke, and that *U* is the last one I have to learn?"

She laughed. "No. Better than that. You now know all the letters you need to know to write your first name." She took his chalk and slate and printed *L-U-K-E* beneath the row of *U*s, then handed it back to him.

"*L-U-K-E.* That's my name, huh?"

His attempt at being blasé failed miserably. She could see he was excited to see his name written down and was champing at the bit to try writing it out for himself.

"Give me your hand." With her hand over his to guide it, they traced the letters together.

He'd come a long way in a week. His hand no longer faltered over the letters, instead his movements were smooth and confident. Truthfully, he didn't need her to help him trace the letters anymore, but she liked to do it.

No doubt a shameless hussy, she enjoyed the warmth of his large capable hand beneath hers, the contrast of her fair skin to his bronze hand. Worse, she liked to hold his hand because it gave her an excuse to sit close to him. It sent lovely little shivers up her spine when her shoulder brushed against his broad shoulder or chest.

And he smelled so good. She wasn't sure why, since they all used the same soap, but Luke smelled different. Better. While he was engrossed in his writing, she'd lean forward, ever so slightly, and breathe deeply, filling her senses with his manly scent.

It was ironic, really. She was the one who'd been so insistent that they have no physical contact, and now she found herself counting the minutes until she could touch him again.

She might be a hussy, but she wasn't a fool. She never let on to Luke that holding his hand was anything more than the obligation of a dutiful teacher. A teacher who'd almost worked herself out of a job. There were only five letters left. She was mightily tempted to add to the original twenty-six.

Case watched Luke writing his name. "That's great. Say, what's your last name? Deborah can show you how to write both."

Luke's hand stopped in midstroke. He raised his eyes to Case.

"Luke's the only name I've got."

"Everybody's got two names, Luke," Case insisted. "Maybe you just forgot the other one."

Luke shook his head. "I've only got one name. You've got to have a father to have two."

"You don't have a father?"

Deborah was aware that, along with her brother, she was staring at Luke, awaiting his answer.

Luke looked down for a minute, as if choosing his words carefully, then spoke. "I don't have a father who claims me."

There was a long, awkward pause before Case said, "Oh."

Poor Luke. Deborah could cry to see the hurt behind his brave expression. His tone had been light as he'd said the words, but it was obvious they pierced him all the way to his heart.

"Tell us about your mother, Luke," she said, trying to steer the conversation to safer, happier ground. "Is she still alive? Does she live nearby?"

His dark eyes took on the strange shuttered look she'd seen before when she'd probed too deeply. "She died when I was five. In Oklahoma, on an Indian reservation."

Case looked stricken. Deborah knew he must be thinking of his own circumstances. "You were just a little boy when she died. Who took care of you?"

"I took care of myself," Luke said with a careless shrug. "Seemed nobody wanted a part-Comanche, part-white kid."

"Did you stay on at the reservation?"

"For a while. As soon as I could, I took off. I traveled around doing odd jobs for a meal or a place to stay." It was obvious by the way he spoke that the memories were uncomfortable, even painful.

"Is that where you met Cyrus?" Deborah asked.

Luke's face brightened. "Yeah. Ol' Cyrus didn't care that I was a half-breed. He told me that the way he figured it, one human was as good as the next." He lapsed into thoughtful silence. Finally he said, "Your uncle Cyrus is a good man."

Deborah resolved to look upon her uncle with a little more charity. He might have exaggerated the charms of his house and left it in a shambles, but he evidently was the first, and maybe the only person to show Luke kindness. She lifted a silent prayer to heaven that God would repay Cyrus's hospitality a hundredfold.

"You know, Luke," Case was saying. "Jesus says the same thing as Uncle Cyrus. He loves everybody the same. Even cripples and half-breeds."

Luke shot him a grin. "Your friend sounds like a real nice guy."

~◆~

Deborah labored with a heavy heart for the rest of the day. No matter what she did, her thoughts returned to the glimpses Luke had given them of his childhood.

Preparing meals reminded her of a little boy forced to work for every scrap of food. As she turned the mattress and changed the linens, she imagined the kind of cold, dirty places a homeless child would be forced to sleep in. When she fussed at her brother for his table manners, or his dirty face and hands, she tried to imagine what it would be like to grow up without anyone to care.

When Luke and Case washed the evening dishes, Deborah slipped into her room to pray. "What do You want me to say, Lord? What comfort do You have to offer a man who's known rejection his whole life?"

Each evening while the men washed the dishes, Deborah put on a kettle of water to heat. After the dishes were put away, she'd add the boiling water to a tub of cold water for evening baths. Without servants to haul and heat the water, hot sink-down-to-your-neck baths were a luxury to be enjoyed once a week. The rest of the time, they made do with the tub of warm water on the kitchen table, a washrag, and soap. A modicum of privacy was achieved by sending the others to another room.

After everyone had washed off the day's grime and Luke had dumped the water out back, they settled in around the stove for Scripture time. Tonight, as Deborah arranged her skirts and opened the Bible on her lap, she was moved to do something different.

"Tonight we're not going to continue where we left off last night in the story of the Israelites."

Luke's disappointment was clearly visible by flickering lamplight.

"I've been thinking about what you told us this morning, Luke, and I was reminded of a psalm where King David describes God's position to the fatherless. It is Psalm 68:5–6." She flipped to the verse and began to read. "'A father of the fatherless, and a judge of the widows, is God in his holy habitation. God setteth the solitary in families: he bringeth out those which are bound with chains: but the rebellious dwell in a dry land.'"

Deborah looked up from the passage. "If my understanding of this is correct, God has been watching out for you all along, as a father to the fatherless. Furthermore, I believe He directed you to us"—she glanced down at the Bible to reread—"God setteth the solitary in families."

"It says all that?"

She nodded.

He was out of his chair and at her side. "Where?"

She pointed to the verses with her finger. He looked down at the words for a moment, but with his still-limited knowledge of letters, it was useless. He heaved an impatient sigh and returned to his chair.

"Maybe you'd better read it again," he suggested. "So I can catch all the words."

Deborah lay awake long after Case's breathing had developed the slow cadence of sleep. Sleep eluded her. Her mind was cluttered with thoughts and impressions of the day. She'd made progress in solving the mystery of Luke and, at the same time, uncovered a new mystery.

His questionable parentage and lack of upbringing seemed to explain his reticent nature. Uncle Cyrus's unprecedented kindness to the unwanted child gave credence to Luke's determination to repay Cyrus by looking after her and Case. He'd learned to work hard from necessity.

When she thought about his childhood, a deep sense of grief and pity welled up within her.

But when she thought of Luke and the man he'd become, she had nothing but admiration for him.

Necessity and rejection might have molded him to a point, but the fact that the hardships he'd faced hadn't defeated him filled her with respect.

Luke was a fine, honorable man she'd come to esteem highly.

The mystery she now faced was, how had he come to mean so much to her and what was she going to do about it?

CHAPTER 11

T hat's all for today, gentlemen. Case, would you please put up the slates? Luke, since you've completed your alphabet, I want you to spend the next few days in review before we start something else." After issuing her instructions, Deborah got up from the table and headed out to the hall.

Luke watched her go, enjoying the gentle sway of her skirts. He was surely going to miss the alphabet lessons. Especially the hand-holding.

While he was delighted to have completed the alphabet, he was sorry there'd be no more reason for Deborah to place her slender hand over his to guide him around a letter. If he hadn't been in such a hurry to learn to read for himself, he'd have told her he couldn't do so many letters each day. At least that way he'd have extended the touching for a few more days.

It wasn't just the hand-holding that made learning so pleasurable. He liked it when she scooted her chair real close to his.

At first the writing part made him break out into a sweat, but after a day or two, it wasn't the letters that got him worked up. It was the woman.

Up close he could appreciate the fine, creamy texture of her skin. He could admire her long, thick lashes and the way the tip of her tongue peeked out from between her lips when she concentrated real hard. Separated by just inches, he could feel the warmth of her body and smell the sweet fragrance of her hair.

It made him sweat just to think about it.

Maybe it was a good thing there were only twenty-six letters. Any more and he'd dehydrate.

Deborah reentered the kitchen, tying on a wide-brimmed straw bonnet over her hair. "I'm going to plant my seeds this morning. Case, do you want to come?"

"Do you need me?"

She looked surprised at the question. "Not really. I just knew you always enjoyed watching me put in a garden."

"If you need my help, I'll be glad to come with you, but if not, I think I'd rather go with Luke." He flashed her a sheepish grin. "That is, if you don't mind."

She laughed. "I don't mind at all. You two go along. But remember to be back by noon for lunch."

⸺⸺❖⸺⸺

Case followed Luke to the barn, like a puppy trailing at his heels. "What are we going to do today, Luke?"

"I thought we'd ride out across the place—check things out."

"You gonna take Horse?"

Luke nodded. "Beats walking."

"You and me are both gonna ride Horse?" Case asked for clarification. "Together?"

Luke nodded again.

"Yippee!" Case hopped up and down like a crazed grasshopper. He chattered excitedly while Luke saddled Horse and led her out of the barn into the sunlight. "She sure is big. She sure has pretty eyes. I wonder if she likes the taste of hay. How much do you think she weighs?"

Luke grinned at the steady stream of talk. "You ready?"

Case's gaze traveled the long distance from the ground to Horse's back, several feet above his head. He swallowed hard. "Yup."

Luke caught him around the waist and gently lifted him up onto the saddle.

Case's green eyes widened. "This is so high."

"You sit up by the horn," Luke instructed him. "I'll ride behind you."

Case moved forward and Luke mounted behind him, putting an arm around either side of the boy. "You take the reins."

Case swiveled to face him. "Me?" he squeaked.

Luke nodded.

Case took the leather straps in his hands with a white-knuckled grip. "So how do I make her go?"

"Give her a little nudge with your leg."

Horse, as well-trained a mare as any Luke ever had, responded to the slight pressure by walking.

"I did it!" Case exclaimed. "I made her go."

What was it about the kid that made the simplest things enjoyable? "Okay now, lead her around the house and out the front gate."

Case lapsed into a rare silence as he directed his full concentration on steering the horse. Once past the gate, Luke instructed him to keep to the dirt road that edged the property.

After they'd walked along for several minutes, Case asked, "Can she go any faster?"

Luke checked over his shoulder. The house stood between them and Deborah. He was certain even her eagle eyes couldn't see them. Seemed prudent she didn't witness them moving along at anything beyond a leisurely pace. "Yeah, she'll go faster. Better give me the reins."

Luke pulled Case closer to brace the boy against his body. "Hold on to the horn. Ready?"

He felt Case nod.

Luke slapped the reins and Horse shot off at a full gallop. As her long strides ate up the road, the force of the speed pushed Case against Luke's chest. Just as he expected, the kid wasn't afraid. Case was laughing and squealing in pure delight.

After a minute or two of flying along at a hard, breathtaking gallop, Luke reined Horse in. "Whoa, now. Easy, girl."

"That was fine," Case declared when they'd slowed to a walk. "Can we do it again?"

Luke laughed. "Later. Let's give Horse a rest."

With his hat pulled down to shield his eyes from the sun, Luke trained his attention on the land, looking for evidence of trespassers. They cantered down the dirt road, kicking up a cloud of dust, then turned east through waist-deep grass to check out the places where the cover of trees would make it an appealing place to camp.

After an hour or so, Luke was satisfied there'd been no suspicious activity. Everything looked unchanged since his vigil several weeks ago.

"Where are we going, Luke?"

He'd almost forgotten the boy was there. Case was uncharacteristically quiet. A sure sign he was tiring. "What do you say we head to the springs?"

"That sounds great," Case said in a weary little voice. He hesitated for a heartbeat before asking, "What springs?"

"Let me show you." Luke chuckled as he reined Horse around. The kid had amazing spirit. Infirmity never got in the way of his enthusiasm. Case was up for anything.

With one arm wrapped securely around Case's waist, Luke steered Horse through the swaying grasses toward the northeast end of Cyrus's land. Luke slowed the horse as they reached the mesquite-ringed pond.

He slid out of the saddle and extended his arms to Case, whose normally pale skin shone a bloodless white. As he leaned heavily into Luke's arms, Luke realized the kid was exhausted. Instead of lowering him to the ground to walk the short distance to the spring, Luke slid an arm under Case's legs and carried him. Case was too tired to protest.

Luke pushed through the low-growing trees, his back to the branches to shield Case, and up to a smooth flat rock the size of the kitchen table at the water's edge. Luke lowered Case onto the rock, then sat beside him.

"Sure is pretty, Luke," Case said, trailing his fingers in the crystal-clear water. "You visit here much?"

"Cyrus and I used to come here when the weather got warm enough to swim. We'd stay in the water until we were nearly frozen, then we'd lie back on this rock and let the sun dry us." Luke crossed his arms behind his head and lay back to demonstrate.

As he expected, Case copied him, lying down with his feet dangling over the edge of the rock. They lay there in silence, enjoying the penetrating heat from the sun-warmed rock and the cheerful burbling of the spring.

Luke had begun to think Case had dropped off to sleep when his little voice piped up, "Looking up at the sky always makes me think of God."

Luke looked up into the wide canopy of blue. "I can see where it might."

"You, too, Luke? Does it make you think of God?"

Luke pondered the question. From childhood he'd been aware that something or someone greater than himself had created the earth. The intricacies of a single flower, the majesty of a rock canyon, the beauty of a lake at dawn all bespoke the craftsmanship of a limitless being. But being raised as neither Indian nor white man, he had never heard the name of the creator.

It wasn't until Deborah opened the Bible and read to him of God, the all-powerful Creator of the universe, that he knew who was behind it all.

"I'd never heard about God before you and your sister came along."

Case sprang up, propping himself on one elbow so that he might look into Luke's face. "No one ever told you about God? Not even in church?"

"Didn't go to church."

"Didn't go—" Case paused. "Then no one's ever introduced you to Jesus, have they?"

"Can't say as they have. Of course, if he's from Louisiana, like you, it's not likely our paths would ever cross."

"From Louisiana?" Case started to giggle. "Oh no, Luke, Jesus isn't a person like you or me. He's a spirit. God's Son."

Luke tipped his hat off his face and sat up. "How was I supposed to know He's not from Louisiana?" he grumbled. "With you yapping about Him all the time, 'bout how He's your friend and everything, I figured He had to be a neighbor."

Case grew serious. "I'm sorry, Luke. I wasn't making fun of you. Honest. I was just so surprised to hear you didn't know about Jesus."

Somewhat mollified, Luke settled back against the rock and recovered his face with his hat.

"Just as soon as God made the world and the people in it, folks began to sin. They turned away from God. But even though they chose their own ways instead of God's ways, God still loved them. He wanted to make a way for sinful people to come back to Him. You see, sin separates us from God."

"Makes sense." Luke remembered the Bible stories Deborah read that spoke of the sacrifices God's people had to offer to cover their sins so that they could be right with God.

"So God sent His only Son, Jesus. Jesus never sinned, not even once. But Jesus loved people so much that He was willing to take the punishment for everyone's sins on Himself so that they could come back to God."

"What was the punishment?"

"Death. They hung Him on a cross."

Luke gave a low whistle. "Seems like mighty serious punishment."

Case nodded. "It is. But then God is seriouser about sin than Debs is about washing behind my ears. The Bible says that the wages of sin are death."

"So this Jesus fella is willing to die in the place of those folks so they can get back on good terms with God?"

"Not just 'those folks.' Anybody. You and me."

Luke sat up. "Why would He die for me? I don't even know Him."

"But He knows you. And He loves you. The Bible says so. When Jesus hung on the cross and died, it was because He loves you."

"So now everybody is right with God?"

Case shook his head. "No. God offers Jesus' sacrifice so folks can get right with Him, but it's a present. A present isn't yours until you accept it."

"How do you accept a gift you can't see, from a God you can't see?"

"By faith. You accept it with your heart. When you truly realize that you want to be right with God and can't do it on your own, then you tell Him. You tell Him you accept His gift of salvation."

Luke cocked a dark brow in skepticism. "Where'd you hear all this?"

"It's in the Bible, Luke. Every word of it. I can show you when we get home."

After lunch, while Deborah tidied the kitchen, Case got his Bible from his bedroom and carried it out to the lean-to. "Luke, you got a minute?" he called from the doorway.

"For you, yeah. What do you need?"

Case limped into the shelter. "I wanted to show you where it says all that stuff about Jesus in the Bible."

They sat side by side on the pallet while Case flipped the pages of his Bible. Luke bit back a sigh of frustration. The words on the pages still looked like nothing more than a jumble of symbols to him. He could make out the individual letters, but he began to despair he'd ever be able to read the words for himself.

"Here's one of the real important ones. It's John 3:16. It says, 'For God so loved the world, that he gave his only begotten Son, that whosoever believeth in him should not perish, but have everlasting life.' "

"What's this 'everlasting life' stuff?"

"It means that after you die, your spirit will live on, forever, with God."

"Oh."

Case flipped a few more pages. "Here's one you and I talked about earlier. It's in Romans 6:23. 'For the wages of sin is death; but the gift of God is eternal life through Jesus Christ our Lord.' " Case looked up. "You see, it's just like I said, salvation is a present from God. He wants to give it to you, because He loves you."

Though he was far from understanding how God could love him, Luke nodded.

"There's one more thing, a verse I think you'll like the best of all." Case's little fingers flew over the pages as he searched. "Ah, here it is. It's in the book of John, chapter one, verse twelve. " 'But as many as received him, to them gave he power to become the sons of God, even to them that believe on his name.' " He beamed up at Luke. "Do you understand what that says?"

"Not exactly."

"It says that when you receive the gift of Jesus as your Savior, then you become a son of God. Don't you see, Luke? You'd never have to feel sad that you didn't have a father, because God would be your father."

CHAPTER 12

Despite only a few hour's sleep, Luke felt better than he'd ever felt in his life. He'd lain awake for hours last night, marveling over the facts Case had shared from his Bible. God loved him.

Deborah had told him before that God looked after widows and orphans, but it was hearing about God's Son, Jesus, that revealed the depth of God's love.

God loved Luke enough that He'd give up His own Son's life to win Luke to Himself. Amazing.

Not only did God love him, but He wanted to call Luke His child. The deepest desire of Luke's heart, the yearning he dared not speak aloud, was to belong to someone. He'd wanted to be not an embarrassing product of a night's passion, but an acknowledged member of the family.

And all this time, God had wanted to call Luke His son.

Luke shifted the weight of the bundle of chopped wood to his left arm so he might open the back door with his right. The mouthwatering smell of freshly baked biscuits and fried ham wafted out to meet him. He stepped inside, pushed the door closed behind him with his booted foot, and started down the hall when Case rounded the corner and barreled into him.

"Whoa there," Luke said, lifting the bundle high so Case wouldn't plow face-first into the wood. "What's the hurry?"

"We're going into town, Luke," Case managed between gasps. "Debs said so. Said she needs to do some shopping on account of my birthday's coming up."

"Birthday, huh?"

Case fell into step beside Luke as he carried the wood into the kitchen and deposited it in the woodbin. "Yup. April 30. I'll be eight years old."

"You'll be an old man for sure."

"We're going to leave as soon as breakfast's over and the team is hitched up. You'll come, won't you?"

Even though things were going pretty well, he wasn't going to take any chances of provoking Deborah's ire by inviting himself where he wasn't wanted. Luke looked over to Deborah, who was standing at the stove, for approval.

She nodded. "We'd like you to join us," she said with a smile. "That is, if you feel you can get away."

If she kept smiling at him like that, she'd have a hard time keeping him away. "Got nothing pressing."

She carried a plate heaped with sliced ham and biscuits to the table. "You all sit down and we'll eat."

Breakfast was accomplished in a hurry. While Deborah cleaned up the breakfast dishes, Luke and Case went outside to hitch up the team.

"So what's a fella turning eight get for his birthday?" Luke asked as they walked across the yard. He needed to be thinking about a present for the kid and didn't figure his own childhood would provide any clues. As a boy of eight, all Luke had wanted was a full stomach and a warm, safe place to sleep.

Case shrugged. "Usually a shirt or a pair of pants."

"That right? That's what you want?"

Case wrinkled his nose. "Naw, but it's the kind of things girls like to give. Deborah won't give me what I really want."

"What's that?"

Case looked over his shoulder to be certain they wouldn't be overheard. "Promise you won't tell?"

Luke tried to match Case's solemn expression. He held up his right hand and vowed, "I promise."

Case looked back once again, then leaned in toward Luke to whisper, "I want a ladder."

"A ladder?"

"Shh!" Case whipped around to be sure his sister wasn't nearby. "You told me you wouldn't tell."

Luke dismissed the suggestion with a careless wave of his hand. "She can't hear us. She's in the house. But I don't understand what in the world you would want with a ladder."

Case's green eyes sparkled. "I'd climb to the loft."

Now Luke began to understand. There was a narrow loft above the "sitting room," as Deborah liked to call it. One of Luke's responsibilities since joining Case and his sister had been to help remove the trash from the room opposite the kitchen and make the place habitable. He'd noticed how Case never missed an opportunity to join him in the sitting room, and once there how he was drawn to the rickety ladder leaning against the wall. Case would stand at the bottom and look up longingly at the loft.

Once Luke had asked Case why he didn't climb up and see what was there, but Case had explained that Deborah had forbidden it. Seemed that a ladder was too risky for a crippled boy.

Since then, Deborah had Luke break up the old relic to use for firewood.

"I'd sleep up there every night," Case said, his eyes alight with the dream. "It would be my own special place, like a tree house high above the world."

"It'd be a fine place for an eight-year-old to sleep."

Reality doused the light in Case's eyes. "Of course, I always need new pants."

His heart broken at the child's resigned acceptance, Luke nodded. "Of course."

Once the team was harnessed, Luke went in to get Deborah. "Wagon's ready, ma'am."

She hurried down the hall toward him, adjusting her hat. "Thank you, Luke."

He gave her a hand up into the wagon, a less than satisfactory experience since both wore gloves, and climbed up onto the bench beside her. She sent him a smile of thanks that warmed him all the way to his boots.

"You okay back there?" he called over his shoulder to Case, who sat behind them, with his back to the side of the wagon.

"You bet," Case called back. "Let's see how fast you can run 'em, Luke."

Luke darted a sheepish glance at Deborah, who met his look with a suspicious tilt of her brow. Luke decided it was in the best interest of peacekeeping to lead the team out at a sedate pace.

Spring was in full bloom in Texas. An ever-present breeze stirred the lush green grasses, giving them the rolling appearance of waves on the sea. Bright clusters of flowers—red clovers, coral Indian paintbrushes, and indigo bluebonnets—grew in colorful abundance. For a time the occupants of the wagon rode in silence, content to bask in the wide-open beauty.

"I suppose I ought to consider purchasing horses," Deborah said as they rattled along the dirt road. "Oxen don't make a very handsome team."

"And horses are *much* faster," Case piped up from the back.

"Thank you, Case," Deborah said repressively. "Luke, what do you think? Should I look into getting a pair of horses? I have some money set aside. Would they be a worthwhile investment or an expensive extravagance?"

"Want my honest opinion?"

"Yes."

"Horses are useful. And the boy"—Luke indicated Case with a jerk of his thumb—"ought to have one of his own. Man's gotta know how to ride and care for a horse."

Case was on his knees behind them. "Oh Debs, I'd love a horse."

Deborah toyed with her reticule as she digested the information. "As to the cost? What would—"

A wonderful idea occurred to Luke. Here was his opportunity to repay some of what Deborah and her brother had given him. It was a rare experience, a heady feeling, to be on equal footing with her. In this he wasn't a hired man. He wasn't a student. He was an equal. "I can get a couple of beauties for you, for free."

"We can afford free, Debs," Case said.

Deborah folded her arms across her chest and sat up even straighter. "Absolutely not. I won't hear of it. I'm sorry I brought the matter up."

"What—?"

She met his bewildered look with an angry one. "I cannot abide horse thieves."

"Horse thieves?" he repeated with a dangerous edge to his voice. "You thought I was going to *steal* the horses for you?"

Her eyes widened at his ominous dark glare, but she proceeded, "Well, yes, I did. What else am I to think? You have your own horse, but to acquire others at no cost—"

"I have several horses," he said coolly. "Horses gained through honest means. I am not a thief."

"No indeed," Case chirped from the back. "What a silly thing to say, Debs. There isn't a finer man than our Luke anywhere." He punctuated his statement with a pat on Luke's back. "You should know that."

"I'm sorry—"

He knew she was looking at him, but he refused to take his eyes from the road. "When we get to town, I'll send word for two horses to be delivered."

"We couldn't accept such a costly gift."

"Consider them payment for my education." Luke spoke with such chilling finality he knew no one would challenge him.

No one spoke at all.

The celebratory air with which they'd begun the excursion disappeared like a vapor. They rode along in uncomfortable silence with only the jangling of harnesses and the rattling of the wagon to disturb the quiet.

Luke was furious. And hurt. He tried to tell himself it didn't matter. It wasn't the first time somebody had mistaken him for a criminal, and it wouldn't be the last.

But it did matter. Other folks took one look at his bronze skin and coal-black hair and thought the worst. He was used to that. But to have been around Deborah all this time and realize she'd never looked beyond the surface, to the man within, cut deeply.

He'd been a fool to believe things were different with Deborah. To let a few warm looks and some hand-holding convince him that she saw him as something more than an ignorant half-breed.

As bad as he was feeling, he felt a hundred times worse to know he'd ruined the kid's trip into town. Instead of his usual nonstop flow of excited chatter, Case was shut up tight. Probably afraid to say anything for fear of setting Luke off.

He'd never hurt the boy. A man couldn't ask for a finer champion. The darkness that had settled over him lifted with the memory of Case's little hand patting him while he defended Luke to his sister. "Couldn't find a finer man," he'd said.

"You still back there?" Luke called over his shoulder.

"Yes, sir."

"Whew. I'm glad to hear it. It was so quiet I was beginning to think a big old crow swooped down and carried you off."

The sound of Case's giggling warmed Luke. "There's a flock of hungry-looking birds in that stand of trees up ahead." He pointed to a pecan grove on the right. "Seems to me that you'd better look lively lest they mistake you for lunch."

Case was back on his knees, looking off in the direction of Luke's gloved finger. "Do you really think so?" he asked in obvious delight at the gruesome prospect.

Luke chuckled.

"Think maybe if I sing it'll warn them off?"

"Seems reasonable."

Case sat back against the wagon wall and began to sing. In the pure, clear tones of a child he sang songs about God's love and faithfulness, songs they'd sung after Deb's Bible reading in the evening. Pretty soon Deborah joined in, adding her voice in perfect harmony. The combination of the heavenly sounds and heart-stirring words raised gooseflesh on Luke's arms. Funny how even songs about God had the power to speak to the hunger in his soul.

The last half hour of the trip passed quickly. Case and Deborah sang. Between songs Case exclaimed over the flowers and birds and everything else they passed along the way.

By the time Luke had slowed the team in front of the general store, he'd almost forgotten Deborah's unflattering accusations. Almost.

"Whoa." He pulled back on the reins then looked to Deborah for instructions.

"Case, dearest, why don't you run inside and see if the shopkeeper has any penny candy." She pulled a coin from her reticule and pressed it into his hand.

Case looked confused. "Aren't you two coming?"

"Yes, in just a minute. Luke and I have something to discuss first."

Case shot Luke a pitying glance. "Are you sure you don't want to come on with me?"

"In a minute. You run along."

Luke hopped down from the wagon to lift Case out. As he did, Case whispered, "Think she means to yell at you? Would you rather I stay?"

Luke grinned as he gently lowered the boy to the ground and waited for him to gain his balance before releasing him. "You go ahead," he whispered back. "I can handle your sister."

Case didn't look convinced. "Don't let her send you away. Remind her she promised you could stay."

Luke ruffled his hair. "I'll remind her."

Case stepped up onto the grayed plank sidewalk and limped up to the store, stopping several times to send an unhappy look to Luke over his shoulder before entering.

Luke walked back around to the front of the wagon and climbed onto the bench. "What is it you want to discuss?"

She kept her eyes downcast, trained on her hands folded in her lap. "I wanted to tell you I'm sorry."

"Forget it."

She raised her eyes to his. "I can't. I spoke without thinking earlier—"

"It's nothing."

Deborah refused to be deterred. "—and I hurt you."

This time it was Luke who looked away.

"I'm truly sorry, Luke. Case was right to scold me. I know better than to think you're a thief."

She reached over to lay her small, gloved hand on his. When he looked up she said, "I haven't known you long, but I am certain that I've never met a more honorable man than you. You are kind, hardworking, gentle, and intelligent, and Case and I are blessed to call you our friend."

As if that wasn't enough to send his senses reeling, Deborah leaned up and planted a quick kiss on his cheek before scrambling down off the bench in a flurry of skirts. Once on the ground, she raised her face to his, her smooth skin flaming beneath her bonnet, and said primly, "Meet us in the store after you've completed your business." With that she turned and darted up into the store.

For a long moment Luke stared after her in mute amazement. A man didn't usually have that many nice things said over him when he was laid to rest. To have heard all that, and get kissed, and still be alive to enjoy it was just about more than he could stand.

Finally he hopped off the bench, secured the team, and headed down the dirt street with the swagger of a man with the world in his pocket. It was an unusual feeling to be appreciated, one he wouldn't mind getting used to.

Luke strode past the livery and the blacksmith, past the saloon, to the sturdy stone office at the end of the street that served as bank and post office. He had his hand on the doorknob and was about to step inside when a man standing by the door of the jail across the street caught his eye.

Luke's hand fell away from the door as he turned around for a closer look. "Adam?"

The man at the jail lifted his head and looked over toward Luke.

Luke stepped down off the sidewalk and started across the street. "Adam Waldrip?" he called, louder this time.

This time the man took a step forward. "Luke? Is that you?"

Both men hurried now, meeting in the middle of the road.

"Luke!" A wide grin split Adam's face as he clapped a hand on Luke's back. "You're a sight for sore eyes. How long has it been?"

Luke smiled back at the one man besides Cyrus he called friend. "Long time, Adam. Too long."

Adam stepped back to study Luke. "The years seem to sit awful well on you." He shook his head with mock dismay. "Must be that savage blood that preserves you so well."

Luke snorted at the oft-repeated jibe. "Wish I could say the same for you. Cryin' shame you get uglier every time I see you. It's a wonder the townsfolk haven't asked you to wear a feed sack over your head to keep from frightening the children and livestock."

Easily the best-looking man west of the Mississippi and un-comfortably aware of it, Adam threw back his head and laughed. "I've missed you, Luke. Have you got a minute? We've got some catching up to do."

When Adam placed a hand on Luke's shoulder and steered him back toward the jail, Luke asked, "Where're we headed?"

Adam nodded toward the jail. "My office."

"The jail?" Belatedly Luke noticed the star on Adam's chest. "You're the law?"

Adam grinned. "Only temporarily."

"I'll bet there's a story that goes along with the badge," Luke said.

Adam swung open the door and stepped aside for Luke to enter. "You can hear the whole thing over a cup of coffee."

Luke pulled up a chair and sat down while Adam went to the back to get the coffee.

Adam returned seconds later and handed Luke a cup. "What're you doing back in Texas? I thought we'd seen the last of you."

Luke shrugged. It was too difficult to try to explain the longing that drove him here, the void that prevented him from set-tling down. "Thought I might come back and check on Cyrus."

"He's gone, Luke. Got a wild hair to move farther west."

Luke nodded. "I know."

"You've been out to his place already?"

"Been living there a couple of weeks."

Adam laughed. "I should have known you were in town when Crandall told me about a tall fellow who appeared out of the shadows like an avenging angel to save him from certain death."

"You know Crandall?"

"Jed Crandall? Big rancher fella? Sure. I must have run into him just days after you did. He's the one who talked me into taking this job." Adam pointed to the badge. "I told him I'd do it until they could find someone else. I'm thinking of settling down here and opening law offices." Adam suddenly frowned. "If you've been out at Cyrus's place for a couple of weeks, how come I haven't seen you before?"

"I haven't been into town. Haven't had any time. Woman's been running me pretty hard."

A predatory gleam lit Adam's eyes as he moved his chair closer to Luke's. "A woman, huh? This is getting interesting. What's a woman doing out at Cyrus's place? With you?"

"She's kin. A niece of his."

"Oh." Adam's face fell. "She look like him?"

Luke chuckled. Cyrus was a kind man with a heart as big as Texas, but he was two shades uglier than sin. Deborah was a vision. Still, it might not be a bad thing for Adam to suspect a family resemblance.

Luke had witnessed firsthand Adam's almost mythical powers over the ladies, and he didn't want him within fifty yards of Deborah for fear she'd fall under his spell. "Definitely family," he said with a deliberately misleading nod.

"Too bad. Why are you hanging around?"

"She and her kid brother are all alone out there. I couldn't very well turn my back on them. Not after all Cyrus did for me."

"It's that code of honor of yours," Adam said with a knowing nod. "Seems it's always getting you into a mess." He chuckled. "Of course, I'm grateful you have it. I'd be a dead man if it wasn't for that sense of honor that makes you stick your nose where it doesn't belong. Still, I hate to see you trapped playing nursemaid to some old spinster."

Luke released the long-suffering sigh of a martyr. "I've got to do it."

Adam wagged his head. "You're a better man than I. Is there anything I can do to help?"

There was something. It was humiliating to have to ask another man to perform such a simple task, even if the man was his friend. "As a matter of fact, there is. She and her brother need horses. I told her I'd get a couple for them, but I really don't have time to ride south to get them. I was on my way to the bank to get someone to write a letter to Juan, asking him to send me a pair. . ."

Adam saved him the embarrassment by suggesting, "Why don't you let me write the letter? Let me get a pen and paper, and you can tell me what to say."

———

It was nearly three-quarters of an hour later when Luke strode up the hard-packed dirt of Main Street toward the general store. Time had gotten away from him as he'd visited with Adam. They'd had over a year of history to catch each other up on.

As he walked, Luke allowed himself the luxury of a daydream. He imagined settling down in one place, with a good woman by his side, a fine boy to raise, and a loyal friend for a neighbor. He was so entrenched in his thoughts he didn't see the man staggering out of the saloon and into his path until he was nearly on top of him.

Luke's arm caught the man's shoulder hard enough to spin him around. Luke tried to catch him, but his reaction was a fraction of a second too late, and the man hit the ground with a thud.

"I'm sorry," Luke said, bending over him to give him a hand up. "I wasn't watching."

The man, pitifully thin and unshaven, squinted up at Luke through the cloud of dust he'd raised when he fell. "An Indian." He cursed, his speech slurred with liquor. "Shoulda known. Indians think they own the West." He cursed again.

Luke ignored the insults. "Here," he said as he reached out his hand, "let me help you up."

The man spat on the ground. "I'm not touchin' no filthy Indian."

The remark was almost funny coming from a man so encrusted with dirt Luke could scarcely tell if he was black or white. "Suit yourself." He left the man lying there and turned to walk away.

"Wait!" The man labored to his hands and knees, stirring up more dust in the process, and after several wobbly false starts, pulled himself to his feet. He stood there, swaying unsteadily, as he tried to focus bloodshot eyes on Luke's face. "I've seen you before," he said at last.

Luke shook his head. He'd never laid eyes on the man before today. The poor drunk was delusional. Luke turned to go.

"I've seen you before," the man insisted.

Luke could see Deborah and Case standing out in front of the store, waiting on him. He walked toward them, picking up his pace to shake the drunk who now followed him, shouting in a raspy voice, "I know you."

"Who is that?" Deborah asked in a nervous whisper when Luke arrived at the front of the store.

Luke cast a careless glance over his shoulder to see the drunk stumbling along some twenty yards away. "Nobody. Just a drunk."

Even so, Luke was determined to be gone before the man caught up to them. His shouting was beginning to draw a crowd, and Luke didn't want Deborah and Case exposed to the crude insults. He took the paper-wrapped packages from Deborah's arms. "Is this all?"

"The rest is already loaded in the wagon."

"Good. Let's go." He caught her elbow and hurried her to the wagon, with Case ambling along behind them.

Luke tossed Case into the back of the well-loaded wagon, then gave Deborah a hand up before going around to climb onto the bench beside her.

The drunk was almost alongside them when Luke took the reins and signaled the team to go. The man shouted something, his words too slurred to understand, as they rolled by him.

"He's creepy, Luke," Case whispered from behind him. "I wish he'd go away."

"He's just a poor old drunk, Case," Luke assured him as he steered the team out of town. "Nothing to worry about."

But even as he spoke the words, Luke knew they were false. His sixth sense told him to worry plenty.

CHAPTER 13

Deborah pulled off her apron and hung it next to Luke's jacket on a wooden peg in the hall. She leaned the handle of her broom against the wall and stepped into the sitting room. Her full skirts whispered across the polished wood floor as she crossed to the silk-covered settee and sat down.

The sitting room was her retreat. She liked to come in here when Case and Luke were busy elsewhere, to be alone with her thoughts.

The settee, a delicately carved mahogany round side table beside it, and the richly patterned oval rug beneath them were all of the rich trappings of her former life that she had brought along. Those few pieces were the only hint of the life that had once been hers.

The elegant furniture looked out of place in the crude log room, but when she sat among the heirlooms, her few connections to her family in Louisiana, she felt a sense of strength and peace. She did her best thinking here.

Not that she came in to lament the changes in her life. The transition from lady to frontier woman had been a difficult one, but well worth the cost. The exchange of her smooth white hands for red hands roughened by hard work was a small price to pay for the rich new life they'd found.

Warm sunlight poured in through the windows. Deborah looked up, smiling at the effect of the cheery yellow calico curtains she and Luke had hung just last night. She'd never made curtains before, but the log room needed something to soften it, and the gathers of fabric did the trick nicely. They gave the room a welcoming feel.

Luke said he would build her some shelves to display knick-knacks. She thought she'd place them on the wall between the windows for a finishing touch.

When she looked around, it was difficult to believe this was the same room they'd discovered a month ago. All the hours of backbreaking work, the hours of hauling and scrubbing and polishing, had unearthed a cozy little haven. A home.

She hadn't realized just how oppressive it had been living under Aunt Mimi's roof, until she discovered the freedom of their little home in Texas. Neither she nor Case would ever be the same.

Deborah could hear Case out in the yard, playing with their new chickens. From the squawking sound of things, the chickens weren't enjoying the game. She stood and walked to the window for a look.

Case was standing next to the new chicken coop he and Luke had built, a flailing chicken clamped to his chest, and an ear-to-ear grin on his face while the other chickens flapped wildly at his feet. She laughed at the sight of her brother trying to cuddle a hen.

This was not the same pale, sickly little boy she'd brought from Louisiana. His color had improved steadily over the month they'd been in Texas. The child positively glowed with health. He was stronger and steadier on his feet than she had ever seen him. Not that she should be surprised. With the enormous amount of food he was putting away at mealtimes, he should be growing in leaps and bounds.

She leaned her forehead against the cool pane to watch him play. While all the physical changes in Case were impressive, the change that most delighted her was his new air of self-assurance.

Her brother had always been treated as an invalid. Because of his handicap, he'd never been allowed to do anything for himself. Though she'd acted out of love, Deborah regretted all the years she'd deprived him of opportunities to accomplish anything. By trying to protect him from harming himself, she'd actually done him harm.

Luke had changed all that. Whether with her approval or not, he'd insisted Case be treated as a normal child with normal responsibilities. Though she might not agree with all his methods—a shudder still ran through her every time she thought of the knife incident—she had to admit that the results were amazing.

By allowing Case to do things for himself, to succeed or fail, Luke had given her brother the thing he needed most: confidence.

She watched a moment more before drifting from the window back to the settee. It wasn't thoughts of Luke's effect on her brother that brought her to the sitting room this afternoon. It was Luke's effect on her.

From the very first time she'd met him, Luke had dominated her thoughts, though the direction of the thoughts had altered radically. In the beginning, she'd feared the tall, fierce-looking Indian. Later, when she realized he meant no harm to Case or her, she'd resented his high-handed, self-appointed guardianship. What's more, she resented Luke's interference with her brother.

She'd even battled some jealousy when she saw the place Luke held in her brother's affection. Case had always looked up to her, always believed she'd hung the moon. How could she compete with a powerful Indian who could do everything she could do and more?

Then, slowly, without her even being aware, things began to change. Luke became less of a fearsome intruder and more of a welcome member of the family.

She wasn't sure just when it happened. One day she'd found herself looking forward to seeing his slow, heart-stopping smile. She wanted to hear his opinions on farming, ranching, and even Case.

When was it she first caught herself watching Luke's handsome face, suddenly alive to every movement of his dark brow or stubborn jaw? When was it that the searching look in his eyes first penetrated to her soul? When did the brush of his arm against her shoulder or the feel of his strong hand in hers begin to ignite sparks?

She couldn't pinpoint precisely when the changes began, but she had a pretty good idea they'd all started with the reading lessons. Suddenly Luke had no longer been perfect. He had been flesh and blood with very human weaknesses and needs. In the face of Luke's vulnerability, Deborah had tossed away her fears and reservations, and in the process, she'd lost her heart.

There. She'd said it. She'd fallen in love with Luke. The admission wasn't so painful as she'd feared.

The only real problem she could foresee was if she tried to do something about it.

"Hey, Debs," Case said, peeking his head around the doorway. "Where's Luke?"

"He said he had an errand to run, dearest. I'm certain he'll be home soon."

"I sure hope so. I miss him." Case paused and sniffed the air appreciatively. "Say, is that my birthday cake I smell?"

Deborah smiled. "It should be just about done. Why don't you help me get it out of the oven?"

———✦———

Dinner was finished and the table set when she heard the back door swing open.

"Luke?" Case was on his feet and racing toward the hall when Luke stepped into the kitchen.

Case pinned him at the doorway. "Where have you been?"

Luke reached down to ruffle his hair. "It's a secret."

Case's eyes lit up. "A secret? That must mean a present. You bought me a birthday present, didn't you? What'd you get me?"

"Stop pestering Luke," Deborah scolded. "Let the poor man come in and sit down."

Luke strode across the kitchen to stand behind Deborah at the stove. "Mmm, something smells mighty good."

Even without turning around she could tell Luke was only inches away. His nearness sent her pulse racing. "You two run along and wash up so we can eat while the food's hot."

She was relieved, yet strangely disappointed when Luke moved away. She knew she was acting like a lovesick fool, but her hands weren't quite steady when she carried the pot of stew to the table.

"Ho boy, Debs," Case said rubbing his hands together. "This looks delicious." He sat down at the end of the table with Luke seated on his right and his sister on his left. "Let's say the blessing quick, so we can eat."

Luke and Case polished off the rabbit stew and corn bread with gratifying speed. Deborah merely picked at her food. She discovered that falling in love killed her appetite.

Over dried-apple cake and coffee, Case and Deborah shared stories of past birthday celebrations with their family in Louisiana. Luke seemed to enjoy the conversation, laughing with them over the memories and prompting them to tell another when they finished.

"What about you, Luke?" Case asked. "Don't you have any funny stories about your birthday?"

Deborah watched an almost imperceptible flicker of pain flash through Luke's dark eyes. Then he smiled. "Sorry, Case. I don't know when my birthday is."

Case looked as though he might argue, as if such a thing was incomprehensible to the child, then stopped himself. "I don't guess the exact day matters a bit. I'd be pleased if you'd share mine."

"Thanks. That's mighty generous of you." Luke's eyes sparkled with mischief. "You know that means I get to share your presents, too."

Case was momentarily taken aback by the suggestion. He seemed to give the matter solemn consideration for an instant, then after darting a quick look at his sister, he said, "That's okay with me, but I doubt they'll fit."

Luke gave a shout of laughter.

Deborah had no idea what her brother said that was so funny as to set Luke off laughing like that. Pretty soon Case started laughing, and that made Luke laugh all the harder. It was so funny to see them laughing that Deborah joined in.

Luke was the first to catch his breath. "With all this talk about presents, I guess you'll be wanting yours."

Case bobbed his head. "You bet."

Luke got up from the table. "Excuse me just a minute. I left your present out in the lean-to."

While he was gone, Deborah collected the two packages she'd hidden in the corner and placed them on the table in front of Case. Luke reentered the kitchen, carrying a feed sack.

"I think you'd best open this one first," he said as he placed the sack in Case's lap. When the sack moved, Case's eyes nearly popped from his head.

Case hurriedly untied the rope at the top of the sack, and out sprang a small black puppy with a spot of white on his left ear and the tip of his tail, and four white paws. "A dog?" Case looked from Luke to Deborah back to Luke. "A dog? For me?"

Luke nodded.

Case looked to Deborah. "Can I keep it?"

She smiled. "Of course. Luke and I talked about it before he went to get him. We thought every eight-year-old boy ought to have a dog."

Case drew the wiggling puppy into his arms and rested his head on top of the soft black one. "It's the best present in the world," he whispered. He turned to Luke. "Thanks, Luke."

"What'll you call him?"

"It's a him?" Case thought for a moment. "I know, I'll name him Luke."

Luke's amused eyes met hers over the top of Case's head. "That's a lovely idea," Deborah said. "But I wonder if it won't make it difficult for us to know which Luke you're talking to."

Case wrinkled his nose. "I hadn't thought of that." He buried his nose in the puppy's soft fur to think. "Maybe I should name him *Blacky* or *Bootsie*."

"You don't have to decide tonight."

"Your sister's right. Puppy's gone without a name this long. Another night won't hurt him."

The puppy slurped his long pink tongue up the side of Case's face. "He kissed me. That means he likes me." He hugged the puppy tighter. "This is the best present I've ever had."

"Looks as if you've got two more waiting on you," Luke said, indicating the two packages on the table.

Case picked up the first, a large flat parcel wrapped in brown paper and tied with string, while balancing the wiggly puppy on his lap. He flashed Luke a knowing grin as he pulled the paper away to expose a pair of pants. "New pants," he said with an unsuccessful effort to sound pleased and surprised.

"I thought you would like a new pair. They're canvas, just like Luke's."

Case giggled as he thanked her while Luke succumbed to a suspicious fit of coughing. Deborah considered asking them just what was going on, but decided to allow them their private joke.

"Open this." She handed him a small rectangular package.

Case picked up the box and shook it. His eyes lit up at the nice solid rattle. He pulled off the paper and opened the box lid. "A knife," he cried, pulling the small folding knife from the box. "A real knife."

Deborah reached over to catch the puppy lest he fall in Case's excitement.

Case reverently turned the knife from side to side in his hand, inspecting every inch before opening and closing the blade several dozen times. "Look, Luke." In the event Luke missed seeing it done, he demonstrated once again how to open and close the three-inch blade.

Luke smiled and nodded his approval. "That's a fine tool. Seems your sister believes you're man enough to handle a blade responsibly. It's up to you to prove her right."

"I'll be careful, Debs. You'll be proud of me."

She leaned over to press a kiss to the top of his head. "I already am."

~◆~

It was late by the time everyone was washed up and they gathered around the stove for the evening's Bible reading. Deborah read several chapters from Deuteronomy and led them in prayers. "Time for bed."

Luke cleared his throat. "I've got one last present for Case."

Deborah looked over at him in surprise.

Case's tired eyes rounded. "What is it, Luke?"

Luke stood up. "Follow me."

Case followed close at Luke's heels as he crossed the hall and entered the sitting room. Deborah trailed behind them.

When she first stepped into the sitting room, she didn't notice anything new. Luke had lit a lamp on the square oak table they kept in the corner, its flickering gold light casting dancing shadows on the log walls. Her eyes inched across the room looking for the surprise.

Her discovery coincided with Case's delighted shout. He let out a shriek worthy of a Comanche war party. "A ladder! Luke, you got me a ladder."

Sure enough, leaned against the far wall, connecting the floor to the loft was a sturdy-looking ladder.

Deborah watched while Case mounted the first rung, then gaining his balance, climbed to the second and third, with Luke standing behind him, poised to catch her brother should he lose his balance and fall.

Perched on the fourth rung, with sheer delight written all over his freckled face, Case seemed suddenly to remember his sister and her feelings about climbing. "Isn't it beautiful?" he asked in an obvious attempt to turn her up sweet. "It looks awfully nice in here, don't you think?"

She said nothing.

His smile faltered and his little face grew solemn. "Is this okay with you, Debs? Can I keep the ladder even though I'm crippled?"

She glanced from her brother's worried look to Luke's thunderous glare. It didn't take a genius to read his mind. He was angry. If she wasn't in love with the man, she might actually be afraid. With his powerful arms folded across his chest and his feet set apart in a fighting stance, he was every inch a fierce warrior ready for battle.

Still, she refused to be intimidated. "Case, I wonder if you would excuse us for just a moment. There's something I need to discuss with Luke."

Slowly, mournfully, Case backed down the ladder and head downcast, shuffled from the room.

Luke didn't move. Not so much as a blink. Deborah felt her previously strong limbs melt to jelly. So much for not being intimidated.

It was only the knowledge that her cause was just that gave her the courage to cross to him. She stood twelve inches from him, close enough to get a bird's-eye view of his unyielding expression. She doubted she could talk to him like this. Perhaps she should try Case's ploy.

"Did you make the ladder?"

"I did." He didn't appear to be softening.

She ran her fingertips along the satiny smooth railing of polished oak. "I should have guessed. The craftsmanship is excellent."

The compliment elicited no reaction. Not even a flicker in those dark eyes.

She inched closer to study him. How did he stand so still? "Are you breathing?" she asked suspiciously.

Deborah detected the tiniest movement, a muscle twitching in his square jaw. "You said there was something you wanted to discuss?" he asked flatly.

Despite his dampening response, she held her ground. "Yes, I did. I wanted to talk about the ladder. Were you aware that I'd told Case he was forbidden to climb to the loft? That I felt it was dangerous for a child in his condition?"

"I was."

He was practically breathing fire. When it came to Case, Luke was truly terrifying and for some odd reason, it delighted her. She bit back a grin. "I believe a weak child, unsteady on his feet, has no place climbing a ladder."

Luke was silent.

"But that is what I wanted to discuss with you. You see, Case isn't a weak child anymore. Just today, when I watched him from the window I noticed how strong he's become. It's a miracle. He's confident and full of energy, just as a normal eight-year-old boy should be."

The direction of the conversation seemed to take Luke by surprise. His defensive posture softened. The avenging gleam in his dark eyes faded. "So what does that have to do with the ladder?"

Deborah gave in to the urge to touch him, to gentle him. She reached out a hand and rested it on his bronze forearm. "I realize that the circumstances have completely changed," she said. "I no longer believe a ladder to be a hazard. The climbing will help build his balance and leg strength, and I'm sure a boy of eight would enjoy having a space of his own." She smiled up at Luke. "I think building Case the ladder was a good idea."

Luke looked baffled. "So why are we having this discussion?"

She withdrew her hand. "Because I disagree with your methods. You gave Case the ladder with the full knowledge that it was against my will. If you thought I was wrong, you should have come to me first, instead of going around me."

"Would you have listened to me?"

A smile lifted the corners of her mouth as she met his eyes and held them. "Yes," she said honestly. "Over the past few weeks, I've come to appreciate your wisdom on a great many things, especially on rearing a young boy. I know you love Case and want the best for him, and I value your opinions."

"Thank you."

"Your insight on the nature of boys is a good balance to my overprotectiveness," she continued. "Together I think we can do a fine job of raising Case. I'd like you to help me."

The dazzling warmth of Luke's sudden smile made her knees wobble. "I'd like that."

As they stood there, separated by mere inches, Deborah felt the atmosphere shift. The warmth mirrored in his dark eyes suddenly burned hotter. He reached out, gently cupping her shoulders in his hands.

Drawn by an irresistible force, Deborah moved toward him, lifting her face to his. As he lowered his mouth to hers, her eyes fluttered shut. Her heart raced in anticipation of his kiss.

"Are you kissing her, Luke?" Case asked, hobbling up beside them with the puppy in his arms. "Does that mean we can keep the ladder?"

They split apart at the untimely intrusion. Ashamed at being discovered in Luke's arms, Deborah took two steps backward and concentrated on smoothing her skirts.

She noted Luke's voice wasn't quite steady as he answered Case. "Yes, Case. You can keep the ladder."

CHAPTER 14

Luke waited until he heard Deborah rattle the bolt on the back door before setting out. He rechecked his rifle, making certain it was loaded, and slid his knife into the sheath on his leg.

He moved from the lean-to to the barn in the dark, his booted feet silent on the packed earth. Horse shifted in her stall as he approached. He didn't light the lantern to saddle her, preferring the cover of darkness.

He led Horse through the yard, not mounting until they were outside the fence. There, he swung up into the saddle and headed out. He figured he'd follow the pattern he'd set patrolling when Deborah and Case first arrived. He'd head to the southwestern point of the land and go from there.

A strong breeze rolled across the grassy plains and stirred Luke's hair. Smelled like rain. He glanced up to see clouds moving in over the full moon. They'd be looking at a pretty good storm come morning.

He and Horse loped along, Luke's eyes alert for any sign of danger. His sixth sense had been working overtime since he'd run into that drunk in town. He couldn't say why, he had no recollection of the man, but Luke knew instinctively he meant trouble.

Luke was accustomed to trouble. Over the years, it'd become as natural as breathing. What he wasn't accustomed to was having someone to protect, someone he loved, whose safety meant more to him than his own.

A picture of Deborah filled his mind. As long as he lived, he'd never forget the look on her face tonight as she told him she valued his opinions. There was such admiration, such—dare he hope?—love in her eyes, he'd been brought to his knees. He was so unworthy, he didn't deserve her slightest consideration.

But he loved her, and he believed she loved him. It felt so right to pull her into his embrace. He knew she wanted his kiss as much as he needed to kiss her.

Luke started at a sharp rustling in the brush on his left, his hand flying instinctively to his gun. When a fox darted from the cover of the grasses, Luke released a long breath. The fox had caught him unaware because he'd allowed his focus to drift from the job at hand.

A careless man didn't live long, certainly not long enough to protect the people he loved. He pushed the picture of Deborah in his arms to the recesses of his mind to savor later. Right now he needed to be one hundred percent alert.

⟶◈⟵

Luke raised his collar against the chill wind as he made his way back to the lean-to. It was still dark and with the thick cover of clouds overhead, he suspected dawn would bring little additional light.

The hours he'd spent in the saddle left him tired, but satisfied. He'd found no sign of trouble.

He lifted the latch on the door of the lean-to and silently pushing the door open, stepped inside. He placed his rifle against the plank wall, within easy reach. He walked to the pallet and started to sit down to pull off his boots, only to halt at the last minute when he noticed two good-sized lumps under the covers.

Luke eased the blanket up for a better look. Case and his new dog were curled up, sound asleep in the middle of the pallet. The puppy lifted his head at the intrusion, sniffed at Luke, then nuzzled up next to Case and closed his eyes to sleep.

Luke grinned. Case and the dog were fast friends already. Every boy ought to have a dog, the presence of another living creature to assure he was never alone. Someone to love him, good times or bad.

Luke picked up his saddlebag from the crate that served as a table, and using it as a pillow, he lay down on the ground beside the pallet to sleep. He folded his arms across his chest and closed his weary eyes.

Outside the wind howled. Luke levered up on his elbow, smoothed the blanket up tight around Case, and lay back to sleep.

———

"Hey, Luke."

Luke's eyes flew open.

Case's freckled face was so close, Luke couldn't focus on it. "Where you been?"

It was too early to engage in such a cheerful conversation. Luke closed his eyes and rolled over on his side. "Out."

Undaunted, Case lay across him, peeking around Luke's shoulder to ask, "Why are you sleeping on the ground?"

Luke didn't bother to open his eyes. "Because somebody was in my bed."

"Oh." Case giggled guiltily. "We came looking for you last night."

By now the puppy had wiggled around to Luke's head and proceeded to lick his face. Luke batted at the dog, covering his face with his arm. "You've found me," Luke mumbled, "so why don't you and your buddy get on into the house and let me sleep?"

"Buddy? Say, Luke, that's a great name for my dog. Buddy. Hey, look, he likes the name. He wagged his tail when I said it."

Luke grunted.

"Okay, Buddy, let's go, Buddy. Follow me, Buddy."

The twosome clambered out of the lean-to, noisily closing the door behind them.

———

Luke awoke several hours later to the sound of raindrops pelting the roof. Though it wasn't raining hard, already moisture was dripping down through the cracks. He hauled himself up off the hard ground and scrubbed his hands over his face. He was hungry and dirty. He looked up at the dripping ceiling. Before he got cleaned up for breakfast, he'd best stash his things someplace dry.

Fifteen minutes later, Luke entered the back door of the house, clean and dressed in a fresh shirt. The smell of hot coffee beckoned him to the kitchen. He took a cup off a shelf and filled it from the pot sitting on the stove.

"Good morning," Deborah called as she came through the doorway. She tied an apron around her waist as she approached him. "Case said you were up late last night and wanted to sleep in. I saved some breakfast for you. Sit down and I'll fix you a plate."

"Thanks." He carried his cup to the table and sat so he could watch Deborah at the stove. Luke was certain he'd never seen a more beautiful sight.

She was wearing a plain white blouse and gray skirt. He'd noted she wasn't the sort of woman who wore a lot of frills, but she always managed to look soft and feminine. Her long hair was pulled off her face with combs and pinned in a loose knot at the nape of her neck. He couldn't count the number of times he'd been tempted to reach out and touch a silken strand.

She turned from the stove, a full plate in her hands, and walked toward him. The smile on her face assured him there would be no awkwardness over last night's near kiss.

She placed the plate in front of him, then slid into the chair across from his. "When Case told me you were out last night, I began to worry. Is there a problem?"

Luke deliberated about how much he should tell her. By suggesting the possibility of danger he risked dampening the feelings he thought he'd seen in her eyes last night. Deborah had strong feelings about violence. If she thought his presence would bring violence down upon their heads, her feelings for him might change.

On the other hand, he must warn them. Until his sixth sense was silenced, they must all be on their guard. "No problem, exactly. Just a feeling. I can't explain except to say when I get this feeling, it always means danger."

Deborah blanched. "Danger?"

He kept his expression neutral, waiting for her to draw the logical conclusion. If it wasn't for him and his "violent lifestyle" she and Case would be safe. His presence brought trouble. Maybe they'd be better off if he left.

Deborah was silent for a long time, the falling rain outside amplifying the quiet. "What do we need to do?" she asked at last.

"*We?*"

She shot him a look of exasperation. "Of course *we*. Did you think you were in this alone?" She frowned. "Never mind answering, I can see the truth in your face. Though it is nothing for you to lay everything aside to protect the relatives of a man you once knew, you believe we'd have no qualms about abandoning you."

"It's not—"

She wouldn't let him finish. "I understand that given your background, it is difficult to look to others for help. You have been on your own your whole life. But things change. You are not alone anymore, and you might as well get used to it."

"Hey, Debs, hey, Luke!" Case called as he burst into the kitchen with Buddy at his heels.

Deborah was out of her chair in a flash. "Case! You're soaked," she scolded.

He grinned. "Buddy had some business outside. I went with him to show him the best places."

She fought an answering smile. "That was very kind of you, I'm sure. Now get out of those wet things and into some dry clothes. You can sit here by the stove and warm up. I'll fix you a cup of tea."

Case grimaced at the mention of tea before limping off to the other room to change. Buddy gave a mighty shake, sending droplets of water flying into the air, then turned three neat circles in front of the stove before settling in with a contented sigh.

Deborah put on a pot of water to boil and rummaged around for the tin of chamomile tea.

Case returned minutes later. He handed his wet clothes to his sister and joined Luke at the table. "Were you surprised to find Buddy and me in your bed last night?"

Luke nodded. "A bit."

"I had something to tell you. Something too wonderful to wait until morning."

"Is that right? And just what is this wonderful thing?"

"I figured out how to get you a birthday. It bothered me a whole lot last night when you said you didn't know when you were born. Everybody ought to have a birthday. I thought about it when I went to bed and I came up with a plan. You've got to be born again."

Up until his last statement, Luke had been following Case's excited chatter. Suddenly he was lost. "Do what?"

Deborah carried a cup of steaming tea to the table and placed it in front of Case before taking a seat across from Luke.

"It doesn't mean be reborn physically," she explained. "That's impossible, of course. Being born again is a term used in the Bible for spiritual rebirth."

"It's like we talked about at the springs. God sent His only Son, Jesus, to die on the cross to take our punishment for sins. Anyone who receives the gift of salvation is born again. See how easy it would be?"

"I don't know—"

"What's not to know?" Case asked. "Don't you want to be born again?"

Did he want to be born again? More than anything. Luke knew beyond a shadow of a doubt that this rebirth was the thing he'd been hungering for his entire life. The void within him, the yearning that would not be quieted, was his soul-seeking connection with his Creator.

God had done His part. Luke would never understand why the Almighty Creator of the universe would want to have anything to do with a sorry half-breed, but He did, and Luke wasn't fool enough to refuse the offer. "But I'm not ready."

Case was incredulous. "How can you not be ready?"

Deborah placed a hand on his arm to silence her brother and turned to Luke. "Why would you want to wait?"

This was going to be tough. He felt foolish spilling his guts. Still, they'd done so much for him. He owed them an explanation. "Once I'm born again, God is going to call me His son, right?"

Both Case and Deborah nodded.

"Well then, I want Him to be proud of me. No father is going to want a half-breed son that's stupid. When I can read the Bible for myself, then I'll accept His salvation."

"No Luke, that's wrong. God doesn't think like that. Goodness, if He waited until we were good enough before He offered us salvation, no one would ever be saved. Don't you see? God is perfect. Unless you become perfect, you'll never be worthy to be called His child.

"But the Bible tells us that God didn't care if we weren't perfect. It says that while we were yet sinners, Christ died for us. God didn't wait until you were good enough to offer His Son's life for yours. You don't have to wait until you're good enough to accept."

Luke hesitated. He supposed if his life had been an ordinary one, with a loving family and a place to call home, the decision would be an easy one. But all his life he'd worked for everything he got—whether food, a place to sleep, or respect. Because he'd earned everything, it went against his nature to take what he hadn't earned, something he was unworthy of.

Deborah must have sensed his quandary. "This is not a decision to be rushed. You see, accepting salvation is only the beginning. By becoming God's child, you are submitting to His authority in your life, to being molded by God's Spirit and through His Word into the person He wants you to be."

Outside, lightning slashed across the sky. Rain pelted the roof and sluiced down the windows in sheets. Inside, the room was cozy and warm, illuminated by the flickering lamp.

The contrast between the quiet of the house and the fury of the storm mirrored Luke's own life. He had a choice to make. Did he want to continue on in the storm, or was he ready to take shelter in the God who wanted to call him son?

"Tell me how to do it."

Deborah beamed. "All you have to do is pray, Luke. And mean it in your heart."

"I'll pray with you," Case offered. "I can say the words, and you can repeat them after me."

Luke couldn't resist grinning into Case's eager face. "It's a deal."

Case reached across the table to take Luke's hand. They closed their eyes and bowed their heads.

As he waited for Case to begin, Luke was surprised when Deborah slipped her hand into Luke's empty one and gave it a gentle squeeze of support.

"Heavenly Father," Case began, "I know I'm a sinner, completely unworthy to come before You. But I also know that in Your grace and mercy You made a way for me to be Your child, through Your Son, Jesus. I accept Your salvation through Jesus. I make Him Lord of my life, and I thank You for making me Your child. In Jesus' name I pray, amen."

"Welcome to the family, Luke," Deborah whispered.

Case hopped up and threw his arms around Luke's neck. "Happy birthday!"

⎯⎯✦⎯⎯

Deborah declared it a day of celebration. She baked another cake, this one in honor of Luke's "rebirthday." While she cooked, Case and Luke did only the chores that must be done: gathering eggs, milking the cow, and feeding the livestock. They determined the rest could wait until tomorrow.

The storm raged throughout the day. The winds howled and rattled the glass in the windows and a soaking rain continued to fall. Lightning flashed across the leaden sky, and thunder crashed through the roiling heavens. It was a good day to stay inside.

Luke built a roaring fire in the huge stone fireplace in the sitting room to chase away the damp chill. Case dragged a small rag rug from the storage room and placed it in front of the fire so Buddy might join them.

They gathered around the square oak table to play cards and checkers. When they tired of games, Deborah and Case sang and told stories. Deborah got out the Bible and reread God's promises to believers. Luke sat back in his chair to listen, arms folded across his chest, in complete contentment.

He was no longer a fatherless son. Finally, after all the years of loneliness and rejection, he had a Father who claimed him as His own. A Father who so treasured Luke that He would pay the highest price to bring Luke to Himself.

Luke didn't figure he'd ever understand it all. But he knew for sure that he'd found what he'd been seeking his whole life. He belonged to God. And he was loved.

Deborah and Case had taken to the floor to dance. Deborah's eyes gleamed as precious jewels in the firelight as she and Case laughed and whirled around the room. He smiled as Buddy joined in their graceless antics, barking and jumping at their feet.

As he watched them spin by, he wondered if it was wrong for a man who'd finally found the thing he'd looked for his whole life to suddenly want more. Was it greedy to aspire beyond having a father of his own? To want a woman and family to love?

<hr />

"Bedtime, Case."

Case looked up from his noisy wrestling match with the dog. "Already?"

Deborah nodded. "It's late."

Case yawned. "I guess I am pretty tired. It sure has been a fun day." He hugged Buddy, kissed his furry head, and bid him good night. He limped over to the table to hug and kiss Luke and Deborah, then headed for the ladder. He was halfway to the loft when he turned to ask, "Where's Luke gonna sleep tonight?"

Deborah frowned. "I hadn't thought about that. It'll be wet in the lean-to—"

"I'll sleep in the barn."

Deborah shook her head. "No indeed. You'd get soaked just going from the house to the barn. Soaked and covered in mud. Besides, it's cold out there."

Luke wasn't sure he'd ever get used to people caring about him, but he was willing to try.

"Why doesn't he sleep in your room, Debs? I've got plenty of space in my bed up here. You can sleep in the loft with me."

"That's a wonderful idea." Deborah turned to Luke, "I'll just collect the few things I'll need for the night, and the room's yours."

After Case was tucked in, Luke followed Deborah to her room, hanging back at the door while she gathered some clothes.

"Luke," she said, "earlier today you said you thought we were in some sort of danger. Do you still?"

He nodded. "I do. With the bad weather as cover I haven't worried too much today. Man'd be a fool to try anything in a storm like that. But the danger's still there."

"What's the plan?"

He allowed himself a smile into her grave upturned face. "The plan is to keep you and Case safe and dispose of the danger."

"But—"

He placed a finger over her soft pink mouth. "Trust me." When he withdrew his finger, she hopped up on her toes and kissed him lightly on the mouth. Before he could react to the surprise assault, she'd tucked the garments under her arm and darted out of the room.

He leaned back against the door frame and smiled.

CHAPTER 15

Luke's first thought upon awakening was that the storm had finally moved on. The stillness outside meant he'd have plenty to do today, getting things back into shape after yesterday's strong winds and rain, plus seeing to the security of the area.

Worries about Deborah and her brother's safety had kept him awake long into the night. That, and the subtle fragrance of Deborah that clung to the sheets he was wrapped in. Concern for their safety demanded that he leave. The haunting sweetness of her scent begged him to stay.

The long night brought no answers to his dilemma. On the one hand, Deborah and Case needed his protection. They were alone and vulnerable. On the other hand, they wouldn't be exposed to any real danger if he wasn't there to attract it.

While his wasn't the violent lifestyle Deborah had once accused him of, he'd seen his share of trouble. He had no doubt that the danger they now faced could be traced to him.

If he stayed, he risked exposing them to the violence she abhorred. How long would it be before she came to hate him as well?

If he left, he'd lose the two people he'd come to love more

than life. How could he go on without them?

His thoughts once more at a frustrating impasse, Luke sat up and swung his feet around to the floor. The house was quiet. Deborah and Case must be catching a few extra minutes of sleep. He'd go fire up the stove and put some water on for coffee.

Luke dragged on his pants. He pulled on his shirt, fumbling with the buttons as he made his way across the dark hall and into the kitchen, now faintly illuminated with the pearl gray light of dawn.

He got the fire in the stove going and while he waited for the kindling to burn hot enough to add the big wood, he padded over to the window to see how the yard had fared through the storm.

He pressed his face to the glass. A gunshot rang out. Luke started at the sound, reflexively pulling back from the window. At the same moment, a second shot exploded, shattering the glass pane inches from where he stood. Luke dropped to the floor, his heart pounding, his mind racing.

"Luke?"

Deborah and Case. Crouching down to avoid detection, Luke raced from the kitchen to the sitting room. Deborah and Case peered nervously over the side of the loft.

"What was that?" Deborah asked.

"Sounded like gunfire," Case said with more curiosity than fear.

Luke kept his voice low and even. "It *was* gunfire. It came from outside the kitchen. I'm going out to investigate. I want you to stay in the loft until I tell you it's safe to come down."

"But Luke—"

"Don't come down until I say so."

Deborah looked as though she might argue. Case reached over and wrapped an arm around her shoulders. "Don't worry. I'll protect Debs. You get the bad guy. And remember to be careful, Luke."

Luke allowed himself one last look, memorizing the faces of the two people he loved most, before turning to go. As he rounded the corner he thought he heard Deborah whisper, "Take care of him, Lord. I love him."

Luke grabbed his rifle and with a quick glance toward the front of the house to be certain the door was secure, he darted down the hall and eased open the back door just enough to slip out.

The gunshots appeared to have come from the north. Luke knew of several good-sized oaks in the northern corner of the yard that would provide cover for an assailant. He'd check there first. If the gunman was in the trees, Luke could exit the back of the house and come around the side of the lean-to without being spotted. With the woodpile on the end of the lean-to for protection, he could draw out the man. The key was to keep him away from the house.

Luke kept low to the ground, pressed against the damp walls of the house as he moved. Slowly, silently, he eased off the back porch and around to the lean-to. When he came to the end of the woodpile, stacked some four feet off the ground, he stopped.

Carefully, he peered around the sodden logs, his gaze trained on the oaks. Nothing. No sign of movement. Still, instinct told him the gunman waited there.

By now, the sun had started its ascent, dispelling the shadows of dawn. The air held a slight chill and the earth beneath Luke's bare feet was damp and cold.

An unnatural silence hung in the air. Nothing stirred. Luke shifted back on his haunches and waited.

"Hey, Indian!"

Luke stiffened. The voice he heard was that of the drunk he'd knocked over in town.

"Hey, Indian," the taunting cry continued, "why don't you come on out? I've got something for you."

Luke sat forward slightly, scanning the trees. He thought he saw movement behind the trunks. He raised his rifle, the trunk in his sights. When he moved again, Luke had him.

"Yeah, I've got a present for you. Just like the present you gave my brother. Remember him? The one you shot down in cold blood?"

The raspy voice triggered memories beyond their recent run-in in town. It all came flooding back.

An attempted robbery. The gunman and his brother hiding out in mesquites to hold up Jed Crandall. When the brother had drawn on Luke, he'd killed him.

Luke sighed. It was almost a relief to know who it was that wanted to kill him.

"You killed my brother," he shouted. "He was all I had left, and you killed him. Now I'm going to kill you."

Luke shifted the gun slightly to the left and put his finger on the trigger.

"Luke?"

Luke's heart ground to a halt as he heard Case's loud whisper. "Luke?"

Luke lowered his gun as he saw Case's head appear in the kitchen window not four feet from where Luke crouched. *Please, God, don't let the gunman see Case.* "Get down," Luke hissed.

Case didn't hear. "Hey, Luke, where are you?" He bobbed around at the window, trying to locate Luke outside.

Luke saw the assailant move out from behind the trees, the barrel of his gun directed at Case.

Time seemed to slow. Each sound dragged eerily, each movement became an exaggerated pantomime.

The man was going to kill Case.

"No!" Luke shouted as he jumped from behind the woodpile. He saw the gunman pivot, and an evil smile lit his face as he redirected his gun at Luke.

Luke heard the shot and the screams.

He waited for the pain.

The gunman jerked backward and collapsed on the ground in a heap.

Luke looked at the fallen man, then to his gun hanging uselessly in his right hand, then back to the gunman.

Adam Waldrip swaggered around the side of the house. "What in the world did you think you were doing?" he demanded. "In my entire life I've never seen anything so stupid. Were you hoping his gun wasn't loaded?"

"The kid—" Luke was so shaken he could scarcely speak, much less defend himself. For a long moment he stared at his friend. Finally he found his voice. "Where did you come from?"

Adam shrugged. "I was delivering your horses. I'd have brought them out yesterday, but the weather was lousy, so I figured I'd wait and bring them out this morning." He glanced back over his shoulder toward the gunman. "Seems like you're lucky I waited until today."

"You saved my life, Adam."

"Forget it. I owed you one."

"Luke? Luke? My heavens, are you all right?" Deborah rounded the corner of the house, skirts flying, and threw herself into his arms.

Luke dropped his rifle and pulled her to his chest, stroking her head with a not-quite-steady hand.

"I was so afraid," she cried into his shirt. "I thought he was going to kill you."

Case limped around the corner of the house to join them, his freckled face wreathed in smiles. "Hey, Luke, did you wonder why I was at the window instead of in the loft like you told me to be? It's because I saw him ride up." Case pointed to Adam. "I figured you'd want to know."

Suddenly the whole thing struck Luke as funny. Deborah weeping with relief in his arms, Case chattering away as though his life hadn't been on the line minutes ago, and Adam staring at the three of them as though they were mad. Luke threw back his head and laughed.

Deborah stepped back, out of his arms, to stare at him with a tear-streaked face. "What is so funny?"

He couldn't answer. He could only shake his head and laugh harder.

She looked to Adam. "What is he laughing about?"

"I couldn't say, ma'am." He doffed his hat. "By the way, I'm Adam Waldrip."

"How do you do, Mr. Waldrip. I'm Deborah Marbury. This is my brother, Case."

"Pleased to meet you." Adam's handsome smile faded. "You're not the lady who lives here, are you?"

Deborah didn't seem to know what to make of his odd

question. "My brother and I live here."

"You're Cyrus's people?"

She nodded. "Yes. We've just moved here from Louisiana."

"But Luke said—I thought you'd be—" Adam stopped himself, and after shooting a killing glare at Luke, he began to laugh.

"Tell me, Mr. Waldrip, where do you two know each other from?" Deborah asked as she delivered a cup of coffee to Adam at the kitchen table.

"Luke and I go back a long way, ma'am. First time we met, I was being chased by a half-dozen desperadoes. Luke joined up with me and helped even out the odds."

Case's eyes glowed with admiration. "You and Luke fought six men? Did you win?"

"Did we win?" Adam caught the censorious look in Deborah's eyes and moderated his answer. "Yes, Case, we won."

"We spent some time out in California," Luke said, "then we lost touch with each other when I returned to Texas after the war. I didn't know Adam was back until I ran into him in town last week."

"Luke told me he was here looking after Cyrus's people." Adam shot Luke a look that told him just what he thought of Luke's leading him to believe Deborah to be an old spinster instead of the beautiful woman she was. "I'd been wanting to get out here to meet you, so when Juan brought the horses into town two days ago, I volunteered to bring them out the rest of the way." Adam turned the full power of his smile on Deborah. "And I'm very glad I did."

Luke was shocked and delighted to see Deborah appeared unaffected by Adam's good looks. She kept her warm gaze on Luke, as it had been since they'd come inside, as she answered, "Any friend of Luke's is a friend of ours."

Deborah was standing in front of the small oval mirror she'd finally gotten around to hanging on the wall of her bedroom, putting the finishing touches on her hair, when she heard the back door open.

"Hey, Debs!" Case called. "We're home. And hungry. What's for supper?"

She met her brother in the hall. "Chicken and dumplings." She looked past him toward the closed door. "Where's Luke?"

"He's putting up Horse." Case hung his hat on a peg in the hall and followed her into the kitchen. "Was that Adam I just saw riding out?"

Even with her back to him, there was no mistaking the disapproval in his voice. "Yes. He stopped in for a visit."

"Seems he's been out to visit several times over the last few weeks."

She lifted the lid on the pot and stirred the bubbling contents. "He's a good friend of Luke's, dearest."

"Well then, why is he visiting when Luke ain't around?" Case hobbled up to the stove to look her straight in the eyes. "Are you sweet on him, Debs?"

"What a thing to say," she scolded. The back door swung open and she called out, "Hello, Luke."

"Evening, Deborah. Something smells mighty fine." Luke hung his hat next to Case's and combed his long fingers through his hair before joining them in the kitchen. She noted he was wearing his red shirt tonight, the one that set off his dark good looks so well. It was enough to make her heart flutter to her throat.

She deliberately turned her back to him, so she could concentrate. "Supper's all ready. If you and Case will sit down, we'll eat."

Conversation over supper centered mainly on the day's activities. Deborah reported on the progress of her garden, Case entertained them with stories of Buddy's adventures, and Luke bragged on Case's riding skills. On the surface everything seemed light and cheerful, but Deborah couldn't help feeling the atmosphere was a bit strained.

Fact was, things hadn't been the same since last month when

that terrible man had ridden out to kill Luke.

She couldn't put her finger on the problem; there'd been no obvious changes, but she sensed Luke had pulled back. He worked as hard as ever, maybe harder, and he spent lots of time with Case, but he seemed to avoid spending any time alone with her.

"Hey, Luke, you want to go outside with me while I teach Buddy to catch a ball?" Case asked as he dried the last supper dish and placed it on the stack.

"Sure—"

"No!"

Both sets of eyes widened at her abrupt response. "I'd like Luke to stay inside with me," Deborah explained. "There's something we need to discuss."

"Aw, Debs."

"Never mind the fussing, young man. You and Buddy run along outside. And keep him away from the chickens."

Case whistled, and Buddy raced to his side. When Deborah heard the back door close behind them, she turned to Luke. "Adam was here this afternoon."

"So I saw." Without sparing her a glance, Luke picked up the tub of soapy water and stepped around her to carry it out to the back porch.

"Don't you want to know why he rode out all this way?" she asked, following at his heels.

He tossed the water off the porch and tucked the tub under his arm. "I've got a pretty good idea."

Frustration mounted as she trailed him back to the kitchen. He avoided her gaze as he replaced the tub under the cabinet. She couldn't take it anymore. "Luke! What is the matter with you?"

"Nothing."

She jumped into his path so he couldn't escape. "Oh no, you don't. We've let this go on long enough. It's time for it to stop."

She thought she saw pain flicker through his dark eyes, but his voice was free of emotion as he said, "I understand."

She slapped her hands on her hips. "Well, I'm glad somebody

does. I, for one, don't understand anything. One minute you're looking at me as though you might gobble me up, and the next minute you won't look at me at all. And what about the touching?" she demanded.

He looked truly perplexed. "What touching? I haven't come near you in weeks."

"Exactly. You've been avoiding me, and I don't like it." The astonishment on his face told her she'd gone too far to turn back. "I love you, Luke." Suddenly her nerve deserted her and she dropped her gaze. "And I thought you loved me."

"I do." His deep voice was barely a whisper. "I love you with all my heart."

She was right. He loved her. She did think he could try sounding more cheerful when he said so. Still her heart soared with hope. She took a step closer and stared up into his handsome face. "Then why are you acting like this? If you love me, why don't you do something about it?"

He stared at his booted feet. "Because I love you."

For some reason the bleak resignation in his voice made her angry. "And I'm supposed to understand that? You love me so you're going to treat me like a stranger?"

He caught her by the shoulders, his eyes searing her with their intensity. "I have nothing to give you."

"Is that what this is all about?" she asked with a relieved laugh. "You're worried that you're poor and can't take on a family?"

"I'm not poor." .

"You're not?"

He shook his head. "Not at all. I was very successful out in California. I've made some good investments, I've got a good-sized herd of cattle south of here—"

It was her turn to look perplexed. "You have all that and yet you say you have nothing to give me?"

He laughed mirthlessly. "I could have all the wealth I could ever want, and it wouldn't matter. I still don't have what I need to make you my wife. Deborah, I don't have a name."

"But—"

"It's no use. For a while I allowed myself to dream that

somehow we could be together. I saw us building a ranch, raising Case and more children of our own. But it's impossible. I love you too much to ever ask you to be mine."

The light of understanding finally dawned. "So you did the honorable thing. You pulled back from me so I wouldn't get the wrong idea."

He cupped her face tenderly in his hand, stroking her cheek with his thumb. "How long would you be satisfied with a handy-man who can only love you from afar? You deserve so much more."

"Like Adam?"

He dropped his hands and stepped back. "Adam is a good man. He's honest, kind—"

"—and he's got a last name," she finished for him.

Luke nodded. "And he's got a last name."

"Well, so do you." From her pocket she pulled the document she'd read and reread a thousand times since Adam delivered it earlier. She unfolded it and waved it in his face. "Happy birthday, Luke Godson."

Luke snatched the paper from her hands and squinted at the tiny lines of writing. She knew he could make out the occasional word, but his skills weren't enough to decipher the missive. After a second or two he raised his eyes to hers. "What is this?"

"It's your new name. Case and I wanted to get you some-thing special for your birthday. We couldn't think of anything you wanted more than a name so we got you one."

Luke stared at her as though she were mad.

"I'm serious." She plucked the paper from his shock-stiffened hands and began to read, "In response to the formal petition sub-mitted to the State of Texas for consideration on May 1, 1867, and after due—"

She glanced up from her reading to see Luke's expression, something between wild hope and abject confusion. He looked as though he might explode at any minute. She took pity on him and skimmed down the page. "Okay, here's the good part. By decree of the Governor of Texas, the petitioner is hereby granted the name Luke Godson—"

"Me? I'm Luke Godson?"

She nodded.

"How?" Luke was too overcome to continue.

"Adam. When Case and I told him what we wanted to do, it was Adam who suggested we petition the state. It took forever to hear back from them, but Adam finally received it today." She grinned up at him. "That's why he came out this afternoon, to deliver your new name."

"He hasn't been coming out here to court you?"

The understanding and relief on his face made her smile as she shook her head. "Adam's been keeping us posted on the progress of our petition. He knows the only person I'm interested in courting is you."

"Luke Godson." Luke repeated as he looked down at the paper she held. "You sure it's legal?"

"Absolutely. It's signed by the governor." She pointed to the flourished signature as proof. "You're Luke Godson."

Luke cocked his head. "It has a nice ring to it, don't you think?"

She nodded.

"Do you like it well enough to make it your own? Will you marry me and become Mrs. Luke Godson?"

"Yes and yes."

He pulled her into his arms and kissed her with all the love in his heart. Just when she thought she might incinerate in his passionate embrace, he lifted his head. "When?"

She wasn't quite ready for the kissing to end. She wrapped her arms around his neck, and tugged him back. The second before their lips met, she whispered, "The sooner the better."

Nancy Lavo is a gifted author from the big state of Texas where she lives with her husband and three children. She is a light-hearted person who loves adding touches of comedy to her stories to balance with the more serious message of salvation.

To See His Way

by Kathleen Paul

DEDICATION

In memory of Jan Wayne Paul, a modern adventurer.

CHAPTER 1

I t's hot, Tildie," Marilyn complained.

"That's the truth, Mari." Tildie reached over to wipe the sweat from the little brown face with an old faded scrap of calico. "You're getting darker, and your hair's getting lighter every day."

"I want my hair to be blond and curly like yours."

"It's not such a blessing as you'd think, Cousin. And I don't turn a golden tan, but rather red—like a ripe tomato."

Marilyn giggled and squeezed her rag doll closer. Her legs hung over the back of the wooden seat and swung merrily. The worn canvas tarp covering the bowed frame of the buckboard provided blessed shade. Even so, the sun blazed in the sky, and they found it more and more difficult to ignore the discomfort of the wind, the heat, and the hard surface they sat upon.

The wagon lurched, and Tildie grabbed both the wooden seat and the shoulder of her littlest cousin, Evelyn, at the same time. How could the little cherub sleep with the sweltering heat and the unmerciful, jostling wagon wheels hitting every rut and ridge in the dirt trail?

The heat of Colorado's summer sun permeated even the interior of their wagon. In the distance, the Rocky Mountains rose majestically, looking as if they could be reached by nightfall. It was an illusion. The lone wagon had many miles to travel before it even reached the foothills. Four days would just bring them to their destination, a fort on the Arkansas River.

The wagon hit a deep rut, and everyone held tight to keep from falling out. Marilyn turned a stormy face to scowl at her stepfather's back. He drove the wagon in a slumped position, growling at the horses from time to time and never speaking to the woman who sat beside him.

Tildie followed her gaze, and her own lips thinned to a stern line. She had not expected the unhappy home she found after traveling to Aunt Matilda's. Maybe she'd made a mistake in coming. She shook her head over her selfishness. It wasn't the ideal situation she'd dreamed of, but she'd found love from the children and felt she helped her despairing aunt.

When she left Indiana, Tildie expected to join the only family she had. The situation in Lafayette was bleak, the memories hard to deal with. She'd been alone and desperate to be within the warm circle of family once more. Unfortunately, the decision to travel west had brought her to an even more unsatisfactory situation.

Aunt Matilda's three little ones perched with Tildie on the wide shelf across the back tailgate of the old buckboard. The wind blew sporadically from the west, and each cloud of dirt kicked up by horses and wagon swirled away before it could settle on the children. Tildie braced herself against the pole that supported the covering. Evelyn's wet little head rested on her lap. The toddler's short, tawny curls clung in tight rings darkened by sweat. Tildie kept a hand on the babe's shoulder for fear a bounce would toss the sleeping child to the hard, stony ground.

Four-year-old Marilyn, called Mari for her sweet, merry temperament, sat as a mirror image across from her grown cousin. The cousins favored each other with the same golden tresses, dark lashes and brows, small even features, and sparkling blue eyes. Once, they had gone to the Breakdon settlement and strangers had assumed Mari was Tildie's little girl. Aunt Matilda didn't care, or perhaps, she didn't even notice. Nothing much penetrated the weary despondency that surrounded the older woman.

Tildie reached across to help Mari arrange her rag doll on the bench to lay much the way her sister Evelyn lay against Tildie. Mari patted her dolly's shoulder and grinned at her big cousin.

Between the little girls sat Boister, whose real name was Henry. His father had been Aunt Matilda's first husband—a kind and sturdy man who objected to his namesake being called Little Henry and called him Mister. Aunt Matilda laughingly called him Beau. Somehow, Beau and Mister got mixed and slurred together. The resulting "Boister" had been a good appellation for the energetic child full of rambunctious fun before his pa died.

A sudden jolt rocked them, and Tildie grabbed Evelyn into her arms. Marilyn screeched and clung to the seat. Her doll fell into the wagon. Boister fell in as well, but he scrambled back. The normally placid team lurched wildly before the wagon. The horses reared and backed erratically, causing the buckboard to pitch. They flailed their legs in the air and voiced their terror in high-pitched whinnies. Masters's rough voice could be heard above the clamor as he fought for control. One last mighty jolt sent the four passengers in back tumbling to the ground. The horses bolted, leaving them in the dust.

"Snake!" Boister's voice cracked.

Tildie's head jerked around as her arms froze in their reach for Mari's still form.

A large, menacing snake coiled by the trail ahead of them. The distinct buzzing of his rattle warned the humans to stay away. He unwound, stretching out to his full five feet. Evidently he'd had enough of the trail, horses, wagons, and humans. He slithered off into the brush, leaving the petrified cousins.

Tildie shuddered at the sight of the snake's rattled tail disappearing under a bush. Closing her eyes, she inhaled deeply to calm herself and whispered, "*Thank You, Lord.*"

She dismissed her bruises. The fall had shaken her up but caused no permanent damage. Boister stood beside her. She handed him the crying Evelyn and crawled over to Mari. The child gasped for air, and Tildie hoped she'd find nothing more seriously wrong other than having the wind knocked out of her. Tildie spoke soothing words to the frightened child as she ran her hands over little arms and legs to feel for broken bones. Finally, the breathing became regular with only hiccuping sobs. Tildie, convinced that the injuries consisted of bumps, bruises, and a scare, rocked Mari gently in her arms.

She peered down the road after the disappearing wagon. Nothing blocked her view. They sat on the grasslands where nothing higher than thimbleweed, spring larkspur, and bristly crowfoot waved above the blue grama grasses. In a short distance the land changed abruptly. But for now, through the cloud of dust, she could see the wagon bouncing wildly behind the runaway team.

The trail rose on an incline. Surely the horses would tire and stop soon. Her assessment of her surroundings transpired in a breath of time.

Boister dumped the other wailing sister in her lap and sat down on a boulder to wait. He scowled after the disappearing wagon. "Didn't want to go to Fort Reynald, anyway," he said.

"Me needer." Marilyn stuck out her lower lip in a childish pout. She squirmed around in Tildie's lap to face her cousin on this very important issue. "I don't want you to marry that man. I want you to stay with us."

"I haven't said I'm going to marry the man your stepfather picked out, but he might be nice." Tildie tried to sound hopeful. In her heart, she knew any associate of John Masters could not be a suitable husband.

"Don't you like being our cousin? Don't you want to stay with us?" asked Marilyn.

Boister snorted. He knew better than to ask those baby questions. Wasn't much any of them could do now that John Masters had made his decision.

His little sister ignored him and persisted in pestering her cousin. "How come you don't have real children?"

"Not my time yet, Mari. And I shall always be your cousin." Tildie planted a kiss on her cousin's damp forehead.

She enjoyed mothering the children. With their own mother lost in a world of despondency, the children had adopted Tildie as the one to run to for everything from a torn sleeve to a hurting splinter.

"God will give me a husband first, then all the little ones I could possibly want." She smiled with more assurance than she felt. John Masters's attempt to interfere with God's order might succeed. Between the two, Tildie would count on God to come out the stronger. It was just that sometimes it was hard to remember when, for all intents and purposes, it sure looked like she was heading down a dusty trail in the hot sun toward a mighty unpleasant future.

She shook her head, turning to God with her perplexing thoughts. *I don't see Your hand in this, Lord. Let me have faith in the things I cannot see.*

"If you have babies will they be my sisters?" Mari demanded her attention.

"They'll be your cousins," Tildie answered with a brief smile. Mari's chatter brought up the disturbing picture of a husband she might not like. She'd be sharing her life with a stranger if she wasn't careful. John Masters's schemes could be difficult to thwart, but God was on her side. No one could force her to marry anybody. She could get a job and just stay in Fort Reynald. That would mean being separated from these children, but that was a certainty anyway. John Masters had made it clear she was not welcome on the homestead any longer.

Tildie set Mari and Evie on their feet and scrambled up herself. The wagon had disappeared, clean out of sight. They might as well start walking. Sitting here in the sun with no shade might scorch them clear through. They'd just follow the tracks. Before long they'd be able to spot the wagon lumbering back to get them.

The trail barely distinguished itself from the rough terrain around it. The deep ruts held an overgrowth of thistle, weeds, and porcupine grass. In spite of this, Tildie felt confident that following the wagon was better than waiting in the searing sun.

"Come on, we'll walk to meet them," Tildie said with what

cheerfulness she could muster. She looked over at Boister, still slumped on top of his rock. The boy looked too sober. He always looked too sober. He often acted like a grumpy old man instead of a six-year-old boy. He had his reasons, she figured.

Big Henry had died in a rockslide, and Boister had been the first to reach him. The little boy had found his father's large familiar hand sticking out of the rubble and pulled with all his might. It took grown men two hours to remove the boulders that had crushed the life out of Henry Baskerman. Boister had been crushed in spirit, and the somber, haunted look masked a once-vital personality. Aunt Matilda's letters had been full of the little pistol's derring-do adventures before the death of her husband. Tildie wondered which was the greater tragedy: losing his father, or acquiring Masters as a stepfather.

Matilda had married John Masters within six months. She couldn't handle adversity and thought John would take the weight of grief off her shoulders. She was mistaken. John Masters proved a burden of grief in himself, and he broke what little courage the widow had left. He acted surly to the children who were not his and later showed no more tolerance of the squalling babe that came out of his own union with Matilda.

The promising spread failed without Henry's energetic enthusiasm for tilling the soil. Masters sold off the cattle to buy whiskey and poker chips. The sparkle of admiration in Masters's eye as he courted Matilda turned out to be the gleam of greed. When his plans for a life of ease on an already established bit of land failed, he blamed everyone but himself. The children often took the brunt of his wrath.

Tildie tried an encouraging smile and held a hand out to Boister. "Come on. I'm glad you're not still in the wagon. At least we have one strong man to protect us."

Boister shot her a look, not accepting her false dependence on him. He didn't outwardly scorn her puny attempt to make things seem better, but he didn't take the offered hand. He started off without speaking, plodding ahead of the girls and Tildie.

Tildie sighed and took hold of each little girl's hand. So far she hadn't been able to soften Boister's hardened heart. She would just keep trying and praying.

"Look." She pointed to a bird in the dust several yards away from their path. "That's a meadowlark. See his yellow vest and black cravat? Watch him bend over to touch the ground. Doesn't it look like he's bowing?"

They stopped in the trail to watch this strange performance.

"What's he doing?" asked Mari.

"I don't really know, but I've always thought he's hiding. See, his back blends in with the dirt and dry plants. With his yellow front ducked down, he almost disappears."

"You think he thought that out himself?" Boister sounded doubtful.

Tildie laughed. "No, not really. With that little bitty head there must be a little bitty brain within. God gives His creatures an instinct to protect themselves."

"He's not very well hidden," Boister scoffed.

"Sometimes God lets humans laugh at His creatures' funny ways," she continued. "It's all right to laugh. God says He gives us joy."

Boister cast her one of his tolerant looks. He was telling her as clearly as if he had spoken that her nonsense wasn't for him. He marched on.

As they returned to their hot walk, Tildie fell into her own thoughts. She'd been with the children six months. Orphaned in Indiana, she'd written to the aunt she was named after. Her mother's sister lived in southern Colorado territory, near Kansas. Tildie longed to go to the aunt she remembered from her childhood. She didn't get the letter that said *not* to come. She knew it existed, had known since the moment she walked across the wooden porch and knocked on the door. John Masters told her.

"Do you want to marry the grocer?" asked Mari, coming back to the topic than most disturbed her.

Her question startled Tildie.

"I don't know if I do, or I don't," she answered truthfully. "Reckon I'll decide that once I've met this Mr. Armand des Reaux."

"I don't want you to marry him. You'll never get to visit us."

Marilyn couldn't quite keep the whine out of her voice.

Tildie closed her eyes and prayed against the pain in her heart. How could she desert these children? Tildie knew what her absence would mean to them. It was she who sang at her chores. She told funny stories as they lay in bed at night. She hugged them, laughed, and said out loud she loved them. Tildie imitated her aunt Matilda as she had been years ago on an Indiana farm. Tildie had been the happy child. Matilda had been the almost grown playmate.

Now, Tildie's aunt spoke rarely. She never laughed. She walked in a daze through the house. She sat in her rocker while Tildie did the chores. It made Tildie's heart ache to think of her aunt, but a worse pain grabbed her when she considered the life the children would have in that house with John Masters and no one to act as a buffer.

Boister turned around and walked backwards. He'd listened to the three he pretended to ignore. Now he looked from his sister to his cousin. He spoke words to his sister, but his eyes bore a hole in Tildie. "She don't have no reason to want to visit us. *I* wouldn't come visit us."

"Boister," said Tildie earnestly, "if Mr. des Reaux turns out to be an agreeable man, I'll ask him if you and your sisters can stay with me."

"Won't be," Boister stated flatly. "He be a friend of *him*." He jerked his head in the direction the wagon had taken.

The image of John Masters's unkempt, hulking figure towering in rage over her aunt's diminished form sprang up in Tildie's mind. She shuddered. Secretly, she agreed with Boister's estimate of the circumstance.

She'd been praying with all her might since John Masters returned from a trip with news he was getting rid of the extra mouth dumped on him. He told her he got her a husband, a Frenchie who owned his own store at a new fort established by some fur traders. It was close to the foothills of the Rockies on the Arkansas River.

Tildie yearned to see the mountains. She selfishly wanted to escape the atmosphere of oppression in her aunt's home. She liked the idea of being somewhere where people came and went, providing more variety in company than her family, the drunken head of it, and a few cowhands. However, she had no desire to take up residence in a fort where she would very likely be the only white woman. She thought the Mexican and Indian women would be interesting, but she doubted they would speak English. What kind of fellowship could you have with someone you couldn't talk to?

Her fear of traveling in the company of her uncouth uncle disappeared the day he announced the whole family was making the trip. Suspicion replaced her fear. Why would he bother taking everyone? He certainly never put himself out for anyone else's pleasure. The mystery vanished when she heard him tell a silent Aunt Matilda that he'd show her he could provide for her and her brats. The Frenchie would give them clothes and winter supplies when they delivered the bride.

Tildie sighed and her eyes fell on the little boy trudging along a few feet ahead of them. He'd turned back around and stalwartly tramped in the heat. She called after him. "If Mr. des Reaux is impossible, Boister, then I won't marry him, and I'll get a job. It may take time, but you're my family, and someday we'll be together. Maybe Fort Reynald will have places I can work. I worked in a boardinghouse to get the money to come to you."

"You'd better pray about that," said Mari, her little voice echoing the exact tone Tildie often used.

Tildie smiled. She marveled at Marilyn. Mari absorbed the comfort of a loving Father God and the friendship and protection of His Son. Boister believed, too, but so far, the joy of the Lord had not released him from his sorrow. Tildie knew it would, but she was impatient, especially now that it looked like they would be separated. She wouldn't be there to nourish the little ones with the Word of God.

Her faith had provoked this scheme to marry her off. John Masters might grumble about an extra mouth to feed, but his real complaint railed against the Lord Tildie knew so well. She received banishment from her aunt's home because she stood for something which was vinegar and gall to her new uncle. John

Masters enjoyed someone else doing the work, and Tildie did plenty. He might have kept her on for that reason, but Tildie's love of God nearly drove him wild.

He had called her every name he could think of. His vocabulary did not extend to fancy words. In his raving, he couldn't quite bring up the high-sounding names he needed to express his disgust. Tildie got the message, though. He thought her sanctimonious, self-righteous, and interfering.

The children loved her and flourished in the sunshine of her faith. She whispered prayers to them in the morning after they stretched, before they threw off the covers. She prayed with them when they ate, got hurt, or lost something. She tucked them in with a prayer. She even sang hymns.

As John Masters's intolerance became louder and more abrasive, Tildie had tried to be less demonstrative in his presence, not wishing to bring on the distressing bouts of fury. But Masters chafed against her quietness, as well.

"I've been praying," Tildie assured her little cousin. "Remember, God listens to your prayers, too. No matter what happens, you must talk to Him."

Marilyn nodded, but Boister who had glanced back at them firmly turned his face to look away.

Troubled, Tildie prayed, *Oh Father, please, I want them with me. I want to reach Boister.*

"Let's pray for God to direct our steps," she said aloud. "Then I'll tell you about some stepping-stones back in Lafayette, Indiana, that take you across a little creek to a lush meadow where fireflies blink at the end of day."

"What's fireflies?" asked Mari.

"First, we pray," said Tildie.

CHAPTER 2

How could the wagon have gotten so far ahead? Didn't they stop? They couldn't have just gone on. Surely John Masters would turn the wagon and come back for them. After all, she was the cargo he was taking to market.

Tildie and the children trudged up the rocky path. Evie perched on her back, legs wrapped around her waist, arms encircling her neck. Tildie had stopped talking, saving her energy for walking. Sweat beaded on her forehead and trickled into her eyes, making them sting and water. Her legs felt heavy. Muscles protested, both from the fall off the wagon and this abominable trek.

Freshly scarred rocks on the trail marked where the metal rim of the wagon wheel or horse's iron-shod hoof had struck. However, no sight or sound of the wagon itself appeared. Tildie fought an increasing sense of uneasiness.

The terrain had altered considerably as they walked, always trudging uphill. They approached the summit, walking on the twenty foot wide rock and earth shelf. The road dropped off steeply at one side and rose just as abruptly on the other. They kept to the middle, avoiding the cliff-like edge.

A cluster of elm trees offered welcome shade, and they

stopped to rest. In spite of the heat, the little girls leaned close to their cousin as she sat against the largest tree trunk. Boister tried to stretch out in a patch of grass a little ways off. The rocks dug into his back and he sat up immediately. Tildie shut her eyes, resting and praying against the unease building in her.

"What's that?" Boister sprang to his feet. "Do you hear it?" He ran toward the top of the rise.

"Boister, wait!" cried Tildie as she scrambled up.

The trail turned abruptly at the top of the ridge. Boister stood gazing over the edge. His little form froze in a rigid attitude. Even before she reached him, she knew by his stance that something horrible lay before him. Tildie wrapped her arms around him and drew him away before she looked herself. When she saw the scene below, she gasped, turning the stiff boy away from the sight and pressing his face against her dress futilely blocking the view.

At the bottom of the steep ravine the wagon lay shattered. One horse lay lifeless. The other horse struggled to rise, then fell still, only to repeat the pathetic attempt a moment later. Halfway down among the rocks sprawled the still figure of Matilda Masters, only recognizable by the color of her dress. A brilliant red stain flowed from her shattered form, across the rocks. Masters was nowhere to be seen.

Boister suddenly wrenched away from her and ran to the other side of the trail. Bending over, he threw up, then crumpled into a sobbing huddle. Tildie scooped him up in her arms. Tears blinded her as she stumbled back down the trail. Mari approached, her hand firmly clasping Evie's. They looked so small and helpless.

Dear God, this can't be! Tildie's anguish turned her to her heavenly Father. She reached the smaller children and knelt in the dirt, gathering them all as close to her as she could. She and Boister wept, and the little girls joined them, not really knowing why except that something was terribly wrong.

Eventually, the emotional storm subsided. They clung together, weary. Tildie wondered if she would be able to creep down that sheer drop to her aunt's body. What if she were only injured?

Could she move her to safety if she was? Were there ropes in the wagon? Surely, she'd seen some. Threads of a plan began to form in her mind. She must do *something*.

A small sound startled her, and she looked up. The children felt her tense, and they, too, looked up from where their heads were buried against her.

"Indians," whispered Mari.

Three stood on the trail, their black, serious eyes studying the children without emotion. Tildie looked over her shoulder, seeking an escape route. Two more of the bronzed men stood about the same distance behind her, and another two on horseback waited at the turn of the trail. Some of the strange men had circles tattooed on their chests. Others had numerous straight lined scars on their arms. One had what looked like a stuffed crow dangling from his waist.

Three men came forward in long easy strides. The oldest passed without a word. The two younger stopped beside Tildie and the huddled children.

"Be calm, children," she whispered. "Remember Jesus is always with us. He will never leave us nor forsake us." Tildie's voice shook, and she tightened her hold on Evie as one of the Indian men reached for her.

The second man put a hand on her shoulder. She looked up into his face. His serene expression waylaid her fear. She saw sympathy in his eyes. Shocked to find an underlying kindness in one she thought of as a savage, Tildie didn't know what to think. He placed his hand under her arm and, with no visible effort, lifted her to her feet.

One Indian took Evelyn, who whimpered softly. Tildie saw him pat her back. The second released her arm and swooped up Mari. Mari gasped and terrified little blue eyes peered over the Indian's shoulder as the men started up the hill. Tildie shook herself from her trance, grabbed Boister's hand, and started after them. Wherever they took her girls, she would follow.

Around the bend, several more Indians patiently waited with a group of quiet, unsaddled horses. An Indian efficiently threw Tildie up on a dappled pony. The same Indian hoisted Boister up with another young man. No, not a man, but an adolescent boy. He looked so hard and serious. Tildie gulped down the fear rising in her throat. These people hadn't threatened them. . .perhaps they even meant to help.

As one unit, they started moving. The Indians carrying Mari and Evie rode on either side of Tildie, so close that her horse needed no guidance from her hand. The men didn't speak. Tildie prayed.

Lord, protect us. Further prayer tumbled through Tildie's bewildered mind. She trembled over words for her unhappy aunt. Her thoughts rambled, mixing with her prayers. Was Aunt Matilda still alive? Where was John Masters? Did the Indians intend to harm them? *God, are You watching out for us? I promised the children that You would. Your Word says You will. Oh God, I'm scared.*

They reached a descending path and turned aside to follow it. At the base, a few of the men separated and headed back. Surely they were going to see about the wagon. Was it possible that they would bring her aunt to her? Could she have survived? Was Masters alive?

Her band picked up speed and Tildie concentrated on staying astride the swift pony. If she fell, she would fall under the other horses' hooves. She began to wish that she rode with one of their Indian captors. *Were* they captors, or were they rescuers? What did these men intend? She had only a hazy knowledge of Indians. Was this one of the ferocious tribes, bloodthirsty and inflamed by revenge? How could she know? They were not exactly friendly, neither did they seem hostile.

Tildie swayed and felt herself slipping. A strong hand steadied her. She looked into the face of the man next to her. The same Indian who had first placed a hand on her shoulder gazed steadily into her eyes. She drew strength from his solemn demeanor. He had saved her from a fall. His face registered no emotion. He released her and turned to watch the way they traveled.

Was this God's answer to her fearful questions? Was this action by the stoic Indian meant to relieve her worries? *God, speak to me. I'm scared!* She looked over at Evelyn, riding with an Indian's strong arm around her little body. A big grin brightened her face as they sped along. Her fair hair, the sweat dried now by the wind, flowed back against the Indian's dark chest, spreading over the dark tattoos.

Okay, I'll trust, promised Tildie.

The village surprised her. She had not expected the neatly erected tepees, the smell of dinner cooking, or the curious stares of the little children.

When she slid off the pony, her knees buckled. Again, the same silent Indian reached to steady her. The older man spoke, and a woman came forward to guide Tildie and the children into a tepee. The woman gave them water to drink.

Even in her anxious state, Tildie stared in fascination at the inside of the Indian's home. Spaced about four feet apart, the framework of twenty-one pine poles made a twenty-foot circle. About two-and-a-half inches in diameter at the base, the poles tapered off as they extended their twenty foot length. The thinner tops rested together as they crossed in a narrow bunch where a hole in the hide covering had a small flap. A shallow hole dug in the middle of the earthen floor smoldered with a small fire. A larger fire had been directly outside the tepee. Bedding, buffalo robes, and various household items were piled in neat order around the sides.

An Indian woman bathed little Evie and chattered to the child in soothing, incomprehensible syllables. An older woman with long braids heavy with gray hair brought water, soothing potions, and a change of clothes. When Tildie and the children were physically more comfortable, the older woman brought them food.

Tildie thanked her. Then, she and the children joined hands to pray. They must have been a strange sight, sitting cross-legged in an Indian tepee, wearing Indian clothing, but praying as they did around the kitchen table of the wooden house on the homestead. The Indian woman watched with serious eyes. When they finished praying and began to eat, she gave a decisive nod as if she understood something from the little scene. She abruptly walked out of the tepee.

Left alone, Tildie and the children relaxed and enjoyed the surprisingly tasty stew.

"When are we going home?" Mari asked. With her hunger satisfied, she had thoughts of something besides her stomach.

"I don't know," answered Tildie. Evie curled up in her lap. The long dusk of summer finally deepened into night. The wind stilled as it often did at twilight and insects tuned up just as they did back home. Evie hugged Tildie and seemed almost content.

Boister cast her a worried look, and Tildie started speaking quickly for fear he would say something upsetting to the girls. He was perfectly capable of predicting their death by some means of torture. "They've been very nice to us, haven't they? I wonder if any of them speak English."

"Is Mama dead?" asked Mari.

Tildie looked at her small, sad face and longed for a better answer. "I think so," was all she could say.

"Did she go to heaven?" Mari asked solemnly.

"Yes."

"Then she's dead, Tildie. She wouldn't go to heaven unless Jesus called her. Jesus called Pa. Now he's called Mama. She'll be happy, Tildie, don't worry."

Tildie stared at her little cousin. She hadn't told the children these things. Apparently, before their mother withdrew into her shell of despair, she had talked to them of God and heaven. Tildie nodded, "That's right, Mari. Your ma and pa are in heaven."

"He isn't," said Boister. Clearly the response indicted John Masters. Boister never referred to the man by any name if he could help it.

The boy's cold expression clutched at her heart. Remembering his tears at the scene of the accident, Tildie sighed. Perhaps those tears signified something good. Boister so very rarely showed emotion. The apathetic attitude resembled his mother's too much. A shiver ran down Tildie's spine in spite of the warmth of the night air.

She bowed her head, closed her eyes, and rested her cheek against Evie's curly head. *God, this is too much for me. I can't take care of these children. Boister hurts so badly. Inside, he's hurt. I don't know what to say or do. Are we going to die here? Will I be able to keep little Evie, Mari, and Boister if we get out? Where will we live? How will I provide for them? Oh God, this is impossible. You must truly be able to achieve the impossible this time. I have no choice but to leave it all in Your hands.*

Evie gave a soft muzzled snore in her sleep, and Tildie gently placed her on a mat next to the buffalo skin wall. Marilyn took her place in Tildie's lap, and even Boister scooted closer. Tildie sang softly. She wandered through the tunes without any order. Sometimes she sang one through, and others, she skipped from verse to verse, using the words of the old hymns to soothe her own heart as well as the children's.

Horses came into the camp. Voices murmured in low, urgent tones. Even knowing that she could not understand, Tildie strained to hear the words. Finally, she heard a shifting of feet and horses being led away. The older Indian woman came into the tepee. She handed Mari's rag doll to her. To Tildie, she handed Aunt Matilda's Bible.

"Thank you, thank you," Tildie said through the tears, clutching the precious Book.

Some of the Indians had been to the wagon. They'd brought these items to her. In light of the language barrier, questions were futile. Tildie looked at the old woman and saw understanding and compassion in her face. Tildie gratefully accepted the comfort God sent for this moment.

⁓

The old Indian woman apparently lived alone in the tepee. She made no attempt to verbally communicate with her guests. With kind eyes and firm nudges, she prodded the newcomers into doing what she wanted. The first day, she showed them how to help with the chores, beginning with building up the fire for their cooking. None of the village Indians seemed to be much interested in the little family and let the old woman be in charge of all their doings.

"Couldn't we just leave?" asked Boister at midday.

"I'm too sore to walk very far," answered Tildie. "And I don't know where we are, or where we should go."

"We should head for the mountains. That's the way we were headed before. Or we could turn away and keep the mountains to our backs. That's the way to go home," Boister said, then fell silent.

A horrible prospect crossed Tildie's mind, and she hastened to say something that would keep Boister from striking out on his own in some attempt to find help. "We should stay together, Boister. I need you to help me be brave. I mean it. God will send us help or show us how to get back home. Meanwhile, we *must* take care of each other."

Boister nodded, and Tildie took a measure of comfort from the small gesture.

"Who's that old lady?" Mari pointed to the Indian woman who cared for them. "Is she the tribe's grandma?"

"I don't know who she is, Mari, but we should be grateful she's kind to us."

"What should I call her?" asked the little girl with big eyes.

"Older One," said Boister promptly. "If you look around the camp, you won't see anyone older. She has more wrinkles on her face than any I ever saw anywhere."

"The others seem to treat her with a great deal of respect," said Tildie. "Until we learn her name, I guess it would be all right to call her Older One."

⸺⸺❖⸺⸺

Late in the day, more Indians arrived. At the far side of the village, Tildie saw them surrounded by her new neighbors. Through the crowd, she got glimpses of the newcomers. The Indians who had just arrived had a litter with an injured man strapped to it. Older One went over to the crowd, speaking to first one, and then another of her tribe. She waved them impatiently away from her tepee. She obviously did not want the man in addition to her other white guests.

The Indians brought the litter closer, carrying it past Older One's tepee. Tildie gasped as she recognized John Masters's clothing more than his bloody features. She followed the men. The children also started after them, but Older One would not allow it. She turned them back sternly.

The grim Indians placed John Masters in a tepee quite a distance from Older One's. They put him down gently, spoke not a word, and left the tepee quickly. One man stayed to cradle Masters's head and dribble water between his battered lips. Tildie did not think her aunt's husband even swallowed. The Indian stood and walked out.

Tildie knelt beside Masters and looked him over. Dried blood caked one side of his face. His swollen, discolored features bloated with bruises. Loosening the binds which held him to the litter, she saw his broken legs. One mangled hand lay tied with a cloth to stop the bleeding. His raspy breathing pushed a trickle of bloody drool from his mouth. His wounds were too massive for Tildie's few nursing skills. She wondered if even a doctor could save him.

The tepee flap drew back, and an Indian elder walked in. Tildie moved aside as the man knelt beside John Masters, assessing his wounds in a thorough manner. If there were a healer in the village, Tildie felt sure this was the man.

He sat back on his heels and studied the patient in silence. In the end, he stood and walked out without doing anything to aid the wounded man.

Tildie bathed Masters's face and squeezed water into his mouth as she had seen the first Indian do. After some time, another Indian came into the tepee and indicated she must leave. Tildie left feeling inadequate. John Masters was going to die.

CHAPTER 3

During the night, Tildie worried. The children snuggled beside her in the pile of animal skins which served as their bed. Older One snored softly from across the way. The stars twinkled through the hole at the top of the tepee where poles crossed and smoke could drift out. Her prayers seemed to go around in circles rising no higher than the little opening to the sky visible above her. The worry weighed them down.

It all boiled down to whether or not she could trust the almighty God who had given her work when her parents and brother died, guided her to Aunt Matilda's home, and given her strength to put up with John Masters's taunts. God had stood close in times of trouble before, but now He seemed distant. Present troubles cast menacing shadows so that she could not see Him. Reason told her that her thinking was faulty, but fear told her there was no help, no end to this predicament. Sleep came eventually, without her soul settling into peace.

❦

The morning surprised Tildie. It mocked her with cheerfulness. Older One chanted a sing-song melody. Birds twittered in the trees. The bustle of the Indian camp echoed the busy noises she had heard the previous morning. Evie chattered her toddler nonsense to the doll Older One had made for her. Mari hurried to help stir the pot of mash. Boister followed another lad down to the stream.

Surely there should be some sign that a man had died, or lay dying. Tildie's eyes turned to the tepee harboring John Masters. Had he made it through the night? She started toward the tepee, but Older One turned her back, just as she had turned the children back the day before. Older One put a bowl before her, and Tildie knew she was to grind the corn. She sighed and sat down in the shade of a tree. As her hands worked the round grinding stone across the rough stone bowl, her mind kept returning to the injured man in the tepee.

After several tries, Tildie escaped Older One's interference and reached the tepee where John Masters lay. She went in cautiously. An old woman sat in the gloomy space and nodded solemnly at her entrance. She did not, however, offer anything more than the acknowledgment of her presence. Tildie knelt beside the broken man.

"John," she spoke after a moment. "John, do you hear me?"

He groaned and stirred slightly.

Contradictory feelings overwhelmed her. This despicable man had caused so much misery. She'd tried not to hate him, but now that he lay helpless before her she realized how great her anger and resentment had grown. She blamed him for taking over her uncle's home and making it a place full of strife. She blamed him for her loving aunt's withdrawal and neglect of the children. She blamed him for every uncomfortable moment she had experienced since she arrived, uninvited, on his doorstep. She even blamed him that they were prisoners in this Indian village. This accusation skittered around the fact that she didn't really believe they were prisoners.

Still, John Masters was despicable, and that was his own fault. He was hateful, proud, a bully, and a lazy, foul-smelling vermin. He deserved to die, and she knew he would go to hell. She looked at the miserable shell that struggled to breathe, sweated with fever, and smelled of death. Her emotions battered against the cold hatred she felt for him. The careful reserve she had used to deal with this man crumbled, and she cried.

"John, can you hear me?"

"Curse you, girl," he muttered. "Nobody asked you to come."

"John, you're going to die," she sobbed. "Aunt Matilda is already dead."

His eyes opened and he looked at her, really looked at her. She knew he saw her and his mind was clear.

"You're going to die, John, and you are the lowest man I have ever met. I'm sure there's someone out there worse than you, but I never met him. You took advantage of a widow's grief. You stole her homestead and ran it down to nothing. You treated her badly, you treated her kids badly, and you even treated your own little girl badly. You're scum."

"Thought you was all goodness," John protested with just a touch of irony in his whispery voice. "Ain't right to talk to a dying man like that."

"You're going to go to hell."

"Reckon so," he gasped.

"You don't have to," she whispered.

"You gonna preach?" The scornful twist to his lips reminded Tildie how often he'd belittled her faith. Still, she was compelled to speak.

"Aren't you scared? Aren't you ashamed? How can you die and face God, knowing He's going to toss you in hell? It's not make-believe or women's talk, John. You're going to find out too late that all the religion you've been scoffing at is true."

Tildie wiped the back of her hand across her eyes, not knowing why she even stayed beside this worthless man who had caused her nothing but grief, who had been the ruin of her aunt's family.

"Too late," his voice bubbled as he repeated the phrase. A trickle of blood oozed out of the corner of his mouth.

"It's not," said Tildie firmly. "You're still breathing. Just admit you're bad and ask for forgiveness. Christ died for you—even you. You can go to heaven if you just say it."

Tildie clenched her fists in her lap. Tears ran down her cheeks, and she no longer tried to stop their flow. He looked at her again. A searching look, but she couldn't meet his eyes. She crossed her arms over her middle, and rocked back and forth as she sobbed.

She saw his eyes close and watched him through blurry vision. His lips moved but no sound came out. He coughed. He seemed unconscious, then his lips moved again. His hand moved toward her, but she cringed away, and it fell limp by his side.

Tildie angrily wiped the tears from her face. She did not want to cry for this man. She took deep breaths, trying to stop this ridiculous emotional outburst. Why was she bawling over this reprobate? She hated him. She felt glad he was dying. She screwed her eyes shut and willed herself to stop, holding her breath and tensing every muscle in her body. She tried to call out to God and found there were no words. *Pray for me, Holy Spirit,* she demanded. *I can't. I can't.*

At last peace descended on her. With slow, calming breaths she returned to her surroundings and opened her eyes to look down on John Masters's face. He was dead, and in his death, the perpetual sneer that had marred his features vanished. He looked calm, at peace.

As she looked at his face, she knew. He had taken Christ as his Savior at the last possible moment. He wasn't going to be punished for all the pain he'd inflicted on Aunt Matilda and the children. He'd escaped punishment. He'd cheated. That's what she felt, even though her mind told her she was wrong to feel that way. God had chosen to be merciful to another wretched sinner.

Tildie rose to her feet and turned away. God was good. His ways were right. She should be happy. Instead, she felt cold and alone.

Chapter 4

In the weeks that followed, Tildie wondered what they did with his body. As far as she could tell, it just disappeared the next day.

The Indians' way of expressing their condolences left her confused. They did not speak to her or show any sympathy, yet she sensed they knew of her loss and respected her grief.

In her unsettled state of emotions, it was a good thing that they could not exchange comments. From time to time she found herself crying. How could she have explained that she cried for her aunt, not John Masters? She cried because she had never gotten to visit with the aunt she remembered from her youth. That woman was destroyed by the time she reached Colorado.

She cried because she was angry with herself for the bitter feelings she had about John Masters's salvation. She cried because she was afraid. She was hounded by the responsibility of caring for her little cousins. She feared being among the Indians, even in the face of Older One's kindness. She feared going back to the white settlement where the good citizens would undoubtedly want to take the children from her and place them in homes where they could be cared for. She cried because those good citizens were probably right; she wouldn't be able to provide for the children adequately.

She cried because, in all of this, she should have depended on God and been strong in her faith. Instead, she slipped away from the children so she could cry without alarming them or cried quietly in the night, thinking no one would know.

When her parents and brother had died, the pastor and church members bolstered her faith. On her own, she apparently had no perseverance. Fear dogged her every waking moment, and this disappointed her. Surely she could be strong in the Lord through adversity. When she analyzed her situation, she carefully counted her blessings. She and the children were housed, fed, and treated well. Yet, she dwelled on what might happen and could not turn her mind as she should to think of things that were good and lovely. It was only through a conscious effort to turn everything over to God in prayer that she kept her sanity. Gradually, the turmoil subsided and the routines of life filled the great inner void.

Mari and Boister began to understand the Indians and spoke words of their language. Tildie made very little progress and had to laugh each time Older One threw up her hands in despair over her stupidity. The impatient Indian hostess would haul one of the children over to Tildie's side, speak to Boister or Mari, then wait for the child to translate. Her expression clearly indicated that she thought the mother was the slowest of the white guests in her tepee.

The days lengthened, and Tildie began to notice the individuals in the Indian village. A young Indian boy, White Feather, took Boister under his wing. They went out together, and although Tildie had trepidation over just where they went and what they did, they came back, dirty and content. Boister learned to fish and hunt with the help of his new friend. Mari played with the other little girls, but she also spent time doing chores for Older One. Little Evie toddled among the women and children and gathered the same tolerant affection as the other toddlers of the tribe.

Slowly, Tildie became aware of one Indian who watched her. This strong young man often stood close by. His serious face held dark, piercing eyes, following her every movement. When he came close to the tepee, Older One scolded him and shooed him away. Once she pushed Tildie into the tepee and would not let her come back out until the men rode off from camp.

This new worry occupied Tildie's mind. Obviously, the man thought a young white woman would make a good wife. Tildie began to think less of her confused grief over the deaths of Matilda and John Masters and began to concentrate on what went on around her. She had no desire to be claimed by this Indian. She stayed closer to Older One or with a group of the other Indian women.

Older One showed Tildie how to cut fresh venison into strips and lay it out to dry in the sun. Tildie's hands ached from the hours of tedious labor. As in many cases before, she found herself admiring the older woman for her skill and stamina. No stranger to hard work herself, she marveled how these Indian women worked endlessly. They laughed, as well. Often running chatter between the ladies merrily lightened their mood as they diligently repeated a monotonous chore. Listening to the rhythm of their talk, Tildie could almost imagine her white neighbors in Lafayette sitting around a quilting frame, exchanging the same peaceful banter.

The day had been long. Tildie took off her work dress and put on another Older One provided. She carried the soiled dress down to the creek along with several other items that Older One thrust into her arms. Tildie enjoyed this one chore. In the shade of an elm tree, she sat on the outcrop of flat rock, dangling her feet in the water as she scrubbed the clothes in the gently flowing stream. Mari and Evie had tagged along behind her, and they played by the water's edge.

Just as the thought crossed her mind that Boister was turning into a little fish from his daily swims with his friend, she heard a splash. Evie floundered in shallow, slow-moving water. Mari gave a cry of alarm and jumped in after her. Tildie tossed aside the shirt she held and scrambled down the bank. With a leap and two strides through the cold water, she had hold of Mari, but Evie moved beyond her reach. Tildie turned quickly and shoved the older child toward the shore, urging her to climb out. Frantic, Tildie swung back to catch Evie only to see the child doing a fair dog paddle. Unfortunately, she paddled away from Tildie and the bank.

"Evie, come back!" cried Tildie. She hurried after her, but the smooth rocks in the stream bed turned under her feet. With each slip, her little cousin got farther away.

A splash downstream alerted Tildie to the presence of the solemn Indian who shadowed her in camp. He stood in the path of the oncoming child and scooped her into his arms. With confident strides, he came upstream. Evie clung happily to her rescuer. The Indian reached Tildie and put a hand under her arm to steady her as they made their way to the bank.

Dancing and clapping, Mari laughed at them. The Indian put Evie down next to her sister and helped Tildie up the slight incline. Tildie hugged the children and laughed with them, grateful that nothing serious had befallen them. She stood up, wringing the water from the skirt of her Indian gown and shyly looked up at their rescuer.

He stood watching, a glimmer of humor brightening his eyes and bringing a softness to his normally aloof expression. Tildie had learned that these Indians had a well-developed sense of humor, even to the point of some very uproarious practical jokes. She smiled at him, recognizing that he, too, found the escapade amusing.

"Thank you," Tildie said. His expression sobered, and he looked deep into her eyes. She turned away. Tildie had no desire to offend the man, but his gaze was warm and too intimate. His interest frightened her.

"Thank you," she said again, quickly picking up the laundry.

"Come, girls," she commanded. "We must get you out of those wet clothes."

"We'll dry," Mari pointed out.

"Come," she answered abruptly and hurried toward camp. Mari helped Evie up and took hold of her chubby hand. The girls gave the Indian one more parting grin. They'd enjoyed the dunking and hastened after Tildie only because they were accustomed to obeying.

That night as Tildie lay in bed with her three cousins, she prayed in earnest—something that had been hard since John Marshall's death.

Thank You, Father, for keeping Mari and Evie safe. Forgive me for being such a weakling. I am trying to trust You. I know that You will provide for us. I admit I'm afraid of just how You'll provide, but I trust You. I'll try not to be such a coward. I'll try not to demand things my way. But, please, Father, let us stay together. Please, let us be a family. Please, don't take the little ones from me. I trust You. I trust You. I want to trust You.

Morning came with the usual tasks Tildie had learned to expect. She was stirring a pot when a shadow fell across her, and she looked up to see an elder with the Indian who followed her standing at his shoulder. She quickly rose and faced them.

The elder looked her over and nodded his approval.

"You need a man," he stated flatly, surprising her by speaking English.

Oh God, give me the right words. I must answer carefully.

Assurance came to her. She did not need a man. As a child of God, she was in His care. Even though her faith had been weak of late, she knew that His care was far superior to the care of any man.

Confidently she shook her head and spoke softly. "No, I have Someone."

The older man turned and spoke briefly to the younger Indian. They walked away, leaving Tildie relieved that it had taken so little to turn them from their purpose.

CHAPTER 5

Tildie looked up as the other women began to stand and prattle. She followed a pointing finger to a giant white man striding into the village beside an Indian.

A Swede, thought Tildie immediately as she observed him. *No other race towers over others in that golden aura like the Swedish people back home in Indiana.*

A large, reddish-gold dog followed the two travelers. The dog had a peculiar backpack, carrying part of the load for his master.

The white man smiled easily as he exchanged greetings with many of the tribe. Several children dashed out to pet the dog, exclaiming happily as they trotted beside the two men and the dog.

Tildie had never seen a man so stunning. His straight blond hair hung down over his collar. With a healthy tan, he was still fair beside the swarthy Indians. Straight nose, firm lips, and squarish chin, he was handsome. His expression radiated warmth. His light-colored eyes smiled on those around him. Dressed in buckskins and homespun cloth, with dark leather boots nearly to his knees, he looked magnificent.

Tildie started walking toward him, vaguely thinking that this was a white man, and a white man would surely speak

English. He would help her and the children. She caught Evie up in her arms as she passed and reached out to take Mari's hand to pull her along. By the time he reached the chief's tepee, she'd broken into a run.

Something one of the Indians said drew his attention to her. He turned, watching her. She came to a halt, suddenly unsure. Her eyes searched his. Would this stranger help? Could he get them out of the Indian village? He smiled, and she recognized the smile.

Odd, but her brother had had just that kind of smile, thin lips that tilted into a crooked smile, full of charm and good humor. Tildie felt as if her own brother had come to rescue her. She ran again as fast as she could, encumbered by the little girls. The crowd of Indians to one side parted, allowing Boister to join her. He ran, too.

Tildie crossed the last few yards, hurling herself into the white man's arms. Distrustful, Boister shed his wariness and grabbed one of the giant's legs and Mari, the other. Tildie buried her face against his chest. She cried with relief.

It felt right to be in his strong arms. His tall frame provided a bulwark to cling to. Larger, sturdier, safer than any man she could recall, he must have stooped to embrace them. She felt his chin upon her head. She heard him laugh and wondered how it could all be so natural.

Finally embarrassed, she leaned back. He wiped tears from her face with gentle fingertips. The villagers crowded around them, rejoicing as they witnessed what appeared to them a happy reunion. The Indians' smiling faces, their strange words of joy surrounded her. She looked up with bewilderment at the white man.

"I came as soon as I heard you were here," he explained.

"I don't understand."

"These are my friends. I learned their language when I lived with them four winters ago. I wasn't very fluent back then. When I tried to tell them that I didn't want one of their Indian maidens, that my God had chosen a woman for me, they thought I already had a wife, not that I was waiting to find her. When you knelt to pray as they'd seen me do, they decided you were my woman. They haven't seen many people kneel to pray.

"My name is Jan Borjesson. You have a boy named Boister?" At her nod, he continued. "They decided he's my son because the names sound alike. That would make sense to them. Moving Waters came to my cabin with the wonderful news that my woman had arrived from the East."

Tildie's head went down. She couldn't look the handsome stranger in the face. She stared at his feet and felt herself blushing. She knew it wasn't a delicate flush, but a searing red, covering her neck and cheeks. She could feel the warmth of her embarrassment and was embarrassed even more by the rosy betrayal of her emotions. The stranger, Jan Borjesson, squeezed her shoulders and laughed.

"I'm a missionary, and I'll get you and your children out of here. We'll talk later about where you want to go. Now, I must sit with the elders of the tribe and talk. They'll probably want me to stay a few days to tell them stories from the Book, then I'll take you to the nearest white settlement. Take your children back to your tepee." He gave her a little shake at the same time using a finger to raise her chin. She had to look at him. "Everything is going to be all right."

He smiled, and Tildie felt that everything would, indeed, be all right. She thanked God as she herded the children away from the center of the village.

"Who is he?" asked Boister.

"Could you call him Pa till we get out of here, Boister?" Tildie asked. She knew he'd been listening so that he really knew as much as she did. The important thing was to aid the stranger in their release from the Indians. Surely the Indians would let the little family go peacefully. They'd never shown any hostility toward her or the children.

Boister looked over his shoulder and studied the white man. He stood taller than the tallest of the warriors.

Boister's solemn face reflected the seriousness of his thoughts. He'd never given John Masters the privilege of being called Pa. This stranger had done nothing to deserve the honor. He looked up at Tildie's expectant face.

"If you do, the little ones will," she explained. "It'll make it easier for the Indians to let us go."

"He's going to take us away?" he asked.

Tildie nodded. "Back to a white settlement."

Boister looked down at the dirt, studying his scuffed moccasins. He shrugged. "Guess so," he said and started moving towards Older One's tepee.

They ate supper with Older One while the white man, Jan Borjesson, stayed with his Indian friends. Tildie hoped to talk to him soon. She sat brooding over her bowl of venison stew. Was this missionary an answer to her sporadic prayers? Had God honored her with this blessed rescue even when she had displayed so little faith? Humbly, Tildie prayed her thanks. God again demonstrated His grace, for surely she was not worthy of this delivery. Knowing God loved her even in her weakness spread warmth through Tildie's heart.

In contrast to Tildie's pensive mood, Older One rejoiced. She grinned at Tildie until Tildie realized what the old woman was thinking and blushed. Older One patted her shoulder and looked into her eyes with such a knowing expression that Tildie blushed again. Each time her eyes met the old woman's, Tildie felt her cheeks grow warm. Each blush set Older One off in a cackling giggle.

The fire died down. The children slept in their bed. Older One brought in a new dress of soft, smooth leather for Tildie to wear. The eager Indian woman combed and braided Tildie's blond locks, all the time whispering in her native language words which Tildie could only guess referred to the time when the blond giant would come to the tepee. Older One's grins and chortling heightened Tildie's embarrassment.

Tildie ignored Older One, but still she grew impatient for the Swede to come. She wanted information—when they would leave and where he would take them.

At last Older One snored softly. The tepee flap pulled back and Jan Borjesson's huge form blocked the moonlight.

"Are you asleep?" he whispered.

"No," Tildie answered, just as quietly.

He extended his hand. "Come and walk with me."

Tildie rose from the pallet, crossed the small space, and took his hand naturally. His large dog greeted her, and she dropped the man's hand to pet behind the dog's soft ears.

"Her name is Gladys," offered Jan.

"Gladys?" The oddly proper name for a furry beast startled a nervous giggle out of her.

Borjesson nodded his head, smiling down at her with the crooked grin that made him look so like her brother.

"After a schoolteacher from my youth. I was madly in love with her through two and a half grades. She married the blacksmith."

Tildie looked up at him shyly, wondering if he was teasing her. His face gave nothing away.

They walked through the quiet Indian village. No matter what time of night, there always seemed to be a few Indians awake and watchful. Borjesson nodded to them as they passed, and they returned his nonverbal greeting with grunts and grins. Tildie suspected she knew what they were thinking, and again, she blushed. Perhaps in the moonlight, that telltale red stain would not be noticed by her companion.

At last he indicated they could stop. He offered a seat on a smooth boulder. Gladys sat beside Tildie and rested her chin in her lap. When Tildie did not take the hint, the dog nudged her hand indicating she would gladly accept a good rub behind the ears.

"S'pose you could tell me your name?" asked Jan. "I can't exactly call you, 'wife.'"

"Tildie, Matilda Harris."

"Well, Matilda Harris, you must tell me how best to help you. Where do you wish to go? Where are your people?"

"I have none. I don't know where to go."

"Who were the couple who died in the accident?" He then explained, "My friends have given me a full account of how they found you."

"My aunt and her husband," she answered readily. "They

were taking me to Fort Reynald to marry a grocer named Armand des Reaux."

The tall man turned abruptly toward her, "You're to marry des Reaux?" A note of disbelief sharpened his tone.

"I've never met him," she hurried to explain. "My aunt's husband arranged the marriage. John Masters said he couldn't afford to keep me."

"Well, you must certainly *not* go to Fort Reynald. Des Reaux is a mean, uncouth character. We'll just cross that off your list of possibilities." He sat quietly for a moment. "You say your aunt's husband, not your uncle. Why is that?"

"I came out from Lafayette, Indiana, after the last of my family died. I didn't realize my aunt's second husband would be so different from Uncle Henry. I remembered him as generous and warmhearted. They lived near us when I was small.

"At the time it seemed a wise move, and even though the last six months have been difficult, I believe I helped my aunt some and made parts of her life more bearable."

"Are there relatives from the other side of the children's family?" Tildie shook her head. "It's just me and the three children now."

Tildie looked away trying to hide her discomfort. She realized this gentle giant thought the children were her own. She didn't ordinarily lie to someone who'd been kind to her. The blatant falsehood made her tense. Her parents had trained deceit out of her as any Christian parents would. She must tell him the truth, yet she feared he'd then devise some plan for their well-being that would mean separating them all.

Her conscience battled against her fears. Emotionally, she clung to the reasoning that the circumstances justified the lie. Adding to her guilt, his next words proved he wasn't comfortable with lying, either.

"I'll have to consider this, Tildie." He spoke slowly, "I've never lied to these people. I worked hard to gain their trust. I don't like pretending that we're man and wife, and I would have put an end to it immediately except for a warning from Moving Waters. He believes you're my woman and he hurried me here because Bear Standing Tall wants you for his own."

Tildie nodded. "I know which one that must be." She thought of the man who followed her and helped her with the girls when they fell into the stream.

"Fighting for the right to take you to your own people didn't seem wise. Identified as my woman, you're free to go with me."

She nodded again. So, he was hedging in order to prevent an unpleasant circumstance as well. Somehow, that thought did little to alleviate her own burdened conscience.

"I can take you and the children out of here," Jan continued, "but I'm not sure where to take you. They would think it most peculiar if I just took you to a nearby town and dumped you."

"Would they know?"

"Ah, yes, they would know. They are an astute people, and this is their country. They are very aware of all the white men's movements."

"How do they explain the three children when you have been in this area for over four years?"

"I travel a lot. Gladys and I have explored thousands of miles. I've often been beyond their territory."

At the mention of her name, Gladys left Tildie's side to sit at her master's feet. Jan affectionately petted her, and Tildie noticed for the first time the heavy frosting of white hair around the dog's muzzle. Man and dog had been companions for a long time. This man knew the country, the Indians, the way of the land. She must trust him, putting their lives in his hand and trusting that this was what her heavenly Father desired.

"What do you think we should do about leaving here?" she asked.

"First, I'll take you to my cabin. I need to do a few things to leave it for the winter. Then, I'll take you back to Kansas City. From there you should be able to travel back East."

"There's nothing there for us. The children have, I mean, my aunt has. . .had, a ranch in Colorado close to the Kansas and Texas borders. The land would be ours now. We're the only relatives."

"You wish to return there?"

"Yes, I think so."

"A woman with three children, running a ranch alone. Forgive me, but it doesn't sound very practical."

"A woman with three children returning East to no home, with no money or friends *does* sound practical?"

He grinned. In the moonlight, his teeth shone in that crooked smile. She waited.

He shook his head slowly.

"I don't have an answer for that one. Can you give me twenty-four hours?"

"I don't see that there is a point to it. You may try to make up a reason to dissuade me, but the fact is if God is going to introduce more trials in my life, I'd rather be tried in a place familiar to me than tried in a strange place among strangers."

"You have friends at the ranch?"

"I lived there for six months before John Masters decided to take me to Fort Reynald."

He was quiet for a moment, looking up to the stars. When he finally spoke, the question startled her. "What happened to your husband?"

"I've never had a husband, Mr. Borjesson."

He turned to look at her then. Although she hadn't planned to tell him, she was relieved that she had. The deception had made her uneasy, and she knew that God would honor truth.

"I'm only eighteen. I would have had to marry when I was eleven to be Boister's mother." Tildie smiled as she saw his face in the moonlight. His expression held no hint of condemnation. "The children are my aunt's. The Indians assumed they were mine."

"This does get more complicated, doesn't it?" The missionary smiled, and she noticed the crinkle lines around his eyes. She was glad she'd told the truth. She nodded, waiting to see what he would say.

"Well, there's no sense making plans without prayer and a good night's sleep. God will make the path clear if we don't rush it. Are you content with that?"

"Yes."

"I'm still here to help you. Do you trust me?"

"As long as you don't try to separate me from the children or the children from each other."

"Now, why would I try to do that?"

"Because it's more practical?"

"I don't see that tearing a family apart would be God's way."

Overwhelming relief flooded through Tildie. She grabbed the giant around the waist and hugged him.

"Thank you. Thank you."

He laughed and awkwardly patted her on the back. "I haven't done anything yet."

CHAPTER 6

Jan contentedly sat with the men and told them stories from the Good Book. It pleased him that the Indians asked questions about the great God who cared for all people. He referred to what Paul said in Acts about the Unknown God, stressing that even if God were unknown to a tribe, that did not mean He did not exist.

In the evening, the people of the village gathered around the fire, and he preached to the women and children as well as the men. The custom of the Indians was to relate their stories with a rhythm. There was a cadence of speech reserved just for the great stories of old. Jan, while living with the Indians, had cultivated this method of delivery into his own style. Now he spoke not only in their native tongue, but with the same inflection and flow of their traditional stories.

Jan talked with the medicine man who had been hostile to his words on previous visits. In their legends, the Arapaho people revered a being called Creator who made earth. The old man showed interest in the Bible stories as he had never done before. Jan prayed that his Indian friend would truly hear the Gospel message.

"Tell me if the creator of my people will die if I turn to your

God," said the old man as he sat with the missionary in the evening.

"I don't believe that is the way it is." Jan replied earnestly. "You are a man who has always sought the truth. You have spoken to the one you call Creator whom you believe to have power over man and the world. I say that you have talked to God but did not know His name or the things He has revealed to us through His Son.

"When you spoke to the Creator of Rain, you were speaking to Jehovah, because He is the God of Rain. When you spoke to the Creator of Light, you were speaking to Jehovah, because He not only is the God of Light, but He created light, and the Book says He *is* Light. You have often spoken to the Creator, but now He has sent me to tell you that there is but one God, the one and only, true and living Jehovah."

"And the evil spirits?"

"There is no God but the good and just Jehovah. Evil spirits would like us to believe that they have the power of God, but they do not. They have the power of fear. In God there is no darkness at all. God does not give us a spirit of fear, but of love, truth, and a sound mind. God casts out all fear."

"I will think on these things, Jan Borjesson," the man promised. Jan prayed that he would also remember what he had told him about the purpose of God's Son's journey to the people of the earth.

Another time he told the man, "God is fair. He does not want His people to be ignorant of Him. He sends someone to tell what He has revealed to others. If you were to walk for a hundred years, you would come near the land where His Son visited the earth." He drew a small circle in the dirt and pointed to it as he spoke. "God did not want just these people so far away to possess the great knowledge of Him. He sent people out, here and here and here." Jan drew more rings around the first circle. "These people were told about God. Then, more people went out at God's command to tell of His greatness."

Jan drew more rings around the original.

"You see the Truth of God is spreading." He drew the circles farther and farther away from the center. "Now, I am here," he said, pointing to the outermost circle. "It is because God wants the Arapaho to know."

"It is like a pebble dropped in the pond," said the old medicine man solemnly.

"Yes," said Jan, knowing that it was often best to let the Indian think rather than to continue talking. After a few moments, the old man nodded, rose to his feet, and left Jan to wonder how much the man believed.

~·~

Three days after Jan had walked into the village, he left with his newly acquired "family." They had little to carry as they set out on foot. Rolled blankets held meager supplies. Each carried a bundle and the Indian equivalent to a canteen. Gladys had her saddlebag pouches packed.

Jan explained that the Arapaho expected Tildie to bear the bulk of their burden. Women and dogs traditionally carried all as the semi-nomadic tribe moved around. He chortled. "The women particularly like when I tell how Jesus often honored women and sought to make their burdens less onerous. They are in favor of following our God in this area."

Jan provided each of his fellow travelers with a walking stick. The girls' had animal heads carved at the top knob. Little Evie soon found herself carried by the big Swede in a sling much like the Indians used to carry their smallest children.

They marched toward the mountains for several hours, then Jan called a halt under a shade tree next to a brook. They ate the bread Older One had given them and settled in for a nap. While the hot September sun beat down on the dry land and the winds flowed down off the mountainside, they would rest.

In the tepee of Older One, Jan slept with the little family group. He had nestled between Mari and Boister. Next to Mari had been Evie with Tildie near the outside wall. Now, as they prepared to sleep in the shade of the elm, Mari plopped down beside Jan. Evie and Tildie took up the other blanket.

Tildie watched Boister stand undecided. Obviously, he

didn't want to lie on a blanket with the girls nor settle beside Jan Borjesson. Finally, he sat between the two blankets with his back against the tree trunk.

When Tildie awoke hours later, he was a crumpled figure, alone at the base of the tree. Her heart stirred with helplessness. Nothing she did seemed to bring Boister back to his childhood. He never fully interacted with anyone. She had thought that in the Indian village, he was showing some signs of attachment to the men and boys who included him in their daily lives.

He must feel sad over parting from his Indian friends. He had found something there with the other boys, despite their cultural differences. He'd been accepted. Even though he seldom spoke, or maybe, because he *was* such a little stoic, the Indian boys had included him in their games as well as their forages out into the countryside. Boister had brought with him a bow and set of arrows, a knife, and several other things Indian boys valued. Tildie didn't know exactly how he had acquired them. Perhaps the Indian men had given them to him as he learned alongside their sons.

Now Boister slept and he looked vulnerable like any other little six-year-old boy. The hard lines of his face were relaxed. He didn't look tough. Tildie knew he must grow up to be a man in this harsh world, but she regretted his loss of childish delight. She had never seen him giggle with abandon like the girls. She closed her eyes to pray and drifted from the comfort of the Father's presence into a peaceful sleep.

She awoke to the smell of dinner. Jan Borjesson grinned at her as she stretched and sat up. He crouched by a small fire, sitting on his heels and stirring the pot Boister had carried.

"Hmm, that's smells good."

"It's jerky and wild onions. Boister and I found a patch there by the stream. It still isn't cool enough to travel comfortably, so I figured we'd eat a bite first."

The breeze rustled the leaves above and played with the wisps of curly blond hair that framed Tildie's face. Her cheeks and the tip of her nose were red from the sun. Tildie reached up and pulled out the braid that hung down her back. With her fingers, she combed through the tangles and proceeded to redo the braid in a more orderly fashion.

The girls busily constructed a house out of sticks and leaves. Boister sat on a rock by the stream.

"There's a trading post two days west," said Jan, watching her as he stirred. "I have some credit there. We'll get a horse and some supplies. Think you can fashion a bonnet out of whatever material old Jake has available?"

"I'll certainly try." She looked down at her deerskin dress. "I don't look like an Indian or a white woman. Much longer in the sun and I'll be red and blistering."

"I was just thinking how nice it was to have company," Jan said with an admiring glance. His next words ruined any illusion Tildie had of her attractive appearance. "I guess I'm not too particular on what my company looks like, whether you're burnt or not. I've lived out here now for six years, and in that time, I've seen two white women. One was old Jake's wife. She died four winters ago. The other was a Frenchwoman traveling with a trapper. She didn't speak any English, Swedish, or Indian. Her trapper friend didn't want her talking to anyone, anyway. Jealous type."

Tildie smiled, thinking how the trapper had cause to be jealous. Jan Borjesson was a man who would turn any woman's head.

"So you're Swedish. I thought so. We had a Swedish community in Lafayette."

"My grandparents came from Sweden and lived in Ohio. My parents live in the same farmhouse my grandpa built. I'm the oldest of thirteen children."

"The Indian women only have three or four children each. I thought that odd."

"Not when you consider that a man might have three wives. Then he is supporting nine to twelve children."

Tildie's eyes grew big. "I hadn't noticed that." She thought for a moment. "The Indian who wanted me, did he have other wives?"

Jan laughed. "You would've been wife number four. The elders weren't too happy with his greed."

Tildie blushed. Jan continued, ignoring her discomfort. "He also had a passel of kids. He must have admired you quite a bit to be willing to take on three more."

He laughed again, but the thought sobered Tildie. She looked over to where the children sat happily engaged in their own activities.

"That's going to be a problem." She sighed. "They're good children, but I can't imagine how I'm going to provide for them. The homestead was profitable when Uncle Henry was alive, but John Masters pretty much ruined it. I'll have to depend on the foreman to turn it back into a working ranch."

"There's a foreman taking care of things?"

"Yes, George Taylor. He's probably getting more done without John Masters underfoot."

"Tell me about the ranch."

Tildie began with what she knew from the letters they had received from her aunt and uncle after the two headed west to settle. Boister came over to sit beside her, soaking up the information about his parents' early life.

"Uncle Henry had a way about him," said Tildie. "He was a friend to everyone. He was strong and ready to lend a helping hand to anyone. There were just a handful of settlers in their group, and he became their leader.

"He was helping with a load of rock. They were gathering the stones from a streambed to make a chimney in a neighbor's house. The load tipped, and he and the wagon went down the bank in a landslide."

Boister took hold of her hand. "I got to him first," he said. "Everyone was yelling, 'stay back,' but I didn't mind 'em. Pa was dead."

Tildie gave him a squeeze with the arm she draped across his back. His scrawny frame tensed as he leaned against her. It was the first time she'd ever heard him say anything about the accident. She knew it was a monumental step for the little boy but wasn't sure how to respond. He probably didn't want her to make a fuss, so she plunged on with the story.

"Aunt Matilda had never been without someone to guide

her. First it was her father, my grandpa. Then when he died, it was her brother. She married Uncle Henry when she was eighteen. They lived in Lafayette for two years before he decided to move west.

"After he died, she needed someone to help her. Unfortunately, John Masters came along and sweet-talked her into believing he was the answer to her prayers. He wanted the house Uncle Henry had already built, fields that were already plowed and sown, and the thriving cattle spread Henry already started.

"Once they were married, John showed his true colors and browbeat my aunt and the children. He got drunk regularly and drove off most of the hands.

"When I came, there was no help in the house anymore. Aunt Matilda had Evelyn, who was almost a year old. Aunt Matilda had given up, just quit."

Tildie stared off into the distance remembering the woman who came to the door when she knocked. Thin, aged, with vacant eyes, she stood there, not recognizing her favorite niece. Her face and demeanor were so altered, Tildie thought she had come to the wrong house. With dawning horror, she realized this pathetic woman was the aunt who had played with her when she was young. This was the vibrant young woman whose earlier kindness had won a place in Tildie's heart forever.

She had reached out and taken the thin, rough hands of her aunt. "Aunt Matilda, it's Tildie. . . ."

The guide she'd hired to bring her from the nearest settlement realized something was wrong. "Miss, this is the right place. Weren't you expected?"

"I wrote a letter. . ."

The door opened wider and John Masters pushed Matilda aside to stand in the doorway. His feet apart, his arms crossed over his chest, he looked at the uninvited guest with barefaced contempt. "We wrote back, 'don't come,'" he growled. "I got enough mouths to feed. I took on two brats when I married your aunt, and we have a gal of our own. You're not needed here. If you could ride a horse and work the cattle, that'd be different. Can't keep decent help out here." He turned, pushing Matilda out of the way again, and stomped back into the dark house.

"You want me to take you back to the way station? A stage will be coming through next week. Take you back East," offered the guide.

"No."

The word was but a whisper. It didn't come from his passenger, but from the woman in the door. Aunt Matilda took hold of Tildie's arm and looked her full in the face. Her eyes filled with tears and the grip on Tildie's arm tightened. "Stay. Please stay."

"Yes, Aunt Matilda, I'll stay."

Chapter 7

Jan handed Tildie a bowl of soup. She took it absentmindedly. Evie toddled over to thump herself down on the ground next to her cousin. The tousle-headed charmer held her chubby hands out to Jan with a irresistible smile and said, "Please."

"You want some soup, too?"

Jan dipped out the broth and handed it to the little girl. "Be careful. It's hot!" he warned.

"Hot. Blow," she commanded and held the bowl in front of Tildie's face. Tildie turned from her memories to involve herself in helping Evie cool her soup. Evie handled her spoon very well, even though she hadn't seen her second birthday yet.

"Hot. Blow," she said repeatedly, making them laugh as she dipped the spoon into the crude bowl, then held it out for different people to blow. Some soup was spilled, but not enough to cry over.

Tildie admired Jan's way with Evie. Some men didn't know how to handle a toddler's enthusiasm. Jan took it as a matter of course that Evie's soup needed to be blown, and some spoonfuls required a blow from each and every one of her dinner partners. He had as much fun joining in her foolishness as the family.

Eventually, they had to resume their long trek. They

watched the sun set over the Rockies as they followed it west. Jan informed them that the mountains originally had been called 'Shining Mountains,' and Tildie agreed it was more than appropriate.

Evie soon rode in the sling again, hanging on Jan's side. When Mari got tired, they stopped to shift the loads. Tildie got Evie and the sling. Jan hoisted Mari onto his back. He shortened his long stride so Boister and Tildie had to do less scurrying to keep up with him.

As they walked, he told stories. Some were of his travels in the wild, unsettled plains. Others were of his childhood. His Swedish grandmother had a store of Old World folktales, and Jan related them with a heavy Swedish accent. The accent alone sent the children into peals of laughter. The travel seemed easy with the merry sound of laughter and eager questions.

Tildie was distracted. She barely listened and didn't join in. Her mind dwelt on the time she spent living with her aunt and John Masters. Again, she felt the cold fury toward the man who had come into her aunt's life and made a bad situation so much worse. She stewed on his meanness and missed the humor in the stories Jan told.

Silver clouds scuttered across the moon. The night breeze gentled after the blustery day. They walked with only short rests until the travelers began to stumble over their own feet.

In spite of the long nap in the afternoon, the children settled down as soon as Jan and Tildie had the blankets rolled out. Tildie lay down as well, but she found it impossible to sleep. After a time, she gave up and went to sit on the trunk of a fallen tree, gazing out over the moon-drenched landscape. Gladys plopped at her feet, quickly going back to sleep with her chin on Tildie's bare toes. When the dog raised her head sharply and gave a muffled *woof* of greeting, Tildie looked over her shoulder to see the huge form of the Swede coming toward her.

"Can't sleep?" He sat beside her.

"I'm sorry if I woke you."

"I'm used to Gladys being tucked up beside me. When she moved, I wondered why."

"It's beautiful, isn't it?" She waved a hand gesturing to the slightly rolling hills and the towering mountains beyond.

"It is." They sat in silence for a while.

Out of the stillness of the night came an owl's call, "Who cooks for you? Who cooks for you all?"

"What was that?" asked Tildie, brought out of her reflective mood by the strange, mellow sound.

"It's a barred owl. It could be almost a mile away."

"Who cooks for you? Who cooks for you all?" the owl repeated.

"It's eerie," observed Tildie. "Are you sure it's far away? It sounds so near."

"No, I'm not sure. The sound carries so well, he could be in one of the trees above us or clear across the field."

"It sounds like he asked who's cooking."

Jan chuckled. "He has another cry." Just as he finished his sentence, a shrill, cat-like scream rent the air. Tildie jumped and grabbed Jan's arm.

"That's it," laughed Jan.

"Did he kill something? Wasn't that the cry of his victim?"

"No, that was his other call. I always thought he was venting his frustration because no one answers when he asks who's cooking."

"Who cooks for you? Who cooks for you all?" came the call on the still night air.

Tildie laughed. "We should answer him. I don't want him getting frustrated again."

They were silent for a while, listening to the night sounds. A slight breeze whispered through the leaves above. The brook bubbled over the round stones. A *plop* in the water sounded nearby, and Tildie lifted an inquiring eyebrow at Jan.

"Toad, most probably."

She nodded, confident that Jan would be able to identify any of the mysterious night sounds.

Jan watched her as though puzzled. "Why are you disturbed? You've been quiet since you told me about John Masters's and your aunt's spread. The children joined in the talk as we walked, but you seemed far away."

Tildie turned her face from his scrutiny. He was a missionary, a man of God. Would he understand the torment she'd felt since the day John Masters died?

"You tell people about Christ, don't you?" Her words were a bare whisper hovering among the quiet sounds of the night. "You tell them how to be saved?"

"Yes."

"How do you feel when someone believes in Jesus, accepts Him?"

"I feel good." Jan shrugged, baffled by her question.

"Have you ever hated the one who accepted Christ? Have you ever wanted to take the words back, wished you hadn't spoken, wanted the man in hell?" Tildie voice remained low, vibrating with the pent-up rage she'd been hiding.

"Who, Tildie?"

"John Masters." She drew her knees up until her feet rested on the wide log and her arms wrapped tightly around her legs. She bowed her head against her knees, hiding her face. "I hate him. I can't let go of the feelings. While he was alive, we just tried to get through each day without having more trouble than we needed. I didn't realize how much I hated him.

"He destroyed what my uncle had built. He destroyed my aunt. Boister has never recovered from his father's death, and that can be laid at John Masters's door, too. The girls were mistreated. He even hit them when he was drunk. Once he swung at me. I ducked and he fell into the fireplace. He hit his head and was out cold. I pulled him out, and Aunt Matilda and I wrapped his burned hand with salve and clean linen strips. We left him to sleep it off on the hearth rug.

"I didn't feel the anger then, but when he was lying there, dying in the Indian tepee, rage surged inside of me."

She turned her face to rest her cheek on her knees, and Jan saw wet streaks. Until that moment, he hadn't realized she was crying. Her cold, dispassionate voice hid the tears.

He laid a hand on her back, and she closed her eyes, relaxing somewhat in the comfort of his touch. Taking a deep breath, she let it out slowly. It came in a shudder, and her lovely features tightened into a grimace as she tried to control her feelings. Jan's hand stroked up and down her back in a soothing motion.

"Tell me about it, Tildie."

She couldn't face him as she spoke, so Tildie lifted her head to stare off and away from the lonely spot where they sat. "I don't know what I was thinking I would say when I managed to sneak away from Older One and crossed the village. I knew he was dying. I had to see him, but really didn't know why.

"He was mangled, and the smell was horrid. He looked so dirty and disgusting. All the times he was drunk, I never felt pity for him, and all of a sudden, I was sorry for him." She paused, remembering the confusion of strong feelings.

"I hated him. Aunt Matilda was already dead. He was supposed to take care of her. He didn't, and she was dead. He was supposed to take care of the children, and he was going to die and leave them and me alone in that Indian village. Any minute he would slip away. I starting telling him how horrid he was, how mean and low-down. He was dying, and I was railing at him."

She paused again, almost too ashamed to go on. Jan waited.

"He heard me. He said I shouldn't talk to a dying man like that, and then I was telling him to repent because he was going to hell. I didn't hear him say the words, but I know he did. I could see it on his face when he was dead. That despicable, low-down worm of a man had a look of complete and utter peace on his face, and I was angrier than ever. He'd made so many people suffer, and he didn't get punished. I didn't want him to get off scot-free."

The last words came out in sobs and Jan put his arm around her. First she stiffened and drew away, but the emotion had too hard a grip on her. She leaned against him, trying to stifle the sobs against his chest.

She thought of the sleeping children and didn't want them to waken. As in the lonely nights in the Indian encampment, she desperately did not want them to see her weak. She must be strong for them. . .and how could she explain the bitter tears of hatred for their stepfather? How could she be an example of a strong and loving Christian when she was so weak and full of hatred?

"There, there, Tildie. Cry it all out." Jan spoke softly into her hair, rocking her gently in his arms. After a bit, the violent, racking sobs subsided. She rested within the curve of his arm.

"You know, he did suffer," Jan said.

"He was in terrible pain from his injuries," agreed Tildie. The shame of her verbal attack on a dying man softened her voice.

"Yes, but I was meaning every day of his life."

Tildie pulled back from him and took out the scrap of calico she still used as a handkerchief. She blew her nose and wiped her tears.

"What do you mean?" she asked.

"If you know a person who acts like he did, you can walk away from him. Some of them, you can walk away and never deal with again. Some of them, you can at least have a moment's peace from time to time away from their distemper. But imagine *being* that person. You could never get away for even a moment. Even in your dreams, you would still be the despicable character everyone hates."

She leaned against him again, and he held her close to his side.

"I never thought of that." Tildie sighed.

"There must have been a lot of hate in that man, and as much as he aimed his hatred at you and his family, he aimed more at himself. He knew he wasn't as good a man as your uncle Henry. That probably made him meaner. Even in his evil intent to take over the ranch and live a life of ease, he failed. Do you think he ever succeeded at anything?"

"Probably not," she admitted.

"Do you think he liked himself for taking a good thing and making it bad?"

"He said it was the lazy hands, bad weather, and coyotes. He had an excuse for every failure."

"And did you believe the excuses?"

"No," she said strongly.

"Do you think he really believed them?"

"No," she said quietly.

"He was a miserable man, and he suffered every day of his life just because he was stuck being himself. He knew of no way to change. He didn't have our Savior to ease his pain and lead him to a better way."

"I haven't been a good Christian, Jan. In the Indian camp, I asked God to help me and didn't expect Him to listen. God knows He had to force me to talk to John about salvation. I didn't want to, and God knows how angry I am that John didn't go to hell." She hiccuped on another sob. "Jan, that sounds so horrible. Everytime the thought goes through my head, I'm ashamed. How can God even stand for me to call on His Name?"

"Well, let's count your sins. One, you hated a hateful man. Two, you begrudgingly helped him to heaven. Three, you're angry with God for forgiving him. Four, you doubt God is good enough to forgive you of your sins. Five, you doubt God is strong enough to help you conquer the resentment and hatred and provide for you and the kids all at the same time. Maybe, the last one should count as three. One for resentment, one for hatred, and one for thinking He wouldn't take care of you. That makes seven."

Tildie leaned back to look at his face, uncertain as to where his list would lead her.

"How many times did Christ say we were to forgive?" he asked.

"Seventy times seven."

"Uh-huh. Maybe because He figured that was about all we were capable of. Personally, I think He just meant not to be keeping score." Jan shifted and gave her shoulders a squeeze. "Now God, being God, should be able to forgive a whole lot more sins than a human's puny four hundred and ninety. Doesn't that figure?"

"Yes."

"And, since He doesn't keep count, having lost previous sins in the depths of the ocean, it figures He could handle your seven sins."

Tildie nodded.

"Now, taking under consideration that you're going to repent of these seven sins, what we have left is how you're going to deal with them in the future."

She nodded again.

"Number one, hating the hateful man. Best just say you're sorry for taking over God's job of being judge and jury. Then, forget about that one. Number two, telling the Gospel through clenched teeth, so to speak. Thank Him for using you anyway and move on to number three. What was Number three?"

Tildie thought for a moment.

"Being angry with God for forgiving John."

Jan nodded and was silent for a moment. "Best just say you're working on getting over it and ask for some help. Number four, doubting God is ready and willing to forgive you of your sins. Thank Him for waiting for you like the father waited for the prodigal son and tell Him you're ready for any fatted calves with your name on them. Might say you're sorry again. It'll make you feel better.

"Numbers five, six, and seven—anger, resentment, and lack of trust. Phew! Guess you're just a lowly, no-good follower like Peter, Paul, doubting Thomas, Barnabas, and Mark to name a few."

Tildie gasped. She looked at his earnest face and saw kindness there. Shyly, a smile warmed her face. He was right. She had been trying so hard to overcome her weaknesses, she'd been so busy browbeating herself for her failures, she'd forgotten how great God is.

"Thank you, Jan." She hugged him. "Sometimes when you talk to me, I feel like my own father is giving me advice."

"Your father?" Jan's eyebrows rose an inch.

"Yes, he was a schoolteacher and a strong Christian. He always seemed to have words of wisdom from the Bible. He was so mature and stable. With him around, I felt secure."

"You feel secure with me?"

"Yes, I trust you. More than I would have trusted my own big brother, Daniel. Daniel was good with figures. He worked in a bank, but he wouldn't have known how to handle this, and he certainly wouldn't have walked across the plains of Colorado."

Jan sat quietly for a moment. "So, what happened to your big brother?"

"Influenza. My parents, too. It took almost one third of the population of Lafayette in seven weeks."

His arms tightened around her. There was so much sadness in her past. He wanted to protect her, make the days ahead comfortable and easy for her. Maybe he was feeling protective like a father. Her warm compact body fit so snugly against his side. No, he definitely was not feeling fatherly. He let her go and slapped his hands on his knees. "Well, since I remind you of your father and older brother, I best act like one of 'em and shoo you to bed. We have a long walk ahead of us tomorrow."

She stood up and looked down at him. "Thank you again, Jan. I feel much better."

"Sure," he said as she turned and walked back to the blankets where the little ones slept.

Jan stooped to ruffle the fur around Gladys's neck and spoke so only his canine companion could hear. "Seems like I'm not much interested in being like a father or an older brother to Miss Matilda Harris."

He sighed and looked out into the vast starry sky.

"Father in heaven," he prayed. "What are You proposing I do about this?" Taking advice he'd handed out to others, Jan decided to pray and sleep on it.

CHAPTER 8

Tildie stood on the hill overlooking a man-made structure that barely marred the landscape. They'd reached the trading post. Disappointment dragged at her steps as she followed the skipping children down the gentle slope. They were excited to reach anyplace. Jan said this hovel held a wonderment of goods. Tildie swallowed hard against the tears. She chided herself. Had she expected Brenner's Mercantile on Main Street Lafayette?

The building proved to be little more than a man's sod house with shelves lining the only room. She found no material she could use to make a skirt, blouse, bonnet, or anything that would get her out of the Indian garb. This didn't bother her as much as it would have three months earlier. She liked the feel of the heavy leather. It was actually cooler than cotton, which would have clung to her as she perspired. As they walked through the brush, her Indian dress and leggings didn't catch in the branches as a white woman's clothing would.

With no bonnets available, Jan bought her a comb and a man's hat from the three men's hats on the shelf. Her image in the warped shiny tin piece Jake used as a mirror made her grin. She looked a vision with her pale deerskin dress, two long blond braids hanging down, topped with a black felt hat. Jan also bought a hat for Boister. Boister's face was a nut brown. Tildie's was beet red, having burned, peeled, and burned again. Jake recommended some ointment for her burnt skin.

Jan bought three horses. Since he'd made no purchases just for the little girls, he told them they could name the horses.

Mari named hers Charger, remembering a story Tildie had told her about knights in England who rode noble steeds. An undistinguished roan with a sway back, but good teeth, Charger hardly looked the part his name implied. Soon they fell to calling him Charlie.

Evie insisted her horse be called "Horse."

When Jan turned to Boister with a question in his eye, Boister walked over to the third horse, a bay, and stroked her shoulder and neck as high as he could reach.

"Do you want to name her?" asked Jan.

The horse bent her head and nuzzled Boister around the neck and down the front of his shirt, looking for a treat.

"Greedy Gert." Boister smiled. He reached in his pocket and pulled out a dried apple slice he'd gotten from Jake. Greedy Gert lipped it out of his palms and scarfed it down quickly.

Two old saddles came with the horses. The harnesses looked decrepit, but Jan thought them usable. Boister rode Greedy Gert with only an Indian girth. Tildie held Evie in front of her on Horse, and Jan carried Mari on Charlie. They made good time on the trail, bypassed Fort Reynald, and headed up a canyon beyond Manitou Springs in just a couple of days.

"We've got to get up into that tree line." Jan came back from leading their little procession to ride beside her.

Tildie looked up the steep embankment to the thick fir trees. It would be a hard climb and once there, the going would be rough.

"Why? The way is easier here," she protested.

"Air's cooled off considerable in the last few minutes. Look at the sky—clouds are gathering from the west. It's raining in the mountains. The reason there's no tall growth in this canyon is it's a run-off. Down here we could be caught in a flash flood.

We're going up to be safe."

Tildie nodded her head, thanking God Jan knew these things. She never would have picked up the signs. She'd been daydreaming about the ranch, wondering what life would be like in the little house with just her and the children—and without Jan. She was getting used to having him around.

Jan dismounted and led Mari on the horse up the side of the incline. Boister followed with Evie and Tildie bringing up the rear.

They progressed slowly. The wind picked up as they neared the crest, and Tildie became aware of a steady roar distinctly different from the bluster of the wind.

"Jan, I hear something."

"I hear it, too. Concentrate on where you're going."

Gladys stood at the top watching their climb. She added her encouragement in urgent, sharp barks.

A few heavy raindrops pelted them in huge drops. The cadence of their sharp *ping* against the rocks picked up. Soon the torrent forced Tildie to duck her head and bend over Evie to protect the child with her body. Horse blew through her nostrils expressing her displeasure and Charlie answered. Horse tossed her head and tried to push past the middle horse.

Jan quickened the pace. The noise grew louder and, although Tildie had never had experience with the sound, she knew it was deadly and coming down the canyon. She could no longer hear Gladys's bark. She couldn't hear the horses or Jan—nothing but the deafening roar of rampaging water and great rumblings of thunder.

Jan and Mari climbed over the edge. He tied the reins around a branch and lifted Mari down, then turned to hasten Boister's mount. "Dismount and tie him off, Boister," he shouted over the roar.

The rain dissolved the ground into a slippery mass. A crack of thunder broke above them, and Horse reared, lost her footing, then fell sideways against the rocks. Tildie let go of the reins and, with both arms around Evie, tried to clear the falling horse. She flew backward and to the side, fortunately next to the mountain, not the drop to the crevasse below. She twisted so Evie was on top of her, trying not to let go or fall on her. Tildie heard the horse scream in terror and sensed Horse's hooves scrabbling for purchase right beside her. A hoof caught her on the side, and as she rolled, her head struck something. A flash of light, immediately followed by a crash of thunder, echoed the pain within her skull. Evelyn screeched.

Through a haze of pain, Tildie saw Jan above her. He wrenched Evie from her hold and turned to pass the little girl to her brother right behind him. Jan pulled Tildie to her feet. She gasped as pain enveloped her right side. The Swede took no notice and half-dragged her up the last few feet to safety. She could hear nothing but the roar. A great wall of muddy water, carrying logs, small boulders, and other debris passed beneath them. With the swirling waters just inches from their feet, Jan pulled her higher over the ridge.

The noise level dropped immediately. Tildie heard Evie and Mari crying. She turned from Jan's arms to reach them. A pain pierced her back high between the shoulder blades, and blackness engulfed her.

Vaguely, she became aware of sounds and movement beside her. Rain splashed on her face, but she couldn't lift her hands to wipe it away. The rain and wind still pounded the earth, but the thunder muttered in the distance. A small, cold rivulet of rain ran through the mud by her side. Tildie could feel it, knew it was there, but couldn't move away. She tried to open her eyes, to speak, but the effort was too much. She slipped again into oblivion.

She was cold. She could hear a fire crackling, but she couldn't move toward it. She tried to open her eyes. She couldn't. There was something warm on each side of her. The girls. She was between the girls. It was so cold. She gave up trying. It was better to sleep.

"Tildie, drink this," a voice commanded her. Someone lifted her head and shoulders. It hurt. *Please*, she begged. *Leave me alone*. No words came. The warm broth dribbled down her throat and down her chin. She tried to swallow. *Leave me alone*, she wanted to cry. She swallowed.

The voices. Sometimes she recognized the voices. Evie chanting her version of a lullaby. Mari asking for something. A cup? Her supper? Tildie couldn't quite hear.

Quiet. The world smelled wet. Smoke drifted from a fire, filled with the acrid odor of soggy wood trying to burn. The wool of the wet blanket stank. She wanted to move.

Someone moved her gently, but it felt like she was being tossed from side to side. *Don't*, she screamed but knew there was no sound. *Please, please, please let me be.*

Warmer. The sun beat down on her. Now the blanket smelled musty. Mari repeated a counting rhyme in a sing-song voice.

"Pick it up. Lay it out. One for baby. Don't you pout. Pick it up. Lay it out. Two for brother, inside out. Pick it up. Lay it out. One for sister. She can't count."

The sun was gone. A voice mumbled in her ear. On one side the warmth of a small figure curled against her side. On the other, a body stretched full-length beside her. A warm arm rested over her stomach. A heavy thigh nestled against her own. She could feel his breath on her cheek. She heard the words.

"Heavenly Father, bring her through this. Heal her, Lord. I've done all I can. Give her strength. Give her life. Give her healing. Bless her. I thank You for bringing her into my life. I thank you for Marilyn, Evelyn, and Boister. They need her, Lord. Heal her. Make her recover." The words went on, and Tildie slept.

She opened her eyes. Over her was an impromptu lean-to fashioned out of cut and woven branches. She moved her head to the side. A neat, small fire blazed inside a circle of smooth round stones. Boister fed it sticks. Mari attempted to comb her own hair as she sat on a log, a little behind her brother. Beyond that, three horses were tied to a rope suspended between two trees.

So Horse had not plummeted to her death, nor bolted and run. With that thought came a conglomeration of memories, some distinct, others hazy and dreamlike. Tildie lay still, trying to sort them out.

The horses moved restlessly. One snorted, and one whinnied

softly. Tildie heard Evie's chatter right before Jan strode into the little clearing with Evie riding his shoulders and Gladys trotting beside him. He tossed a dead rabbit to Boister, who caught it and held it up to admire. Jan reached up and, with one motion, grabbed a giggling Evie and swung her down to sit beside her sister. Tildie noted Evie's hair was cut in a rather ragtag style, close to her head. With two long strides, Jan crossed the clearing and crouched beside her. His huge form blocked the sun and she couldn't see his face with the light behind him.

"You're awake." He waited for her to respond. When she didn't, he continued. "Are you thirsty? Do you want a drink?"

"Yes." The whisper was hardly audible.

"Mari, bring a cup of water," he called and sat down beside Tildie. He lifted her to a sitting position, her back against his chest. The pain seared through her, and even as it threatened to turn her stomach, she realized that the pain was not as intense as it had been during the long hours she'd slept and roused, barely conscious.

Mari brought the cup.

"Is she all right?" she asked.

Tildie had closed her eyes against the pain. She opened them to look into Mari's dear, little, concerned face. She tried to smile.

"Tildie, we thought you would die. We prayed," Mari whispered.

"I'm not going to die," she managed to say.

"Drink this." Jan had taken the cup. One of his strong arms supported her around the waist. The other hand held the cup to her lips. She drank, but even swallowing caused the pain to rise and ebb away. She paused.

"More," she whispered. The next sip brought less pain. She leaned her head back against Jan's shoulder and relaxed. It was then the blanket slipped, just enough to expose her bare shoulder. The cool air hit her skin, and she realized her dress was gone. She was wrapped in blankets. Her eyes grew wide, and she stared around the campsite. It had the look of a place that had been inhabited for a while.

"How long?" she croaked.

"Eight days."

"My dress?"

"It was wet through, and you were cold."

"Evie's hair?"

"She cried when I combed it and it got more and more tangled. I cut it off." With the last admission, Jan's voice filled with regret.

" 'Sall right." The words came out slurred. "Grow."

"Is she all right?" asked Mari again. Boister seemed to just come aware of the activity in the lean-to. He'd been cleaning the rabbit. He came to the lean-to with bloody hands, holding a bloody knife.

"Is she awake? Will she live?" he asked.

Before Jan could answer, Tildie struggled to lean away from him.

"Sick," she muttered as she turned away from the gruesome sight of her cousin's hands. She fought the nausea and felt Jan's hand on her back.

"Go wash up, Boister. Yes, I think she's going to make it."

CHAPTER 9

Now she was used to sleeping in Jan's arms. For days, she had been getting stronger. The pain still hovered, but only as a ghost of its former self with sharp reminders when she breathed too deeply or suddenly moved.

At night, the children all nestled between her and the back of the lean-to. Jan lay down between her and the outside. He cradled her gently, and she relished the warmth that came through the blankets. He offered her no consideration for her modesty as she became better. He uninhibitedly helped her to slip the Indian dress over her head and gently lifted her while Marilyn pulled it down over her hips. He strapped the leggings back on her legs, and it was he who supported her when she was able to get up and go relieve herself in the woods. Several times, she fainted when the pain grabbed her after an ill-advised movement. He caught her and held her until she revived.

Once she woke up in the middle of the night, whimpering in his arms.

"Hush now, honey," he crooned soothingly. "You're going to be all right. The pain will go away. You're going to live. You're going to get over this. Hush, now. I'm here." His voice calmed her as he spoke, some to her and some in entreaties to their heavenly Father for mercy on her, healing, and strength.

Another week went by. She awoke one morning to frigid air and a dusting of powdery white snow on the ground.

Boister stirred the pot over the fire. The girls still huddled in their blankets at the back of the lean-to. Jan bent over a tree-pole construction.

"Jan," she called. He left his project immediately.

"Do you need to get up?" He knelt beside her.

"No, not yet. What are you doing?"

"I'm building a travois, an Indian litter for carrying you to my cabin. We can't stay here any longer."

"How far is it?"

"Not far as the crow flies, but we aren't crows." He smiled down at her, and she decided not to press him for answers.

She was better. She could almost put her weight on her legs, but she still couldn't take a step. She'd asked what he thought was wrong.

"I think a couple of broken ribs. You have a massive bruise on your back. There's even the outline of Horse's foot in deep purple. There may be some injury to your spine, though thank God, you don't seem to be paralyzed. Also, you had a concussion, and one leg was bruised from the knee up to your hip. I couldn't find sign of a broken bone, but it sure was one ugly bruise."

She was embarrassed that he had examined her so closely and turned the subject away from herself. "The children were all right?"

"Scared, cold, and worried, but no injuries. They've been real troopers, helping me to take care of you and not complaining." He paused. "They've been praying hard, too. We didn't know if you'd live."

"Jan, I'm so grateful."

He cut her off. "No, not a word. I'm just glad you're alive. Hey!" he lightened his tone. "After a week of being mother and father to three small kids, I'd have given you a good shake and told you to come back and help me out if you'd died."

"I'm sorry."

"No, don't be. Remember, I'm the oldest of thirteen. I know

how to change diapers. By the way, Evie is now totally independent in that area."

"You trained her?" said Tildie, incredulous.

"Well, I took off the nappies completely and encouraged her to lift up her dress and squat. She's gotten very good at it."

Tildie started to laugh, but the pain caused her to groan instead—albeit with a smile on her lips.

When they started out, Evie and Mari rode double on the back of Horse with the travois attached behind. Jan led the horse, and Gladys trotted beside Tildie's travois as if she had appointed herself guardian. Next, Boister held Charlie's reins. Greedy Gert followed docilely behind.

The travois consisted of two long poles attached to a harness over Horse's shoulders. The free ends dragged behind the horse with a blanket secured in a sling-like fashion between them. Tildie was strapped in and surrounded by most of their belongings.

It was two days' travel, and the days became a blur of jostling and pain for Tildie. She awoke the third night inside a cabin, lying on a pine needle bed with a heavy blanket beneath her and a quilt on top. She could hear the sound of the others' breathing and saw dimly a dying fire glowing in a fireplace across the room. Beyond that she could see the horses. She was confused. Was she in a cabin or a barn?

"Jan," she whispered into the dark.

There was a stirring beside the bed, and Jan's head appeared inches from hers.

"Are you all right? Do you need something?"

"We're at your cabin?"

"Yes."

"Where is everybody?

"Mari and Evie are over there on a pallet. Gladys and Boister are there." He pointed them out in the dim light. "Do you want a drink?"

"Yes."

He rose from his pallet in one fluid movement. She was astonished again at how well such a big man moved. He moved more like an Indian than a white man. Now that she had lived among the Arapaho, she could appreciate the difference. Very few white men had such grace.

He returned with the cup, handed it to her, and laughed softly when he had to rescue the cup before she dropped it. He helped her sit up, and she drank it all.

"Thank you."

He lowered her and put the cup on the floor. "Are you all right?" he asked again. "You feel feverish."

"I ache," she said but chose not to elaborate. "It feels strange to be sleeping by myself. After all, there have been six bodies in the lean-to for weeks."

"Six?"

"I was counting Gladys." She could feel herself getting sleepy again. "Are there horses in your living room?" she asked, not sure to trust her vision.

"Yes."

She looked at his strong face. He was smiling. "Jan, don't go away. I'm frightened tonight."

"Why?" He held her hand and smoothed the hair back from her hot, dry forehead.

"I think something's wrong. Inside. I don't think I'm going to live."

"Don't say that, Tildie."

She sighed, and the effort made her wince.

"You *are* going to live. You would've died by now if you were going to. Every day you're stronger."

"Not tonight, Jan. Something's wrong."

"Please, Tildie, don't talk like that. Rest."

"Jan, I'm glad you came to get us. I'm sorry I'm such a burden."

He leaned over and kissed her forehead. If possible, she was hotter than she had been only a few minutes before. "Tildie, don't do this. Don't die. You have to fight."

She was unconscious, and he stood abruptly, his hands clenched at his sides. His chin came up, and he stared at the ceiling.

"Lord, I want this woman. Don't let her die. I feel like she's always been a part of my life. I loved her before I met her. She's the woman I knew I'd meet one day. God, You understand. She's my other part. She's kind and brave and laughs like a child when she's happy. Don't let her die. Tell me what to do for her. Don't take her away. Let me be her husband. Let me take care of her. Give her into my hands, Lord. Let me cherish her. God, don't take her."

The fever raged during the night. Jan brought snow in from outside and barely let it melt before dipping a rag into it and wiping her face, neck, and arms. When Boister awoke in the morning he helped. When Mari joined them a few minutes later, Jan took off the blanket that had been kicked about as she struggled against the fever. "Here, each of you take a rag and wash her legs with the cool water."

"Is she going to die now?" asked Mari.

"Is it because we moved her?" asked Boister.

"We had to leave," answered Jan. "Heavy snow fell last night. We got to the cabin just in time. God was with us in making that trip. He'll be with us through this."

The eyes of the two small children looked at him. They were scared, and he was, too. He knelt on the floor and gestured for them to come to him. They walked into his arms and held on to one another, taking comfort in the agony and hope that they shared.

"Pray, Mari. Pray, Boister." He had meant for them to pray throughout the day, but Mari took him literally. She folded her little hands in front of her. Still leaning heavily against him, she began, "God, we love Tildie. You already have Pa and Mama. We want Tildie to stay here. Please don't take her." Her little face screwed up, and she buried it in Jan's shoulder.

"God," said Boister. "I promise not to hate You for taking Pa and sending John Masters. I promise to listen to Jan's stories and learn to read the Bible. I won't hide when it's chore time. I won't tease Mari and Evie. I won't give Tildie a hard time when she wants me to practice my sums. I'll be good. Always. Please, don't let Tildie die."

Jan squeezed them, fighting the tears in his eyes. "You don't have to make a bargain with God, Boister. He wants to give us good things without making deals."

"I've been telling Him bad things in my head. I told Him He's no good 'cause He didn't do right by my family. I told Him He's mean and awful. He's going to take Tildie because I'm bad."

"No, Boister, no. That's not the way God works. People may act like that because people aren't holy like God, but God is bigger and better than people. God loves us, and He will take care of us. Even when we don't understand, He is faithful. He is just. He's in control. We must trust Him. We have to, Boister. He wants to bless us. I don't understand why all this has happened. I do know that I love your cousin. If you hadn't been in that Indian camp, I never would have met her."

"If He kills her now, it don't mean much," sobbed Boister.

"God doesn't kill people." Jan sounded desperate now. How could he explain so the little boy would understand? What was Mari thinking? Was she just as confused? "Sometimes He takes people to heaven because it would be too hard on them down here. Think of all the pain Tildie's been in. What if that were to go on forever? In heaven, she won't hurt any more. She'll be well."

"Do you want her to die?" Boister's voice was small and choked.

"No, I want her to live. But that's what I want. That isn't necessarily what God wants. Maybe that isn't what's best for Tildie. We have to give up what we want and ask God to do what's best for her. It's not your fault she's sick."

"I pushed the wagon." His voice was so low, Jan almost couldn't make out the words.

"What?"

"The wagon with the rocks. One wheel was stuck. I pushed it to get it over the rock, and I stumbled and hit it sideways. It slid over the edge. It killed my pa."

"How old were you, Boister?"

"Three."

"And you remember this?"

Boister nodded his downcast head. "I dream about it. I think about it every day. I can hear the men shouting. I hear the rocks and the wagon creaking."

"Boister, you were three. Look at Mari, how little she is. You were a little boy. That wagon must have weighed a ton. Boister, you couldn't have knocked it off the path with your puny little shove. It was going anyway. You didn't do it. You were too little."

"I did it. I fell and it slid away, down the bank. I did it."

There was desperation in his voice and Jan knew it was important to get through to him. "Boister, no. You didn't do it." Jan sent up a quick plea for help. What could he say to relieve this child's anguish? "Boister, remember the rock at the camp—the one you climbed on? You couldn't move that rock, could you?"

Boister shook his head.

"*I* couldn't even move that rock, Boister. Even if we got it in a wagon, I couldn't move the wagon. If you took all the smaller rocks that your Pa and those men had been moving that day, and put them together, they would have been about as big as that rock. Boister, you didn't knock the wagon over. You couldn't have. It's just a coincidence that you bumped it just as it was going over anyway." Jan, with one arm still securely around Mari, tilted his head to look at Boister's partially hidden face. "Do you understand, Boister? You could *not* have moved that wagon."

Boister's shoulders shook, and Jan held him closer. Soon, the sobs broke out, and the little boy shuddered as all the pent-up guilt released.

Evie woke and Mari slipped over to talk quietly to her as Jan rocked Boister in his arms.

Later as they ate breakfast, Boister stirred his mash with little enthusiasm. Jan watched him but said nothing. To his eye, the boy looked more relaxed. Jan could only pray the talk had done him good.

For a day and a half more, Tildie was delirious, fighting the fever and sometimes lashing out at Jan as he put the cooling cloths on her forehead. During the second night, the fever broke. The children awoke to find both Jan and Tildie sleeping soundly.

Boister told the girls to be quiet, and he sliced them biscuits from two days before and gave them warmed water to drink.

The girls quietly played with their two dolls while Boister attempted to clean up. They needed more firewood, so he bundled up, admonished the girls to be quiet, and took Gladys out to gather what he could find.

CHAPTER 10

"W e're cold." Mari tugged at Jan's sleeve.

"Code," agreed Evie, bobbing her head up and down.

Jan stretched and looked over at Tildie. She was sleeping restfully on the pine needle mattress. He reached for his boots and pulled them on. The room was chilly, the fire almost out.

"I'll go out and get some firewood."

"Boister already did."

Jan looked quickly about the cabin. Boister was nowhere in sight. He sprang to his feet and grabbed his heavy blanket coat.

"How long has he been gone?"

"Since we ate breakfast."

Gladys was gone, too. Maybe nothing was wrong. Gladys could lead him back to the cabin. Jan wrapped a scarf around his neck and pulled a knitted cap down over his ears. He opened the door to the blaring light of sun on mountain snow.

He hurried around the corner, kicked the snow off a couple of smaller logs and brought them in. Repeating the process several times, he soon had the fire blazing.

"Mari, I have to leave you in charge of Evie and Tildie. Keep Evie away from the fire. If Tildie wakes up, give her some water and a biscuit to chew on." The little girl nodded solemnly. Jan kissed her good-bye on the forehead and ruffled her hair. He gave Evie a quick peck and looked one last time at Tildie.

"I'll be back as soon as I can." He opened the door and plunged into the deep snow, following the tracks left by Boister and Gladys.

No new snowfall obscured their tracks into the woods. With Jan's long stride reaching over the heavy snow, he quickly covered the territory Boister had plowed through in his meandering.

When Jan found Boister, he had the strong urge to yank him up by the back of his pants and blister him good. All manner of disasters had plagued his thoughts as possible explanations for the boy not returning.

Boister and Gladys lay in the snow, scrutinizing the most makeshift rabbit trap Jan had ever seen. Built with the Indian snare in mind, it had some imaginative white boy innovations that would not have held a weak, blind rabbit for the time it took it to turn around, but boy and dog were entranced with the contraption.

Jan did nothing to cover the sound of his approach and Boister and Gladys turned eagerly to greet him, jumping up to run to him.

"Look, Jan," Boister pointed to his trap. "If we wait awhile, we'll have rabbit stew for dinner. I thought some rabbit meat would make Tildie feel better. You know, give her the broth."

"That's a good idea, son, but I need you back at the cabin. We'll hunt up some meat for dinner for sure. Come on, now. Tildie's better, and if she wakes to find us gone, she'll be worried."

Boister abandoned his trap immediately. "I was gathering twigs for kindling and then I got to thinking how they would bend and make a trap. It's not exactly how White Feather taught me, but. . ." He looked over his shoulder at the trap. "Can we check it tomorrow? Or should we take it apart? I don't want a rabbit to get stuck in it and die if we aren't going to eat it."

Jan didn't have the heart to tell him the first stiff wind

would collapse the contraption, so he shrugged. "We'll check it tomorrow."

They went back to the house to find Tildie still asleep and the girls playing their never-ending game of putting dolls to bed, waking them up to feed them, and putting them back to bed.

In the evening, Tildie awoke. She sipped on venison broth, courtesy of Jan's afternoon hunt. The next day, she sat up on her bed. A few days later, she sat in a chair.

"Jan, these children *smell*," she said, wrinkling her nose over Evie's shorn head.

Jan looked up from the snare he was helping Boister craft. His head shook slightly from side to side in bewilderment.

"Didn't your mother make all twelve of your sisters and brothers take a bath from time to time?" Tildie's eyebrows arched over her eyes.

"Yes, but we had a tub and towels and something beside old lye soap."

"Jan, you and I stink as well."

"What do you propose we do about it?"

"We'll give the children a standing bath."

"A standing bath?"

"We need two pails."

Jan looked over at the area beside the fireplace where he put together his food. He wouldn't exactly call it a kitchen, but it had a pretty good-sized kettle. His mind wandered over his meager possessions.

"There's a bucket I use to feed the horses."

Tildie looked toward the stable end of the cabin. In an economy of heating, it attached to the house with only a half wall between the main room and the stalls. The children thought this was marvelous and visited with the horses regularly.

Jan explained that the heat of the horses' bodies helped warm the cabin, and in the dead of winter, he didn't have to worry about them being in a drafty stable freezing to death. Of course, the stable room had originally been built for a horse and a pack mule, but the three new tenants were comfortable, if crowded.

"What became of the original tenants?" Tildie had asked.

"Traded them."

"For what?"

"Books."

"Books?"

He shrugged. "Winter before last, I read to the animals every book I owned two or three times each. Gladys and I don't mind walking. We didn't really need the horse and mule once we were settled in.

"Gladys is good company during the winter months, but the books truly were better companions than the horses, and I didn't have to feed them every day and clean out their stalls."

Boister laughed. He threw back his head and laughed. The girls looked up in surprise, and they laughed too, more to be joining in the merriment than realizing what had struck their big brother as funny. Tildie who had never seen her cousin laugh, smiled with tears in her eyes. Gladys began to bounce around him and added her bark to the hullabaloo. Jan swept down on the boy and tickled him until Boister begged him to stop. Mari and Evie joined in by tackling Jan and claiming they could save their brother.

Eventually the fun subsided, and the four lay in mock exhaustion on the floor.

"I haven't forgotten the baths," said Tildie.

"Our babies need a bath, too." Mari reached out to rescue her doll, which had been carelessly thrown aside.

Evie bobbed her head in agreement and crawled over to where her doll lay upside down against the wall.

"So does Gladys, Tildie," pointed out Boister.

Jan drew the line at the dog. "Only humans are getting bathed this winter," he declared.

Mari's lower lip came out in a pout. "Sarah is 'uman." She squeezed her beloved playmate.

Jan looked to Tildie for advice.

"The dollies can take a bath with you. Just hold on to them, and they'll get plenty clean." She hoped this would suffice. It was going to be a chore just washing bodies and clothes.

They heated the water in the kettle, then they stripped down

Evie first, standing her in the horses' feed bucket. With Tildie's supervision from her chair, Mari and Jan wet down the giggling girl, soaped her up, and sponged her off. She was wrapped in a large piece of blanket and relegated to Tildie's lap while the process was repeated for Marilyn.

As long as Evie did not wiggle too much, Tildie enjoyed having her in her lap. The little girl settled quietly, with only a reminder that too much bouncing hurt her cousin.

Boister did his own wetting down, but Jan declared he wasn't energetic enough in the application of the soap and ended up scrubbing him.

"My skin's gonna come off!" Boister declared as he turned pink under the scant bubbles of the lye soap.

The girls laughed, and Jan showed no mercy.

"Your turn," Boister declared as he hunkered by the fire in his blanket. His eye was on Tildie.

She turned pink, but declared, "Yes, I must have my turn. If you gentlemen will put up a blanket for privacy, Marilyn will help me."

"Me, too," insisted Evie. "Wash Tildie. I scrub, scrub, scrub-a-dub."

"You'll have to be gentle, Evie," Jan said, gazing at Tildie's blush. "Remember, your cousin got hurt and has been sick."

"You better let me do the scrubbing," said Mari, importantly. "You can wrap her in the blanket."

"Well then," said Tildie, thoroughly embarrassed. "Shall we get started?"

Her bath took a while and there was a lot of giggling behind the makeshift screen. Jan concentrated on keeping a fresh supply of water warm and studiously avoided watching the blanket being bumped by the figures behind it.

With all the bodies washed except Jan and Gladys, Tildie instructed from her bed that their clothing must be washed. The dollies were set on the hearth to observe the proceedings as they, themselves, dried. With only the small bucket and kitchen kettle to use for washing, laundry was an all-afternoon project. During the process, Mari and Evie managed to get their cloth dolls soaking wet again, and they were laid farther from the hubbub of activity to dry.

The children were draped in their blankets with ropes binding their garments to them. Jan said they looked like Romans in togas and spent an hour explaining about the customs of early Greece and Italy while they labored over the soapy project. Tildie fell asleep directly after dinner which was cooked amidst garments hanging about, drying in the cabin's fireplace heat.

She awoke to a darkened room. The blanket still hung over the space in front of her bed. Jan was there straightening the pallet he slept on beside her. "Jan."

"Sorry, I didn't mean to wake you."

"I can't see you."

He leaned over the bed so his face was close to hers. She felt his nearness, but it was so dark she still couldn't see.

"It's snowing again," he said.

She touched the side of his face.

"Your hair's wet."

"I took a bath after the children were in bed."

"Thank you."

"Oh, you're welcome. I couldn't be the only human in the cabin who smelled." She could hear the laughter in his voice.

"No, I meant, thank you for going to all the trouble. For the children, for me."

"We're going to be here a long time, Tildie—maybe until spring. You can't travel now, and by the time you can, hard winter will have set in."

"Are we going to be all right? Is there enough food, enough fuel?"

He took her hand, the one with which she unconsciously stroked the side of his face, feeling the smoothness of his just shaved cheek.

"Yes, that's no problem. I'll hunt now, and we can dry the meat or let it freeze in the cave I use for storage. There are trees all around us for firewood. It may be difficult to get enough hay in for the stock, but I'll manage. It would be nice if we had a cow."

"A cow?"

"Milk and cheese for the little ones."

"The children will get bored."

"If they're bored, we'll give 'em baths. That took all day, and they loved running around in their togas, playing chase between the hanging clothes."

"Do you mind them?"

"Last year, I was nearly crazy with loneliness. No, I don't mind them." She liked his tone of voice. She could listen to him talk this way every night. It was nice to have him there.

"There is something else, Tildie." He sounded serious. Was he going to talk about her injuries? Did he have something to say about why it was taking her so long to recover?

"What?" she whispered in her anxiety.

"I don't think of you as one of the children. I think of you as a woman—a warm, beautiful, kind, sweet woman."

She started to cry.

It alarmed him. "I wouldn't hurt you, Tildie. I'd never do that, but it's going to be a long winter in this cabin, and I've got my heart set on marrying you."

"But I'm sick and maybe a cripple...and until today, I smelled like a goat."

"You're brave, and you're going to get well. And until today, I smelled like a buffalo."

She giggled through the tears.

"I don't know if I love you," she admitted. "Sometimes, I think I'd die if you walked away and left us. I've thought about when we get back to the ranch and you've fulfilled your promise to see us safely away from the Indians. Then, you'd leave us. I don't want that."

He stroked her hair back from her face, and she felt warm and secure.

"I've never been in love, Jan. I don't know if I can be a good wife. All I've thought about the last two years is keeping a roof over my head, then keeping the children safe and happy."

He kissed her then, interrupting her ramblings. When his lips released hers, she gasped a tiny little breath of air that tickled his lips so close to hers.

"Jan," she whispered.

"You talk too much." He kissed her again.

When he pulled away, he stared at her, barely making out her features in the dark.

"Do you think you could love me?" he asked.

"Yes." The answer came without hesitation. He smiled. He shifted, deliberately moving away from her but retaining her hand in his. He sat on his pallet with his back against the wall.

"We'll have to get married," he said huskily.

"How can we do that?"

"I'll marry us. When the spring comes, we'll register the wedding in the nearest town that has a courthouse. That may be clear back in Oklahoma. Can you handle that? We'll be married in the eyes of God. The children will be our witnesses. It's unusual, but out in the wilderness, that's how some couples have to do it."

"Have you married people before?" This thought fascinated her.

"Yes, I was a regular preacher before I came west to be a missionary."

"I didn't know that. Jan, there's an awful lot I don't know about you."

"We've got a long, cold winter ahead of us. By spring we should be pretty well acquainted."

"When will we get married?"

"Let's say. . .when you're strong enough to stand up for the ceremony."

"How long do you think that will take?"

He rose up on his knees and came to kiss her again, trailing light, feathery kisses over her forehead, down her cheeks, and settling on her lips. He pulled himself away abruptly.

"Go to sleep now, Tildie. Rest, so you can get well quickly."

"Good night, Jan."

"Good night, honey."

Chapter 11

A new parson came to the village parish," said Jan. From her bed, Tildie smiled at the thick Swedish accent he adopted for the telling of one of his grandmother's tales.

"He asked how there came to be in the church cemetery a lifelike, stone statue of a man of humble means. Why 'tis a man of two centuries past who, while walking through the grounds on a beautiful spring day, had the insensitivity to make a cruel remark regarding the dead. Instead of the proper respect, he said they'd done what they did in life to earn where they slept in death. He was instantly turned to stone, whereas his companion, who had doffed his hat, and said, 'God's peace to all who rest here,' marched on without feeling so much as a twinge in his overworked limbs."

"Limbs in a tree?" asked Mari.

"No, your arms and legs are limbs," explained Boister with scant tolerance for his little sister's ignorance. "Means he didn't have a charlie horse or cramp or nothing."

"Charlie? Horse?" Evie's big eyes turned toward the stable end of the cabin.

"Oh, forget it," said Boister, at the end of his patience. "Tell the story, Jan."

"The parson said the statue should've been prayed over to release the poor, unfortunate man now that he had learned the error of his ways. The townsfolk said, indeed, the man had been prayed over by every parson since."

The wide-eyed children sat, listening to every word, Boister on his pallet with Gladys, Mari and Evie on their own. Jan sat in his chair between them, leaning forward as he told one of the many bedtime stories they indulged in every night.

"Well, the parson was a man who liked a challenge, so he had three strong men from the parish carry the stone statue and set it in the corner of his study where it would be within hearing of the many prayers he said each day.

"It was this parson's custom to end his evening prayers with these words, 'And by Your grace, heavenly Father, banish all that is evil from this house. Amen.' As the weeks went by, the parson began to think that there was a flurry of activity in the room each night after he said this prayer. It was nothing he could hear or see but rather a stirring of the air.

"He was a practical man who didn't worry too much about it, figuring if it was something beyond him to deal with, then his mighty God was taking care of it. One night he heard a small noise like a chuckle from the corner of the room where stood the statue. It was such a small tittering sound that he was not quite sure he heard it. The next night he heard it again, and it was more distinct. He took up his candle and peered about in the corner. Nothing, so he went to bed. The next night he heard it even more plainly, and since there was nothing in the corner besides the statue, he determined that it was the statue who had laughed.

" 'Now,' he says to the statue, 'If I can hear you laugh, then I can hear you talk. Be so kind as to tell me what makes you laugh each night.' Considering the state of the man in a statue-like pose, he thought there could not be much to laugh at."

"How can a statue talk?" asked Marilyn.

"It's a story," answered Boister. "Be quiet."

Jan continued. "The statue spoke very courteously to the parson. Remember, he has had a long time to repent of harsh words.

He said that the parson was a very kind man, a very learned man, a very good counselor to his parishioners, and a very witty man behind the pulpit telling very worthy accounts from the Bible. However, he quarreled a little too much with his headstrong wife. 'Every night you call upon God to banish all evil from the house,' explained the voice from the statue, 'and a thousand little imps dance out the door. With each cross and contrary word that passes between wife and husband the next day, they come back in one by one.'

"The statue went on to explain that among these imps was a little fellow 'who wiggles about so, and does such tricks on his merry way out the door' that the statue could not help but laugh at his antics and funny faces.

"The parson had a heavy heart from hearing this. He went to his wife and explained that when stones began to speak in his study, it was wise for them to listen. They agreed to speak more kindly to one another and not be quick to anger, nor insensitive to each other's feelings.

"The wife was particularly unhappy to think of impish creatures free in her home throughout the day. Husband and wife behaved more seemly and soon began to enjoy each other as they had when first they were married.

"The statue was silent, and after many months when the parson and his wife were truly happy once again, the parson thought to ask the statue had he not seen the little imps, and particularly the one who made him laugh?

"The statue declared that he had upon occasion seen him lurking outside the door, peeping in, and being very impatient about it. The imp had finally given up and gone—no doubt to find a more quarrelsome household.

"The parson called his wife to rejoice with him, and thanked God together for ending their petty disagreements. The wife asked how it was with the statue, considering they were so happy and he was still stone.

"The statue replied that he was very nearly at peace, for he had done the kind parson a good deed. When the parson said his prayers that very night, the stone became flesh, drew his first breath in a three hundred years and his last throughout eternity. The parson and his wife saw that he had a very nice funeral, for they were glad of the man's release from his penance and grateful that their own entrapment in hasty words was ended."

"Tildie always says, 'and they lived happily ever after.'" Mari informed Jan. "That way we know the story is over and we have to lie down."

"Well, my grandmother never said it, but I don't think it will ruin her stories." Having told the story with the heavy Swedish accent, now that he was just talking, the inflection lingered upon his words. Tildie liked the sound of it, and she listened carefully as he continued. "The parson and his wife lived happily ever after. Now, put your heads on your pillows and go to sleep."

"Jan, do you tell your grandmother's stories to the Indians?" asked Boister.

"No, I only tell them stories from the Good Book. I think I might confuse them since they're just learning facts from the Bible. I wouldn't want them to expect to pray a person out of a stone statue."

"Don't you think we might get confused?" Boister asked. "I mean, I never would, but the little girls might."

"No, you don't have a language problem and are here to ask me or Tildie questions any time you want. Also, since you already know so much, it is good for you to use your brain and decide which is a fun story and which is the truth from God's Holy Word. You're a stronger Christian because you can think these things through."

"I want a kiss good night," declared Mari.

"Kiss, too," added Evie.

Before Jan could answer, the girls scrambled out of their covers and gave Jan a hug and kiss. They next stormed Tildie's bed, remembering just in time to carefully climb up instead of madly scrambling to kiss her. Jan watched them with a big grin on his face. When they came back, he knelt beside their pallet and carefully tucked them in, pausing to pray their good-night prayers with them.

He blew out the candle. Turning away, he was surprised to

find Boister standing beside him. He looked at the boy and saw there was something he wanted to say.

"Boister?" he inquired softly.

There was no response. Jan, who was still on his knees, leaned back so he sat on his heels. The flickering light from the fire revealed the little boy's features tightened in a mask of indecision. With an expelled breath of tension, Boister leapt at Jan, threw his arms around his neck, and gave him a quick, convulsive hug. Then just as quickly, he let go and darted across the room to dive into his blankets, turned his back to the room, and lay very still as if he had instantly gone to sleep.

Jan slowly rose to his feet and walked to the boy's pallet. He leaned over, pulled the blanket up more securely around his shoulders, then laid his big hand on the boy's small head for an instant. He said no words but across his face the look of tenderness Boister evoked was clearly evident. He moved then to settle on his pallet on the floor beside Tildie's bed.

After a few minutes, he reached up over the side of the bed to find Tildie's hand and hold it.

"Why are you sniffling?" he asked.

"I'm happy."

"Boister?"

"Yes, he's going to be all right. You've helped him where I couldn't. Thank God John Masters was taking us to Fort Reynald. Thank God for the accident. My aunt would have been happy to know that her son was better. She truly loved her children, you know. She was just incapable of fighting the circumstances. She gave up."

"We won't give up, Tildie. We have the strength of our Savior to draw upon."

"She did, too, Jan. She just forgot to use it. I think she always counted on Uncle Henry to seek God, so she just benefited secondhand from his strength. When he was gone, she had no personal connection to God."

"I don't want that to happen to you, Tildie. We must teach the children well."

"Yes, Jan." Tildie turned on her side and smiled into the

darkness. She was happy with how God had changed her life. If asked to choose this road, she never would have taken it, not being able to see this place she had come to from the beginning. This, however, was good. She knew the truth of the verse that says all things work together for good to them who love God.

CHAPTER 12

Tildie stood behind the chair, marveling that she was doing so without hurting. She let go and stood with her hands out to her sides.

"Very good," said a voice in back of her. She jumped and grabbed for the chair as she lost her balance. Strong arms caught her and swept her up. Jan held her against his chest. "Does this mean I finally have a bride?" He kissed her nose.

Tildie giggled. "Put me down. I want to try a step."

Boister, Mari, and Evie gathered around. Evie clapped her hands as Jan set Tildie on her feet and steadied her. When he let go she started to sink, so he wrapped his arms around her middle and stood close.

"Okay, Tildie, I'll support your weight, and you walk. Right foot first." She felt his right thigh pushing against the back of her right leg. She concentrated and managed to work with him, moving the heavy leg forward in a slow, dragging step. For some reason, her toes didn't want to lift off the floor.

"Great. Now the other side," urged Jan.

Six steps and she was exhausted. He kissed the back of her ear as she slumped against him. "We've got all winter. Before spring we'll have you turned around, facing me, and we'll be dancing."

Tildie laughed softly at his optimism. He made it seem possible.

"Dancing!" Evie squealed.

"You don't even know what dancing is," scoffed Boister.

"She saw the Arapahos do the Sun Dance," said Mari in defense of her little sister.

"She never saw a square dance."

"You never saw a square dance either." Mari's jaw set in a defiant line.

"I did," said Boister. "You just don't remember."

"That's enough. You'll have little imps dancing all over the house with your contentious words." Jan's voice interrupted their debate. "Let me put your cousin in her chair, and I'll tell you an Arapaho Indian tale."

Boister pushed the chair they had padded with deer skins over closer to the fireplace, and the girls pulled their pallet over as well. Instead of placing Tildie in the chair, Jan sat in it and kept her in his lap.

"Many years ago, the buffalo left the Arapaho. The women of the Arapaho frowned with worry. The children of the Arapaho cried with hunger. The chiefs of the Arapaho turned to Black Robe, a medicine man of great power. Black Robe didn't have the magic to call the buffalo back to the plains without at least one buffalo to use his magic on. He decided to ask Cedar Tree for help and sent the mighty warrior west to hunt the buffalo.

"Cedar Tree hunted for many days and finally he saw black forms upon the horizon. He traveled eagerly toward what he hoped would be buffalo, but as he got closer, he began to doubt that he had found the buffalo. Then one of them spread wings and flew into the sky. Soon all the black forms sprouted wings. Clearly, they were ravens taking flight.

"Discouraged, Cedar Tree returned to the village and told Black Robe what he'd seen. The medicine man was greatly displeased.

" 'Don't you know, Cedar Tree, that you have been tricked by your own thoughts. You did see buffalo. If you had remained firm in your belief, you could have walked among them and slain the biggest to save our tribe from starvation. Instead, you let them trick you into thinking they were black birds. You allowed them to fly away.'

"The Arapaho village suffered. One old woman took off her moccasins and boiled them to make soup. Her uncle, Trying Bear, an even older Indian, did not like the taste of his dinner and set off to find something else to put in the pot. He was so old he did not even have weapons.

"Trying Bear passed Black Robe sitting on a rock. Black Robe gave the old man a bow and arrow and told him he was to hunt until he found something, even if it was only the carcass of a buffalo long dead with only scraps of dried flesh clinging to the bone.

"Trying Bear hunted a long time and did find a dried buffalo carcass. He had no need to shoot it with an arrow, so he shot the arrow straight into the sky in celebration. The arrow landed back in the camp and Black Robe knew the old man had found what was needed.

"Black Robe painted his black pony white because this was part of his magic. Many Arapaho warriors followed Black Robe because they wanted to see what he would do. The medicine man traveled until the sun was high in the sky, then he came upon Trying Bear waiting patiently beside the dead buffalo. Black Robe took his magic eagle feather and threw it, point first, into the bones of the dried buffalo. Immediately, a live buffalo rose out of the dead one.

"Black Robe turned to Trying Bear, impatient because the old man just sat there.

" 'Shoot it,' he commanded.

"Trying Bear shot it.

"Black Robe turned to the Arapaho who had followed him. 'Do you see the ravens flying down to land in the field beyond the hill? Go shoot the buffalo you find there.'

"The men went over the hill and found the buffalo that had so long hidden from them. There was a great feast of thanksgiving in the village lasting many days."

"Did they see the dead buffalo turn into the live one?" asked Boister.

"They said so," answered Jan.

"Is it real?" asked Mari.

"What do you think?" asked Jan.

Marilyn turned to her big brother for his verdict.

"Only God can do a miracle. It's a story."

Jan nodded. "What truth is in that story? Why tell it?"

Boister scrunched up his face while he thought. "If you want to help, you can help even if you aren't the best hunter. You have to do what you're told to do."

Jan smiled and roughed up Boister's hair. "Right, and I told those Indians who told me that tale that God has many stories in His Book that says that God uses the weak to dumbfound the mighty."

"Like Joshua," said Boister, "at the Battle of Jericho."

"And Gideon leading a handful of men to defeat an army," added Tildie.

"David," said Mari, "and Go-li-uff."

"Jesus," Evie said and clapped her hands.

"Yes," said Jan. "Even Jesus came as a poor baby, not a mighty warrior. That confused the Jews."

Evie stood up and went to stand beside Jan. She pushed at Tildie with her little hand.

"My turn," she said, sticking her lower lip out in a pronounced pout. "Tildie, get up!"

Jan laughed. "You don't really want to sit tamely in my lap." He stood up and gently placed Tildie in the chair. "Since Tildie can't dance yet, why don't you and I do a jig?"

He lifted the little girl into his arms and twirled her around the room while singing a lively song in Swedish. Boister grabbed Mari by the hands, and the two spun around and 'round, not really keeping step to the music.

Tildie clapped her hands and hummed along. Happy, she considered the many good times between them. Now, if she could only get up out of the chair and help more in the cabin.

Their days began to take on a routine. Jan carved shallow

trays from a slab of wood and filled them with sandy dirt. Daily, Tildie taught the children to write their letters in the trays. Jan read from his books or told stories. Tildie exercised her legs with Jan's help, then with two crutches Jan and Boister made for her. Slowly, she gained enough strength to stand on her own and walk.

⁓

"I'm going down to Fort Reynald to get some supplies," Jan announced one night as they lay in bed, he on the pallet, and she on the pine needle mattress.

"How long will you be gone?" Tildie didn't like the idea, and a plaintive tone invaded her voice.

"About a week."

"Jan, what do we need so badly?"

"Flour, salt, and I'll try to get Christmas presents for the children. Maybe there'll be some material and you can make dresses for the girls."

"Is it really necessary?"

"I wouldn't leave if I didn't think so, and I trust you'll be all right. The weather's been so warm, there's little snow on the ground. It's best that I go now, while I still can." He reached up and patted her hand reassuringly. "Boister's become right handy. You're strong enough now almost to walk without those crutches. I'll even leave Gladys with you."

She grasped his hand. "Jan, come up here. Please. I don't want to talk to you when you're so far away."

"All of two feet."

"Please."

"No, honey, it's *not* a good idea."

"Jan," she pleaded.

"Enough, Tildie. Be quiet, or I'll go to sleep with the horses."

"They'd step on you."

"As you're stepping on my heart right now. Don't ask such a thing of me, Tildie."

"I'm sorry."

He rose and gathered her in his arms to kiss her with all

the longing that drove him crazy. He released her and sat back as far away from her as the tiny space would allow. "Do you understand, Tildie? I'll be wanting us to marry just as soon as I get back."

"I understand."

"I'm going to sleep out with Boister and Gladys." He quickly rolled up his pallet. "Good night, honey."

"Good night, Jan."

In the morning, they helped him get his things together. He readied Horse and Greedy Gert. He would ride on Gert and use Horse to pack out furs they had ready, but didn't need to use themselves.

He kissed Tildie and the girls good-bye, then gave Boister a sturdy hug. "Take care of them for me. If the weather turns bad, it may take me a little longer to return. You're not to worry, and don't let the women worry either."

Boister grinned, accepting the responsibility eagerly.

Jan rode off into the sunshine, following the path that led to a game trail down the mountain. The fine day begged Tildie to bring her chair outside, so they did their letters and sums in the dirt together. Evie drew pictures with her stick beside her older brother and sister. They were so peaceful in their endeavors that two chipmunks scampered on a log near the door with no fear.

Tildie gave thanks for the beauty that surrounded them and prayed safety for Jan.

CHAPTER 13

Established by fur traders, raucous Fort Reynald held not a single woman within its walls. Situated on the Arkansas River at the best ford for miles up or down the river, it catered to the rugged mountain men and traded with Indians for buffalo skins.

Jan went to trade his furs at the long, low shack with the hand-scrawled sign claiming, "Mercantile." He found brightly colored material for the girls' dresses. Since the Indians favored the pretty calicoes, the dealer had a good variety. Jan got plenty to make the girls' dresses and maybe a shirt for Boister. He also bought a rifle, intending to take the boy hunting.

The owner also had an assortment of oddities gathered when the mountain men traded for supplies. Jan looked them over, searching for a ring to surprise Tildie when they wed. There was none. He bought a knife for Boister, a hair ornament worked in leather for Marilyn, and a little copper pot with a lid for Evie. He bought enough forks and spoons so all of them could have their own when they sat down to dinner. They'd been using wooden spoons that he had whittled.

One spoon stood out among all the others. It was obviously silver with a slender handle and a floral design at its end.

Although tarnished, Jan knew it would serve the function he had in mind. He smiled as he added it to his selections.

Next, he went over to the side of the building that stored the grocer goods.

"You be the preaching Swede, be you not?" asked a man with a thick French accent. He sat on a barrel behind the counter, his feet propped up on a stack of boxes marked "salt." A heavy-set man, not fat, his short frame bulged with massive muscles. His dark beard straggled from a swarthy face. His greasy hair matched his old, worn clothes in filth. He'd whittled a toothpick and passed it back and forth across his row of yellowed teeth as he spoke.

Jan looked into the small, shifty eyes of Armand des Reaux. "My name's Jan Borjesson. I've traded here before."

"Heard you lived with the Indians." The grocer's voice held a note of disdain.

"I've lived with several tribes."

"Arapaho?" Des Reaux spit out the word.

"Yes."

"You being an Indian-lover, I suppose they'd give you something valuable if it came their way?"

"I don't know what you mean?"

"A white woman, say a young white woman." Des Reaux rose from his seat and leaned menacingly over the makeshift counter.

His attitude drew the attention of the men swapping tales around the potbellied stove. They stopped to listen to the exchange at the counter. Many of them had heard des Reaux brag about how his bed would be warmed this winter.

"I've just collected my family from Chief Two Bear's camp. Is that what you're referring to?" Jan responded quietly, seemingly undisturbed by the questions.

Des Reaux snorted. "Seems improbable a man who lives in the mountains, travels over the plains living with Injuns, does a little fur trading on the side, should all of a sudden acquire a wife and three shavers."

The dirty Frenchman shrugged as if he was merely relating an interesting bit of speculation, but Jan knew better. Menace underlined every word.

"Now, I was expecting a bride this summer," continued des Reaux. He stood polishing one of the many knives from his display case. "She was being brought to me by a friend." He paused and looked directly at Jan. "A friend who never made it."

Des Reaux carefully put the knife down and picked up a bigger, wicked-looking blade before he spoke again. "I traded with Drescher a while back, and he's friendly with your Arapaho."

Jan nodded. "I know Drescher."

"He tells me that the Arapaho took on a young white woman with three kids. This most unusual event happened just about the time my bride was to come. Very unusual, don't you think?"

"My friend Moving Waters," Jan said distinctly, "came to get me. He recognized whose family had come to their camp."

"Not many white women in this territory." The words dismissed Jan's explanation as if he hadn't even spoken. The Frenchman suddenly leaned back, but rather than easing the tension, the move charged the air. In the same way a mountain lion drawn back to spring on his prey flexes his muscles, he turned the knife in his hand over and over in a rhythmic motion.

"Was your bride bringing you three children to rear?" asked Jan.

"Maybe yes, maybe no." Des Reaux sneered.

"And the name of your bride?" asked Jan, wondering just how much the man knew about John Masters' niece.

Des Reaux's eyes narrowed with hatred. "What would be the name of this woman you got from the Arapaho?"

"Tildie. The children are Henry, Marilyn, and Evelyn. Have you any more questions before we get around to the salt, flour, salt pork, and beans I came for?"

Des Reaux reached behind him and Jan tensed for action, but the Frenchman merely put down the knife and pulled out a pad of paper, slamming it down on the countertop.

"I don't know you. I'll want hard cash for your goods." The words delivered implied an insult but Jan ignored them and got down to the business of acquiring the things he wanted. The grocer scratched out the charges on his paper and totaled the sum.

It seemed high to Jan, and he asked to see the list. The men behind him once more abandoned their talk to watch the next episode. A fight would relieve the monotony.

Jan found an error in addition and pointed it out. He was on the alert. The Frenchman might have made an honest mistake, but it was more likely he meant to cheat him or provoke a fight. Des Reaux shook his head and smiled. Somehow the smile was not reassuring.

"I have made a mistake. We all make mistakes. Is it not so, Monsieur? Some mistakes, however, are more costly than others."

Jan felt a frisson of warning and prayed that God's angels would protect him from this wicked man, for now Jan was sure that the trader was not merely unpleasant, but truly evil. He prayed to be alert to the danger and ready to protect himself. The Frenchman was plotting some revenge. Even if he was unsure that Jan had taken the woman he planned to marry, he hadn't liked being pointed out in error over the bill.

Jan took his purchases to one of the outer buildings where he expected to spend the night. Still within the compound of the fort, the boardinghouse had several rooms where lodgers slept side by side on the floor. After looking over the accommodations, he decided to sleep with the horses in the livery. The bedding was filthier than the last time he'd been in Reynald, and he didn't wish to itch all night and carry bed bugs back with him.

"Now, I don't mind the company," said the young man who ran the stable. His speech was more formal than the usual in the west. He delivered it with great precision and a thick British accent. "But I'll be charging you for the stall just as if you put another horse in here."

Jan laughed, for the small Englishman had a cocky smile on his unlined face and was friendlier than most of the inhabitants of Reynald. He was by far cleaner, as well, than the old codgers around the fort.

"I don't mind paying. The hay here is cleaner than the blankets at the house."

"I've been told that before. It might not be as warm here as it is in the house, but few of the horses snore."

"My name is Jan Borjesson. I don't believe you were here the last time I was through."

"My name's Henderson. I came to the territory in late March, and now I shall most likely reside here forever." He sighed as if admitting a great sorrow in his life.

"Why is that?" asked Jan, intrigued by the man's sudden gloom.

"Have a seat, and I'll tell you a sad story."

Jan pulled up a small, empty nail barrel, sat down, and leaned back against the stall door where Greedy Gert ate her dinner. He noted that the Englishman had perked up at his interest and didn't look particularly despondent about the prospect of telling his sad tale.

"Cup of tea?" Henderson offered.

"Thanks." Jan took the warm mug of strong, sweetened tea.

"My story starts in London. I was the butler to the Earl of Dredonshire as was my father before me. The earl died and the new earl was a bit of a scoundrel. I had it in my mind that I didn't want to settle down to the same life my father had. I decided to cross the Atlantic and start fresh in a new country.

"I was seasick to the point of offering fellow passengers all my worldly goods if they'd just end my life in a quick and painless way. One more day at sea, and there would have been no need to employ their services."

"Can't say I've ever been plagued with that particular ailment," commiserated Jan. "Of course, I've never been on the ocean—just Lake Erie."

"Please, let us not mention any body of water bigger than a mud puddle."

Jan laughed.

"I lay torpid—"

"Torpid?" Jan interrupted.

"Oh, definitely torpid, dear sir," said the ex-butler.

Jan saw the gleam of subtle humor in the young Englishman's eye and liked him better for it.

"I lay torpid in New York City," Henderson began again, "until I could stand once more. Then, I felt the inclination to come deeper into the country. I heard of prairies so wide, you could walk days and not come across another human."

Jan nodded for that was certainly true.

"Unfortunately, I got sick on the train. Indeed, it was not as bad as when I was on the ship, but my constitution just isn't made for traveling.

"Next, I rode in a wagon. I surmised that that conveyance would be slower and wouldn't cause me much discomfort." The Englishman shook his head mournfully. "A wagon proved to be irrevocably and too frequently plagued by great jostling. I decided a horse might prove acceptable to my contrary stomach. This, too, proved to be disastrous.

"Mr. Borjesson, I *walked* the last three hundred miles to this fort, and I am ashamed to say I was stricken with yet another malady."

"Surely, you weren't nauseated while walking?" Jan asked incredulously.

Henderson stared down at his boot tips and sighed wearily. "No, I discovered a phobia, a weakness of character, that has doomed me to stay within the confines of this rudimentary settlement."

"Rattlesnakes?" guessed Jan, thoroughly understanding how one could be terrified of the venomous beasts.

"No," said Henderson wearily. "Perhaps you will understand if you know a little of my background. I was born in London. Never traveled until the day I set out for America. The most grass I'd seen at one time was in the London parks. The aristocrats prefer beautifully kept, tidy bits of lawn. Groomed, you might say, to match the cosmopolitan style of the populace.

"On the ship, I rarely came above deck. Those few times I did, the sight of the expanse of ocean quickly heaved my stomach. In New York, there were buildings to which I was accustomed. On the train, I rarely looked out the window since the countryside speeding by adversely affected my internal organs.

"I rode inside the wagon, and I stayed mounted on the horse

for less than a day. At this point, I was bound to my companions by the sheer circumstance that I could *not* return east on my own, not knowing anything about the country or how to survive. For weeks I walked in utter agony, every moment fighting as panic rose within my breast, threatening to drive me mad. Once within these wooden barricades, I was able to resume a more equable demeanor."

"I don't understand," said Jan. "Were you afraid of Indians, wild beasts, renegades?"

"The open space, Mr. Borjesson. The great endless expanse. The complete infinity of the horizon. It is a completely irrational fear. Totally beyond my abilities to subdue."

CHAPTER 14

Jan watched the Englishman's display of total dejection. The man used a great deal of self-effacing humor in the telling of his tale, but there was an underlying melancholy that rang true. Jan tried to imagine the grip of such a terror and found it difficult. To fear being out in the open? Preposterous!

Of course, he knew many a man who broke out in a cold sweat at the sound of a rattler. Jan, himself, got a chill up his spine whenever he encountered a snake. He didn't particularly like scaling cliffs, either. . .but to be paralyzed with dread? The closest he could recall being in that kind of panic was when he thought Tildie might slip out of his grasp into the torrential waters of the flash flood.

Henderson jumped up, startling Jan. "Enough of this! They tell me you are a family man, and des Reaux has taken a dislike to you."

"I did get that impression," agreed Jan.

"Not an enviable place to be," sympathized the Englishman. "Des Reaux is a frustrated man and therefore, dangerous. He does not have the power over the fur traders he imagined when he embarked on this enterprise."

"How do you know this?" asked Jan.

"The Frenchman drinks, and when he drinks, he talks. Since no man is his friend, he comes out to the livery and talks to his mule. A very sad state of affairs, don't you think?"

Jan nodded his agreement, noting again the humor on Henderson's face.

"Des Reaux is disappointed to have a man of integrity sharing his place of business. Across the room, Rodgers, in the mercantile, will not cooperate in the Frenchman's schemes to turn a bigger profit. Des Reaux is affronted daily by the gall of honesty.

"And des Reaux ran a saloon in St. Joe. He misses the excitement. Unfortunately, he had to leave that establishment quickly. A situation turned sour over the lamentable death of one of his clients.

"A particularly unpleasant part of his exile is the lack of female companionship, and he thought that rectified. Something went wrong. The white female was not delivered. He advanced fifty dollars to an imbecile—this is the word he uses—eager for the supplies. Des Reaux made an error in judgement.

"The Frenchman is a dangerous man because he is angry over too many things. His life is full of irritations."

"You're saying the Frenchman bought a wife."

Henderson shrugged, "An arranged marriage. I tell you, his heart was not engaged. He was discussing the woman with his mule one night, and he could not even remember her name. Only that it started with an M—Mary, Martha, Melissa, Margaret. He guessed them all, and none sounded right to his intoxicated brain."

The Englishman sat abruptly on a bale of hay.

"Now," he said, "you have heard too much about me and too much about the despicable des Reaux. I am interested in you. Do I discern in you a kindred spirit? I have heard of you, the Swedish preacher who lives among the Indians. Tell me of your adventures. I may never walk out onto the plains again, but you shall free me in my mind. I shall see the things you have seen. I shall know those whom you have known."

"That's a pretty tall order."

"First then, tell me of the friends you have made among the

Indians. They fascinate me."

The two men enjoyed each other's company and talked late into the night. Henderson shared his dinner with Jan and gave him an extra blanket to put between him and the itchy straw. In the morning, they continued their discussion while Henderson used his small forge to fashion the silver spoon handle into a ring, a Christmas present for Tildie.

Jan thought it was worthwhile to remain an extra day. Henderson began questioning what the preacher told the Indians and the opportunity arose to share the gospel with this displaced English butler.

"Henderson, you're needed over at the boardinghouse." A rough-looking trader interrupted their talk in the early morning.

"What is it?"

"Knifing."

"You must excuse me, Jan," apologized the liveryman. "I have some skill in taking care of wounds and am called upon at least twice a week to stitch up someone, pull a tooth, or remove a bullet. Please stay. I shall return as soon as is possible."

Henderson returned an hour later and busied himself about the livery taking care of chores. Jan joined him, helping out where he could.

"My suspicions have been aroused over this knifing," admitted Henderson. "There was no reason for the attack. No one knew of any grudge against the victim. He was a man who has often slept in one of the rooms, but this night he chose to sleep in a different room because he was finally, 'fed up' were the words he used, with a fellow boarder's snoring. He was the new man in a room usually given to those who do not sleep there for more than one night."

"I don't see what you're getting at, Henderson."

"Your disagreement with the French grocer. Of course, I admit to a healthy English prejudice against all things French, but Jan, the man who was knifed was of the same build as you. A very tall, lean giant of a man. Not as young or with hair as fair, but in the dark this would be indiscernible."

"You think des Reaux was out to murder me?"

"Oh, he would not have gone himself, but he is a disreputable villain."

"I can't take this seriously, Henderson. How could the man profit by my death?"

"To some, it is not always necessary to profit monetarily. He may believe that your lovely Tildie is his lost betrothed. You have therefore cheated him. Too, he did not care for your easy detection of the extra profit he hoped to make by misrepresenting your bill. Such a man would relish revenge even of an imagined insult."

"I think you're being highly dramatic, Henderson." Jan raised his hand to ward off Henderson's sputtering objection. "I'll watch my back, and I thank you for the warning, but I'm not convinced that an innocent man was stabbed because he happened to be lying in a place where I *might* be sleeping."

Henderson was slightly affronted by the disregard of his supposition. He became a very haughty Englishman for all of ten minutes, and Jan got a glimpse of how very proper an English butler could be. Henderson thawed in a short time.

Late in the evening, after several hours of spiritual talk, Henderson admitted his need for a Savior and bowed his head in submission and acceptance of the Master's plan.

The following morning, Jan presented him with a gift. Jan tore a few pages out of an old Bible.

"I'm tearing out the book of Acts, Henderson. I'm sorry but I've already ripped out the gospels and given them away. You'll find much to think on from this account of the young church. Here's an address you can write to, and the good people I know there will send you a whole Bible."

"Thank you, Jan." The Englishman held the pages carefully.

Jan swung up into the saddle and, with a promise to see Henderson at the next opportunity, bid the man farewell.

"Watch your back, Mr. Borjesson," Henderson said as he waved good-bye. "It is an American expression that I think is very apropos to your situation."

Jan grinned over the prim and proper young man's concern.

Two hours later he was no longer amused. He lay beside the

trail with both horses gone, pressing his wadded-up shirt to a bullet hole in his shoulder.

On the plus side, he wasn't so far from the fort that he couldn't walk back. On the minus side, the bushwhacker had hit him twice, once in the shoulder and a crease along his scalp. He had bound the head wound with his bandanna, but it bled profusely and was slow to stop. The other bullet lodged in his shoulder and, if he was not mistaken, had broken his collarbone.

Jan leaned against the rock and wished some of his gear had fallen off the horse when he had. A canteen would be nice. The new rifle he'd purchased for Boister would be handy.

He reached in his pocket and retrieved his pocket knife. First cutting the sleeves off of his shirt, he rewadded the already soaked shirt and tied it on tight against the bullet hole. Next, he dragged himself over to what little shade an outcrop of rock and straggly scrub brush provided. He knew he was near collapse and didn't want to wake up in worse shape. Even though the winter sun didn't have the strength to fry him, lying unconscious beneath it at this altitude would be two more strikes against his chance of survival.

When he came to, the sun had disappeared behind the Rockies. The evening sky was still light, having taken on the aquamarine hue that would deepen to purple before the tiny pinpoints of starlight showed. The air had taken on a distinct chill and it helped clear his head.

Jan grimaced as he pulled himself to a sitting position. He maneuvered himself to sit on one of the lower rocks and looked about him for anything that would help. Jan reached out to pluck the old stems of a mountain dandelion. The dried plant could be chewed like gum, and he needed the little nourishment it would provide.

It wasn't cold enough for him to freeze to death during the night, but he would certainly lose energy staying warm. He'd had a rest, and it probably behooved him to make progress toward the fort while he could. Jan plucked another stem and searched around for a stick to make some kind of crutch. He found one long enough to use as a cane. It was better than nothing.

Closing his eyes, Jan prayed before he hoisted his considerable frame to his feet and started the trek back to the relative safety of the fort. He owed an apology to Henderson for scoffing at his concern and hoped he'd be able to deliver it.

Think, he ordered himself. *You've got to think straight, or you won't get out of this.* Sitting down before he fell down, Jan rested on a boulder. His mind drifted.

It had been a couple of hours, as near as he could figure. He'd concentrated on keeping his right shoulder to the mountains, not wanting to get turned around and lose time wandering.

Where was Camel Rock? Did he cross that stream by the stand of blue spruce? Jan swiped a shaky hand across his face. *All the landmarks couldn't have been swallowed up by the night. Am I passing them without seeing them? Am I lost?*

Oh Father, guide my steps.

Jan moved on, forcing each foot to step forward as it came its turn.

Again, he slumped against an incline. It had been necessary to sit. For some time, he'd been fighting the dizziness. It wouldn't be wise to fall hard upon his shoulder and start the bleeding once again. With an effort, he formed words of a prayer in his head. He needed strength. He needed guidance. He needed endurance. He needed help. Fleetingly, he thought how desperately he needed to get back to Tildie and the children before winter set in—but that was trouble for another day. Tonight, he needed to stay alive.

The morning birds brought him back to his senses. Shivering, he struggled to his feet. He must make a few miles before he ground down to a complete halt. One foot in front of the other. One step at a time.

CHAPTER 15

If watching out the window could bring him back, thought Tildie, *Jan would be drawn here like a moth to the lantern.* She turned from the window and hobbled across to the table where the children shaped biscuit dough into odd clumps to drop in the fat to fry.

"That's too big, Boister," Mari said with authority. She often did kitchen chores with Tildie and felt that in this one area she had an advantage over her older brother. Since the last deep snow, Boister had joined them out of boredom.

"It'll be all soft and gooshy in the middle, even if the outside is nice and crisp." Mari continued to display her superior knowledge.

"I like the middle doughy," claimed Boister. He set his lump of dough aside and pinched off another.

"Snake," proclaimed Evie enthusiastically as she put her long piece with those to be fried.

"That's nothing but a fat worm," taunted Boister.

"You let imps in the house all the time," said Mari with a fierce scowl at her brother. "Remember Jan's story. There's no need to be ugly to Evie. Her snakes are as good as your great lumps that'll never cook through."

Tildie drew out the chair and sat down at the table. She laid her crutches on the floor. She could get by in the morning without using them, but they became necessary as the day wore on and she got tired. It irked her, and she deliberately turned to distract the children from their quarrel in hopes it would also distract her from the pain in her back that ran through her hip and down the right leg. Tildie picked up a lump of dough.

"They say in Africa there are animals as big as a house. They're called elephants and the only thing about them that is a normal size is their tail. An elephant has a tail much like a cow, only it is stuck to a body as big as this room." She fashioned a huge lump and stuck on a tiny tail.

"His legs are like tree trunks." She added four sturdy legs.

"He has a great, huge head, but tiny eyes." She picked up another pinch of dough, shaping the head and putting indentations for the eyes. "And he has flapping ears on each side of his head." The children giggled at the creature she held in her hand. "But the strangest thing is his nose, which comes out and out and out." She pulled and pinched until she had a trunk formed. "He can use it to pick up things, squirt water he sucks up from the river, or pat his baby elephant on the head."

"Can we fry him?" asked Boister.

"No, he'd fall apart," said Tildie. "I'm not as good as God at making wondrous creatures. Mine won't hold up under wear and tear."

"It isn't a real animal anyway," said Boister.

"Oh, but it is," declared Tildie. "Maybe it's the animal the Bible refers to as the behemoth or the leviathan."

"I thought that was a water animal," said Boister.

"Maybe, it is. I'm not sure." Tildie looked doubtfully at the elephant. She stood it on the table, and the weight of his body caused the legs to buckle. His head fell forward and was in danger of dropping off.

"I wish Jan were here. He would know." Mari sighed.

"He won't come back now," Boister announced. "Not 'til the snow melts."

"Is that true, Tildie? Is Jan not coming back?" Mari turned

to her cousin and her eyes reflected the fear she was feeling. "Will he never come back? Will he come when the snow melts? Will he come at all?" The questions tumbled one after the other in an avalanche of apprehension. The last word came out with a sob.

Tildie reached across and gathered Mari in her arms, dropping bits of dough and shedding flour down her dress.

"He'll come back as soon as he can, Mari, as soon as he can."

"What if he fell off like Mama and. . ." She choked on the thought.

"He's used to traveling alone. He can take care of himself. He'd want us to be brave and look after ourselves, too. We can do that," said Tildie. She leaned away from the little girl. Still disregarding her floured hands, she took Mari's face between her palms. "We can do that, can't we?" Tildie looked the girl straight in the eye.

Mari stared back for a moment to gather the strength Tildie hoped she saw there. Nodding her head firmly, Mari answered, "Yes, we can!"

When the darkness came and the children were sound asleep the confidence that Tildie had manufactured for them disappeared. She lay in the bed Jan had given her and cried quietly, praying through the tears that her big Swede was not hurt, suffering someplace out on the trail. It never occurred to her that he might have just decided he didn't want a wife and family. She knew something had happened, because Jan Borjesson had promised to come back—and so far, he hadn't.

Mentally, she took stock of what provisions they had in the cabin. They could make it. With only one horse to feed instead of three, there was probably enough of the long meadow grass stacked for hay in the crib outside. Of course, they would have to stretch out the flour by making biscuits every other day. Would that be enough? Maybe she should say twice a week. The meat would last a long time, but they had no vegetables. Water was no problem, either. They had meat and water.

It might not be a very interesting diet, but they could live on it. They could live on it until Jan came back, and he would come back. He was not dead, just delayed. The very thought of him being dead caught at her heart, and she refused to entertain the notion.

The wind began to howl. Surely it was mocking her fears, trying to make her scream with terror. She would not! She would pray and be strong. God had seen her through the weeks at the Indian camp. God would be with her now.

It was a daily struggle. There wasn't enough to do to ward off the gnawing consternation. She invented things to keep busy. The children learned verses from the Bible. They acted out parts of the books Jan had on his bookshelf. They made up a song to learn Boister's addition and subtraction facts. Soon Mari, and even Evie, could sing facts from one plus one to nine minus nine. Tildie made up a story about a happy little imp who tried to steal ideas from them that they could use to keep from getting bored.

And Tildie walked. She paced back and forth in the little cabin, strengthening her legs. She'd march with the children, singing their numbers song and singing the songs her own father had sung when he sawed wood back in Indiana. In the back of her mind was the possibility that come springtime, she and the children would have to walk out of the mountains by themselves.

They'd just be going down to find Jan. It wasn't that he wasn't there. He wasn't dead. He couldn't come to them, but they would go to him. They just had to pass the time 'til the spring thaw. It was only a matter of time. *Oh dear God, let it only be a matter of time.*

She wasn't tired enough. That was the problem. The little they did to occupy their time wasn't enough to wear her out so that when she laid her head down at night she could sleep.

Boister shoveled out the stall, kept Charlie provided with a clean stable, and brought in the hay for feed. Boister also took Charlie out into the yard and gave his little sisters rides, exercising the horse and pleasing the girls to no end. Boister brought in the wood, hauled out the ashes, and trudged through the snow with Gladys to the cave where meat was stored.

Tildie genuinely praised him for his efforts. Without him, she and the girls would be uncomfortable to say the least. Finally,

Boister acted more like a normal boy, showing pride over his responsibilities, grumbling at his little sisters, and affectionately hugging Tildie when the notion struck him. She thanked God for rescuing Boister from that false guilt.

Many times when the sun shone, Tildie bundled up the children and let them roll snowballs to make snowmen in front of the cabin. She could only sit by the door. Her crippled legs couldn't forge through the snow.

How she would love to be so tired that she would sleep as soon as she crawled under the heavy blanket! She delayed going to bed. Once she lay down on that pine needle mattress, her mind began to churn. All the suppressed fears raised their ugly heads and hissed at her in the dark. The prayers she said in the morning to help her face the day sounded hollow and meaningless at night. . .and the nights were so long.

She hadn't conserved the candles until too late. She realized that the oil in the lamps wouldn't last forever, that the candles wouldn't burn all winter. They started to keep the candles and the lantern for special occasions and spent most of their time in what light the fire provided. Jan probably could have told her to be more careful. Jan would have known how to make more candles, but he wasn't here.

Then the noises began. It wasn't her imagination. Charlie shifted nervously in his stall. He whinnied his uneasiness. Gladys came awake and crouched next to the wall, growling in her throat. Outside, something clawed at the shutters, at the door, at the wall. For what seemed like hours, it wandered outside the cabin, coming back again and again to scrabble at the wood. Boister woke and came to sit in the bed with Tildie. Neither spoke. Perhaps if it didn't hear anything, it would go away.

In the morning, they looked at the tracks in the snow. They examined the deep claw marks in the soft pine wood around the door and windows.

"Do you know what that track is?" asked Tildie.

"Maybe bear," guessed Boister. "Jan never showed me that track, or I'd know."

"I thought bears slept through the winter," said Mari.

"Hibernate," said Tildie, "yes, bears hibernate."

"It's big," said Evie.

"Must be a bear," said Boister.

"Well, we'll just have to pray that bear goes to bed real soon." Tildie ushered her little tribe back into the cabin.

"He's been in the meat," Boister whispered to her that afternoon when he came in with a load of wood.

"We have Jan's rifle, and you can trap a rabbit. We won't starve, Boister—even if the bear eats all the meat. God will take care of us."

The bear was back again that night. He returned every night, and as Tildie examined the damage he did on the windows, she wondered how long it would be before he broke through.

Now she lay awake with new fears. She'd wait for the clawing to begin. Sometimes it was long in coming. She would think that he would skip a night, but just as she was drifting off, the persistent clawing began. She prayed that the thick walls and door would hold against the onslaught. She knew if the bear was in a rage, he could probably force his way in.

Every morning they surveyed the incredible damage, but the bear didn't seem intent on entering the cabin. Every night, he toyed with the windows and doors. Every night, either before or after, he would raid the cave and haul away some of the frozen meat.

One day Gladys roamed away from the cabin and didn't return.

"I've got to find her, Tildie. Jan left me in charge of taking care of you. That includes Gladys. Gladys is special. She's been Jan's dog forever. Jan will be so angry with me that she's gone."

Tildie had a hard time convincing Boister that he couldn't take off at dusk and search for the missing dog.

"Jan will understand. He'd be much madder if you did something you knew to be foolish. Going out in the dark on this mountain with a bear prowling about is foolish! Gladys has lived in the wilderness a lot longer than we have, and she probably knows more about how to take care of herself than we do."

"But she could be hurt someplace," protested Boister.

"I know," said Tildie softly, looking off toward the woods, wishing the dog would suddenly come bounding toward them.

"Jan won't be mad, Boister. He wouldn't lay the responsibility on you for what Gladys got in her head to do. Maybe she decided he's been gone too long, and she's gone off to find him."

"Do you really think so?" asked Boister.

Tildie shook her head. "I don't know what to think, except she's a pretty smart old dog. We just have to hope nothing bad has happened to her."

Gladys didn't return the next day. In looking for the old dog, Tildie suspected Boister explored as far away from the cabin as he dared.

The dog was a link to Jan. She'd been a comfort in one way or another to each member of the family. She went with Boister whenever he ventured outdoors. She lay with the girls when they took their naps or were playing quietly on their pallets, and she acted as a watchdog giving Tildie a confidence she needed. Now, with Gladys not around to bark her warnings, Tildie was even more concerned. They all missed her terribly, and the little girls cried at the loss of their friend.

CHAPTER 16

I f she had Boister haul the meat into the cabin, would the bear become more determined to break in? They gathered up a good deal of the meat and hung it in bags of skin from branches high in a Ponderosa pine. The bear could climb as high as Boister. Three days after they'd hidden the stash, the bear discovered it. Boister thought maybe he'd followed his scent to the tree. Tildie admitted they didn't know enough about bears to even guess what was going on in the animal's head. All they could do was pray, and she didn't admit to the children how futile the exercise seemed to her.

A sunny day enticed them outside. Although the temperature was low, the high, dry mountain air made it almost comfortable. Tildie sat in the door of the cabin with mending in her hands. It was easier to stitch out in the sunlight than by the light of the fire. The girls strapped their dolls to flat pieces of wood they used as miniature sleds. Climbing up the small embankment, they let their dollies ride down, squealing as if they were the ones enjoying the sensation of speeding down the hill.

Maybe Tildie and Boister could rig up some kind of sleigh for the girls' Christmas present. Tildie mulled over the possibilities. Boister was out in the woods now, gathering what he recognized as edible. Tildie marveled at how much he'd learned while they spent the few months in the Indian village. He must have listened as well as watched for he brought things home from his foraging that the Indians had told him about but never shown him.

Shouting in the distance brought Tildie's head up. She rose to her feet. Was it Jan returning? No! As the hullabaloo came nearer, she caught the distress of Boister's shouts. The sound brought fear to her heart, clamping the muscles in her chest until she almost stopped breathing. She peered into the trees but could see nothing from the direction of his frantic yells.

"Get inside," Tildie ordered the girls, but they both froze. "Mari, Evie, inside, now!"

Evie started to cry, and Mari ran over to take her hand, trying to pull her toward the door. Evie sat down, still crying, and Mari started crying with her.

Boister broke through the last few bushes and started across the open space to the cabin. Behind him lumbered the bear. Tildie pushed the chair aside and rushed into the cabin to grab Jan's rifle. She'd never shot a gun before, but now was not the time to debate over whether she could or not. She ran out again.

Tildie raised the gun to her shoulder. She sighted down the barrel and squeezed the trigger. The explosion knocked her off her feet and back into the cabin. She lay there for a second with the smoking gun beside her. As she sat up, Boister came through the door with wailing Evie under his arm. Mari screeched as she followed him. Boister yelled to close and bar the door. Over the commotion the children made, Tildie could hear the roar of the angry bear.

Tildie scrambled out of the way as Boister threw Evie into her lap. Mari pushed at the door while Boister grabbed the bar. As he put his shoulder to the door and swung it shut, Tildie saw the bear within feet of entering the cabin. She pushed Evie off her lap and hurled herself against the door with Mari and Boister. The boy jammed the bar in place, and they all froze in their positions against the door.

Nothing happened. Evie cried loudly. Mari sobbed as she

gasped for air. Tears rang down Boister's cheeks, and he panted from his long run. Tildie slid to the floor, still leaning heavily against the plank door.

There was no assault upon the door. No pounding, no clawing, no enraged bear growling and snarling to get in. Where was he? Tildie looked at the window where both the inside shutters and outside shutters stood open.

She touched Boister's arm and pointed. He understood immediately and scrambled over to close and bar the shutters. He moved quickly to the two other windows, and then to the stable door. When all was secure, he came back to Tildie's side and sat down next to her.

"Are you hurt?" she asked as he moved as close to her as he could. Evie crawled across the floor and over Boister to get into Tildie's lap. "Are you hurt?" she repeated.

"No." His denial caught on a sob. He turned his face into her shoulder, and she knew he was crying quietly. His fists tightened on her sleeve, but he couldn't bring himself to speak. Tildie squeezed his shoulders and turned to the girls. "Mari, are you okay?"

Mari paused in her whimpering to nod. She sniffed and rubbed her nose on her sleeve. "Where is he?"

"I don't know," answered Tildie.

Evie reached up and put a little hand on Tildie's cheek. "Okay?" she asked. Her little face was tear-streaked, her eyes red from crying.

"Yes." Tildie laughed softly. "I'm okay, are you?"

Evie smiled and nodded. The tension eased from their bodies, and Mari gave a nervous giggle. "I was scared," she admitted.

"Me, too," Evie said and gave her sister a comforting pat.

Boister shuddered next to Tildie.

"We were all scared," said Tildie. "Boister was the bravest of all. He got us all into the cabin and barred the door."

"We all helped," said Mari.

Boister lifted his face and scrubbed at his eyes and cheeks. Evie stretched out her arms to him, and he grabbed her, holding her tight against his small chest. Mari crawled across Tildie to hug both of them. For a moment the four of them embraced in a family hug until Tildie spoke softly. "I have to get up off the floor. I don't know how much damage I did when I fell, but I'm beginning to hurt."

The children clambered off. Boister and Mari helped her rise and move awkwardly to the chair by the table. Evie helpfully pushed from behind.

The children stood close around her. Tildie sat in the chair, panting over the exertion. Mari reached over and took her big brother's hand. "Where did the bear go, Boister?"

Evie looked up at him, waiting for him to say. Tildie put a hand on his shoulder. "We have to look," she said quietly.

He nodded. Mari handed Tildie her crutches, and they moved solemnly to the front window. They stood in the dim light, listening. . .but heard no sound other than the wind from outside.

"Maybe we should load the gun again," suggested Boister.

Tildie nodded, and Boister ran to pick it up. He took care as he loaded it just as Jan had shown him.

"Girls, stand back," he ordered as he handed the rifle to Tildie. They scurried over to their pallet, and Tildie stood a few feet back as she aimed the gun at the window. Boister quietly pulled up the bar and lowered it to the floor. He eased one shutter open a crack and peered through.

He shut it and turned back to Tildie.

"I don't see anything."

"Listen," she instructed. "Maybe you'll hear him."

Boister opened the shutter a crack again and listened. He opened it wider and looked with more daring. Finally he opened both sides and pressed his face against the greased paper.

"I see a dark shape in front of the door!" he exclaimed. "I think it's him. I think he's dead. You must've hit him, Tildie. He's lying right in front of the door."

"Bears don't play possum, do they?" asked Mari from where she sat hugging Evie in their bed.

Tildie lowered the gun. "I don't think so."

Boister ran to the door.

"Wait, Boister. What if he's only stunned?" objected Tildie.

"Then let's get the door open and finish him off before he comes to," answered Boister.

He hauled off the bar and waited for Tildie to stand ready, taking aim before he swung the door open.

The bear lay before the door with his nose barely a foot from the opening. His great arms stretched out beside him. The claws looked yellow and vicious even as he lay still.

"I don't think he's breathing," said Boister.

The girls began to whimper.

Boister started to take a step outside.

"Be careful," urged Tildie. "And don't get between the gun and the bear."

Boister nodded and crept toward the huge animal, keeping to the side. He bent over to examine it, and Tildie held her breath, realizing she was praying without having thought out the need.

Suddenly, Boister stood upright, put forth his foot, and carefully nudged the bear. "He's dead," he declared.

The girls cheered, and Tildie staggered backward to land in the chair by the table. Tears rolled down her cheeks, and the girls came to hug her.

"Why are you crying now?" asked Mari. "Now we're safe."

Boister came over and gave Tildie a pat on the shoulder. "That's just the way women are sometimes," he said sagely to his little sisters. He went back to examine the bear.

"I don't see where you hit him, Tildie." He grabbed the beast by the ears making Tildie shudder and look away.

"The eye, Tildie," he crowed. "You shot him right in the eye."

Tildie looked back, and with the girls' help, picked up her crutches to go see for herself.

"That's mighty fine shooting, Tildie," said Boister. "Wait until Jan hears. That's great. I didn't think you'd ever fired a gun before."

"I haven't, Boister." Tildie gave him a weak smile. "I think we'll have to thank God for my marksmanship. I aimed for his chest."

Boister looked at her, wide-eyed and speechless. He started to grin, then he laughed. Soon, all four of them roared, tears of relief running down their cheeks. They held their aching sides and reveled in the sheer joy of having been delivered from the bear.

When he could talk again, Boister said, "You know what else, Tildie?"

"No, what?" She wiped her apron over her cheeks.

"God also delivered fresh meat and a bearskin rug to our doorstep. If we'd killed this bear someplace else, I couldn't have dragged him home."

Tildie smiled and looked at the bear, trying to see him as a gift left on the doorstep. Suddenly her face brightened. "Boister, I think I remember you can make candles from the tallow off of a bear's fat."

"Hurray!" cried Mari. She grabbed Evie's hands and started bouncing up and down. The two girls did a little dance around the cabin.

Tildie hobbled out to stand next to Boister as he stared admiringly at the bagged bear.

"Tildie?" He tilted his head back to look up at his cousin. "Do you happen to know how to dress a bear?"

Tildie shook her head. "Not one single idea," she admitted.

Boister sighed and looked back down at the huge beast. He put a hand to his head and scratched his scalp with his fingertips. He shrugged and grinned.

"Can't be much more than skinning a deer, and that's just a bit fancier than skinning a rabbit or a squirrel." He put his hand in Tildie's and gave it a squeeze. "We'll manage."

CHAPTER 17

Jan would be eternally grateful to the trapper who picked him up, even if the smell that emanated from the old coot was enough to make Jan lose what little was still in his stomach. To be fair, the vomiting might have been due to the crease the bullet had laid across his head. The trapper also gave him a drink from his canteen. That was vastly appreciated. Even if the trapper was not precisely careful with his injuries, he did throw Jan up on the horse and let him ride.

Jan thanked Henderson for not letting him die. The Englishman tended his wounds, dug out the bullet, and declared the bone not broken, only bruised. He fought the fever that threatened to overcome Jan's resolve to live, forced water and broth down him, and prayed over him. He even pulled Jan's Bible out during one of Jan's lucid moments and read to him from Psalms as he was instructed.

Nonetheless, Jan was not grateful for Henderson's interference once he could sit up on the bales of hay serving as his sick bed. "What do you mean I can't go yet?" Jan growled at his nurse. "My family's up there without sufficient provisions. Winter's here. I can't stay down in Fort Reynald with them alone in the cabin."

"Neither can you travel safely," insisted the Englishman. "Your wounds are not sufficiently healed. You haven't regained your strength. The only thing I can say is you've been without fever for all of twenty-four hours. It would be suicide, sir, and what good would you be to your wife and children, dead on the trail?"

Jan threw the tin cup he held across the room.

"And there is the matter of the identity of who ambushed you," continued Henderson, undaunted by Jan's display of temper. "Your pack horse came back here with its full load. I know, I watched you fasten each item on with my own eyes, and I unloaded those same items with a foreboding in my heart.

"It was because the horse showed up at the fort's gate that I knew you were in trouble. I know you will forgive me for not setting out to search for you, myself, but I have not yet overcome my disability. Therefore, I sent one of the trappers I know to be a good man in my stead."

Jan lowered his head carefully back down to what was serving as his pillow. The Englishman's rhetoric was making the headache worse, if that were possible.

"Your bay is missing, it's true," continued Henderson, ignoring the groan from his patient. "I can't believe someone shot you and left you for dead for one horse and didn't take the one loaded with supplies."

"He just didn't catch Horse," muttered Jan.

"Couldn't catch Horse? Which was the steadier of the two when you stayed with me before? Gert or Horse? Horse! She's the more domesticated of the two. It was Horse who turned around and headed for the nearest stable when she found herself loose."

"Go away, Henderson," groaned Jan. "I bow to your superior judgment for today."

He had to bow to the Englishman's judgment for more than one day. When he did rise from the bed, he swayed. Henderson told him it was loss of blood. His vision blurred. Henderson said it was due to a concussion. His knees buckled. Henderson said it was weakness from the fever. Jan threw a boot at him. Henderson said he was getting better.

———❖———

Few of the trappers were in the habit of visiting with the stuffy ex-butler. Instead, they congregated around the potbellied stove of the main mercantile building. Most of these men would spend the entire winter in the relative comfort of the fort, gambling, drinking, and occasionally having what they called fandangos where the men got liquored up enough to dance wildly to the Mexican guitars even without female partners. In early spring, those men would disperse into the mountains to trap the furs at their peak of splendor.

Jan and Henderson had plenty of time to talk and, since he was good for little else, Jan began telling stories as he was in the habit of doing with the children. Henderson found them amusing and eventually asked another man to join them. By the end of the second week, Jan entertained a room full of men. It was one form of entertainment available at the fort.

Most mountain men practiced telling tall tales. They enjoyed having someone with stories they hadn't heard before—someone who also appreciated the telling of their outlandish yarns. When Jan began to end the evening storytelling sessions with preaching, they stayed to listen.

Predicted heavy snowfall was a topic of much speculation. Determining whether or not it would be an especially hard winter depended upon woolly worms and how high off the ground the hornets had nested that year. Jan listened to all these conjectures with growing alarm. Although skeptical of the old sayings, he wanted to return to Tildie and the children with all possible speed. One night, he announced to Henderson that he was leaving the next day. In the morning there was two feet of snow on the ground.

"It'll melt quick," advised one of the trappers. "First snow never stays."

Jan was frustrated, but knew the foolishness of starting off in uncertain weather. Two gray cold days followed, spitting snow out of the clouds in frequent flurries. On the third day, a burst of sunshine and a quick thaw surprised the fort. Jan made plans to borrow a riding horse from Henderson and repack Horse.

He was determined to set out before yet another spell of bad weather delayed him.

"I don't want you brought back across a saddle, sir," said Henderson.

"Then we won't make it known that I'm leaving", answered Jan. "I'll slip out at first light tomorrow morning."

The only difference in their nightly routine was that when Jan presented the gospel that night to the trappers, he made a more obvious push for the men to make a decision for accepting Christ.

In the morning, he left before most of the fort's populace awoke.

CHAPTER 18

Boister and Mari struggled under the weight of the huge skin. They'd cleared a place in the snow where they intended to stretch and peg the hide, hair side down. Scraps of fat and tissue still adhered to the hide, and their next job was to remove them by scraping the inner surface with smooth rocks. But for now, they were having a time of it trying to drag the heavy skin over to the prepared spot.

"Need some help?"

"Jan!" squealed Mari. She dropped her end of the bearskin, and ran through the snow.

"Tildie, Tildie!" yelled Boister, abandoning the skin. "Jan's back."

Evie and Tildie rushed out of the cabin, running to throw their arms around Jan. He kissed them all around, even Boister, then kissed Tildie once more for good measure.

"Oh Jan," exclaimed Tildie. "You're so thin and pale. What happened?"

"Where's Gert?" asked Boister. Boister looked with disdain upon the borrowed horse and then beyond, to the trees expecting his Gert to come through the thicket.

"Gert's probably running with some Indians' herd by now,"

explained Jan.

"You lost Gert?" Boister sounded hurt. His face began to crumple. "We lost Gladys, too. She just went off one day and didn't come back. I looked for her, Jan. I tried to follow her tracks, but I lost them in a thick wood."

"She's an old dog, Boister," Jan began.

"She never would've run off," Boister said through a sniffle.

"No, son, you're right," agreed Jan. "She knew a lot about taking care of herself, but sometimes things happen even to those who are good at taking care of themselves. She may be dead, and if she never returns, we have to remember what a happy life she led."

"Let's take Jan inside and have his story," suggested Tildie. "It looks to me like we almost lost him."

They led Jan into the cabin, where Tildie'd been slicing thin strips of bear meat to dip in boiling salt water in preparation for drying.

Jan gladly sat and rested while Boister took the horses into the stable and unloaded them.

"Don't you be looking too closely at those bundles, Boister," instructed Jan. "I've got surprises in there that'll have to keep 'til Christmas."

"Presents, Evie," Mari explained.

The little girls' eyes perked up as they turned to carefully watch their brother, hoping something would accidentally fall open. They even rushed to help carry the different bundles when Jan began directing Boister as to where to put them. Tildie sat on Jan's lap, where he'd pulled her when he first sat in the chair by the table.

"Here," Jan said as he shifted her from one side to the other. "Sit facing this way and lean against the other shoulder."

"Why?" asked Tildie, looking closely at his face. She didn't like the lines of pain she saw around his mouth. She tried to get up, but he held her.

"No, Tildie, be still." He firmly gripped her. "I've waited over a month to hold you again, and as long as you don't squirm, I'm okay."

"Jan," she spoke softly. "Tell me what happened."

Before he could begin Boister and Mari launched into the tale of the bear, starting with his marauding around the cabin and stealing their meat.

"I'm glad you're back, Jan," said Boister with a big grin. "Now I don't have to do all the work around here anymore."

"Shame!" exclaimed Tildie in mock indignation. "As if that were the only reason we're glad he's back."

"Stories!" Evie clapped her hands together.

Mari was silent. She came to stand beside Jan and put her little hand on his big arm. "I'm glad you're back 'cause I love you. You don't have to tell stories if you don't want to." Big tears welled up in her eyes. "You don't have to do work. Just, please, never go away again. I missed you."

Jan wrapped his free arm around her little shoulders and kissed her on the top of her head. "I don't ever want to go away again, Mari," he said. "But I can't promise that. I may need to go for supplies. But I want you to know that I missed you, too. I tried my best to get back here as soon as I could."

Evie moved closer and gave Tildie a push as she had often done before. "Tildie, move. Evie's turn."

Tildie relinquished her spot on Jan's lap. As soon as Tildie sat in her chair next to him, Boister surprised her by coming to stand close. He leaned against her leg, moving it aside, and then sat on the edge of her chair with her. Mari crawled into Jan's lap to sit with her little sister.

"Now tell us," Mari commanded.

Jan laughed, happy to be with his adopted family. He told of his uneventful trip to the fort, then listed some of the things he had purchased. He left out his unpleasant encounter with des Reaux, but detailed an account of his friendship with Henderson. He told how Henderson feared open spaces and mimicked his English accent making them all laugh as he relayed how often Henderson had served him tea. Then he told how he'd been shot and minimized the painful trip back to the fort and the days of being weak and helpless.

"But all the time I was away from you, I wanted very much

to hurry back. And while I was sick, I thought of a plan. It's really an extension of a plan I already had, but I want to put it before you and see if it meets with your approval."

Three little heads bobbed up and down. Tildie tilted hers with a look of inquiry.

"I've asked Tildie to marry me," continued Jan. "That means she'd be my wife and the mother of my children."

Mari clapped her hands. Boister cheered.

"But I feel like you three are already my children. I love you and want us to be a family. If we would agree to be a family, then I'd be your pa and Tildie'd be your mama. We'd live together until you're all grown up and want homes of your own. When I go away on a trip, Mari, you'll know that I'll come back because I'd be your pa, and a pa would do anything possible to get back to his children."

Mari had no second thoughts. She put her arms around Jan's neck, making him wince a bit as she hugged tightly against his sore shoulder.

"Yes," she pronounced enthusiastically. "Can I call you Pa?"

Jan smiled and nodded.

Mari released him and jumped off his lap to climb into Tildie's and hug her. "You can be my mama," she said.

Evie looked at the grown-ups with a puzzled frown between her eyes.

Jan spoke to her carefully, looking into her trusting eyes. "Evie, can I be your pa?"

She still looked unsure as to what was going on. "Pa," she tried the word. Then she looked at Tildie, and a smile grew on her face. "Tildie-ma." She laughed.

That seemed to settle that vote. Jan, Tildie, and Mari turned to look at Boister. He pulled away from Tildie and stood straight, a wary look on his face.

Mari watched him anxiously, then turned with a question for Jan. "Jan," she asked. "Will my real mama and pa be mad because we got a new mama and a new pa?"

"No, Mari," said Jan with confidence. "They'd be happy because families are a good thing, and God likes families."

She turned to Tildie with the same question in her eyes.

"Your mama would be pleased," said Tildie. "She was my very special aunt, and she helped take care of me when I was your age. She taught me how to love children, and she would be happy to know I was taking care of you as your mama."

Mari's face relaxed with relief, and she slid down to go to her brother. Cautiously, she took his hand in her own.

"It's okay, Boister," she spoke quietly. "We don't have to say Mama and Pa unless we want to. But will you please say it's okay? I want to be a family and we can't without you. There's nobody else to be the brother. You *have* to say yes."

Boister didn't jerk away from her or reply quickly with a harsh answer. He looked first at her, then at the others in the room, waiting. He nodded solemnly. "It's okay," he said.

"Hallelujah!" shouted Jan. He plopped Evie on the floor next to her sister and stood. "Let's have a wedding."

Everyone laughed. Mari grabbed her sister's hands and began her own wild version of a polka with her willing partner. Jan pulled Tildie to her feet. He looked down at her with such ardent eyes that Tildie blushed. She ducked her head.

"Jan Borjesson, you said we wouldn't wed until I could stand at the ceremony," she objected with teasing in her voice.

Boister surprised them by answering, "Tildie, you were walking around the cabin without your crutches until the gun knocked you over yesterday. You can't use that as an excuse. The real problem is the cake. You gotta have cake at a wedding."

"How do you know that?" asked Mari.

"'Cause Mama told me about her cake and the dancing and the party at her wedding."

"It's too late to bake a cake tonight," explained Tildie. "And I don't know how tasty a cake would be without any eggs. We could wait until tomorrow to have the wedding."

"No, we can't." Jan vetoed that idea.

"I could set the dough tonight, and we could have fried bread with sugar coating for breakfast," suggested Tildie.

"Hurray!" cried Mari and Boister together.

"Jan, what am I going to wear?" asked Tildie.

"I brought you a whole bunch of material," he answered.

"Jan, I cannot make a dress in an hour," she objected.

"Don't make a dress out of it," he declared. "Just kinda wrap it around."

"A toga, a toga," squealed Mari happily.

"I'm going to get married in a toga, without a cake or a preacher, with a half-skinned bear on the table."

"Not half-skinned, Tildie," said Boister indignantly. "His whole skin is outside."

"I'll clean up the mess while you wash and fashion some kind of wedding dress," promised Jan. "The girls and Boister will help me, and we'll have bear steak for dinner. I'll cook."

"You really want to get married tonight, don't you?" she asked.

He looked in her eyes and nodded slowly. She blushed.

"All right," she said in a voice of resignation. "If this family is going to insist, I guess my only choice is to comply." She stole a look at Jan, who was still watching her, and blushed again. "Where's the material for my wedding dress, Jan Borjesson?"

CHAPTER 19

As a religious ceremony of proper decorum and solemnity, the wedding failed completely. As a joyous celebration, it excelled everyone's expectations.

Of the three pieces of material, Tildie chose the golden calico over the red or the more somber blue. She suddenly insisted that she wash her hair, and the bath took longer than pleased Jan. He and Boister finished what they could of the bear meat and cleaned up the remnants of that messy business. Then the little girls giggled as Jan took a bath in the stable with Boister carrying the pots of warm water to him.

The sun set before they stood together in front of the fireplace. Jan read words from his Bible, and they exchanged their vows quietly, looking into each other's faces and perfectly content with what they saw there. The silver ring was just a little loose, but Tildie and the children exclaimed over its beauty.

Afterward, they danced to Jan's loud renditions of old Swedish folk songs. Tildie sang several of the songs she'd learned from her father. The children sang along when they knew the words. Mari insisted that they sing the sums song that they'd made up to learn their addition facts. Finally, they sat down to the wedding feast, which included pieces of hard candy Jan had brought up from the fort.

The overexcited children resisted going to their beds. Jan insisted they go. In his rich baritone, Jan sang a lullaby his grandmother and mother had sung to him while Tildie sat on his lap in the deerskin-covered chair. When the children were still restless, he and Tildie harmonized melodious hymns. Finally, the children finished their squirming and slept. The newlyweds watched the flickering light of the fireplace.

"Our voices sound good together," commented Jan.

"Uh-huh," Tildie responded dreamily.

"Are you tired?"

"I haven't slept well while you were gone—especially since the bear started worrying us. Since we shot him. . .my goodness, was that only yesterday? It's been a busy two days."

"Are you happy?"

"Yes," said Tildie. "It wasn't the wedding I dreamed of, but it sure is chock-full of good memories."

He ran a finger down the edge of the material that formed the neckline of her toga. "I thought my bride was beautiful. Your gown is beautiful." He buried his face in her hair. "Your hair is beautiful. Your eyes are beautiful. Your smile is. . ."

"I know," said Tildie, "beautiful."

"No," said Jan. "I mean, it's beautiful, but I thought of another word. Your smile is charming."

Tildie giggled and rested her head against his uninjured shoulder. "You look tired, Jan."

"I am," he admitted. "Henderson said I was foolish to travel, but he didn't know what was waiting for me here." He kissed her.

"Jan, when we get back to a settlement with a preacher, would you mind if we got married again?"

"You don't feel married."

"I don't know," admitted Tildie. "It's so different from what I imagined." Another giggle escaped her. "You know, I actually think our wedding was better."

Jan nuzzled her neck and she squirmed. "That tickles," she objected.

"Tildie, I'd like to pick you up and carry you to our bed, but I don't think I can."

"Are you too tired?" she asked with real concern. She had gotten a glimpse over the half wall of the ugly red scar high on his chest when he'd stood up in the stable. She touched the scar on his forehead where the bullet had just missed ending his life.

"I admit my shoulder is aching something fierce, but I'm not too tired to love you."

She didn't speak.

"What about you, Tildie?" he asked softly. "Are you recovered enough to be my wife?"

She tensed, her back straightening as she unconsciously pulled away from his embrace. She took a deep breath and made herself relax. Purposefully she nestled down in his arms. "I'm a little nervous."

He put his lips against her ear. "So am I," he whispered.

"Let's go to bed," she suggested and stood. He came up right after her and wrapped her in his arms. After kissing her one more time, he lost the nervousness. Now she smiled at him with no shyness at all, and they walked over to the little niche that contained the pine needle mattress. Jan had hung a blanket across the opening to give Tildie the privacy she needed for her bath. He pushed an edge aside and led his bride through.

———

"Get up, get up." An insistent voice roused the sleeping adults. "You promised to make fried bread."

Tildie opened her eyes to find Mari and Evie standing on one side of the bed and Boister on the other. She blushed at the three pairs of eyes staring at her intently and burrowed down further in the covers.

Jan sat up and looked groggily at the invaders.

"Rule Number One for the Borjesson family: The mother and father are to be left alone in their bed until they wake up. You children get on the other side of that blanket."

His voice of authority sent them scurrying around the edge

of the blanket.

"Now," said Jan. "One of you call to wake us up. We're now asleep again." He lay back down and took Tildie in his arms.

There was some giggling and whispered consultation from the other side. Mari's voice piped up. "Mama, Pa, can we have breakfast now?"

Jan turned a grinning face to Tildie's. "Yes, daughter," he answered. "Put some wood on the fire, and I'll be out as soon as I'm dressed."

"We already put the wood on," said Boister. "We've been waiting an awful long time."

"Mama?" Evie's voice sounded plaintive.

"I'll be out in a minute, Evie," answered Tildie past the lump in her throat. "Sit in Mama's chair and wait patiently."

Jan leaned over to kiss her as he got out of bed.

"No need to hurry, honey. I'll take care of them."

"She called me mama," Tildie whispered.

"Well, don't cry about it," he admonished her with a laugh. "Pretty soon they'll be mama-ing you to death."

Tildie smiled at the prospect.

While Jan and Boister took care of the chores, Tildie, Evie, and Mari made the fried bread. First, they took out a starter from their crock of sourdough to set aside for the next batch of dough. Then the girls pinched off dime-sized pieces, and Tildie dropped them into a deep kettle of smoking-hot fat. When the pieces rose to the surface, Tildie turned them with a long, forked stick. When they glistened golden brown on all sides and smelled heavenly, she lifted them out, and the girls waited until they drained and cooled a bit before rolling them in sugar. The little puffs of sweet dough were a treat. They'd not had enough sugar to lavish on these delicacies for quite a while.

There was plenty of work to do that first morning. The bear meat and skin must be taken care of without delay. With Jan to help, the whole procedure took less time. Soon the skin was staked and scraped. The meat hung in strips in a smokehouse, and they put big hunks away in the cave. Jan and Boister worked to make the storage cave more secure.

"Black bears don't hibernate as the grizzly does," explained Jan. "They sleep most of the winter away, but they can wake up two or three times or maybe more and wander away from their den. This one just didn't see any reason to settle down when he had such interesting folk to investigate every night. Perhaps later in the winter he would have settled in for longer naps.

"This bear will make our winter more luxurious," he continued. "Why, we'll have grease to waterproof our boots and use on our hands when they get chapped by the cold, dry air. It makes a good throat rub and hair oil. Mighty good thing Tildie shot this bear." Jan grinned at Boister. They both knew it was only the hand of God that directed the bullet to the right place. Tildie really didn't deserve much credit when it came to slaying the beast. She'd been brave to stand before the charging bear, but it was a blessing her shot hit the target.

Inside, Tildie and the girls rendered the fat in preparation for making candles. They'd save some of the fat for cooking and making soap. Tildie encouraged the girls to be speedy with their chores.

"As soon as we're finished with this old bear, I can make you some dresses," she explained.

The girls wanted new dresses, so they swept and washed dishes. Even little Evie helped as best she could with all the little chores that would have kept Tildie away from her hot kettle. Their new mama guarded the boiling grease and wouldn't let them near.

The days that followed brought the new family closer together. Through the cold November, they played games, heard stories, sang songs, and did lessons with both Tildie and Jan. Jan began teaching Boister to shoot his rifle, but held off telling the boy that the gun was his until Christmas. Tildie sewed new dresses and shirts. The material that had been her wedding gown made a beautiful dress and her favorite to wear. She made shirts for both Jan and Boister out of the more somber blue, and the little girls had three dresses apiece plus new petticoats and aprons.

For a Christmas surprise, she stitched matching dresses out of the scraps for the little girls' dolls, and hemmed handkerchiefs for the whole family. Boister and Jan worked on a secret in the stable. It was easy to tell that their project involved wood, but the ladies of the household refrained from snooping.

The isolated family had no idea what the date was on the calendar, so when the projects were near completion, Jan announced that Christmas would be celebrated in exactly seven days. That sent the little cabin's occupants into a flurry of last-minute preparations including decorating, baking, and finishing their gifts.

"Why didn't you just say that tomorrow would be Christmas?" asked Tildie.

"What, Tildie?" he exclaimed. "Were you never a child? Part of the fun of Christmas is waiting and it seeming like it'll never come."

Their Christmas morning was simple, but filled with the kind of things that make memories sweet. Even Evie, with Jan's help, had made a trivet for Tildie so she could put the hot kettle on the table. Jan's gifts from the fort were exclaimed over. They donned the clothes quickly and paraded before the others. Jan told story after story, some from the Bible, and some that were sentimental Christmas happenings from his own past.

In the evening after all the gaiety had wound down and there was a cozy atmosphere in the cabin, Boister read the Christmas story from Luke with some help from Jan. He'd been practicing all week, but he still tripped over some words.

"A very satisfying Christmas," Jan murmured to Tildie that night as they lay in bed. "Last year, I was all alone except for Gladys. Somehow, having a family to share the celebration with makes the whole thing more beautiful."

"I suppose that's because God's intention in having His Son come to earth was to share the Good News with all people."

"A lonely vigil is just not in keeping with the spirit of Christmas," agreed Jan.

"When you think that the shepherds shouted for joy, and the

skies filled with angels praising His Name. . . ."

"It just seems impossible to make it a sober, quiet occasion, doesn't it?"

"Yes, impossible," agreed Tildie.

CHAPTER 20

In February, Tildie was sure that there would be an additional member of their family. A few mornings of nausea confirmed her suspicions, and Jan seemed pleased with the news.

"Remember a long time ago when you asked if my babies would be your sisters, Mari?" Tildie introduced the subject one morning as they did lessons.

Mari frowned for a minute in contemplation, then smiled as she recalled. "You said they'd be my cousins."

"Yes, I said that then, but now—because we've decided to be a family with Jan—it's different. Next fall, you'll have a baby brother or a baby sister."

"You're going to have a baby?" asked Boister.

Tildie smiled at them all. "Yes."

Boister looked at Jan and grinned. "I hope it's a boy, Pa. We're already outnumbered."

Jan looked astonished. In the three months since the wedding, Boister had always avoided calling Jan anything. When he had to relay a message to someone in the house he would say, *your Pa* wants you, or *he* says to. . . Now Jan had finally been called Pa and he wanted to shout with joy. Instead he grinned back at Boister and said, "Yep, but if God gives us another girl to take care of, we'll just have to figure it's because we've been doing such a good job with the ones we've already got."

Jan did take good care of his new family. Tildie had mostly recovered from her accident. She still limped noticeably but only occasionally became overtired and ached in her bones. She joked that she would be one of those people who would be able to predict a spell of bad weather by the pain in her legs. Tildie felt confident that God had ordained this marriage, that her life was just as it should be, and God was pleased.

***

Tildie and Jan sat out in the yard of their cabin, enjoying the cool night air and watching for shooting stars. They sat on a blanket on the ground with their backs against a pile of logs. With Jan's arm around her, Tildie felt comfortable and secure.

"As I see it, Mrs. Borjesson," said Jan, "we have numerous options as to where to live and raise our family."

Tildie tilted up her head where it rested on his shoulder so she could see his face.

"Pray tell." She grinned.

"We can live here, go back and live with the Arapaho, take over the children's ranch, or go back to Ohio, where my family would welcome you with open arms."

"Which do you prefer?" she asked, trying not to be anxious. She had her own desires but realized she'd never be happy if Jan went where she preferred and then wasn't happy, himself.

"I'm a little tired of wilderness living to tell the truth," Jan explained. "I'd like to settle where there are some other people."

Tildie held her breath. The Arapaho Indians were "other people," and as much as she'd grown to like and respect Older One, she did not regard living the nomadic and difficult life of the Indians as a pleasant future. Still, if God had called Jan to be a missionary to the Indians, she must comply.

She slowly let out the breath she had been holding. As the air left her lungs, she tried to mentally let go of her will to dictate the future.

"The passion I had to tell the Indians of our Lord," continued her husband, "seems to have transferred to another area of service."

"What's that, Jan?"

"Part of it's raising the children," he said seriously. "I haven't completely come to understand, but it seems to revolve around preparing the next generation of Christians. I feel the need to be a part of a community, to preach regularly, to be in a church every week."

Tildie merely nodded, not wanting to interrupt his thoughts as he strove to share them with her.

"The ranch is waiting for the children to return, and you said there was a settlement close by. I think I would like to go to the children's ranch, keep it going so Boister would have that as his heritage from his parents, and serve as pastor in that community. Do they have a church?"

"No," admitted Tildie. The homestead held no fond memories for her. The little prairie house had been a home of unhappiness. She wasn't sure this was the best plan, but she held her peace. Jan would change the atmosphere of the run-down ranch. Under his guidance, it would again prosper and be a new place, different from what it had been. She had confidence in Jan.

It wasn't until the next day while she was busy with some mundane chore that the little voice of doubt crept in. John Masters had married her aunt merely to have possession of a prime piece of land, but that had nothing to do with Jan.

As more of the snow thawed, Jan took Boister out a couple of times each week to check the passes they'd need to traverse to get down out of the mountains. The woolly worms had been right and the footage of snow collected in shaded spots was remarkable. In April, Jan finally announced they would be leaving as soon as Tildie said they were packed up.

"No need to take everything, Tildie," Jan informed her. "We'll leave the cabin so that if somebody stumbles on to it, they can use it. Dishes and blankets can all be replaced easier than we can tote them with us. Leave whatever staples that will keep, too. It might save somebody's life." They also left wood cut and stacked, candles, and a flint box, some heavy pans, and of course, all the furniture.

"The ranch has all we'll need," said Jan and left the cabin to see about the meat in the cave that would not keep.

"How does he know the ranch has all we need?" Tildie asked herself.

"Mama, Mama," Mari's voice called urgently from far away. Tildie dropped the blanket she'd folded and ran to the door, her heart in her throat. The last time a child had called like that, a bear had been right at his heels.

She stood in the doorway of the cabin and looked directly at the place Boister had broken through the brush on the run. Sure enough, Mari stumbled out of the woods in almost exactly the same spot, but she wasn't running, and she held a golden, furry bundle in her arms. Tildie took several steps out of the cabin.

Following Mari, several clumsy pups bounced through the short weeds. The last out of the thicket was Gladys. Gladys! Tildie began to run in her awkward gait. Out of the corner of her eye, she saw Jan and Boister descending the hill from the cave, hurrying to meet the lost dog.

Gladys barked joyously and ran from one member to the next, licking faces. When the greetings subsided, Tildie asked, "Mari, where did you find her?"

"She found me!" exclaimed the happy child. "Look, she has puppies." She did, indeed. Puppies surrounded Jan as if they recognized their mother's master.

"Five," shouted Boister. "Five puppies!"

Jan roughed the fur around Gladys's neck. "Well, old girl, who'd have thought you'd be a mother again at this late date? Let's look at these puppies and see if we can distinguish what kind of dog you've been friendly with."

He sat down on the grass amidst the dogs and kids. Evie promptly plopped in his lap, and Boister captured a puppy for him to inspect.

Jan examined the fluffy fur, rounded ears, squarish muzzle, and short body. "I don't see any wolf in these pups," he announced.

"Where did she find a father for them, then?" asked Tildie.

"Remember, the Indians keep dogs."

Tildie did remember that the Arapaho kept dogs for eating, among other things. The thought had bothered her.

"Are there Indians close by?" asked Tildie who had thought they were rather remote from any other humans.

"Some," said Jan, vaguely. "There's a winter camp near Manitou Springs. That's pretty far for Gladys to have gone visiting. Well, if she spoke English, she might tell us, but we'll probably never know."

He rose from the ground easily and hoisted Evie up to his shoulder. "I suppose you want to take the dogs with us on our journey."

Tildie gasped. How could he even think of leaving them behind?

The children began to clamor their insistence, and Tildie looked at Jan closely. A twinkle in his eye as he looked down at the mass of kids and dogs at his feet gave him away. He intended all along to take the pups. He was enjoying Boister's and Mari's claims that the dogs would be no trouble, that they would each personally take care of them, and make sure the pups weren't in the way.

At last Jan took pity on them and gracefully acquiesced to their request. Gladys and her brood would travel with them.

In the morning they set out. Evie and the pups rode on the travois when they were tired. Mari preferred to ride on Charlie. Boister walked more than he had on their previous trip, and Tildie was struck with how mature he was becoming. *He's almost seven*, she thought. Yet, he marched alongside Jan as if he were twice that age. Tildie walked some too, but her back and legs began to ache and Jan insisted she ride, so she stretched out on the travois.

"This isn't much better," she complained as Evie nestled down beside her and the pups tried to lick her face. Jan just laughed.

Tildie was surprised to learn they were going to Fort Reynald.

"Why?" she asked. She had no desire to meet the Frenchman

who could have become her husband.

"I want to check on Henderson," replied Jan. "You'll enjoy meeting him. Remember, he saved my life. You might think of something you need before we start out across the prairie. Also, it's a good idea to check on the mood of the Indians before we cross their territory."

"You mean they might be hostile?"

"Probably not," said Jan. "Or at least, no more than usual. But they have feuds between the tribes, and it's smart to know where the disputes are festering."

Tildie closed her eyes in prayer. She just wanted to get home, wherever that might be. She hoped it was someplace where they wouldn't be constantly afraid of wild things—whether they were bears or renegades.

CHAPTER 21

Tildie entered the gates of Fort Reynald with trepidation. They immediately went to the livery. There, the genuine friendliness of Henderson, combined with his interesting accent, did much to alleviate her uneasiness. It was decided that they would accept his humble hospitality for the evening meal and camp outside the walls of the fort with many other visitors.

About thirty tepees gathered around the decrepit wooden structure passing for a fort. Some were occupied by Arapaho, some by Cheyenne, and several by trappers. An uneasy peace reigned between the Indians and trappers. The natives tolerated the traders because they obliged them in their own passion to dicker and barter. Most Indians looked down upon the trappers as interlopers.

When Henderson offered them tea, Jan, standing behind the Englishman, smiled at Tildie with an I-told-you-so look in his eye. The children enjoyed taking tea with the man who spoke so oddly. They giggled because he sounded just as Jan had imitated, and Boister went so far as to say that a "cup of tea would be most welcome." His imitation of Jan's imitation of Henderson's accent made them all laugh. Henderson knew he was being made sport of and took it good-naturedly.

"I have a request of you, my giant friend," he said when the children finished their tea and scooted outside.

"What is it?" asked Jan. "You know I'm willing to oblige if it's within my ability."

"I want to go back East."

"Cross the prairie?" Jan could not hide the incredulous tone that invaded his voice.

"I think I can do it in your company and with the strength of Jesus."

"You're welcome to come with us, but we plan to travel only as far as the North Fork of the Cimarron in western Kansas territory. Why do you want to leave?"

"Rumor has it that the new inspector for Indian affairs will be more thorough this summer. None of the traders at this fort have a license, and with the unscrupulous competition of the Bent brothers, business is failing anyway. Most of the Indians have gone to trade either south, at Fort El Pueblo; or east, at Bent's Fort. Fort Reynald will surely fold before the end of the summer and then I would be stuck here with my own company. I'd rather try to make my way east with you."

Jan looked over at Tildie, who nodded her head slightly, indicating she had no objection.

"Fine, Henderson," said Jan, "you're welcome to join us."

"I feel compelled to issue a warning," Henderson continued.

"What about?"

"Des Reaux is in a black mood. He took a Mexican woman to wife this winter, and she grew tired of him quickly. She left him with a knife wound in his side when she departed at the first opportunity.

"He's not pleased at being forced out of business by the Bents. Then, too, several traders drank a bit too much one evening just last week and decided to display their dislike of the Frenchman before they left for the summer. They tied him up and trashed his side of the mercantile building, leaving the other side in fairly decent order. In short, des Reaux is spoiling for a fight."

"We'll stay out of his way," commented Jan.

Henderson nodded.

"I do have something you might consider valuable for our journey," offered Henderson.

Jan merely lifted his eyebrows in inquiry.

"I had a small wagon given to me in lieu of payment. Perhaps Mrs. Borjesson will ride more comfortably in it."

Jan smiled at Tildie. Her small frame showed the bulge of a baby. Henderson was right about the wagon.

Tired, Tildie longed to lie down on something that did not bounce, jolt, and sway. Henderson laughed with understanding at her request to stretch out on his motionless hay, but quickly gave his permission. Jan went to see that the children remained out of trouble while his pregnant wife rested.

Boister played with two Arapaho children. The white children amazed the Indians with their knowledge of the Arapaho language. Soon Jan heard Boister telling an elaborate account of their encounter with the bear.

Jan only interrupted once to make sure the listeners knew it was a black bear, not a grizzly. He didn't want them thinking that any bear was to be toyed with, and especially they should not expect to stop a grizzly with one bullet. After the exciting tale had been told and Boister had answered many questions, the boys began the serious business of trading.

Mari knew that both in the telling of tales and the trading of goods, she was to stay in the background—for as a girl and a child, she did not have Boister's status. Evie was treated with more tolerance, but Mari did not chafe. Evidently, she and Boister had a system set up where she could signal her wishes to him. He acquired a pair of moccasins for her as well as a Green River Knife for himself.

When Tildie emerged from the livery after her nap, she sat beside Jan. "They've made friends," she stated, watching the boys play at an Indian sport involving a ball-like sack of rawhide.

"No," said Jan. "These people don't give their friendship so easily. Once you're truly accepted, neither do they abandon you without good cause. Perhaps it's a more stable system than our own."

She leaned against him. Lately she'd had doubts as to whether Jan really wanted her as a wife. She seemed so inferior to his standard. She knew she hadn't the Christian maturity he had. She was always to be a cripple it seemed. She knew that there were many women back East who were prettier, wittier, and more educated than she. He'd been lonely and obviously enjoyed the family atmosphere he had inherited with the responsibility of her. Now, she was cranky, clumsy, and lethargic most of the time. How could any man as fine as Jan feel blessed with such a burden as she? She sighed with the weight of her unhappy thoughts.

His arm came around her. "Are you okay?"

She sniffled, but didn't answer.

"Why don't you tell me what's on your mind?"

She shook her head slightly, ashamed that she should be so close to tears when there was nothing definite to warrant such gloom.

"Is it that Henderson is coming with us? I think you'll find him an agreeable traveling companion. I do wonder how he'll react once we're outside the walls of the fort."

She shook her head again.

"Tildie," he said earnestly, "You must remember that I'm the eldest of thirteen children. What I'm going to say is no reflection on you, but just something I noticed and my father gave me to believe was true."

She said nothing.

"My mother, when she was expecting, would sometimes cry. She said herself that there was nothing specific to cause her tears, but that there were a multitude of little things that weighed her down."

"You're saying it's all right to be a crybaby?"

"I'm saying when you feel like everything is wrong, come lean on me. I love you." He kissed her quickly, mindful of the public place they sat. She dug out her scrap of calico, wiped her eyes, and blew her nose.

"What are you grinning at?" she asked petulantly.

"My beautiful wife."

"Humph!" She looked away, embarrassed. "Your beautiful wife has a red nose, puffy eyes, and a swollen body."

Jan grinned and nodded. "Looks great to me."

Tildie turned back to him, and a smile broke through her tears. Jan had a way of banishing all her doubts. She could believe he honestly loved her when he sat beside her and looked at her with that warmth in his eyes.

Many of the men at the fort smelled from the lack of personal hygiene, but a rancid odor suddenly invaded the quiet talk between Jan and his wife and wrenched them out of their self-absorption.

Jan stood as soon as the shadow touched him. "Des Reaux," he acknowledged the man's presence.

"Borjesson." The Frenchman nodded, seemingly undaunted by the fact that Jan towered over him. He worked the toothpick from one corner of his mouth to the other while staring boldly at Tildie. "This is your wife?"

"Tildie," Jan spoke as he put a hand on her arm and drew her to stand beside him. He put a protective arm around her shoulders. "This is Armand des Reaux, the grocer at Fort Reynald."

Tildie knew she must remain calm. She fought the feeling of disgust that rose in her throat as she assessed the repellent nature of the man before her. This was the man John Masters had expected her to marry? This repulsive, malodorous, vulgar pig was his idea of a husband for her? She now realized how truly John Masters must have despised her.

She nodded, acknowledging the introduction but unable to voice any suitable pleasantries.

The Frenchman's eyes narrowed, and he insolently looked her over.

"Amazing, Borjesson," he spoke with false congeniality. "Your wife looks so young to be the mother of three children."

Jan's grip on her shoulders tightened.

"I take good care of her, des Reaux."

The coldness in her husband's voice sent a shiver down her spine. Surely, the Frenchman would get the message. Jan stood between her and des Reaux. A flood of gratitude filled her as she realized that God had given her a giant Swede to protect her from this unsavory person.

"Welcome to the fort, my little friend." The congenial tone of des Reaux's words still contained an underlying threat. "The sunshine of your presence is long overdue in this godforsaken hole. An entire year overdue, *mon cherie*."

Tildie felt the rigidity intensify in her husband's stance. The last thing she wanted to see was a fight between these two men. Jan was undoubtedly the stronger of the two, but the Frenchman impressed her as the type to use a knife instead of settling their disagreement with just their fists. She found the courage to speak.

"Thank you for your welcome, Mr. des Reaux." She smiled up at Jan's face, ignoring the rigid set of his jaw and the thin line of his lips. Determinedly, she went on. "I'm happy to be with my husband here in Colorado. I, too, thought this area might be godforsaken, until Jan reminded me of God's goodness."

She turned innocent eyes upon the antagonistic Frenchman. "Perhaps you don't know the promise God gives His children. In the Bible it says He will never leave us nor forsake us, no matter what the circumstances. I lost sight of that while waiting in the Indian camp."

"Spoken like a true wife of a preacher," conceded the Frenchman. His eyes lost none of the hard glitter that chilled her heart. He removed the crude toothpick from his mouth and grinned widely, showing his yellowed teeth.

In an effort to find something legitimate to focus on other than this despicable man, Tildie shifted her gaze to the children. They stood in a line behind the man, having abandoned their game. The solemn faces of the Indian children told their hatred for the Frenchman. Their narrowed eyes bored holes in the back of the grocer. They watched his every move intently, showing their distrust. Boister had taken Mari's hand. Mari held Evie's.

Do they remember? wondered Tildie. *Do they realize this is the man their stepfather intended me to marry?* Boister's stony expression could mean he remembered or just recognized this Frenchman as the same type of evil man as John Masters.

"Mama," whimpered Evie.

Tildie held out her hand. "Come, Evelyn. Let's go see about fixing dinner."

Evie ran to grab her hand.

"Good day, Mr. des Reaux." Tildie turned a disinterested shoulder on the Frenchman and marched away with a straight back and head held high.

"A truly magnificent woman." Des Reaux watched her as she departed. Suddenly, a large hand grabbed the shirtfront below the man's leering face, lifting him off the ground.

"Be careful how you look at my wife, des Reaux." Jan's voice was a low growl. "My God orders men to treat their wives as He treats His church. I understand that to mean I should be willing to die for my family. *This* preacher knows how to fight."

Des Reaux made a deprecating movement with his hands and gasped out a disclaimer as best he could. "I have no interest in your wife."

The Swede dropped des Reaux, and he collapsed in the dirt. Jan clenched his fists at his side, determined not to pound the little weasel into the ground.

"Come, children," he ordered and turned on his heel, leaving the angry Frenchman muttering in the dust.

CHAPTER 22

"W e can leave tomorrow." Jan held a supply list the three adults and three children had labored over the night before. They sat at Henderson's table, but Tildie and Mari had made the breakfast. Now, as Jan reached for the last of Tildie's tasty biscuits, he told Boister to put a skip in his step and get ready to go to the mercantile.

"I want to go," begged Mari. "Please."

"No," said Jan as he pushed the last bite in his mouth and wiped his hands on his pant legs. "The men in the fort don't have the manners I'd expect to be shown before my daughters." He took a mug from Henderson's table and lifted it to his lips. With his head tipped back, he drained it and set it back down with a thud. He then rubbed his forearm across his mouth wiping away any wetness.

The sight of the expression on Tildie's face arrested the movement in mid-swipe. One of her finely drawn eyebrows arched in mock indignation, and a smile quivered at the corner of her mouth.

"What?" he asked.

"The trappers have no manners?" She looked pointedly at the arm that still rested against his mouth.

At that moment, Henderson came in from the other room. "Would you care for more tea, Madame?" he asked, holding the tin pot he used for brewing with the same elegance he would have held a teapot of Wedgwood china.

Jan dropped both arms to his sides and looked from the former butler to his wife. "Tildie, you're not comparing me to Henderson here."

The look of absolute horror on his face brought laughter bubbling out of Tildie. She laughed until her side hurt and tears ran down her face. Long before she could recover, Jan shot her a disgusted look, waved at Boister to "come on," and left to buy the supplies they would need on the trail.

⚜

"That's about all we can do to make it comfortable," Jan said as he moved a barrel to the side and began strapping it to the wooden arch that held the canvas over the wagon bed. "With those boxes padded with buffalo robes and blankets, it should make a fairly comfortable bed."

Tildie stood on tiptoe with her hands on the back of the wagon, trying to see in. Jan turned her toward him and lifted, holding her snug against his chest.

"Can you see better now?" He laughed at her prim expression as she looked around quickly to see who might be watching.

"I see fine," she sputtered.

"You haven't even looked in the wagon," he pointed out.

"Jan, put me down." She struggled weakly.

He kissed her cheek as she turned her face back and forth, still trying to see if anyone was watching them.

"How 'bout I put you down in the wagon and you can stretch out on that makeshift bed to see how it feels?"

"Why?" She quit struggling to admire the fine lines at the corners of his eyes that crinkled so attractively when he smiled at her.

"Henderson and I will be finishing up loading the donkey cart. You need your afternoon nap, and if you're in the wagon, you'll be out of our way as we move around the livery."

"Who will watch the children?"

"Henderson and I can watch the children, and when Evie gets cranky, I'll bring her to the wagon and tell her to take a nap with Mama." He gave her a hug, kissed her lightly on the lips, and swung her up and over the back of the wagon.

"I'll be easier in my mind if you're close to where Henderson and I are working instead of on the outside of the fort where we've been camping."

"Are you worried about des Reaux?"

"I've been praying for protection, but that doesn't mean I'm going to be careless with what God has entrusted to me."

"You're worried about that man?"

Jan looked seriously into her eyes. "Honey, we must be as harmless as doves and as wise as serpents. I believe Armand des Reaux to be evil." He leaned forward and kissed her again. "You take a nap. Tomorrow, we'll be on the trail, and we needn't worry about the Frenchman again."

—⋙⋘—

An hour later, Jan lifted Evie over the tailgate of the wagon. He put a finger to his lips and pointed to Tildie.

"Shh! Little girl," he cautioned, "crawl in next to your mama and try not to wake her. Take a nice nap, and when both my pretty girls get up, we'll fix supper. Tonight, we'll get to hear Pennsylvania Paterson play his fiddle."

Evie leaned out of the wagon and gave her pa a squeezing hug and a big kiss on the cheek before she turned and crawled over the barrels, boxes, and gunnysacks to where Tildie lay napping. She pulled herself onto the buffalo robes and turned to wave good-bye. She blew another kiss, put her finger to her little lips, and hissed a loud "Sh," giggled, and snuggled down. Jan shook his head, grinning at her antics, and returned to the work in the barn. They'd discovered weak boards in the bottom of the cart, and those had to be repaired before they could finish loading it.

"Fire!" The shout was followed by more bellows and the sounds of men running. Henderson and Jan dropped what they were doing and raced out of the livery, into the open square around which the buildings of the fort were built.

The smell of smoke and the sound of the flames crackling as they consumed canvas assaulted the men.

"The wagon," Henderson exclaimed.

Two burly mountain men slashed at the canvas on the Borjesson wagon, ripped it from the frame, and threw it to the ground. Two other men stood beside the wooden wagon and beat the flames with horse blankets. Another man ran up with a bucket of water and emptied it on the flames. He immediately ran back from where he'd come.

"Tildie, Evie!" Jan ran to the end of the wagon and tried to look inside. Heavy smoke choked him and stung his eyes. He could see nothing even as the men pulled off the canvas covering. "Tildie," he shouted again and started to climb in.

Two hands grabbed him from behind. "I'm here. I'm here."

Jan twirled around and grabbed her into a strong embrace. "Evie?" he gasped.

"She's here, too."

He felt the child wrapped around one of his legs before he looked down and saw her. He let Tildie go in order to bend over and peel the frightened child from his leg. He hoisted her into his arms to hold her tightly and pat her back, murmuring words of comfort. He moved them away from the wagon. "I just left her with you."

Tildie smiled through her tears and nodded. "Yes," she agreed, "but you forgot little girls should go potty before they go down for their naps. She woke me and we left the wagon."

Jan looked down at his wife. "Thank God, Tildie!"

She nodded and leaned against him.

The noise around the wagon subsided, and they looked to see the men had put out the fire. They had acted quickly. A fire in the fort of dried wooden structures was a serious threat.

Several of the men came over to where the family had gathered. Boister stood with Mari. Henderson stood behind them with a hand on each of their shoulders.

"Thanks," said Jan to the crowd.

The men signaled their acknowledgment with curt nods.

"You okay?" one of them asked Tildie.

"Yes, thank you."

"Did you see the dirt was on fire underneath the wagon?" asked a tall, dark man. He'd been beating the flames.

"What does that mean?" asked another. "Dirt don't burn."

"Kerosene." The man spat in the dirt. "Someone poured it on the canvas, and it dripped on the dirt. You can smell it, too."

"It was des Reaux," said the man who had carried the bucket. "I saw him walking fast toward his place with something under his coat just before I saw the fire."

An angry murmur ran through the group of men. Nobody liked the Frenchman. A fire endangered all of them. Jan sensed that at any moment the men would decide justice was needed, and they were the ones to administer it.

He held up a hand, stopping them just as they were about to turn *en masse* and storm through the fort to the Frenchman's store. "Wait!" he ordered. "First of all, we only *think* he did this. Did anyone see him pour the kerosene? Light the wagon?"

"The swine did it," proclaimed one of the men loudly. "None of us did it, so it must've been him."

"No one else had a reason," agreed another.

"Fine," said Jan. "We'll go talk to him about it. Did you hear what I said? We will *talk* to him."

Jan handed Evie into Tildie's arms and pushed her toward Henderson. "Stay here," he advised and put himself at the front of the band of men marching to the mercantile.

There were seven men behind Jan, and he prayed that he would be able to control the situation. Wrath thrummed through his veins like a tympani. Still the Holy Spirit dampened his anger. This devil had almost hurt Tildie and Evie, but he had no desire to see the Frenchman dangling from a rope, pierced with knives, or whatever else these rough men could think of as "just punishment."

They entered the store, bursting through the wooden door with such force it slammed back against the wall.

Des Reaux dangled from the grip of two mountain men who had evidently followed him without waiting to discuss the matter. The short man's face was bloodied.

Jan stopped, as did the others behind him. With one look at what had already transpired, the men surged forward, eager to finish the job.

"Stop!" yelled Jan. "I don't want to be as low as this worm."

The other men turned to look at him. This strange statement arrested their attention. Relieved, Jan saw confusion on their faces. He needed to make them think before they plowed ahead, running purely on mindless revenge.

"He's a weasel, an unscrupulous beast," said the preaching Swede. "He's not a human. He's an animal." The two men holding the limp Frenchman aloft lowered him to the floor, but didn't let him go.

Jan took a few steps forward so he could snarl into des Reaux's face. He saw the terror in his eyes and knew the man recognized these mountain men wanted to kill him.

"This is a snake." Jan hissed the words in the frightened man's dirty face. "Like the serpent in the Garden of Eden, he crawls on his belly and brings destruction. This is not a man, but a creature of evil."

Jan turned suddenly to look his listeners in the eye. His steady gaze went from one man to the next. "We recognize him for what he is, because we're not the low, cowardly brute that he is. No man here would douse a man's property with kerosene and torch it. Maybe he thought my wife was in there, or maybe he saw her leave and only wanted to destroy what belonged to me. Either way, his evil jeopardized this entire encampment."

The men grunted agreement and pressed forward. Jan again held up his hand. "But," he exclaimed, "I don't wish to be identified with this scum. I won't join him in his wickedness. I stand apart."

"We'll take care of him for you," volunteered one of the men.

"You don't have to take care of him for me. 'Vengeance is mine, sayeth the Lord.' God Almighty will deal with this man. I pity him. We might hang him, and that few moments of agony would be all that des Reaux had to pay for his crime—but God tells us that for men like des Reaux, He has a lake of fire, a place of never-ending torment. God says He'll throw this man into the outer darkness where there shall be wailing and gnashing of teeth, agony we cannot understand. Do you see why I don't want to be like him?" Jan stopped to gauge how his audience responded. He didn't often rail on about hell and damnation, but he was a preacher, and he knew how to get his point across.

⁕

Three hours later, at Tildie's insistence, Henderson went over to see what was happening. He returned to say that it appeared her husband was conducting a revival.

"Can I go listen, Mama?" asked Boister.

Tildie looked at him with a blank expression. She couldn't quite comprehend what had happened. Jan had left with a small mob of men bent on violence. Now he was preaching! Reserved Boister had called her, "Mama," as if it were the most natural thing in the world, and he was hopping from one foot to the other waiting for her to give him permission to go listen to a sermon. She turned questioning eyes to Henderson.

"It would be all right, Madame, if the young man were to sit on the edge of the crowd."

"Crowd?" she whispered.

Henderson smiled. "Jan is standing on the roof of the mercantile, and most of the people in the fort and from the surrounding encampment are gathered in the square. He moved out of the building some time ago when it became too crowded. He must have realized there were people outside who could not hear."

Tildie walked over to the barn door and pushed it open. She saw the backs of people who pressed closer to be able to see and hear her husband. She heard the familiar cadence of his speech but couldn't make out the words.

"Please, Mama," Boister begged.

"I'll watch after the boy," offered Henderson.

"Yes, go," she answered. Boister and Henderson bolted out the door.

"What's Pa doing?" asked Mari.

"He's telling the people about God."

"Like he tells us?"

"Yes," answered Tildie.

"Uh-uh," disagreed Evie from where she stood in the door at Tildie's feet.

Tildie swung her up in her arms. "What do you mean 'uh-uh,' little one?"

Evie giggled and covered her ears. "Pa yelling!" she exclaimed.

CHAPTER 23

W ell," said Tildie when Jan crawled in beside her, "What happened?"

Jan chuckled. "You know when I headed across that square toward the mercantile, I never expected that I was going to see God working. I thought I had a pretty fair chance of seeing some miserable men claim justice their own way. I was praying mighty hard with every step."

Jan stroked her arm absentmindedly. He sighed with contentment. "It's always a pleasure to watch the Master at work, to see Him turn things around, working all things together for good. To see His way plow through a situation gone sour and turn it up sweet.

"Over thirty—I lost count—of those rough men accepted Christ as their Savior. Seven of the Arapaho decided the same. I tried to keep count so I'd know how many Bibles to send here."

"What about des Reaux?"

"He had the smell of kerosene on the inside of his jacket. Made a perfect example of how sin clings to you and there's nothing you can do to remove the stain, get rid of the smell. Next step was to introduce them to Jesus, who washes all their sins away."

"So what's going to happen to des Reaux?" asked Tildie impatiently.

"He's going to be escorted to Bent's Fort, where the U.S. Calvary will take him in hand." Like Fort Reynald, Bent's Fort was actually a privately owned establishment, not a military outpost. It, however, was on the Santa Fe Trail, and the U.S. Calvary found its location convenient.

"What about us?" asked Tildie.

"Well, I don't think we'll be leaving tomorrow, but we should be heading out by the middle of next week. Des Reaux generously donated any supplies we lost in the fire out of his stock."

"He did?"

"Well, I think he thought that would barter him out of his predicament."

Tildie thought this over and decided she wouldn't inquire as to how that came about. She didn't want to waste any more time on the Frenchman. Other questions had been stirring in her mind. "Do you want to stay here and shepherd the flock?"

Jan laughed again and pulled her closer to snuggle her back against his front. "Where'd you ever hear a phrase like that?"

"From you," she answered, trying to ignore the nuzzling he was doing to her ear. "You said you wanted to have a church and a congregation, and you wanted to 'shepherd the flock,' teaching them to be strong in the Word."

"Mmm." He began nibbling on her ear and then down her neck.

"Jan," she spoke as sharply as she could in a whisper, not wanting to wake the others who slept in the barn.

"What?"

"I'm trying to talk to you."

"Tildie, I've been talking for hours. I don't want to talk right now."

He turned her toward him and kissed her eyes, her cheeks, and her lips. She sighed and gave up trying to get any more information out of him.

Jan spent most of his time talking to people while Henderson and his family repacked the repaired wagon. Henderson had bartered with some Indians for a large piece of leather formerly used for a teepee. He began cutting it to replace the burned canvas. Due to the men of the fort's quick action, not much had been damaged under the canvas. A barrel was charred, and they had to put the blankets and buffalo hides out to air. The buffalo hides were cured in what amounted to an Indian smokehouse, so they didn't smell much worse than before.

"Tildie, come with me." Jan stood at the door of the barn, holding out his hand. She took note of how serious he looked and immediately crossed over to take his hand. With a look over her shoulder to see that the children were supervised by Henderson, she went with him.

"What is it?" she asked.

They passed through the front gate of the compound, and he strolled off toward the river. When they reached the huge cottonwood tree, he sat down and pulled her down beside him.

"The men who took des Reaux to Bent's Fort just got back."

"Did they kill him?" she asked with her eyes wide. The despicable man had a talent for provoking people, and he wouldn't be smart enough not to antagonize his captors.

"No." Jan shook his head. "He got there all right. The men brought back some disturbing news."

"What?"

"Comanches are terrorizing the lower part of the Kansas territory, down through Texas and in parts of Oklahoma."

"The ranch? The settlement—Breakdon?"

"Breakdon was wiped out."

"Oh no!" Tildie gasped. Pictures of the dusty main street, the clapboard buildings, the hitching rails flitted through her mind. Individual faces of people she had met on the rare occasions she'd gone to town sprang up. She saw the owner of the general store carrying a sack of flour to a buckboard outside the front door of his establishment. She saw three children running after a dog down the main street. She leaned against Jan and closed her eyes trying to block out those images. Those people were most probably dead. Were the men left behind on the ranch also dead? Would they ever know?

"What are we going to do?" she whispered.

"I want to go home to Ohio," he said without preamble.

"Ohio?"

"Yes." He squeezed her shoulders. "I never really wanted to settle at the homestead. I thought it best for the children, so I was willing. My real desire is to go back East. My brothers are working to help colored people get to Canada."

"Runaway slaves?" Tildie breathed the question, eyes wide with apprehension.

Jan merely nodded.

"That's very dangerous."

He nodded again.

"What do you want to do, Tildie?" he finally asked when her silence stretched too long.

Tildie leaned back and looked at him. Tears coursed down her cheeks. He reached out callused fingers and gently wiped them away.

"Yes, Jan, I want to go, too. I didn't want to go to Uncle Henry's. It doesn't hold any good memories for me, and I don't think it does for Boister, either."

"Why didn't you tell me?"

"Because I didn't think you really loved me."

His mouth fell open and for a moment, he didn't speak. "You didn't think. . .?"

She dropped her chin so she wouldn't have to look at his incredulous expression.

"*Didn't* think," he repeated. "What do you think now?"

"I thought you chose me because I was the only one around, and if more women had been available, you wouldn't have picked me."

"And what do you think now?" he repeated.

"I thought you were lonely and you liked having the children because it reminded you of your family growing up."

"And what do you think now?"

"I think I love you so much that I can't stand the thought of you not loving me."

"But you're not sure I love you." His calm voice cut through her, and she folded up as much as she could over her round belly and cried into her hands.

He put his arms around her and stroked her spine, hugging her and rocking her back and forth.

"Tildie, does God love you?"

She sniffed and nodded affirmative against his chest.

"Is He always saying 'I love you,' day in and day out, in ways you can see, hear, and feel?"

She shook her head, still not raising it from the comfortable position where she could hear his heartbeat and his voice rumble.

"But you know He loves you?"

She nodded yes again.

"Well, Matilda Borjesson, I love you. I'm only human, and I can't do near the things God has done to prove His love for you, but you're just going to have to *believe* I love you and *know* I love you." He tilted her head back and began kissing the tears away. "And when we get back to a place where there's a preacher other than myself, I'm going to marry you again. Not because we aren't married already in the eyes of God, but because you want it. And, if you want me to marry you once a year, I'll do it. If you want me to marry you once a month or once a week, I'll do it. But Tildie, my love, for all that marrying, I won't mean the vows one bit more than I do right now. The words will stay the same, but the love is going to grow."

He captured her lips then and kissed her with the commitment binding them together.

She believed.

EPILOGUE

G et up! Get up!" Mari bounced on the bed.

Tildie forced her eyes open. Blurry figures stood all around. Startled at the sight of so many people in her room, she reached one hand over and found Jan's place empty in the big feather bed.

Astrid, Jan's sister, stepped forward with a bundled baby in her arms. Her words came pouring forth in the same rush that characterized everything she did.

"Tomi is impatient for his breakfast. And Mother is beside herself, thinking of all the details for your wedding. Jan has gone to the church to help with the decorations Aunt Julee is determined to see hung from the rafters. She's stripped the woods of ivy and woven a garland with lovely white flowers. You must see for yourself. She's been up half the night. If you don't stir yourself out of this bed, the next delegation of in-laws will be the brawny brothers."

Tildie sat up with a grin and took her squirming son. With a practiced flip of the small blanket and rearrangement of her gown, she soon had the sturdy four-month-old baby nestled against her breast. Tildie still wasn't use to this Swedish sisterhood who invaded her room without a thought. She modestly covered Tomi's bald head and her shoulder with the blanket.

Born before they reached St. Jo, Missouri, Tomi was always impatient to get done what needed to be done, including eating. If a meal were two minutes later than he expected, he would raise a holler that could be heard in three states—or that's what his proud grandpa claimed. Now that Tildie was awake, Jan's seven sisters and her own Mari and Evie crowded to find seats on every available spot on the huge bed. Talking and laughing with no sense of order to the conversation, the girls relayed every bit of information they could recall on the preparations for the wedding.

Suddenly, the room fell silent as a good-natured "Ach!" boomed from the doorway. Jan's mother entered waving a wooden spoon in one hand and flapping her long white apron much as she did when she shooed the chickens. "Out of here, out of here. Go! There's work to be done. I send one of you up to get Jan's Tildie out of bed, and here all of you are. How can she get up when you have her pinned by her sheets to the bed? Get up. Get out. Shoo."

Giggling and scuffling as they left, the sisters pushed out of the narrow door, taking Evie and Mari with them. When the last skirt had swung past the door frame, Ingrid closed the door with a firm hand.

She came over to the bed and plopped down in one of the places just vacated by one of her frivolous daughters.

"Now." She patted Tildie's blanket-covered leg. "Are you ready for this big day?"

"Yes, Mother Borjesson." Tildie grinned at the short, stout woman who'd taken to mothering her just as soon as she'd stepped through the farmhouse door.

"If your mother were here on the morning of your wedding day, she'd likely take the time to give you some godly advice."

Tildie nodded as she efficiently shifted her son to nurse from the other side.

"I'll tell you to read Proverbs, one chapter for every day of the month. All the advice in there is what keeps a marriage together. Turning away wrath with a soft answer and such. But you notice, dear Tildie, that some of the months only have thirty days and that leaves out chapter thirty-one. I know in my bones that God has ordained a wife and mother as a special minister to His families, but I also know we women can get to thinking too highly of ourselves. On the one hand, He probably was giving us a break from stewing over just how much work it is to keep a family going, and on the other. . ." Her blue eyes twinkled with merry humor. "He didn't think we needed to hear how important we are every single month."

They both chortled over the thought.

Ingrid reached for Tomi. "Is that boy finished? I'll burp him and take him downstairs. You get ready," she ordered, already halfway to the door. "Eleven o'clock. All the family, all the neighbors, everyone from the church. We'll have the wedding of the year. It's not everyone who gets to marry one of the handsome Borjesson men twice. Hurry, girl."

A few minutes after her mother-in-law had disappeared with her baby, Tildie heard Jan's voice calling her name from outside. She went over to the open window and looked down to where he stood below.

"I thought you were hanging decorations at the church," Tildie said.

"I was. They're hung. Aunt Julee is stretched out in the back pew, sleeping. Snoring, too."

"You left her there?"

"Her house is one block from the church in town."

Jan looked perturbed.

"What's wrong?" asked Tildie.

"I'm just thanking God I married you in Colorado."

"Any particular reason?"

"Because now that you've met my family, you might have said no." He ran a hand through his hair. "Tildie?"

"Yes?"

"My mother is having the time of her life. She says I can't see you until after the wedding. Ridiculous!" He paused and looked up at her with such tenderness, she almost climbed down the trellis to give him a morning hug and kiss. He sighed. "Thanks for not getting upset."

"Jan?"

"Yes?"

"Are we going to move into the parsonage as of tonight?"

"Yes."

She grinned, knowing he would understand exactly why she wanted to be private in their own little house after two weeks in the bustling Borjesson household.

"Then I have no reason to be upset."

His answering expression of delight told her he, too, was ready to be a smaller family again. He blew her a kiss before turning to walk away.

"Meet me at the church, Matilda Harris Borjesson."

"Yes, sir!"

Kathleen Paul retired early from teaching school, but soon got bored! The result: a determination to start a new career. Now she is an award-winning novelist writing Christian romance and fantasy. She says, "I feel blessed to be doing what I like best." She mentors all ages, teaching teenagers and weekly adult writing workshops. "God must have imprinted 'teacher' on me clear down to the bone. I taught in public school, then home schooled my children, and worked in private schools. Now my writing week isn't very productive unless I include some time with kids." Her two grown children make her proud, and her two grandsons make her laugh.

Available from Barbour Publishing

GI *Brides*

Letters from home give three soldiers
something to live for and come home to.